A TRI

MW01139197

By

Elizabeth von Arnim

The Enchanted April

The Solitary Summer

Vera

Cover Illustration: © Awenart | Dreamstime.com

ISBN-13: 978-1482357585
ISBN-10: 1482357585
This Edition: © 2013 verneysbooks

The Enchanted April

by

Elisabeth von Arnim

Chapter 1

It began in a Woman's Club in London on a February afternoon—an uncomfortable club, and a miserable afternoon—when Mrs. Wilkins, who had come down from Hampstead to shop and had lunched at her club, took up The Times from the table in the smoking-room, and running her listless eye down the Agony Column saw this:

To Those Who Appreciate Wistaria and Sunshine. Small mediaeval Italian Castle on the shores of the Mediterranean to be Let furnished for the month of April. Necessary servants remain. Z, Box 1000, The Times.

That was its conception; yet, as in the case of many another, the conceiver was unaware of it at the moment.

So entirely unaware was Mrs. Wilkins that her April for that year had then and there been settled for her that she dropped the newspaper with a gesture that was both irritated and resigned, and went over to the window and stared drearily out at the dripping street.

Not for her were mediaeval castles, even those that are specially described as small. Not for her the shores in April of the Mediterranean, and the wisteria and sunshine. Such delights were only for the rich. Yet the advertisement had been addressed to persons who appreciate these things, so that it had been, anyhow addressed too to her, for she certainly appreciated them; more than anybody knew; more than she had ever told. But she was poor. In the whole world she possessed of her very own only ninety pounds, saved from year to year, put by carefully pound by pound, out of her dress allowance. She had scraped this sum together at the suggestion of her husband as a shield and refuge against a rainy day. Her dress allowance, given her by her father, was £100 a year, so that Mrs. Wilkins's clothes were what her husband, urging her to save, called modest and becoming, and her acquaintance to each other, when they spoke of her at all, which was seldom for she was very negligible, called a perfect sight.

Mr. Wilkins, a solicitor, encouraged thrift, except that branch of it which got into his food. He did not call that thrift, he called it bad housekeeping. But for the thrift which, like moth, penetrated into

Mrs. Wilkins's clothes and spoilt them, he had much praise. "You never know," he said, "when there will be a rainy day, and you may bevery glad to find you have a nest-egg. Indeed we both may."

Looking out of the club window into Shaftesbury Avenue—hers was an economical club, but convenient for Hampstead, where she lived, and for Shoolbred's, where she shopped—Mrs. Wilkins, having stood there some time very drearily, her mind's eye on the Mediterranean in April, and the wisteria, and the enviable opportunities of the rich, while her bodily eye watched the really extremely horrible sooty rain falling steadily on the hurrying umbrellas and splashing omnibuses, suddenly wondered whether perhaps this was not the rainy day Mellersh—Mellersh was Mr. Wilkins—had so often encouraged her to prepare for, and whether to get out of such a climate and into the small mediaeval castle wasn't perhaps what Providence had all along intended her to do with her savings. Part of her savings, of course; perhaps quite a small part. The castle, being mediaeval, might also be dilapidated, and dilapidations were surely cheap. She wouldn't in the least mind a few of them, because you didn't pay for dilapidations which were already there, on the contrary—by reducing the price you had to pay they really paid you. But what nonsense to think of it . . .

She turned away from the window with the same gesture of mingled irritation and resignation with which she had laid down The Times, and crossed the room towards the door with the intention of getting her mackintosh and umbrella and fighting her way into one of the overcrowded omnibuses and going to Shoolbred's on her way home and buying some soles for Mellersh's dinner—Mellersh was difficult with fish and liked only soles, except salmon—when she beheld Mrs. Arbuthnot, a woman she knew by sight as also living in Hampstead and belonging to the club, sitting at the table in the middle of the room on which the newspapers and magazines were kept, absorbed, in her turn, in the first page of The Times.

Mrs. Wilkins had never yet spoken to Mrs. Arbuthnot, who belonged to one of the various church sets, and who analysed, classified, divided and registered the poor; whereas she and Mellersh, when they did go out, went to the parties of impressionist painters, of whom in Hampstead there were many. Mellersh had a sister who had married one of them and lived up on the Heath, and because of this alliance Mrs. Wilkins was drawn into a circle which was highly unnatural to her, and she had learned to dread pictures.

She had to say things about them, and she didn't know what to say. She used to murmur, "marvelous," and feel that it was not enough. But nobody minded. Nobody listened. Nobody took any notice of Mrs. Wilkins. She was the kind of person who is not noticed at parties. Her clothes, infested by thrift, made her practically invisible; her face was non-arresting; her conversation was reluctant; she was shy. And if one's clothes and face and conversation are all negligible, thought Mrs. Wilkins, who recognized her disabilities, what, at parties, is there left of one?

Also she was always with Wilkins, that clean-shaven, fine-looking man, who gave a party, merely by coming to it, a great air. Wilkins was very respectable. He was known to be highly thought of by his senior partners. His sister's circle admired him. He pronounced adequately intelligent judgments on art and artists. He was pithy; he was prudent; he never said a word too much, nor, on the other had, did he ever say a word too little. He produced the impression of keeping copies of everything he said; and he was so obviously reliable that it often happened that people who met him at these parties became discontented with their own solicitors, and after a period of restlessness extricated themselves and went to Wilkins.

Naturally Mrs. Wilkins was blotted out. "She," said his sister, with something herself of the judicial, the digested, and the final in her manner, "should stay at home." But Wilkins could not leave his wife at home. He was a family solicitor, and all such have wives and show them. With his in the week he went to parties, and with his on Sundays he went to church. Being still fairly young—he was thirty-nine—and ambitious of old ladies, of whom he had not yet acquired in his practice a sufficient number, he could not afford to miss church, and it was there that Mrs. Wilkins became familiar, though never through words, with Mrs. Arbuthnot.

She saw her marshalling the children of the poor into pews. She would come in at the head of the procession from the Sunday School exactly five minutes before the choir, and get her boys and girls neatly fitted into their allotted seats, and down on their little knees in their preliminary prayer, and up again on their feet just as, to the swelling organ, the vestry door opened, and the choir and clergy, big with the litanies and commandments they were presently to roll out, emerged. She had a sad face, yet she was evidently efficient. The combination used to make Mrs. Wilkins wonder, for she had been told my Mellersh, on days when she had only been able to get plaice, that if one were efficient one wouldn't be depressed, and that if one does one's job well one becomes automatically bright and brisk.

About Mrs. Arbuthnot there was nothing bright and brisk, though much in her way with the Sunday School children that was automatic; but when Mrs. Wilkins, turning from the window, caught sight of her in the club she was not being automatic at all, but was looking fixedly at one portion of the first page of The Times, holding the paper quite still, her eyes not moving. She was just staring; and her face, as usual, was the face of a patient and disappointed Madonna.

Mrs. Wilkins watched her a minute, trying to screw up courage to speak to her. She wanted to ask her if she had seen the advertisement. She did not know why she wanted to ask her this, but she wanted to. How stupid not to be able to speak to her. She looked so kind. She looked so unhappy. Why couldn't two unhappy people refresh each other on their way through this dusty business of life by a little talk—real, natural talk, about what they felt, what they would have liked, what they still tried to hope? And she could not help thinking that Mrs. Arbuthnot, too, was reading that very same advertisement. Her eyes were on the very part of the paper. Was she, too, picturing what it would be like—the colour, the fragrance, the light, the soft lapping of the sea among little hot rocks? Colour, fragrance, light, sea; instead of Shaftesbury Avenue, and the wet omnibuses, and the fish department at Shoolbred's, and the Tube to Hampstead, and dinner, and to-morrow the same and the day after the same and always the same . . .

Suddenly Mrs. Wilkins found herself leaning across the table. "Are you reading about the mediaeval castle and the wisteria?" she heard herself asking.

Naturally Mrs. Arbuthnot was surprised; but she was not half so much surprised as Mrs. Wilkins was at herself for asking.

Mrs. Arbuthnot had not yet to her knowledge set eyes on the shabby, lank, loosely-put-together figure sitting opposite her, with its small freckled face and big grey eyes almost disappearing under a smashed-down wet-weather hat, and she gazed at her a moment without answering. She was reading about the mediaeval castle and the wisteria, or rather had read about it ten minutes before, and since then had been lost in dreams—of light, of colour, of fragrance, of the soft lapping of the sea among little hot rocks . . .

"Why do you ask me that?" she said in her grave voice, for her training of and by the poor had made her grave and patient.

Mrs. Wilkins flushed and looked excessively shy and frightened. "Oh, only because I saw it too, and I thought perhaps—I thought somehow—" she stammered.

Whereupon Mrs. Arbuthnot, her mind being used to getting people into lists and divisions, from habit considered, as she gazed thoughtfully at Mrs. Wilkins, under what heading, supposing she had to classify her, she could most properly be put.

"And I know you by sight," went on Mrs. Wilkins, who, like all the shy, once she was started; lunged on, frightening herself to more and more speech by the sheer sound of what she had said last in her ears. "Every Sunday—I see you every Sunday in church—"

"In church?" echoed Mrs. Arbuthnot.

"And this seems such a wonderful thing—this advertisement about the wisteria—and—"

Mrs. Wilkins, who must have been at least thirty, broke off and wriggled in her chair with the movement of an awkward and embarrassed schoolgirl.

"It seems so wonderful," she went on in a kind of burst, "and—it is such a miserable day . . ."

And then she sat looking at Mrs. Arbuthnot with the eyes of an imprisoned dog.

"This poor thing," thought Mrs. Arbuthnot, whose life was spent in helping and alleviating, "needs advice."

She accordingly prepared herself patiently to give it.

"If you see me in church," she said, kindly and attentively, "I suppose you live in Hampstead too?"

"Oh yes," said Mrs. Wilkins. And she repeated, her head on its long thin neck drooping a little as if the recollection of Hampstead bowed her, "Oh yes."

"Where?" asked Mrs. Arbuthnot, who, when advice was needed, naturally first proceeded to collect the facts.

But Mrs. Wilkins, laying her hand softly and caressingly on the part of The Times where the advertisement was, as though the mere printed words of it were precious, only said, "Perhaps that is why this seems so wonderful."

"No—I think that's wonderful anyhow," said Mrs. Arbuthnot, forgetting facts and faintly sighing.

"Then you were reading it?"

"Yes," said Mrs. Arbuthnot, her eyes going dreamy again.

"Wouldn't it be wonderful?" murmured Mrs. Wilkins.

"Wonderful," said Mrs. Arbuthnot. Her face, which had lit up, faded into patience again. "Very wonderful," she said. "But it's no use wasting one's time thinking of such things."

"Oh, but it is," was Mrs. Wilkins's quick, surprising reply; surprising because it was so much unlike the rest of her—the characterless coat and skirt, the crumpled hat, the undecided wisp of hair straggling out, "And just the considering of them is worth while in itself—such a change from Hampstead—and sometimes I believe—I really do believe—if one considers hard enough one gets things."

Mrs. Arbuthnot observed her patiently. In what category would she, supposing she had to, put her?

"Perhaps," she said, leaning forward a little, "you will tell me your name. If we are to be friends"—she smiled her grave smile—"as I hope we are, we had better begin at the beginning."

"Oh yes—how kind of you. I'm Mrs. Wilkins," said Mrs. Wilkins. "I don't expect," she added, flushing, as Mrs. Arbuthnot said nothing, "that it conveys anything to you. Sometimes it—it doesn't seem to convey anything to me either. But"—she looked round with a movement of seeking help—"I am Mrs. Wilkins."

She did not like her name. It was a mean, small name, with a kind of facetious twist, she thought, about its end like the upward curve of a pugdog's tail. There it was, however. There was no doing anything with it. Wilkins she was and Wilkins she would remain; and though her husband encouraged her to give it on all occasions as Mrs. Mellersh-Wilkins she only did that when he was within earshot, for she thought Mellersh made Wilkins worse, emphasizing it in the way Chatsworth on the gate-posts of a villa emphasizes the villa.

When first he suggested she should add Mellersh she had objected for the above reason, and after a pause—Mellersh was much too prudent to speak except after a pause, during which presumably he was taking a careful mental copy of his coming observation—he said, much displeased, "But I am not a villa," and looked at her as he looks who hopes, for perhaps the hundredth time, that he may not have married a fool.

Of course he was not a villa, Mrs. Wilkins assured him; she had never supposed he was; she had not dreamed of meaning . . . she was only just thinking . . .

The more she explained the more earnest became Mellersh's hope, familiar to him by this time, for he had then been a husband for two years, that he might not by any chance have married a fool; and they had a prolonged quarrel, if that can be called a quarrel which is conducted with dignified silence on one side and earnest apology on the other, as to whether or no Mrs. Wilkins had intended to suggest that Mr. Wilkins was a villa.

"I believe," she had thought when it was at last over—it took a long while—"that anybody would quarrel about anything when they've not left off being together for a single day for two whole years. What we both need is a holiday."

"My husband," went on Mrs. Wilkins to Mrs. Arbuthnot, trying to throw some light on herself, "is a solicitor. He—" She cast about for something she could say elucidatory of Mellersh, and found: "He's very handsome."

"Well," said Mrs. Arbuthnot kindly, "that must be a great pleasure to you."

"Why?" asked Mrs. Wilkins.

"Because," said Mrs. Arbuthnot, a little taken aback, for constant intercourse with the poor had accustomed her to have her pronouncements accepted without question, "because beauty—handsomeness—is a gift like any other, and if it is properly used—"

She trailed off into silence. Mrs. Wilkins's great grey eyes were fixed on her, and it seemed suddenly to Mrs. Arbuthnot that perhaps she was becoming crystallized into a habit of exposition, and of exposition after the manner of nursemaids, through having an audience that couldn't but agree, that would be afraid, if it wished, to interrupt, that didn't know, that was, in fact, at her mercy.

But Mrs. Wilkins was not listening; for just then, absurd as it seemed, a picture had flashed across her brain, and there were two figures in it sitting together under a great trailing wisteria that stretched across the branches of a tree she didn't know, and it was herself and Mrs. Arbuthnot—she saw them—she saw them. And behind them, bright in sunshine, were old grey walls—the mediaeval castle—she saw it—they were there . . .

She therefore stared at Mrs. Arbuthnot and did not hear a word she said. And Mrs. Arbuthnot stared too at Mrs. Wilkins, arrested by the expression on her face, which was swept by the excitement of what she saw, and was as luminous and tremulous under it as water in sunlight when it is ruffled by a gust of wind. At this moment, if she had been at a party, Mrs. Wilkins would have been looked at with interest.

They stared at each other; Mrs. Arbuthnot surprised, inquiringly, Mrs. Wilkins with the eyes of some one who has had a revelation. Of course. That was how it could be done. She herself, she by herself, couldn't afford it, and wouldn't be able, even if she could afford it, to go there all alone; but she and Mrs. Arbuthnot together . . .

She leaned across the table, "Why don't we try and get it?" she whispered.

Mrs. Arbuthnot became even more wide-eyed. "Get it?" she repeated.

"Yes," said Mrs. Wilkins, still as though she were afraid of being overheard. "Not just sit here and say How wonderful, and then go home to Hampstead without having put out a finger—go home just as usual and see about the dinner and the fish just as we've been doing for years and years and will go on doing for years and years. In fact," said Mrs. Wilkins, flushing to the roots of her hair, for the sound of what she was saying, of what was coming pouring out, frightened her, and yet she couldn't stop, "I see no end to it. There is no end to it. So that there ought to be a break, there ought to be intervals—in everybody's interests. Why, it would really be being unselfish to go away and be happy for a little, because we would come back so much nicer. You see, after a bit everybody needs a holiday."

"But—how do you mean, get it?" asked Mrs. Arbuthnot.

"Take it," said Mrs. Wilkins.

"Take it?"

"Rent it. Hire it. Have it."

"But—do you mean you and I?"

"Yes. Between us. Share. Then it would only cost half, and you look so—you look exactly as if you wanted it just as much as I do—as if you ought to have a rest—have something happy happen to you."

"Why, but we don't know each other."

"But just think how well we would if we went away together for a month! And I've saved for a rainy day—look at it—"

"She is unbalanced," thought Mrs. Arbuthnot; yet she felt strangely stirred.

"Think of getting away for a whole month—from everything—to heaven—"

"She shouldn't say things like that," thought Mrs. Arbuthnot. "The vicar—" Yet she felt strangely stirred. It would indeed be wonderful to have a rest, a cessation.

Habit, however, steadied her again; and years of intercourse with the poor made her say, with the slight though sympathetic superiority of the explainer, "But then, you see, heaven isn't somewhere else. It is here and now. We are told so."

She became very earnest, just as she did when trying patiently to help and enlighten the poor. "Heaven is within us," she said in her gentle low voice. "We are told that on the very highest authority. And you know the lines about the kindred points, don't you—"

"Oh yes, I know them," interrupted Mrs. Wilkins impatiently.

"The kindred points of heaven and home," continued Mrs. Arbuthnot, who was used to finishing her sentences. "Heaven is in our home."

"It isn't," said Mrs. Wilkins, again surprisingly.

Mrs. Arbuthnot was taken aback. Then she said gently, "Oh, but it is. It is there if we choose, if we make it."

"I do choose, and I do make it, and it isn't," said Mrs. Wilkins.

Then Mrs. Arbuthnot was silent, for she too sometimes had doubts about homes. She sat and looked uneasily at Mrs. Wilkins, feeling more and more the urgent need to getting her classified. If she could only classify Mrs. Wilkins, get her safely under her proper heading, she felt that she herself would regain her balance, which did seem very strangely to be slipping all to one side. For neither had she had a holiday for years, and the advertisement when she saw it had set her dreaming, and Mrs. Wilkins's excitement about it was infectious, and she had the sensation, as she listened to her impetuous, odd talk and watched her lit-up face, that she was being stirred out of sleep.

Clearly Mrs. Wilkins was unbalanced, but Mrs. Arbuthnot had met the unbalanced before—indeed she was always meeting them— and they had no effect on her own stability at all; whereas this one was making her feel quite wobbly, quite as though to be off and away, away from her compass points of God, Husband, Home and Duty—she didn't feel as if Mrs. Wilkins intended Mr. Wilkins to

13

come too—and just for once be happy, would be both good and desirable. Which of course it wasn't; which certainly of course it wasn't. She, also, had a nest-egg, invested gradually in the Post Office Savings Bank, but to suppose that she would ever forget her duty to the extent of drawing it out and spending it on herself was surely absurd. Surely she couldn't, she wouldn't ever do such a thing? Surely she wouldn't, she couldn't ever forget her poor, forget misery and sickness as completely as that? No doubt a trip to Italy would be extraordinarily delightful, but there were many delightful things one would like to do, and what was strength given to one for except to help one not to do them?

Steadfast as the points of the compass to Mrs. Arbuthnot were the great four facts of life: God, Husband, Home, Duty. She had gone to sleep on these facts years ago, after a period of much misery, her head resting on them as on a pillow; and she had a great dread of being awakened out of so simple and untroublesome a condition. Therefore it was that she searched with earnestness for a heading under which to put Mrs. Wilkins, and in this way illumine and steady her own mind; and sitting there looking at her uneasily after her last remark, and feeling herself becoming more and more unbalanced and infected, she decided pro tem, as the vicar said at meetings, to put her under the heading Nerves. It was just possible that she ought to go straight into the category Hysteria, which was often only the antechamber to Lunacy, but Mrs. Arbuthnot had learned not to hurry people into their final categories, having on more than one occasion discovered with dismay that she had made a mistake; and how difficult it had been to get them out again, and how crushed she had been with the most terrible remorse.

Yes. Nerves. Probably she had no regular work for others, thought Mrs. Arbuthnot; no work that would take her outside herself. Evidently she was rudderless—blown about by gusts, by impulses. Nerves was almost certainly her category, or would be quite soon if no one helped her. Poor little thing, thought Mrs. Arbuthnot, her own balance returning hand in hand with her compassion, and unable, because of the table, to see the length of Mrs. Wilkins's legs. All she saw was her small, eager, shy face, and her thin shoulders, and the look of childish longing in her eyes for something that she was sure was going to make her happy. No; such things didn't make people happy, such fleeting things. Mrs. Arbuthnot had learned in her long life with Frederick—he was her

14

husband, and she had married him at twenty and was not thirty-three—where alone true joys are to be found. They are to be found, she now knew, only in daily, in hourly, living for others; they are to be found only—hadn't she over and over again taken her disappointments and discouragements there, and come away comforted?—at the feet of God.

Frederick had been the kind of husband whose wife betakes herself early to the feet of God. From him to them had been a short though painful step. It seemed short to her in retrospect, but I had really taken the whole of the first year of their marriage, and every inch of the way had been a struggle, and every inch of it was stained, she felt at the time, with her heart's blood. All that was over now. She had long since found peace. And Frederick, from her passionately loved bridegroom, from her worshipped young husband, had become second only to God on her list of duties and forbearances. There he hung, the second in importance, a bloodless thing bled white by her prayers. For years she had been able to be happy only by forgetting happiness. She wanted to stay like that. She wanted to shut out everything that would remind her of beautiful things, that might set her off again long, desiring . . .

"I'd like so much to be friends," she said earnestly. "Won't you come and see me, or let me come to you sometimes? Whenever you feel as if you wanted to talk. I'll give you my address"—she searched in her handbag—"and then you won't forget." And she found a card and held it out.

Mrs. Wilkins ignored the card.

"It's so funny," said Mrs. Wilkins, just as if she had not heard her, "But I see us both—you and me—this April in the mediaeval castle."

Mrs. Arbuthnot relapsed into uneasiness. "Do you?" she said, making an effort to stay balanced under the visionary gaze of the shining grey eyes. "Do you?"

"Don't you ever see things in a kind of flash before they happen?" asked Mrs. Wilkins.

"Never," said Mrs. Arbuthnot.

She tried to smile; she tried to smile the sympathetic yet wise and tolerant smile with which she was accustomed to listen to the necessarily biased and incomplete view of the poor. She didn't succeed. The smile trembled out.

15

"Of course," she said in a low voice, almost as if she were afraid the vicar and the Savings Bank were listening, "it would be most beautiful—most beautiful—"

"Even if it were wrong," said Mrs. Wilkins, "it would only be for a month."

"That—" began Mrs. Arbuthnot, quite clear as to the reprehensibleness of such a point of view; but Mrs. Wilkins stopped her before she could finish.

"Anyhow," said Mrs. Wilkins, stopping her, "I'm sure it's wrong to go on being good for too long, till one gets miserable. And I can see you've been good for years and years, because you look so unhappy"—Mrs. Arbuthnot opened her mouth to protest—"and I— I've done nothing but duties, things for other people, ever since I was a girl, and I don't believe anybody loves me a bit—a bit—the b- better—and I long—oh, I long—for something else—something else—"

Was she going to cry? Mrs. Arbuthnot became acutely uncomfortable and sympathetic. She hoped she wasn't going to cry. Not there. Not in that unfriendly room, with strangers coming and going.

But Mrs. Wilkins, after tugging agitatedly at a handkerchief that wouldn't come out of her pocket, did succeed at last in merely apparently blowing her nose with it, and then, blinking her eyes very quickly once or twice, looked at Mrs. Arbuthnot with a quivering air of half humble, half frightened apology, and smiled.

"Will you believe," she whispered, trying to steady her mouth, evidently dreadfully ashamed of herself, "that I've never spoken to any one before in my life like this? I can't think, I simply don't know, what has come over me."

"It's the advertisement," said Mrs. Arbuthnot, nodding gravely.

"Yes," said Mrs. Wilkins, dabbing furtively at her eyes, "and us both being so—"—she blew her nose again a little—"miserable."

Chapter 2

Of Course Mrs. Arbuthnot was not miserable—how could she be, she asked herself, when God was taking care of her?—but she let that pass for the moment unrepudiated, because of her conviction that here was another fellow-creature in urgent need of her help; and not just boots and blankets and better sanitary arrangements this time, but the more delicate help of comprehension, of finding the exact right words.

The exact right words, she presently discovered, after trying various ones about living for others, and prayer, and the peace to be found in placing oneself unreservedly in God's hands—to meet all these words Mrs. Wilkins had other words, incoherent and yet, for the moment at least, till one had had more time, difficult to answer—the exact right words were a suggestion that it would do no harm to answer the advertisement. Non-committal. Mere inquiry. And what disturbed Mrs. Arbuthnot about this suggestion was that she did not make it solely to comfort Mrs. Wilkins; she made it because of her own strange longing for the mediaeval castle.

This was very disturbing. There she was, accustomed to direct, to lead, to advise, to support—except Frederick; she long since had learned to leave Frederick to God—being led herself, being influenced and thrown off her feet, by just an advertisement, by just an incoherent stranger. It was indeed disturbing. She failed to understand her sudden longing for what was, after all, self-indulgence, when for years no such desire had entered her heart.

"There's no harm in simply asking," she said in a low voice, as if the vicar and the Savings Bank and all her waiting and dependent poor were listening and condemning.

"It isn't as if it committed us to anything," said Mrs. Wilkins, also in a low voice, but her voice shook.

They got up simultaneously—Mrs. Arbuthnot had a sensation of surprise that Mrs. Wilkins should be so tall—and went to a writing-table, and Mrs. Arbuthnot wrote to Z, Box 1000, The Times, for particulars. She asked for all particulars, but the only one they really wanted was the one about the rent. They both felt that it was Mrs. Arbuthnot who ought to write the letter and do the business part. Not only was she used to organizing and being practical, but she also was older, and certainly calmer; and she herself had no doubt too that she was wiser. Neither had Mrs. Wilkins any doubt of this; the very way Mrs. Arbuthnot parted her hair suggested a great calm that could only proceed from wisdom.

But if she was wiser, older and calmer, Mrs. Arbuthnot's new friend nevertheless seemed to her to be the one who impelled. Incoherent, she yet impelled. She appeared to have, apart from her need of help, an upsetting kind of character. She had a curious infectiousness. She led one on. And the way her unsteady mind leaped at conclusions—wrong ones, of course; witness the one that she, Mrs. Arbuthnot, was miserable—the way she leaped at conclusions was disconcerting.

Whatever she was, however, and whatever her unsteadiness, Mrs. Arbuthnot found herself sharing her excitement and her longing; and when the letter had been posted in the letter-box in the hall and actually was beyond getting back again, both she and Mrs. Wilkins felt the same sense of guilt.

"It only shows," said Mrs. Wilkins in a whisper, as they turned away from the letter-box, "how immaculately good we've been all our lives. The very first time we do anything our husbands don't know about we feel guilty."

"I'm afraid I can't say I've been immaculately good," gently protested Mrs. Arbuthnot, a little uncomfortable at this fresh example of successful leaping at conclusions, for she had not said a word about her feeling of guilt.

"Oh, but I'm sure you have—I see you being good—and that's why you're not happy."

"She shouldn't say things like that," thought Mrs. Arbuthnot. "I must try and help her not to."

Aloud she said gravely, "I don't know why you insist that I'm not happy. When you know me better I think you'll find that I am. And I'm sure you don't mean really that goodness, if one could attain it, makes one unhappy."

"Yes, I do," said Mrs. Wilkins. "Our sort of goodness does. We have attained it, and we are unhappy. There are miserable sorts of goodness and happy sorts—the sort we'll have at the mediaeval castle, for instance, is the happy sort."

"That is, supposing we go there," said Mrs. Arbuthnot restrainingly. She felt that Mrs. Wilkins needed holding on to. "After all, we've only written just to ask. Anybody may do that. I think it quite likely we shall find the conditions impossible, and even if they were not, probably by to-morrow we shall not want to go."

"I see us there," was Mrs. Wilkins's answer to that.

All this was very unbalancing. Mrs. Arbuthnot, as she presently splashed though the dripping streets on her way to a meeting she was to speak at, was in an unusually disturbed condition of mind. She had, she hoped, shown herself very calm to Mrs. Wilkins, very practical and sober, concealing her own excitement. But she was really extraordinarily moved, and she felt happy, and she felt guilty, and she felt afraid, and she had all the feelings, though this she did not know, of a woman who was come away from a secret meeting with her lover. That, indeed, was what she looked like when she arrived late on her platform; she, the open-browed, looked almost furtive as her eyes fell on the staring wooden faces waiting to hear her try and persuade them to contribute to the alleviation of the urgent needs of the Hampstead poor, each one convinced that they needed contributions themselves. She looked as though she were hiding something discreditable but delightful. Certainly her customary clear expression of candor was not there, and its place was taken by a kind of suppressed and frightened pleasedness, which would have led a more worldly-minded audience to the instant conviction of recent and probably impassioned lovemaking.

Beauty, beauty, beauty . . . the words kept ringing in her ears as she stood on the platform talking of sad things to the sparsely attended meeting. She had never been to Italy. Was that really what her nest-egg was to be spent on after all? Though she couldn't approve of the way Mrs. Wilkins was introducing the idea of predestination into her immediate future, just as if she had no choice, just as if to struggle, or even to reflect, were useless, it yet influenced her. Mrs. Wilkins's eyes had been the eyes of a seer. Some people were like that, Mrs. Arbuthnot knew; and if Mrs. Wilkins had actually seen her at the mediaeval castle it did seem probable that struggling would be a waste of time. Still, to spend her nest-egg on self-indulgence— The origin of this egg had been corrupt, but she had at least supposed its end was to be creditable. Was she to deflect it from its intended destination, which alone had appeared to justify her keeping it, and spend it on giving herself pleasure?

Mrs. Arbuthnot spoke on and on, so much practiced in the kind of speech that she could have said it all in her sleep, and at the end

19

of the meeting, her eyes dazzled by her secret visions, she hardly noticed that nobody was moved in any way whatever, least of all in the way of contributions.

But the vicar noticed. The vicar was disappointed. Usually his good friend and supporter Mrs. Arbuthnot succeeded better than this. And, what was even more unusual, she appeared, he observed, not even to mind.

"I can't imagine," he said to her as they parted, speaking irritably, for he was irritated both by the audience and by her, "what these people are coming to. Nothing seems to move them."

"Perhaps they need a holiday," suggested Mrs. Arbuthnot; an unsatisfactory, a queer reply, the vicar thought.

"In February?" he called after her sarcastically.

"Oh no—not till April," said Mrs. Arbuthnot over her shoulder.

"Very odd," thought the vicar. "Very odd indeed." And he went home and was not perhaps quite Christian to his wife.

That night in her prayers Mrs. Arbuthnot asked for guidance. She felt she ought really to ask, straight out and roundly, that the mediaeval castle should already have been taken by some one else and the whole thing thus be settled, but her courage failed her. Suppose her prayer were to be answered? No; she couldn't ask it; she couldn't risk it. And after all—she almost pointed this out to God—if she spent her present nest-egg on a holiday she could quite soon accumulate another. Frederick pressed money on her; and it would only mean, while she rolled up a second egg, that for a time her contributions to the parish charities would be less. And then it could be the next nest-egg whose original corruption would be purged away by the use to which it was finally put.

For Mrs. Arbuthnot, who had no money of her own, was obliged to live on the proceeds of Frederick's activities, and her very nest-egg was the fruit, posthumously ripened, of ancient sin. The way Frederick made his living was one of the standing distresses of her life. He wrote immensely popular memoirs, regularly, every year, of the mistresses of kings. There were in history numerous kings who had had mistresses, and there were still more numerous mistresses who had had kings; so that he had been able to publish a book of memoirs during each year of his married life, and even so there were greater further piles of these ladies waiting to be dealt with. Mrs. Arbuthnot was helpless. Whether she liked it or not, she was obliged to live on the proceeds. He gave her a dreadful sofa once, after the success of his Du Barri memoir, with swollen cushions and soft, receptive lap, and it seemed to her a miserable thing that there, in her very home, should flaunt this re-incarnation of a dead old French sinner.

Simply good, convinced that morality is the basis of happiness, the fact that she and Frederick should draw their sustenance from guilt, however much purged by the passage of centuries, was one of the secret reasons of her sadness. The more the memoired lady had forgotten herself, the more his book about her was read and the more free-handed he was to his wife; and all that he gave her was spent, after adding slightly to her nest-egg—for she did hope and believe that some day people would cease to want to read of wickedness, and then Frederick would need supporting—on helping the poor. The parish flourished because, to take a handful at random, of the ill-behavior of the ladies Du Barri, Montespan, Pompadour, Ninon de l'Enclos, and even of learned Maintenon. The poor were the filter through which the money was passed, to come out, Mrs. Arbuthnot hoped, purified. She could do no more. She had tried in days gone by to think the situation out, to discover the exact right course for her to take, but had found it, as she had found Frederick, too difficult, and had left it, as she had left Frederick, to God. Nothing of this money was spent on her house or dress; those remained, except for the great soft sofa, austere. It was the poor who profited. Their very boots were stout with sins. But how difficult it had been. Mrs. Arbuthnot, groping for guidance, prayed about it to exhaustion. Ought she perhaps to refuse to touch the money, to avoid it as she would have avoided the sins which were its source? But then what about the parish's boots? She asked the vicar what he thought, and through much delicate language, evasive and cautious, it did finally appear that he was for the boots.

At least she had persuaded Frederick, when first he began his terrible successful career—he only began it after their marriage; when she married him he had been a blameless official attached to the library of the British Museum—to publish the memoirs under another name, so that she was not publicly branded. Hampstead read the books with glee, and had no idea that their writer lived in its midst. Frederick was almost unknown, even by sight, in Hampstead. He never went to any of its gatherings. Whatever it was he did in the way of recreation was done in London, but he never spoke of what he did or whom he saw; he might have been perfectly friendless for any mention he ever made of friends to his wife. Only the vicar knew where the money for the parish came from, and he regarded it, he told Mrs. Arbuthnot, as a matter of honour not to mention it.

And at least her little house was not haunted by the loose lived ladies, for Frederick did his work away from home. He had two rooms near the British Museum, which was the scene of his exhumations, and there he went every morning, and he came back long after his wife was asleep. Sometimes he did not come back at all. Sometimes she did not see him for several days together. Then he would suddenly appear at breakfast, having let himself in with his latchkey the night before, very jovial and good-natured and free-handed and glad if she would allow him to give her something—a well-fed man, contented with the world; a jolly, full-blooded, satisfied man. And she was always gentle, and anxious that his coffee should be as he liked it.

He seemed very happy. Life, she often thought, however much one tabulated was yet a mystery. There were always some people it was impossible to place. Frederick was one of them. He didn't seem to bear the remotest resemblance to the original Frederick. He didn't seem to have the least need of any of the things he used to say were so important and beautiful—love, home, complete communion of thoughts, complete immersion in each other's interests. After those early painful attempts to hold him up to the point from which they had hand in hand so splendidly started, attempts in which she herself had got terribly hurt and the Frederick she supposed she had married was mangled out of recognition, she hung him up finally by her bedside as the chief subject of her prayers, and left him, except for those, entirely to God. She had loved Frederick too deeply to be able now to do anything but pray for him. He had no idea that he never went out of the house without her blessing going with him too, hovering, like a little echo of finished love, round that once dear head. She didn't dare think of him as he used to be, as he had seemed to her to be in those marvelous first days of their love-making, of their marriage. Her child had died; she had nothing, nobody of her own to lavish herself on. The poor became her children, and God the object of her love. What could be happier than such a life, she sometimes asked herself; but her face, and particularly her eyes, continued sad.

"Perhaps when we're old . . . perhaps when we are both quite old . . ." she would think wistfully.

Chapter 3

The owner of the mediaeval castle was an Englishman, a Mr. Briggs, who was in London at the moment and wrote that it had beds enough for eight people, exclusive of servants, three sitting-rooms, battlements, dungeons, and electric light. The rent was £60 for the month, the servants' wages were extra, and he wanted references—he wanted assurances that the second half of his rent would be paid, the first half being paid in advance, and he wanted assurances of respectability from a solicitor, or a doctor, or a clergyman. He was very polite in his letter, explaining that his desire for references was what was usual and should be regarded as a mere formality.

Mrs. Arbuthnot and Mrs. Wilkins had not thought of references, and they had not dreamed a rent could be so high. In their minds had floated sums like three guineas a week; or less, seeing that the place was small and old.

Sixty pounds for a single month.

It staggered them.

Before Mrs. Arbuthnot's eyes rose up boots: endless vistas, all the stout boots that sixty pounds would buy; and besides the rent there would be the servants' wages and the food, and the railway journeys out and home. While as for references, these did indeed seem a stumbling-block; it did seem impossible to give any without making their plan more public than they had intended.

They had both—even Mrs. Arbuthnot, lured for once away from perfect candour by the realization of the great saving of trouble and criticism an imperfect explanation would produce—they had both thought it would be a good plan to give out, each to her own circle, their circles being luckily distinct, that each was going to stay with a friend who had a house in Italy. It would be true as far as it went—Mrs. Wilkins asserted that it would be quite true, but Mrs. Arbuthnot thought it wouldn't be quite—and it was the only way, Mrs. Wilkins said, to keep Mellersh even approximately quiet. To spend any of her money just on the mere getting to Italy would cause him indignation; what he would say if he knew she was renting part of a mediaeval castle on her own account Mrs. Wilkins preferred not to think. It would take him days to say it all; and this although it was her very own money, and not a penny of it had ever been his.

"But I expect," she said, "your husband is just the same. I expect all husbands are alike in the long run."

Mrs. Arbuthnot said nothing, because her reason for not wanting Frederick to know was the exactly opposite one—Frederick would by only to pleased for her to go, he would not mind it in the very least; indeed, he would hail such a manifestation of self-indulgence and worldliness with an amusement that would hurt, and urge her to have a good time and not to hurry home with a crushing detachment. Far better, she thought, to be missed by Mellersh than to be sped by Frederick. To be missed, to be needed, from whatever motive, was, she thought, better than the complete loneliness of not being missed or needed at all.

She therefore said nothing, and allowed Mrs. Wilkins to leap at her conclusions unchecked. But they did, both of them, for a whole day feel that the only thing to be done was to renounce the mediaeval castle; and it was in arriving at this bitter decision that they really realized how acute had been their longing for it.

Then Mrs. Arbuthnot, whose mind was trained in the finding of ways out of difficulties, found a way out of the reference difficulty; and simultaneously Mrs. Wilkins had a vision revealing to her how to reduce the rent.

Mrs. Arbuthnot's plan was simple, and completely successful. She took the whole of the rent in person to the owner, drawing it out of her Savings Bank—again she looked furtive and apologetic, as if the clerk must know the money was wanted for purposes of self-indulgence—and, going up with the six ten pound notes in her hand-bag to the address near the Brompton Oratory where the owner lived, presented them to him, waiving her right to pay only half. And when he saw her, and her parted hair and soft dark eyes and sober apparel, and heard her grave voice, he told her not to bother about writing round for those references.

"It'll be all right," he said, scribbling a receipt for the rent. "Do sit down, won't you? Nasty day, isn't it? You'll find the old castle has lots of sunshine, whatever else it hasn't got. Husband going?"

Mrs. Arbuthnot, unused to anything but candour, looked troubled at this question and began to murmur inarticulately, and the owner at once concluded that she was a widow—a war one, of course, for other widows were old—and that he had been a fool not to guess it.

"Oh, I'm sorry," he said, turning red right up to his fair hair. "I didn't mean—h'm, h'm, h'm—"

He ran his eye over the receipt he had written. "Yes, I think that's all right," he said, getting up and giving it to her. "Now," he added, taking the six notes she held out and smiling, for Mrs. Arbuthnot was agreeable to look at, "I'm richer, and you're happier. I've got money, and you've got San Salvatore. I wonder got is best."

"I think you know," said Mrs. Arbuthnot with her sweet smile.

He laughed and opened the door for her. It was a pity the interview was over. He would have liked to ask her to lunch with him. She made him think of his mother, of his nurse, of all things kind and comforting, besides having the attraction of not being his mother or his nurse.

"I hope you'll like the old place," he said, holding her hand a minute at the door. The very feel of her hand, even through its glove, was reassuring; it was the sort of hand, he thought, that children would like to hold in the dark. "In April, you know, it's simply a mass of flowers. And then there's the sea. You must wear white. You'll fit in very well. There are several portraits of you there."

"Portraits?"

"Madonnas, you know. There's one on the stairs really exactly like you."

Mrs. Arbuthnot smiled and said good-bye and thanked him. Without the least trouble and at once she had got him placed in his proper category: he was an artist and of an effervescent temperament.

She shook hands and left, and he wished she hadn't. After she was gone he supposed that he ought to have asked for those references, if only because she would think him so unbusiness-like not to, but he could as soon have insisted on references from a saint in a nimbus as from that grave, sweet lady.

Rose Arbuthnot.

Her letter, making the appointment, lay on the table.

Pretty name.

That difficulty, then, was overcome. But there still remained the other one, the really annihilating effect of the expense on the nest-eggs, and especially on Mrs. Wilkins's, which was in size, compared with Mrs. Arbuthnot's, as the egg of the plover to that of the duck; and this in its turn was overcome by the vision vouchsafed to Mrs.

Wilkins, revealing to her the steps to be taken for its overcoming. Having got San Salvatore—the beautiful, the religious name, fascinated them—they in their turn would advertise in the Agony Column of The Times, and would inquire after two more ladies, of similar desires to their own, to join them and share the expenses.

At once the strain of the nest-eggs would be reduced from half to a quarter. Mrs. Wilkins was prepared to fling her entire egg into the adventure, but she realized that if it were to cost even sixpence over her ninety pounds her position would be terrible. Imagine going to Mellersh and saying, "I owe." It would be awful enough if some day circumstances forced her to say, "I have no nest-egg," but at least she would be supported in such a case by the knowledge that the egg had been her own. She therefore, though prepared to fling her last penny into the adventure, was not prepared to fling into it a single farthing that was not demonstrably her own; and she felt that if her share of the rent was reduced to fifteen pounds only, she would have a safe margin for the other expenses. Also they might economise very much on food—gather olives off their own trees and eat them, for instance, and perhaps catch fish.

Of course, as they pointed out to each other, they could reduce the rent to an almost negligible sum by increasing the number of sharers; they could have six more ladies instead of two if they wanted to, seeing that there were eight beds. But supposing the eight beds were distributed in couples in four rooms, it would not be altogether what they wanted, to find themselves shut up at night with a stranger. Besides they thought that perhaps having so many would not be quite so peaceful. After all, they were going to San Salvatore for peace and rest and joy, and six more ladies, especially if they got into one's bedroom, might a little interfere with that.

However, there seemed to be only two ladies in England at that moment who had any wish to join them, for they had only two answers to their advertisement.

"Well, we only want two," said Mrs. Wilkins, quickly recovering, for she had imagined a great rush.

"I think a choice would have been a good thing," said Mrs. Arbuthnot.

"You mean because then we needn't have had Lady Caroline Dester."

"I didn't say that," gently protested Mrs. Arbuthnot.

"We needn't have her," said Mrs. Wilkins. "Just one more person would help us a great deal with the rent. We're not obliged to have two."

"But why should we not have her? She seems really quite what we want."

"Yes—she does from her letter," said Mrs. Wilkins doubtfully.

She felt she would be terribly shy of Lady Caroline. Incredible as it may seem, seeing how they get into everything, Mrs. Wilkins had never come across any members of the aristocracy.

They interviewed Lady Caroline, and they interviewed the other applicant, a Mrs. Fisher.

Lady Caroline came to the club in Shaftesbury Avenue, and appeared to be wholly taken up by one great longing, a longing to get away from everybody she had ever known. When she saw the club, and Mrs. Arbuthnot, and Mrs. Wilkins, she was sure that here was exactly what she wanted. She would be in Italy—a place she adored; she would not be in hotels—places she loathed; she would not be staying with friends—persons she disliked; and she would be in the company of strangers who would never mention a single person she knew, for the simple reason that they had not, could not have, and would not come across them. She asked a few questions about the fourth woman, and was satisfied with the answers. Mrs. Fisher, of Prince of Wales Terrace. A widow. She too would be unacquainted with any of her friends. Lady Caroline did not even know where Prince of Wales Terrace was.

"It's in London," said Mrs. Arbuthnot.

"Is it?" said Lady Caroline.

It all seemed most restful.

Mrs. Fisher was unable to come to the club because, she explained by letter, she could not walk without a stick; therefore Mrs. Arbuthnot and Mrs. Wilkins went to her.

"But if she can't come to the club how can she go to Italy?" wondered Mrs. Wilkins, aloud.

"We shall hear that from her own lips," said Mrs. Arbuthnot.

From Mrs. Fisher's lips they merely heard, in reply to delicate questioning, that sitting in trains was not walking about; and they knew that already. Except for the stick, however, she appeared to be a most desirable fourth—quiet, educated, elderly. She was much older than they or Lady Caroline—Lady Caroline had informed them she was twenty-eight—but not so old as to have ceased to be

27

active-minded. She was very respectable indeed, and still wore a complete suit of black though her husband had died, she told them, eleven years before. Her house was full of signed photographs of illustrious Victorian dead, all of whom she said she had known when she was little. Her father had been an eminent critic, and in his house she had seen practically everybody who was anybody in letters and art. Carlyle had scowled at her; Matthew Arnold had held her on his knee; Tennyson had sonorously rallied her on the length of her pig-tail. She animatedly showed them the photographs, hung everywhere on her walls, pointing out the signatures with her stick, and she neither gave any information about her own husband nor asked for any about the husbands of her visitors; which was the greatest comfort. Indeed, she seemed to think that they also were widows, for on inquiring who the fourth lady was to be, and being told it was a Lady Caroline Dester, she said, "Is she a widow too?" And on their explaining that she was not, because she had not yet been married, observed with abstracted amiability, "All in good time."

But Mrs. Fisher's very abstractedness—and she seemed to be absorbed chiefly in the interesting people she used to know and in their memorial photographs, and quite a good part of the interview was taken up by reminiscent anecdote of Carlyle, Meredith, Matthew Arnold, Tennyson, and a host of others—her very abstractedness was a recommendation. She only asked, she said, to be allowed to sit quiet in the sun and remember. That was all Mrs. Arbuthnot and Mrs. Wilkins asked of their sharers. It was their idea of a perfect sharer that she should sit quiet in the sun and remember, rousing herself on Saturday evenings sufficiently to pay her share. Mrs. Fisher was very fond, too, she said, of flowers, and once when she was spending a week-end with her father at Box Hill—

"Who lived at Box Hill?" interrupted Mrs. Wilkins, who hung on Mrs. Fisher's reminiscences, intensely excited by meeting somebody who had actually been familiar with all the really and truly and undoubtedly great—actually seen them, heard them talking, touched them.

Mrs. Fisher looked at her over the top of her glasses in some surprise. Mrs. Wilkins, in her eagerness to tear the heart out quickly of Mrs. Fisher's reminiscences, afraid that at any moment Mrs. Arbuthnot would take her away and she wouldn't have heard half, had already interrupted several times with questions which appeared ignorant to Mrs. Fisher.

"Meredith of course," said Mrs. Fisher rather shortly. "I remember a particular week-end"—she continued. "My father often took me, but I always remember this week-end particularly—"

"Did you know Keats?" eagerly interrupted Mrs. Wilkins.

Mrs. Fisher, after a pause, said with sub-acid reserve that she had been unacquainted with both Keats and Shakespeare.

"Oh of course—how ridiculous of me!" cried Mrs. Wilkins, flushing scarlet. "It's because"—she floundered—"it's because the immortals somehow still seem alive, don't they—as if they were here, going to walk into the room in another minute—and one forgets they are dead. In fact one knows perfectly well that they're not dead—not nearly so dead as you and I even now," she assured Mrs. Fisher, who observed her over the top of her glasses.

"I thought I saw Keats the other day," Mrs. Wilkins incoherently proceeded, driven on by Mrs. Fisher's look over the top of her glasses. "In Hampstead—crossing the road in front of that house—you know—the house where he lived—"

Mrs. Arbuthnot said they must be going.

Mrs. Fisher did nothing to prevent them.

"I really thought I saw him," protested Mrs. Wilkins, appealing for belief first to one and then to the other while waves of colour passed over her face, and totally unable to stop because of Mrs. Fisher's glasses and the steady eyes looking at her over their tops. "I believe I did see him—he was dressed in a—"

Even Mrs. Arbuthnot looked at her now, and in her gentlest voice said they would be late for lunch.

It was at this point that Mrs. Fisher asked for references. She had no wish to find herself shut up for four weeks with somebody who saw things. It is true that there were three sitting-rooms, besides the garden and the battlements at San Salvatore, so that there would be opportunities of withdrawal from Mrs. Wilkins; but it would be disagreeable to Mrs. Fisher, for instance, if Mrs. Wilkins were suddenly to assert that she saw Mr. Fisher. Mr. Fisher was dead; let him remain so. She had no wish to be told he was walking about the garden. The only reference she really wanted, for she was much too old and firmly seated in her place in the world for questionable associates to matter to her, was one with regard to Mrs. Wilkins's health. Was her health quite normal? Was she an ordinary, everyday, sensible woman? Mrs. Fisher felt that if she were given even one address she would be able to find out what she needed. So she asked for references, and her visitors appeared to be so much taken aback—Mrs. Wilkins, indeed, was instantly sobered—that she added, "It is usual."

Mrs. Wilkins found her speech first. "But," she said "aren't we the ones who ought to ask for some from you?"

And this seemed to Mrs. Arbuthnot too the right attitude. Surely it was they who were taking Mrs. Fisher into their party, and not Mrs. Fisher who was taking them into it?

For answer Mrs. Fisher, leaning on her stick, went to the writing-table and in a firm hand wrote down three names and offered them to Mrs. Wilkins, and the names were so respectable, more, they were so momentous, they were so nearly august, that just to read them was enough. The President of the Royal Academy, the Archbishop of Canterbury, and the Governor of the Bank of England—who would dare disturb such personages in their meditations with inquires as to whether a female friend of theirs was all she should be?

"They have know me since I was little," said Mrs. Fisher—everybody seemed to have known Mrs. Fisher since or when she was little.

"I don't think references are nice things at all between—between ordinary decent women," burst out Mrs. Wilkins, made courageous by being, as she felt, at bay; for she very well knew that the only reference she could give without getting into trouble was Shoolbred, and she had little confidence in that, as it would be entirely based on Mellersh's fish. "We're not business people. We needn't distrust each other—"

And Mrs. Arbuthnot said, with a dignity that yet was sweet, "I'm afraid references do bring an atmosphere into our holiday plan that isn't quite what we want, and I don't think we'll take yours up or give you any ourselves. So that I suppose you won't wish to join us."

And she held out her hand in good-bye.

Then Mrs. Fisher, her gaze diverted to Mrs. Arbuthnot, who inspired trust and liking even in Tube officials, felt that she would be idiotic to lose the opportunity of being in Italy in the particular conditions offered, and that she and this calm-browed woman between them would certainly be able to curb the other one when

30

she had her attacks. So she said, taking Mrs. Arbuthnot's offered hand, "Very well. I waive references."

She waived references.

The two as they walked to the station in Kensington High Street could not help thinking that this way of putting it was lofty. Even Mrs. Arbuthnot, spendthrift of excuses for lapses, thought Mrs. Fisher might have used other words; and Mrs. Wilkins, by the time she got to the station, and the walk and the struggle on the crowded pavement with other people's umbrellas had warmed her blood, actually suggested waiving Mrs. Fisher.

"If there is any waiving to be done, do let us be the ones who waive," she said eagerly.

But Mrs. Arbuthnot, as usual, held on to Mrs. Wilkins; and presently, having cooled down in the train, Mrs. Wilkins announced that at San Salvatore Mrs. Fisher would find her level. "I see her finding her level there," she said, her eyes very bright.

Whereupon Mrs. Arbuthnot, sitting with her quiet hands folded, turned over in her mind how best she could help Mrs. Wilkins not to see quite so much; or at least, if she must see, to see in silence.

Chapter 4

It had been arranged that Mrs. Arbuthnot and Mrs. Wilkins, traveling together, should arrive at San Salvatore on the evening of March 31st—the owner, who told them how to get there, appreciated their disinclination to begin their time in it on April 1st—and Lady Caroline and Mrs. Fisher, as yet unacquainted and therefore under no obligations to bore each other on the journey, for only towards the end would they find out by a process of sifting who they were, were to arrive on the morning of April 2nd. In this way everything would be got nicely ready for the two who seemed, in spite of the equality of the sharing, yet to have something about them of guests.

There were disagreeable incidents towards the end of March, when Mrs. Wilkins, her heart in her mouth and her face a mixture of guilt, terror and determination, told her husband that she had been invited to Italy, and he declined to believe it. Of course he declined to believe it. Nobody had ever invited his wife to Italy before. There was no precedent. He required proofs. The only proof was Mrs. Arbuthnot, and Mrs. Wilkins had produced her; but after what entreaties, what passionate persuading! Mrs. Arbuthnot had not imagined she would have to face Mr. Wilkins and say things to him that were short of the truth, and it brought home to her what she had for some time suspected, that she was slipping more and more away from God.

Indeed, the whole of March was filled with unpleasant, anxious moments. It was an uneasy month. Mrs. Arbuthnot's conscience, made super-sensitive by years of pampering, could not reconcile what she was doing with its own high standard of what was right. It gave her little peace. It nudged her at her prayers. It punctuated her entreaties for divine guidance with disconcerting questions, such as, "Are you not a hypocrite? Do you really mean that? Would you not, frankly, be disappointed if that prayer were granted?"

The prolonged wet, raw weather was on the side too of her conscience, producing far more sickness than usual among the poor. They had bronchitis; they had fevers; there was no end to the distress. And here she was going off, spending precious money on going off, simply and solely to be happy. One woman. One woman being happy, and these piteous multitudes . . .

She was unable to look the vicar in the face. He did not know, nobody knew, what she was going to do, and from the very beginning she was unable to look anybody in the face. She excused herself from making speeches appealing for money. How could she stand up and ask people for money when she herself was spending so much on her own selfish pleasure? Nor did it help her or quiet her that, having actually told Frederick, in her desire to make up for what she was squandering, that she would be grateful if he would let her have some money, he instantly gave her a cheque for £100. He asked no questions. She was scarlet. He looked at her a moment and then looked away. It was a relief to Frederick that she should take some money. She gave it all immediately to the organization she worked with, and found herself more tangled in doubts than ever.

Mrs. Wilkins, on the contrary, had no doubts. She was quite certain that it was a most proper thing to have a holiday, and altogether right and beautiful to spend one's own hard-collected savings on being happy.

"Think how much nicer we shall be when we come back," she said   to Mrs. Arbuthnot, encouraging that pale lady.

No, Mrs. Wilkins had no doubts, but she had fears; and March was for her too an anxious month, with the unconscious Mr. Wilkins coming back daily to his dinner and eating his fish in the silence of imagined security.

Also things happened so awkwardly. It really is astonishing, how awkwardly they happen. Mrs. Wilkins, who was very careful all this month to give Mellersh only the food he liked, buying it and hovering over its cooking with a zeal more than common, succeeded so well the Mellersh was pleased; definitely pleased; so much pleased that he began to think that he might, after all, have married the right wife instead of, as he had frequently suspected, the wrong one. The result was that on the third Sunday in the month—Mrs. Wilkins had made up her trembling mind that on the fourth Sunday, there being five in that March and it being on the fifth of them that she and Mrs. Arbuthnot were to start, she would tell Mellersh of her invitation—on the third Sunday, then, after a very well-cooked lunch in which the Yorkshire pudding had melted in his mouth and the apricot tart had been so perfect that he ate it all, Mellersh, smoking his cigar by the brightly burning fire the while hail gusts banged on the window, said "I am thinking of taking you to Italy for

Easter." And paused for her astounded and grateful ecstasy.

None came. The silence in the room, except for the hail hitting the windows and the gay roar of the fire, was complete. Mrs. Wilkins could not speak. She was dumbfounded. The next Sunday was the day she had meant to break her news to him, and she had not yet even prepared the form of words in which she would break it.

Mr. Wilkins, who had not been abroad since before the war, and was noticing with increasing disgust, as week followed week of wind and rain, the peculiar persistent vileness of the weather, and slowly conceived a desire to get away from England for Easter. He was doing very well in his business. He could afford a trip. Switzerland was useless in April. There was a familiar sound about Easter in Italy. To Italy he would go; and as it would cause comment if he did not take his wife, take her he must—besides, she would be useful; a second person was always useful in a country whose language one did not speak for holding things, for waiting with the luggage.

He had expected an explosion of gratitude and excitement. The absence of it was incredible. She could not, he concluded, have heard. Probably she was absorbed in some foolish day-dream. It was regrettable how childish she remained.

He turned his head—their chairs were in front of the fire—and looked at her. She was staring straight into the fire, and it was no doubt the fire that made her face so red.

"I am thinking," he repeated, raising his clear, cultivated voice and speaking with acerbity, for inattention at such a moment was deplorable, "of taking you to Italy for Easter. Did you not hear me?"

Yes, she had heard him, and she had been wondering at the extraordinary coincidence—really most extraordinary—she was just going to tell him how—how she had been invited—a friend had invited her—Easter, too—Easter was in April, wasn't it?—-her friend had a—had a house there.

In fact Mrs. Wilkins, driven by terror, guilt and surprise, had been more incoherent if possible than usual.

It was a dreadful afternoon. Mellersh, profoundly indignant, besides having his intended treat coming back on him like a blessing to roost, cross-examined her with the utmost severity. He demanded that she refuse the invitation. He demanded that, since she had so outrageously accepted it without consulting him, she should write and cancel her acceptance. Finding himself up against an unsuspected, shocking rock of obstinacy in her, he then declined to believe she had been invited to Italy at all. He declined to believe in this Mrs. Arbuthnot, of whom till that moment he had never heard; and it was only when the gentle creature was brought round—with such difficulty, with such a desire on her part to throw the whole thing up rather than tell Mr. Wilkins less than the truth—and herself endorsed his wife's statements that he was able to give them credence. He could not but believe Mrs. Arbuthnot. She produced the precise effect on him that she did on Tube officials. She hardly needed to say anything. But that made no difference to her conscience, which knew and would not let her forget that she had given him an incomplete impression. "Do you," asked her conscience, "see any real difference between an incomplete impression and a completely stated lie? God sees none."

The remainder of March was a confused bad dream. Both Mrs. Arbuthnot and Mrs. Wilkins were shattered; try as they would not to, both felt extraordinarily guilty; and when on the morning of the 30th they did finally get off there was no exhilaration about the departure, no holiday feeling at all.

"We've been too good—much too good," Mrs. Wilkins kept on murmuring as they walked up and down the platform at Victoria, having arrived there an hour before they need have, "and that's why we feel as though we're doing wrong. We're brow-beaten—we're not any longer real human beings. Real human beings aren't ever as good as we've been. Oh"—she clenched her thin hands—"to think that we ought to be so happy now, here on the very station, actually starting, and we're not, and it's being spoilt for us just simply because we've spoilt them! What have we done—what have we done, I should like to know," she inquired of Mrs. Arbuthnot indignantly, "except for once want to go away by ourselves and have a little rest from them?"

Mrs. Arbuthnot, patiently pacing, did not ask who she meant by them, because she knew. Mrs. Wilkins meant their husbands, persisting in her assumption that Frederick was as indignant as Mellersh over the departure of his wife, whereas Frederick did not even know his wife had gone.

Mrs. Arbuthnot, always silent about him, had said nothing of this to Mrs. Wilkins. Frederick went too deep into her heart for her to talk about him. He was having an extra bout of work finishing another of those dreadful books, and had been away practically continually the last few weeks, and was away when she left. Why should she tell him beforehand? Sure as she so miserably was that he would have no objection to anything she did, she merely wrote him a note and put it on the hall-table ready for him if and when he should come home. She said she was going for a month's holiday as she needed a rest and she had not had one for so long, and that Gladys, the efficient parlourmaid, had orders to see to his comforts. She did not say where she was going; there was no reason why she should; he would not be interested, he would not care.

The day was wretched, blustering and wet; the crossing was atrocious, and they were very sick. But after having been very sick, just to arrive at Calais and not be sick was happiness, and it was there that the real splendour of what they were doing first began to warm their benumbed spirits. It got hold of Mrs. Wilkins first, and spread from her like a rose-coloured flame over her pale companion. Mellersh at Calais, where they restored themselves with soles because of Mrs. Wilkins's desire to eat a sole Mellersh wasn't having—Mellersh at Calais had already begun to dwindle and seem less important. None of the French porters knew him; not a single official at Calais cared a fig for Mellersh. In Paris there was no time to think of him because their train was late and they only just caught the Turin train at the Gare de Lyons; and by the afternoon of the next day when they got into Italy, England, Frederick, Mellersh, the vicar, the poor, Hampstead, the club, Shoolbred, everybody and everything, the whole inflamed sore dreariness, had faded to the dimness of a dream.

Chapter 5

It was Cloudy in Italy, which surprised them. They had expected brilliant sunshine. But never mind: it was Italy, and the very clouds looked fat. Neither of them had ever been there before. Both gazed out of the windows with rapt faces. The hours flew as long as it was daylight, and after that there was the excitement of getting nearer, getting quite near, getting there. At Genoa it had begun to rain—Genoa! Imagine actually being at Genoa, seeing its name written up in the station just like any other name—at Nervi it was pouring, and when at last towards midnight, for again the train was late, they got to Mezzago, the rain was coming down in what seemed solid sheets. But it was Italy. Nothing it did could be bad. The very rain was different—straight rain, falling properly on to one's umbrella; not that violently blowing English stuff that got in everywhere. And it did leave off; and when it did, behold the earth would be strewn with roses.

Mr. Briggs, San Salvatore's owner, had said, "You get out at Mezzago, and then you drive." But he had forgotten what he amply knew, that trains in Italy are sometimes late, and he had imagined his tenants arriving at Mezzago at eight o'clock and finding a string of flys to choose from.

The train was four hours late, and when Mrs. Arbuthnot and Mrs. Wilkins scrambled down the ladder-like high steps of their carriage into the black downpour, their skirts sweeping off great pools of sooty wet because their hands were full of suit-cases, if it had not been for the vigilance of Domenico, the gardener at San Salvatore, they would have found nothing for them to drive in. All ordinary flys had long since gone home. Domenico, foreseeing this, had sent his aunt's fly, driven by her son his cousin; and his aunt and her fly lived in Castagneto, the village crouching at the feet of San Salvatore, and therefore, however late the train was, the fly would not dare come home without containing that which it had been sent to fetch.

Domenico's cousin's name was Beppo, and he presently emerged out of the dark where Mrs. Arbuthnot and Mrs. Wilkins stood, uncertain what to do next after the train had gone on, for they could see no porter and they thought from the feel of it that they were

37

standing not so much on a platform as in the middle of the permanent way.

Beppo, who had been searching for them, emerged from the dark with a kind of pounce and talked Italian to them vociferously. Beppo was a most respectable young man, but he did not look as if he were, especially not in the dark, and he had a dripping hat slouched over one eye. They did not like the way he seized their suit-cases. He could not be, they thought, a porter. However, they presently from out of his streaming talk discerned the words San Salvatore, and after that they kept on saying them to him, for it was the only Italian they knew, as they hurried after him, unwilling to lose sight of their suit-cases, stumbling across rails and through puddles out to where in the road a small, high fly stood.

Its hood was up, and its horse was in an attitude of thought. They climbed in, and the minute they were in—Mrs. Wilkins, indeed, could hardly be called in—the horse awoke with a start from its reverie and immediately began going home rapidly; without Beppo; without the suit-cases.

Beppo darted after him, making the night ring with his shouts, and caught the hanging reins just in time. He explained proudly, and as it seemed to him with perfect clearness, that the horse always did that, being a fine animal full of corn and blood, and cared for by him, Beppo, as if he were his own son, and the ladies must be alarmed—he had noticed they were clutching each other; but clear, and loud, and profuse of words though he was, they only looked at him blankly.

He went on talking, however, while he piled the suit-cases up round them, sure that sooner or later they must understand him, especially as he was careful to talk very loud and illustrate everything he said with the simplest elucidatory gestures, but they both continued only to look at him. They both, he noticed sympathetically, had white faces, fatigued faces, and they both had big eyes, fatigued eyes. They were beautiful ladies, he thought, and their eyes, looking at him over the tops of the suit-cases watching his every movement—there were no trunks, only numbers of suit-cases—were like the eyes of the Mother of God. The only thing the ladies said, and they repeated it at regular intervals, even after they had started, gently prodding him as he sat on his box to call his attention to it, was, "San Salvatore?"

And each time he answered vociferously, encouragingly, "Si, si—
San Salvatore."

"We don't know of course if he's taking us there," said Mrs. Arbuthnot at last in a low voice, after they had been driving as it seemed to them a long while, and had got off the paving-stones of the sleep-shrouded town and were out on a winding road with what they could just see was a low wall on their left beyond which was a great black emptiness and the sound of the sea. On their right was something close and steep and high and black—rocks, they whispered to each other; huge rocks.

They felt very uncomfortable. It was so late. It was so dark. The road was so lonely. Suppose a wheel came off. Suppose they met Fascisti, or the opposite of Fascisti. How sorry they were now that they had not slept at Genoa and come on the next morning in daylight.

"But that would have been the first of April," said Mrs. Wilkins, in a low voice.

"It is that now," said Mrs. Arbuthnot beneath her breath.

"So it is," murmured Mrs. Wilkins.

They were silent.

Beppo turned round on his box—a disquieting habit already noticed, for surely his horse ought to be carefully watched—and again addressed them with what he was convinced was lucidity—no patois, and the clearest explanatory movements.

How much they wished their mothers had made them learn Italian when they were little. If only now they could have said, "Please sit round the right way and look after the horse." They did not even know what horse was in Italian. It was contemptible to be so ignorant.

In their anxiety, for the road twisted round great jutting rocks, and on their left was only the low wall to keep them out of the sea should anything happen, they too began to gesticulate, waving their hands at Beppo, pointing ahead. They wanted him to turn round again and face his horse, that was all. He thought they wanted him to drive faster; and there followed a terrifying ten minutes during which, as he supposed, he was gratifying them. He was proud of his horse, and it could go very fast. He rose in his seat, the whip cracked, the horse rushed forward, the rocks leaped towards them, the little fly swayed, the suit-cases heaved, Mrs. Arbuthnot and Mrs. Wilkins clung. In this way they continued, swaying, heaving, clattering, clinging, till at a point near Castagneto there was a rise in the road, and on reaching the foot of the rise the horse, who knew every inch of the way, stopped suddenly, throwing everything in the fly into a heap, and then proceeded up at the slowest of walks.

Beppo twisted himself round to receive their admiration, laughingwith pride in his horse.

There was no answering laugh from the beautiful ladies. Their eyes, fixed on him, seemed bigger than ever, and their faces against the black of the night showed milky.

But here at least, once they were up the slope, were houses. The rocks left off, and there were houses; the low wall left off, and there were houses; the sea shrunk away, and the sound of it ceased, and the loneliness of the road was finished. No lights anywhere, of course, nobody to see them pass; and yet Beppo, when the houses began, after looking over his shoulder and shouting "Castagneto" at the ladies, once more stood up and cracked his whip and once more made his horse dash forward.

"We shall be there in a minute," Mrs. Arbuthnot said to herself, holding on.

"We shall soon stop now," Mrs. Wilkins said to herself, holding on. They said nothing aloud, because nothing would have been heard above the whip-cracking and the wheel-clattering and the boisterous inciting noises Beppo was making at his horse.

Anxiously they strained their eyes for any sight of the beginning of San Salvatore.

They had supposed and hoped that after a reasonable amount of village a mediaeval archway would loom upon them, and through it they would drive into a garden and draw up at an open, welcoming door, with light streaming from it and those servants standing in it who, according to the advertisement, remained.

Instead the fly suddenly stopped.

Peering out they could see they were still in the village street, with small dark houses each side; and Beppo, throwing the reins over the horse's back as if completely confident this time that he would not go any farther, got down off his box. At the same moment, springing as it seemed out of nothing, a man and several half-grown boys appeared on each side of the fly and began dragging out the suit-cases.

"No, no—San Salvatore, San Salvatore"—exclaimed Mrs. Wilkins, trying to hold on to what suit-cases she could.

"Si, si—San Salvatore," they all shouted, pulling.

"This can't be San Salvatore," said Mrs. Wilkins, turning to Mrs. Arbuthnot, who sat quite still watching her suit-cases being taken from her with the same patience she applied to lesser evils. She knew she could do nothing if these men were wicked men determined to have her suit-cases.

"I don't think it can be," she admitted, and could not refrain from a moment's wonder at the ways of God. Had she really been brought here, she and poor Mrs. Wilkins, after so much trouble in arranging it, so much difficulty and worry, along such devious paths of prevarication and deceit, only to be—

She checked her thoughts, and gently said to Mrs. Wilkins, while the ragged youths disappeared with the suit-cases into the night and the man with the lantern helped Beppo pull the rug off her, that they were both in God's hands; and for the first time on hearing this, Mrs. Wilkins was afraid.

There was nothing for it but to get out. Useless to try to go on sitting in the fly repeating San Salvatore. Every time they said it, and their voices each time were fainter, Beppo and the other man merely echoed it in a series of loud shouts. If only they had learned Italian when they were little. If only they could have said, "We wish to be driven to the door." But they did not even know what door was in Italian. Such ignorance was not only contemptible, it was, they now saw, definitely dangerous. Useless, however, to lament it now. Useless to put off whatever it was that was going to happen to them by trying to go on sitting in the fly. They therefore got out.

The two men opened their umbrellas for them and handed them to them. From this they received a faint encouragement, because they could not believe that if these men were wicked they would pause to open umbrellas. The man with the lantern then made signs to them to follow him, talking loud and quickly, and Beppo, they noticed, remained behind. Ought they to pay him? Not, they thought, if they were going to be robbed and perhaps murdered. Surely on such an occasion one did not pay. Besides, he had not after all brought them to San Salvatore. Where they had got to was evidently somewhere else. Also, he did not show the least wish to be paid; he let them go away into the night with no clamour at all. This, they could not help thinking, was a bad sign. He asked for nothing because presently he was to get so much.

They came to some steps. The road ended abruptly in a church and some descending steps. The man held the lantern low for them to see the steps.

"San Salvatore?" said Mrs. Wilkins once again, very faintly, before committing herself to the steps. It was useless to mention it now, of course, but she could not go down steps in complete silence. No mediaeval castle, she was sure, was ever built at the bottom of steps.

Again, however, came the echoing shout—"Si, si—San Salvatore."

They descended gingerly, holding up their skirts just as if they would be wanting them another time and had not in all probability finished with skirts for ever.

The steps ended in a steeply sloping path with flat stone slabs down the middle. They slipped a good deal on these wet slabs, and the man with the lantern, talking loud and quickly, held them up. His way of holding them up was polite.

"Perhaps," said Mrs. Wilkins in a low voice to Mrs. Arbuthnot, "It is all right after all."

"We're in God's hands," said Mrs. Arbuthnot again; and again Mrs.
Wilkins was afraid.

They reached the bottom of the sloping path, and the light of the lantern flickered over an open space with houses round three sides. The sea was the fourth side, lazily washing backwards and forwards on pebbles.

"San Salvatore," said the man pointing with his lantern to a black mass curved round the water like an arm flung about it.

They strained their eyes. They saw the black mass, and on the top of it a light.

"San Salvatore?" they both repeated incredulously, for where were the suit-cases, and why had they been forced to get out of the fly?

"Si, si—San Salvatore."

They went along what seemed to be a quay, right on the edge of the water. There was not even a low wall here—nothing to prevent the man with the lantern tipping them in if he wanted to. He did not, however, tip them in. Perhaps it was all right after all, Mrs. Wilkins again suggested to Mrs. Arbuthnot on noticing this, who this time was herself beginning to think that it might be, and said no more about God's hands.

The flicker of the lantern danced along, reflected in the wet pavement of the quay. Out to the left, in the darkness and evidently at the end of a jetty, was a red light. They came to an archway with a heavy iron gate. The man with the lantern pushed the gate open. This time they went up steps instead of down, and at the top of them was a little path that wound upwards among flowers. They could not see the flowers, but the whole place was evidently full of them.

It here dawned on Mrs. Wilkins that perhaps the reason why the fly had not driven them up to the door was that there was no road, only a footpath. That also would explain the disappearance of the suit-cases. She began to feel confident that they would find their suit-cases waiting for them when they got up to the top. San Salvatore was, it seemed, on the top of a hill, as a mediaeval castle should be. At a turn of the path they saw above them, much nearer now and shining more brightly, the light they had seen from the quay. She told Mrs. Arbuthnot of her dawning belief, and Mrs. Arbuthnot agreed that it was very likely a true one.

Once more, but this time in a tone of real hopefulness, Mrs. Wilkins said, pointing upwards at the black outline against the only slightly less black sky, "San Salvatore?" And once more, but this time comfortingly, encouragingly, came back the assurance, "Si, si—San Salvatore."

They crossed a little bridge, over what was apparently a ravine, and then came a flat bit with long grass at the sides and more flowers. They felt the grass flicking wet against their stockings, and the invisible flowers were everywhere. Then up again through trees, along a zigzag path with the smell all the way of the flowers they could not see. The warm rain was bringing out all the sweetness. Higher and higher they went in this sweet darkness, and the red light on the jetty dropped farther and farther below them.

The path wound round to the other side of what appeared to be a little peninsula; the jetty and the red light disappeared; across the emptiness on their left were distant lights.

"Mezzago," said the man, waving his lantern at the lights.

"Si, si," they answered, for they had by now learned si, si. Upon which the man congratulated them in a great flow of polite words, not one of which they understood, on their magnificent Italian; for this was Domenico, the vigilant and accomplished gardener of San

Salvatore, the prop and stay of the establishment, the resourceful, the gifted, the eloquent, the courteous, the intelligent Domenico. Only they did not know that yet; and he did in the dark, and even sometimes in the light, look, with his knife-sharp swarthy features and swift, panther movements, very like somebody wicked.

They passed along another flat bit of path, with a black shape like a high wall towering above them on their right, and then the path went up again under trellises, and trailing sprays of scented things caught at them and shook raindrops on them, and the light of the lantern flickered over lilies, and then came a flight of ancient steps worn with centuries, and then another iron gate, and then they were inside, though still climbing a twisting flight of stone steps with old walls on either side like the walls of dungeons, and with a vaulted roof.

At the top was a wrought-iron door, and through it shone a flood of electric light.

"Ecco," said Domenico, lithely running up the last few steps ahead and pushing the door open.

And there they were, arrived; and it was San Salvatore; and their suit-cases were waiting for them; and they had not been murdered.

They looked at each other's white faces and blinking eyes very solemnly.

It was a great, a wonderful moment. Here they were, in their mediaeval castle at last. Their feet touched its stones.

Mrs. Wilkins put her arm round Mrs. Arbuthnot's neck and kissed her.

"The first thing to happen in this house," she said softly, solemnly, "shall be a kiss."

"Dear Lotty," said Mrs. Arbuthnot.

"Dear Rose," said Mrs. Wilkins, her eyes brimming with gladness.

Domenico was delighted. He liked to see beautiful ladies kiss. He made them a most appreciative speech of welcome, and they stood arm in arm, holding each other up, for they were very tired, blinking smilingly at him, and not understanding a word.

Chapter 6

When Mrs. Wilkins woke next morning she lay in bed a few minutes before getting up and opening the shutters. What would she see out of her window? A shining world, or a world of rain? But it would be beautiful; whatever it was would be beautiful.

She was in a little bedroom with bare white walls and a stone floor and sparse old furniture. The beds—there were two—were made of iron, enameled black and painted with bunches of gay flowers. She lay putting off the great moment of going to the window as one puts off opening a precious letter, gloating over it. She had no idea what time it was; she had forgotten to wind up her watch ever since, centuries ago, she last went to bed in Hampstead. No sounds were to be heard in the house, so she supposed it was very early, yet she felt as if she had slept a long while—so completely rested, so perfectly content. She lay with her arms clasped round her head thinking how happy she was, her lips curved upwards in a delighted smile. In bed by herself: adorable condition. She had not been in a bed without Mellersh once now for five whole years; and the cool roominess of it, the freedom of one's movements, the sense of recklessness, of audacity, in giving the blankets a pull if one wanted to, or twitching the pillows more comfortably! It was like the discovery of an entirely new joy.

Mrs. Wilkins longed to get up and open the shutters, but where she was was really so very delicious. She gave a sigh of contentment, and went on lying there looking round her, taking in everything in her room, her own little room, her very own to arrange just as she pleased for this one blessed month, her room bought with her own savings, the fruit of her careful denials, whose door she could bolt if she wanted to, and nobody had the right to come in. It was such a strange little room, so different from any she had known, and so sweet. It was like a cell. Except for the two beds, it suggested a happy austerity. "And the name of the chamber," she thought, quoting and smiling round at it, "was Peace."

Well, this was delicious, to lie there thinking how happy she was, but outside those shutters it was more delicious still. She jumped up, pulled on her slippers, for there was nothing on the stone floor but one small rug, ran to the window and threw open the shutters.

"Oh!" cried Mrs. Wilkins.

All the radiance of April in Italy lay gathered together at her feet. The sun poured in on her. The sea lay asleep in it, hardly stirring. Across the bay the lovely mountains, exquisitely different in colour, were asleep too in the light; and underneath her window, at the bottom of the flower-starred grass slope from which the wall of the castle rose up, was a great cypress, cutting through the delicate blues and violets and rose-colours of the mountains and the sea like a great black sword.

She stared. Such beauty; and she there to see it. Such beauty; and she alive to feel it. Her face was bathed in light. Lovely scents came up to the window and caressed her. A tiny breeze gently lifted her hair. Far out in the bay a cluster of almost motionless fishing boats hovered like a flock of white birds on the tranquil sea. How beautiful, how beautiful. Not to have died before this . . . to have been allowed to see, breathe, feel this. . . . She stared, her lips parted. Happy? Poor, ordinary, everyday word. But what could one say, how could one describe it? It was as though she could hardly stay inside herself, it was as though she were too small to hold so much of joy, it was as though she were washed through with light. And how astonishing to feel this sheer bliss, for here she was, not doing and not going to do a single unselfish thing, not going to do a thing she didn't want to do. According to everybody she had ever some across she ought at least to have twinges. She had not one twinge. Something was wrong somewhere. Wonderful that at home she should have been so good, so terribly good, and merely felt tormented. Twinges of every sort had there been her portion; aches, hurts, discouragements, and she the whole time being steadily unselfish. Now she had taken off all her goodness and left it behind her like a heap in rain-sodden clothes, and she only felt joy. She was naked of goodness, and was rejoicing in being naked. She was stripped, and exulting. And there, away in the dim mugginess of Hampstead, was Mellersh being angry.

She tried to visualize Mellersh, she tried to see him having breakfast and thinking bitter things about her; and lo, Mellersh himself began to shimmer, became rose-colour, became delicate violet, became an enchanting blue, became formless, became iridescent. Actually Mellersh, after quivering a minute, was lost in light.

"Well," thought Mrs. Wilkins, staring, as it were, after him. How extraordinary not to be able to visualize Mellersh; and she who used to know every feature, every expression of his by heart. She simply could not see him as he was. She could only see him resolved into beauty, melted into harmony with everything else. The familiar words of the General Thanksgiving came quite naturally into her mind, and she found herself blessing God for her creation, preservation, and all the blessings of this life, but above all for His inestimable Love; out loud; in a burst of acknowledgment. While Mellersh, at that moment angrily pulling on his boots before going out into the dripping streets, was indeed thinking bitter things about her.

She began to dress, choosing clean white clothes in honour of the summer's day, unpacking her suit-cases, tidying her adorable little room. She moved about with quick, purposeful steps, her long thin body held up straight, her small face, so much puckered at home with effort and fear, smoothed out. All she had been and done before this morning, all she had felt and worried about, was gone. Each of her worries behaved as the image of Mellersh had behaved, and dissolved into colour and light. And she noticed things she had not noticed for years—when she was doing her hair in front of the glass she noticed it, and thought, "Why, what pretty stuff." For years she had forgotten she had such a thing as hair, plaiting it in the evening and unplaiting it in the morning with the same hurry and indifference with which she laced and unlaced her shoes. Now she suddenly saw it, and she twisted it round her fingers before the glass, and was glad it was so pretty. Mellersh couldn't have seen it either, for he had never said a word about it. Well, when she got home she would draw his attention to it. "Mellersh," she would say, "look at my hair. Aren't you pleased you've got a wife with hair like curly honey?"

She laughed. She had never said anything like that to Mellersh yet, and the idea of it amused her. But why had she not? Oh yes— she used to be afraid of him. Funny to be afraid of anybody; and especially of one's husband, whom one saw in his more simplified moments, such as asleep, and not breathing properly through his nose.

When she was ready she opened her door to go across to see if Rose, who had been put the night before by a sleepy maidservant into a cell opposite, were awake. She would say good-morning to her, and then she would run down and stay with that cypress tree till breakfast was ready, and after breakfast she wouldn't so much as

47

look out of a window till she had helped Rose get everything ready for Lady Caroline and Mrs. Fisher. There was much to be done that day, settling in, arranging the rooms; she mustn't leave Rose to do it alone. They would make it all so lovely for the two to come, have such an entrancing vision ready for them of little cells bright with flowers. She remembered she had wanted Lady Caroline not to come; fancy wanting to shut some one out of heaven because she thought she would be shy of her! And as though it mattered if she were, and as though she would be anything so self-conscious as shy. Besides, what a reason. She could not accuse herself of goodness over that. And she remembered she had wanted not to have Mrs. Fisher either, because she had seemed lofty. How funny of her. So funny to worry about such little things, making them important.

The bedrooms and two of the sitting-rooms at San Salvatore were on the top floor, and opened into a roomy hall with a wide glass window at the north end. San Salvatore was rich in small gardens in different parts and on different levels. The garden this window looked down on was made on the highest part of the walls, and could only be reached through the corresponding spacious hall on the floor below. When Mrs. Wilkins came out of her room this window stood wide open, and beyond it in the sun was a Judas tree in full flower. There was no sign of anybody, no sound of voices or feet. Tubs of arum lilies stood about on the stone floor, and on a table flamed a huge bunch of fierce nasturtiums. Spacious, flowery, silent, with the wide window at the end opening into the garden, and the Judas tree absurdly beautiful in the sunshine, it seemed to Mrs. Wilkins, arrested on her way across to Mrs. Arbuthnot, too good to be true. Was she really going to live in this for a whole month? Up to now she had had to take what beauty she could as she went along, snatching at little bits of it when she came across it—a patch of daisies on a fine day in a Hampstead field, a flash of sunset between two chimney pots. She had never been in definitely, completely beautiful places. She had never been even in a venerable house; and such a thing as a profusion of flowers in her rooms was unattainable to her. Sometimes in the spring she had bought six tulips at Shoolbred's, unable to resist them, conscious that Mellersh if he knew what they had cost would think it inexcusable; but they had soon died, and then there were no more. As for the Judas tree, she hadn't an idea what it was, and gazed at it out there against the sky with the rapt expression of one who sees a heavenly vision.

Mrs. Arbuthnot, coming out of her room, found her there like that, standing in the middle of the hall staring.

"Now what does she think she sees now?" thought Mrs. Arbuthnot.

"We are in God's hands," said Mrs. Wilkins, turning to her, speaking with extreme conviction.

"Oh!" said Mrs. Arbuthnot quickly, her face, which had been covered with smiles when she came out of her room, falling. "Why, what has happened?"

For Mrs. Arbuthnot had woken up with such a delightful feeling of security, of relief, and she did not want to find she had not after all escaped from the need of refuge. She had not even dreamed of Frederick. For the first time in years she had been spared the nightly dream that he was with her, that they were heart to heart, and its miserable awakening. She had slept like a baby, and had woken up confident; she had found there was nothing she wished to say in her morning prayer, except Thank you. It was disconcerting to be told she was after all in God's hands.

"I hope nothing has happened?" she asked anxiously.

Mrs. Wilkins looked at her a moment, and laughed. "How funny," she said, kissing her.

"What is funny?" asked Mrs. Arbuthnot, her face clearing because
Mrs. Wilkins laughed.

"We are. This is. Everything. It's all so wonderful. It's so funny and so adorable that we should be in it. I daresay when we finally reach heaven—the one they talk about so much—we shan't find it a bit more beautiful."

Mrs. Arbuthnot relaxed to smiling security again. "Isn't it divine?" she said?

"Were you ever, ever in your life so happy?" asked Mrs. Wilkins, catching her by the arm.

"No," said Mrs. Arbuthnot. Nor had she been; not ever; not even in her first love-days with Frederick. Because always pain had been close at hand in that other happiness, ready to torture with doubts, to torture even with the very excess of her love; while this was the simple happiness of complete harmony with her surroundings, the happiness that asks for nothing, that just accepts, just breathes, just is.

"Let's go and look at that tree close," said Mrs. Wilkins. "I don't believe it can only be a tree."

And arm in arm they went along the hall, and their husbands would not have known them their faces were so young with eagerness, and together they stood at the open window, and when their eyes, having feasted on the marvelous pink thing, wandered farther among the beauties of the garden, they saw sitting on the low wall at the east edge of it, gazing out over the bay, her feet in lilies, Lady Caroline.

They were astonished. They said nothing in their astonishment, but stood quite still, arm in arm, staring down at her.

She too had on a white frock, and her head was bare. They had had no idea that day in London, when her hat was down to her nose and her furs were up to her ears, that she was so pretty. They had merely thought her different from the other women in the club, and so had the other women themselves, and so had all the waitresses, eyeing her sideways and eyeing her again as they passed the corner where she sat talking; but they had had no idea she was so pretty. She was exceedingly pretty. Everything about her was very much that which it was. Her fair hair was very fair, her lovely grey eyes were very lovely and grey, her dark eyelashes were very dark, her white skin was very white, her red mouth was very red. She was extravagantly slender—the merest thread of a girl, though not without little curves beneath her thin frock where little curves should be. She was looking out across the bay, and was sharply defined against the background of empty blue. She was full in the sun. Her feet dangled among the leaves and flowers of the lilies just as if it did not matter that they should be bent or bruised.

"She ought to have a headache," whispered Mrs. Arbuthnot at last, "sitting there in the sun like that."

"She ought to have a hat," whispered Mrs. Wilkins.

"She is treading on lilies."

"But they're hers as much as ours."

"Only one-fourth of them."

Lady Caroline turned her head. She looked up at them a moment, surprised to see them so much younger than they had seemed that day at the club, and so much less unattractive. Indeed, they were really almost quite attractive, if any one could ever be really quite attractive in the wrong clothes. Her eyes, swiftly glancing over them, took in every inch of each of them in the half second before she smiled and waved her hand and called out Good-morning. There was nothing, she saw at once to be hoped for in the way of interest from their clothes. She did not consciously think this, for she was having a violent reaction against beautiful clothes and the slavery they impose on one, her experience being that the instant one had got them they took one in hand and gave one no peace till they had been everywhere and been seen by everybody. You didn't take your clothes to parties; they took you. It was quite a mistake to think that a woman, a really well-dressed woman, wore out her clothes; it was the clothes that wore out the woman—dragging her about at all hours of the day and night. No wonder men stayed younger longer. Just new trousers couldn't excite them. She couldn't suppose that even the newest trousers ever behaved like that, taking the bit between their teeth. Her images were disorderly, but she thought as she chose, she used what images she like. As she got off the wall and came towards the window, it seemed a restful thing to know she was going to spend an entire month with people in dresses made as she dimly remembered dresses used to be made five summers ago.

"I got here yesterday morning," she said, looking up at them and smiling. She really was bewitching. She had everything, even a dimple.

"It's a great pity," said Mrs. Arbuthnot, smiling back, "because we were going to choose the nicest room for you."

"Oh, but I've done that," said Lady Caroline. "At least, I think it's the nicest. It looks two ways—I adore a room that looks two ways, don't you? Over the sea to the west, and over this Judas tree to the north."

"And we had meant to make it pretty for you with flowers," said Mrs. Wilkins.

"Oh, Domenico did that. I told him to directly I got here. He's the gardener. He's wonderful."

"It's a good thing, of course," said Mrs. Arbuthnot a little hesitatingly, "to be independent, and to know exactly what one wants."

"Yes, it saves trouble," agreed Lady Caroline.

"But one shouldn't be so independent," said Mrs. Wilkins, "as to leave no opportunity for other people to exercise their benevolences on one."

Lady Caroline, who had been looking at Mrs. Arbuthnot, now looked at Mrs. Wilkins. That day at the queer club she had had

51

merely a blurred impression of Mrs. Wilkins, for it was the other one who did all the talking, and her impression had been of somebody so shy, so awkward that it was best to take no notice of her. She had not even been able to say good-bye properly, doing it in an agony, turning red, turning damp. Therefore she now looked at her in some surprise; and she was still more surprised when Mrs. Wilkins added, gazing at her with the most obvious sincere admiration, speaking indeed with a conviction that refused to remain unuttered, "I didn't realize you were so pretty."

She stared at Mrs. Wilkins. She was not usually told this quite so immediately and roundly. Abundantly as she was used to it—impossible not to be after twenty-eight solid years—it surprised her to be told it with such bluntness, and by a woman.

"It's very kind of you to think so," she said.

"Why, you're very lovely," said Mrs. Wilkins. "Quite, quite lovely."

"I hope," said Mrs. Arbuthnot pleasantly, "you make the most of it."

Lady Caroline then stared at Mrs. Arbuthnot. "Oh yes," she said. "I make the most of it. I've been doing that ever since I can remember."

"Because," said Mrs. Arbuthnot, smiling and raising a warning forefinger, "it won't last."

Then Lady Caroline began to be afraid these two were originals. If so, she would be bored. Nothing bored her so much as people who insisted on being original, who came and buttonholed her and kept her waiting while they were being original. And the one who admired her—it would be tiresome if she dogged her about in order to look at her. What she wanted of this holiday was complete escape from all she had had before, she wanted the rest of complete contrast. Being admired, being dogged, wasn't contrast, it was repetition; and as for originals, to find herself shut up with two on the top of a precipitous hill in a medieval castle built for the express purpose of preventing easy goings out and in, would not, she was afraid, be especially restful. Perhaps she had better be a little less encouraging. They had seemed such timid creatures, even the dark one—she couldn't remember their names—that day at the club, that she had felt it quite safe to be very friendly. Here they had come out of their shells; already; indeed, at once. There was no sign of timidity about either of them here. If they had got out of their shells so immediately, at the very first contact, unless she checked them they would soon begin to press upon her, and then good-bye to her dream of thirty restful, silent days, lying unmolested in the sun, getting her feathers smooth again, not being spoken to, not waited on, not grabbed at and monopolized, but just recovering from the fatigue, the deep and melancholy fatigue, of the too much.

Besides, there was Mrs. Fisher. She too must be checked. Lady Caroline had started two days earlier than had been arranged for two reasons: first, because she wished to arrive before the others in order to pick out the room or rooms she preferred, and second, because she judged it likely that otherwise she would have to travel with Mrs. Fisher. She did not want to travel with Mrs. Fisher. She did not want to arrive with Mrs. Fisher. She saw no reason whatever why for a single moment she should have to have anything at all to do with Mrs. Fisher.

But unfortunately Mrs. Fisher also was filled with a desire to get to San Salvatore first and pick out the room or rooms she preferred, and she and Lady Caroline had after all traveled together. As early as Calais they began to suspect it; in Paris they feared it; at Modane they knew it; at Mezzago they concealed it, driving out to Castagneto in two separate flys, the nose of the one almost touching the back of the other the whole way. But when the road suddenly left off at the church and the steps, further evasion was impossible; and faced by this abrupt and difficult finish to their journey there was nothing for it but to amalgamate.

Because of Mrs. Fisher's stick Lady Caroline had to see about everything. Mrs. Fisher's intentions, she explained from her fly when the situation had become plain to her, were active, but her stick prevented their being carried out. The two drivers told Lady Caroline boys would have to carry the luggage up to the castle, and she went in search of some, while Mrs. Fisher waited in the fly because of her stick. Mrs. Fisher could speak Italian, but only, she explained, the Italian of Dante, which Matthew Arnold used to read with her when she was a girl, and she thought this might be above the heads of boys. Therefore Lady Caroline, who spoke ordinary Italian very well, was obviously the one to go and do things.

"I am in your hands," said Mrs. Fisher, sitting firmly in her fly. "You must please regard me as merely an old woman with a stick."

And presently, down the steps and cobbles to the piazza, and along the quay, and up the zigzag path, Lady Caroline found herself as much obliged to walk slowly with Mrs. Fisher as if she were her own grandmother.

"It's my stick," Mrs. Fisher complacently remarked at intervals.

And when they rested at those bends of the zigzag path where seats were, and Lady Caroline, who would have liked to run on and get to the top quickly, was forced in common humanity to remain with Mrs. Fisher because of her stick, Mrs. Fisher told her how she had been on a zigzag path once with Tennyson.

"Isn't his cricket wonderful?" said Lady Caroline absently.

"The Tennyson," said Mrs. Fisher, turning her head and observing her a moment over her spectacles.

"Isn't he?" said Lady Caroline.

"And it was a path, too," Mrs. Fisher went on severely, "curiously like this. No eucalyptus tree, of course, but otherwise curiously like this. And at one of the bends he turned and said to me—I see him now turning and saying to me—"

Yes, Mrs. Fisher would have to be checked. And so would these two up at the window. She had better begin at once. She was sorry she had got off the wall. All she need have done was to have waved her hand, and waited till they came down and out into the garden to her.

So she ignored Mrs. Arbuthnot's remark and raised forefinger, and said with marked coldness—at least, she tried to make it sound marked—that she supposed they would be going to breakfast, and that she had had hers; but it was her fate that however coldly she sent forth her words they came out sounding quite warm and agreeable. That was because she had a sympathetic and delightful voice, due entirely to some special formation of her throat and the roof of her mouth, and having nothing whatever to do with what she was feeling. Nobody in consequence ever believed they were being snubbed. It was most tiresome. And if she stared icily it did not look icy at all, because her eyes, lovely to begin with, had the added loveliness of very long, soft, dark eyelashes. No icy stare could come out of eyes like that; it got caught and lost in the soft eyelashes, and the persons stared at merely thought they were being regarded with a flattering and exquisite attentiveness. And if ever she was out of humour or definitely cross—and who would not be sometimes in such a world?—she only looked so pathetic that people all rushed to comfort her, if possible by means of kissing. It was more than tiresome, it was maddening. Nature was determined

54

that she should look and sound angelic. She could never be disagreeable or rude without being completely misunderstood.

"I had my breakfast in my room," she said, trying her utmost to sound curt. "Perhaps I'll see you later."

And she nodded, and went back to where she had been sitting on the wall, with the lilies being nice and cool round her feet.

Chapter 7

Their eyes followed her admiringly. They had no idea they had been snubbed. It was a disappointment, of course, to find she had forestalled them and that they were not to have the happiness of preparing for her, of watching her face when she arrived and first saw everything, but there was till Mrs. Fisher. They would concentrate on Mrs. Fisher, and would watch her face instead; only, like everybody else, they would have preferred to watch Lady Caroline's.

Perhaps, then, as Lady Caroline had talked of breakfast, they had better begin by going and having it, for there was too much to be done that day to spend any more time gazing at the scenery—servants to be interviewed, the house to be gone through and examined, and finally Mrs. Fisher's room to be got ready and adorned.

They waved their hands gaily at Lady Caroline, who seemed absorbed in what she saw and took no notice, and turning away found the maidservant of the night before had come up silently behind them in cloth slippers with string soles.

She was Francesca, the elderly parlour-maid, who had been with the owner, he had said, for years, and whose presence made inventories unnecessary; and after wishing them good-morning and hoping they had slept well, she told them breakfast was ready in the dining-room on the floor below, and if they would follow her she would lead.

They did not understand a single word of the very many in which Francesca succeeded in clothing this simple information, but they followed her, for it at least was clear that they were to follow, and going down the stairs, and along the broad hall like the one above except for glass doors at the end instead of a window opening into the garden, they were shown into the dining-room; where, sitting at the head of the table having her breakfast, was Mrs. Fisher.

This time they exclaimed. Even Mrs. Arbuthnot exclaimed, though her exclamation was only "Oh."

Mrs. Wilkins exclaimed at greater length. "Why, but it's like having the bread taken out of one's mouth!" exclaimed Mrs. Wilkins.

"How do you do," said Mrs. Fisher. "I can't get up because of my stick." And she stretched out her hand across the table.

They advanced and shook it.

"We had no idea you were here," said Mrs. Arbuthnot.

"Yes," said Mrs. Fisher, resuming her breakfast. "Yes. I am here." And with composure she removed the top of her egg.

"It's a great disappointment," said Mrs. Wilkins. "We had meant to give you such a welcome."

This was the one, Mrs. Fisher remembered, briefly glancing at her, who when she came to Prince of Wales Terrace said she had seen Keats. She must be careful with this one—curb her from the beginning.

She therefore ignored Mrs. Wilkins and said gravely, with a downward face of impenetrable calm bent on her egg, "Yes. I arrived yesterday with Lady Caroline."

"It's really dreadful," said Mrs. Wilkins, exactly as if she had not been ignored. "There's nobody left to get anything ready for now. I fee thwarted. I feel as if the bread had been taken out of my mouth just when I was going to be happy swallowing it."

"Where will you sit?" asked Mrs. Fisher of Mrs. Arbuthnot— markedly of Mrs. Arbuthnot; the comparison with the bread seemed to her most unpleasant.

"Oh, thank you—" said Mrs. Arbuthnot, sitting down rather suddenly next to her.

There were only two places she could sit down in, the places laid on either side of Mrs. Fisher. She therefore sat down in one, and Mrs. Wilkins sat down opposite her in the other.

Mrs. Fisher was at the head of the table. Round her was grouped the coffee and the tea. Of course they were all sharing San Salvatore equally, but it was she herself and Lotty, Mrs. Arbuthnot mildly reflected, who had found it, who had had the work of getting it, who had chosen to admit Mrs. Fisher into it. Without them, she could not help thinking, Mrs. Fisher would not have been there. Morally Mrs. Fisher was a guest. There was no hostess in this party, but supposing there had been a hostess it would not have been Mrs. Fisher, nor Lady Caroline, it would have been either herself or Lotty. Mrs. Arbuthnot could not help feeling this as she sat down, and Mrs. Fisher, the hand which Ruskin had wrung suspended over the pots before her, inquired, "Tea or coffee?" She could not help feeling it even more definitely when Mrs. Fisher touched a small gong on the

57

table beside her as though she had been used to that gong and that table ever since she was little, and, on Francesca's appearing, bade her in the language of Dante bring more milk. There was a curious air about Mrs. Fisher, thought Mrs. Arbuthnot, of being in possession; and if she herself had not been so happy she would have perhaps minded.

Mrs. Wilkins noticed it too, but it only made her discursive brain think of cuckoos. She would no doubt immediately have begun to talk of cuckoos, incoherently, unrestrainably and deplorably, if she had been in the condition of nerves and shyness she was in last time she saw Mrs. Fisher. But happiness had done away with shyness—she was very serene; she could control her conversation; she did not have, horrified, to listen to herself saying things she had no idea of saying when she began; she was quite at her ease, and completely natural. The disappointment of not going to be able to prepare a welcome for Mrs. Fisher had evaporated at once, for it was impossible to go on being disappointed in heaven. Nor did she mind her behaving as hostess. What did it matter? You did not mind things in heaven. She and Mrs. Arbuthnot, therefore, sat down more willingly than they otherwise would have done, one on either side of Mrs. Fisher, and the sun, pouring through the two windows facing east across the bay, flooded the room, and there was an open door leading into the garden, and the garden was full of many lovely things, especially freesias.

The delicate and delicious fragrance of the freesias came in through the door and floated round Mrs. Wilkins's enraptured nostrils. Freesias in London were quite beyond her. Occasionally she went into a shop and asked what they cost, so as just to have an excuse for lifting up a bunch and smelling them, well knowing that it was something awful like a shilling for about three flowers. Here they were everywhere—bursting out of every corner and carpeting the rose beds. Imagine it—having freesias to pick in armsful if you wanted to, and with glorious sunshine flooding the room, and in your summer frock, and its being only the first of April!

"I suppose you realize, don't you, that we've got to heaven?" she said, beaming at Mrs. Fisher with all the familiarity of a fellow-angel.

"They are considerably younger than I had supposed," thought Mrs. Fisher, "and not nearly so plain." And she mused a moment, while she took no notice of Mrs. Wilkins's exuberance, on their instant and agitated refusal that day at Prince of Wales Terrace to have anything to do with the giving or the taking of references.

Nothing could affect her, of course; nothing that anybody did. She was far too solidly seated in respectability. At her back stood massively in a tremendous row those three great names she had offered, and they were not the only ones she could turn to for support and countenance. Even if these young women—she had no grounds for believing the one out in the garden to be really Lady Caroline Dester, she had merely been told she was—even if these young women should all turn out to be what Browning used to call—how well she remembered his amusing and delightful way of putting things—Fly-by-Nights, what could it possibly, or in any way matter to her? Let them fly by night if they wished. One was not sixty-five for nothing. In any case there would only be four weeks of it, at the end of which she would see no more of them. And in the meanwhile there were plenty of places where she could sit quietly away from them and remember. Also there was her own sitting-room, a charming room, all honey-coloured furniture and pictures, with windows to the sea towards Genoa, and a door opening on to the battlements. The house possessed two sitting-rooms, and she explained to that pretty creature Lady Caroline—certainly a pretty creature, whatever else she was; Tennyson would have enjoyed taking her for blows on the downs—who had seemed inclined to appropriate the honey-colored one, that she needed some little refuge entirely to herself because of her stick.

"Nobody wants to see an old woman hobbling about everywhere," she had said. "I shall be quite content to spend much of my time by myself in here or sitting out on these convenient battlements."

And she had a very nice bedroom, too; it looked two ways, across the bay in the morning sun—she liked the morning sun—and onto the garden. There were only two of these bedrooms with cross-views in the house, she and Lady Caroline had discovered, and they were by far the airiest. They each had two beds in them, and she and Lady Caroline had had the extra beds taken out at once and put into two of the other rooms. In this way there was much more space and comfort. Lady Caroline, indeed, had turned hers into a bed-sitting-room, with the sofa out of the bigger drawing-room and the writing-table and the most comfortable chair, but she herself had not had to do that because she had her own sitting-room, equipped with what was necessary. Lady Caroline had thought at first of taking the bigger sitting-room entirely for her own, because the dining-room on the floor below could quite well be used between meals to sit in by the two others, and was a very pleasant room with nice chairs, but she had not liked the bigger sitting-room's shape—it was a round room in the tower, with deep slit windows pierced through the massive walls, and a domed and ribbed ceiling arranged to look like an open umbrella, and it seemed a little dark. Undoubtedly Lady Caroline had cast covetous glances at the honey-coloured room, and if she Mrs. Fisher, had been less firm would have installed herself in it. Which would have been absurd.

"I hope," said Mrs. Arbuthnot, smilingly making an attempt to convey to Mrs. Fisher that though she, Mrs. Fisher, might not be exactly a guest she certainly was not in the very least a hostess, "your room is comfortable."

"Quite," said Mrs. Fisher. "Will you have some more coffee?"

"No, thank you. Will you?"

"No, thank you. There were two beds in my bedroom, filling it up unnecessarily, and I had one taken out. It has made it much more convenient."

"Oh that's why I've got two beds in my room!" exclaimed Mrs. Wilkins, illuminated; the second bed in her little cell had seemed an unnatural and inappropriate object from the moment she saw it.

"I gave no directions," said Mrs. Fisher, addressing Mrs. Arbuthnot, "I merely asked Francesca to remove it."

"I have two in my room as well," said Mrs. Arbuthnot.

"Your second one must be Lady Caroline's. She had hers removed too," said Mrs. Fisher. "It seems foolish to have more beds in a room than there are occupiers."

"But we haven't got husbands here either," said Mrs. Wilkins, "and I don't see any use in extra beds in one's room if one hasn't got husbands to put in them. Can't we have them taken away too?"

"Beds," said Mrs. Fisher coldly, "cannot be removed from one room after another. They must remain somewhere."

Mrs. Wilkins's remarks seemed to Mrs. Fisher persistently unfortunate. Each time she opened her mouth she said something best left unsaid. Loose talk about husbands had never in Mrs. Fisher's circle been encouraged. In the 'eighties, when she chiefly flourished, husbands were taken seriously, as the only real obstacles to sin. Beds too, if they had to be mentioned, were approached with caution; and a decent reserve prevented them and husbands ever being spoken of in the same breath.

She turned more markedly than ever to Mrs. Arbuthnot. "Do let me give you a little more coffee," she said.

"No, thank you. But won't you have some more?"

"No indeed. I never have more than two cups at breakfast. Would you like an orange?"

"No thank you. Would you?"

"No, I don't eat fruit at breakfast. It is an American fashion which I am too old now to adopt. Have you had all you want?"

"Quite. Have you?"

Mrs. Fisher paused before replying was this a habit, this trick of answering a simple question with the same question? If so it must be curbed, for no one could live for four weeks in any real comfort with somebody who had a habit.

She glanced at Mrs. Arbuthnot, and her parted hair and gentle brow reassured her. No; it was accident, not habit, that had produced those echoes. She could as soon imagine a dove having tiresome habits as Mrs. Arbuthnot. Considering her, she thought what a splendid wife she would have been for poor Carlyle. So much better than that horrid clever Jane. She would have soothed him.

"Then shall we go?" she suggested.

"Let me help you up," said Mrs. Arbuthnot, all consideration.

"Oh, thank you—I can manage perfectly. It's only sometimes that my stick prevents me—"

Mrs. Fisher got up quite easily; Mrs. Arbuthnot had hovered over her for nothing.

"I'm going to have one of these gorgeous oranges," said Mrs. Wilkins, staying where she was and reaching across to a black bowl piled with them. "Rose, how can you resist them. Look—have this one.

Do have this beauty—" And she held out a big one.

"No, I'm going to see to my duties," said Mrs. Arbuthnot, moving towards the door. "You'll forgive me for leaving you, won't you," she added politely to Mrs. Fisher.

Mrs. Fisher moved towards the door too; quite easily; almost quickly; her stick did not hinder her at all. She had no intention of being left with Mrs. Wilkins.

"What time would you like to have lunch?" Mrs. Arbuthnot asked her, trying to keep her head as at least a non-guest, if not

61

precisely a hostess, above water.

"Lunch," said Mrs. Fisher, "is at half-past twelve."

"You shall have it at half-past twelve then," said Mrs. Arbuthnot. "I'll tell the cook. It will be a great struggle," she continued, smiling, "but I've brought a little dictionary—"

"The cook," said Mrs. Fisher, "knows."

"Oh?" said Mrs. Arbuthnot.

"Lady Caroline has already told her," said Mrs. Fisher.

"Oh?" said Mrs. Arbuthnot.

"Yes. Lady Caroline speaks the kind of Italian cooks understand. I am prevented going into the kitchen because of my stick. And even   if I were able to go, I fear I shouldn't be understood."

"But—" began Mrs. Arbuthnot.

"But it's too wonderful," Mrs. Wilkins finished for her from the table, delighted with these unexpected simplifications in her and Rose's lives. "Why, we've got positively nothing to do here, either of us, except just be happy. You wouldn't believe," she said, turning her head and speaking straight to Mrs. Fisher, portions of orange in either hand, "how terribly good Rose and I have been for years without stopping, and how much now we need a perfect rest."

And Mrs. Fisher, going without answering her out the room, said to herself, "She must, she shall be curbed."

Chapter 8

Presently, when Mrs. Wilkins and Mrs. Arbuthnot, unhampered by any duties, wandered out and down the worn stone steps and under the pergola into the lower garden, Mrs. Wilkins said to Mrs. Arbuthnot, who seemed pensive, "Don't you see that if somebody else does the ordering it frees us?"

Mrs. Arbuthnot said she did see, but nevertheless she thought it rather silly to have everything taken out of their hands.

"I love things to be taken out of my hands," said Mrs. Wilkins.

"But we found San Salvatore," said Mrs. Arbuthnot, "and it is rather silly that Mrs. Fisher should behave as if it belonged only to her."

"What is rather silly," said Mrs. Wilkins with much serenity, "is to mind. I can't see the least point in being in authority at the price of one's liberty."

Mrs. Arbuthnot said nothing to that for two reasons—first, because she was struck by the remarkable and growing calm of the hitherto incoherent and excited Lotty, and secondly because what she was looking at was so very beautiful.

All down the stone steps on either side were periwinkles in full flower, and she could now see what it was that had caught at her the night before and brushed, wet and scented, across her face. It was wistaria. Wistaria and sunshine . . . she remembered the advertisement. Here indeed were both in profusion. The wistaria was tumbling over itself in its excess of life, its prodigality of flowering; and where the pergola ended the sun blazed on scarlet geraniums, bushes of them, and nasturtiums in great heaps, and marigolds so brilliant that they seemed to be burning, and red and pink snapdragons, all outdoing each other in bright, fierce colour. The ground behind these flaming things dropped away in terraces to the sea, each terrace a little orchard, where among the olives grew vines on trellises, and fig-trees, and peach-trees, and cherry-trees. The cherry-trees and peach-trees were in blossom— lovely showers of white and deep rose-colour among the trembling delicacy of the olives; the fig-leaves were just big enough to smell of figs, the vine-buds were only beginning to show. And beneath these trees were groups of blue and purple irises, and bushes of lavender, and grey, sharp cactuses, and the grass was thick with dandelions and daisies, and right down at the bottom was the sea. Colour seemed flung down anyhow, anywhere; every sort of colour, piled up in heaps, pouring along in rivers—the periwinkles looked exactly as if they were being poured down each side of the steps—and flowers that grow only in borders in England, proud flowers keeping themselves to themselves over there, such as the great blue irises and the lavender, were being jostled by small, shining common things like dandelions and daisies and the white bells of the wild onion, and only seemed the better and the more exuberant for it.

They stood looking at this crowd of loveliness, this happy jumble, in silence. No, it didn't matter what Mrs. Fisher did; not here; not in such beauty. Mrs. Arbuthnot's discomposure melted out of her. In the warmth and light of what she was looking at, of what to her was a manifestation, and entirely new side of God, how could one be discomposed? If only Frederick were with her, seeing it too, seeing as he would have seen it when first they were lovers, in the days when he saw what she saw and loved what she loved. . .

She sighed.

"You mustn't sigh in heaven," said Mrs. Wilkins. "One doesn't."

"I was thinking how one longs to share this with those one loves," said Mrs. Arbuthnot.

"You mustn't long in heaven," said Mrs. Wilkins. "You're supposed to be quite complete there. And it is heaven, isn't it, Rose? See how everything has been let in together—the dandelions and the irises, the vulgar and the superior, me and Mrs. Fisher—all welcome, all mixed up anyhow, and all so visibly happy and enjoying ourselves."

"Mrs. Fisher doesn't seem happy—not visibly, anyhow," said Mrs. Arbuthnot, smiling.

"She'll begin soon, you'll see."

Mrs. Arbuthnot said she didn't believe that after a certain age people began anything.

Mrs. Wilkins said she was sure no one, however old and tough, could resist the effects of perfect beauty. Before many days, perhaps only hours, they would see Mrs. Fisher bursting out into every kind of exuberance. "I'm quite sure," said Mrs. Wilkins, "that we've got to heaven, and once Mrs. Fisher realizes that that's where she is, she's bound to be different. You'll see. She'll leave off being ossified, and go all soft and able to stretch, and we shall get quite—

why, I shouldn't be surprised if we get quite fond of her."

The idea of Mrs. Fisher bursting out into anything, she who seemed so particularly firmly fixed inside her buttons, made Mrs. Arbuthnot laugh. She condoned Lotty's loose way of talking of heaven, because in such a place, on such a morning, condonation was in the very air. Besides, what an excuse there was.

And Lady Caroline, sitting where they had left her before breakfast on the wall, peeped over when she heard laughter, and saw them standing on the path below, and thought what a mercy it was they were laughing down there and had not come up and done it round her. She disliked jokes at all times, but in the morning she hated them; especially close up; especially crowding in her ears. She hoped the originals were on their way out for a walk, and not on their way back from one. They were laughing more and more. What could they possibly find to laugh at?

She looked down on the tops of their heads with a very serious face, for the thought of spending a month with laughers was a grave one, and they, as though they felt her eyes, turned suddenly and looked up.

The dreadful geniality of those women. . .

She shrank away from their smiles and wavings, but she could not shrink out of sight without falling into the lilies. She neither smiled nor waved back, and turning her eyes to the more distant mountains surveyed them carefully till the two, tired of waving, moved away along the path and turned the corner and disappeared.

This time they both did notice that they had been met with, at least, unresponsiveness.

"If we weren't in heaven," said Mrs. Wilkins serenely, "I should say we had been snubbed, but as nobody snubs anybody there of course we can't have been."

"Perhaps she is unhappy," said Mrs. Arbuthnot.

"Whatever it is she is she'll get over it here," said Mrs. Wilkins with conviction.

"We must try and help her," said Mrs. Arbuthnot.

"Oh, but nobody helps anybody in heaven. That's finished with. You don't try to be, or do. You simply are."

Well, Mrs. Arbuthnot wouldn't go into that—not here, not to-day. The vicar, she knew, would have called Lotty's talk levity, if not profanity. How old he seemed from here; an old, old vicar.

They left the path, and clambered down the olive terraces, down and down, to where at the bottom the warm, sleepy sea heaved gently among the rocks. There a pine-tree grew close to the water, and they sat under it, and a few yards away was a fishing-boat lying motionless and green-bellied on the water. The ripples of the sea made little gurgling noises at their feet. They screwed up their eyes to be able to look into the blaze of light beyond the shade of their tree. The hot smell from the pine-needles and from the cushions of wild thyme that padded the spaces between the rocks, and sometimes a smell of pure honey from a clump of warm irises up behind them in the sun, puffed across their faces. Very soon Mrs. Wilkins took her shoes and stockings off, and let her feet hang in the water. After watching her a minute Mrs. Arbuthnot did the same. Their happiness was then complete. Their husbands would not have known them. They left off talking. They ceased to mention heaven. They were just cups of acceptance.

Meanwhile Lady Caroline, on her wall, was considering her position. The garden on the top of the wall was a delicious garden, but its situation made it insecure and exposed to interruptions. At any moment the others might come and want to use it, because both the hall and the dining-room had doors opening straight into it. Perhaps, thought Lady Caroline, she could arrange that it should be solely hers. Mrs. Fisher had the battlements, delightful with flowers, and a watch-tower all to herself, besides having snatched the one really nice room in the house. There were plenty of places the originals could go to—she had herself seen at least two other little gardens, while the hill the castle stood on was itself a garden, with walks and seats. Why should not this one spot be kept exclusively for her? She liked it; she liked it best of all. It had the Judas tree and an umbrella pine, it had the freesias and the lilies, it had a tamarisk beginning to flush pink, it had the convenient low wall to sit on, it had from each of its three sides the most amazing views—to the east the bay and mountains, to the north the village across the tranquil clear green water of the little harbour and the hills dotted with white houses and orange groves, and to the west was the thin thread of land by which San Salvatore was tied to the mainland, and then the open sea and the coast line beyond Genoa reaching away into the blue dimness of France. Yes, she would say she wanted to have this entirely to herself. How obviously sensible if each of them had their own special place to sit in apart. It was essential to her comfort that she should be able to be apart, left alone, not talked to. The others ought to like it best too. Why herd? One had enough of that in England, with one's relations and friends—oh, the numbers of them!—pressing on one continually. Having successfully escaped them for four weeks why continue, and with persons having no earthly claim on one, to herd?

She lit a cigarette. She began to feel secure. Those two had gone for a walk. There was no sign of Mrs. Fisher. How very pleasant this was.

Somebody came out through the glass doors, just as she was drawing a deep breath of security. Surely it couldn't be Mrs. Fisher, wanting to sit with her? Mrs. Fisher had her battlements. She ought to stay on them, having snatched them. It would be too tiresome if she wouldn't, and wanted not only to have them and her sitting-room but to establish herself in this garden as well.

No; it wasn't Mrs. Fisher, it was the cook.

She frowned. Was she going to have to go on ordering the food? Surely one or other of those two waving women would do that now.

The cook, who had been waiting in increasing agitation in the kitchen, watching the clock getting nearer to lunch—time while she still was without knowledge of what lunch was to consist of, had gone at last to Mrs. Fisher, who had immediately waved her away. She then wandered about the house seeking a mistress, any mistress, who would tell her what to cook, and finding none; and at last, directed by Francesca, who always knew where everybody was, came out to Lady Caroline.

Dominica had provided this cook. She was Costanza, the sister of that one of his cousins who kept a restaurant down on the piazza. She helped her brother in his cooking when she had no other job, and knew every sort of fat, mysterious Italian dish such as the workmen of Castagneto, who crowded the restaurant at midday, and the inhabitants of Mezzago when they came over on Sundays, loved to eat. She was a fleshless spinster of fifty, grey-haired, nimble, rich of speech, and thought Lady Caroline more beautiful than anyone she had ever seen; and so did Domenico; and so did the boy Giuseppe who helped Domenico and was, besides, his nephew; and so did the girl Angela who helped Francesca and was, besides, Domenico's niece; and so did Francesca herself. Domenico and Francesca, the only two who had seen them, thought the two ladies who arrived last very beautiful, but compared to the fair young lady who arrived first they were as candles to the electric light that had lately been installed, and as the tin tubs in the bedrooms to the wonderful new bathroom their master had had arranged on his last visit.

Lady Caroline scowled at the cook. The scowl, as usual, was transformed on the way into what appeared to be an intent and beautiful gravity, and Costanza threw up her hands and took the saints aloud to witness that here was the very picture of the Mother of God.

Lady Caroline asked her crossly what she wanted, and Costanza's head went on one side with delight at the sheer music of her voice. She said, after waiting a moment in case the music was going to continue, for she didn't wish to miss any of it, that she wanted orders; she had been to the Signorina's mother, but in vain.

"She is not my mother," repudiated Lady Caroline angrily; and her anger sounded like the regretful wail of a melodious orphan.

Costanza poured forth pity. She too, she explained, had no mother—

Lady Caroline interrupted with the curt information that her mother was alive and in London.

Costanza praised God and the saints that the young lady did not yet know what it was like to be without a mother. Quickly enough did misfortunes overtake one; no doubt the young lady already had a husband.

"No," said Lady Caroline icily. Worse than jokes in the morning did she hate the idea of husbands. And everybody was always trying to press them on her—all her relations, all her friends, all the evening papers. After all, she could only marry one, anyhow; but you would think from the way everybody talked, and especially those persons who wanted to be husbands, that she could marry at least a dozen.

Her soft, pathetic "No" made Costanza, who was standing close to her, well with sympathy.

"Poor little one," said Costanza, moved actually to pat her encouragingly on the shoulder, "take hope. There is still time."

"For lunch," said Lady Caroline freezingly, marveling as she spoke that she should be patted, she who had taken so much trouble to come to a place, remote and hidden, where she could be sure that among other things of a like oppressive nature pattings also were not, "we will have—"

Costanza became business-like. She interrupted with suggestions, and her suggestions were all admirable and all expensive.

Lady Caroline did not know they were expensive, and fell in with them at once. They sounded very nice. Every sort of young vegetables and fruits came into them, and much butter and a great deal of cream and incredible numbers of eggs. Costanza said enthusiastically at the end, as a tribute to this acquiescence, that of the many ladies and gentlemen she had worked for on temporary jobs such as this she preferred the English ladies and gentlemen. She more than preferred them—they roused devotion in her. For they knew what to order; they did not skimp; they refrained from grinding down the faces of the poor.

From this Lady Caroline concluded that she had been extravagant, and promptly countermanded the cream.

Costanza's face fell, for she had a cousin who had a cow, and the cream was to have come from them both.

"And perhaps we had better not have chickens," said Lady Caroline.

Costanza's face fell more, for her brother at the restaurant kept chickens in his back-yard, and many of them were ready for killing.

"Also do not order strawberries till I have consulted with the other ladies," said Lady Caroline, remembering that it was only the first of April, and that perhaps people who lived in Hampstead might be poor; indeed, must be poor, or why live in Hampstead? "It is not I who am mistress here."

"Is it the old one?" asked Costanza, her face very long.

"No," said Lady Caroline.

"Which of the other two ladies is it?"

"Neither," said Lady Caroline.

Then Costanza's smiles returned, for the young lady was having fun with her and making jokes. She told her so, in her friendly Italian way, and was genuinely delighted.

"I never make jokes," said Lady Caroline briefly. "You had better go, or lunch will certainly not be ready by half-past twelve."

And these curt words came out sounding so sweet that Costanza felt as if kind compliments were being paid her, and forgot her disappointment about the cream and the chickens, and went away all gratitude and smiles.

"This," thought Lady Caroline, "will never do. I haven't come here to housekeep, and I won't."

She called Costanza back. Costanza came running. The sound of her name in that voice enchanted her.

"I have ordered the lunch for to-day," said Lady Caroline, with the serious angel face that was hers when she was annoyed, "and I have also ordered the dinner, but from now on you will go to one of the other ladies for orders. I give no more."

The idea that she would go on giving orders was too absurd. She never gave orders at home. Nobody there dreamed of asking her to do anything. That such a very tiresome activity should be thrust upon her here, simply because she happened to be able to talk Italian, was ridiculous. Let the originals give orders if Mrs. Fisher refused to. Mrs. Fisher, of course, was the one Nature intended for such a purpose. She had the very air of a competent housekeeper. Her clothes were the clothes of a housekeeper, and so was the way she did her hair.

Having delivered herself of her ultimatum with an acerbity that turned sweet on the way, and accompanied it by a peremptory gesture of dismissal that had the grace and loving-kindness of a benediction, it was annoying that Costanza should only stand still with her head on one side gazing at her in obvious delight.

"Oh, go away!" exclaimed Lady Caroline in English, suddenly exasperated.

There had been a fly in her bedroom that morning which had stuck just as Costanza was sticking; only one, but it might have been a myriad it was so tiresome from daylight on. It was determined to settle on her face, and she was determined it should not. Its persistence was uncanny. It woke her, and would not let her go to sleep again. She hit at it, and it eluded her without fuss or effort and with an almost visible blandness, and she had only hit herself. It came back again instantly, and with a loud buzz alighted on her cheek. She hit at it again and hurt herself, while it skimmed gracefully away. She lost her temper, and sat up in bed and waited, watching to hit at it and kill it. She kept on hitting at it at last with fury and with all her strength, as if it were a real enemy deliberately trying to madden her; and it elegantly skimmed in and out of her blows, not even angry, to be back again the next instant. It succeeded every time in getting on to her face, and was quite indifferent how often it was driven away. That was why she had dressed and come out so early. Francesca had already been told to put a net over her bed, for she was not going to allow herself to be annoyed twice like that. People were exactly like flies. She wished there were nets for keeping them off too. She hit at them with words and frowns, and like the fly they slipped between her blows and were untouched. Worse than the fly, they seemed unaware that she had even tried to hit them. The fly at least did for a moment go away. With human beings the only way to get rid of them was to go away herself. That was what, so tired, she had done this April; and having got here, having got close up to the details of life at San Salvatore, it appeared that here, too, she was not to be let alone.

Viewed from London there had seemed to be no details. San Salvatore from there seemed to be an empty, a delicious blank. Yet, after only twenty-four hours of it, she was discovering that it was not a blank at all, and that she was having to ward off as actively as ever. Already she had been much stuck to. Mrs. Fisher had stuck nearly the whole of the day before, and this morning there had been no peace, not ten minutes uninterruptedly alone.

Costanza of course had finally to go because she had to cook, but hardly had she gone before Domenico came. He came to water and tie up. That was natural, since he was the gardener, but he watered and tied up all the things that were nearest to her; he hovered closer and closer; he watered to excess; he tied plants that were as straight and steady as arrows. Well, at least he was a man, and therefore not quite so annoying, and his smiling good-morning was received with an answering smile; upon which Domenico forgot his family, his wife, his mother, his grown-up children and all his duties, and only wanted to kiss the young lady's feet.

He could not do that, unfortunately, but he could talk while he worked, and talk he did; voluminously; pouring out every kind of information, illustrating what he said with gestures so lively that he had to put down the watering-pot, and thus delay the end of the watering.

Lady Caroline bore it for a time but presently was unable to bear it, and as he would not go, and she could not tell him to, seeing that he was engaged in his proper work, once again it was she who had to.

She got off the wall and moved to the other side of the garden, where in a wooden shed were some comfortable low cane chairs. All she wanted was to turn one of these round with its back to Domenico and its front to the sea towards Genoa. Such a little thing to want. One would have thought she might have been allowed to do that unmolested. But he, who watched her every movement, when he saw her approaching the chairs darted after her and seized one and asked to be told where to put it.

Would she never get away from being waited on, being made comfortable, being asked where she wanted things put, having to say thank you? She was short with Domenico, who instantly concluded the sun had given her a headache, and ran in and fetched her a sunshade and a cushion and a footstool, and was skilful, and was wonderful, and was one of Nature's gentlemen.

She shut her eyes in a heavy resignation. She could not be unkind to Domenico. She could not get up and walk indoors as she would have done if it had been one of the others. Domenico was intelligent and very competent. She had at once discovered that it was he who really ran the house, who really did everything. And his manners were definitely delightful, and he undoubtedly was a charming person. It was only that she did so much long to be let alone. If only, only she could be left quite quiet for this one month, she felt that she might perhaps make something of herself after all.

She kept her eyes shut, because then he would think she wanted to sleep and would go away.

Domenico's romantic Italian soul melted within him at the sight, for having her eyes shut was extraordinarily becoming to her. He stood entranced, quite still, and she thought he had stolen away, so she opened them again.

No; there he was, staring at her. Even he. There was no getting away from being stared at.

"I have a headache," she said, shutting them again.

"It is the sun," said Domenico, "and sitting on the wall without a hat."

"I wish to sleep."

"Si signorina," he said sympathetically; and went softly away.

She opened her eyes with a sigh of relief. The gentle closing of the glass doors showed her that he had not only gone quite away but had shut her out in the garden so that she should be undisturbed. Now perhaps she would be alone till lunch-time.

It was very curious, and no one in the world could have been more surprised than she herself, but she wanted to think. She had never wanted to do that before. Everything else that it is possible to do without too much inconvenience she had either wanted to do or had done at one period or another of her life, but not before had she

72

wanted to think. She had come to San Salvatore with the single intention of lying comatose for four weeks in the sun, somewhere where her parents and friends were not, lapped in forgetfulness, stirring herself only to be fed, and she had not been there more than a few hours when this strange new desire took hold of her.

There had been wonderful stars the evening before, and she had gone out into the top garden after dinner, leaving Mrs. Fisher alone over her nuts and wine, and, sitting on the wall at the place where the lilies crowded their ghost heads, she had looked out into the gulf of the night, and it had suddenly seemed as if her life had been a noise all about nothing.

She had been intensely surprised. She knew stars and darkness did produce unusual emotions because, in others, she had seen them being produced, but they had not before done it in herself. A noise all about nothing. Could she be quite well? She had wondered. For a long while past she had been aware that her life was a noise, but it had seemed to be very much about something; a noise, indeed, about so much that she felt she must get out of earshot for a little or she would be completely, and perhaps permanently, deafened. But suppose it was only a noise about nothing?

She had not had a question like that in her mind before. It had made her feel lonely. She wanted to be alone, but not lonely. That was very different; that was something that ached and hurt dreadfully right inside one. It was what one dreaded most. It was what made one go to so many parties; and lately even the parties had seemed once or twice not to be a perfectly certain protection. Was it possible that loneliness had nothing to do with circumstances, but only with the way one met them? Perhaps, she had thought, she had better go to bed. She couldn't be very well.

She went to bed; and in the morning, after she had escaped the fly and had her breakfast and got out again into the garden, there was this same feeling again, and in broad daylight. Once more she had that really rather disgusting suspicion that her life till now had not only been loud but empty. Well, if that were so, and if her first twenty-eight years—the best ones—had gone just in meaningless noise, she had better stop a moment and look round her; pause, as they said in tiresome novels, and consider. She hadn't got many sets of twenty-eight years. One more would see her growing very like Mrs. Fisher. Two more— She averted her eyes.

73

Her mother would have been concerned if she had known. Her mother doted. Her father would have been concerned too, for he also doted. Everybody doted. And when, melodiously obstinate, she had insisted on going off to entomb herself in Italy for a whole month with queer people she had got out of an advertisement, refusing even to take her maid, the only explanation her friends could imagine was that poor Scrap—such was her name among them—had overdone it and was feeling a little nervy.

Her mother had been distressed at her departure. It was such an odd thing to do, such a sign of disappointment. She encouraged the general idea of the verge of a nervous breakdown. If she could have seen her adored Scrap, more delightful to look upon than any other mother's daughter had ever yet been, the object of her utmost pride, the source of all her fondest hopes, sitting staring at the empty noonday Mediterranean considering her three possible sets of twenty-eight years, she would have been miserable. To go away alone was bad; to think was worse. No good could come out of the thinking of a beautiful young woman. Complications could come out of it in profusion, but no good. The thinking of the beautiful was bound to result in hesitations, in reluctances, in unhappiness all round. And here, if she could have seen her, sat her Scrap thinking quite hard. And such things. Such old things. Things nobody ever began to think till they were at least forty.

Chapter 9

That one of the two sitting-rooms which Mrs. Fisher had taken for her own was a room of charm and character. She surveyed it with satisfaction on going into it after breakfast, and was glad it was hers. It had a tiled floor, and walls the colour of pale honey, and inlaid furniture the colour of amber, and mellow books, many in ivory or lemon-coloured covers. There was a big window overlooking the sea towards Genoa, and a glass door through which she could proceed out on to the battlements and walk along past the quaint and attractive watch-tower, in itself a room with chairs and a writing table, to where on the other side of the tower the battlements ended in a marble seat, and one could see the western bay and the point round which began the Gulf of Spezia. Her south view, between these two stretches of sea, was another hill, higher than San Salvatore, the last of the little peninsula, with the bland turrets of a smaller and uninhabited castle on the top, on which the setting sun still shone when everything else was sunk in shadow. Yes, she was very comfortably established here; and receptacles—Mrs. Fisher did not examine their nature closely, but they seemed to be small stone troughs, or perhaps little sarcophagi—ringed round the battlements with flowers.

These battlements, she thought, considering them, would have been a perfect place for her to pace up and down gently in moments when she least felt the need of her stick, or to sit in on the marble seat, having first put a cushion on it, if there had not unfortunately been a second glass door opening on to them, destroying their complete privacy, spoiling her feeling that the place was only for her. The second door belonged to the round drawing-room, which both she and Lady Caroline had rejected as too dark. That room would probably be sat in by the women from Hampstead, and she was afraid they would not confine themselves to sitting in it, but would come out through the glass door and invade her battlements. This would ruin the battlements. It would ruin them as far as she was concerned if they were to be overrun; or even if, not actually overrun, they were liable to be raked by the eyes of persons inside the room. No one could be perfectly at ease if they were being watched and knew it. What she wanted, what she surely had a right to, was privacy. She had no wish to intrude on the others; why then

75

should they intrude on her? And she could always relax her privacy if, when she became better acquainted with her companions, she should think it worth while, but she doubted whether any of the three would so develop as to make her think it worth while.

Hardly anything was really worth while, reflected Mrs. Fisher, except the past. It was astonishing, it was simply amazing, the superiority of the past to the present. Those friends of hers in London, solid persons of her own age, knew the same past that she knew, could talk about it with her, could compare it as she did with the tinkling present, and in remembering great men forget for a moment the trivial and barren young people who still, in spite of the war, seemed to litter the world in such numbers. She had not come away from these friends, these conversable ripe friends, in order to spend her time in Italy chatting with three persons of another generation and defective experience; she had come away merely to avoid the treacheries of a London April. It was true what she had told the two who came to Prince of Wales Terrace, that all she wished to do at San Salvatore was to sit by herself in the sun and remember. They knew this, for she had told them. It had been plainly expressed and clearly understood. Therefore she had a right to expect them to stay inside the round drawing-room and not to emerge interruptingly on to her battlements.

But would they? The doubt spoilt her morning. It was only towards lunch-time that she saw a way to be quite safe, and ringing for Francesca, bade her, in slow and majestic Italian, shut the shutters of the glass door of the round drawing-room, and then, going with her into the room, which had become darker than ever in consequence, but also, Mrs. Fisher observed to Francesca, who was being voluble, would because of this very darkness remain agreeably cool, and after all there were the numerous slit-windows in the walls to let in light and it was nothing to do with her if they did not let it in, she directed the placing of a cabinet of curios across the door on its inside.

This would discourage egress.

Then she rang for Domenico, and caused him to move one of the flower-filled sarcophagi across the door on its outside.

This would discourage ingress.

"No one," said Domenico, hesitating, "will be able to use the door."

"No one," said Mrs. Fisher firmly, "will wish to."

76

She then retired to her sitting-room, and from a chair placed where she could look straight on to them, gazed at her battlements, secured to her now completely, with calm pleasure.

Being here, she reflected placidly, was much cheaper than being in an hotel and, if she could keep off the others, immeasurably more agreeable. She was paying for her rooms—extremely pleasant rooms, now that she was arranged in them—£3 a week, which came to about eight shillings a day, battlements, watch-tower and all. Where else abroad could she live as well for so little, and have as many baths as she like, for eight shillings a day? Of course she did not yet know what her food would cost, but she would insist on carefulness over that, though she would also insist on its being carefulness combined with excellence. The two were perfectly compatible if the caterer took pains. The servants' wages, she had ascertained, were negligible, owing to the advantageous exchange, so that there was only the food to cause her anxiety. If she saw signs of extravagance she would propose that they each hand over a reasonable sum every week to Lady Caroline which should cover the bills, any of it that was not used to be returned, and if it were exceeded the loss to be borne by the caterer.

Mrs. Fisher was well off and had the desire for comforts proper to her age, but she disliked expenses. So well off was she that, had she so chosen, she could have lived in an opulent part of London and driven from it and to it in a Rolls-Royce. She had no such wish. It needed more vitality than went with true comfort to deal with a house in an opulent spot and a Rolls-Royce. Worries attended such possessions, worries of every kind, crowned by bills. In the sober gloom of Prince of Wales Terrace she could obscurely enjoy inexpensive yet real comfort, without being snatched at by predatory men-servants or collectors for charities, and a taxi stand was at the end of the road. Her annual outlay was small. The house was inherited. Death had furnished it for her. She trod in the dining-room on the Turkey carpet of her fathers; she regulated her day by the excellent black marble clock on the mantelpiece which she remembered from childhood; her walls were entirely covered by the photographs her illustrious deceased friends had given either herself or her father, with their own handwriting across the lower parts of their bodies, and the windows, shrouded by the maroon curtains of all her life, were decorated besides with the selfsame aquariums to which she owed her first lessons in sealore, and in which still swam slowly the goldfishes of her youth.

Were they the same goldfish? She did not know. Perhaps, like carp, they outlived everybody. Perhaps, on the other hand, behind the deep-sea vegetation provided for them at the bottom, they had from time to time as the years went by withdrawn and replaced themselves. Were they or were they not, she sometimes wondered, contemplating them between the courses of her solitary means, the same goldfish that had that day been there when Carlyle—how well she remembered it—angrily strode up to them in the middle of some argument with her father that had grown heated, and striking the glass smartly with his fist had put them to flight, shouting as they fled, "Och, ye deaf devils! Och, ye lucky deaf devils! Ye can't hear anything of the blasted, blethering, doddering, glaikit fool-stuff yer maister talks, can ye?" Or words to that effect.

Dear, great-souled Carlyle. Such natural gushings forth; such true freshness; such real grandeur. Rugged, if you will—yes, undoubtedly sometimes rugged, and startling in a drawing-room, but magnificent. Who was there now to put beside him? Who was there to mention in the same breath? Her father, than whom no one had had more flair, said: "Thomas is immortal." And here was this generation, this generation of puniness, raising its little voice in doubts, or, still worse, not giving itself the trouble to raise it at all, not—it was incredible, but it had been thus reported to her—even reading him. Mrs. Fisher did not read him either, but that was different. She had read him; she had certainly read him. Of course she had read him. There was Teufelsdröck—she quite well remembered a tailor called Teufelsdröck. So like Carlyle to call him that. Yes, she must have read him, though naturally details escaped her.

The gong sounded. Lost in reminiscence Mrs. Fisher had forgotten time, and hastened to her bedroom to wash her hands and smoothe her hair. She did not wish to be late and set a bad example, and perhaps find her seat at the head of the table taken. One could put no trust in the manners of the younger generation; especially not in those of that Mrs. Wilkins.

She was, however, the first to arrive in the dining-room. Francesca in a white apron stood ready with an enormous dish of smoking hot, glistening macaroni, but nobody was there to eat it.

Mrs. Fisher sat down, looking stern. Lax, lax.

"Serve me," she said to Francesca, who showed a disposition to wait for the others.

Francesca served her. Of the party she liked Mrs. Fisher least, in fact she did not like her at all. She was the only one of the four ladies who had not yet smiled. True she was old, true she was unbeautiful, true she therefore had no reason to smile, but kind ladies smiled, reason or no. They smiled, not because they were happy but because they wished to make happy. This one of the four ladies could not then, Francesca decided, be kind; so she handed her the macaroni, being unable to hide any of her feelings, morosely.

It was very well cooked, but Mrs. Fisher had never cared for maccaroni, especially not this long, worm-shaped variety. She found it difficult to eat—slippery, wriggling off her fork, making her look, she felt, undignified when, having got it as she supposed into her mouth, ends of it yet hung out. Always, too, when she ate it she was reminded of Mr. Fisher. He had during their married life behaved very much like maccaroni. He had slipped, he had wriggled, he had made her feel undignified, and when at last she had got him safe, as she thought, there had invariably been little bits of him that still, as it were, hung out.

Francesca from the sideboard watched Mrs. Fisher's way with macaroni gloomily, and her gloom deepened when she saw her at last take her knife to it and chop it small.

Mrs. Fisher really did not know how else to get hold of the stuff. She was aware that knives in this connection were improper, but one did finally lose patience. Maccaroni was never allowed to appear on her table in London. Apart from its tiresomeness she did not even like it, and she would tell Lady Caroline not to order it again. Years of practice, reflected Mrs. Fisher, chopping it up, years of actual living in Italy, would be necessary to learn the exact trick. Browning managed maccaroni wonderfully. She remembered watching him one day when he came to lunch with her father, and a dish of it had been ordered as a compliment to his connection with Italy. Fascinating, the way it went in. No chasing round the plate, no slidings off the fork, no subsequent protrusions of loose ends—just one dig, one whisk, one thrust, one gulp, and lo, yet another poet had been nourished.

"Shall I go and seek the young lady?" asked Francesca, unable any longer to look on a good maccaroni being cut with a knife.

79

Mrs. Fisher came out of her reminiscent reflections with difficulty. "She knows lunch is at half-past twelve," she said. "They all know."

"She may be asleep," said Francesca. "The other ladies are further away, but this one is not far away."

"Beat the gong again then," said Mrs. Fisher.

What manners, she though; what, what manners. It was not an hotel, and considerations were due. She must say she was surprised at Mrs. Arbuthnot, who had not looked like somebody unpunctual. Lady Caroline, too—she had seemed amiable and courteous, whatever else she might be. From the other one, of course, she expected nothing.

Francesca fetched the gong, and took it out into the garden and advanced, beating it as she advanced, close up to Lady Caroline, who, still stretched in her low chair, waited till she had done, and then turned her head and in the sweetest tones poured forth what appeared to be music but was really invective.

Francesca did not recognize the liquid flow as invective; how was she to, when it came out sounding like that? And with her face all smiles, for she could not but smile when she looked at this young lady, she told her the maccaroni was getting cold.

"When I do not come to meals it is because I do not wish to come to meals," said the irritated Scrap, "and you will not in future disturb me."

"Is She ill?" asked Francesca, sympathetic but unable to stop smiling. Never, never had she seen hair so beautiful. Like pure flax; like the hair of northern babes. On such a little head only blessing could rest, on such a little head the nimbus of the holiest saints could fitly be placed.

Scrap shut her eyes and refused to answer. In this she was injudicious, for its effect was to convince Francesca, who hurried away full of concern to tell Mrs. Fisher, that she was indisposed. And Mrs. Fisher, being prevented, she explained, from going out to Lady Caroline herself because of her stick, sent the two others instead, who had come in at that moment heated and breathless and full of excuses, while she herself proceeded to the next course, which was a very well-made omelette, bursting most agreeably at both its ends with young green peas.

"Serve me," she directed Francesca, who again showed a disposition to wait for the others.

"Oh, why won't they leave me alone?" Scrap asked herself when she heard more scrunchings on the little pebbles which took the place of grass, and therefore knew some one else was approaching.

She kept her eyes tight shut this time. Why should she go in to lunch if she didn't want to? This wasn't a private house; she was in no way tangled up in duties towards a tiresome hostess. For all practical purposes San Salvatore was an hotel, and she ought to be let alone to eat or not to eat exactly as if she really had been in an hotel.

But the unfortunate Scrap could not just sit still and close her eyes without rousing that desire to stroke and pet in her beholders with which she was only too familiar. Even the cook had patted her. And now a gentle hand—how well she knew and how much she dreaded gentle hands—was placed on her forehead.

"I'm afraid you're not well," said a voice that was not Mrs. Fisher's, and therefore must belong to one of the originals.

"I have a headache," murmured Scrap. Perhaps it was best to say that; perhaps it was the shortest cut to peace.

"I'm so sorry," said Mrs. Arbuthnot softly, for it was her hand being gentle.

"And I," said Scrap to herself, "who thought if I came here I would escape mothers."

"Don't you think some tea would do you good?" asked Mrs. Arbuthnot tenderly.

"Tea? The idea was abhorrent to Scrap. In this heat to be drinking tea in the middle of the day. . .

"No," she murmured.

"I expect what would really be best for her," said another voice, "is to be left quiet."

How sensible, thought Scrap; and raised the eye-lashes of one eye just enough to peep through and see who was speaking.

It was the freckled original. The dark one, then, was the one with the hand. The freckled one rose in her esteem.

"But I can't bear to think of you with a headache and nothing being done for it," said Mrs. Arbuthnot. "Would a cup of strong black coffee—?"

Scrap said no more. She waited, motionless and dumb, till Mrs. Arbuthnot should remove her hand. After all, she couldn't stand there all day, and when she went away she would have to take her hand with her.

"I do think," said the freckled one, "that she wants nothing except quiet."

And perhaps the freckled one pulled the one with the hand by the sleeve, for the hold on Scrap's forehead relaxed, and after a minute's silence, during which no doubt she was being contemplated—she was always being contemplated—the footsteps began to scrunch the pebbles again, and grew fainter, and were gone.

"Lady Caroline has a headache," said Mrs. Arbuthnot, re-entering the dining-room and sitting down in her place next to Mrs. Fisher. "I can't persuade her to have even a little tea, or some black coffee. Do you know what aspirin is in Italian?"

"The proper remedy for headaches," said Mrs. Fisher firmly, "is castor oil."

"But she hasn't got a headache," said Mrs. Wilkins.

"Carlyle," said Mrs. Fisher, who had finished her omelette and had leisure, while she waited for the next course, to talk, "suffered at one period terribly from headaches, and he constantly took castor oil as a remedy. He took it, I should say, almost to excess, and called it, I remember, in his interesting way the oil of sorrow. My father said it coloured for a time his whole attitude to life, his whole philosophy. But that was because he took too much. What Lady Caroline wants is one dose, and one only. It is a mistake to keep on taking castor oil."

"Do you know the Italian for it?" asked Mrs. Arbuthnot.

"Ah, that I'm afraid I don't. However, she would know. You can ask her."

"But she hasn't got a headache," repeated Mrs. Wilkins, who was struggling with the maccaroni. "She only wants to be let alone."

They both looked at her. The word shovel crossed Mrs. Fisher's mind in connection with Mrs. Wilkins's actions at that moment.

"Then why should she say she has?" asked Mrs. Arbuthnot.

"Because she is still trying to be polite. Soon she won't try, when the place has got more into her—she'll really be it. Without trying. Naturally."

"Lotty, you see," explained Mrs. Arbuthnot, smiling to Mrs. Fisher, who sat waiting with a stony patience for her next course, delayed because Mrs. Wilkins would go on trying to eat the maccaroni, which must be less worth eating than ever now that it was cold; "Lotty, you see, has a theory about this place—"

But Mrs. Fisher had no wish to hear any theory of Mrs. Wilkins's.

"I am sure I don't know," she interrupted, looking severely at Mrs. Wilkins, "why you should assume Lady Caroline is not telling the truth."

"I don't assume—I know." said Mrs. Wilkins.

"And pray how do you know?" asked Mrs. Fisher icily, for Mrs. Wilkins was actually helping herself to more maccaroni, offered her officiously and unnecessarily a second time by Francesca.

"When I was out there just now I saw inside her."

Well, Mrs. Fisher wasn't going to say anything to that; she wasn't going to trouble to reply to downright idiocy. Instead she sharply rapped the little table-gong by her side, though there was Francesca standing at the sideboard, and said, for she would wait no longer for her next course, "Serve me."

And Francesca—it must have been wilful—offered her the maccaroni again.

Chapter 10

There was no way of getting into or out of the top garden at San Salvatore except through the two glass doors, unfortunately side by side, of the dining-room and the hall. A person in the garden who wished to escape unseen could not, for the person to be escaped from could be met on the way. It was a small, oblong garden, and concealment was impossible. What trees there were—the Judas tree, the tamarisk, the umbrella-pine—grew close to the low parapets. Rose bushes gave no real cover; one step to right or left of them, and the person wishing to be private was discovered. Only the north-west corner was a little place jutting out from the great wall, a kind of excrescence or loop, no doubt used in the old distrustful days for observation, where it was possible to sit really unseen, because between it and the house was a thick clump of daphne.

Scrap, after glancing round to see that no one was looking, got up and carried her chair into this place, stealing away as carefully on tiptoe as those steal whose purpose is sin. There was another excrescence on the walls just like it at the north-east corner, but this, though the view from it was almost more beautiful, for from it you could see the bay and the lovely mountains behind Mezzago, was exposed. No bushes grew near it, nor had it any shade. The north-west loop then was where she would sit, and she settled into it, and nestling her head in her cushion and putting her feet comfortably on the parapet, from whence they appeared to the villagers on the piazza below as two white doves, thought that now indeed she would be safe.

Mrs. Fisher found her there, guided by the smell of her cigarette. The incautious Scrap had not thought of that. Mrs. Fisher did not smoke herself, and all the more distinctly could she smell the smoke of others. The virile smell met her directly she went out into the garden from the dining-room after lunch in order to have her coffee. She had bidden Francesca set the coffee in the shade of the house just outside the glass door, and when Mrs. Wilkins, seeing a table being carried there, reminded her, very officiously and tactlessly Mrs. Fisher considered, that Lady Caroline wanted to be alone, she retorted—and with what propriety—that the garden was for everybody.

Into it accordingly she went, and was immediately aware that Lady Caroline was smoking. She said to herself, "These modern young women," and proceeded to find her; her stick, now that lunch was over, being no longer the hindrance to action that it was before her meal had been securely, as Browning once said—surely it was Browning? Yes, she remembered how much diverted she had been—roped in.

Nobody diverted her now, reflected Mrs. Fisher, making straight for the clump of daphne; the world had grown very dull, and had entirely lost its sense of humour. Probably they still had their jokes, these people—in fact she knew they did, for Punch still went on; but how differently it went on, and what jokes. Thackeray, in his inimitable way, would have made mincemeat of this generation. Of how much it needed the tonic properties of that astringent pen it was of course unaware. It no longer even held him—at least, so she had been informed—in any particular esteem. Well, she could not give it eyes to see and ears to hear and a heart to understand, but she could and would give it, represented and united in the form of Lady Caroline, a good dose of honest medicine.

"I hear you are not well," she said, standing in the narrow entrance of the loop and looking down with the inflexible face of one who is determined to do good at the motionless and apparently sleeping Scrap.

Mrs. Fisher had a deep voice, very like a man's, for she had been overtaken by that strange masculinity that sometimes pursues a woman during the last laps of her life.

Scrap tried to pretend that she was asleep, but if she had been her cigarette would not have been held in her fingers but would have been lying on the ground.

She forgot this. Mrs. Fisher did not, and coming inside the loop, sat down on a narrow stone seat built out of the wall. For a little she could sit on it; for a little, till the chill began to penetrate.

She contemplated the figure before her. Undoubtedly a pretty creature, and one that would have had a success at Farringford. Strange how easily even the greatest men were moved by exteriors. She had seen with her own eyes Tennyson turn away from everybody—turn, positively, his back on a crowd of eminent people assembled to do him honour, and withdraw to the window with a young person nobody had ever heard of, who had been brought there by accident and whose one and only merit—if it be a merit, that which is conferred by chance—was beauty. Beauty! All over before you can turn round. An affair, one might almost say, of minutes. Well, while it lasted it did seem able to do what it liked with men. Even husbands were not immune. There had been passages in the life of Mr. Fisher . . .

"I expect the journey has upset you," she said in her deep voice. "What you want is a good dose of some simple medicine. I shall ask Domenico if there is such a thing in the village as castor oil."

Scrap opened her eyes and looked straight at Mrs. Fisher.

"Ah," said Mrs. Fisher, "I knew you were not asleep. If you had been you would have let your cigarette fall to the ground."

"Waste," said Mrs. Fisher. "I don't like smoking for women, but I still less like waste."

"What does one do with people like this?" Scrap asked herself, her eyes fixed on Mrs. Fisher in what felt to her an indignant stare but appeared to Mrs. Fisher as really charming docility.

"Now you'll take my advice," said Mrs. Fisher, touched, "and not neglect what may very well turn into an illness. We are in Italy, you know, and one has to be careful. You ought, to begin with, to go to bed."

"I never go to bed," snapped Scrap; and it sounded as moving, as forlorn, as that line spoken years and years ago by an actress playing the part of Poor Jo in dramatized version of Bleak House—"I'm always moving on," said Poor Jo in this play, urged to do so by a policeman; and Mrs. Fisher, then a girl, had laid her head on the red velvet parapet of the front row of the dress circle and wept aloud.

It was wonderful, Scrap's voice. It had given her, in the ten years since she came out, all the triumphs that intelligence and wit can have, because it made whatever she said seem memorable. She ought, with a throat formation like that, to have been a singer, but in every kind of music Scrap was dumb except this one music of the speaking voice; and what a fascination, what a spell lay in that. Such was the liveliness of her face and the beauty of her colouring that there was not a man into whose eyes at the sight of her there did not leap a flame of intensest interest; but, when he heard her voice, the flame in that man's eyes was caught and fixed. It was the same with every man, educated and uneducated, old, young, desirable themselves or undesirable, men of her own world and bus-conductors, generals and Tommies—during the war she had had a perplexing time—bishops equally with vergers—round about her

86

confirmation startling occurrences had taken place—wholesome and unwholesome, rich and penniless, brilliant or idiotic; and it made no difference at all what they were, or how long and securely married: into the eyes of every one of them, when they saw her, leapt this flame, and when they heard her it stayed there.

Scrap had had enough of this look. It only led to difficulties. At first it had delighted her. She had been excited, triumphant. To be apparently incapable of doing or saying the wrong thing, to be applauded, listened to, petted, adored wherever she went, and when she came home to find nothing there either but the most indulgent proud fondness—why, how extremely pleasant. And so easy, too. No preparation necessary for this achievement, no hard work, nothing to learn. She need take no trouble. She had only to appear, and presently say something.

But gradually experiences gathered round her. After all, she had to take trouble, she had to make efforts, because, she discovered with astonishment and rage, she had to defend herself. That look, that leaping look, meant that she was going to be grabbed at. Some of those who had it were more humble than others, especially if they were young, but they all, according to their several ability, grabbed; and she who had entered the world so jauntily, with her head in the air and the completest confidence in anybody whose hair was grey, began to distrust, and then to dislike, and soon to shrink away from, and presently to be indignant. Sometimes it was just as if she didn't belong to herself, wasn't her own at all, but was regarded as a universal thing, a sort of beauty-of-all-work. Really men . . . And she found herself involved in queer vague quarrels, being curiously hated. Really women . . . And when the war came, and she flung herself into it along with everybody else, it finished her. Really generals . . .

The war finished Scrap. It killed the one man she felt safe with, whom she would have married, and it finally disgusted her with love. Since then she had been embittered. She was struggling as angrily in the sweet stuff of life as a wasp got caught in honey. Just as desperately did she try to unstick her wings. It gave her no pleasure to outdo other women; she didn't want their tiresome men. What could one do with men when one had got them? None of them would talk to her of anything but the things of love, and how foolish and fatiguing that became after a bit. It was as though a healthy person with a normal hunger was given nothing whatever to eat but sugar. Love, love . . . the very word made her want to slap somebody. "Why should I love you? Why should I?" she would ask amazed sometimes when somebody was trying—somebody was always trying—to propose to her. But she never got a real answer, only further incoherence.

A deep cynicism took hold of the unhappy Scrap. Her inside grew hoary with disillusionment, while her gracious and charming outside continued to make the world more beautiful. What had the future in it for her? She would not be able, after such a preparation, to take hold of it. She was fit for nothing; she had wasted all this time being beautiful. Presently she wouldn't be beautiful, and what then? Scrap didn't know what then, it appalled her to wonder even. Tired as she was of being conspicuous she was at least used to that, she had never known anything else; and to become inconspicuous, to fade, to grow shabby and dim, would probably be most painful. And once she began, what years and years of it there would be! Imagine, thought Scrap, having most of one's life at the wrong end. Imagine being old for two or three times as long as being young. Stupid, stupid. Everything was stupid. There wasn't a thing she wanted to do. There were thousands of things she didn't want to do. Avoidance, silence, invisibility, if possible unconsciousness—these negations were all she asked for a moment; and here, even here, she was not allowed a minute's peace, and this absurd woman must come pretending, merely because she wanted to exercise power and make her go to bed and make her—hideous—drink castor oil, that she thought she was ill.

"I'm sure," said Mrs. Fisher, who felt the cold of the stone beginning to come through and knew she could not sit much longer, "you'll do what is reasonable. Your mother would wish—have you a mother?"

A faint wonder came into Scrap's eyes. Have you a mother? If ever anybody had a mother it was Scrap. It had not occurred to her that there could be people who had never heard of her mother. She was one of the major marchionesses—there being, as no one knew better than Scrap, marchionesses and marchionesses—and had held high positions at Court. Her father, too, in his day had been most prominent. His day was a little over, poor dear, because in the war he had made some important mistakes, and besides he was now grown old; still, there he was, an excessively well-known person. How restful, how extraordinarily restful to have found some one who had never heard of any of her lot, or at least had not yet connected her with them.

She began to like Mrs. Fisher. Perhaps the originals didn't know anything about her either. When she first wrote to them and signed her name, that great name of Dester which twisted in and out of English history like a bloody thread, for its bearers constantly killed, she had taken it for granted that they would know who she was; and at the interview of Shaftesbury Avenue she was sure they did know, because they hadn't asked, as they otherwise would have, for references.

Scrap began to cheer up. If nobody at San Salvatore had ever heard of her, if for a whole month she could shed herself, get right away from everything connected with herself, be allowed really to forget the clinging and the clogging and all the noise, why, perhaps she might make something of herself after all. She might really think; really clear up her mind; really come to some conclusion.

"What I want to do here," she said, leaning forward in her chair and clasping her hands round her knees and looking up at Mrs. Fisher, whose seat was higher than hers, almost with animation, so much pleased was she that Mrs. Fisher knew nothing about her, "is to come to a conclusion. That's all. It isn't much to want, is it? Just that."

She gazed at Mrs. Fisher, and thought that almost any conclusion would do; the great thing was to get hold of something, catch something tight, cease to drift.

Mrs. Fisher's little eyes surveyed her. "I should say," she said, "that what a young woman like you wants is a husband and children."

"Well, that's one of the things I'm going to consider," said Scrap amiably. "But I don't think it would be a conclusion."

"And meanwhile," said Mrs. Fisher, getting up, for the cold of the stone was now through, "I shouldn't trouble my head if I were you with considerings and conclusions. Women's heads weren't made for thinking, I assure you. I should go to bed and get well."

"I am well," said Scrap.

"Then why did you send a message that you were ill?"

"I didn't."

"Then I've had all the trouble of coming out here for nothing."

"But wouldn't you prefer coming out and finding me well than coming out and finding me ill?" asked Scrap, smiling?

Even Mrs. Fisher was caught by the smile.

"Well, you're a pretty creature," she said forgivingly. "It's a pity you weren't born fifty years ago. My friends would have liked looking at you."

"I'm very glad I wasn't," said Scrap. "I dislike being looked at."

"Absurd," said Mrs. Fisher, growing stern again. "That's what you are made for, young women like you. For what else, pray? And I assure you that if my friends had looked at you, you would have been looked at by some very great people."

"I dislike very great people," said Scrap, frowning. There had been an incident quite recently—really potentates. . .

"What I dislike," said Mrs. Fisher, now as cold as that stone she had got up from, "is the pose of the modern young woman. It seems to me pitiful, positively pitiful, in its silliness."

And, her stick crunching the pebbles, she walked away.

"That's all right," Scrap said to herself, dropping back into her comfortable position with her head in the cushion and her feet on the parapet; if only people would go away she didn't in the least mind why they went.

"Don't you think darling Scrap is growing a little, just a little, peculiar?" her mother had asked her father a short time before that latest peculiarity of the flight to San Salvatore, uncomfortably struck by the very odd things Scrap said and the way she had taken to slinking out of reach whenever she could and avoiding everybody except—such a sign of age—quite young men, almost boys.

"Eh? What? Peculiar? Well, let her be peculiar if she likes. A woman with her looks can be any damned thing she pleases," was the infatuated answer.

"I do let her," said her mother meekly; and indeed if she did not, what difference would it make?

Mrs. Fisher was sorry she had bothered about Lady Caroline. She went along the hall towards her private sitting-room, and her stick as she went struck the stone floor with a vigour in harmony with her feelings. Sheer silliness, these poses. She had no patience with them. Unable to be or do anything of themselves, the young of the present generation tried to achieve a reputation for cleverness by decrying all that was obviously great and obviously good and by praising everything, however obviously bad, that was different. Apes, thought Mrs. Fisher, roused. Apes. Apes. And in her sitting-room she found more apes, or what seemed to her in her present mood more, for there was Mrs. Arbuthnot placidly drinking coffee, while at the writing-table, the writing-table she already looked upon as sacred, using her pen, her own pen brought for her hand alone from Prince of Wales Terrace, sat Mrs. Wilkins writing; at the table; in her room; with her pen.

"Isn't this a delightful place?" said Mrs. Arbuthnot cordially. "We have just discovered it."

"I'm writing to Mellersh," said Mrs. Wilkins, turning her head and also cordially—as though, Mrs. Fisher thought, she cared a straw who she was writing to and anyhow knew who the person she called Mellersh was. "He'll want to know," said Mrs. Wilkins, optimism induced by her surroundings, "that I've got here safely."

Chapter 11

The sweet smells that were everywhere in San Salvatore were alone enough to produce concord. They came into the sitting-room from the flowers on the battlements, and met the ones from the flowers inside the room, and almost, thought Mrs. Wilkins, could be seen greeting each other with a holy kiss. Who could be angry in the middle of such gentlenesses? Who could be acquisitive, selfish, in the old rasped London way, in the presence of this bounteous beauty?

Yet Mrs. Fisher seemed to be all three of these things.

There was so much beauty, so much more than enough for every one, that it did appear to be a vain activity to try and make a corner in it.

Yet Mrs. Fisher was trying to make a corner in it, and had railed off a portion for her exclusive use.

Well, she would get over that presently; she would get over it inevitably, Mrs. Wilkins was sure, after a day or two in the extraordinary atmosphere of peace in that place.

Meanwhile she obviously hadn't even begun to get over it. She stood looking at her and Rose with an expression that appeared to be one of anger. Anger. Fancy. Silly old nerve-racked London feelings, thought Mrs. Wilkins, whose eyes saw the room full of kisses, and everybody in it being kissed, Mrs. Fisher as copiously as she herself and Rose.

"You don't like us being in here," said Mrs. Wilkins, getting up and at once, after her manner, fixing on the truth. "Why?"

"I should have thought," said Mrs. Fisher leaning on her stick, "you could have seen that it is my room."

"You mean because of the photographs," said Mrs. Wilkins.

Mrs. Arbuthnot, who was a little red and surprised, got up too.

"And the notepaper," said Mrs. Fisher. "Notepaper with my London address on it. That pen—"

She pointed. It was still in Mrs. Wilkins's hand.

"Is yours. I'm very sorry," said Mrs. Wilkins, laying it on the table. And she added smiling, that it had just been writing some very amiable things.

"But why," asked Mrs. Arbuthnot, who found herself unable to acquiesce in Mrs. Fisher's arrangements without at least a gentle struggle, "ought we not to be here? It's a sitting-room."

"There is another one," said Mrs. Fisher. "You and your friend cannot sit in two rooms at once, and if I have no wish to disturb you in yours I am unable to see why you should wish to disturb me in mine."

"But why—" began Mrs. Arbuthnot again.

"It's quite natural," Mrs. Wilkins interrupted, for Rose was looking stubborn; and turning to Mrs. Fisher she said that although sharing things with friends was pleasant she could understand that Mrs. Fisher, still steeped in the Prince of Wales Terrace attitude to life, did not yet want to, but that she would get rid of that after a bit and feel quite different. "Soon you'll want us to share," said Mrs. Wilkins reassuringly. "Why, you may even get so far as asking me to use your pen if you knew I hadn't got one."

Mrs. Fisher was moved almost beyond control by this speech. To have a ramshackle young woman from Hampstead patting her on the back as it were, in breezy certitude that quite soon she would improve, stirred her more deeply than anything had stirred her since her first discovery that Mr. Fisher was not what he seemed. Mrs. Wilkins must certainly be curbed. But how? There was a curious imperviousness about her. At that moment, for instance, she was smiling as pleasantly and with as unclouded a face as if she were saying nothing in the least impertinent. Would she know she was being curbed? If she didn't know, if she were too tough to feel it, then what? Nothing, except avoidance; except, precisely, one's own private sitting-room.

"I'm an old woman," said Mrs. Fisher, "and I need a room to myself. I cannot get about, because of my stick. As I cannot get about I have to sit. Why should I not sit quietly and undisturbed, as I told you in London I intended to? If people are to come in and out all day long, chattering and leaving doors open, you will have broken the agreement, which was that I was to be quiet."

"But we haven't the least wish—" began Mrs. Arbuthnot, who was again cut short by Mrs. Wilkins.

"We're only too glad," said Mrs. Wilkins, "for you to have this room if it makes you happy. We didn't know about it, that's all. We wouldn't have come in if we had—not till you invited us, anyhow. I expect," she finished looking down cheerfully at Mrs. Fisher, "you soon will." And picking up her letter she took Mrs. Arbuthnot's hand and drew her towards the door.

Mrs. Arbuthnot did not want to go. She, the mildest of women, was filled with a curious and surely unchristian desire to stay and fight. Not, of course, really, nor even with any definitely aggressive words. No; she only wanted to reason with Mrs. Fisher, and to reason patiently. But she did feel that something ought to be said, and that she ought not to allow herself to be rated and turned out as if she were a schoolgirl caught in ill behaviour by Authority.

Mrs. Wilkins, however, drew her firmly to and through the door, and once again Rose wondered at Lotty, at her balance, her sweet and equable temper—she who in England had been such a thing of gusts. From the moment they got into Italy it was Lotty who seemed the elder. She certainly was very happy; blissful, in fact. Did happiness so completely protect one? Did it make one so untouchable, so wise? Rose was happy herself, but not anything like so happy. Evidently not, for not only did she want to fight Mrs. Fisher but she wanted something else, something more than this lovely place, something to complete it; she wanted Frederick. For the first time in her life she was surrounded by perfect beauty, and her one thought was to show it to him, to share it with him. She wanted Frederick. She yearned for Frederick. Ah, if only, only Frederick . . .

"Poor old thing," said Mrs. Wilkins, shutting the door gently on Mrs. Fisher and her triumph. "Fancy on a day like this."

"She's a very rude old thing," said Mrs. Arbuthnot.

"She'll get over that. I'm sorry we chose just her room to go and sit in."

"It's much the nicest," said Mrs. Arbuthnot. "And it isn't hers."

"Oh but there are lots of other places, and she's such a poor old thing. Let her have the room. Whatever does it matter?"

And Mrs. Wilkins said she was going down to the village to find out where the post-office was and post her letter to Mellersh, and would Rose go too.

"I've been thinking about Mellersh," said Mrs. Wilkins as they walked, one behind the other, down the narrow zigzag path up which they had climbed in the rain the night before.

She went first. Mrs. Arbuthnot, quite naturally now, followed. In England it had been the other way about—Lotty, timid, hesitating, except when she burst out so awkwardly, getting behind the calm

94

and reasonable Rose whenever she could.

"I've been thinking about Mellersh," repeated Mrs. Wilkins over her shoulder, as Rose seemed not to have heard.

"Have you?" said Rose, a faint distaste in her voice, for her experiences with Mellersh had not been of a kind to make her enjoy remembering him. She had deceived Mellersh; therefore she didn't like him. She was unconscious that this was the reason of her dislike, and thought it was that there didn't seem to be much, if any, of the grace of god about him. And yet how wrong to feel that, she rebuked herself, and how presumptuous. No doubt Lotty's husband was far, far nearer to God than she herself was ever likely to be. Still, she didn't like him.

"I've been a mean dog," said Mrs. Wilkins.

"A what?" asked Mrs. Arbuthnot, incredulous of her hearing.

"All this coming away and leaving him in that dreary place while I rollick in heaven. He had planned to take me to Italy for Easter himself. Did I tell you?"

"No," said Mrs. Arbuthnot; and indeed she had discouraged talk about husbands. Whenever Lotty had begun to blurt out things she had swiftly changed the conversation. One husband led to another, in conversation as well as in life, she felt, and she could not, she would not, talk of Frederick. Beyond the bare fact that he was there, he had not been mentioned. Mellersh had had to be mentioned, because of his obstructiveness, but she had carefully kept him from overflowing outside the limits of necessity.

"Well, he did," said Mrs. Wilkins. "He had never done such a thing in his life before, and I was horrified. Fancy—just as I had planned to come to it myself."

She paused on the path and looked up at Rose.

"Yes," said Rose, trying to think of something else to talk about.

"Now you see why I say I've been a mean dog. He had planned a holiday in Italy with me, and I had planned a holiday in Italy leaving him at home. I think," she went on, her eyes fixed on Rose's face, "Mellersh has every reason to be both angry and hurt."

Mrs. Arbuthnot was astonished. The extraordinary quickness with which, hour by hour, under her very eyes, Lotty became more selfless, disconcerted her. She was turning into something surprisingly like a saint. Here she was now being affectionate about Mellersh—Mellersh, who only that morning, while they hung their feet into the sea, had seemed a mere iridescence, Lotty had told her,

95

a thing of gauze. That was only that morning; and by the time they had had lunch Lotty had developed so far as to have got him solid enough again to write to, and to write to at length. And now, a few minutes later, she was announcing that he had every reason to be angry with her and hurt, and that she herself had been—the language was unusual, but it did express real penitence—a mean dog.

Rose stared at her astonished. If she went on like this, soon a nimbus might be expected round her head, was there already, if one didn't know it was the sun through the tree-trunks catching her sandy hair.

A great desire to love and be friends, to love everybody, to be friends with everybody, seemed to be invading Lotty—a desire for sheer goodness. Rose's own experience was that goodness, the state of being good, was only reached with difficulty and pain. It took a long time to get to it; in fact one never did get to it, or, if for a flashing instant one did, it was only for a flashing instant. Desperate perseverance was needed to struggle along its path, and all the way was dotted with doubts. Lotty simply flew along. She had certainly, thought Rose, not got rid of her impetuousness. It had merely taken another direction. She was now impetuously becoming a saint. Could one really attain goodness so violently? Wouldn't there be an equally violent reaction?

"I shouldn't," said Rose with caution, looking down into Lotty's bright eyes—the path was steep, so that Lotty was well below her— "I shouldn't be sure of that too quickly."

"But I am sure of it, and I've written and told him so."

Rose stared. "Why, but only this morning—" she began.

"It's all in this," interrupted Lotty, tapping the envelope and looking pleased.

"What—everything?"

"You mean about the advertisement and my savings being spent? Oh no—not yet. But I'll tell him all that when he comes."

"When he comes?" repeated Rose.

"I've invited him to come and stay with us."

Rose could only go on staring.

"It's the least I could do. Besides—look at this." Lotty waived her hand. "Disgusting not to share it. I was a mean dog to go off and leave him, but no dog I've every heard of was ever as mean as I'd be if I didn't try and persuade Mellersh to come out and enjoy this too.

96

It's barest decency that he should have some of the fun out of my nest-egg. After all, he has housed me and fed me for years. One shouldn't be churlish."

"But—do you think he'll come?

"Oh, I hope so," said Lotty with the utmost earnestness; and added, "Poor lamb."

At that Rose felt she would like to sit down. Mellersh a poor lamb? That same Mellersh who a few hours before was mere shimmer? There was a seat at the bend of the path, and Rose went to it and sat down. She wished to get her breath, gain time. If she had time she might perhaps be able to catch up the leaping Lotty, and perhaps be able to stop her before she committed herself to what she probably presently would be sorry for. Mellersh at San Salvatore? Mellersh, from whom Lotty had taken such pains so recently to escape?

"I see him here," said Lotty, as if in answer to her thoughts.

Rose looked at her with real concern: for every time Lotty said in that convinced voice, "I see," what she saw came true. Then it was to be supposed that Mr. Wilkins too would presently come true.

"I wish," said Rose anxiously, "I understood you."

"Don't try," said Lotty, smiling.

"But I must, because I love you."

"Dear Rose," said Lotty, swiftly bending down and kissing her.

"You're so quick," said Rose. "I can't follow your developments. I can't keep touch. It was what happened with Freder—"

She broke off and looked frightened.

"The whole idea of our coming here," she went on again, as Lotty didn't seem to have noticed, "was to get away, wasn't it? Well, we've got away. And now, after only a single day of it, you want to write to the very people—"

She stopped.

"The very people we were getting away from," finished Lotty. "It's quite true. It seems idiotically illogical. But I'm so happy, I'm so well, I feel so fearfully wholesome. This place—why, it makes

me feel flooded with love."

And she stared down at Rose in a kind of radiant surprise.

Rose was silent a moment. Then she said, "And do you think it will have the same effect on Mr. Wilkins?"

Lotty laughed. "I don't know," she said. "But even if it doesn't, there's enough love about to flood fifty Mr. Wilkinses, as you call him. The great thing is to have lots of love about. I don't see," she went on, "at least I don't see here, though I did at home, that it matters who loves as long as somebody does. I was a stingy beast at home, and used to measure and count. I had a queer obsession about justice. As though justice mattered. As though justice can really be distinguished from vengeance. It's only love that's any good. At home I wouldn't love Mellersh unless he loved me back, exactly as much, absolute fairness. Did you ever. And as he didn't, neither did I, and the aridity of that house! The aridity . . ."

Rose said nothing. She was bewildered by Lotty. One odd effect of San Salvatore on her rapidly developing friend was her sudden free use of robust words. She had not used them in Hampstead. Beast and dog were more robust than Hampstead cared about. In words, too, Lotty had come unchained.

But how she wished, oh how Rose wished, that she too could write to her husband and say "Come." The Wilkins ménage, however pompous Mellersh might be, and he had seemed to Rose pompous, was on a healthier, more natural footing than hers. Lotty could write to Mellersh and would get an answer. She couldn't write to Frederick, for only too well did she know he wouldn't answer. At least, he might answer—a hurried scribble, showing how much bored he was at doing it, with perfunctory thanks for her letter. But that would be worse than no answer at all; for his handwriting, her name on an envelope addressed by him, stabbed her heart. Too acutely did it bring back the letters of their beginnings together, the letters from him so desolate with separation, so aching with love and longing. To see apparently one of these very same letters arrive, and open it to find:

Dear Rose—Thanks for letter. Glad you're having a good time. Don't hurry back. Say if you want any money. Everything going splendidly here—
Yours, Frederick.

—no, it couldn't be borne.

"I don't think I'll come down to the village with you to-day," she said, looking up at Lotty with eyes suddenly gone dim. "I think I want to think."

"All right," said Lotty, at once starting off briskly down the path. "But don't think too long," she called back over her shoulder. "Write and invite him at once."

"Invite whom?" asked Rose, startled.

"Your husband."

Chapter 12

At the evening meal, which was the first time the whole four sat round the dining-room table together, Scrap appeared.

She appeared quite punctually, and in one of those wrappers or tea-gowns which are sometimes described as ravishing. This one really was ravishing. It certainly ravished Mrs. Wilkins, who could not take her eyes off the enchanting figure opposite. It was a shell-pink garment, and clung to the adorable Scrap as though it, too, loved her.

"What a beautiful dress!" exclaimed Mrs. Wilkins eagerly.

"What—this old rag?" said Scrap, glancing down at it as if to see which one she had got on. "I've had it a hundred years." And she concentrated on her soup.

"You must be very cold in it," said Mrs. Fisher, thin-lipped; for it showed a great deal of Scrap—the whole of her arms, for instance, and even where it covered her up it was so thin that you still saw her.

"Who—me?" said Scrap, looking up a moment. "Oh, no."

And she continued her soup.

"You mustn't catch a chill, you know," said Mrs. Arbuthnot, feeling that such loveliness must at all costs be preserved unharmed. "There's a great difference here when the sun goes down."

"I'm quite warm," said Scrap, industriously eating her soup.

"You look as if you had nothing at all on underneath," said Mrs. Fisher.

"I haven't. At least, hardly anything," said Scrap, finishing her soup.

"How every imprudent," said Mrs. Fisher, "and how highly improper."

Whereupon Scrap stared at her.

Mrs. Fisher had arrived at dinner feeling friendly towards Lady Caroline. She at least had not intruded into her room and sat at her table and written with her pen. She did, Mrs. Fisher had supposed, know how to behave. Now it appeared that she did not know, for was this behaving, to come dressed—no, undressed—like that to a meal? Such behaviour was not only exceedingly improper but also most inconsiderate, for the indelicate creature would certainly catch a chill, and then infect the entire party. Mrs. Fisher had a great objection to other people's chills. They were always the fruit of folly; and then they were handed on to her, who had done nothing at all to deserve them.

"Bird-brained," though Mrs. Fisher, sternly contemplating Lady Caroline. "Not an idea in her head except vanity."

"But there are no men here," said Mrs. Wilkins, "so how can it be improper? Have you noticed," she inquired of Mrs. Fisher, who endeavoured to pretend she did not hear, "How difficult it is to be improper without men?"

Mrs. Fisher neither answered her not looked at her; but Scrap looked at her, and did that with her mouth which in any other mouth would have been a fain grin. Seen from without, across the bowl of nasturtiums, it was the most beautiful of brief and dimpled smiles.

She had a very alive sort of face, that one, thought Scrap, observing Mrs. Wilkins with a dawn of interest. It was rather like a field of corn swept by lights and shadows. Both she and the dark one, Scrap noticed, had changed their clothes, but only in order to put on silk jumpers. The same amount of trouble would have been enough to dress them properly, reflected Scrap. Naturally they looked like nothing on earth in the jumpers. It didn't matter what Mrs. Fisher wore; indeed, the only thing for her, short of plumes and ermine, was what she did wear. But these others were quite young still, and quite attractive. They really definitely had faces. How different life would be for them if they made the most of themselves instead of the least. And yet—Scrap was suddenly bored, and turned away her thoughts and absently ate toast. What did it matter? If you did make the most of yourself, you only collected people round you who ended by wanting to grab.

"I've had the most wonderful day," began Mrs. Wilkins, her eyes shining.

Scrap lowered hers. "Oh," she thought, "she's going to gush."

"As though anybody were interested in her day," thought Mrs. Fisher, lowering hers also.

In fact, whenever Mrs. Wilkins spoke Mrs. Fisher deliberately cast down her eyes. Thus would she mark her disapproval. Besides, it seemed the only safe thing to do with her eyes, for no one could tell what the uncurbed creature would say next. That which she had just said, for instance, about men—addressed too, to her—what could she mean? Better not conjecture, thought Mrs. Fisher; and her eyes, though cast down, yet saw Lady Caroline stretch out her hand to the Chianti flask and fill her glass again.

Again. She had done it once already, and the fish was only just going out of the room. Mrs. Fisher could see that the other respectable member of the party, Mrs. Arbuthnot, was noticing it too. Mrs. Arbuthnot was, she hoped and believed, respectable and well-meaning. It is true she also had invaded her sitting-room, but no doubt she had been dragged there by the other one, and Mrs. Fisher had little if anything against Mrs. Arbuthnot, and observed with approval that she only drank water. That was as it should be. So, indeed, to give her her dues, did the freckled one; and very right at their age. She herself drank wine, but with what moderation: one meal, one glass. And she was sixty-five, and might properly, and even beneficially, have had a least two.

"That," she said to Lady Caroline, cutting right across what Mrs. Wilkins was telling them about her wonderful day and indicating the wine-glass, "is very bad for you."

Lady Caroline, however, could not have heard, for she continued to sip, her elbow on the table, and listen to what Mrs. Wilkins was saying.

And what was it she was saying? She had invited somebody to come and stay? A man?

Mrs. Fisher could not credit her ears. Yet it evidently was a man, for she spoke of the person as he.

Suddenly and for the first time—but then this was most important—Mrs. Fisher addressed Mrs. Wilkins directly. She was sixty-five, and cared very little what sorts of women she happened to be with for a month, but if the women were to be mixed with men it was a different proposition altogether. She was not going to be made a cat's-paw of. She had not come out there to sanction by her presence what used in her day to be called fast behaviour. Nothing had been said at the interview in London about men; if there had been she would have declined, of course to come.

"What is his name?" asked Mrs. Fisher, abruptly interposing.

Mrs. Wilkins turned to her with a slight surprise. "Wilkins," she said.

"Wilkins?"

"Yes,"

"Your name?"

"And his."

"A relation?"

"Not blood."

"A connection?"

"A husband."

Mrs. Fisher once more cast down her eyes. She could not talk to Mrs. Wilkins. There was something about the things she said. . . "A husband." Suggesting one of many. Always that unseemly twist to everything. Why could she not say "My husband"? Besides, Mrs. Fisher had, she herself knew not for what reason, taken both the Hampstead young women for widows. War ones. There had been an absence of mention of husbands at the interview which would not, she considered, be natural if such persons did after all exist. And if a husband was not a relation, who was? "Not blood." What a way to talk. Why, a husband was the first of all relations. How well she remembered Ruskin—no, it was not Ruskin, it was the Bible that said a man should leave his father and mother and cleave only to his wife; showing that she became by marriage an even more than blood relation. And if the husband's father and mother were to be nothing to him compared to his wife, how much less than nothing ought the wife's father and mother be to her compared to her husband. She herself had been unable to leave her father and mother in order to cleave to Mr. Fisher because they were no longer, when she married, alive, but she certainly would have left them if they had been there to leave. Not blood, indeed. Silly talk.

The dinner was very good. Succulence succeeded succulence. Costanza had determined to do as she chose in the matter of cream and eggs the first week, and see what happened at the end of it when the bills had to be paid. Her experience of the English was that they were quiet about bills. They were shy of words. They believed readily. Besides, who was the mistress here? In the absence of a definite one, it occurred to Costanza that she might as well be the mistress herself. So she did as she chose about the dinner, and it was very good.

The four, however, were so much preoccupied by their own conversation that they ate it without noticing how good it was. Even Mrs. Fisher, she who in such matters was manly, did not notice. The entire excellent cooking was to her as though it were not; which shows how much she must have been stirred.

She was stirred. It was that Mrs. Wilkins. She was enough to stir anybody. And she was undoubtedly encouraged by Lady Caroline, who, in her turn, was no doubt influenced by the Chianti.

Mrs. Fisher was very glad there were no men present, for they certainly would have been foolish about Lady Caroline. She was precisely the sort of young woman to unbalance them; especially, Mrs. Fisher recognized, at that moment. Perhaps it was the Chianti momentarily intensifying her personality, but she was undeniably most attractive; and there were few things Mrs. Fisher disliked more than having to look on while sensible, intelligent men, who the moment before were talking seriously and interestingly about real matters, became merely foolish and simpering—she had seen them actually simpering—just because in walked a bit of bird-brained beauty. Even Mr. Gladstone, that great wise statesman, whose hand had once rested for an unforgettable moment solemnly on her head, would have, she felt, on perceiving Lady Caroline left off talking sense and horribly embarked on badinage.

"You see," Mrs. Wilkins said—a silly trick that, with which she mostly began her sentences; Mrs. Fisher each time wished to say, "Pardon me—I do not see, I hear"—but why trouble?—"You see," said Mrs. Wilkins, leaning across towards Lady Caroline, "we arranged, didn't we, in London that if any of us wanted to we could each invite one guest. So now I'm doing it."

"I don't remember that," said Mrs. Fisher, her eyes on her plate.

"Oh yes, we did—didn't we, Rose?"

"Yes—I remember," said Lady Caroline. "Only it seemed so incredible that one could every want to. One's whole idea was to get away from one's friends."

"And one's husbands."

Again that unseemly plural. But how altogether unseemly, thought Mrs. Fisher. Such implications. Mrs. Arbuthnot clearly thought so too, for she had turned red.

"And family affection," said Lady Caroline—or was it the Chianti speaking? Surely it was the Chianti.

"And the want of family affection," said Mrs. Wilkins—what a light she was throwing on her home life and real character.

"That wouldn't be so bad," said Lady Caroline. "I'd stay with that. It would give one room."

"Oh no, no—it's dreadful," cried Mrs. Wilkins. "It's as if one had no clothes on."

"But I like that," said Lady Caroline.

"Really—" said Mrs. Fisher.

"It's a divine feeling, getting rid of things," said Lady Caroline, who was talking altogether to Mrs. Wilkins and paid no attention to the other two.

"Oh, but in a bitter wind to have nothing on and know there never will be anything on and you going to get colder and colder till at last you die of it—that's what it was like, living with somebody who didn't love one."

These confidences, thought Mrs. Fisher . . . and no excuse whatever for Mrs. Wilkins, who was making them entirely on plain water. Mrs. Arbuthnot, judging from her face, quite shared Mrs. Fisher's disapproval; she was fidgeting.

"But didn't he?" asked Lady Caroline—every bit as shamelessly unreticent as Mrs. Wilkins.

"Mellersh? He showed no signs of it."

"Delicious," murmured Lady Caroline.

"Really—" said Mrs. Fisher.

"I didn't think it was at all delicious. I was miserable. And now, since I've been here, I simply stare at myself being miserable. As miserable as that. And about Mellersh."

"You mean he wasn't worth it."

"Really—" said Mrs. Fisher.

"No, I don't. I mean I've suddenly got well."

Lady Caroline, slowly twisting the stem of her glass in her fingers, scrutinized the lit-up face opposite.

"And now I'm well I find I can't sit here and gloat all to myself. I can't be happy, shutting him out. I must share. I understand exactly what the Blessed Damozel felt like.

"What was the Blessed Damozel?" asked Scrap.

"Really—" said Mrs. Fisher; and with such emphasis this time that Lady Caroline turned to her.

"Ought I to know?" she asked. "I don't know any natural history. It sounds like a bird."

"It is a poem," said Mrs. Fisher with extraordinary frost.

"Oh," said Scrap.

"I'll lend it to you," said Mrs. Wilkins, over whose face laughter rippled.

"No," said Scrap.

"And its author," said Mrs. Fisher icily, "though not perhaps quite what one would have wished him to be, was frequently at my father's table."

"What a bore for you," said Scrap. "That's what mother's always doing—inviting authors. I hate authors. I wouldn't mind them so much if they didn't write books. Go on about Mellersh," she said, turning to Mrs. Wilkins.

"Really—" said Mrs. Fisher.

"All those empty beds," said Mrs. Wilkins.

"What empty beds?" asked Scrap.

"The ones in this house. Why, of course they each ought to have somebody happy inside them. Eight beds, and only four people. It's dreadful, dreadful to be so greedy and keep everything just for oneself. I want Rose to ask her husband out too. You and Mrs. Fisher haven't got husbands, but why not give some friend a glorious time?"

Rose bit her lip. She turned red, she turned pale. If only Lotty would keep quiet, she thought. It was all very well to have suddenly become a saint and want to love everybody, but need she be so tactless? Rose felt that all her poor sore places were being danced on. If only Lotty would keep quiet . . .

And Mrs. Fisher, with even greater frostiness than that with which she had received Lady Caroline's ignorance of the Blessed Damozel, said, "There is only one unoccupied bedroom in this house."

"Only one?" echoed Mrs. Wilkins, astonished. "Then who are in all the others?"

"We are," said Mrs. Fisher.

"But we're not in all the bedrooms. There must be at least six. That leaves two over, and the owner told us there were eight beds—didn't he Rose?"

"There are six bedrooms," said Mrs. Fisher; for both she and Lady Caroline had thoroughly searched the house on arriving, in order to see which part of it they would be most comfortable in, and they both knew that there were six bedrooms, two of which were very small, and in one of these small ones Francesca slept in the company of a chair and a chest of drawers, and the other, similarly furnished, was empty.

Mrs. Wilkins and Mrs. Arbuthnot had hardly looked at the house, having spent most of their time out-of-doors gaping at the scenery, and had, in the agitated inattentiveness of their minds when first they began negotiating for San Salvatore, got into their heads that the eight beds of which the owner spoke were the same as eight bedrooms; which they were not. There were indeed eight beds, but four of them were in Mrs. Wilkins's and Mrs. Arbuthnot's rooms.

"There are six bedrooms," repeated Mrs. Fisher. "We have four, Francesca has the fifth, and the sixth is empty."

"So that," said Scrap, "However kind we feel we would be if we could, we can't. Isn't it fortunate?"

"But then there's only room for one?" said Mrs. Wilkins, looking round at the three faces.

"Yes—and you've got him," said Scrap.

Mrs. Wilkins was taken aback. This question of the beds was unexpected. In inviting Mellersh she had intended to put him in one of the four spare-rooms that she imagined were there. When there were plenty of rooms and enough servants there was no reason why they should, as they did in their small, two-servanted house at home, share the same one. Love, even universal love, the kind of love with which she felt herself flooded, should not be tried. Much patience and self-effacement were needed for successful married sleep. Placidity; a steady faith; these too were needed. She was sure she would be much fonder of Mellersh, and he not mind her nearly so much, if they were not shut up together at night, if in the morning they could meet with the cheery affection of friends between whom lies no shadow of differences about the window or the washing arrangements, or of absurd little choked-down resentments at something that had seemed to one of them unfair. Her happiness, she felt, and her ability to be friends with everybody, was the result of her sudden new freedom and its peace. Would there be that sense of freedom, that peace, after a night shut up with Mellersh? Would she be able in the morning to be full towards him, as she was at that moment full, of nothing at all but loving-kindness? After all, she hadn't been very long in heaven. Suppose she hadn't been in it long enough for her to have become fixed in blandness? And only that morning what an extraordinary joy it had been to find herself alone when she woke, and able to pull the bed-clothes any way she liked!

Francesca had to nudge her. She was so much absorbed that she did not notice the pudding.

"If," thought Mrs. Wilkins, distractedly helping herself, "I share my room with Mellersh I risk losing all I now feel about him. If on the other hand I put him in the one spare-room, I prevent Mrs. Fisher and Lady Caroline from giving somebody a treat. True they don't seem to want to at present, but at any moment in this place one or the other of them may be seized with a desire to make somebody happy, and then they wouldn't be able to because of Mellersh."

"What a problem," she said aloud, her eyebrows puckered.

"What is?" asked Scrap.

"Where to put Mellersh."

Scrap stared. "Why, isn't one room enough for him?" she asked?

"Oh yes, quite. But then there won't be any room left at all—any room for somebody you may want to invite."

"I shan't want to," said Scrap.

"Or you," said Mrs. Wilkins to Mrs. Fisher. "Rose, of course, doesn't count. I'm sure she would like sharing her room with her husband. It's written all over her."

"Really—" said Mrs. Fisher.

"Really what?" asked Mrs. Wilkins, turning hopefully to her, for she thought the word this time was the preliminary to a helpful suggestion.

It was not. It stood by itself. It was, as before, mere frost.

Challenged, however, Mrs. Fisher did fasten it on to a sentence. "Really am I to understand," she asked, "that you propose to reserve the one spare-room for the exclusive use of your own family?"

"He isn't my own family," said Mrs. Wilkins. "He's my husband. You see—"

"I see nothing," Mrs. Fisher could not this time refrain from interrupting—for what an intolerable trick. "At the most I hear, and that reluctantly."

But Mrs. Wilkins, as impervious to rebuke as Mrs. Fisher had feared, immediately repeated the tiresome formula and launched out into a long and excessively indelicate speech about the best place for the person she called Mellersh to sleep in.

Mellersh—Mrs. Fisher, remembering the Thomases and Johns and Alfreds and Roberts of her day, plain names that yet had all become glorious, thought it sheer affection to be christened Mellersh—was, it seemed, Mrs. Wilkins's husband, and therefore his place was clearly indicated. Why this talk? She herself, as if foreseeing his arrival, had had a second bed put in Mrs. Wilkins's room. There were certain things in life which were never talked about but only done. Most things connected with husbands were not talked about; and to have a whole dinner-table taken up with a discussion as to where one of them should sleep was an affront to the decencies. How and where husbands slept should be known only to their wives. Sometimes it was not known to them, and then the marriage had less happy moments; but these moments were not talked about either; the decencies continued to be preserved. At least, it was so in her day. To have to hear whether Mr. Wilkins should or should not sleep with Mrs. Wilkins, and the reasons why he should and the reasons why he shouldn't, was both uninteresting and indelicate.

She might have succeeded in imposing propriety and changing the conversation if it had not been for Lady Caroline. Lady Caroline encouraged Mrs. Wilkins, and threw herself into the discussion with every bit as much unreserve as Mrs. Wilkins herself. No doubt she was impelled on this occasion by Chianti, but whatever the reason there it was. And, characteristically, Lady Caroline was all for Mr. Wilkins being given the solitary spare-room. She took that for granted. Any other arrangement would be impossible, she said; her expression was, Barbarous. Had she never read her Bible, Mrs. Fisher was tempted to inquire—And they two shall be one flesh? Clearly also, then, one room. But Mrs. Fisher did not inquire. She did not care even to allude to such texts to some one unmarried.

However, there was one way she could force Mr. Wilkins into his proper place and save the situation: she could say she herself intended to invite a friend. It was her right. They had all said so. Apart from propriety, it was monstrous that Mrs. Wilkins should want to monopolise the one spare-room, when in her own room was everything necessary for her husband. Perhaps she really would invite somebody—not invite, but suggest coming. There was Kate Lumley, for instance. Kate could perfectly afford to come and pay her share; and she was of her own period and knew, and had known, most of the people she herself knew and had known. Kate, of course, had only been on the fringe; she used to be asked only to the big parties, not to the small ones, and she still was only on the fringe. There were some people who never got off the fringe, and Kate was one. Often, however, such people were more permanently agreeable to be with than the others, in that they remained grateful.

Yes; she might really consider Kate. The poor soul had never married, but then everybody could not expect to marry, and she was quite comfortably off—not too comfortably, but just comfortably enough to pay her own expenses if she came and yet be grateful. Yes; Kate was the solution. If she came, at one stroke, Mrs. Fisher saw, would the Wilkinses be regularized and Mrs. Wilkins be prevented from having more than her share of the rooms. Also, Mrs. Fisher would save herself from isolation; spiritual isolation. She desired physical isolation between meals, but she disliked that isolation which is of the spirit. Such isolation would, she feared, certainly be hers with these three alien-minded young women. Even Mrs. Arbuthnot was, owing to her friendship with Mrs. Wilkins, necessarily alien-minded. In Kate she would have a support. Kate, without intruding on her sitting-room, for Kate was tractable, would be there at meals to support her.

Mrs. Fisher said nothing at the moment; but presently in the drawing-room, when they were gathered round the wood fire—she had discovered there was no fireplace in her own sitting-room, and therefore she would after all be forced, so long as the evenings remained cool, to spend them in the other room—presently, while Francesca was handing coffee round and Lady Caroline was poisoning the air with smoke, Mrs. Wilkins, looking relieved and pleased, said: "Well, if nobody really wants that room, and wouldn't use it anyhow, I shall be very glad if Mellersh may have it."

"Of course he must have it," said Lady Caroline.

Then Mrs. Fisher spoke.

"I have a friend," she said in her deep voice; and sudden silence fell upon the others.

"Kate Lumley," said Mrs. Fisher.

Nobody spoke.

"Perhaps," continued Mrs. Fisher, addressing Lady Caroline, "you know her?"

No, Lady Caroline did not know Kate Lumley; and Mrs. Fisher, without asking the others if they did, for she was sure they knew no one, proceeded. "I wish to invite her to join me," said Mrs. Fisher.

Complete silence.

Then Scrap said, turning to Mrs. Wilkins, "That settles Mellersh, then."

"It settles the question of Mr. Wilkins," said Mrs. Fisher, "although I am unable to understand that there should ever have been a question, in the only way that is right."

"I'm afraid you're in for it, then," said Lady Caroline, again to Mrs. Wilkins. "Unless," she added, "he can't come."

But Mrs. Wilkins, her brow perturbed—for suppose after all she were not yet quite stable in heaven?—could only say, a little uneasily, "I see him here."

110

Chapter 13

The uneventful days—only outwardly uneventful—slipped by in floods of sunshine, and the servants, watching the four ladies, came to the conclusion there was very little life in them.

To the servants San Salvatore seemed asleep. No one came to tea, nor did the ladies go anywhere to tea. Other tenants in other springs had been far more active. There had been stir and enterprise; the boat had been used; excursions had been made; Beppo's fly was ordered; people from Mezzago came over and spent the day; the house rang with voices; even sometimes champagne had been drunk. Life was varied, life was interesting. But this? What was this? The servants were not even scolded. They were left completely to themselves. They yawned.

Perplexing, too, was the entire absence of gentlemen. How could gentlemen keep away from so much beauty? For, added up, and even after the subtraction of the old one, the three younger ladies produced a formidable total of that which gentlemen usually sought.

Also the evident desire of each lady to spend long hours separated from the other ladies puzzled the servants. The result was a deathly stillness in the house, except at meal-times. It might have been as empty as it had been all the winter, for any sounds of life there were. The old lady sat in her room, alone; the dark-eyed lady wandered off alone, loitering, so Domenico told them, who sometimes came across her in the course of his duties, incomprehensibly among the rocks; the very beautiful fair lady lay in her low chair in the top garden, alone; the less, but still beautiful fair lady went up the hills and stayed up them for hours, alone; and every day the sun blazed slowly round the house, and disappeared at evening into the sea, and nothing at all had happened.

The servants yawned.

Yes the four visitors, while their bodies sat—that was Mrs. Fisher's—or lay—that was Lady Caroline's—or loitered—that was Mrs. Arbuthnot's—or went in solitude up into the hills—that was Mrs. Wilkins's—were anything but torpid really. Their minds were unusually busy. Even at night their minds were busy, and the dreams they had were clear, thin, quick things, entirely different from the heavy dreams of home. There was that in the atmosphere of San Salvatore which produced active-mindedness in all except

111

the natives. They, as before, whatever the beauty around them, whatever the prodigal seasons did, remained immune from thoughts other than those they were accustomed to. All their lives they had seen, year by year, the amazing recurrent spectacle of April in the gardens, and custom had made it invisible to them. They were as blind to it, as unconscious of it, as Domenico's dog asleep in the sun.

The visitors could not be blind to it—it was too arresting after London in a particularly wet and gloomy March. Suddenly to be transported to that place where the air was so still that it held its breath, where the light was so golden that the most ordinary things were transfigured—to be transported into that delicate warmth, that caressing fragrance, and to have the old grey castle as the setting, and, in the distance, the serene clear hills of Perugini's backgrounds, was an astonishing contrast. Even Lady Caroline, used all her life to beauty, who had been everywhere and seen everything, felt the surprise of it. It was, that year, a particularly wonderful spring, and of all the months at San Salvatore April, if the weather was fine, was best. May scorched and withered; March was restless, and could be hard and cold in its brightness; but April came along softly like a blessing, and if it were a fine April it was so beautiful that it was impossible not to feel different, not to feel stirred and touched.

Mrs. Wilkins, we have seen, responded to it instantly. She, so to speak, at once flung off all her garments and dived straight into glory, unhesitatingly, with a cry of rapture.

Mrs. Arbuthnot was stirred and touched, but differently. She had odd sensations—presently to be described.

Mrs. Fisher, being old, was of a closer, more impermeable texture, and offered more resistance; but she too had odd sensations, also in their place to be described.

Lady Caroline, already amply acquainted with beautiful houses and climates, to whom they could not come quite with the same surprise, yet was very nearly as quick to react as Mrs. Wilkins. The place had an almost instantaneous influence on her as well, and of one part of this influence she was aware: it had made her, beginning on the very first evening, want to think, and acted on her curiously like a conscience. What this conscience seemed to press upon her notice with an insistence that startled her—Lady Caroline hesitated to accept the word, but it would keep on coming into her head—was that she was tawdry.

She must think that out.

The morning after the first dinner together, she woke up in a condition of regret that she should have been so talkative to Mrs. Wilkins the night before. What had made her be, she wondered. Now, of course, Mrs. Wilkins would want to grab, she would want to be inseparable; and the thought of a grabbing and an inseparableness that should last four weeks made Scrap's spirit swoon within her. No doubt the encouraged Mrs. Wilkins would be lurking in the top garden waiting to waylay her when she went out, and would hail her with morning cheerfulness. How much she hated being hailed with morning cheerfulness—or indeed, hailed at all. She oughtn't to have encouraged Mrs. Wilkins the night before. Fatal to encourage. It was bad enough not to encourage, for just sitting there and saying nothing seemed usually to involve her, but actively to encourage was suicidal. What on earth had made her? Now she would have to waste all the precious time, the precious, lovely time for thinking in, for getting square with herself, in shaking Mrs. Wilkins off.

With great caution and on the tips of her toes, balancing herself carefully lest the pebbles should scrunch, she stole out when she was dressed to her corner; but the garden was empty. No shaking off was necessary. Neither Mrs. Wilkins nor anybody else was to be seen. She had it entirely to herself. Except for Domenico, who presently came and hovered, watering his plants, again especially all the plants that were nearest her, no one came out at all; and when, after a long while of following up thoughts which seemed to escape her just as she had got them, and dropping off exhausted to sleep in the intervals of this chase, she felt hungry and looked at her watch and saw that it was past three, she realized that nobody had even bothered to call her in to lunch. So that, Scrap could not but remark, if any one was shaken off it was she herself.

Well, but how delightful, and how very new. Now she would really be able to think, uninterruptedly. Delicious to be forgotten.

Still, she was hungry; and Mrs. Wilkins, after that excessive friendliness the night before, might at least have told her lunch was ready. And she had really been excessively friendly—so nice about Mellersh's sleeping arrangements, wanting him to have the spare-room and all. She wasn't usually interested in arrangements, in fact she wasn't ever interested in them; so that Scrap considered she might be said almost to have gone out of her way to be agreeable to

Mrs. Wilkins. And, in return, Mrs. Wilkins didn't even bother whether or not she had any lunch.

Fortunately, though she was hungry, she didn't mind missing a meal. Life was full of meals. They took up an enormous proportion of one's time; and Mrs. Fisher was, she was afraid, one of those persons who at meals linger. Twice now had she dined with Mrs. Fisher, and each time she had been difficult at the end to dislodge, lingering on slowly cracking innumerable nuts and slowly drinking a glass of wine that seemed as if it would never be finished. Probably it would be a good thing to make a habit of missing lunch, and as it was quite easy to have tea brought out to her, and as she breakfasted in her room, only once a day would she have to sit at the dining-room table and endure the nuts.

Scrap burrowed her head comfortably in the cushions, and with her feet crossed on the low parapet gave herself up to more thought. She said to herself, as she had said at intervals throughout the morning: Now I'm going to think. But, never having thought out anything in her life, it was difficult. Extraordinary how one's attention wouldn't stay fixed; extraordinary how one's mind slipped sideways. Settling herself down to a review of her past as a preliminary to the consideration of her future, and hunting in it to begin with for any justification of that distressing word tawdry, the next thing she knew was that she wasn't thinking about this at all, but had somehow switched on to Mr. Wilkins.

Well, Mr. Wilkins was quite easy to think about, though not pleasant. She viewed his approach with misgivings. For not only was it a profound and unexpected bore to have a man added to the party, and a man, too, of the kind she was sure Mr. Wilkins must be, but she was afraid—and her fear was the result of a drearily unvarying experience—that he might wish to hang about her.

This possibility had evidently not yet occurred to Mrs. Wilkins, and it was not one to which she could very well draw her attention; not, that is, without being too fatuous to live. She tried to hope that Mr. Wilkins would be a wonderful exception to the dreadful rule. If only he were, she would be so much obliged to him that she believed she might really quite like him.

But—she had misgivings. Suppose he hung about her so that she was driven from her lovely top garden; suppose the light in Mrs. Wilkins's funny, flickering face was blown out. Scrap felt she would particularly dislike this to happen to Mrs. Wilkins's face, yet she had never in her life met any wives, not any at all, who had been able to understand that she didn't in the least want their husbands. Often she had met wives who didn't want their husbands either, but that made them none the less indignant if they thought somebody else did, and none the less sure, when they saw them hanging round Scrap, that she was trying to get them. Trying to get them! The bare thought, the bare recollection of these situations, filled her with a boredom so extreme that it instantly sent her to sleep again.

When she woke up she went on with Mr. Wilkins.

Now if, thought Scrap, Mr. Wilkins were not an exception and behaved in the usual way, would Mrs. Wilkins understand, or would it just simply spoil her holiday? She seemed quick, but would she be quick about just this? She seemed to understand and see inside one, but would she understand and see inside one when it came to Mr. Wilkins?

The experienced Scrap was full of doubts. She shifted her feet on the parapet; she jerked a cushion straight. Perhaps she had better try and explain to Mrs. Wilkins, during the days still remaining before the arrival—explain in a general way, rather vague and talking at large—her attitude towards such things. She might also expound to her her peculiar dislike of people's husbands, and her profound craving to be, at least for this one month, let alone.

But Scrap had her doubts about this too. Such talk meant a certain familiarity, meant embarking on a friendship with Mrs. Wilkins; and if, after having embarked on it and faced the peril it contained of too much Mrs. Wilkins, Mr. Wilkins should turn out to be artful—and people did get very artful when they were set on anything—and manage after all to slip through into the top garden, Mrs. Wilkins might easily believe she had been taken in, and that she, Scrap, was deceitful. Deceitful! And about Mr. Wilkins. Wives were really pathetic.

At half-past four she heard sounds of saucers on the other side of the daphne bushes. Was tea being sent out to her?

No; the sounds came no closer, they stopped near the house. Tea was to be in the garden, in her garden. Scrap considered she might at least have been asked if she minded being disturbed. They all knew she sat there.

Perhaps some one would bring hers to her in her corner.

No; nobody brought anything.

115

Well, she was too hungry not to go and have it with the others to-day, but she would give Francesca strict orders for the future.

She got up, and walked with that slow grace which was another of her outrageous number of attractions towards the sounds of tea. She was conscious not only of being very hungry but of wanting to talk to Mrs. Wilkins again. Mrs. Wilkins had not grabbed, she had left her quite free all day in spite of the rapprochement the night before. Of course she was an original, and put on a silk jumper for dinner, but she hadn't grabbed. This was a great thing. Scrap went towards the tea-table quite looking forward to Mrs. Wilkins; and when she came in sight of it she saw only Mrs. Fisher and Mrs. Arbuthnot.

Mrs. Fisher was pouring out the tea, and Mrs. Arbuthnot was offering Mrs. Fisher macaroons. Every time Mrs. Fisher offered Mrs. Arbuthnot anything—her cup, or milk, or sugar—Mrs. Arbuthnot offered her macaroons—pressed them on her with an odd assiduousness, almost with obstinacy. Was it a game? Scrap wondered, sitting down and seizing a macaroon.

"Where is Mrs. Wilkins?" asked Scrap.

They did not know. At least, Mrs. Arbuthnot, on Scrap's inquiry, did not know; Mrs. Fisher's face, at the name, became elaborately uninterested.

It appeared that Mrs. Wilkins had not been seen since breakfast. Mrs. Arbuthnot thought she had probably gone for a picnic. Scrap missed her. She ate the enormous macaroons, the best and biggest she had ever come across, in silence. Tea without Mrs. Wilkins was dull; and Mrs. Arbuthnot had that fatal flavour of motherliness about her, of wanting to pet one, to make one very comfortable, coaxing one to eat—coaxing her, who was already so frankly, so even excessively, eating—that seemed to have dogged Scrap's steps through life. Couldn't people leave one alone? She was perfectly able to eat what she wanted unincited. She tried to quench Mrs. Arbuthnot's zeal by being short with her. Useless. The shortness was not apparent. It remained, as all Scrap's evil feelings remained, covered up by the impenetrable veil of her loveliness.

Mrs. Fisher sat monumentally, and took no notice of either of them. She had had a curious day, and was a little worried. She had been quite alone, for none of the three had come to lunch, and none of them had taken the trouble to let her know they were not coming; and Mrs. Arbuthnot, drifting casually into tea, had behaved oddly

116

till Lady Caroline joined them and distracted her attention.

Mrs. Fisher was prepared not to dislike Mrs. Arbuthnot, whose parted hair and mild expression seemed very decent and womanly, but she certainly had habits that were difficult to like. Her habit of instantly echoing any offer made her of food and drink, of throwing the offer back on one, as it were, was not somehow what one expected of her. "Will you have some more tea?" was surely a question to which the answer was simply yes or no; but Mrs. Arbuthnot persisted in the trick she had exhibited the day before at breakfast, of adding to her yes or no the words, "Will you?" She had done it again that morning at breakfast and here she was doing it at tea—the two meals at which Mrs. Fisher presided and poured out. Why did she do it? Mrs. Fisher failed to understand.

But this was not what was worrying her; this was merely by the way. What was worrying her was that she had been quite unable that day to settle to anything, and had done nothing but wander restlessly from her sitting-room to her battlements and back again. It had been a wasted day, and how much she disliked waste. She had tried to read, and she had tried to write to Kate Lumley; but no—a few words read, a few lines written, and up she got again and went out on to the battlements and stared at the sea.

It did not matter that the letter to Kate Lumley should not be written. There was time enough for that. Let the others suppose her coming was definitely fixed. All the better. So would Mr. Wilkins be kept out of the spare-room and put where he belonged. Kate would keep. She could be held in reserve. Kate in reserve was just as potent as Kate in actuality, and there were points about Kate in reserve which might be missing from Kate in actuality. For instance, if Mrs. Fisher were going to be restless, she would rather Kate were not there to see. There was a want of dignity about restlessness, about trotting backwards and forwards. But it did matter that she could not read a sentence of any of her great dead friends' writings; no, not even of Browning's, who had been so much in Italy, nor of Ruskin's, whose Stones of Venice she had brought with her to re-read so nearly on the very spot; nor even a sentence of a really interesting book like the one she had found in her sitting-room about the home life of the German Emperor, poor man—written in the nineties, when he had not yet begun to be more sinned against than sinning, which was, she was firmly convinced, what was the matter with him now, and full of exciting things about his birth and his right arm and accoucheurs—without having to put it down and go and stare at the sea.

Reading was very important; the proper exercise and development of one's mind was a paramount duty. How could one read if one were constantly trotting in and out? Curious, this restlessness. Was she going to be ill? No, she felt well; indeed, unusually well, and she went in and out quite quickly—trotted, in fact—and without her stick. Very odd that she shouldn't be able to sit still, she thought, frowning across the tops of some purple hyacinths at the Gulf of Spezia glittering beyond a headland; very odd that she, who walked so slowly, with such dependence on her stick, should suddenly trot.

It would be interesting to talk to some one about it, she felt. Not to Kate—to a stranger. Kate would only look at her and suggest a cup of tea. Kate always suggested cups of tea. Besides, Kate had a flat face. That Mrs. Wilkins, now—annoying as she was, loose-tongued as she was, impertinent, objectionable, would probably understand, and perhaps know what was making her be like this. But she could say nothing to Mrs. Wilkins. She was the last person to whom one would admit sensations. Dignity alone forbade it. Confide in Mrs. Wilkins? Never.

And Mrs. Arbuthnot, while she wistfully mothered the obstructive Scrap at tea, felt too that she had had a curious day. Like Mrs. Fisher's, it had been active, but, unlike Mrs. Fisher's, only active in mind. Her body had been quite still; her mind had not been still at all, it had been excessively active. For years she had taken care to have no time to think. Her scheduled life in the parish had prevented memories and desires from intruding on her. That day they had crowded. She went back to tea feeling dejected, and that she should feel dejected in such a place with everything about her to make her rejoice, only dejected her the more. But how could she rejoice alone? How could anybody rejoice and enjoy and appreciate, really appreciate, alone? Except Lotty. Lotty seemed able to. She had gone off down the hill directly after breakfast, alone yet obviously rejoicing, for she had not suggested that Rose should go too, and she was singing as she went.

Rose had spent the day by herself, sitting with her hands clasping her knees, staring straight in front of her. What she was staring at were the grey swords of the agaves, and, on their tall stalks, the pale irises that grew in the remote place she had found, while beyond them, between the grey leaves and the blue flowers, she saw the sea. The place she had found was a hidden corner where the sun-baked stones were padded with thyme, and nobody was likely to come. It was out of sight and sound of the house; it was off any path; it was near the end of the promontory. She sat so quiet that presently lizards darted over her feet, and some tiny birds like finches, frightened away at first, came back again and flitted among the bushes round her just as if she hadn't been there. How beautiful it was. And what was the good of it with no one there, no one who loved being with one, who belonged to one, to whom one could say, "Look." And wouldn't one say, "Look—dearest?" Yes, one would say dearest; and the sweet word, just to say it to somebody who loved one, would make one happy.

She sat quite still, staring straight in front of her. Strange that in this place she did not want to pray. She who had prayed so constantly at home didn't seem able to do it here at all. The first morning she had merely thrown up a brief thank you to heaven on getting out of bed, and had gone straight to the window to see what everything looked like—thrown up the thank you as carelessly as a ball, and thought no more about it. That morning, remembering this and ashamed, she had knelt down with determination; but perhaps determination was bad for prayers, for she had been unable to think of a thing to say. And as for her bedtime prayers, on neither of the nights had she said a single one. She had forgotten them. She had been so much absorbed in other thoughts that she had forgotten them; and, once in bed, she was asleep and whirling along among bright, thin swift dreams before she had so much time as to stretch herself out.

What had come over her? Why had she let go the anchor of prayer? And she had difficulty, too, in remembering her poor, in remembering even that there were such things as poor. Holidays, of course, were good, and were recognized by everybody as good, but ought they so completely to blot out, to make such havoc of, the realities? Perhaps it was healthy to forget her poor; with all the greater gusto would she go back to them. But it couldn't be healthy to forget her prayers, and still less could it be healthy not to mind.

Rose did not mind. She knew she did not mind. And, even worse, she knew she did not mind not minding. In this place she was indifferent to both the things that had filled her life and made it seem as if it were happy for years. Well, if only she could rejoice in her wonderful new surroundings, have that much at least to set against the indifference, the letting go—but she could not. She had no work; she did not pray; she was left empty.

Lotty had spoilt her day that day, as she had spoilt her day the day before—Lotty, with her invitation to her husband, with her suggestion that she too should invite hers. Having flung Frederick into her mind again the day before, Lotty had left her; for the whole afternoon she had left her alone with her thoughts. Since then they had been all of Frederick. Where at Hampstead he came to her only in her dreams, here he left her dreams free and was with her during the day instead. And again that morning, as she was struggling not to think of him, Lotty had asked her, just before disappearing singing down the path, if she had written yet and invited him, and again he was flung into her mind and she wasn't able to get him out.

How could she invite him? It had gone on so long, their estrangement, such years; she would hardly know what words to use; and besides, he would not come. Why should he come? He didn't care about being with her. What could they talk about? Between them was the barrier of his work and her religion. She could not—how could she, believing as she did in purity, in responsibility for the effect of one's actions on others—bear his work, bear living by it; and he she knew, had at first resented and then been merely bored by her religion. He had let her slip away; he had given her up; he no longer minded; he accepted her religion indifferently, as a settled fact. Both it and she—Rose's mind, becoming more luminous in the clear light of April at San Salvatore, suddenly saw the truth—bored him.

Naturally when she saw this, when that morning it flashed upon her for the first time, she did not like it; she liked it so little that for a space the whole beauty of Italy was blotted out. What was to be done about it? She could not give up believing in good and not liking evil, and it must be evil to live entirely on the proceeds of adulteries, however dead and distinguished they were. Besides, if she did, if she sacrificed her whole past, her bringing up, her work for the last ten years, would she bore him less? Rose felt right down at her very roots that if you have once thoroughly bored somebody it is next to impossible to unbore him. Once a bore always a bore—certainly, she thought, to the person originally bored.

Then, thought she, looking out to sea through eyes grown misty, better cling to her religion. It was better—she hardly noticed the reprehensibleness of her thought—than nothing. But oh, she wanted to cling to something tangible, to love something living, something that one could hold against one's heart, that one could see and touch and do things for. If her poor baby hadn't died . . . babies didn't get bored with one, it took them a long while to grow up and find one out. And perhaps one's baby never did find one out; perhaps one would always be to it, however old and bearded it grew, somebody special, somebody different from every one else, and if for no other reason, precious in that one could never be repeated.

Sitting with dim eyes looking out to sea she felt an extraordinary yearning to hold something of her very own tight to her bosom. Rose was slender, and as reserved in figure as in character, yet she felt a queer sensation of—how could she describe it?—bosom. There was something about San Salvatore that made her feel all bosom. She wanted to gather to her bosom, to comfort and protect, soothing the dear head that should lie on it with softest strokings and murmurs of love. Frederick, Frederick's child—come to her, pillowed on her, because they were unhappy, because they had been hurt. . . They would need her then, if they had been hurt; they would let themselves be loved then, if they were unhappy.

Well, the child was gone, would never come now; but perhaps Frederick—some day—when he was old and tired . . .

Such were Mrs. Arbuthnot's reflections and emotions that first day at San Salvatore by herself. She went back to tea dejected as she had not been for years. San Salvatore had taken her carefully built-up semblance of happiness away from her, and given her nothing in exchange. Yes—it had given her yearnings in exchange, this ache and longing, this queer feeling of bosom; but that was worse than nothing. And she who had learned balance, who never at home was irritated but always able to be kind, could not, even in her dejection, that afternoon endure Mrs. Fisher's assumption of the position as hostess at tea.

One would have supposed that such a little thing would not have touched her, but it did. Was her nature changing? Was she to be not only thrown back on long—stifled yearnings after Frederick, but also turned into somebody who wanted to fight over little things? After tea, when both Mrs. Fisher and Lady Caroline had disappeared again—it was quite evident that nobody wanted her—she was more dejected than ever, overwhelmed by the discrepancy between the splendour outside her, the warm, teeming beauty and self-sufficiency of nature, and the blank emptiness of her heart.

Then came Lotty, back to dinner, incredibly more freckled, exuding the sunshine she had been collecting all day, talking, laughing, being tactless, being unwise, being without reticence; and Lady Caroline, so quiet at tea, woke up to animation, and Mrs. Fisher was not so noticeable, and Rose was beginning to revive a little, for Lotty's spirits were contagious as she described the delights of her day, a day which might easily to any one else have had nothing in it but a very long and very hot walk and sandwiches, when she suddenly said catching Rose's eye, "Letter gone?"

Rose flushed. This tactlessness . . .

"What letter?" asked Scrap, interested. Both her elbows were on the table and her chin was supported in her hands, for the nut-stage had been reached, and there was nothing for it but to wait in as comfortable as position as possible till Mrs. Fisher had finished cracking.

"Asking her husband here," said Lotty.

Mrs. Fisher looked up. Another husband? Was there to be no end to them? Nor was this one, then, a widow either; but her husband was no doubt a decent, respectable man, following a decent, respectable calling. She had little hope of Mr. Wilkins; so little, that she had refrained from inquiring what he did.

"Has it?" persisted Lotty, as Rose said nothing.

"No," said Rose.

"Oh, well—to-morrow then," said Lotty.

Rose wanted to say No again to this. Lotty would have in her place, and would, besides, have expounded all her reasons. But she could not turn herself inside out like that and invite any and everybody to come and look. How was it that Lotty, who saw so many things, didn't see stuck on her heart, and seeing keep quiet about it, the sore place that was Frederick?

"Who is your husband?" asked Mrs. Fisher, carefully adjusting another nut between the crackers.

"Who should he be," said Rose quickly, roused at once by Mrs. Fisher to irritation, "except Mr. Arbuthnot?"

"I mean, of course, what is Mr. Arbuthnot?"

And Rose, gone painfully red at this, said after a tiny pause, "My husband."

Naturally, Mrs. Fisher was incensed. She couldn't have believed it of this one, with her decent hair and gentle voice, that she too should be impertinent.

Chapter 14

That first week the wistaria began to fade, and the flowers of the Judas-tree and peach-trees fell off and carpeted the ground with rose-colour. Then all the freesias disappeared, and the irises grew scarce. And then, while these were clearing themselves away, the double banksia roses came out, and the big summer roses suddenly flaunted gorgeously on the walls and trellises. Fortune's Yellow was one of them; a very beautiful rose. Presently the tamarisk and the daphnes were at their best, and the lilies at their tallest. By the end of the week the fig-trees were giving shade, the plum-blossom was out among the olives, the modest weigelias appeared in their fresh pink clothes, and on the rocks sprawled masses of thick-leaved, star-shaped flowers, some vivid purple and some a clear, pale lemon.

By the end of the week, too, Mr. Wilkins arrived; even as his wife had foreseen he would, so he did. And there were signs almost of eagerness about his acceptance of her suggestion, for he had not waited to write a letter in answer to hers, but had telegraphed.

That, surely, was eager. It showed, Scrap thought, a definite wish for reunion; and watching his wife's happy face, and aware of her desire that Mellersh should enjoy his holiday, she told herself that he would be a very unusual fool should he waste his time bothering about anybody else. "If he isn't nice to her," Scrap thought, "he shall be taken to the battlements and tipped over." For, by the end of the week, she and Mrs. Wilkins had become Caroline and Lotty to each other, and were friends.

Mrs. Wilkins had always been friends, but Scrap had struggled not to be. She had tried hard to be cautious, but how difficult was caution with Mrs. Wilkins! Free herself from every vestige of it, she was so entirely unreserved, so completely expansive, that soon Scrap, almost before she knew what she was doing, was being unreserved too. And nobody could be more unreserved than Scrap, once she let herself go.

The only difficulty about Lotty was that she was nearly always somewhere else. You couldn't catch her; you couldn't pin her down to come and talk. Scrap's fears that she would grab seemed grotesque in retrospect. Why, there was no grab in her. At dinner and after dinner were the only times one really saw her. All day long she was invisible, and would come back in the late afternoon looking a perfect sight, her hair full of bits of moss, and her freckles worse than ever. Perhaps she was making the most of her time before Mellersh arrived to do all the things she wanted to do, and meant to devote herself afterwards to going about with him, tidy and in her best clothes.

Scrap watched her, interested in spite of herself, because it seemed so extraordinary to be as happy as all that on so little. San Salvatore was beautiful, and the weather was divine; but scenery and weather had never been enough for Scrap, and how could they be enough for somebody who would have to leave them quite soon and go back to life in Hampstead? Also, there was the imminence of Mellersh, of that Mellersh from whom Lotty had so lately run. It was all very well to feel one ought to share, and to make a beau geste and do it, but the beaux gestes Scrap had known hadn't made anybody happy. Nobody really liked being the object of one, and it always meant an effort on the part of the maker. Still, she had to admit there was no effort about Lotty; it was quite plain that everything she did and said was effortless, and that she was just simply, completely happy.

And so Mrs. Wilkins was; for her doubts as to whether she had had time to become steady enough in serenity to go on being serene in Mellersh's company when she had it uninterruptedly right round the clock, had gone by the middle of the week, and she felt that nothing now could shake her. She was ready for anything. She was firmly grafted, rooted, built into heaven. Whatever Mellersh said or did, she would not budge an inch out of heaven, would not rouse herself a single instant to come outside it and be cross. On the contrary, she was going to pull him up into it beside her, and they would sit comfortably together, suffused in light, and laugh at how much afraid of him she used to be in Hampstead, and at how deceitful her afraidness had made her. But he wouldn't need much pulling. He would come in quite naturally after a day or two, irresistibly wafted on the scented breezes of that divine air; and there he would sit arrayed in stars, thought Mrs. Wilkins, in whose mind, among much other débris, floated occasional bright shreds of poetry. She laughed to herself a little at the picture of Mellersh, that top-hatted, black-coated, respectable family solicitor, arrayed in stars, but she laughed affectionately, almost with a maternal pride in how splendid he would look in such fine clothes. "Poor lamb," she murmured to herself affectionately. And added, "What he wants is a thorough airing."

This was during the first half of the week. By the beginning of the last half, at the end of which Mr. Wilkins arrived, she left off even assuring herself that she was unshakeable, that she was permeated beyond altering by the atmosphere, she no longer thought of it or noticed it; she took it for granted. If one may say so, and she certainly said so, not only to herself but also to Lady Caroline, she had found her celestial legs.

Contrary to Mrs. Fisher's idea of the seemly—but of course contrary; what else would one expect of Mrs. Wilkins?—she did not go to meet her husband at Messago, but merely walked down to the point where Beppo's fly would leave him and his luggage in the street of Castagneto. Mrs. Fisher disliked the arrival of Mr. Wilkins, and was sure that anybody who could have married Mrs. Wilkins must be at least of an injudicious disposition, but a husband, whatever his disposition, should be properly met. Mr. Fisher had always been properly met. Never once in his married life had he gone unmet at a station, nor had he ever not been seen off. These observances, these courtesies, strengthened the bonds of marriage, and made the husband feel he could rely on his wife's being always there. Always being there was the essential secret for a wife. What would have become of Mr. Fisher if she had neglected to act on this principle she preferred not to think. Enough things became of him as it was; for whatever one's care in stopping up, married life yet seemed to contain chinks.

But Mrs. Wilkins took no pains. She just walked down the hill singing—Mrs. Fisher could hear her—and picked up her husband in the street as casually as if he were a pin. The three others, still in bed, for it was not nearly time to get up, heard her as she passed beneath their windows down the zigzag path to meet Mr. Wilkins, who was coming by the morning train, and Scrap smiled, and Rose sighed, and Mrs. Fisher rang her bell and desired Francesca to bring her her breakfast in her room. All three had breakfast that day in their rooms, moved by a common instinct to take cover.

Scrap always breakfasted in bed, but she had the same instinct for cover, and during breakfast she made plans for spending the whole day where she was. Perhaps, though, it wouldn't be as necessary that day as the next. That day, Scrap calculated, Mellersh would be provided for. He would want to have a bath, and having a

126

bath at San Salvatore was an elaborate business, a real adventure if one had a hot one in the bathroom, and it took a lot of time. It involved the attendance of the entire staff—Domenico and the boy Giuseppe coaxing the patent stove to burn, restraining it when it burnt too fiercely, using the bellows to it when it threatened to go out, relighting it when it did go out; Francesca anxiously hovering over the tap regulating its trickle, because if it were turned on too full the water instantly ran cold, and if not full enough the stove blew up inside and mysteriously flooded the house; and Costanza and Angela running up and down bringing pails of hot water from the kitchen to eke out what the tap did.

This bath had been put in lately, and was at once the pride and the terror of the servants. It was very patent. Nobody quite understood it. There were long printed instructions as to its right treatment hanging on the wall, in which the word pericoloso recurred. When Mrs. Fisher, proceeding on her arrival to the bathroom, saw this word, she went back to her room again and ordered a sponge-bath instead; and when the others found what using the bathroom meant, and how reluctant the servants were to leave them alone with the stove, and how Francesca positively refused to, and stayed with her back turned watching the tap, and how the remaining servants waited anxiously outside the door till the bather came safely out again, they too had sponge-baths brought into their rooms instead.

Mr. Wilkins, however, was a man, and would be sure to want a big bath. Having it, Scrap calculated, would keep him busy for a long while. Then he would unpack, and then, after his night in the train, he would probably sleep till the evening. So would he be provided for the whole of that day, and not be let loose on them till dinner.

Therefore Scrap came to the conclusion she would be quite safe in the garden that day, and got up as usual after breakfast, and dawdled as usual through her dressing, listening with a slight cocked ear to the sounds of Mr. Wilkins's arrival, of his luggage being carried into Lotty's room on the other side of the landing, of his educated voice as he inquired of Lotty, first, "Do I give this fellow anything?" and immediately afterwards, "Can I have a hot bath?"—of Lotty's voice cheerfully assuring him that he needn't give the fellow anything because he was the gardener, and that yes, he could have a hot bath; and soon after this the landing was filled with the familiar noises of wood being brought, of water being brought, of feet running, of tongues vociferating—-in fact, with the preparation of the bath.

Scrap finished dressing, and then loitered at her window, waiting till she should hear Mr. Wilkins go into the bathroom. When he was safely there she would slip out and settle herself in her garden and resume her inquiries into the probable meaning of her life. She was getting on with her inquiries. She dozed much less frequently, and was beginning to be inclined to agree that tawdry was the word to apply to her past. Also she was afraid that her future looked black.

There—she could hear Mr. Wilkins's educated voice again. Lotty's door had opened, and he was coming out of it asking his way to the bathroom.

"It's where you see the crowd," Lotty's voice answered—still a cheerful voice, Scrap was glad to notice.

His steps went along the landing, and Lotty's steps seemed to go downstairs, and then there seemed to be a brief altercation at the bathroom door—hardly so much an altercation as a chorus of vociferations on one side and wordless determination, Scrap judged, to have a bath by oneself on the other.

Mr. Wilkins knew no Italian, and the expression pericoloso left him precisely as it found him—or would have if he had seen it, but naturally he took no notice of the printed matter on the wall. He firmly closed the door on the servants, resisting Domenico, who tried to the last to press through, and locked himself in as a man should for his bath, judicially considering, as he made his simple preparations for getting in, the singular standard of behaviour of these foreigners who, both male and female, apparently wished to stay with him while he bathed. In Finland, he had heard, the female natives not only were present on such occasions but actually washed the bath-taking traveler. He had not heard, however, that this was true too of Italy, which somehow seemed much nearer civilization— perhaps because one went there, and did not go to Finland.

Impartially examining this reflection, and carefully balancing the claims to civilization of Italy and Finland, Mr. Wilkins got into the bath and turned off the tap. Naturally he turned off the tap. It was what one did. But on the instructions, printed in red letters, was a paragraph saying that the tap should not be turned off as long as there was still fire in the stove. It should be left on—not much on, but on—until the fire was quite out; otherwise, and here again was

128

the word pericoloso, the stove would blow up.

Mr. Wilkins got into the bath, turned off the tap, and the stove blew up, exactly as the printed instructions said it would. It blew up, fortunately, only in its inside, but it blew up with a terrific noise, and Mr. Wilkins leapt out of the bath and rushed to the door, and only the instinct born of years of training made him snatch up a towel as he rushed.

Scrap, half-way across the landing on her way out of doors, heard the explosion.

"Good heavens," she thought, remembering the instruction, "there goes Mr. Wilkins!"

And she ran toward the head of the stairs to call the servants, and as she ran, out ran Mr. Wilkins clutching his towel, and they ran into each other.

"That damned bath!" cried Mr. Wilkins, imperfectly concealed in his towel, his shoulders exposed at one end and his legs at the other, and Lady Caroline Dester, to meet whom he had swallowed all his anger with his wife and come out to Italy.

For Lotty in her letter had told him who was at San Salvatore besides herself and Mrs. Arbuthnot, and Mr. Wilkins at once had perceived that this was an opportunity which might never recur. Lotty had merely said, "There are two other women here, Mrs. Fisher and Lady Caroline Dester," but that was enough. He knew all about the Droitwiches, their wealth, their connections, their place in history, and the power they had, should they choose to exert it, of making yet another solicitor happy by adding him to those they already employed. Some people employed one solicitor for one branch of their affairs, and another for another. The affairs of the Droitwiches must have many branches. He had also heard—for it was, he considered, part of his business to hear, and having heard to remember—of the beauty of their only daughter. Even if the Droitwiches themselves did not need his services, their daughter might. Beauty led one into strange situations; advice could never come amiss. And should none of them, neither parents nor daughter nor any of their brilliant sons, need him in his professional capacity, it yet was obviously a most valuable acquaintance to make. It opened up vistas. It swelled with possibilities. He might go on living in Hampstead for years, and not again come across such another chance.

Directly his wife's letter reached him he telegraphed and packed. This was business. He was not a man to lose time when it came to business; nor was he a man to jeopardize a chance by neglecting to be amiable. He met his wife perfectly amiably, aware that amiability under such circumstances was wisdom. Besides, he actually felt amiable—very. For once, Lotty was really helping him. He kissed her affectionately on getting out of Beppo's fly, and was afraid she must have got up extremely early; he made no complaints of the steepness of the walk up; he told her pleasantly of his journey, and when called upon, obediently admired the views. It was all neatly mapped out in his mind, what he was going to do that first day— have a shave, have a bath, put on clean clothes, sleep a while, and then would come lunch and the introduction to Lady Caroline.

In the train he had selected the words of his greeting, going over them with care—some slight expression of his gratification in meeting one of whom he, in common with the whole world, had heard—but of course put delicately, very delicately; some slight reference to her distinguished parents and the part her family had played in the history of England—made, of course, with proper tact; a sentence or two about her eldest brother Lord Winchcombe, who had won his V.C. in the late war under circumstances which could only cause—he might or might not add this—every Englishman's heart to beat higher than ever with pride, and the first steps towards what might well be the turning-point in his career would have been taken.

And here he was . . . no, it was too terrible, what could be more terrible? Only a towel on, water running off his legs, and that exclamation. He knew at once the lady was Lady Caroline—the minute the exclamation was out he knew it. Rarely did Mr. Wilkins use that word, and never, never in the presence of a lady or a client. While as for the towel—why had he come? Why had he not stayed in Hampstead? It would be impossible to live this down.

But Mr. Wilkins was reckoning without Scrap. She, indeed, screwed up her face at the first flash of him on her astonished sight in an enormous effort not to laugh, and having choked the laughter down and got her face serious again, she said as composedly as if he had had all his clothes on, "How do you do."

What perfect tact. Mr. Wilkins could have worshipped her. This exquisite ignoring. Blue blood, of course, coming out.

Overwhelmed with gratitude he took her offered hand and said "How do you do," in his turn, and merely to repeat the ordinary words seemed magically to restore the situation to the normal. Indeed, he was so much relieved, and it was so natural to be shaking hands, to be conventionally greeting, that he forgot he had only a towel on and his professional manner came back to him. He forgot what he was looking like, but he did not forget that this was Lady Caroline Dester, the lady he had come all the way to Italy to see, and he did not forget that it was in her face, her lovely and important face, that he had flung his terrible exclamation. He must at once entreat her forgiveness. To say such a word to a lady—to any lady, but of all ladies to just this one . . .

"I'm afraid I used unpardonable language," began Mr. Wilkins very earnestly, as earnestly and ceremoniously as if he had had his clothes on.

"I thought it most appropriate," said Scrap, who was used to damns.

Mr. Wilkins was incredibly relieved and soothed by this answer. No offence, then, taken. Blue blood again. Only blue blood could afford such a liberal, such an understanding attitude.

"It is Lady Caroline Dester, is it not, to whom I am speaking?" he asked, his voice sounding even more carefully cultivated than usual, for he had to restrain too much pleasure, too much relief, too much of the joy of the pardoned and the shriven from getting into it.

"Yes," said Scrap; and for the life of her she couldn't help smiling. She couldn't help it. She hadn't meant to smile at Mr. Wilkins, not ever; but really he looked—and then his voice was the top of the rest of him, oblivious of the towel and his legs, and talking just like a church.

"Allow me to introduce myself," said Mr. Wilkins, with the ceremony of the drawing-room. "My name is Mellersh-Wilkins."

And he instinctively held out his hand a second time at the words.

"I thought perhaps it was," said Scrap, a second time having hers shaken and a second time unable not to smile.

He was about to proceed to the first of the graceful tributes he had prepared in the train, oblivious, as he could not see himself, that he was without his clothes, when the servants came running up the stairs and, simultaneously, Mrs. Fisher appeared in the doorway of her sitting-room. For all this had happened very quickly, and the servants away in the kitchen, and Mrs. Fisher pacing her battlements, had not had time on hearing the noise to appear before the second handshake.

The servants when they heard the dreaded noise knew at once what had happened, and rushed straight into the bathroom to try and staunch the flood, taking no notice of the figure on the landing in the towel, but Mrs. Fisher did not know what the noise could be, and coming out of her room to inquire stood rooted on the door-sill.

It was enough to root anybody. Lady Caroline shaking hands with what evidently, if he had had clothes on, would have been Mrs. Wilkins's husband, and both of them conversing just as if—

Then Scrap became aware of Mrs. Fisher. She turned to her at once. "Do let me," she said gracefully, "introduce Mr. Mellersh-Wilkins. He has just come. This," she added, turning to Mr. Wilkins, "is Mrs. Fisher."

And Mr. Wilkins, nothing if not courteous, reacted at once to the conventional formula. First he bowed to the elderly lady in the doorway, then he crossed over to her, his wet feet leaving footprints as he went, and having got to her he politely held out his hand.

"It is a pleasure," said Mr. Wilkins in his carefully modulated voice, "to meet a friend of my wife's."

Scrap melted away down into the garden.

Chapter 15

The strange effect of this incident was that when they met that evening at dinner both Mrs. Fisher and Lady Caroline had a singular feeling of secret understanding with Mr. Wilkins. He could not be to them as other men. He could not be to them as he would have been if they had met him in his clothes. There was a sense of broken ice; they felt at once intimate and indulgent; almost they felt to him as nurses do—as those feel who have assisted either patients or young children at their baths. They were acquainted with Mr. Wilkins's legs.

What Mrs. Fisher said to him that morning in her first shock will never be known, but what Mr. Wilkins said to her in reply, when reminded by what she was saying of his condition, was so handsome in its apology, so proper in its confusion, that she had ended by being quite sorry for him and completely placated. After all, it was an accident, and nobody could help accidents. And when she saw him next at dinner, dressed, polished, spotless as to linen and sleek as to hair, she felt this singular sensation of a secret understanding with him and, added to it, of a kind of almost personal pride in his appearance, now that he was dressed, which presently extended in some subtle way to an almost personal pride in everything he said.

There was no doubt whatever in Mrs. Fisher's mind that a man was infinitely preferable as a companion to a woman. Mr. Wilkins's presence and conversation at once raised the standard of the dinner-table from that of a bear garden—yes, a bear garden—to that of a civilized social gathering. He talked as men talk, about interesting subjects, and, though most courteous to Lady Caroline, showed no traces of dissolving into simpers and idiocy whenever he addressed her. He was, indeed, precisely as courteous to Mrs. Fisher herself; and when for the first time at that table politics were introduced, he listened to her with the proper seriousness on her exhibiting a desire to speak, and treated her opinions with the attention they deserved. He appeared to think much as she did about Lloyd George, and in regard to literature he was equally sound. In fact there was real conversation, and he liked nuts. How he could have married Mrs. Wilkins was a mystery.

Lotty, for her part, looked on with round eyes. She had expected Mellersh to take at least two days before he got to this stage, but the

133

San Salvatore spell had worked instantly. It was not only that he was pleasant at dinner, for she had always seen him pleasant at dinners with other people, but he had been pleasant all day privately—so pleasant that he had complimented her on her looks while she was brushing out her hair, and kissed her. Kissed her! And it was neither good-morning nor good-night.

Well, this being so, she would put off telling him the truth about her nest-egg, and about Rose not being his hostess after all, till next day. Pity to spoil things. She had been going to blurt it out as soon as he had had a rest, but it did seem a pity to disturb such a very beautiful frame of mind as that of Mellersh this first day. Let him too get more firmly fixed in heaven. Once fixed he wouldn't mind anything.

Her face sparkled with delight at the instantaneous effect of San Salvatore. Even the catastrophe of the bath, of which she had been told when she came in from the garden, had not shaken him. Of course all that he had needed was a holiday. What a brute she had been to him when he wanted to take her himself to Italy. But this arrangement, as it happened, was ever so much better, though not through any merit of hers. She talked and laughed gaily, not a shred of fear of him left in her, and even when she said, struck by his spotlessness, that he looked so clean that one could eat one's dinner off him, and Scrap laughed, Mellersh laughed too. He would have minded that at home, supposing that at home she had had the spirit to say it.

It was a successful evening. Scrap, whenever she looked at Mr. Wilkins, saw him in his towel, dripping water, and felt indulgent. Mrs. Fisher was delighted with him. Rose was a dignified hostess in Mr. Wilkins's eyes, quiet and dignified, and he admired the way she waived her right to preside at the head of the table—as a graceful compliment, of course, to Mrs. Fisher's age. Mrs. Arbuthnot was, opined Mr. Wilkins, naturally retiring. She was the most retiring of the three ladies. He had met her before dinner alone for a moment in the drawing-room, and had expressed in appropriate language his sense of her kindness in wishing him to join her party, and she had been retiring. Was she shy? Probably. She had blushed, and murmured as if in deprecation, and then the others had come in. At dinner she talked least. He would, of course, become better acquainted with her during the next few days, and it would be a pleasure, he was sure.

Meanwhile Lady Caroline was all and more than all Mr. Wilkins had imagined, and had received his speeches, worked in skillfully between the courses, graciously; Mrs. Fisher was the exact old lady he had been hoping to come across all his professional life; and Lotty had not only immensely improved, but was obviously au mieux—Mr. Wilkins knew what was necessary in French—with Lady Caroline. He had been much tormented during the day by the thought of how he had stood conversing with Lady Caroline forgetful of his not being dressed, and had at last written her a note most deeply apologizing, and beseeching her to overlook his amazing, his incomprehensible obliviousness, to which she had replied in pencil on the back of the envelop, "Don't worry." And he had obeyed her commands, and had put it from him. The result was he was now in great contentment. Before going to sleep that night he pinched his wife's ear. She was amazed. These endearments . . .

What is more, the morning brought no relapse in Mr. Wilkins, and he kept up to his high level through out the day, in spite of its being the first day of the second week, and therefore pay day.

It being pay day precipitated Lotty's confession, which she had, when it came to the point, been inclined to put off a little longer. She was not afraid, she dared anything, but Mellersh was in such an admirable humour—why risk clouding it just yet? When, however, soon after breakfast Costanza appeared with a pile of very dirty little bits of paper covered with sums in pencil, and having knocked at Mrs. Fisher's door and been sent away, and at Lady Caroline's door and been sent away, and at Rose's door and had no answer because Rose had gone out, she waylaid Lotty, who was showing Mellersh over the house, and pointed to the bits of paper and talked very rapidly and loud, and shrugged her shoulders a great deal, and kept on pointing at the bits of paper, Lotty remembered that a week had passed without anybody paying anything to anyone, and that the moment had come to settle up.

"Does this good lady want something?" inquired Mr. Wilkins mellifluously.

"Money," said Lotty.

"Money?"

"It's the housekeeping bills."

"Well, you have nothing to do with those," said Mr. Wilkins serenely.

"Oh yes, I have—"

And the confession was precipitated.

It was wonderful how Mellersh took it. One would have imagined that his sole idea about the nest-egg had always been that it should be lavished on just this. He did not, as he would have done at home, cross-examine her; he accepted everything as it came pouring out, about her fibs and all, and when she had finished and said, "You have every right to be angry, I think, but I hope you won't be and will forgive me instead," he merely asked, "What can be more beneficial than such a holiday?"

Whereupon she put her arm through his and held it tight and said, "Oh, Mellersh, you really are too sweet!"—her face red with pride in him.

That he should so quickly assimilate the atmosphere, that he should at once become nothing but kindness, showed surely what a real affinity he had with good and beautiful things. He belonged quite naturally in this place of heavenly calm. He was—extraordinary how she had misjudged him—by nature a child of light. Fancy not minding the dreadful fibs she had gone in for before leaving home; fancy passing even those over without comment. Wonderful. Yet not wonderful, for wasn't he in heaven? In heaven nobody minded any of those done-with things, one didn't even trouble to forgive and forget, one was much too happy. She pressed his arm tight in her gratitude and appreciation; and though he did not withdraw his, neither did he respond to her pressure. Mr. Wilkins was of a cool habit, and rarely had any real wish to press.

Meanwhile, Costanza, perceiving that she had lost the Wilkinses' ear had gone back to Mrs. Fisher, who at least understood Italian, besides being clearly in the servants' eyes the one of the party marked down by age and appearance to pay the bills; and to her, while Mrs. Fisher put the final touches to her toilette, for she was preparing, by means of putting on a hat and veil and feather boa and gloves, to go for her first stroll in the lower garden—positively her first since her arrival—she explained that unless she was given money to pay the last week's bills the shops of Castagneto would refuse credit for the current week's food. Not even credit would they give, affirmed Costanza, who had been spending a great deal and was anxious to pay all her relations what was owed them and also to find out how her mistresses took it, for that day's meals. Soon it would be the hour of colazione, and how could there be colazione without meat, without fish, without eggs, without—

Mrs. Fisher took the bills out of her hand and looked at the total; and she was so much astonished by its size, so much horrified by the extravagance to which it testified, that she sat down at her writing-table to go into the thing thoroughly.

Costanza had a very bad half-hour. She had not supposed it was in the English to be so mercenary. And then la Vecchia, as she was called in the kitchen, knew so much Italian, and with a doggedness that filled Costanza with shame on her behalf, for such conduct was the last one expected from the noble English, she went through item after item, requiring and persisting till she got them, explanations.

There were no explanations, except that Costanza had had one glorious week of doing exactly as she chose, of splendid unbridled licence, and that this was the result.

Costanza, having no explanations, wept. It was miserable to think she would have to cook from now on under watchfulness, under suspicion; and what would her relations say when they found the orders they received were whittled down? They would say she had no influence; they would despise her.

Costanza wept, but Mrs. Fisher was unmoved. In slow and splendid Italian, with the roll of the cantos of the Inferno, she informed her that she would pay no bills till the following week, and that meanwhile the food was to be precisely as good as ever, and at a quarter the cost.

Costanza threw up her hands.

Next week, proceeded Mrs. Fisher unmoved, if she found this had been so she would pay the whole. Otherwise—she paused; for what she would do otherwise she did not know herself. But she paused and looked impenetrable, majestic and menacing, and Costanza was cowed.

Then Mrs. Fisher, having dismissed her with a gesture, went in search of Lady Caroline to complain. She had been under the impression that Lady Caroline ordered the meals and therefore was responsible for the prices, but now it appeared that the cook had been left to do exactly as she pleased ever since they got there, which of course was simply disgraceful.

Scrap was not in her bedroom, but the room, on Mrs. Fisher's opening the door, for she suspected her of being in it and only pretending not to hear the knock, was still flowerlike from her presence.

137

"Scent," sniffed Mrs. Fisher, shutting it again; and she wished Carlyle could have had five minutes' straight talk with this young woman. And yet—perhaps even he—

She went downstairs to go into the garden in search of her, and in the hall encountered Mr. Wilkins. He had his hat on, and was lighting a cigar.

Indulgent as Mrs. Fisher felt towards Mr. Wilkins, and peculiarly and even mystically related after the previous morning's encounter, she yet could not like a cigar in the house. Out of doors she endured it, but it was not necessary, when out of doors was such a big place, to indulge the habit indoors. Even Mr. Fisher, who had been, she should say, a man originally tenacious of habits, had quite soon after marriage got out of this one.

However, Mr. Wilkins, snatching off his hat on seeing her, instantly threw the cigar away. He threw it into the water a great jar of arum lilies presumably contain, and Mrs. Fisher, aware of the value men attach to their newly-lit cigars, could not but be impressed by this immediate and magnificent amende honorable.

But the cigar did not reach the water. It got caught in the lilies, and smoked on by itself among them, a strange and depraved-looking object.

"Where are you going to, my prett—" began Mr. Wilkins, advancing towards Mrs. Fisher; but he broke off just in time.

Was it morning spirits impelling him to address Mrs. Fisher in the terms of a nursery rhyme? He wasn't even aware that he knew the thing. Most strange. What could have put it, at such a moment, into his self-possessed head? He felt great respect for Mrs. Fisher, and would not for the world have insulted her by addressing her as a maid, pretty or otherwise. He wished to stand well with her. She was a woman of parts, and also, he suspected, of property. At breakfast they had been most pleasant together, and he had been struck by her apparent intimacy with well-known persons. Victorians, of course; but it was restful to talk about them after the strain of his brother-in-law's Georgian parties on Hampstead Heath. He and she were getting on famously, he felt. She already showed all the symptoms of presently wishing to become a client. Not for the world would he offend her. He turned a little cold at the narrowness of his escape.

She had not, however, noticed.

"You are going out," he said very politely, all readiness should she confirm his assumption to accompany her.

"I want to find Lady Caroline," said Mrs. Fisher, going towards the glass door leading into the top garden.

"An agreeable quest," remarked Mr. Wilkins, "May I assist in the search? Allow me—" he added, opening the door for her.

"She usually sits over in that corner behind the bushes," said Mrs. Fisher. "And I don't know about it being an agreeable quest. She has been letting the bills run up in the most terrible fashion, and needs a good scolding."

"Lady Caroline?" said Mr. Wilkins, unable to follow such an attitude. "What has Lady Caroline, if I may inquire, to do with the bills here?"

"The housekeeping was left to her, and as we all share alike it ought to have been a matter of honour with her—"

"But—Lady Caroline housekeeping for the party here? A party which includes my wife? My dear lady, you render me speechless. Do you not know she is the daughter of the Droitwiches?"

"Oh, is that who she is," said Mrs. Fisher, scrunching heavily over the pebbles towards the hidden corner. "Well, that accounts for it. The muddle that man Droitwich made in his department in the war was a national scandal. It amounted to misappropriation of the public funds."

"But it is impossible, I assure you, to expect the daughter of the Droitwiches—" began Mr. Wilkins earnestly.

"The Droitwiches," interrupted Mrs. Fisher, "are neither here nor there. Duties undertaken should be performed. I don't intend my money to be squandered for the sake of any Droitwiches."

A headstrong old lady. Perhaps not so easy to deal with as he had hoped. But how wealthy. Only the consciousness of great wealth would make her snap her fingers in this manner at the Droitwiches. Lotty, on being questioned, had been vague about her circumstances, and had described her house as a mausoleum with gold-fish swimming about in it; but now he was sure she was more than very well off. Still, he wished he had not joined her at this moment, for he had no sort of desire to be present at such a spectacle as the scolding of Lady Caroline Dester.

Again, however, he was reckoning without Scrap. Whatever she felt when she looked up and beheld Mr. Wilkins discovering her corner on the very first morning, nothing but angelicness appeared on her face. She took her feet off the parapet on Mrs. Fisher's sitting down on it, and listening gravely to her opening remarks as to her not having any money to fling about in reckless and uncontrolled household expenditure, interrupted her flow by pulling one of the cushions from behind her head and offering it to her.

"Sit on this," said Scrap, holding it out. "You'll be more comfortable."

Mr. Wilkins leapt to relieve her of it.

"Oh, thanks," said Mrs. Fisher, interrupted.

It was difficult to get into the swing again. Mr. Wilkins inserted the cushion solicitously between the slightly raised Mrs. Fisher and the stone of the parapet, and again she had to say "Thanks." It was interrupted. Besides, Lady Caroline said nothing in her defence; she only looked at her, and listened with the face of an attentive angel.

It seemed to Mr. Wilkins that it must be difficult to scold a Dester who looked like that and so exquisitely said nothing. Mrs. Fisher, he was glad to see, gradually found it difficult herself, for her severity slackened, and she ended by saying lamely, "You ought to have told me you were not doing it."

"I didn't know you thought I was," said the lovely voice.

"I would now like to know," said Mrs. Fisher, "what you propose to do for the rest of the time here."

"Nothing," said Scrap, smiling.

"Nothing? Do you mean to say—"

"If I may be allowed, ladies," interposed Mr. Wilkins in his suavest professional manner, "to make a suggestion"—they both looked at him, and remembering him as they first saw him felt indulgent— "I would advise you not to spoil a delightful holiday with worries over housekeeping."

"Exactly," said Mrs. Fisher. "It is what I intend to avoid."

"Most sensible," said Mr. Wilkins. "Why not, then," he continued, "allow the cook—an excellent cook, by the way—so much a head per diem"—Mr. Wilkins knew what was necessary in Latin—"and tell her that for this sum she must cater for you, and not only cater but cater as well as ever? One could easily reckon it out. The charges of a moderate hotel, for instance, would do as a basis, halved, or perhaps even quartered."

"And this week that has just passed?" asked Mrs. Fisher. "The terrible bills of this first week? What about them?"

"They shall be my present to San Salvatore," said Scrap, who didn't like the idea of Lotty's nest-egg being reduced so much beyond what she was prepared for.

There was a silence. The ground was cut from under Mrs. Fisher's feet.

"Of course if you choose to throw your money about—" she said at last, disapproving but immensely relieved, while Mr. Wilkins was rapt in the contemplation of the precious qualities of blue blood. This readiness, for instance, not to trouble about money, this free-handedness—it was not only what one admired in others, admired in others perhaps more than anything else, but it was extraordinarily useful to the professional classes. When met with it should be encouraged by warmth of reception. Mrs. Fisher was not warm. She accepted—from which he deduced that with her wealth went closeness—but she accepted grudgingly. Presents were presents, and one did not look them in this manner in the mouth, he felt; and if Lady Caroline found her pleasure in presenting his wife and Mrs. Fisher with their entire food for a week, it was their part to accept gracefully. One should not discourage gifts.

On behalf of his wife, then, Mr. Wilkins expressed what she would wish to express, and remarking to Lady Caroline—with a touch of lightness, for so should gifts be accepted in order to avoid embarrassing the donor—that she had in that case been his wife's hostess since her arrival, he turned almost gaily to Mrs. Fisher and pointed out that she and his wife must now jointly write Lady Caroline the customary latter of thanks for hospitality. "A Collins," said Mr. Wilkins, who knew what was necessary in literature. "I prefer the name Collins for such a letter to either that of Board and Lodging or Bread and Butter. Let us call it a Collins."

Scrap smiled, and held out her cigarette case. Mrs. Fisher could not help being mollified. A way out of waste was going to be found, thanks to Mr. Wilkins, and she hated waste quite as much as having to pay for it; also a way was found out of housekeeping. For a moment she had thought that if everybody tried to force her into housekeeping on her brief holiday by their own indifference (Lady Caroline), or inability to speak Italian (the other two), she would have to send for Kate Lumley after all. Kate could do it. Kate and she had learnt Italian together. Kate would only be allowed to come on condition that she did do it.

But this was much better, this way of Mr. Wilkins's. Really a most superior man. There was nothing like an intelligent, not too young man for profitable and pleasurable companionship. And when she got up, the business for which she had come being settled, and said she now intended to take a little stroll before lunch, Mr. Wilkins did not stay with Lady Caroline, as most of the men she had known would, she was afraid, have wanted to—he asked to be permitted to go and stroll with her; so that he evidently definitely preferred conversation to faces. A sensible, companionable man. A clever, well-read man. A man of the world. A man. She was very glad indeed she had not written to Kate the other day. What did she want with Kate? She had found a better companion.

But Mr. Wilkins did not go with Mrs. Fisher because of her conversation, but because, when she got up and he got up because she got up, intending merely to bow her out of the recess, Lady Caroline had put her feet up on the parapet again, and arranging her head sideways in the cushions had shut her eyes.

The daughter of the Droitwiches desired to go to sleep.

It was not for him, by remaining, to prevent her.

Chapter 16

And so the second week began, and all was harmony. The arrival of Mr. Wilkins, instead of, as three of the party had feared and the fourth had only been protected from fearing by her burning faith in the effect on him of San Salvatore, disturbing such harmony as there was, increased it. He fitted in. He was determined to please, and he did please. He was most amiable to his wife—not only in public, which she was used to, but in private, when he certainly wouldn't have been if he hadn't wanted to. He did want to. He was so much obliged to her, so much pleased with her, for making him acquainted with Lady Caroline, that he felt really fond of her. Also proud; for there must be, he reflected, a good deal more in her than he had supposed, for Lady Caroline to have become so intimate with her and so affectionate. And the more he treated her as though she were really very nice, the more Lotty expanded and became really very nice, and the more he, affected in his turn, became really very nice himself; so that they went round and round, not in a vicious but in a highly virtuous circle.

Positively, for him, Mellersh petted her. There was at no time much pet in Mellersh, because he was by nature a cool man; yet such was the influence on him of, as Lotty supposed, San Salvatore, that in this second week he sometimes pinched both her ears, one after the other, instead of only one; and Lotty, marveling at such rapidly developing affectionateness, wondered what he would do, should he continue at this rate, in the third week, when her supply of ears would have come to an end.

He was particularly nice about the washstand, and genuinely desirous of not taking up too much of the space in the small bedroom. Quick to respond, Lotty was even more desirous not to be in his way; and the room became the scene of many an affectionate combat de générosité, each of which left them more pleased with each other than ever. He did not again have a bath in the bathroom, though it was mended and ready for him, but got up and went down every morning to the sea, and in spite of the cool nights making the water cold early had his dip as a man should, and came up to breakfast rubbing his hands and feeling, as he told Mrs. Fisher, prepared for anything.

Lotty's belief in the irresistible influence of the heavenly atmosphere of San Salvatore being thus obviously justified, and Mr. Wilkins, whom Rose knew as alarming and Scrap had pictured as icily unkind, being so evidently a changed man, both Rose and Scrap began to think there might after all be something in what Lotty insisted on, and that San Salvatore did work purgingly on the character.

They were the more inclined to think so in that they too felt a working going on inside themselves: they felt more cleared, both of them, that second week—Scrap in her thoughts, many of which were now quite nice thoughts, real amiable ones about her parents and relations, with a glimmer in them of recognition of the extraordinary benefits she had received at the hands of—what? Fate? Providence?—anyhow of something, and of how, having received them, she had misused them by failing to be happy; and Rose in her bosom, which though it still yearned, yearned to some purpose, for she was reaching the conclusion that merely inactively to yearn was no use at all, and that she must either by some means stop her yearning or give it at least a chance—remote, but still a chance—of being quieted by writing to Frederick and asking him to come out.

If Mr. Wilkins could be changed, thought Rose, why not Frederick? How wonderful it would be, how too wonderful, if the place worked on him too and were able to make them even a little understand each other, even a little be friends. Rose, so far had loosening and disintegration gone on in her character, now was beginning to think her obstinate strait-lacedness about his books and her austere absorption in good works had been foolish and perhaps even wrong. He was her husband, and she had frightened him away. She had frightened love away, precious love, and that couldn't be good. Was not Lotty right when she said the other day that nothing at all except love mattered? Nothing certainly seemed much use unless it was built up on love. But once frightened away, could it ever come back? Yes, it might in that beauty, it might in the atmosphere of happiness Lotty and San Salvatore seemed between them to spread round like some divine infection.

She had, however, to get him there first, and he certainly couldn't be got there if she didn't write and tell him where she was.

She would write. She must write; for if she did there was at least a chance of his coming, and if she didn't there was manifestly none.

And then, once here in this loveliness, with everything so soft and kind and sweet all round, it would be easier to tell him, to try and explain, to ask for something different, for at least an attempt at something different in their lives in the future, instead of the blankness of separation, the cold—oh, the cold—of nothing at all but the great windiness of faith, the great bleakness of works. Why, one person in the world, one single person belonging to one, of one's very own, to talk to, to take care of, to love, to be interested in, was worth more than all the speeches on platforms and the compliments of chairmen in the world. It was also worth more— Rose couldn't help it, the thought would come—than all the prayers.

These thoughts were not head thoughts, like Scrap's, who was altogether free from yearnings, but bosom thoughts. They lodged in the bosom; it was in the bosom that Rose ached, and felt so dreadfully lonely. And when her courage failed her, as it did on most days, and it seemed impossible to write to Frederick, she would look at Mr. Wilkins and revive.

There he was, a changed man. There he was, going into that small, uncomfortable room every night, that room whose proximities had been Lotty's only misgiving, and coming out of it in the morning, and Lotty coming out of it too, both of them as unclouded and as nice to each other as when they went in. And hadn't he, so critical at home, Lotty had told her, of the least thing going wrong, emerged from the bath catastrophe as untouched in spirit as Shadrach, Meshach and Abednego were untouched in body when they emerged from the fire? Miracles were happening in this place. If they could happen to Mr. Wilkins, why not to Frederick?

She got up quickly. Yes, she would write. She would go and write to him at once.

But suppose—

She paused. Suppose he didn't answer. Suppose he didn't even answer.

And she sat down again to think a little longer.

In these hesitations did Rose spend most of the second week.

Then there was Mrs. Fisher. Her restlessness increased that second week. It increased to such an extent that she might just as well not have had her private sitting-room at all, for she could no longer sit. Not for ten minutes together could Mrs. Fisher sit. And added to the restlessness, as the days of the second week proceeded on their way, she had a curious sensation, which worried her, of rising sap. She knew the feeling, because she had sometimes had it in childhood in specially swift springs, when the lilacs and the syringes seemed to rush out into blossom in a single night, but it was strange to have it again after over fifty years. She would have liked to remark on the sensation to some one, but she was ashamed. It was such an absurd sensation at her age. Yet oftener and oftener, and every day more and more, did Mrs. Fisher have a ridiculous feeling as if she were presently going to burgeon.

Sternly she tried to frown the unseemly sensation down. Burgeon, indeed. She had heard of dried staffs, pieces of mere dead wood, suddenly putting forth fresh leaves, but only in legend. She was not in legend. She knew perfectly what was due to herself. Dignity demanded that she should have nothing to do with fresh leaves at her age; and yet there it was—the feeling that presently, that at any moment now, she might crop out all green.

Mrs. Fisher was upset. There were many things she disliked more than anything else, and one was when the elderly imagined they felt young and behaved accordingly. Of course they only imagined it, they were only deceiving themselves; but how deplorable were the results. She herself had grown old as people should grow old—steadily and firmly. No interruptions, no belated after-glows and spasmodic returns. If, after all these years, she were now going to be deluded into some sort of unsuitable breaking-out, how humiliating.

Indeed she was thankful, that second week, that Kate Lumley was not there. It would be most unpleasant, should anything different occur in her behaviour, to have Kate looking on. Kate had known her all her life. She felt she could let herself go—here Mrs. Fisher frowned at the book she was vainly trying to concentrate on, for where did that expression come from?—much less painfully before strangers than before an old friend. Old friends, reflected Mrs. Fisher, who hoped she was reading, compare one constantly with what one used to be. They are always doing it if one develops. They are surprised at development. They hark back; they expect motionlessness after, say, fifty, to the end of one's days.

That, thought Mrs. Fisher, her eyes going steadily line by line down the page and not a word of it getting through into her consciousness, is foolish of friends. It is condemning one to a premature death. One should continue (of course with dignity) to develop, however old one may be. She had nothing against developing, against further ripeness, because as long as one was

146

alive one was not dead—obviously, decided Mrs. Fisher, and development, change, ripening, were life. What she would dislike would be unripening, going back to something green. She would dislike it intensely; and this is what she felt she was on the brink of doing.

Naturally it made her very uneasy, and only in constant movement could she find distraction. Increasingly restless and no longer able to confine herself to her battlements, she wandered more and more frequently, and also aimlessly, in and out of the top garden, to the growing surprise of Scrap, especially when she found that all Mrs. Fisher did was to stare for a few minutes at the view, pick a few dead leaves off the rose-bushes, and go away again.

In Mr. Wilkins's conversation she found temporary relief, but though he joined her whenever he could he was not always there, for he spread his attentions judiciously among the three ladies, and when he was somewhere else she had to face and manage her thoughts as best she could by herself. Perhaps it was the excess of light and colour at San Salvatore which made every other place seem dark and black; and Prince of Wales Terrace did seem a very dark black spot to have to go back to—a dark, narrow street, and her house dark and narrow as the street, with nothing really living or young in it. The goldfish could hardly be called living, or at most not more than half living, and were certainly not young, and except for them there were only the maids, and they were dusty old things.

Dusty old things. Mrs. Fisher paused in her thoughts, arrested by the strange expression. Where had it come from? How was it possible for it to come at all? It might have been one of Mrs. Wilkins's, in its levity, its almost slang. Perhaps it was one of hers, and she had heard her say it and unconsciously caught it from her.

If so, this was both serious and disgusting. That the foolish creature should penetrate into Mrs. Fisher's very mind and establish her personality there, the personality which was still, in spite of the harmony apparently existing between her and her intelligent husband, so alien to Mrs. Fisher's own, so far removed from what she understood and liked, and infect her with her undesirable phrases, was most disturbing. Never in her life before had such a sentence come into Mrs. Fisher's head. Never in her life before had she though of her maids, or of anybody else, as dusty old things. Her maids were not dusty old things; they were most respectable, neat women, who were allowed the use of the bathroom every Saturday night. Elderly, certainly, but then so was she, so was her house, so was her furniture, so were her goldfish. They were all elderly, as they should be, together. But there was a great difference between being elderly and being a dusty old thing.

How true it was what Ruskin said, that evil communications corrupt good manners. But did Ruskin say it? On second thoughts she was not sure, but it was just the sort of thing he would have said if he had said it, and in any case it was true. Merely hearing Mrs. Wilkins's evil communications at meals—she did not listen, she avoided listening, yet it was evident she had heard—those communications which, in that they so often were at once vulgar, indelicate and profane, and always, she was sorry to say, laughed at by Lady Caroline, must be classed as evil, was spoiling her own mental manners. Soon she might not only think but say. How terrible that would be. If that were the form her breaking-out was going to take, the form of unseemly speech, Mrs. Fisher was afraid she would hardly with any degree of composure be able to bear it.

At this stage Mrs. Fisher wished more than ever that she were able to talk over her strange feelings with some one who would understand. There was, however, no one who would understand except Mrs. Wilkins herself. She would. She would know at once, Mrs. Fisher was sure, what she felt like. But this was impossible. It would be as abject as begging the very microbe that was infecting one for protection against its disease.

She continued, accordingly, to bear her sensations in silence, and was driven by them into that frequent aimless appearing in the top garden which presently roused even Scrap's attention.

Scrap had noticed it, and vaguely wondered at it, for some time before Mr. Wilkins inquired of her one morning as he arranged her cushions for her—he had established the daily assisting of Lady Caroline into her chair as his special privilege—whether there was anything the matter with Mrs. Fisher.

At that moment Mrs. Fisher was standing by the eastern parapet, shading her eyes and carefully scrutinizing the distant white houses of Mezzago. They could see her through the branches of the daphnes.

"I don't know," said Scrap.

"She is a lady, I take it," said Mr. Wilkins, "who would be unlikely to have anything on her mind?"

"I should imagine so," said Scrap, smiling.

"If she has, and her restlessness appears to suggest it, I should be more than glad to assist her with advice."

"I am sure you would be most kind."

"Of course she has her own legal adviser, but he is not on the spot. I am. And a lawyer on the spot," said Mr. Wilkins, who endeavoured to make his conversation when he talked to Lady Caroline light, aware that one must be light with young ladies, "is worth two in—we won't be ordinary and complete the proverb, but say London."

"You should ask her."

"Ask her if she needs assistance? Would you advise it? Would it not be a little—a little delicate to touch on such a question, the question whether or no a lady has something on her mind?"

"Perhaps she will tell you if you go and talk to her. I think it must be lonely to be Mrs. Fisher."

"You are all thoughtfulness and consideration," declared Mr. Wilkins, wishing, for the first time in his life, that he were a foreigner so that he might respectfully kiss her hand on withdrawing to go obediently and relieve Mrs. Fisher's loneliness.

It was wonderful what a variety of exits from her corner Scrap contrived for Mr. Wilkins. Each morning she found a different one, which sent him off pleased after he had arranged her cushions for her. She allowed him to arrange the cushions because she instantly had discovered, the very first five minutes of the very first evening, that her fears lest he should cling to her and stare in dreadful admiration were baseless. Mr. Wilkins did not admire like that. It was not only, she instinctively felt, not in him, but if it had been he would not have dared to in her case. He was all respectfulness. She could direct his movements in regard to herself with the raising of an eyelash. His one concern was to obey. She had been prepared to like him if he would only be so obliging as not to admire her, and she did like him. She did not forget his moving defencelessness the first morning in his towel, and he amused her, and he was kind to Lotty. It is true she liked him most when he wasn't there, but then she usually liked everybody most when they weren't there. Certainly he did seem to be one of those men, rare in her experience, who never looked at a woman from the predatory angle. The comfort of this, the simplification it brought into the relations of the party, was immense. From this point of view Mr. Wilkins was simply ideal; he was unique and precious. Whenever she thought of him, and was

149

perhaps inclined to dwell on the aspects of him that were a little boring, she remembered this and murmured, "But what a treasure."

Indeed it was Mr. Wilkins's one aim during his stay at San Salvatore to be a treasure. At all costs the three ladies who were not his wife must like him and trust him. Then presently when trouble arose in their lives—and in what lives did not trouble sooner or later arise?—they would recollect how reliable he was and how sympathetic, and turn to him for advice. Ladies with something on their minds were exactly what he wanted. Lady Caroline, he judged, had nothing on hers at the moment, but so much beauty—for he could not but see what was evident—must have had its difficulties in the past and would have more of them before it had done. In the past he had not been at hand; in the future he hoped to be. And meanwhile the behaviour of Mrs. Fisher, the next in importance of the ladies from the professional point of view, showed definite promise. It was almost certain that Mrs. Fisher had something on her mind. He had been observing her attentively, and it was almost certain.

With the third, with Mrs. Arbuthnot, he had up to this made least headway, for she was so very retiring and quiet. But might not this very retiringness, this tendency to avoid the others and spend her time alone, indicate that she too was troubled? If so, he was her man. He would cultivate her. He would follow her and sit with her, and encourage her to tell him about herself. Arbuthnot, he understood from Lotty, was a British Museum official—nothing specially important at present, but Mr. Wilkins regarded it as his business to know all sorts and kinds. Besides, there was promotion. Arbuthnot, promoted, might become very much worth while.

As for Lotty, she was charming. She really had all the qualities he had credited her with during his courtship, and they had been, it appeared, merely in abeyance since. His early impressions of her were now being endorsed by the affection and even admiration Lady Caroline showed for her. Lady Caroline Dester was the last person, he was sure, to be mistaken on such a subject. Her knowledge of the world, her constant association with only the best, must make her quite unerring. Lotty was evidently, then, that which before marriage he had believed her to be—she was valuable. She certainly had been most valuable in introducing him to Lady Caroline and Mrs. Fisher. A man in his profession could be immensely helped by a clever and attractive wife. Why had she not been attractive sooner? Why this sudden flowering?

Mr. Wilkins began too to believe there was something peculiar, as Lotty had almost at once informed him, in the atmosphere of San Salvatore. It promoted expansion. It brought out dormant qualities. And feeling more and more pleased, and even charmed, by his wife, and very content with the progress he was making with the two others, and hopeful of progress to be made with the retiring third, Mr. Wilkins could not remember ever having had such an agreeable holiday. The only thing that might perhaps be bettered was the way they would call him Mr. Wilkins. Nobody said Mr. Mellersh-Wilkins. Yet he had introduced himself to Lady Caroline—he flinched a little on remembering the circumstances—as Mellersh-Wilkins.

Still, this was a small matter, not enough to worry about. He would be foolish if in such a place and such society he worried about anything. He was not even worrying about what the holiday was costing, and had made up his mind to pay not only his own expenses but his wife's as well, and surprise her at the end by presenting her with her nest-egg as intact as when she started; and just the knowledge that he was preparing a happy surprise for her made him feel warmer than ever towards her.

In fact Mr. Wilkins, who had begun by being consciously and according to plan on his best behaviour, remained on it unconsciously, and with no effort at all.

And meanwhile the beautiful golden days were dropping gently from the second week one by one, equal in beauty with those of the first, and the scent of beanfields in flower on the hillside behind the village came across to San Salvatore whenever the air moved. In the garden that second week the poet's eyed narcissus disappeared out the long grass at the edge of the zigzag path, and wild gladiolus, slender and rose-coloured, came in their stead, white pinks bloomed in the borders, filing the whole place with their smoky-sweet smell, and a bush nobody had noticed burst into glory and fragrance, and it was a purple lilac bush. Such a jumble of spring and summer was not to be believed in, except by those who dwelt in those gardens. Everything seemed to be out together—all the things crowded into one month which in England are spread penuriously over six. Even primroses were found one day by Mrs. Wilkins in a cold corner up in the hills; and when she brought them down to the geraniums and heliotrope of San Salvatore they looked quite shy.

Chapter 17

On the first day of the third week Rose wrote to Frederick.

In case she should again hesitate and not post the letter, she gave it to Domenico to post; for if she did not write now there would be no time left at all. Half the month at San Salvatore was over. Even if Frederick started directly he got the letter, which of course he wouldn't be able to do, what with packing and passport, besides not being in a hurry to come, he couldn't arrive for five days.

Having done it, Rose wished she hadn't. He wouldn't come. He wouldn't bother to answer. And if he did answer, it would just be giving some reason which was not true, and about being too busy to get away; and all that had been got by writing to him would be that she would be more unhappy than before.

What things one did when one was idle. This resurrection of Frederick, or rather this attempt to resurrect him, what was it but the result of having nothing whatever to do? She wished she had never come away on a holiday. What did she want with holidays? Work was her salvation; work was the only thing that protected one, that kept one steady and one's values true. At home in Hampstead, absorbed and busy, she had managed to get over Frederick, thinking of him latterly only with the gentle melancholy with which one thinks of some one once loved but long since dead; and now this place, idleness in this soft place, had thrown her back to the wretched state she had climbed so carefully out of years ago. Why, if Frederick did come she would only bore him. Hadn't she seen in a flash quite soon after getting to San Salvatore that that was really what kept him away from her? And why should she suppose that now, after such a long estrangement, she would be able not to bore him, be able to do anything but stand before him like a tongue-tied idiot, with all the fingers of her spirit turned into thumbs? Besides, what a hopeless position, to have as it were to beseech: Please wait a little—please don't be impatient—I think perhaps I shan't be a bore presently.

A thousand times a day Rose wished she had let Frederick alone. Lotty, who asked her every evening whether she had sent her letter yet, exclaimed with delight when the answer at last was yes, and threw her arms round her. "Now we shall be completely happy!" cried the enthusiastic Lotty.

But nothing seemed less certain to Rose, and her expression became more and more the expression of one who has something on her mind.

Mr. Wilkins, wanting to find out what it was, strolled in the sun in his Panama hat, and began to meet her accidentally.

"I did not know," said Mr. Wilkins the first time, courteously raising his hat, "that you too liked this particular spot." And he sat down beside her.

In the afternoon she chose another spot; and she had not been in it half an hour before Mr. Wilkins, lightly swinging his cane, came round the corner.

"We are destined to meet in our rambles," said Mr. Wilkins pleasantly. And he sat down beside her.

Mr. Wilkins was very kind, and she had, she saw, misjudged him in Hampstead, and this was the real man, ripened like fruit by the beneficent sun of San Salvatore, but Rose did want to be alone. Still, she was grateful to him for proving to her that though she might bore Frederick she did not bore everybody; if she had, he would not have sat talking to her on each occasion till it was time to go in. True he bored her, but that wasn't anything like so dreadful as if she bored him. Then indeed her vanity would have been sadly ruffled. For now that Rose was not able to say her prayers she was being assailed by every sort of weakness: vanity, sensitiveness, irritability, pugnacity—strange, unfamiliar devils to have coming crowding on one and taking possession of one's swept and empty heart. She had never been vain or irritable or pugnacious in her life before. Could it be that San Salvatore was capable of opposite effects, and the same sun that ripened Mr. Wilkins made her go acid?

The next morning, so as to be sure of being alone, she went down, while Mr. Wilkins was still lingering pleasantly with Mrs. Fisher over breakfast, to the rocks by the water's edge where she and Lotty had sat the first day. Frederick by now had got her letter. To-day, if he were like Mr. Wilkins, she might get a telegram from him.

She tried to silence the absurd hope by jeering at it. Yet—if Mr. Wilkins had telegraphed, why not Frederick? The spell of San Salvatore lurked even, it seemed, in notepaper. Lotty had not dreamed of getting a telegram, and when she came in at lunch-time there it was. It would be too wonderful if when she went back at lunch-time she found one there for her too. . .

Rose clasped her hands tight round her knees. How passionately she longed to be important to somebody again—not important on platforms, not important as an asset in an organization, but privately important, just to one other person, quite privately, nobody else to know or notice. It didn't seem much to ask in a world so crowded with people, just to have one of them, only one out of all the millions, to oneself. Somebody who needed one, who thought of one, who was eager to come to one—oh, oh how dreadfully one wanted to be precious!

All the morning she sat beneath the pine-tree by the sea. Nobody came near her. The great hours passed slowly; they seemed enormous. But she wouldn't go up before lunch, she would give the telegram time to arrive. . .

That day Scrap, egged on by Lotty's persuasions and also thinking that perhaps she had sat long enough, had arisen from her chair and cushions and gone off with Lotty and sandwiches up into the hills till evening. Mr. Wilkins, who wished to go with them, stayed on Lady Caroline's advice with Mrs. Fisher in order to cheer her solitude, and though he left off cheering her about eleven to go and look for Mrs. Arbuthnot, so as for a space to cheer her too, thus dividing himself impartially between these solitary ladies, he came back again presently mopping his forehead and continued with Mrs. Fisher where he had left off, for this time Mrs. Arbuthnot had hidden successfully. There was a telegram, too, for her he noticed when he came in. Pity he did not know where she was.

"Ought we to open it?" he said to Mrs. Fisher.

"No," said Mrs. Fisher.

"It may require an answer."

"I don't approve of tampering with other people's correspondence."

"Tampering! My dear lady—"

Mr. Wilkins was shocked. Such a word. Tampering. He had the greatest possible esteem for Mrs. Fisher, but he did at times find her a little difficult. She liked him, he was sure, and she was in a fair way, he felt, to become a client, but he feared she would be a headstrong and secretive client. She was certainly secretive, for though he had been skilful and sympathetic for a whole week, she had as yet given him no inkling of what was so evidently worrying her.

154

"Poor old thing," said Lotty, on his asking her if she perhaps could throw light on Mrs. Fisher's troubles. "She hasn't got love."

"Love?" Mr. Wilkins could only echo, genuinely scandalized. "But surely, my dear—at her age—"

"Any love," said Lotty.

That very morning he had asked his wife, for he now sought and respected her opinion, if she could tell him what was the matter with Mrs. Arbuthnot, for she too, though he had done his best to thaw her into confidence, had remained persistently retiring.

"She wants her husband," said Lotty.

"Ah," said Mr. Wilkins, a new light shed on Mrs. Arbuthnot's shy and modest melancholy. And he added, "Very proper."

And Lotty said, smiling at him, "One does."

And Mr. Wilkins said, smiling at her, "Does one?"

And Lotty said, smiling at him, "Of course."

And Mr. Wilkins, much pleased with her, though it was still quite early in the day, a time when caresses are sluggish, pinched her ear.

Just before half-past twelve Rose came slowly up through the pergola and between the camellias ranged on either side of the old stone steps. The rivulets of periwinkles that flowed down them when first she arrived were gone, and now there were these bushes, incredibly rosetted. Pink, white, red, striped—she fingered and smelt them one after the other, so as not to get to her disappointment too quickly. As long as she hadn't seen for herself, seen the table in the hall quite empty except for its bowl of flowers, she still could hope, she still could have the joy of imagining the telegram lying on it waiting for her. But there is no smell in a camellia, as Mr. Wilkins, who was standing in the doorway on the look-out for her and knew what was necessary in horticulture, reminded her.

She started at his voice and looked up.

"A telegram has come for you," said Mr. Wilkins.

She stared at him, her mouth open.

"I searched for you everywhere, but failed—"

Of course. She knew it. She had been sure of it all the time. Bright and burning, Youth in that instant flashed down again on Rose. She flew up the steps, red as the camellia she had just been fingering, and was in the hall and tearing open the telegram before Mr. Wilkins had finished his sentence. Why, but if things could happen like this—why, but there was no end to—why, she and Frederick—they were going to be—again—at last—

"No bad news, I trust?" said Mr. Wilkins who had followed her, for when she had read the telegram she stood staring at it and her face went slowly white. Curious to watch how her face went slowly white.

She turned and looked at Mr. Wilkins as if trying to remember him.

"Oh no. On the contrary—"

She managed to smile. "I'm going to have a visitor," she said, holding out the telegram; and when he had taken it she walked away towards the dining-room, murmuring something about lunch being ready.

Mr. Wilkins read the telegram. It had been sent that morning from Mezzago, and was:

Am passing through on way to Rome. May I pay my respects this afternoon?

Thomas Briggs.

Why should such a telegram make the interesting lady turn pale? For her pallor on reading it had been so striking as to convince Mr. Wilkins she was receiving a blow.

"Who is Thomas Briggs?" he asked, following her into the dining-room.

She looked at him vaguely. "Who is—?" she repeated, getting her thoughts together again.

"Thomas Briggs."

"Oh. Yes. He is the owner. This is his house. He is very nice. He is coming this afternoon."

Thomas Briggs was at that very moment coming. He was jogging along the road between Mezzago and Castagneto in a fly, sincerely hoping that the dark-eyed lady would grasp that all he wanted was to see her, and not at all to see if his house were still there. He felt that an owner of delicacy did not intrude on a tenant. But—he had been thinking so much of her since that day. Rose Arbuthnot. Such a pretty name. And such a pretty creature—mild, milky, mothery in the best sense; the best sense being that she wasn't his mother and couldn't have been if she had tried, for parents were the only things impossible to have younger than oneself. Also, he was passing so near. It seemed absurd not just to look in and see if she were comfortable. He longed to see her in his house. He longed to see it as her background, to see her sitting in his chairs, drinking out of his cups, using all his things. Did she put the big crimson brocade

156

cushion in the drawing-room behind her little dark head? Her hair and the whiteness of her skin would look lovely against it. Had she seen the portrait of herself on the stairs? He wondered if she liked it. He would explain it to her. If she didn't paint, and she had said nothing to suggest it, she wouldn't perhaps notice how exactly the moulding of the eyebrows and the slight hollow of the cheek—

He told the fly to wait in Castagneto, and crossed the piazza, hailed by children and dogs, who all knew him and sprang up suddenly from nowhere, and walking quickly up the zigzag path, for he was an active young man not much more than thirty, he pulled the ancient chain that range the bell, and waited decorously on the proper side of the open door to be allowed to come in.

At the sight of him Francesca flung up every bit of her that would fling up—eyebrows, eyelids, and hands, and volubly assured him that all was in perfect order and that she was doing her duty.

"Of course, of course," said Briggs, cutting her short. "No one doubts it."

And he asked her to take in his card to her mistress.

"Which mistress?" asked Francesca.

"Which mistress?"

"There are four," said Francesca, scenting an irregularity on the part of the tenants, for her master looked surprised; and she felt pleased, for life was dull and irregularities helped it along at least a little.

"Four?" he repeated surprised. "Well, take it to the lot then," he said, recovering himself, for he noticed her expression.

Coffee was being drunk in the top garden in the shade of the umbrella pine. Only Mrs. Fisher and Mr. Wilkins were drinking it, for Mrs. Arbuthnot, after eating nothing and being completely silent during lunch, had disappeared immediately afterwards.

While Francesca went away into the garden with his card, her master stood examining the picture on the staircase of that Madonna by an early Italian painter, name unknown, picked up by him at Orvieto, who was so much like his tenant. It really was remarkable, the likeness. Of course his tenant that day in London had had her hat on, but he was pretty sure her hair grew just like that off her forehead. The expression of the eyes, grave and sweet, was exactly the same. He rejoiced to think that he would always have her portrait.

He looked up at the sound of footsteps, and there she was, coming down the stairs just as he had imagined her in that place, dressed in white.

She was astonished to see him so soon. She had supposed he would come about tea-time, and till then she had meant to sit somewhere out of doors where she could be by herself.

He watched her coming down the stairs with the utmost eager interest. In a moment she would be level with her portrait.

"It really is extraordinary," said Briggs.

"How do you do," said Rose, intent only on a decent show of welcome.

She did not welcome him. He was here, she felt, the telegram bitter in her heart, instead of Frederick, doing what she had longed Frederick would do, taking his place.

"Just stand still a moment—"

She obeyed automatically.

"Yes—quite astonishing. Do you mind taking off your hat?"

Rose, surprised, took it off obediently.

"Yes—I thought so—I just wanted to make sure. And look— have you noticed—"

He began to make odd swift passes with his hand over the face in the picture, measuring it, looking from it to her.

Rose's surprise became amusement, and she could not help smiling.

"Have you come to compare me with my original?" she asked.

"You do see how extraordinarily alike—"

"I didn't know I looked so solemn."

"You don't. Not now. You did a minute ago, quite as solemn. Oh yes—how do you do," he finished suddenly, noticing her outstretched hand. And he laughed and shook it, flushing—a trick of his—to the roots of his hair.

Francesca came back. "The Signora Fisher," she said, "will be pleased to see Him."

"Who is the Signora Fisher?" he asked Rose.

"One of the four who are sharing your house."

"Then there are four of you?"

"Yes. My friend and I found we couldn't afford it by ourselves."

"Oh, I say—" began Briggs in confusion, for he would best have liked Rose Arbuthnot—pretty name—not to have to afford anything, but to stay at San Salvatore as long as she liked as his guest.

"Mrs. Fisher is having coffee in the top garden," said Rose. "I'll take you to her and introduce you."

"I don't want to go. You've got your hat on, so you were going for a walk. Mayn't I come too? I'd immensely like being shown round by you."

"But Mrs. Fisher is waiting for you."

"Won't she keep?"

"Yes," said Rose, with the smile that had so much attracted him the first day. "I think she will keep quite well till tea."

"Do you speak Italian?"

"No," said Rose. "Why?"

On that he turned to Francesca, and told her at a great rate, for in Italian he was glib, to go back to the Signora in the top garden and tell her he had encountered his old friend the Signora Arbuthnot, and was going for a walk with her and would present himself to her later.

"Do you invite me to tea?" he asked Rose, when Francesca had gone.

"Of course. It's your house."

"It isn't. It's yours."

"Till Monday week," she smiled.

"Come and show me all the views," he said eagerly; and it was plain, even to the self-depreciatory Rose, that she did not bore Mr. Briggs.

159

Chapter 18

They had a very pleasant walk, with a great deal of sitting down in warm, thyme-fragrant corners, and if anything could have helped Rose to recover from the bitter disappointment of the morning it would have been the company and conversation of Mr. Briggs. He did help her to recover, and the same process took place as that which Lotty had undergone with her husband, and the more Mr. Briggs thought Rose charming the more charming she became.

Briggs was a man incapable of concealments, who never lost time if he could help it. They had not got to the end of the headland where the lighthouse is—Briggs asked her to show him the lighthouse, because the path to it, he knew, was wide enough for two to walk abreast and fairly level—before he had told her of the impression she made on him in London.

Since even the most religious, sober women like to know they have made an impression, particularly the kind that has nothing to do with character or merits, Rose was pleased. Being pleased, she smiled. Smiling, she was more attractive than ever. Colour came into her cheeks, and brightness into her eyes. She heard herself saying things that really sounded quite interesting and even amusing. If Frederick were listening now, she thought, perhaps he would see that she couldn't after all be such a hopeless bore; for here was a man, nice-looking, young, and surely clever—he seemed clever, and she hoped he was, for then the compliment would be still greater—who was evidently quite happy to spend the afternoon just talking to her.

And indeed Mr. Briggs seemed very much interested. He wanted to hear all about everything she had been doing from the moment she got there. He asked her if she had seen this, that, and the other in the house, what she liked best, which room she had, if she were comfortable, if Francesca was behaving, if Domenico took care of her, and whether she didn't enjoy using the yellow sitting-room— the one that got all the sun and looked out towards Genoa.

Rose was ashamed how little she had noticed in the house, and how few of the things he spoke of as curious or beautiful in it she had even seen. Swamped in thought of Frederick, she appeared to have lived in San Salvatore blindly, and more than half the time had gone, and what had been the good of it? She might just as well have been sitting hankering on Hampstead Heath. No, she mightn't; through all her hankerings she had been conscious that she was at least in the very heart of beauty; and indeed it was this beauty, this longing to share it, that had first started her off hankering.

Mr. Briggs, however, was too much alive for her to be able to spare any attention at this moment for Frederick, and she praised the servants in answer to his questions, and praised the yellow sitting-room without telling him she had only been in it once and then was ignominiously ejected, and she told him she knew hardly anything about art and curiosities, but thought perhaps if somebody would tell her about them she would know more, and she said she had spent every day since her arrival out-of-doors, because out-of-doors there was so very wonderful and different from anything she had ever seen.

Briggs walked by her side along his paths that were yet so happily for the moment her paths, and felt all the innocent glows of family life. He was an orphan and an only child, and had a warm, domestic disposition. He would have adored a sister and spoilt a mother, and was beginning at this time to think of marrying; for though he had been very happy with his various loves, each of whom, contrary to the usual experience, turned ultimately into his devoted friend, he was fond of children and thought he had perhaps now got to the age of settling if he did not wish to be too old by the time his eldest son was twenty. San Salvatore had latterly seemed a little forlorn. He fancied it echoed when he walked about it. He had felt lonely there; so lonely that he had preferred this year to miss out a spring and let it. It wanted a wife in it. It wanted that final touch of warmth and beauty, for he never thought of his wife except in terms of warmth and beauty—she would of course be beautiful and kind. It amused him how much in love with this vague wife he was already.

At such a rate was he making friends with the lady with the sweet name as he walked along the path towards the lighthouse, that he was sure presently he would be telling her everything about himself and his past doings and his future hopes; and the thought of such a swiftly developing confidence made him laugh.

"Why are you laughing?" she asked, looking at him and smiling.

"It's so like coming home," he said.

"But it is coming home for you to come here."

"I mean really like coming home. To one's—one's family. I never had a family. I'm an orphan."

"Oh, are you?" said Rose with the proper sympathy. "I hope you've not been one very long. No—I don't mean I hope you have been one very long. No—I don't know what I mean, except that I'm sorry."

He laughed again. "Oh I'm used to it. I haven't anybody. No sisters or brothers."

"Then you're an only child," she observed intelligently.

"Yes. And there's something about you that's exactly my idea of a—of a family."

She was amused.

"So—cosy," he said, looking at her and searching for a word.

"You wouldn't think so if you saw my house in Hampstead," she said, a vision of that austere and hard-seated dwelling presenting itself to her mind, with nothing soft in it except the shunned and neglected Du Barri sofa. No wonder, she thought, for a moment clear-brained, that Frederick avoided it. There was nothing cosy about his family.

"I don't believe any place you lived in could be anything but exactly like you," he said.

"You're not going to pretend San Salvatore is like me?"

"Indeed I do pretend it. Surely you admit that it is beautiful?"

He said several things like that. She enjoyed her walk. She could not recollect any walk so pleasant since her courting days.

She came back to tea, bringing Mr. Briggs, and looking quite different, Mr. Wilkins noticed, from what she had looked till then. Trouble here, trouble here, thought Mr. Wilkins, mentally rubbing his professional hands. He could see himself being called in presently to advise. On the one hand there was Arbuthnot, on the other hand here was Briggs. Trouble brewing, trouble sooner or later. But why had Briggs's telegram acted on the lady like a blow? If she had turned pale from excess of joy, then trouble was nearer than he had supposed. She was not pale now; she was more like her name than he had yet seen her. Well, he was the man for trouble. He regretted, of course, that people should get into it, but being in he was their man.

And Mr. Wilkins, invigorated by these thoughts, his career being very precious to him, proceeded to assist in doing the honours to Mr. Briggs, both in his quality of sharer in the temporary ownership of San Salvatore and of probable helper out of difficulties, with great hospitality, and pointed out the various features of the place to him, and led him to the parapet and showed him Mezzago across the bay.

Mrs. Fisher too was gracious. This was this young man's house. He was a man of property. She liked property, and she liked men of property. Also there seemed a peculiar merit in being a man of property so young. Inheritance, of course; and inheritance was more respectable than acquisition. It did indicate fathers; and in an age where most people appeared neither to have them nor to want them she liked this too.

Accordingly it was a pleasant meal, with everybody amiable and pleased. Briggs thought Mrs. Fisher a dear old lady, and showed he thought so; and again the magic worked, and she became a dear old lady. She developed benignity with him, and a kind of benignity which was almost playful—actually before tea was over including in some observation she made him the words "My dear boy."

Strange words in Mrs. Fisher's mouth. It is doubtful whether in her life she had used them before. Rose was astonished. Now nice people really were. When would she leave off making mistakes about them? She hadn't suspected this side of Mrs. Fisher, and she began to wonder whether those other sides of her with which alone she was acquainted had not perhaps after all been the effect of her own militant and irritating behaviour. Probably they were. How horrid, then, she must have been. She felt very penitent when she saw Mrs. Fisher beneath her eyes blossoming out into real amiability the moment some one came along who was charming to her, and she could have sunk into the ground with shame when Mrs. Fisher presently laughed, and she realized by the shock it gave her that the sound was entirely new. Not once before had she or any one else there heard Mrs. Fisher laugh. What an indictment of the lot of them! For they had all laughed, the others, some more and some less, at one time or another since their arrival, and only Mrs. Fisher had not. Clearly, since she could enjoy herself as she was now enjoying herself, she had not enjoyed herself before. Nobody had cared whether she did or not, except perhaps Lotty. Yes; Lotty had cared, and had wanted her to be happy; but Lotty seemed to produce

163

a bad effect on Mrs. Fisher, while as for Rose herself she had never been with her for five minutes without wanting, really wanting, to provoke and oppose her.

How very horrid she had been. She had behaved unpardonably. Her penitence showed itself in a shy and deferential solicitude towards Mrs. Fisher which made the observant Briggs think her still more angelic, and wish for a moment that he were an old lady himself in order to be behaved to by Rose Arbuthnot just like that. There was evidently no end, he thought, to the things she could do sweetly. He would even not mind taking medicine, really nasty medicine, if it were Rose Arbuthnot bending over him with the dose.

She felt his bright blue eyes, the brighter because he was so sunburnt, fixed on her with a twinkle in them, and smiling asked him what he was thinking about.

But he couldn't very well tell her that, he said; and added, "Some day."

"Trouble, trouble," thought Mr. Wilkins at this, again mentally rubbing his hands. "Well, I'm their man."

"I'm sure," said Mrs. Fisher benignly, "you have no thoughts we may not hear."

"I'm sure," said Briggs, "I would be telling you every one of my secrets in a week."

"You would be telling somebody very safe, then," said Mrs. Fisher benevolently—just such a son would she have liked to have had. "And in return," she went on, "I daresay I would tell you mine."

"Ah no," said Mr. Wilkins, adapting himself to this tone of easy badinage, "I must protest. I really must. I have a prior claim, I am the older friend. I have known Mrs. Fisher ten days, and you, Briggs, have not yet known her one. I assert my right to be told her secrets first. That is," he added, bowing gallantly, "if she has any—which I beg leave to doubt."

"Oh, haven't I!" exclaimed Mrs. Fisher, thinking of those green leaves. That she should exclaim at all was surprising, but that she should do it with gaiety was miraculous. Rose could only watch her in wonder.

"Then I shall worm them out," said Briggs with equal gaiety.

"They won't need much worming out," said Mrs. Fisher. "My difficulty is to keep them from bursting out."

It might have been Lotty talking. Mr. Wilkins adjusted the single eyeglass he carried with him for occasions like this, and examined Mrs. Fisher carefully. Rose looked on, unable not to smile too since Mrs. Fisher seemed so much amused, though Rose did not quite know why, and her smile was a little uncertain, for Mrs. Fisher amused was a new sight, not without its awe-inspiring aspects, and had to be got accustomed to.

What Mrs. Fisher was thinking was how much surprised they would be if she told them of her very odd and exciting sensation of going to come out all over buds. They would think she was an extremely silly old woman, and so would she have thought as lately as two days ago; but the bud idea was becoming familiar to her, she was more apprivoisée now, as dear Matthew Arnold used to say, and though it would undoubtedly be best if one's appearance and sensations matched, yet supposing they did not—and one couldn't have everything—was it not better to feel young somewhere rather than old everywhere? Time enough to be old everywhere again, inside as well as out, when she got back to her sarcophagus in Prince of Wales Terrace.

Yet it is probable that without the arrival of Briggs Mrs. Fisher would have gone on secretly fermenting in her shell. The others only knew her as severe. It would have been more than her dignity could bear suddenly to relax—especially towards the three young women. But now came the stranger Briggs, a stranger who at once took to her as no young man had taken to her in her life, and it was the coming of Briggs and his real and manifest appreciation—for just such a grandmother, thought Briggs, hungry for home life and its concomitants, would he have liked to have—that released Mrs. Fisher from her shell; and here she was at last, as Lotty had predicted, pleased, good-humoured and benevolent.

Lotty, coming back half an hour later from her picnic, and following the sound of voices into the top garden in the hope of still finding tea, saw at once what had happened, for Mrs. Fisher at that very moment was laughing.

"She's burst her cocoon," thought Lotty; and swift as she was in all her movements, and impulsive, and also without any sense of propriety to worry and delay her, she bent over the back of Mrs. Fisher's chair and kissed her.

"Good gracious!" cried Mrs. Fisher, starting violently, for such a thing had not happened to her since Mr. Fisher's earlier days, and then only gingerly. This kiss was a real kiss, and rested on Mrs. Fisher's cheek a moment with a strange, soft sweetness.

When she saw whose it was, a deep flush spread over her face. Mrs. Wilkins kissing her and the kiss feeling so affectionate. . . Even if she had wanted to she could not in the presence of the appreciative Mr. Briggs resume her cast-off severity and begin rebuking again; but she did not want to. Was it possible Mrs. Wilkins like her—had liked her all this time, while she had been so much disliking her herself? A queer little trickle of warmth filtered through the frozen defences of Mrs. Fisher's heart. Somebody young kissing her—somebody young wanting to kiss her. . . Very much flushed, she watched the strange creature, apparently quite unconscious she had done anything extraordinary, shaking hands with Mr. Briggs, on her husband's introducing him, and immediately embarking on the friendliest conversation with him, exactly as if she had known him all her life. What a strange creature; what a very strange creature. It was natural, she being so strange, that one should have, perhaps, misjudged her. . .

"I'm sure you want some tea," said Briggs with eager hospitality to Lotty. He thought her delightful,—freckles, picnic-untidiness and all. Just such a sister would he—

"This is cold," he said, feeling the teapot. "I'll tell Francesca to make you some fresh—"

He broke off and blushed. "Aren't I forgetting myself," he said, laughing and looking round at them.

"Very natural, very natural," Mr. Wilkins reassured him.

"I'll go and tell Francesca," said Rose, getting up.

"No, no," said Briggs. "Don't go away." And he put his hands to his mouth and shouted.

"Francesca!" shouted Briggs.

She came running. No summons in their experience had been answered by her with such celerity.

"'Her Master's voice,'" remarked Mr. Wilkins; aptly, he considered.

"Make fresh tea," ordered Briggs in Italian. "Quick—quick—" "And then remembering himself he blushed again, and begged everybody's pardon.

"Very natural, very natural," Mr. Wilkins reassured him.

Briggs then explained to Lotty what he had explained twice already, once to Rose and once to the other two, that he was on his way to Rome and thought he would get out at Mezzago and just look in to see if they were comfortable and continue his journey the next day, staying the night in an hotel at Mezzago.

"But how ridiculous," said Lotty. "Of course you must stay here. It's your house. There's Kate Lumley's room," she added, turning to Mrs. Fisher. "You wouldn't mind Mr. Briggs having it for one night?

Kate Lumley isn't in it, you know," she said turning to Briggs again and laughing.

And Mrs. Fisher to her immense surprise laughed too. She knew that any other time this remark would have struck her as excessively unseemly, and yet now she only thought it funny.

No indeed, she assured Briggs, Kate Lumley was not in that room. Very fortunately, for she was an excessively wide person and the room was excessively narrow. Kate Lumley might get into it, but that was about all. Once in, she would fit it so tightly that probably she would never be able to get out again. It was entirely at Mr. Briggs's disposal, and she hoped he would do nothing so absurd as go to an hotel—he, the owner of the whole place.

Rose listened to this speech wide-eyed with amazement. Mrs. Fisher laughed very much as she made it. Lotty laughed very much too, and at the end of it bent down and kissed her again—kissed her several times.

"So you see, my dear boy," said Mrs. Fisher, "you must stay here and give us all a great deal of pleasure."

"A great deal indeed," corroborated Mr. Wilkins heartily.

"A very great deal," repeated Mrs. Fisher, looking exactly like a please mother.

"Do," said Rose, on Briggs's turning inquiringly to her.

"How kind of you all," he said, his face broad with smiles. "I'd love to be a guest here. What a new sensation. And with three such—"

He broke off and looked round. "I say," he asked, "oughtn't I to have a fourth hostess? Francesca said she had four mistresses."

"Yes. There's Lady Caroline," said Lotty.

"Then hadn't we better find out first if she invites me too?"

"Oh, but she's sure—" began Lotty.

"The daughter of the Droitwiches, Briggs," said Mr. Wilkins, "is not likely to be wanting in the proper hospitable impulses."

167

"The daughter of the—" repeated Briggs; but he stopped dead, for there in the doorway was the daughter of the Droitwiches herself; or rather, coming towards him out of the dark doorway into the brightness of the sunset, was that which he had not in his life yet seen but only dreamed of, his ideal of absolute loveliness.

Chapter 19

And then when she spoke . . . what chance was there for poor Briggs? He was undone. All Scrap said was, "How do you do," on Mr.
Wilkins presenting him, but it was enough; it undid Briggs.

From a cheerful, chatty, happy young man, overflowing with life and friendliness, he became silent, solemn, and with little beads on his temples. Also he became clumsy, dropping the teaspoon as he handed her her cup, mismanaging the macaroons, so that one rolled on the ground. His eyes could not keep off the enchanting face for a moment; and when Mr. Wilkins, elucidating him, for he failed to elucidate himself, informed Lady Caroline that in Mr. Briggs she beheld the owner of San Salvatore, who was on his way to Rome, but had got out at Mezzago, etc. etc., and that the other three ladies had invited him to spend the night in what was to all intents and purposes his own house rather than an hotel, and Mr. Briggs was only waiting for the seal of her approval to this invitation, she being the fourth hostess—when Mr. Wilkins, balancing his sentences and being admirably clear and enjoying the sound of his own cultured voice, explained the position in this manner to Lady Caroline, Briggs sat and said never a word.

A deep melancholy invaded Scrap. The symptoms of the incipient grabber were all there and only too familiar, and she knew that if Briggs stayed her rest-cure might be regarded as over.

Then Kate Lumley occurred to her. She caught at Kate as at a straw.

"It would have been delightful," she said, faintly smiling at Briggs—she could not in decency not smile, at least a little, but even a little betrayed the dimple, and Briggs's eyes became more fixed than ever—"I'm only wondering if there is room."

"Yes, there is," said Lotty. "There's Kate Lumley's room."

"I thought," said Scrap to Mrs. Fisher, and it seemed to Briggs that he had never heard music till now, "your friend was expected immediately."

"Oh, no," said Mrs. Fisher—with an odd placidness, Scrap thought.

"Miss Lumley," said Mr. Wilkins, "—or should I," he inquired of Mrs. Fisher, "say Mrs.?"

169

"Nobody has ever married Kate," said Mrs. Fisher complacently.

"Quite so. Miss Lumley does not arrive to-day in any case, Lady Caroline, and Mr. Briggs has—unfortunately, if I may say so—to continue his journey to-morrow, so that his staying would in no way interfere with Miss Lumley's possible movements."

"Then of course I join in the invitation," said Scrap, with what was to Briggs the most divine cordiality.

He stammered something, flushing scarlet, and Scrap thought, "Oh," and turned her head away; but that merely made Briggs acquainted

with her profile, and if there existed anything more lovely than Scrap's full face it was her profile.

Well, it was only for this one afternoon and evening. He would leave, no doubt, the first thing in the morning. It took hours to get to Rome. Awful if he hung on till the night train. She had a feeling that the principal express to Rome passed through at night. Why hadn't that woman Kate Lumley arrived yet? She had forgotten all about her, but now she remembered she was to have been invited a fortnight ago. What had become of her? This man, once let in, would come and see her in London, would haunt the places she was likely to go to. He had the makings, her experienced eye could see, of a passionately persistent grabber.

"If," thought Mr. Wilkins, observing Briggs's face and sudden silence, "any understanding existed between this young fellow and Mrs. Arbuthnot, there is now going to be trouble. Trouble of a different nature from the kind I feared, in which Arbuthnot would have played a leading part, in fact the part of petitioner, but trouble that may need help and advice none the less for its not being publicly scandalous. Briggs, impelled by his passions and her beauty, will aspire to the daughter of the Droitwiches. She, naturally and properly, will repel him. Mrs. Arbuthnot, left in the cold, will be upset and show it. Arbuthnot, on his arrival will find his wife in enigmatic tears. Inquiring into their cause, he will be met with an icy reserve. More trouble may then be expected, and in me they will seek and find their adviser. When Lotty said Mrs. Arbuthnot wanted her husband, she was wrong. What Mrs. Arbuthnot wants is Briggs, and it looks uncommonly as if she were not going to get him. Well, I'm their man."

"Where are your things, Mr. Briggs?" asked Mrs. Fisher, her voice round with motherliness. "Oughtn't they to be fetched?" For the sun was nearly in the sea now, and the sweet-smelling April dampness that followed immediately on its disappearance was beginning to steal into the garden.

Briggs started. "My things?" he repeated. "Oh yes—I must fetch them. They're in Mezzago. I'll send Domenico. My fly is waiting in the village. He can go back in it. I'll go and tell him."

He got up. To whom was he talking? To Mrs. Fisher, ostensibly, yet his eyes were fixed on Scrap, who said nothing and looked at no one.

Then, recollecting himself, he stammered, "I'm awfully sorry—I keep on forgetting—I'll go down and fetch them myself."

"We can easily send Domenico," said Rose; and at her gentle voice he turned his head.

Why, there was his friend, the sweet-named lady—but how had she not in this short interval changed! Was it the failing light making her so colourless, so vague-featured, so dim, so much like a ghost? A nice good ghost, of course, and still with a pretty name, but only a ghost.

He turned from her to Scrap again, and forgot Rose Arbuthnot's existence. How was it possible for him to bother about anybody or anything else in this first moment of being face to face with his dream come true?

Briggs had not supposed or hoped that any one as beautiful as his dream of beauty existed. He had never till now met even an approximation. Pretty women, charming women by the score he had met and properly appreciated, but never the real, the godlike thing itself. He used to think "If ever I saw a perfectly beautiful woman I should die"; and though, having now met what to his ideas was a perfectly beautiful woman, he did not die, he became very nearly as incapable of managing his own affairs as if he had.

The others were obliged to arrange everything for him. By questions they extracted from him that his luggage was in the station cloakroom at Mezzago, and they sent for Domenico, and, urged and prompted by everybody except Scrap, who sat in silence and looked at no one, Briggs was induced to give him the necessary instructions for going back in the fly and bringing out his things.

It was a sad sight to see the collapse of Briggs. Everybody noticed it, even Rose.

"Upon my word," thought Mrs. Fisher, "the way one pretty face can turn a delightful man into an idiot is past all patience."

And feeling the air getting chilly, and the sight of the enthralled Briggs painful, she went in to order his room to be got ready, regretting now that she had pressed the poor boy to stay. She had forgotten Lady Caroline's kill-joy face for the moment, and the more completely owing to the absence of any ill effects produced by it on Mr. Wilkins. Poor boy. Such a charming boy too, left to himself. It was true she could not accuse Lady Caroline of not leaving him to himself, for she was taking no notice of him at all, but that did not help. Exactly like foolish moths did men, in other respects intelligent, flutter round the impassive lighted candle of a pretty face. She had seen them doing it. She had looked on only too often. Almost she laid a mother hand on Briggs's fair head as she passed him. Poor boy.

Then Scrap, having finished her cigarette, got up and went indoors too. She saw no reason why she should sit there in order to gratify Mr. Briggs's desire to stare. She would have liked to stay out longer, to go to her corner behind the daphne bushes and look at the sunset sky and watch the lights coming out one by one in the village below and smell the sweet moistness of the evening, but if she did Mr. Briggs would certainly follow her.

The old familiar tyranny had begun again. Her holiday of peace and liberation was interrupted—perhaps over, for who knew if he would go away, after all, to-morrow? He might leave the house, driven out of it by Kate Lumley, but that was nothing to prevent his taking rooms in the village and coming up every day. This tyranny of one person over another! And she was so miserably constructed that she wouldn't even be able to frown him down without being misunderstood.

Scrap, who loved this time of the evening in her corner, felt indignant with Mr. Briggs who was doing her out of it, and she turned her back on the garden and him and went towards the house without a look or a word. But Briggs, when he realized her intention, leapt to his fee, snatched chairs which were not in her way out of it, kicked a footstool which was not in her path on one side, hurried to the door, which stood wide open, in order to hold it open, and followed her through it, walking by her side along the hall.

What was to be done with Mr. Briggs? Well, it was his hall; she couldn't prevent his walking along it.

"I hope," he said, not able while walking to take his eyes off her, so that he knocked against several things he would otherwise have

172

avoided—the corner of a bookcase, an ancient carved cupboard, the table with the flowers on it, shaking the water over—"that you are quite comfortable here? If you're not I'll—I'll flay them alive."

His voice vibrated. What was to be done with Mr. Briggs? She could of course stay in her room the whole time, say she was ill, not appear at dinner; but again, the tyranny of this . . .

"I'm very comfortable indeed," said Scrap.

"If I had dreamed you were coming—" he began.

"It's a wonderful old place," said Scrap, doing her utmost to sound detached and forbidding, but with little hope of success.

The kitchen was on this floor, and passing its door, which was open a crack, they were observed by the servants, whose thoughts, communicated to each other by looks, may be roughly reproduced by such rude symbols as Aha and Oho—symbols which represented and included their appreciation of the inevitable, their foreknowledge of the inevitable, and their complete understanding and approval.

"Are you going upstairs?" asked Briggs, as she paused at the foot of them.

"Yes."

"Which room do you sit in? The drawing-room, or the small yellow room?"

"In my own room."

So then he couldn't go up with her; so then all he could do was to wait till she came out again.

He longed to ask her which was her own room—it thrilled him to hear her call any room in his house her own room—that he might picture her in it. He longed to know if by any happy chance it was his room, for ever after to be filled with her wonder; but he didn't dare. He would find that out later from some one else—Francesca, anybody.

"Then I shan't see you again till dinner?"

"Dinner is at eight," was Scrap's evasive answer as she went upstairs.

He watched her go.

She passed the Madonna, the portrait of Rose Arbuthnot, and the dark-eyed figure he had thought so sweet seemed to turn pale, to shrivel into insignificance as she passed.

She turned the bend of the stairs, and the setting sun, shining through the west window a moment on her face, turned her to glory.

She disappeared, and the sun went out too, and the stairs were dark and empty.

He listened till her footsteps were silent, trying to tell from the sound of the shutting door which room she had gone into, then wandered aimlessly away through the hall again, and found himself back in the top garden.

Scrap from her window saw him there. She saw Lotty and Rose sitting on the end parapet, where she would have liked to have been, and she saw Mr. Wilkins buttonholing Briggs and evidently telling him to story of the oleander tree in the middle of the garden.

Briggs was listening with a patience she thought rather nice, seeing that it was his oleander and his own father's story. She knew Mr. Wilkins was telling him the story by his gestures. Domenico had told it her soon after her arrival, and he had also told Mrs. Fisher, who had told Mr. Wilkins. Mrs. Fisher thought highly of this story, and often spoke of it. It was about a cherrywood walking-stick. Briggs's father had thrust this stick into the ground at that spot, and said to Domenico's father, who was then the gardener, "Here we will have an oleander." And Briggs's father left the stick in the ground as a reminder to Domenico's father, and presently— how long afterwards nobody remembered—the stick began to sprout, and it was an oleander.

There stood poor Mr. Briggs being told all about it, and listening to the story he must have known from infancy with patience.

Probably he was thinking of something else. She was afraid he was. How unfortunate, how extremely unfortunate, the determination that seized people to get hold of and engulf other people. If only they could be induced to stand more on their own feet. Why couldn't Mr. Briggs be more like Lotty, who never wanted anything of anybody, but was complete in herself and respected other people's completeness? One loved being with Lotty. With her one was free, and yet befriended. Mr. Briggs looked so really nice, too. She thought she might like him if only he wouldn't so excessively like her.

Scrap felt melancholy. Here she was shut up in her bedroom, which was stuffy from the afternoon sun that had been pouring into it, instead of out in the cool garden, and all because of Mr. Briggs.

Intolerably tyranny, she thought, flaring up. She wouldn't endure it; she would go out all the same; she would run downstairs while Mr. Wilkins—really that man was a treasure—held Mr. Briggs down telling him about the oleander, and get out of the house by the front door, and take cover in the shadows of the zigzag path. Nobody could see her there; nobody would think of looking for her there.

She snatched up a wrap, for she did not mean to come back for a long while, perhaps not even to dinner—it would be all Mr. Briggs's fault if she went dinnerless and hungry—and with another glance out of the window to see if she were still safe, she stole out and got away to the sheltering trees of the zigzag path, and there sat down on one of the seats placed at each bend to assist the upward journey of those who were breathless.

Ah, this was lovely, thought Scrap with a sigh of relief. How cool. How good it smelt. She could see the quiet water of the little harbour through the pine trunks, and the lights coming out in the houses on the other side, and all round her the green dusk was splashed by the rose-pink of the gladioluses in the grass and the white of the crowding daisies.

Ah, this was lovely. So still. Nothing moving—not a leaf, not a stalk. The only sound was a dog barking, far away somewhere up on the hills, or when the door of the little restaurant in the piazza below was opened and there was a burst of voices, silenced again immediately by the swinging to of the door.

She drew in a deep breath of pleasure. Ah, this was—

Her deep breath was arrested in the middle. What was that?

She leaned forward listening, her body tense.

Footsteps. On the zigzag path. Briggs. Finding her out.

Should she run?

No—the footsteps were coming up, not down. Some one from the village. Perhaps Angelo, with provisions.

She relaxed again. But the steps were not the steps of Angelo, that swift and springy youth; they were slow and considered, and they kept on pausing.

"Some one who isn't used to hills," thought Scrap.

The idea of going back to the house did not occur to her. She was afraid of nothing in life except love. Brigands or murderers as such held no terrors for the daughter of the Droitwiches; she only would have been afraid of them if they left off being brigands and murderers and began instead to try and make love.

The next moment the footsteps turned the corner of her bit of path, and stood still.

"Getting his wind," thought Scrap, not looking round.

Then as he—from the sounds of the steps she took them to belong to a man—did not move, she turned her head, and beheld with astonishment a person she had seen a good deal of lately in London, the well-known writer of amusing memoirs, Mr. Ferdinand Arundel.

She stared. Nothing in the way of being followed surprised her any more, but that he should have discovered where she was surprised her. Her mother had promised faithfully to tell no one.

"You?" she said, feeling betrayed. "Here?"

He came up to her and took off his hat. His forehead beneath the hat was wet with the beads of unaccustomed climbing. He looked ashamed and entreating, like a guilty but devoted dog.

"You must forgive me," he said. "Lady Droitwich told me where you were, and as I happened to be passing through on my way to Rome I thought I would get out at Mezzago and just look in and see how you were."

"But—didn't my mother tell you I was doing a rest-cure?"

"Yes. She did. And that's why I haven't intruded on you earlier in the day. I thought you would probably sleep all day, and wake up about now so as to be fed."

"But—"

"I know. I've got nothing to say in excuse. I couldn't help myself."

"This," thought Scrap, "comes of mother insisting on having authors to lunch, and me being so much more amiable in appearance than I really am."

She had been amiable to Ferdinand Arundel; she liked him—or rather she did not dislike him. He seemed a jovial, simple man, and had the eyes of a nice dog. Also, though it was evident that he admired her, he had not in London grabbed. There he had merely been a good-natured, harmless person of entertaining conversation, who helped to make luncheons agreeable. Now it appeared that he too was a grabber. Fancy following her out there—daring to. Nobody else had. Perhaps her mother had given him the address because she considered him so absolutely harmless, and thought he might be useful and see her home.

Well, whatever he was he couldn't possibly give her the trouble an active young man like Mr. Briggs might give her. Mr. Briggs, infatuated, would be reckless, she felt, would stick at nothing, would lose his head publicly. She could imagine Mr. Briggs doing things with rope-ladders, and singing all night under her window—being really difficult and uncomfortable. Mr. Arundel hadn't the figure for any kind of recklessness. He had lived too long and too well. She was sure he couldn't sing, and wouldn't want to. He must be at least forty. How many good dinners could not a man have eaten by the time he was forty? And if during that time instead of taking exercise he had sat writing books, he would quite naturally acquire the figure Mr. Arundel had in fact acquired—the figure rather for conversation than adventure.

Scrap, who had become melancholy at the sight of Briggs, became philosophical at the sight of Arundel. Here he was. She couldn't send him away till after dinner. He must be nourished.

This being so, she had better make the best of it, and do that with a good grace which anyhow wasn't to be avoided. Besides, he would be a temporary shelter from Mr. Briggs. She was at least acquainted with Ferdinand Arundel, and could hear news from him of her mother and her friends, and such talk would put up a defensive barrier at dinner between herself and the approaches of the other one. And it was only for one dinner, and he couldn't eat her.

She therefore prepared herself for friendliness. "I'm to be fed," she said, ignoring his last remark, "at eight, and you must come up and be fed too. Sit down and get cool and tell me how everybody is."

"May I really dine with you? In these travelling things?" he said, wiping his forehead before sitting down beside her.

She was too lovely to be true, he thought. Just to look at her for an hour, just to hear her voice, was enough reward for his journey and his fears.

"Of course. I suppose you've left your fly in the village, and will be going on from Mezzago by the night train."

"Or stay in Mezzago in an hotel and go on to-morrow. But tell me," he said, gazing at the adorable profile, "about yourself. London has been extraordinarily dull and empty. Lady Droitwich said you were with people here she didn't know. I hope they've been kind to you? You look—well, as if your cure had done everything a cure should."

"They've been very kind," said Scrap. "I got them out of an advertisement."

"An advertisement?"

"It's a good way, I find, to get friends. I'm fonder of one of these than I've been of anybody in years."

"Really? Who is it?"

"You shall guess which of them it is when you see them. Tell me about mother. When did you see her last? We arranged not to write to each other unless there was something special. I wanted to have a month that was perfectly blank."

"And now I've come and interrupted. I can't tell you how ashamed
I am—both of having done it and of not having been able to help it."

"Oh, but," said Scrap quickly, for he could not have come on a better day, when up there waiting and watching for her was, she knew, the enamoured Briggs, "I'm really very glad indeed to see you. Tell me about mother."

Chapter 20

Scrap wanted to know so much about her mother that Arundel had presently to invent. He would talk about anything she wished if only he might be with her for a while and see her and hear her, but he knew very little of the Droitwiches and their friends really— beyond meeting them at those bigger functions where literature is also represented, and amusing them at luncheons and dinners, he knew very little of them really. To them he had always remained Mr. Arundel; no one called him Ferdinand; and he only knew the gossip also available to the evening papers and the frequenters of clubs. But he was, however, good at inventing; and as soon as he had come to an end of first-hand knowledge, in order to answer her inquires and keep her there to himself he proceeded to invent. It was quite easy to fasten some of the entertaining things he was constantly thinking on to other people and pretend they were theirs. Scrap, who had that affection for her parents which warms in absence, was athirst for news, and became more and more interested by the news he gradually imparted.

At first it was ordinary news. He had met her mother here, and seen her there. She looked very well; she said so and so. But presently the things Lady Droitwich had said took on an unusual quality: they became amusing.

"Mother said that?" Scrap interrupted, surprised.

And presently Lady Droitwich began to do amusing things as well as say them.

"Mother did that?" Scrap inquired, wide-eyed.

Arundel warmed to his work. He fathered some of the most entertaining ideas he had lately had on to Lady Droitwich, and also any charming funny things that had been done—or might have been done, for he could imagine almost anything.

Scrap's eyes grew round with wonder and affectionate pride in her mother. Why, but how funny—fancy mother. What an old darling. Did she really do that? How perfectly adorable of her. And did she really say—but how wonderful of her to think of it. What sort of a face did Lloyd George make?

She laughed and laughed, and had a great longing to hug her mother, and the time flew, and it grew quite dusk, and it grew nearly dark, and Mr. Arundel still went on amusing her, and it was a quarter to eight before she suddenly remembered dinner.

"Oh, good heavens!" she exclaimed, jumping up.

"Yes. It's late," said Arundel.

"I'll go on quickly and send the maid to you. I must run, or I'll never be ready in time—"

And she was gone up the path with the swiftness of a young, slender deer.

Arundel followed. He did not wish to arrive too hot, so had to go slowly. Fortunately he was near the top, and Francesca came down the pergola to pilot him indoors, and having shown him where he could wash she put him in the empty drawing-room to cool himself by the crackling wood fire.

He got as far away from the fire as he could, and stood in one of the deep window-recesses looking out at the distant lights of Mezzago. The drawing-room door was open, and the house was quiet with the hush that precedes dinner, when the inhabitants are all shut up in their rooms dressing. Briggs in his room was throwing away spoilt tie after spoilt tie; Scrap in hers was hurrying into a black frock with a vague notion that Mr. Briggs wouldn't be able to see her so clearly in black; Mrs. Fisher was fastening the lace shawl, which nightly transformed her day dress into her evening dress, with the brooch Ruskin had given her on her marriage, formed of two pearl lilies tied together by a blue enamel ribbon on which was written in gold letters Esto perpetua; Mr. Wilkins was sitting on the edge of his bed brushing his wife's hair—thus far in this third week had he progressed in demonstrativeness—while she, for her part, sitting on a chair in front of him, put his studs in a clean shirt; and Rose, ready dressed, sat at her window considering her day.

Rose was quite aware of what had happened to Mr. Briggs. If she had had any difficulty about it, Lotty would have removed it by the frank comments she made while she and Rose sat together after tea on the wall. Lotty was delighted at more love being introduced into San Salvatore, even if it were only one-sided, and said that when once Rose's husband was there she didn't suppose, now that Mrs. Fisher too had at last come unglued—Rose protested at the expression, and Lotty retorted that it was in Keats—there would be another place in the world more swarming with happiness than San Salvatore.

"Your husband," said Lotty, swinging her feet, "might be here quite soon, perhaps to-morrow evening if he starts at once, and there'll be a glorious final few days before we all go home refreshed for life. I don't believe any of us will ever be the same again—and I wouldn't be a bit surprised if Caroline doesn't end by getting fond of the young man Briggs. It's in the air. You have to get fond of people here."

Rose sat at her window thinking of these things. Lotty's optimism . . . yet it had been justified by Mr. Wilkins; and look, too, at Mrs. Fisher. If only it would come true as well about Frederick! For Rose, who between lunch and tea had left off thinking about Frederick, was now, between tea and dinner, thinking of him harder than ever.

It has been funny and delightful, that little interlude of admiration, but of course it couldn't go on once Caroline appeared. Rose knew her place. She could see as well as any one the unusually, the unique loveliness of Lady Caroline. How warm, though, things like admiration and appreciation made one feel, how capable of really deserving them, how different, how glowing. They seemed to quicken unsuspected faculties into life. She was sure she had been a thoroughly amusing woman between lunch and tea, and a pretty one too. She was quite certain she had been pretty; she saw it in Mr. Briggs's eyes as clearly as in a looking-glass. For a brief space, she thought, she had been like a torpid fly brought back to gay buzzing by the lighting of a fire in a wintry room. She still buzzed, she still tingled, just at the remembrance. What fun it had been, having an admirer even for that little while. No wonder people liked admirers. They seemed, in some strange way, to make one come alive.

Although it was all over she still glowed with it and felt more exhilarated, more optimistic, more as Lotty probably constantly felt, than she had done since she was a girl. She dressed with care, though she knew Mr. Briggs would no longer see her, but it gave her pleasure to see how pretty, while she was about it, she could make herself look; and very nearly she stuck a crimson camellia in her hair down by her ear. She did hold it there for a minute, and it looked almost sinfully attractive and was exactly the colour of her mouth, but she took it out again with a smile and a sigh and put it in the proper place for flowers, which is water. She mustn't be silly, she thought. Think of the poor. Soon she would be back with them again, and what would a camellia behind her ear seem like then? Simply fantastic.

But on one thing she was determined: the first thing she would do when she got home would be to have it out with Frederick. If he didn't come to San Salvatore that is what she would do—the very first thing. Long ago she ought to have done this, but always she had been handicapped, when she tried to, by being so dreadfully fond of him and so much afraid that fresh wounds were going to be given her wretched, soft heart. But now let him wound her as much as he chose, as much as he possibly could, she would still have it out with him. Not that he ever intentionally wounded her; she knew he never meant to, she knew he often had no idea of having done it. For a person who wrote books, thought Rose, Frederick didn't seem to have much imagination. Anyhow, she said to herself, getting up from the dressing-table, things couldn't go on like this. She would have it out with him. This separate life, this freezing loneliness, she had had enough of it. Why shouldn't she too be happy? Why on earth—the energetic expression matched her mood of rebelliousness—shouldn't she too be loved and allowed to love?

She looked at her little clock. Still ten minutes before dinner. Tired of staying in her bedroom she thought she would go on to Mrs.
Fisher's battlements, which would be empty at this hour, and watch the
moon rise out of the sea.

She went into the deserted upper hall with this intention, but was attracted on her way along it by the firelight shining through the open door of the drawing-room.

How gay it looked. The fire transformed the room. A dark, ugly room in the daytime, it was transformed just as she had been transformed by the warmth of—no, she wouldn't be silly; she would think of the poor; the thought of them always brought her down to sobriety at once.

She peeped in. Firelight and flowers; and outside the deep slits of windows hung the blue curtain of the night. How pretty. What a sweet place San Salvatore was. And that gorgeous lilac on the table—she must go and put her face in it . . .

But she never got to the lilac. She went one step towards it, and then stood still, for she had seen the figure looking out of the window in the farthest corner, and it was Frederick.

All the blood in Rose's body rushed to her heart and seemed to stop its beating.

She stood quite still. He had not heard her. He did not turn round. She stood looking at him. The miracle had happened, and he had come.

She stood holding her breath. So he needed her, for he had come instantly. So he too must have been thinking, longing . . .

Her heart, which had seemed to stop beating, was suffocating her now, the way it raced along. Frederick did love her then—he must love her, or why had he come? Something, perhaps her absence, had made him turn to her, want her . . . and now the understanding she had made up her mind to have with him would be quite—would be quite—easy—

Her thoughts wouldn't go on. Her mind stammered. She couldn't think. She could only see and feel. She didn't know how it had happened. It was a miracle. God could do miracles. God had done this one. God could—God could—could—

Her mind stammered again, and broke off.

"Frederick—" she tried to say; but no sound came, or if it did the crackling of the fire covered it up.

She must go nearer. She began to creep towards him—softly, softly.

He did not move. He had not heard.

She stole nearer and nearer, and the fire crackled and he heard nothing.

She stopped a moment, unable to breathe. She was afraid. Suppose he—suppose he—oh, but he had come, he had come.

She went on again, close up to him, and her heart beat so loud that she thought he must hear it. And couldn't he feel—didn't he know—

"Frederick," she whispered, hardly able even to whisper, choked by the beating of her heart.

He spun round on his heels.

"Rose!" he exclaimed, staring blankly.

But she did not see his stare, for her arms were round his neck, and her cheek was against his, and she was murmuring, her lips on his ear, "I knew you would come—in my very heart I always, always knew you would come—"

Chapter 21

Now Frederick was not the man to hurt anything if he could help it; besides, he was completely bewildered. Not only was his wife here—here, of all places in the world—but she was clinging to him as she had not clung for years, and murmuring love, and welcoming him. If she welcomed him she must have been expecting him. Strange as this was, it was the only thing in the situation which was evident—that, and the softness of her cheek against his, and the long-forgotten sweet smell of her.

Frederick was bewildered. But not being the man to hurt anything if he could help it he too put his arms round her, and having put them round her he also kissed her; and presently he was kissing her almost as tenderly as she was kissing him; and presently he was kissing her quite as tenderly; and again presently he was kissing her more tenderly, and just as if he had never left off.

He was bewildered, but he still could kiss. It seemed curiously natural to be doing it. It made him feel as if he were thirty again instead of forty, and Rose were his Rose of twenty, the Rose he had so much adored before she began to weigh what he did with her idea of right, and the balance went against him, and she had turned strange, and stony, and more and more shocked, and oh, so lamentable. He couldn't get at her in those days at all; she wouldn't, she couldn't understand. She kept on referring everything to what she called God's eyes—in God's eyes it couldn't be right, it wasn't right. Her miserable face—whatever her principles did for her they didn't make her happy—her little miserable face, twisted with effort to be patient, had been at last more than he could bear to see, and he had kept away as much as he could. She never ought to have been the daughter of a low-church rector—narrow devil; she was quite unfitted to stand up against such an upbringing.

What had happened, why she was here, why she was his Rose again, passed his comprehension; and meanwhile, and until such time as he understood, he still could kiss. In fact he could not stop kissing; and it was he now who began to murmur, to say love things in her ear under the hair that smelt so sweet and tickled him just as he remembered it used to tickle him.

And as he held her close to his heart and her arms were soft round his neck, he felt stealing over him a delicious sense of—at first he didn't know what it was, this delicate, pervading warmth, and then he recognized it as security. Yes; security. No need now to be ashamed of his figure, and to make jokes about it so as to forestall other people's and show he didn't mind it; no need now to be ashamed of getting hot going up hills, or to torment himself with pictures of how he probably appeared to beautiful young women— how middle-aged, how absurd in his inability to keep away from them. Rose cared nothing for such things. With her he was safe. To her he was her lover, as he used to be; and she would never notice or mind any of the ignoble changes that getting older had made in him and would go on making more and more.

Frederick continued, therefore, with greater and greater warmth and growing delight to kiss his wife, and the mere holding of her in his arms caused him to forget everything else. How could he, for instance, remember or think of Lady Caroline, to mention only one of the complications with which his situation bristled, when here was his sweet wife, miraculously restored to him, whispering with her cheek against his in the dearest, most romantic words how much she loved him, how terribly she had missed him? He did for one brief instant, for even in moments of love there were brief instants of lucid thought, recognize the immense power of the woman present and being actually held compared to that of the woman, however beautiful, who is somewhere else, but that is as far as he got towards remembering Scrap; no farther. She was like a dream, fleeing before the morning light.

"When did you start?" murmured Rose, her mouth on his ear. She couldn't let him go; not even to talk she couldn't let him go.

"Yesterday morning," murmured Frederick, holding her close. He couldn't let her go either.

"Oh—the very instant then," murmured Rose.

This was cryptic, but Frederick said, "Yes, the very instant," and kissed her neck.

"How quickly my letter got to you," murmured Rose, whose eyes were shut in the excess of her happiness.

"Didn't it," said Frederick, who felt like shutting his eyes himself.

So there had been a letter. Soon, no doubt, light would be vouchsafed him, and meanwhile this was so strangely, touchingly sweet, this holding his Rose to his heart again after all the years, that he couldn't bother to try to guess anything. Oh, he had been happy during these years, because it was not in him to be unhappy;

besides, how many interests life had had to offer him, how many friends, how much success, how many women only too willing to help him to blot out the thought of the altered, petrified, pitiful little wife at home who wouldn't spend his money, who was appalled by his books, who drifted away and away from him, and always if he tried to have it out with her asked him with patient obstinacy what he thought the things he wrote and lived by looked in the eyes of God. "No one," she said once, "should ever write a book God wouldn't like to read. That is the test, Frederick." And he had laughed hysterically, burst into a great shriek of laughter, and rushed out of the house, away from her solemn little face—away from her pathetic, solemn little face. . .

But this Rose was his youth again, the best part of his life, the part of it that had had all the visions in it and all the hopes. How they had dreamed together, he and she, before he struck that vein of memoirs; how they had planned, and laughed and loved. They had lived for a while in the very heart of poetry. After the happy days came the happy nights, the happy, happy nights, with her asleep close against his heart, with her when he woke in the morning still close against his heart, for they hardly moved in their deep, happy sleep. It was wonderful to have it all come back to him at the touch of her, at the feel of her face against his—wonderful that she should be able to give him back his youth.

"Sweetheart—sweetheart," he murmured, overcome by remembrance, clinging to her now in his turn.

"Beloved husband," she breathed—the bliss of it—the sheer bliss . . .

Briggs, coming in a few minutes before the gong went on the chance that Lady Caroline might be there, was much astonished. He had supposed Rose Arbuthnot was a widow, and he still supposed it; so that he was much astonished.

"Well I'm damned," thought Briggs, quite clearly and distinctly, for the shock of what he saw in the window startled him so much that for a moment he was shaken free of his own confused absorption.

Aloud he said, very red, "Oh I say—I beg your pardon"—and then stood hesitating, and wondering whether he oughtn't to go back to his bedroom again.

If he had said nothing they would not have noticed he was there, but when he begged their pardon Rose turned and looked at him as

186

one looks who is trying to remember, and Frederick looked at him too without at first quite seeing him.

They didn't seem, thought Briggs, to mind or to be at all embarrassed. He couldn't be her brother; no brother ever brought that look into a woman's face. It was very awkward. If they didn't mind, he did. It upset him to come across his Madonna forgetting herself.

"Is this one of your friends?" Frederick was able after an instant to ask Rose, who made no attempt to introduce the young man standing awkwardly in front of them but continued to gaze at him with a kind of abstracted, radiant goodwill.

"It's Mr. Briggs," said Rose, recognizing him. "This is my husband," she added.

And Briggs, shaking hands, just had time to think how surprising it was to have a husband when you were a widow before the gong sounded, and Lady Caroline would be there in a minute, and he ceased to be able to think at all, and merely became a thing with its eyes fixed on the door.

Through the door immediately entered, in what seemed to him an endless procession, first Mrs. Fisher, very stately in her evening lace shawl and brooch, who when she saw him at once relaxed into smiles and benignity, only to stiffen, however, when she caught sight of the stranger; then Mr. Wilkins, cleaner and neater and more carefully dressed and brushed than any man on earth; and then, tying something hurriedly as she came, Mrs. Wilkins; and then nobody.

Lady Caroline was late. Where was she? Had she heard the gong? Oughtn't it to be beaten again? Suppose she didn't come to dinner after all. . .

Briggs went cold.

"Introduce me," said Frederick on Mrs. Fisher's entrance, touching Rose's elbow.

"My husband," said Rose, holding him by the hand, her face exquisite.

"This," thought Mrs. Fisher, "must now be the last of the husbands, unless Lady Caroline produces one from up her sleeve."

But she received him graciously, for he certainly looked exactly like a husband, not at all like one of those people who go about abroad pretending they are husbands when they are not, and said she supposed he had come to accompany his wife home at the end of the

187

month, and remarked that now the house would be completely full. "So that," she added, smiling at Briggs, "we shall at last really be getting our money's worth."

Briggs grinned automatically, because he was just able to realize that somebody was being playful with him, but he had not heard her and he did not look at her. Not only were his eyes fixed on the door but his whole body was concentrated on it.

Introduced in his turn, Mr. Wilkins was most hospitable and called Frederick "sir."

"Well, sir," said Mr. Wilkins heartily, "here we are, here we are"—and having gripped his hand with an understanding that only wasn't mutual because Arbuthnot did not yet know what he was in for in the way of trouble, he looked at him as a man should, squarely in the eyes, and allowed his look to convey as plainly as a look can that in him would be found staunchness, integrity, reliability—in fact a friend in need. Mrs. Arbuthnot was very much flushed, Mr. Wilkins noticed. He had not seen her flushed like that before. "Well, I'm their man," he thought.

Lotty's greeting was effusive. It was done with both hands. "Didn't I tell you?" she laughed to Rose over her shoulder while Frederick was shaking her hands in both his.

"What did you tell her?" asked Frederick, in order to say something. The way they were all welcoming him was confusing. They had evidently all expected him, not only Rose.

The sandy but agreeable young woman didn't answer his question, but looked extraordinarily pleased to see him. Why should she be extraordinarily pleased to see him?

"What a delightful place this is," said Frederick, confused, and making the first remark that occurred to him.

"It's a tub of love," said the sandy young woman earnestly; which confused him more than ever.

And his confusion became excessive at the next words he heard—spoken, these, by the old lady, who said: "We won't wait. Lady Caroline is always late"—for he only then, on hearing her name, really and properly remembered Lady Caroline, and the thought of her confused him to excess.

He went into the dining-room like a man in a dream. He had come out to this place to see Lady Caroline, and had told her so. He had even told her in his fatuousness—it was true, but how fatuous— that he hadn't been able to help coming. She didn't know he was married. She thought his name was Arundel. Everybody in London thought his name was Arundel. He had used it and written under it so long that he almost thought it was himself. In the short time since she had left him on the seat in the garden, where he told her he had come because he couldn't help it, he had found Rose again, had passionately embraced and been embraced, and had forgotten Lady Caroline. It would be an extraordinary piece of good fortune if Lady Caroline's being late meant she was tired or bored and would not come to dinner at all. Then he could—no, he couldn't. He turned a deeper red even than usual, he being a man of full habit and red anyhow, at the thought of such cowardice. No, he couldn't go away after dinner and catch his train and disappear to Rome; not unless, that is, Rose came with him. But even so, what a running away. No, he couldn't.

When they got to the dining-room Mrs. Fisher went to the head of the table—was this Mrs. Fisher's house? He asked himself. He didn't know; he didn't know anything—and Rose, who in her earlier day of defying Mrs. Fisher had taken the other end as her place, for after all no one could say by looking at a table which was its top and which its bottom, led Frederick to the seat next to her. If only, he thought, he could have been alone with Rose; just five minutes more alone with Rose, so that he could have asked her—

But probably he wouldn't have asked her anything, and only gone on kissing her.

He looked round. The sandy young woman was telling the man they called Briggs to go and sit beside Mrs. Fisher—was the house, then, the sandy young woman's and not Mrs. Fisher's? He didn't know; he didn't know anything—and she herself sat down on Rose's other side, so that she was opposite him, Frederick, and next to the genial man who had said "Here we are," when it was only too evident that there they were indeed.

Next to Frederick, and between him and Briggs, was an empty chair: Lady Caroline's. No more than Lady Caroline knew of the presence in Frederick's life of Rose was Rose aware of the presence in Frederick's life of Lady Caroline. What would each think? He didn't know; he didn't know anything. Yes, he did know something, and that was that his wife had made it up with him—suddenly, miraculously, unaccountably, and divinely. Beyond that he knew nothing. The situation was one with which he felt he could not cope. It must lead him whither it would. He could only drift.

189

In silence Frederick ate his soup, and the eyes, the large expressive eyes of the young woman opposite, were on him, he could feel, with a growing look in them of inquiry. They were, he could see, very intelligent and attractive eyes, and full, apart from the inquiry of goodwill. Probably she thought he ought to talk—but if she knew everything she wouldn't think so. Briggs didn't talk either. Briggs seemed uneasy. What was the matter with Briggs? And Rose too didn't talk, but then that was natural. She never had been a talker. She had the loveliest expression on her face. How long would it be on it after Lady Caroline's entrance? He didn't know; he didn't know anything.

But the genial man on Mrs. Fisher's left was talking enough for everybody. That fellow ought to have been a parson. Pulpits were the place for a voice like his; it would get him a bishopric in six months. He was explaining to Briggs, who shuffled about in his seat—why did Briggs shuffle about in his seat?—that he must have come out by the same train as Arbuthnot, and when Briggs, who said nothing, wriggled in apparent dissent, he undertook to prove it to him, and did prove it to him in long clear sentences.

"Who's the man with the voice?" Frederick asked Rose in a whisper; and the young woman opposite, whose ears appeared to have the quickness of hearing of wild creatures, answered, "He's my husband."

"Then by all the rules," said Frederick pleasantly, pulling himself together, "you oughtn't to be sitting next to him."

"But I want to. I like sitting next to him. I didn't before I came here."

"Frederick could think of nothing to say to this, so he only smiled generally.

"It's this place," she said, nodding at him. "It makes one understand. You've no idea what a lot you'll understand before you've done here."

"I'm sure I hope so," said Frederick with real fervour.

The soup was taken away, and the fish was brought. Briggs, on the other side of the empty chair, seemed more uneasy than ever. What was the matter with Briggs? Didn't he like fish?

Frederick wondered what Briggs would do in the way of fidgets if he were in his own situation. Frederick kept on wiping his moustache, and was not able to look up from his plate, but that was as much as he showed of what he was feeling.

Though he didn't look up he felt the eyes of the young woman opposite raking him like searchlights, and Rose's eyes were on him too, he knew, but they rested on him unquestioningly, beautifully, like a benediction. How long would they go on doing that once Lady Caroline was there? He didn't know; he didn't know anything.

He wiped his moustache for the twentieth unnecessary time, and could not quite keep his hand steady, and the young woman opposite saw his hand not being quite steady, and her eyes raked him persistently. Why did her eyes rake him persistently? He didn't know; he didn't know anything.

Then Briggs leapt to his feet. What was the matter with Briggs? Oh—yes—quite: she had come.

Frederick wiped his moustache and got up too. He was in for it now. Absurd, fantastic situation. Well, whatever happened he could only drift—drift, and look like an ass to Lady Caroline, the most absolute as well as deceitful ass—an ass who was also a reptile, for she might well think he had been mocking her out in the garden when he said, no doubt in a shaking voice—fool and ass—that he had come because he couldn't help it; while as for what he would look like to his Rose—when Lady Caroline introduced him to her—when Lady Caroline introduced him as her friend whom she had invited in to dinner—well, God alone knew that.

He, therefore, as he got up wiped his moustache for the last time before the catastrophe.

But he was reckoning without Scrap.

That accomplished and experienced young woman slipped into the chair Briggs was holding for her, and on Lotty's leaning across eagerly, and saying before any one else could get a word in, "Just fancy, Caroline, how quickly Rose's husband has got here!" turned to him without so much as the faintest shadow of surprise on her face, and held out her hand, and smiled like a young angel, and said, "and me late your very first evening."

The daughter of the Droitwiches. . .

Chapter 22

That evening was the evening of the full moon. The garden was an enchanted place where all the flowers seemed white. The lilies, the daphnes, the orange-blossom, the white stocks, the white pinks, the white roses—you could see these as plainly as in the day-time; but the coloured flowers existed only as fragrance.

The three younger women sat on the low wall at the end of the top garden after dinner, Rose a little apart from the others, and watched the enormous moon moving slowly over the place where Shelley had lived his last months just on a hundred years before. The sea quivered along the path of the moon. The stars winked and trembled. The mountains were misty blue outlines, with little clusters of lights shining through from little clusters of homes. In the garden the plants stood quite still, straight and unstirred by the smallest ruffle of air. Through the glass doors the dining-room, with its candle-lit table and brilliant flowers—nasturtiums and marigolds that night—glowed like some magic cave of colour, and the three men smoking round it looked strangely animated figures seen from the silence, the huge cool calm of outside.

Mrs. Fisher had gone to the drawing-room and the fire. Scrap and Lotty, their faces upturned to the sky, said very little and in whispers. Rose said nothing. Her face too was upturned. She was looking at the umbrella pine, which had been smitten into something glorious, silhouetted against stars. Every now and then Scrap's eyes lingered on Rose; so did Lotty's. For Rose was lovely. Anywhere at that moment, among all the well-known beauties, she would have been lovely. Nobody could have put her in the shade, blown out her light that evening; she was too evidently shining.

Lotty bent close to Scrap's ear, and whispered. "Love," she whispered.

Scrap nodded. "Yes," she said, under her breath.

She was obliged to admit it. You only had to look at Rose to know that here was Love.

"There's nothing like it," whispered Lotty.

Scrap was silent.

"It's a great thing," whispered Lotty after a pause, during which they both watched Rose's upturned face, "to get on with one's loving. Perhaps you can tell me of anything else in the world that works such wonders."

But Scrap couldn't tell her; and if she could have, what a night to begin arguing in. This was a night for—

She pulled herself up. Love again. It was everywhere. There was no getting away from it. She had come to this place to get away from it, and here was everybody in its different stages. Even Mrs. Fisher seemed to have been brushed by one of the many feathers of Love's wing, and at dinner was different—full of concern because Mr. Briggs wouldn't eat, and her face when she turned to him all soft with motherliness.

Scrap looked up at the pine-tree motionless among stars. Beauty made you love, and love made you beautiful. . .

She pulled her wrap closer round her with a gesture of defence, of keeping out and off. She didn't want to grow sentimental. Difficult not to, here; the marvelous night stole in through all one's chinks, and brought in with it, whether one wanted them or not, enormous feelings—feelings one couldn't manage, great things about death and time and waste; glorious and devastating things, magnificent and bleak, at once rapture and terror and immense, heart-cleaving longing. She felt small and dreadfully alone. She felt uncovered and defenceless. Instinctively she pulled her wrap closer. With this thing of chiffon she tired to protect herself from the eternities.

"I suppose," whispered Lotty, "Rose's husband seems to you just an ordinary, good-natured, middle-aged man."

Scrap brought her gaze down from the stars and looked at Lotty a moment while she focused her mind again.

"Just a rather red, rather round man," whispered Lotty.

Scrap bowed her head.

"He isn't," whispered Lotty. "Rose sees through all that. That's mere trimmings. She sees what we can't see, because she loves him."

Always love.

Scrap got up, and winding herself very tightly in her wrap moved away to her day corner, and sat down there alone on the wall and looked out across the other sea, the sea where the sun had gone down, the sea with the far-away dim shadow stretching into it which was France.

Yes, love worked wonders, and Mr. Arundel—she couldn't at once get used to his other name—was to Rose Love itself; but it also worked inverted wonders, it didn't invariably, as she well knew, transfigure people into saints and angels. Grievously indeed did it sometimes do the opposite. She had had it in her life applied to her to excess. If it had let her alone, if it had at least been moderate and infrequent, she might, she thought, have turned out a quite decent, generous-minded, kindly, human being. And what was she, thanks to this love Lotty talked so much about? Scrap searched for a just description. She was a spoilt, a sour, a suspicious, and a selfish spinster.

The glass doors of the dining-room opened, and the three men came out into the garden, Mr. Wilkins's voice flowing along in front of them. He appeared to be doing all the talking; the other two were saying nothing.

Perhaps she had better go back to Lotty and Rose; it would be tiresome to be discovered and hemmed into the cul-de-sac by Mr. Briggs.

She got up reluctantly, for she considered it unpardonable of Mr. Briggs to force her to move about like this, to force her out of any place she wished to sit in; and she emerged from the daphne bushes feeling like some gaunt, stern figure of just resentment and wishing that she looked as gaunt and stern as she felt; so would she have struck repugnance into the soul of Mr. Briggs, and been free of him. But she knew she didn't look like that, however hard she might try. At dinner his hand shook when he drank, and he couldn't speak to her without flushing scarlet and then going pale, and Mrs. Fisher's eyes had sought hers with the entreaty of one who asks that her only son may not be hurt.

How could a human being, thought Scrap, frowning as she issued forth from her corner, how could a man made in God's image behave so; and be fitted for better things she was sure, with his youth, his attractiveness, and his brains. He had brains. She had examined him cautiously whenever at dinner Mrs. Fisher forced him to turn away to answer her, and she was sure he had brains. Also he had character; there was something noble about his head, about the shape of his forehead—noble and kind. All the more deplorable that he should allow himself to be infatuated by a mere outside, and waste any of his strength, any of his peace of mind, hanging round just a woman-thing. If only he could see right through her, see through all her skin and stuff, he would be cured, and she might go on sitting undisturbed on this wonderful night by herself.

Just beyond the daphne bushes she met Fredrick, hurrying.

"I was determined to find you first," he said, "before I go to Rose." And he added quickly, "I want to kiss your shoes."

"Do you?" said Scrap, smiling. "Then I must go and put on my new ones. These aren't nearly good enough."

She felt immensely well-disposed towards Frederick. He, at least, would grab no more. His grabbing days, so sudden and so brief, were done. Nice man; agreeable man. She now definitely liked him. Clearly he had been getting into some sort of a tangle, and she was grateful to Lotty for stopping her in time at dinner from saying something hopelessly complicating. But whatever he had been getting into he was out of it now; his face and Rose's face had the same light in them.

"I shall adore you for ever now," said Frederick.

Scrap smiled. "Shall you?" she said.

"I adored you before because of your beauty. Now I adore you because you're not only as beautiful as a dream but as decent as a man."

"When the impetuous young woman," Frederick went on, "the blessedly impetuous young woman, blurted out in the nick of time that I am Rose's husband, you behaved exactly as a man would have behaved to his friend."

"Did I?" said Scrap, her enchanting dimple very evident.

"It's the rarest, most precious of combinations," said Frederick, "to be a woman and have the loyalty of a man."

"Is it?" smiled Scrap, a little wistfully. These were indeed handsome compliments. If only she were really like that . . .

"And I want to kiss your shoes."

"Won't this save trouble?" she asked, holding out her hand.

He took it and swiftly kissed it, and was hurrying away again. "Bless you," he said as he went.

"Where is your luggage?" Scrap called after him.

"Oh, Lord, yes—" said Frederick, pausing. "It's at the station."

"I'll send for it."

He disappeared through the bushes. She went indoors to give the order; and this is how it happened that Domenico, for the second time that evening, found himself journeying into Mezzago and wondering as he went.

Then, having made the necessary arrangements for the perfect happiness of these two people, she came slowly out into the garden again, very much absorbed in thought. Love seemed to bring happiness to everybody but herself. It had certainly got hold of everybody there, in its different varieties, except herself. Poor Mr. Briggs had been got hold of by its least dignified variety. Poor Mr. Briggs. He was a disturbing problem, and his going away next day wouldn't she was afraid solve him.

When she reached the others Mr. Arundel—she kept on forgetting that he wasn't Mr. Arundel—was already, his arm through Rose's, going off with her, probably to the greater seclusion of the lower garden. No doubt they had a great deal to say to each other; something had gone wrong between them, and had suddenly been put right. San Salvatore, Lotty would say, San Salvatore working its spell of happiness. She could quite believe in its spell. Even she was happier there than she had been for ages and ages. The only person who would go empty away would be Mr. Briggs.

Poor Mr. Briggs. When she came in sight of the group he looked much too nice and boyish not to be happy. It seemed out of the picture that the owner of the place, the person to whom they owed all this, should be the only one to go away from it unblessed.

Compunction seized Scrap. What very pleasant days she had spent in his house, lying in his garden, enjoying his flowers, loving his views, using his things, being comfortable, being rested— recovering, in fact. She had had the most leisured, peaceful, and thoughtful time of her life; and all really thanks to him. Oh, she knew she paid him some ridiculous small sum a week, out of all proportion to the benefits she got in exchange, but what was that in the balance? And wasn't it entirely thanks to him that she had come across Lotty? Never else would she and Lotty have met; never else would she have known her.

Compunction laid its quick, warm hand on Scrap. Impulsive gratitude flooded her. She went straight up to Briggs.

"I owe you so much," she said, overcome by the sudden realization of all she did owe him, and ashamed of her churlishness in the afternoon and at dinner. Of course he hadn't known she was being churlish. Of course her disagreeable inside was camouflaged as usual by the chance arrangement of her outside; but she knew it. She was churlish. She had been churlish to everybody for years. Any penetrating eye, thought Scrap, any really penetrating eye, would see her for what she was—a spoilt, a sour, a suspicious and a selfish spinster.

"I owe you so much," therefore said Scrap earnestly, walking straight up to Briggs, humbled by these thoughts.

He looked at her in wonder. "You owe me?" he said. "But it's I who—I who—" he stammered. To see her there in his garden . . . nothing in it, no white flower, was whiter, more exquisite.

"Please," said Scrap, still more earnestly, "won't you clear your mind of everything except just truth? You don't owe me anything. How should you?"

"I don't owe you anything?" echoed Briggs. "Why, I owe you my first sight of—of—"

"Oh, for goodness sake—for goodness sake," said Scrap entreatingly, "do, please, be ordinary. Don't be humble. Why should you be humble? It's ridiculous of you to be humble. You're worth fifty of me."

"Unwise," thought Mr. Wilkins, who was standing there too, while Lotty sat on the wall. He was surprised, he was concerned, he was shocked that Lady Caroline should thus encourage Briggs. "Unwise—very," thought Mr. Wilkins, shaking his head.

Briggs's condition was so bad already that the only course to take with him was to repel him utterly, Mr. Wilkins considered. No half measures were the least use with Briggs, and kindliness and familiar talk would only be misunderstood by the unhappy youth. The daughter of the Droitwiches could not really, it was impossible to suppose it, desire to encourage him. Briggs was all very well, but Briggs was Briggs; his name alone proved that. Probably Lady Caroline did not quite appreciate the effect of her voice and face, and how between them they made otherwise ordinary words seem—well, encouraging. But these words were not quite ordinary; she had not, he feared, sufficiently pondered them. Indeed and indeed she needed an adviser—some sagacious, objective counselor like himself. There she was, standing before Briggs almost holding out her hand to him. Briggs of course ought to be thanked, for they were having a most delightful holiday in his house, but not thanked to excess and not by Lady Caroline alone. That very evening he had been considering the presentation to him next day of a round robin of collective gratitude on his departure; but he should not be thanked like this, in the moonlight, in the garden, by the lady he was so manifestly infatuated with.

197

Mr. Wilkins therefore, desiring to assist Lady Caroline out of this situation by swiftly applied tact, said with much heartiness: "It is most proper, Briggs, that you should be thanked. You will please allow me to add my expressions of indebtedness, and those of my wife, to Lady Caroline's. We ought to have proposed a vote of thanks to you at dinner. You should have been toasted. There certainly ought to have been some—"

But Briggs took no notice of him whatever; he simply continued to look at Lady Caroline as though she were the first woman he had ever seen. Neither, Mr. Wilkins observed, did Lady Caroline take any notice of him; she too continued to look at Briggs, and with that odd air of almost appeal. Most unwise. Most.

Lotty, on the other hand, took too much notice of him, choosing this moment when Lady Caroline needed special support and protection to get up off the wall and put her arm through his and draw him away.

"I want to tell you something, Mellersh," said Lotty at this juncture, getting up.

"Presently," said Mr. Wilkins, waving her aside.

"No—now," said Lotty; and she drew him away.

He went with extreme reluctance. Briggs should be given no rope at all—not an inch.

"Well—what is it?" he asked impatiently, as she led him towards the house. Lady Caroline ought not to be left like that, exposed to annoyance.

"Oh, but she isn't," Lotty assured him, just as if he had said this aloud, which he certainly had not. "Caroline is perfectly all right."

"Not at all all right. That young Briggs is—"

"Of course he is. What did you expect? Let's go indoors to the fire and Mrs. Fisher. She's all by herself."

"I cannot," said Mr. Wilkins, trying to draw back, "leave Lady Caroline alone in the garden."

"Don't be silly, Mellersh—she isn't alone. Besides, I want to tell you something."

"Well tell me, then."

"Indoors."

With reluctance that increased at every step Mr. Wilkins was taken farther and farther away from Lady Caroline. He believed in his wife now and trusted her, but on this occasion he thought she was making a terrible mistake. In the drawing-room sat Mrs. Fisher by the fire, and it certainly was to Mr. Wilkins, who preferred rooms and fires after dark to gardens and moonlight, more agreeable to be in there than out-of-doors if he could have brought Lady Caroline safely in with him. As it was, he went in with extreme reluctance.

Mrs. Fisher, her hands folded on her lap, was doing nothing, merely gazing fixedly into the fire. The lamp was arranged conveniently for reading, but she was not reading. Her great dead friends did not seem worth reading that night. They always said the same things now—over and over again they said the same things, and nothing new was to be got out of them any more for ever. No doubt they were greater than any one was now, but they had this immense disadvantage, that they were dead. Nothing further was to be expected of them; while of the living, what might one not still expect? She craved for the living, the developing—the crystallized and finished wearied her. She was thinking that if only she had had a son—a son like Mr. Briggs, a dear boy like that, going on, unfolding, alive, affectionate, taking care of her and loving her. . .

The look on her face gave Mrs. Wilkins's heart a little twist when she saw it. "Poor old dear," she thought, all the loneliness of age flashing upon her, the loneliness of having outstayed one's welcome in the world, of being in it only on sufferance, the complete loneliness of the old childless woman who has failed to make friends. It did seem that people could only be really happy in pairs—any sorts of pairs, not in the least necessarily lovers, but pairs of friends, pairs of mothers and children, of brothers and sisters—and where was the other half of Mrs. Fisher's pair going to be found?

Mrs. Wilkins thought she had perhaps better kiss her again. The kissing this afternoon had been a great success; she knew it, she had instantly felt Mrs. Fisher's reaction to it. So she crossed over and bent down and kissed her and said cheerfully, "We've come in—" which indeed was evident.

This time Mrs. Fisher actually put up her hand and held Mrs. Wilkins's cheek against her own—this living thing, full of affection, of warm, racing blood; and as she did this she felt safe with the strange creature, sure that she who herself did unusual things so naturally would take the action quite as a matter of course, and not embarrass her by being surprised.

Mrs. Wilkins was not at all surprised; she was delighted. "I believe I'm the other half of her pair," flashed into her mind. "I

199

believe it's me, positively me, going to be fast friends with Mrs. Fisher!"

Her face when she lifted her head was full of laughter. Too extraordinary, the developments produced by San Salvatore. She and Mrs. Fisher . . . but she saw them being fast friends.

"Where are the others?" asked Mrs. Fisher. "Thank you—dear," she added, as Mrs. Wilkins put a footstool under her feet, a footstool obviously needed, Mrs. Fisher's legs being short.

"I see myself throughout the years," thought Mrs. Wilkins, her eyes dancing, "bringing footstools to Mrs. Fisher. . ."

"The Roses," she said, straightening herself, "have gone into the lower garden—I think love-making."

"The Roses?"

"The Fredericks, then, if you like. They're completely merged and indistinguishable."

"Why not say the Arbuthnots, my dear?" said Mr. Wilkins.

"Very well, Mellersh—the Arbuthnots. And the Carolines—"

Both Mr. Wilkins and Mrs. Fisher started. Mr. Wilkins, usually in such complete control of himself, started even more than Mrs. Fisher, and for the first time since his arrival felt angry with his wife.

"Really—" he began indignantly.

"Very well, Mellersh—the Briggses, then."

"The Briggses!" cried Mr. Wilkins, now very angry indeed; for the implication was to him a most outrageous insult to the entire race of Desters—dead Desters, living Desters, and Desters still harmless because they were yet unborn. "Really—"

"I'm sorry, Mellersh," said Mrs. Wilkins, pretending meekness, "if you don't like it."

"Like it! You've taken leave of your senses. Why they've never set eyes on each other before to-day."

"That's true. But that's why they're able now to go ahead."

"Go ahead!" Mr. Wilkins could only echo the outrageous words.

"I'm sorry, Mellersh," said Mrs. Wilkins again, "if you don't like it, but—"

Her grey eyes shone, and her face rippled with the light and conviction that had so much surprised Rose the first time they met.

"It's useless minding," she said. "I shouldn't struggle if I were you. Because—"

She stopped, and looked first at one alarmed solemn face and then at the other, and laughter as well as light flickered and danced over her.

"I see them being the Briggses," finished Mrs. Wilkins.

That last week the syringa came out at San Salvatore, and all the acacias flowered. No one had noticed how many acacias there were till one day the garden was full of a new scent, and there were the delicate trees, the lovely successors to the wistaria, hung all over among their trembling leaves with blossom. To lie under an acacia tree that last week and look up through the branches at its frail leaves and white flowers quivering against the blue of the sky, while the least movement of the air shook down their scent, was a great happiness. Indeed, the whole garden dressed itself gradually towards the end in white pinks and white banksai roses, and the syringe and the Jessamine, and at last the crowning fragrance of the acacias. When, on the first of May, everybody went away, even after they had got to the bottom of the hill and passed through the iron gates out into the village they still could smell the acacias.

The Solitary Summer

By
Elizabeth von Arnim

To the man of wrath
With some apologies and much love

MAY

May 2nd.—Last night after dinner, when we were in the garden, I said, "I want to be alone for a whole summer, and get to the very dregs of life. I want to be as idle as I can, so that my soul may have time to grow. Nobody shall be invited to stay with me, and if any one calls they will be told that I am out, or away, or sick. I shall spend the months in the garden, and on the plain, and in the forests. I shall watch the things that happen in my garden, and see where I have made mistakes. On wet days I will go into the thickest parts of the forests, where the pine needles are everlastingly dry, and when the sun shines I'll lie on the heath and see how the broom flares against the clouds. I shall be perpetually happy, because there will be no one to worry me. Out there on the plain there is silence, and where there is silence I have discovered there is peace."

"Mind you do not get your feet damp," said the Man of Wrath, removing his cigar.

It was the evening of May Day, and the spring had taken hold of me body and soul. The sky was full of stars, and the garden of scents, and the borders of wallflowers and sweet, sly pansies. All day there had been a breeze, and all day slow masses of white clouds had been sailing across the blue. Now it was so still, so motionless, so breathless, that it seemed as though a quiet hand had been laid on the garden, soothing and hushing it into silence.

The Man of Wrath sat at the foot of the verandah steps in that placid after-dinner mood which suffers fools, if not gladly, at least indulgently, and I stood in front of him, leaning against the sun-dial.

"Shall you take a book with you?" he asked.

"Yes, I shall," I replied, slightly nettled by his tone. "I am quite ready to admit that though the fields and flowers are always ready to teach, I am not always in the mood to learn, and sometimes my eyes are incapable of seeing things that at other times are quite plain."

"And then you read?"

"And then I read. Well, dear Sage, what of that?"

But he smoked in silence, and seemed suddenly absorbed by the stars.

"See," he said, after a pause, during which I stood looking at him and wishing he would use longer sentences, and he looked at the sky and did not think about me at all, "see how bright the stars are to-

205

night. Almost as though it might freeze."

"It isn't going to freeze, and I won't look at anything until you have told me what you think of my idea. Wouldn't a whole lovely summer, quite alone, be delightful? Wouldn't it be perfect to get up every morning for weeks and feel that you belong to yourself and to nobody else?" And I went over to him and put a hand on each shoulder and gave him a little shake, for he persisted in gazing at the stars just as though I had not been there. "Please, Man of Wrath, say something long for once," I entreated; "you haven't said a good long sentence for a week."

He slowly brought his gaze from the stars down to me and smiled. Then he drew me on to his knee.

"Don't get affectionate," I urged; "it is words, not deeds, that I want.
But I'll stay here if you'll talk."

"Well then, I will talk. What am I to say? You know you do as you please, and I never interfere with you. If you do not want to have any one here this summer you will not have any one, but you will find it a very long summer."

"No, I won't."

"And if you lie on the heath all day, people will think you are mad."

"What do I care what people think?"

"No, that is true. But you will catch cold, and your little nose will swell."

"Let it swell."

"And when it is hot you will be sunburnt and your skin spoilt."

"I don't mind my skin."

"And you will be dull."

"Dull?"

It often amuses me to reflect how very little the Man of Wrath really knows me. Here we have been three years buried in the country, and I as happy as a bird the whole time. I say as a bird, because other people have used the simile to describe absolute cheerfulness, although I do not believe birds are any happier than any one else, and they quarrel disgracefully. I have been as happy then, we will say, as the best of birds, and have had seasons of solitude at intervals before now during which dull is the last word to describe my state of mind. Everybody, it is true, would not like it, and I had some visitors here a fortnight ago who left after staying about a week and clearly not enjoying themselves. They found it dull, I know, but that of course was their own fault; how can you make a person happy against his will? You can knock a great deal into him in the way of learning and what the schools call extras, but if you try for ever you will not knock any happiness into a being who has not got it in him to be happy. The only result probably would be that you knock your own out of yourself. Obviously happiness must come from within, and not from without; and judging from my past experience and my present sensations, I should say that I have a store just now within me more than sufficient to fill five quiet months.

"I wonder," I remarked after a pause, during which I began to suspect that I too must belong to the serried ranks of the femmes incomprises, "why you think I shall be dull. The garden is always beautiful, and I am nearly always in the mood to enjoy it. Not quite always, I must confess, for when those Schmidts were here" (their name was not Schmidt, but what does that matter?) "I grew almost to hate it. Whenever I went into it there they were, dragging themselves about with faces full of indignant resignation. Do you suppose they saw one of those blue hepaticas overflowing the shrubberies? And when I drove with them into the woods, where the fairies were so busy just then hanging the branches with little green jewels, they talked about Berlin the whole time, and the good savouries their new chef makes."

"Well, my dear, no doubt they missed their savouries. Your garden, I acknowledge, is growing very pretty, but your cook is bad. Poor Schmidt sometimes looked quite ill at dinner, and the beauty of your floral arrangements in no way made up for the inferior quality of the food. Send her away."

"Send her away? Be thankful you have her. A bad cook is more effectual a great deal than Kissingen and Carlsbad and Homburg rolled into one, and very much cheaper. As long as I have her, my dear man, you will be comparatively thin and amiable. Poor Schmidt, as you call him, eats too much of those delectable savouries, and then looks at his wife and wonders why he married her. Don't let me catch you doing that."

"I do not think it is very likely," said the Man of Wrath; but whether he meant it prettily, or whether he was merely thinking of the improbability of his ever eating too much of the local savouries, I cannot tell. I object, however, to discussing cooks in the garden on a starlight night, so I got off his knee and proposed that we should stroll round a little.

It was such a sweet evening, such a fitting close to a beautiful May Day, and the flowers shone in the twilight like pale stars, and the air was full of fragrance, and I envied the bats fluttering through such a bath of scent, with the real stars above and the pansy stars beneath, and themselves so fashioned that even if they wanted to they could not make a noise and disturb the prevailing peace. A great deal that is poetical has been written by English people about May Day, and the impression left on the foreign mind is an impression of posies, and garlands, and village greens, and youths and maidens much be-ribboned, and lambs, and general friskiness. I was in England once on a May Day, and we sat over the fire shivering and listening blankly to the north- east wind tearing down the street and the rattling of the hail against the windows, and the friends with whom I was staying said it was very often so, and that they had never seen any lambs and ribbons. We Germans attach no poetical significance to it at all, and yet we well might, for it is almost invariably beautiful; and as for garlands, I wonder how many villages full of young people could have been provided with them out of my garden, and nothing be missed. It is to-day a garden of wallflowers, and I think I have every colour and sort in cultivation. The borders under the south windows of the house, so empty and melancholy this time last year, are crammed with them, and are finished off in front by a broad strip from end to end of yellow and white pansies. The tea rose beds round the sun-dial facing these borders are sheets of white, and golden, and purple, and wine-red pansies, with the dainty red shoots of the tea roses presiding delicately in their midst. The verandah steps leading down into this pansy paradise have boxes of white, and pink, and yellow tulips all the way up on each side, and on the lawn, behind the roses, are two big beds of every coloured tulip rising above a carpet of forget-me-nots. How very much more charming different-coloured tulips are together than tulips in one colour by itself! Last year, on the recommendation of sundry writers about gardens, I tried beds of scarlet tulips and forget-me-nots. They were pretty enough; but I wish those writers could see my beds of mixed tulips. I never saw anything so sweetly, delicately gay. The only ones I exclude are the rose-coloured ones; but scarlet, gold, delicate pink, and white are all there, and the effect is infinitely enchanting. The forget-me-nots grow taller as the tulips go off, and will presently tenderly engulf them altogether, and so hide the shame of their decay in their kindly little arms. They will be left there, clouds of gentle blue, until the tulips are well withered, and then they will be taken away to make room for the scarlet geraniums that are to occupy these two beds in the summer and flare in the sun as much as they like. I love an occasional mass of fiery colour, and these two will make the lilies look even whiter and more breathless that are to stand sentinel round the semicircle containing the precious tea roses.

The first two years I had this garden, I was determined to do exactly as I chose in it, and to have no arrangements of plants that I had not planned, and no plants but those I knew and loved; so, fearing that an experienced gardener would profit by my ignorance, then about as absolute as it could be, and thrust all his bedding nightmares upon me, and fill the place with those dreadful salad arrangements so often seen in the gardens of the indifferent rich, I would only have a meek man of small pretensions, who would be easily persuaded that I knew as much as, or more than, he did himself. I had three of these meek men one after the other, and learned what I might long ago have discovered, that the less a person knows, the more certain he is that he is right, and that no weapons yet invented are of any use in a struggle with stupidity. The first of these three went melancholy mad at the end of a year; the second was love-sick, and threw down his tools and gave up his situation to wander after the departed siren who had turned his head; the third, when I inquired how it was that the things he had sown never by any chance came up, scratched his head, and as this is a sure sign of ineptitude, I sent him away.

Then I sat down and thought. I had been here two years and worked hard, through these men, at the garden; I had done my best to learn all I could and make it beautiful; I had refused to have more than an inferior gardener because of his supposed more perfect obedience, and one assistant, because of my desire to enjoy the garden undisturbed; I had studied diligently all the gardening books I could lay hands on; I was under the impression that I am an ordinarily intelligent person, and that if an ordinarily intelligent person devotes his whole time to studying a subject he loves, success is very probable; and yet at the end of two years what was my garden like? The failures of the first two summers had been regarded with philosophy; but that third summer I used to go into it sometimes and cry.

As far as I was concerned I had really learned a little, and knew what to buy, and had fairly correct notions as to when and in what soil to sow and plant what I had bought; but of what use is it to buy good seeds and plants and bulbs if you are forced to hand them over to a gardener who listens with ill-concealed impatience to the careful directions you give him, says Jawohl a great many times, and then goes off and puts them in in the way he has always done, which is invariably the wrong way? My hands were tied because of the unfortunate circumstance of sex, or I would gladly have changed places with him and requested him to do the talking while I did the planting, and as he probably would not have talked much there would have been a distinct gain in the peace of the world, which would surely be very materially increased if women's tongues were tied instead of their hands, and those that want to could work with them without collecting a crowd. And is it not certain that the more one's body works the fainter grow the waggings of one's tongue? I sometimes literally ache with envy as I watch the men going about their pleasant work in the sunshine, turning up the luscious damp earth, raking, weeding, watering, planting, cutting the grass, pruning the trees—not a thing that they do from the first uncovering of the roses in the spring to the November bonfires but fills my soul with longing to be up and doing it too. A great many things will have to happen, however, before such a state of popular large-mindedness as will allow of my digging without creating a sensation is reached, so I have plenty of time for further grumblings; only I do very much wish that the tongues inhabiting this apparently lonely and deserted countryside would restrict their comments to the sins, if any, committed by the indigenous females (since sins are fair game for comment) and leave their harmless eccentricities alone. After having driven through vast tracts of forest and heath for hours, and never meeting a soul or seeing a house, it is surprising to be told that on such a day you took such a drive and were at such a spot; yet this has happened to me more than once. And if even this is watched and noted, with what lightning rapidity would the news spread that I had been seen stalking down the garden path with a hoe over my shoulder and a basket in my hand, and weeding written large on every feature! Yet I should love to weed.

210

I think it was the way the weeds flourished that put an end at last to my hesitations about taking an experienced gardener and giving him a reasonable number of helpers, for I found that much as I enjoyed privacy, I yet detested nettles more, and the nettles appeared really to pick out those places to grow in where my sweetest things were planted, and utterly defied the three meek men when they made periodical and feeble efforts to get rid of them. I have a large heart in regard to things that grow, and many a weed that would not be tolerated anywhere else is allowed to live and multiply undisturbed in my garden. They are such pretty things, some of them, such charmingly audacious things, and it is so particularly nice of them to do all their growing, and flowering, and seed-bearing without any help or any encouragement. I admit I feel vexed if they are so officious as to push up among my tea roses and pansies, and I also prefer my paths without them; but on the grass, for instance, why not let the poor little creatures enjoy themselves quietly, instead of going out with a dreadful instrument and viciously digging them up one by one? Once I went into the garden just as the last of the three inept ones had taken up his stand, armed with this implement, in the middle of the sheet of gold and silver that is known for convenience' sake as the lawn, and was scratching his head, as he looked round, in a futile effort to decide where he should begin. I saved the dandelions and daisies on that occasion, and I like to believe they know it. They certainly look very jolly when I come out, and I rather fancy the dandelions dig each other in their little ribs when they see me, and whisper, "Here comes Elizabeth; she's a good sort, ain't she?"—for of course dandelions do not express themselves very elegantly.

But nettles are not to be tolerated. They settled the question on which I had been turning my back for so long, and one fine August morning, when there seemed to be nothing in the garden but nettles, and it was hard to believe that we had ever been doing anything but carefully cultivating them in all their varieties, I walked into the Man of Wrath's den.

"My dear man," I began, in the small caressing voice of one who has long been obstinate and is in the act of giving in, "will you kindly advertise for a head gardener and a proper number of assistants? Nearly all the bulbs and seeds and plants I have squandered my money and my hopes on have turned out to be nettles, and I don't like them. I have had a wretched summer, and never want to see a meek gardener again."

"My dear Elizabeth," he replied, "I regret that you did not take my advice sooner. How often have I pointed out the folly of engaging one incapable person after the other? The vegetables, when we get any, are uneatable, and there is never any fruit. I do not in the least doubt your good intentions, but you are wanting in judgment. When will you learn to rely on my experience?"

I hung my head; for was he not in the pleasant position of being able to say, "I told you so"?—which indeed he has been saying for the last two years. "I don't like relying," I murmured, "and have rather a prejudice against somebody else's experience. Please will you send the advertisement to-day?"

They came in such shoals that half the population must have been head gardeners out of situations. I took all the likely ones round the garden, and I do not think I ever spent a more chastening week than that week of selection. Their remarks were, naturally, of the frankest nature, as I had told them I had had practically only gardeners' assistants since I lived here, and they had no idea, when they were politely scoffing at some arrangement, that it happened to be one of my own. The hot-beds in the kitchen garden with which I had taken such pains were objects of special derision. It appeared that they were all wrong—measurements, preparation, soil, manure, everything that could be wrong, was. Certainly the only crop we had from them was weeds. But I began about half way through the week to grow sceptical, because on comparing their criticisms I found they seldom agreed, and so took courage again. Finally I chose a nice, trim young man, with strikingly intelligent eyes and quick movements, who had shown himself less concerned with the state of chaos existing than with considerations of what might eventually be made of the place. He is very deaf, so he wastes no time in words, and is exceedingly keen on gardening, and knows, as I very soon discovered, a vast amount more than I do, in spite of my three years' application. Moreover, he is filled with that humility and eagerness to learn which is only found in those who have already learned more than their neighbours. He enters into my plans with enthusiasm, and makes suggestions of his own, which, if not always quite in accordance with what are perhaps my peculiar tastes, at least plainly show that he understands his business. We had a very busy winter together altering all the beds, for they none of them had been given a soil in which plants could grow, and next autumn I intend to have all the so-called lawns dug up and levelled, and shall see whether I cannot have decent turf here. I told him he must save the daisy and dandelion roots, and he looked rather crestfallen at that, but he is young, and can learn to like what I like, and get rid of his only fault, a nursery-gardener attitude towards all flowers that are not the fashion. "I shall want a great many daffodils next spring," I shouted one day at the beginning of our acquaintance.

His eyes gleamed. "Ah yes," he said with immediate approval, "they are _sehr modern."

I was divided between amusement at the notion of Spenser's daffadowndillies being *modern*, and indignation at hearing exactly the same adjective applied to them that the woman who sells me my hats bestows on the most appalling examples of her stock.

"They are to be in troops on the grass," I said; whereupon his face grew doubtful. "That is indeed *sehr modern*," I shouted. But he had grown suddenly deafer—a phenomenon I have observed to occur every time my orders are such as he has never been given before. After a time he will, I think, become imbued with my unorthodoxy in these matters; and meanwhile he has the true gardening spirit and loves his work, and love, after all, is the chief thing. I know of no compost so good. In the poorest soil, love alone, by itself, will work wonders.

Down the garden path, past the copse of lilacs with their swelling dark buds, and the great three-cornered bed of tea roses and pansies in front of it, between the rows of china roses and past the lily and foxglove groups, we came last night to the spring garden in the open glade round the old oak; and there, the first to flower of the flowering trees, and standing out like a lovely white naked thing against the dusk of the evening, was a double cherry in full bloom, while close beside it, but not so visible so late, with all their graceful growth outlined by rosy buds, were two Japanese crab apples. The grass just there is filled with narcissus, and at the foot of the oak a colony of tulips consoles me for the loss of the purple crocus patches, so lovely a little while since.

"I must be by myself for once a whole summer through," I repeated, looking round at these things with a feeling of hardly being able to bear their beauty, and the beauty of the starry sky, and the beauty of the silence and the scent—"I must be alone, so that I shall not miss one of these wonders, and have leisure really to *live*."

"Very well, my dear," replied the Man of Wrath, "only do not grumble afterwards when you find it dull. You shall be solitary if you choose, and, as far as I am concerned, I will invite no one. It is always best to allow a woman to do as she likes if you can, and it saves a good deal of bother. To have what she desired is generally an effective punishment."

"Dear Sage," I cried, slipping my hand through his arm, "don't be so wise! I promise you that I won't be dull, and I won't be punished, and I will be happy."

And we sauntered slowly back to the house in great contentment, discussing the firmament and such high things, as though we knew all about them.

May 15th.—There is a dip in the rye-fields about half a mile from my garden gate, a little round hollow like a dimple, with water and reeds at the bottom, and a few water-loving trees and bushes on the shelving ground around. Here I have been nearly every morning lately, for it suits the mood I am in, and I like the narrow footpath to it through the rye, and I like its solitary dampness in a place where everything is parched, and when I am lying on the grass and look down I can see the reeds glistening greenly in the water, and when I look up I can see the rye-fringe brushing the sky. All sorts of beasts come and stare at me, and larks sing above me, and creeping things crawl over me, and stir in the long grass beside me; and here I bring my book, and read and dream away the profitable morning hours, to the accompaniment of the amorous croakings of innumerable frogs.

Thoreau has been my companion for some days past, it having struck me as more appropriate to bring him out to a pond than to read him, as was hitherto my habit, on Sunday mornings in the garden. He is a person who loves the open air, and will refuse to give you much pleasure if you try to read him amid the pomp and circumstance of upholstery; but out in the sun, and especially by this pond, he is delightful, and we spend the happiest hours together, he making statements, and I either agreeing heartily, or just laughing and reserving my opinion till I shall have more ripely considered the thing. He, of course, does not like me as much as I like him, because I live in a cloud of dust and germs produced by wilful superfluity of furniture, and have not the courage to get a match and set light to it: and every day he sees the door-mat on which I wipe my shoes on going into the house, in defiance of his having told me that he had once refused the offer of one on the ground that it is best to avoid even the beginnings of evil. But my philosophy has not yet reached the acute stage that will enable me to see a door-mat in its true character as a hinderer of the development of souls, and I like to wipe my shoes. Perhaps if I had to live with few servants, or if it were possible, short of existence in a cave, to do without them altogether, I should also do without door-mats, and probably in summer without shoes too, and wipe my feet on the grass nature no doubt provides for this purpose; and meanwhile we know that though he went to the woods, Thoreau came back again, and lived for the rest of his days like other people. During his life, I imagine he would have refused to notice anything so fatiguing as an ordinary German woman, and never would have deigned discourse to me on the themes he loved best; but now his spirit belongs to me, and all he thought, and believed, and felt, and he talks as much and as intimately to me here in my solitude as ever he did to his dearest friends years ago in Concord. In the garden he was a pleasant companion, but in the lonely dimple he is fascinating, and the morning hours hurry past at a quite surprising rate when he is with me, and it grieves me to be obliged to interrupt him in the middle of some quaint sentence or beautiful thought just because the sun is touching a certain bush down by the water's edge, which is a sign that it is lunch-time and that I must be off. Back we go together through the rye, he carefully tucked under one arm, while with the other I brandish a bunch of grass to keep off the flies that appear directly we emerge into the sunshine. "Oh, my dear Thoreau," I murmur sometimes, overcome by the fierce heat of the little path at noonday and the persistence of the flies, "did you have flies at Walden to exasperate you? And what became of your philosophy then?" But he never notices my plaints, and I know that inside his covers he is discoursing away like anything on the folly of allowing oneself to be overwhelmed in that terrible rapid and whirlpool called a dinner, which is situated in the meridian shallows, and of the necessity, if one would keep happy, of sailing by it looking another way, tied to the mast like Ulysses. But he gets grimly carried back for all that, and is taken into the house and put on his shelf and left there, because I still happen to have a body attached to my spirit, which, if not fed at the ordinary time, becomes a nuisance. Yet he is right; luncheon is a snare of the tempter, and I would perhaps try to sail by it like Ulysses if I had a biscuit in my pocket to comfort me, but there are the babies to be fed, and the Man of Wrath, and how can a respectable wife and mother sail past any meridian shallows in which those dearest to her have stuck? So I stand by them, and am punished every day by that two-o'clock-in-the-afternoon feeling to which I so much object, and yet cannot avoid. It is mortifying, after the sunshiny morning hours at my pond, when I feel as though I were almost a poet, and very nearly a philosopher, and wholly a joyous animal in an ecstasy of love with life, to come back and live through those dreary luncheon-ridden hours, when the soul is crushed out of sight and sense by cutlets and asparagus and revengeful sweet things. My morning friend turns his back on me when I reenter the library; nor do I ever touch him in the afternoon. Books have their idiosyncrasies as well as people, and will not show me their full beauties unless the place and time in which they are read suits them. If, for instance, I cannot read Thoreau in a drawing-room, how much less would I ever dream of reading Boswell in the grass by a pond! Imagine carrying him off in company with his great friend to a lonely dell in a rye-field, and expecting them to be entertaining. "Nay, my dear lady," the great man would say in mighty tones of rebuke, "this will never do. Lie in a rye-field? What folly is that? And who would converse in a damp hollow that can help it?" So I read and laugh over my Boswell in the library when the lamps are lit, buried in cushions and surrounded by every sign of civilisation, with the drawn curtains shutting out the garden and the country solitude so much disliked by both sage and disciple. Indeed, it is Bozzy who asserts that in the country the only things that make one happy are meals. "I was happy," he says, when stranded at a place called Corrichatachin in the Island of Skye, and unable to get out of it because of the rain,—"I was happy when tea came. Such I take it is the state of those who live in the country. Meals are wished for from the cravings of vacuity of mind, as well as from the desire of eating." And such is the perverseness of human nature that Boswell's wisdom delights me even more than Johnson's, though I love them both very heartily.

In the afternoon I potter in the garden with Goethe. He did not, I am sure, care much really about flowers and gardens, yet he said many lovely things about them that remain in one's memory just as persistently as though they had been inspired expressions of actual feelings; and the intellect must indeed have been gigantic that could so beautifully pretend. Ordinary blunderers have to feel a vast amount before they can painfully stammer out a sentence that will describe it; and when they have got it out, how it seems to have just missed the core of the sensation that gave it birth, and what a poor, weak child it is of what was perhaps a mighty feeling! I read Goethe on a special seat, never departed from when he accompanies me, a seat on the south side of an ice-house, and thus sheltered from the north winds sometimes prevalent in May, and shaded by the low-hanging branches of a great beech-tree from more than flickering sunshine. Through these branches I can see a group of giant poppies just coming into flower, flaming out beyond the trees on the grass, and farther down a huge silver birch, its first spring green not yet deepened out of delicacy, and looking almost golden backed by a solemn cluster of firs. Here I read Goethe—everything I have of his, both what is well known and what is not; here I shed invariable tears over Werther, however often I read it; here I wade through Wilhelm Meister, and sit in amazement before the complications of the Wahlverwandschaften; here I am plunged in wonder and wretchedness by Faust; and here I sometimes walk up and down in the shade and apostrophise the tall firs at the bottom of the glade in the opening soliloquy of Iphigenia. Every now and then I leave the book on the seat and go and have a refreshing potter among my flower beds, from which I return greatly benefited, and with a more just conception of what, in this world, is worth bothering about, and what is not.

In the evening, when everything is tired and quiet, I sit with Walt Whitman by the rose beds and listen to what that lonely and beautiful spirit has to tell me of night, sleep, death, and the stars. This dusky, silent hour is his; and this is the time when I can best hear the beatings of that most tender and generous heart. Such great love, such rapture of jubilant love for nature, and the good green grass, and trees, and clouds, and sunlight; such aching anguish of love for all that breathes and is sick and sorry; such passionate longing to help and mend and comfort that which never can be helped and mended and comforted; such eager looking to death, delicate death, as the one complete and final consolation—before this revelation of yearning, universal pity, every-day selfishness stands awe-struck and ashamed.

When I drive in the forests, Keats goes with me; and if I extend my drive to the Baltic shores, and spend the afternoon on the moss beneath the pines whose pink stems form the framework of the sea,

I take Spenser; and presently the blue waves are the ripples of the Idle Lake, and a tiny white sail in the distance is Phaedria's shallow ship, bearing Cymochles swiftly away to her drowsy little nest of delights. How can I tell why Keats has never been brought here, and why Spenser is brought again and again? Who shall follow the dark intricacies of the elementary female mind? It is safer not to attempt to do so, but by simply cataloguing them collectively under the heading Instinct, have done with them once and for all.

What a blessing it is to love books. Everybody must love something, and I know of no objects of love that give such substantial and unfailing returns as books and a garden. And how easy it would have been to come into the world without this, and possessed instead of an all-consuming passion, say, for hats, perpetually raging round my empty soul! I feel I owe my forefathers a debt of gratitude, for I suppose the explanation is that they too did not care for hats. In the centre of my library there is a wooden pillar propping up the ceiling, and preventing it, so I am told, from tumbling about our ears; and round this pillar, from floor to ceiling, I have had shelves fixed, and on these shelves are all the books that I have read again and again, and hope to read many times more—all the books, that is, that I love quite the best. In the bookcases round the walls are many that I love, but here in the centre of the room, and easiest to get at, are those I love the *best*—the very elect among my favourites. They change from time to time as I get older, and with years some that are in the bookcases come here, and some that are here go into the bookcases, and some again are removed altogether, and are placed on certain shelves in the drawing-room which are reserved for those that have been weighed in the balance and found wanting, and from whence they seldom, if ever, return. Carlyle used to be among the elect. That was years ago, when my hair was very long, and my skirts very short, and I sat in the paternal groves with *Sartor Resartus*, and felt full of wisdom and *Weltschmerz*; and even after I was married, when we lived in town, and the noise of his thunderings was almost drowned by the rattle of droschkies over the stones in the street below, he still shone forth a bright, particular star. Now, whether it is age creeping upon me, or whether it is that the country is very still and sound carries, or whether my ears have grown sensitive, I know not; but the moment I open him there rushes out such a clatter of denunciation, and vehemence, and wrath, that I am completely deafened; and as I easily get bewildered, and love peace, and my chief aim is to follow the apostle's advice and study to be quiet, he has been degraded from his high position round the pillar and has gone into retirement against the wall, where the accident of alphabet causes him to rest in the soothing society of one Carina, a harmless gentleman, whose book on the *Bagni di Lucca* is on his left, and a Frenchman of the name of Charlemagne, whose soporific comedy written at the beginning of the century and called *Le Testament de l'Oncle, ou Les Lunettes Cassees*, is next to him on his right. Two works of his still remain, however, among the elect, though differing in glory—his *Frederick the Great*, fascinating for obvious reasons to the patriotic German mind, and his *Life of Sterling*, a quiet book on the whole, a record of an uneventful life, in which the natural positions of subject and biographer are reversed, the man of genius writing the life of the unimportant friend, and the fact that the friend was exceedingly lovable in no way lessening one's discomfort in the face of such an anomaly. Carlyle stands on an eminence altogether removed from Sterling, who stands, indeed, on no eminence at all, unless it be an eminence, that (happily) crowded bit of ground, where the bright and courageous and lovable stand together. We Germans have all heard of Carlyle, and many of us have read him with due amazement, our admiration often interrupted by groans at the difficulties his style places in the candid foreigner's path; but without Carlyle which of us would ever have heard of Sterling? And even in this comparatively placid book mines of the accustomed vehemence are sprung on the shrinking reader. To the prosaic German, nourished on a literature free from thunderings and any marked acuteness of enthusiasm, Carlyle is an altogether astonishing phenomenon.

And here I feel constrained to inquire sternly who I am that I should talk in this unbecoming manner of Carlyle? To which I reply that I am only a humble German seeking after peace, devoid of the least real desire to criticise anybody, and merely anxious to get out of the way of geniuses when they make too much noise. All I want is to read quietly the books that I at present prefer. Carlyle is shut up now and therefore silent on his comfortable shelf; yet who knows but what in my old age, when I begin to feel really young, I may not once again find comfort in him?

What a medley of books there is round my pillar! Here is Jane Austen leaning against Heine—what would she have said to that, I wonder?—with Miss Mitford and *Cranford* to keep her in countenance on her other side. Here is my Goethe, one of many editions I have of him, the one that has made the acquaintance of the ice-house and the poppies. Here are Ruskin, Lubbock, White's *Selborne*, Izaak Walton, Drummond, Herbert Spencer (only as much of him as I hope I understand and am afraid I do not), Walter Pater, Matthew Arnold, Thoreau, Lewis Carroll, Oliver Wendell Holmes, Hawthorne, *Wuthering Heights*, Lamb's *Essays*, Johnson's *Lives*, Marcus Aurelius, Montaigne, Gibbon, the immortal Pepys, the egregious Boswell, various American children's books that I loved as a child and read and love to this day; various French children's books, loved for the same reason; whole rows of German children's books, on which I was brought up, with their charming woodcuts of quaint little children in laced bodices, and good housemothers cutting bread and butter, and descriptions of the atmosphere of fearful innocence and pure religion and swift judgments and rewards in which they lived, and how the *Finger Gottes* was impressed on everything that happened to them; all the poets; most of the dramatists; and, I verily believe, every gardening book and book about gardens that has been published of late years.

These gardening books are an unfailing delight, especially in winter, when to sit by my blazing peat fire with the snow driving past the windows and read the luscious descriptions of roses and all the other summer glories is one of my greatest pleasures. And then how well I get to know and love those gardens whose gradual development has been described by their owners, and how happily I wander in fancy down the paths of certain specially charming ones in Lancashire, Berkshire, Surrey, and Kent, and admire the beautiful arrangement of bed and border, and the charming bits in unexpected corners, and all the evidences of untiring love! Any book I see advertised that treats of gardens I immediately buy, and thus possess quite a collection of fascinating and instructive garden literature. A few are feeble, and get shunted off into the drawing-room; but the others stay with me winter and summer, and soon lose the gloss of their new coats, and put on the comfortable look of old friends in every-day clothes, under the frequent touch of affection. They are such special friends that I can hardly pass them without a nod and a smile at the well-known covers, each of which has some pleasant association of time and place to make it still more dear.

My spirit too has wandered in one or two French gardens, but has not yet heard of a German one loved beyond everything by its owner. It is, of course, possible that my countrymen do love them and keep quiet about them, but many things are possible that are not probable, and experience compels me to the opinion that this is one of them. We have the usual rich man who has fine gardens laid out regardless of expense, but those are not gardens in the sense I mean; and we have the poor man with his bit of ground, hardly ever treated otherwise than as a fowl-run or a place dedicated to potatoes; and as for the middle class, it is too busy hurrying through life to have time or inclination to stop and plant a rose.

How glad I am I need not hurry. What a waste of life, just getting and spending. Sitting by my pansy beds, with the slow clouds floating leisurely past, and all the clear day before me, I look on at the hot scramble for the pennies of existence and am lost in wonder at the vulgarity that pushes, and cringes, and tramples, untiring and unabashed. And when you have got your pennies, what then? They are only pennies, after all—unpleasant, battered copper things, without a gold piece among them, and never worth the degradation of self, and the hatred of those below you who have fewer, and the derision of those above you who have more. And as I perceive I am growing wise, and what is even worse, allegorical, and as these are tendencies to be fought against as long as possible, I'll go into the garden and play with the babies, who at this moment are sitting in a row on the buttercups, singing what appear to be selections from popular airs.

JUNE

June 3rd.—The Man of Wrath, I observe, is laying traps for me and being deep. He has prophesied that I will find solitude intolerable, and he is naturally desirous that his prophecy should be fulfilled. He knows that continuous rain depresses me, and he is awaiting a spell of it to bring me to a confession that I was wrong after all, whereupon he will make that remark so precious to the married heart, "My dear, I told you so." He begins the day by tapping the barometer, looking at the sky, and shaking his head. If there are any clouds he remarks that they are coming up, and if there are none he says it is too fine to last. He has even gone the length once or twice of starting off to the farm on hot, sunny mornings in his mackintosh, in order to impress on me beyond all doubt that the weather is breaking up. He studiously keeps out of my way all day, so that I may have every opportunity of being bored as quickly as possible, and in the evenings he retires to his den directly after dinner, muttering something about letters. When he has finally disappeared, I go out to the stars and laugh at his transparent wiles.

But how would it be if we did have a spell of wet weather? I do not quite know. As long as it is fine, rainy days in the future do not seem so very terrible, and one, or even two really wet ones are quite enjoyable when they do come—pleasant times that remind one of the snug winter now so far off, times of reading, and writing, and paying one's bills. I never pay bills or write letters on fine summer days. Not for any one will I forego all that such a day rightly spent out of doors might give me; so that a wet day at intervals is almost as necessary for me as for my garden. But how would it be if there were many wet days? I believe a week of steady drizzle in summer is enough to make the stoutest heart depressed. It is to be borne in winter by the simple expedient of turning your face to the fire; but when you have no fire, and very long days, your cheerfulness slowly slips away, and the dreariness prevailing out of doors comes in and broods in the blank corners of your heart. I rather fancy, however, that it is a waste of energy to ponder over what I should do if we had a wet summer on such a radiant day as this. I prefer sitting here on the verandah and looking down through a frame of leaves at all the rosebuds June has put in the beds round the sun-dial, to ponder over nothing, and just be glad that I am alive. The verandah at two o'clock on a summer's afternoon is a place in which to be happy and not decide anything, as my friend Thoreau told me of some other tranquil spot this morning. The chairs are comfortable, there is a table to write on, and the shadows of young leaves flicker across the paper. On one side a Crimson Rambler is thrusting inquisitive shoots through the wooden bars, being able this year for the first time since it was planted to see what I am doing up here, and next to it a Jackmanni clematis clings with soft young fingers to anything it thinks likely to help it up to the goal of its ambition, the roof. I wonder which of the two will get there first. Down there in the rose beds, among the hundreds of buds there is only one full-blown rose as yet, a Marie van Houtte, one of the loveliest of the tea roses, perfect in shape and scent and colour, and in my garden always the first rose to flower; and the first flowers it bears are the loveliest of its own lovely flowers, as though it felt that the first of its children to see the sky and the sun and the familiar garden after the winter sleep ought to put on the very daintiest clothes they can muster for such a festal occasion.

Through the open schoolroom windows I can hear the two eldest babies at their lessons. The village schoolmaster comes over every afternoon and teaches them for two hours, so that we are free from governesses in the house, and once those two hours are over they are free for twenty-four from anything in the shape of learning. The schoolroom is next to the verandah, and as two o'clock approaches their excitement becomes more and more intense, and they flutter up and down the steps, looking in their white dresses like angels on a Jacob's ladder, or watch eagerly among the bushes for a first glimpse of him, like miniature and perfectly proper Isoldes. He is a kind giant with that endless supply of patience so often found in giants, especially when they happen to be village schoolmasters, and judging from the amount of laughter I hear, the babies seem to enjoy their lessons in a way they never did before. Every day they prepare bouquets for him, and he gets more of them than a *prima donna*, or at any rate a more regular supply. The first day he came I was afraid they would be very shy of such a big strange man, and that he would extract nothing from them but tears; but the moment I left them alone together and as I shut the door, I heard them eagerly informing him, by way of opening the friendship, that their heads were washed every Saturday night, and that their hair-ribbons did not match because there had not been enough of the one sort to go round. I went away hoping that they would not think it necessary to tell him how often my head is washed, or any other news of a personal nature about me; but I believe by this time that man knows everything there is to know about the details of my morning toilet, which is daily watched with the greatest interest by the Three. I hope he will be more successful than I was in teaching them Bible stories. I never got farther than Noah, at which stage their questions became so searching as to completely confound me; and as no one likes being confounded, and it is especially regrettable when a parent is placed in such a position, I brought the course to an abrupt end by assuming that owl-like air of wisdom peculiar to infallibility in a corner, and telling them that they were too young to understand these things for the present; and they, having a touching faith in the truth of every word I say, gave three contented little purrs of assent, and proposed that we should play instead at rolling down the grass bank under the south windows—which I did not do, I am glad to remember.

But the schoolmaster, after four weeks' teaching, has got them as far as Moses, and safely past the Noah's ark on which I came to grief, and if glibness is a sign of knowledge then they have learned the story very thoroughly. Yesterday, after he had gone, they emerged into the verandah fresh from Moses and bursting with eagerness to tell me all about it.

"Herr Schenk told us to-day about Moses," began the April baby, making a rush at me.

"Oh?"

"Yes, and a *boser, boser Konig* who said every boy must be deaded, and Moses was the *allerliebster*."

"Talk English, my *dear* baby, and not such a dreadful mixture," I besought.

"He wasn't a cat."

"A cat?"

"Yes, he wasn't a cat, that Moses—a boy was he."

"But of course he wasn't a cat," I said with some severity; "no one ever supposed he was."

"Yes, but mummy," she explained eagerly, with much appropriate hand-action, "the cook's Moses *is* a cat."

"Oh, I see. Well?"

"And he was put in a basket in the water, and that did swim. And then one time they comed, and she said—"

"Who came? And who said?"

"Why, the ladies; and the *Konigstochter* said, '*Ach hormal, daschreit so etwas.*'"

"In German?"

"Yes, and then they went near, and one must take off her shoes and stockings and go in the water and fetch that tiny basket, and then they made it open, and that *Kind* did cry and cry and *strampel* so"—here both the babies gave such a vivid illustration of the *strampeln* that the verandah shook—"and see! it is a tiny baby. And they fetched somebody to give it to eat, and the *Konigstochter* can keep that boy, and further it doesn't go."

"Do you love Moses, mummy?" asked the May baby, jumping into my lap, and taking my face in both her hands—one of the many pretty, caressing little ways of a very pretty, caressing little creature.

"Yes," I replied bravely, "I love him."

"Then I too!" they cried with simultaneous gladness, the seal having thus been affixed to the legitimacy of their regard for him. To be of such authority that your verdict on every subject under heaven is absolute and final is without doubt to be in a proud position, but, like all proud positions, it bristles with pitfalls and drawbacks to the weak-kneed; and most of my conversations with the babies end in a sudden change of subject made necessary by the tendency of their remarks and the unanswerableness of their arguments. Happily, yesterday the Moses talk was brought to an end by the April baby herself, who suddenly remembered that I had not yet seen and sympathised with her dearest possession, a Dutch doll called Mary Jane, since a lamentable accident had bereft it of both its legs; and she had dived into the schoolroom and fished it out of the dark corner reserved for the mangled and thrust it in my face before I had well done musing on the nature and extent of my love for Moses—for I try to be conscientious—and bracing myself to meet the next question.

"See this poor Mary Jane," she said, her voice and hand quivering with tenderness as she lifted its petticoats to show me the full extent of the calamity, "see, mummy, no legs—only twowsers and nothing further."

I wish they would speak English a little better. The pains I take to correct them and weed out the German words that crop up in every sentence are really untiring, and the results discouraging. Indeed, as they get older the German asserts itself more and more, and is threatening to swallow up the little English they have left entirely. I talk English steadily with them, but everybody else, including a small French nurse lately imported, nothing but German. Somebody told me the thing to do was to let children pick up languages when they were babies, at which period they absorb them as easily as food and drink, and are quite unaware that they are learning anything at all; whereupon I immediately introduced this French girl into the family, forgetting how little English they have absorbed, and the result has been that they pass their days delightfully in teaching her German. They were astonished at first on discovering that she could not understand a word they said, and soon set about altering such an uncomfortable state of things; and as they are three to one and very zealous, and she is a meek little person with a profile like a teapot with a twisted black handle of hair, their success was practically certain from the beginning, and she is getting on quite nicely with her German, and has at least already thoroughly learned all the mistakes. She wanders in the garden with a surprised look on her face as of one who is moving about in worlds not realised; and the three cling to her skirts and give her enthusiastic lessons all day long.

Poor Seraphine! What courage to weigh anchor at eighteen and go into a foreign country, to a place where you are among utter strangers, without a friend, unable to speak a word of the language, and not even sure before you start whether you will be given enough to eat. Either it is that saddest of courage forced on the timid by necessity, or, as Doctor Johnson would probably have said, it is stark insensibility; and I am afraid when I look at her I silently agree with the apostle of common sense, and take it for granted that she is incapable of deep feeling, for the altogether inadequate reason that she has a certain resemblance to a teapot. Now is it not hard that a person may have a soul as beautiful as an angel's, a dwelling-place for all sweet sounds and harmonies, and if nature has not thought fit to endow his body with a chin the world will have none of him? The vulgar prejudice is in favour of chins, and who shall escape its influence? I, for one, cannot, though theoretically I utterly reject the belief that the body is the likeness of the soul; for has not each of us friends who, we know, love beyond everything that which is noble and good, and who by no means themselves look noble and good? And what about all the beautiful persons who love nothing on earth except themselves? Yet who in the world cares how perfect the nature may be, how humble, how sweet, how gracious, that dwells in a chinless body? Nobody has time to inquire into natures, and the chinless must be content to be treated in something of the same good-natured, tolerant fashion in which we treat our poor relations until such time as they shall have grown a beard; and those who by their sex are for ever shut out from this glorious possibility will have to take care, should they be of a bright intelligence, how they speak with the tongues of men and of angels, nothing being more droll than the effect of high words and poetic ideas issuing from a face that does not match them.

I wish we were not so easily affected by each other's looks. Sometimes, during the course of a long correspondence with a friend, he grows to be inexpressibly dear to me; I see how beautiful his soul is, how fine his intellect, how generous his heart, and how he already possesses in great perfection those qualities of kindness, and patience, and simplicity, after which I have been so long and so vainly striving. It is not I clothing him with the attributes I love and wandering away insensibly into that sweet land of illusions to which our footsteps turn whenever they are left to themselves, it is his very self unconsciously writing itself into his letters, the very man as he is without his body. Then I meet him again, and all illusions go. He is what I had always found him when we were together, good and amiable; but some trick of manner, some feature or attitude that I do not quite like, makes me forget, and be totally unable to remember, what I know from his letters to be true of him. He, no doubt, feels the same thing about me, and so between us there is a thick veil of something fixed, which, dodge as we may, we never can get round.

"Well, and what do you conclude from all that?" said the Man of Wrath, who had been going out by the verandah door with his gun and his dogs to shoot the squirrels before they had eaten up too many birds, and of whose coat-sleeve I had laid hold as he passed, keeping him by me like a second Wedding Guest, and almost as restless, while I gave expression to the above sentiments.

"I don't know," I replied, "unless it is that the world is very evil and the times are waxing late, but that doesn't explain anything either, because it isn't true."

And he went down the steps laughing and shaking his head and muttering something that I could not quite catch, and I am glad I could not, for the two words I did hear were women and nonsense.

He has developed an unexpected passion for farming, much to my relief, and though we came down here at first only tentatively for a year, three have passed, and nothing has been said about going back to town. Nor will anything be said so long as he is not the one to say it, for no three years of my life can come up to these in happiness, and not even those splendid years of childhood that grow brighter as they recede were more full of delights. The delights are simple, it is true, and of the sort that easily provoke a turning up of the worldling's nose; but who cares for noses that turn up? I am simple myself, and never tire of the blessed liberty from all restraints. Even such apparently indifferent details as being able to walk straight out of doors without first getting into a hat and gloves and veil are full of a subtle charm that is ever fresh, and of which I can never have too much. It is clear that I was born for a placid country life, and placid it certainly is; so much so that the days are sometimes far more like a dream than anything real, the quiet days of reading, and thinking, and watching the changing lights, and the growth and fading of the flowers, the fresh quiet days when life is so full of zest that you cannot stop yourself from singing because you are so happy, the warm quiet days lying on the grass in a secluded corner observing the procession of clouds—this being, I admit, a particularly undignified attitude, but think of the edification! Each morning the simple act of opening my bedroom windows is the means of giving me an ever-recurring pleasure. Just underneath them is a border of rockets in full flower, at that hour in the shadow of the house, whose gables lie sharply defined on the grass beyond, and they send up their good morning of scent the moment they see me leaning out, careful not to omit the pretty German custom of morning greeting. I call back mine, embellished with many endearing words, and then their fragrance comes up close, and covers my face with gentlest little kisses. Behind them, on the other side of the lawn on this west side of the house, is a thick hedge of lilac just now at its best, and what that best is I wish all who love lilac could see. A century ago a man lived here who loved his garden. He loved, however, in his younger years, travelling as well, but in his travels did not forget this little corner of the earth belonging to him, and brought back the seeds of many strange trees such as had never been seen in these parts before, and tried experiments with them in the uncongenial soil, and though many perished, a few took hold, and grew, and flourished, and shade me now at tea-time. What flowers he had, and how he arranged his beds, no one knows, except that the eleven beds round the sun-dial were put there by him; and of one thing he seems to have been inordinately fond, and that was lilac. We have to thank him for the surprising beauty of the garden in May and early June, for he it was who planted the great groups of it, and the banks of it, and massed it between the pines and firs. Wherever a lilac bush could go a lilac bush went; and not common sorts, but a variety of good sorts, white, and purple, and pink, and mauve, and he must have planted it with special care and discrimination, for it grows here as nothing else will, and keeps his memory, in my heart at least, for ever gratefully green. On the wall behind our pew in church there is his monument, he having died here full of years, in the peace that attends the last hours of a good man who has loved his garden; and to the long Latin praises of his virtues and eminence I add, as I pass beneath it on

228

Sundays, a heartiest Amen. Who would not join in the praises of a man to whom you owe your lilacs, and your Spanish chestnuts, and your tulip trees, and your pyramid oaks? "He was a good man, for he loved his garden"—that is the epitaph I would have put on his monument, because it gives one a far clearer sense of his goodness and explains it better than any amount of sonorous Latinities. How could he be anything *but* good since he loved a garden—that divine filter that filters all the grossness out of us, and leaves us, each time we have been in it, clearer, and purer, and more harmless?

June 16th.—Yesterday morning I got up at three o'clock and stole through the echoing passages and strange dark rooms, undid with trembling hands the bolts of the door to the verandah, and passed out into a wonderful, unknown world. I stood for a few minutes motionless on the steps, almost frightened by the awful purity of nature when all the sin and ugliness is shut up and asleep, and there is nothing but the beauty left. It was quite light, yet a bright moon hung in the cloudless grey-blue sky; the flowers were all awake, saturating the air with scent; and a nightingale sat on a hornbeam quite close to me, in loud raptures at the coming of the sun. There in front of me was the sun-dial, there were the rose bushes, there was the bunch of pansies I had dropped the night before still lying on the path, but how strange and unfamiliar it all looked, and how holy— as though God must be walking there in the cool of the day. I went down the path leading to the stream on the east side of the garden, brushing aside the rockets that were bending across it drowsy with dew, the larkspurs on either side of me rearing their spikes of heavenly blue against the steely blue of the sky, and the huge poppies like splashes of blood amongst the greys and blues and faint pearly whites of the innocent, new-born day. On the garden side of the stream there is a long row of silver birches, and on the other side a rye-field reaching across in powdery grey waves to the part of the sky where a solemn glow was already burning. I sat down on the twisted, half-fallen trunk of a birch and waited, my feet in the long grass and my slippers soaking in dew. Through the trees I could see the house with its closed shutters and drawn blinds, the people in it all missing, as I have missed day after day, the beauty of life at that hour. Just behind me the border of rockets and larkspurs came to an end, and, turning my head to watch a stealthy cat, my face brushed against a wet truss of blossom and got its first morning washing. It

229

was wonderfully quiet, and the nightingale on the hornbeam had everything to itself as I sat motionless watching that glow in the east burning redder; wonderfully quiet, and so wonderfully beautiful because one associates daylight with people, and voices, and bustle, and hurryings to and fro, and the dreariness of working to feed our bodies, and feeding our bodies that we may be able to work to feed them again; but here was the world wide awake and yet only for me, all the fresh pure air only for me, all the fragrance breathed only by me, not a living soul hearing the nightingale but me, the sun in a few moments coming up to warm only me, and nowhere a single hard word being spoken, or a single selfish act being done, nowhere anything that could tarnish the blessed purity of the world as God has given it us. If one believed in angels one would feel that they must love us best when we are asleep and cannot hurt each other; and what a mercy it is that once in every twenty-four hours we are too utterly weary to go on being unkind. The doors shut, and the lights go out, and the sharpest tongue is silent, and all of us, scolder and scolded, happy and unhappy, master and slave, judge and culprit, are children again, tired, and hushed, and helpless, and forgiven. And see the blessedness of sleep, that sends us back for a space to our early innocence. Are not our first impulses on waking always good? Do we not all know how in times of wretchedness our first thoughts after the night's sleep are happy? We have been dreaming we are happy, and we wake with a smile, and stare still smiling for a moment at our stony griefs before with a stab we recognise them.

There were no clouds, and presently, while I watched, the sun came up quickly out of the rye, a great, bare, red ball, and the grey of the field turned yellow, and long shadows lay upon the grass, and the wet flowers flashed out diamonds. And then as I sat there watching, and intensely happy as I imagined, suddenly the certainty of grief, and suffering, and death dropped like a black curtain between me and the beauty of the morning, and then that other thought, to face which needs all our courage—the realisation of the awful solitariness in which each of us lives and dies. Often I could cry for pity of our forlornness, and of the pathos of our endeavours to comfort ourselves. With what an agony of patience we build up the theories of consolation that are to protect, in times of trouble, our quivering and naked souls! And how fatally often the elaborate machinery refuses to work at the moment the blow is struck.

I got up and turned my face away from the unbearable, indifferent brightness. Myriads of small suns danced before my eyes as I went along the edge of the stream to the seat round the oak in my spring garden, where I sat a little, looking at the morning from there, drinking it in in long breaths, and determining to think of nothing but just be happy. What a smell of freshly mown grass there was, and how the little heaps into which it had been raked the evening before sparkled with dewdrops as the sun caught them. And over there, how hot the poppies were already beginning to look— blazing back boldly in the face of the sun, flashing back fire for fire. I crossed the wet grass to the hammock under the beech on the lawn, and lay in it awhile trying to swing in time to the nightingale's tune; and then I walked round the ice-house to see how Goethe's corner looked at such an hour; and then I went down to the fir wood at the bottom of the garden where the light was slanting through green stems; and everywhere there was the same mystery, and emptiness, and wonder. When four o'clock drew near I set off home again, not desiring to meet gardeners and have my little hour of quiet talked about, still less my dressing-gown and slippers; so I picked a bunch of roses and hurried in, and just as I softly bolted the door, dreadfully afraid of being taken for a burglar, I heard the first water-cart of the day creaking round the corner. Fearfully I crept up to my room, and when I awoke at eight o'clock and saw the roses in a glass by my side, I remembered what had happened as though it had been years ago.

Now here I have had an experience that I shall not soon forget, something very precious, and private, and close to my soul; a feeling as though I had taken the world by surprise, and seen it as it really is when off its guard—as though I had been quite near to the very core of things. The quiet holiness of that hour seems all the more mysterious now, because soon after breakfast yesterday the wind began to blow from the northwest, and has not left off since, and looking out of the window I cannot believe that it is the same garden, with the clouds driving over it in black layers, and angry little showers every now and then bespattering its harassed and helpless inhabitants, who cannot pull their roots up out of the ground and run for their lives, as I am sure they must long to do. How discouraging for a plant to have just proudly opened its loveliest flowers, the flowers it was dreaming about all the winter and working at so busily underground during the cold weeks of spring, and then for a spiteful shower of five minutes' duration to come and pelt them down, and batter them about, and cover the tender, delicate things with irremediable splashes of mud! Every bed is already filled with victims of the gale, and those that escape one shower go down before the next; so I must make up my mind, I suppose, to the wholesale destruction of the flowers that had reached perfection—that head of white rockets among them that washed my face a hundred years ago—and look forward cheerfully to the development of the younger generation of buds which cannot yet be harmed.

I know these gales. We get them quite suddenly, always from the north-west, and always cold. They ruin my garden for a day or two, and in the summer try my temper, and at all seasons try my skin; yet they are precious because of the beautiful clear light they bring, the intensity of cold blue in the sky and the terrific purple blackness of the clouds one hour and their divine whiteness the next. They fly screaming over the plain as though ten thousand devils with whips were after them, and in the sunny intervals there is nothing in any of nature's moods to equal the clear sharpness of the atmosphere, all the mellowness and indistinctness beaten out of it, and every leaf and twig glistening coldly bright. It is not becoming, a north-westerly gale; it treats us as it treats the garden, but with opposite results, roughly rubbing the softness out of our faces, as I can see when I look at the babies, and avoid the further proof of my own reflection in the glass. But there is life in it, glowing, intense, robust life, and when in October after weeks of serene weather this gale suddenly pounces on us in all its savageness, and the cold comes in a gust, and the trees are stripped in an hour, what a bracing feeling it is, the feeling that here is the first breath of winter, that it is time to pull ourselves together, that the season of work, and discipline, and severity is upon us, the stern season that forces us to look facts in the face, to put aside our dreams and languors, and show what stuff we are made of. No one can possibly love the summer, the dear time of dreams, more passionately than I do; yet I have no desire to prolong it by running off south when the winter approaches and so cheat the year of half its lessons. It is delightful and instructive to potter among one's plants, but it is imperative for body and soul that the pottering should cease for a few months, and that we should be made to realise that grim other side of life. A long hard winter lived through from beginning to end without shirking is one of the most salutary experiences in the world. There is no nonsense about it; you could not indulge in vapours and the finer sentiments in the midst of its deadly earnest if you tried. The thermometer goes down to twenty degrees of frost Reaumur, and down you go with it to the realities, to that elementary state where everything is big—health and sickness, delight and misery, ecstasy and despair. It makes you remember your poorer neighbours, and sends you into their homes to see that they too are fitted out with the armour of warmth and food necessary in the long fight; and in your own home it draws you nearer than ever to each other. Out of doors it is too cold to walk, so you run, and are rewarded by the conviction that you cannot be more than fifteen; or you get into your furs, and dart away in a sleigh over the snow, and are sure there never was music so charming as that of its bells; or you put on your skates, and are off to the lake to which you drove so often on June nights, when it lay rosy in the reflection of the northern glow, and all alive with myriads of wild duck and plovers, and which is now, but for the swish of your skates, so silent, and but for your warmth and jollity, so forlorn. Nor would I willingly miss the early darkness and the pleasant firelight tea and the long evenings among my books. It is then that I am glad I do not live in a cave, as I confess I have in my more godlike moments wished to do; it is then that I feel most capable of attending to the Man of Wrath's exhortations with an open mind; it is then that I actually like to hear the shrieks of the wind, and then that I give my heartiest assent, as I warm my feet at the fire, to the poet's proposition that all which we behold is full of blessings.

But what dreariness can equal the dreariness of a cold gale at midsummer? I have been chilly and dejected all day, shut up behind the streaming window-panes, and not liking to have a fire because of its dissipated appearance in the scorching intervals of sunshine. Once or twice my hand was on the bell and I was going to order one, when out came the sun and it was June again, and I ran joyfully into the dripping, gleaming garden, only to be driven in five minutes later by a yet fiercer squall. I wandered disconsolately round my pillar of books, looking for the one that would lend itself best to the task of entertaining me under the prevailing conditions, but they all looked gloomy, and reserved, and forbidding. So I sat down in a very big chair, and reflected that if there were to be many days like this it might be as well to ask somebody cheerful to come and sit opposite me in all those other big chairs that were looking so unusually gigantic and empty. When the Man of Wrath came in to tea there were such heavy clouds that the room was quite dark, and he peered about for a moment before he saw me. I suppose in the gloom of the big room I must have looked rather lonely, and smaller than usual buried in the capacious chair, for when he finally discovered me his face widened into an inappropriately cheerful smile.

"Well, my dear," he said genially, "how very cold it is."

"Did you come in to say that?" I asked.

"This tempest is very unusual in the summer," he proceeded; to which I made no reply of any sort.

"I did not see you at first amongst all these chairs and cushions. At least, I saw you, but it is so dark I thought you were a cushion."

Now no woman likes to be taken for a cushion, so I rose and began to make tea with an icy dignity of demeanour.

"I am afraid I shall be forced to break my promise not to invite any one here," he said, watching my face as he spoke. My heart gave a distinct leap—so small is the constancy and fortitude of woman. "But it will only be for one night." My heart sank down as though it were lead. "And I have just received a telegram that it will be to-night." Up went my heart with a cheerful bound.

"Who is it?" I inquired. And then he told me that it was the least objectionable of the candidates for the living here, made vacant by our own parson having been appointed superintendent, the highest position in the Lutheran Church; and the gale must have brought me low indeed for the coming of a solitary parson to give me pleasure. The entire race of Lutheran parsons is unpleasing to me,—whether owing to their fault or to mine, it would ill become me to say,—and the one we are losing is the only one I have met that I can heartily respect, and admire, and like. But he is quite one by himself in his extreme godliness, perfect simplicity, and real humility, and though I knew it was unlikely we should find another as good, and I despised myself for the eagerness with which I felt I was looking forward to seeing a new face, I could not stop myself from suddenly feeling cheerful. Such is the weakness of the female mind, and such the unexpected consequences of two months' complete solitude with forty-eight hours' gale at the end of them.

We have had countless applications during the last few weeks for the living, as it is a specially fat one for this part of the country, with a yearly income of six thousand marks, and a good house, and several acres of land. The Man of Wrath has been distracted by the difficulties of choice. According to the letters of recommendation, they were all wonderful men with unrivalled powers of preaching, but on closer inquiry there was sure to be some drawback. One was too old, another not old enough; another had twelve children, and the parsonage only allows for eight; one had a shrewish wife, and another was of Liberal tendencies in politics—a fatal objection; one was in money difficulties because he would spend more than he had, which was not surprising when one heard what he did have; and another was disliked in his parish because he and his wife were too close-fisted and would not spend at all; and at last, the Man of Wrath explained, the moment having arrived when if he did not himself appoint somebody his right to do so would lapse, he had written to the one who was coming, and invited him down that he might look at him, and ask him searching questions as to the faith which is in him.

I forgot my gloom, and my half-formed desperate resolve to break my vow of solitude and fill the house with the frivolous, as I sat listening to the cheerful talk of the little parson this evening. He was so cheerful, yet it was hard to see any cause for it in the life he was leading, a life led by the great majority of the German clergy, fat livings being as rare here as anywhere else. He told us with pleasant frankness all about himself, how he lived on an income of two thousand marks with a wife and six children, and how he was often sorely put to it to keep decent shoes on their feet. "I am continually drawing up plans of expenditure," he said, "but the shoemaker's bill is always so much more than I had expected that it throws my calculations completely out."

His wife, of course, was ailing, but already his eldest child, a girl of ten, took a great deal of the work off her mother's shoulders, poor baby. He was perfectly natural, and said in the simplest way that if the choice were to fall on him it would relieve him of many grinding anxieties; whereupon I privately determined that if the choice did not fall on him the Man of Wrath and I would be strangers from that hour.

"Have you been worrying him with questions about his principles?" I asked, buttonholing the Man of Wrath as he came out from a private conference with him.

"Principles? My dear Elizabeth, how can he have any on that income?"

"If he is not a Conservative will you let that stand in his way, and doom that little child to go on taking work off other people's shoulders?"

"My dear Elizabeth," he protested, "what has my decision for or against him to do with dooming little children to go on doing anything? I really cannot be governed by sentiment."

"If you don't give it to him—" and I held up an awful finger of warning as he retreated, at which he only laughed.

When the parson came to say good-night and good-bye, as he was leaving very early in the morning, I saw at once by his face that all was right. He bent over my hand, stammering out words of thanks and promises of devotion and invocations of blessings in such quantities that I began to feel quite pleased with myself, and as though I had been doing a virtuous deed. This feeling I saw reflected on the Man of Wrath's face, which made me consider that all we had done was to fill the living in the way that suited us best, and that we had no cause whatever to look and feel so benevolent. Still, even now, while the victorious candidate is dreaming of his trebled income and of the raptures of his home-coming to-morrow, the glow has not quite departed, and I am dwelling with satisfaction on the fact that we have been able to raise eight people above those hideous cares that crush all the colour out of the lives of the genteel poor. I am glad he has so many children, because there will be more to be made happy. They will be rich on the little income, and will no doubt dismiss the wise and willing eldest baby to appropriate dolls and pinafores; and everybody will have what they never yet have had, a certain amount of that priceless boon, leisure—leisure to sit down and look at themselves, and inquire what it is they really mean, and really want, and really intend to do with their lives. And this, I may observe, is a beneficial process wholly impossible on 100 pounds a year divided by eight.

But I wonder whether they will be thin-skinned enough ever to discover that other and less delightful side of life only seen by those who have plenty of leisure. Sordid cares may be very terrible to the sensitive, and make them miss the best of everything, but as long as they have them and are busy from morning till night keeping up appearances, they miss also the burden of those fears, and dreads, and realisations that beset him who has time to think. When in the

236

morning I go into my sausage-room and give out sausages, I never think of anything but sausages. My horizon is bounded by them, every faculty is absorbed by them, and they engross me, while I am with them, to the exclusion of the whole world. Not that I love them; as far as that goes, unlike the effect they produce on most of my country-men, they leave me singularly cold; but it is one of my duties to begin the day with sausages, and every morning for the short time I am in the midst of their shining rows, watching my*Mamsell* dexterously hooking down the sleekest with an instrument like a boat-hook, I am practically dead to every other consideration in heaven or on earth. What are they to me, Love, Life, Death, all the mysteries? The one thing that concerns me is the due distribution to the servants of sausages; and until that is done, all obstinate questionings and blank misgivings must wait. If I were to spend my days in their entirety doing such work I should never have time to think, and if I never thought I should never feel, and if I never felt I should never suffer or rapturously enjoy, and so I should grow to be something very like a sausage myself, and not on that account, I do believe, any the less precious to the Man of Wrath.

I know what I would do if I were both poor and genteel—the gentility should go to the place of all good ilities, including utility, respectability, and imbecility, and I would sit, quite frankly poor, with a piece of bread, and a pot of geraniums, and a book. I conclude that if I did without the things erroneously supposed necessary to decency I might be able to afford a geranium, because I see them so often in the windows of cottages where there is little else; and if I preferred such inexpensive indulgences as thinking and reading and wandering in the fields to the doubtful gratification arising from kept-up appearances (always for the bedazzlement of the people opposite, and therefore always vulgar), I believe I should have enough left over to buy a radish to eat with my bread; and if the weather were fine, and I could eat it under a tree, and give a robin some crumbs in return for his cheeriness, would there be another creature in the world so happy? I know there would not.

JULY

July 1st.—I think that after roses sweet-peas are my favourite flowers. Nobody, except the ultra-original, denies the absolute supremacy of the rose. She is safe on her throne, and the only question to decide is which are the flowers that one loves next best. This I have been a long while deciding, though I believe I knew all the time somewhere deep down in my heart that they were sweet-peas; and every summer when they first come out, and every time, going round the garden, that I come across them, I murmur involuntarily, "Oh yes, *you* are the sweetest, you dear, dear little things." And what a victory this is, to be ranked next the rose even by one person who loves her garden. Think of the wonderful beauty triumphed over—the lilies, the irises, the carnations, the violets, the frail and delicate poppies, the magnificent larkspurs, the burning nasturtiums, the fierce marigolds, the smooth, cool pansies. I have a bed at this moment in the full glory of all these things, a little chosen plot of fertile land, about fifteen yards long and of irregular breadth, shutting in at its broadest the east end of the walk along the south front of the house, and sloping away at the back down to a moist, low bit by the side of a very tiny stream, or rather thread of trickling water, where, in the dampest corner, shining in the sun, but with their feet kept cool and wet, is a colony of Japanese irises, and next to them higher on the slope Madonna lilies, so chaste in looks and so voluptuous in smell, and then a group of hollyhocks in tenderest shades of pink, and lemon, and white, and right and left of these white marguerites and evening primroses and that most exquisite of poppies called Shirley, and a little on one side a group of metallic blue delphiniums beside a towering white lupin, and in and out and everywhere mignonette, and stocks, and pinks, and a dozen other smaller but not less lovely plants. I wish I were a poet, that I might properly describe the beauty of this bit as it sparkles this afternoon in the sunshine after rain; but of all the charming, delicate, scented groups it contains, none to my mind is so lovely as the group of sweet-peas in its north-west corner. There is something so utterly gentle and tender about sweet-peas, something so endearing in their clinging, winding, yielding growth; and then the long straight stalk, and the perfect little winged flower at the top, with its soft, pearly texture and wonderful range and combination of colours—all of them pure, all of them satisfying, not an ugly one, or even a less beautiful one among them. And in the house, next to a china bowl of roses, there is no arrangement of flowers so lovely as a bowl of sweet-peas, or a Delf jar filled with them. What a mass of glowing, yet delicate colour it is! How prettily, the moment you open the door, it seems to send its fragrance to meet you! And how you hang over it, and bury your face in it, and love it, and cannot get away from it. I really am sorry for all the people in the world who miss such keen pleasure. It is one that each person who opens his eyes and his heart may have; and indeed, most of the things that are really worth having are within everybody's reach. Any one who chooses to take a country walk, or even the small amount of trouble necessary to get him on to his doorstep and make him open his eyes, may have them, and there are thousands of them thrust upon us by nature, who is for ever giving and blessing, at every turn as we walk. The sight of the first pale flowers starring the copses; an anemone held up against the blue sky with the sun shining through it towards you; the first fall of snow in the autumn; the first thaw of snow in the spring; the blustering, busy winds blowing the winter away and scurrying the dead, untidy leaves into the corners; the hot smell of pines—just like blackberries—when the sun is on them; the first February evening that is fine enough to show how the days are lengthening, with its pale yellow strip of sky behind the black trees whose branches are pearled with raindrops; the swift pang of realisation that the winter is gone and the spring is coming; the smell of the young larches a few weeks later; the bunch of cowslips that you kiss and kiss again because it is so perfect, because it is so divinely sweet, because of all the kisses in the world there is none other so exquisite—who that has felt the joy of these things would exchange them, even if in return he were to gain the whole world, with all its chimney-pots, and bricks, and dust, and dreariness? And we know that the gain of a world never yet made up for the loss of a soul.

One day, in going round the head inspector's garden with his wife, whose care it is, I remarked with surprise that she had no sweet-peas. I called them *Lathyrus odoratus*, and she, having little Latin, did not understand. Then I called them *wohlriechende Wicken*, the German rendering of that which sounds so pretty in English, and she said she had never heard of them. The idea of an existence in a garden yet without sweet-peas, so willing, so modest, and so easily grown, had never presented itself as possible to my imagination. Ever since I can remember, my summers have been filled with them; and in the days when I sat in my own perambulator and they were three times as tall as I was, I well recollect a certain waving hedge of them in the garden of my childhood, and how I stared up longingly at the flowers so far beyond my reach, inaccessibly tossing against the sky. When I grew bigger and had a small garden of my own, I bought their seeds to the extent of twenty pfennings, and trained the plants over the rabbit-hutch that was the chief feature in the landscape. There were other seeds in that garden seeds on which I had laid out all my savings and round which played my fondest hopes, but the sweet-peas were the only ones that came up. The same thing happened here in my first summer, my gardening knowledge not having meanwhile kept pace with my years, and of the seeds sown that first season sweet-peas again were the only ones that came up. I should say they were just the things for people with very little time and experience at their disposal to grow. A garden might be made beautiful with sweet-peas alone, and, with hardly any labour, except the sweet labour of picking to prolong the bloom, be turned into a fairy bower of delicacy and refinement. Yet the Frau Inspector not only had never heard of them, but, on my showing her a bunch, was not in the least impressed, and led me in her garden to a number of those exceedingly vulgar red herbaceous peonies growing among her currant bushes, and announced with conviction that they were her favourite flower. It was on the tip of my tongue to point out that in these days of tree-peonies, and peonies so lovely in their silvery faint tints that they resemble gigantic roses, it is absolutely wicked to suffer those odious red ones to pervert one's taste; that a person who sees nothing but those every time he looks out of his window very quickly has his nice perception for true beauty blunted; that such a person would do well to visit my garden every day during the month of May, and so get himself cured by the sight of my peony bushes covered with huge scented white and blush flowers; and that he would, I was convinced, at the end of the cure, go home and pitch his own on to the dust-heap. But of what earthly use would it have been? Pointing out the difference between what is beautiful and what misses beauty to a Frau Inspector of forty, whose chief business it is to make butter, is likely to be singularly unprolific of good results; and, further, experience has taught me that whenever anything is on the tip of my tongue the best thing to do is to keep it there. I wonder why a woman always wants to interfere.

It is a pity, nevertheless, that this lady should be so wanting in the aesthetic instinct, for her garden is full of possibilities. It lies due south, sheltered on the north, east, and west by farm buildings, and

240

is rich in those old fruit-trees and well-seasoned gooseberry bushes that make such a good basis for the formation of that most delightful type of little garden, the flower-and-fruit-and-vegetable-mixed sort. She has, besides, an inestimable slimy, froggy pond, a perpetual treasure of malodorous water, much pined after by thirsty flowers; and then does she not live in the middle of a farmyard flowing with fertilising properties that only require a bucket and a shovel to transform them into roses? The way in which people miss their opportunities is melancholy.

This pond of hers, by the way, is an object of the liveliest interest to the babies. They do not seem to mind the smell, and they love the slime, and they had played there for several days in great peace before the unfortunate accident of the June baby's falling in and being brought back looking like a green and speckled frog herself, revealed where it was they had persuaded Seraphine to let them spend their mornings. Then there was woe and lamentation, for I was sure they would all have typhoid fever, and I put them mercilessly to bed, and dosed them, as a preliminary, with castor oil—that oil of sorrow, as Carlyle calls it. It was no use sending for the doctor because there is no doctor within reach; a fact which simplifies life amazingly when you have children. During the time we lived in town the doctor was never out of the house. Hardly a day passed but one or other of the Three had a spot, or, as the expressive German has it, a *Pickel*, and what parent could resist sending for a doctor when one lived round the corner? But doctors are like bad habits—once you have shaken them off you discover how much better you are without them; and as for the babies, since they inhabit a garden, prompt bed and the above-mentioned simple remedy have been all that is necessary to keep them robust. I admit I was frightened when I heard where they had been playing, for when the wind comes from that quarter even sitting by my rose beds I have been reminded of the existence of the pond; and I kept them in bed for three days, anxiously awaiting symptoms, and my head full of a dreadful story I had heard of a little boy who had drunk seltzer water and thereupon been seized with typhoid fever and had died, and if, I asked myself with a power of reasoning unusual in a woman, you die after seltzer water, what will you not do after frog-pond? But they did nothing, except be uproarious, and sing at the top of their voices, and clamour for more dinner than I felt would be appropriate for babies who were going to be dangerously ill in a few hours; and so, after due waiting, they were got up and dressed and turned loose again, and from that day to this no symptoms have appeared. The pond was at first strictly forbidden as a playground, but afterwards I made concessions, and now they are allowed to go to a deserted little burying-ground on the west side of it when the wind is in the west; and there at least they can hear the frogs, and sometimes, if they are patient, catch a delightful glimpse of them.

The graveyard is in the middle of a group of pines that bounds the Frau Inspector's garden on that side, and has not been used within the memory of living man. The people here love to make their little burying-grounds in the heart of a wood if they can, and they are often a long way away from the church to which they belong because, while every hamlet has its burying-ground, three or four hamlets have to share a church; and indeed the need for churches is not so urgent as that for graves, seeing that, though we may not all go to church, we all of us die and must be buried. Some of these little cemeteries are not even anywhere near a village, and you come upon them unexpectedly in your drives through the woods—bits of fenced-in forest, the old gates dropping off their hinges, the paths green from long disuse, the unchecked trees casting black, impenetrable shadows across the poor, meek, pathetic graves. I try sometimes, pushing aside the weeds, to decipher the legend on the almost speechless headstones; but the voice has been choked out of them by years of wind, and frost, and snow, and a few stray letters are all that they can utter—a last stammering protest against oblivion.

The Man of Wrath says all women love churchyards. He is fond of sweeping assertions, and is sometimes curiously feminine in his tendency to infer a general principle from a particular instance. The deserted little forest burying-grounds interest and touch me because they are so solitary, and humble, and neglected, and forgotten, and because so many long years have passed since tears were shed over the newly made graves. Nobody cries now for the husband, or father, or brother buried there; years and years ago the last tear that would ever be shed for them was dried—dried probably before the gate was reached on the way home—and they were not missed. Love and sorrow appear to be flowers of civilisation, and most to flourish where life has the broadest margin of leisure and abundance. The primary instincts are always there, and must first be satisfied; and if to obtain the means of satisfying them you have to

242

work from morning till night without rest, who shall find time and energy to sit down and lament? I often go with the babies to the enclosure near the Frau Inspector's pond, and it seems just as natural that they should play there as that the white butterflies should chase each other undisturbed across the shadows. And then the place has a soothing influence on them, and they sober down as we approach it, and on hot afternoons sit quietly enough as close to the pond as they may, content to watch for the chance appearance of a frog while talking to me about angels.

This is their favourite topic of conversation in this particular place. Just as I have special times and places for certain books, so do they seem to have special times and places for certain talk. The first time I took them there they asked me what the mounds were, and by a series of adroit questions extracted the information that the people who had been buried there were now angels (I am not a specialist, and must take refuge in telling them what I was told in my youth), and ever since then they refuse to call it a graveyard, and have christened it the angel-yard, and so have got into the way of discussing angels in all their bearings, sometimes to my confusion, whenever we go there.

"But what *are>* angels, mummy?" said the June baby inconsequently this afternoon, after having assisted at the discussions for several days and apparently listening with attention.

"*Such* a silly baby!" cried April, turning upon her with contempt, "don't you know they are *lieber Gott's* little girls?"

Now I protest I had never told those babies anything of the sort. I answer their questions to the best of my ability and as conscientiously as I can, and then, when I hear them talking together afterwards, I am staggered by the impression they appear to have received. They live in a whole world of independent ideas in regard to heaven and the angels, ideas quite distinct from other people's, and, as far as I can make out, believe that the Being they call *lieber Gott* pervades the garden, and is identical with, among other things, the sunshine and the air on a fine day. I never told them so, nor, I am sure, did Seraphine, and still less Seraphine's predecessor Miss Jones, whose views were wholly material; yet if, on bright mornings, I forget to immediately open all the library windows on coming down, the April baby runs in, and with quite a worried look on her face cries, "Mummy, won't you open the windows and let the *lieber Gott* come in?"

If they were less rosy and hungry, or if I were less prosaic, I might have gloomy forebodings that such keen interest in things and beings celestial was prophetic of a short life; and in books, we know, the children who talk much on these topics invariably die, after having given their reverential parents a quantity of advice. Fortunately such children are confined to books, and there is nothing of the ministering child—surely a very uncomfortable form of infant—about my babies. Indeed, I notice that in their conversations together on such matters a healthy spirit of contradiction prevails, and this afternoon, after having accepted April's definition of angels with apparent reverence, the June baby electrified the other two (always more orthodox and yielding) by remarking that she hoped she would never go to heaven. I pretended to be deep in my book and not listening; April and May were sitting on the grass sewing ("needling" they call it) fearful-looking woolwork things for Seraphine's birthday, and June was leaning idly against a pine trunk, swinging a headless doll round and round by its one remaining leg, her heels well dug into the ground, her sun-bonnet off, and all the yellow tangles of her hair falling across her sunburnt, grimy little face.

"No," she repeated firmly, with her eyes fixed on her sisters' startled faces, "I don't want to. There's nothing there for babies to play with."

"Nothing to play with?" exclaimed the other two in a breath—and throwing down their needle-work they made a simultaneous rush for me.

"Mummy, did you hear? June says she doesn't want to go into the*Himmel*!" cried April, horror-stricken.

"Because there's nothing to play with there, she says," cried May, breathlessly; and then they added with one voice, as though the subject had long ago been threshed out and settled between them, "Why, she can play at ball there with all the *Sternleins* if she likes!"

The idea of the June baby striding across the firmament and hurling the stars about as carelessly as though they were tennis-balls was so magnificent that it sent shivers of awe through me as I read.

"But if you break all your dolls," added April, turning severely to June, and eyeing the distorted remains in her hand, "I don't think*lieber Gott* will let you in at all. When you're big and have tiny Junes—real live Junes—I think you'll break them too, and *lieberGott* doesn't love mummies what breaks their babies."

"But I *must* break my dolls," cried June, stung into indignation by what she evidently regarded as celestial injustice; "*lieber Gott* made me that way, so I can't help doing it, can I, mummy?"

On these occasions I keep my eyes fixed on my book, and put on an air of deep abstraction; and indeed, it is the only way of keeping out of theological disputes in which I am invariably worsted.

July 15th.—Yesterday, as it was a cool and windy afternoon and not as pleasant in my garden as it has lately been, I thought I would go into the village and see how my friends the farm hands were getting on. Philanthropy is intermittent with me as with most people, only they do not say so, and seize me like a cold in the head whenever the weather is chilly. On warm days my bump of benevolence melts away entirely, and grows bigger in proportion as the thermometer descends. When the wind is in the east it is quite a decent size, and about January, in a north-easterly snowstorm, it is plainly visible to the most casual observer. For a few weeks from then to the end of February I can hold up my head and look our parson in the face, but during the summer, if I see him coming my mode of progression in getting out of the way is described with perfect accuracy by the verb "to slink."

The village consists of one street running parallel to the outer buildings of the farm, and the cottages are one-storied, each with rooms for four families—two in front, looking on to the wall of the farmyard, which is the fashionable side, and two at the back, looking on to nothing more exhilarating than their own pigstyes. Each family has one room and a larder sort of place, and shares the kitchen with the family on the opposite side of the entrance; but the women prefer doing their cooking at the grate in their own room rather than expose the contents of their pots to the ill-natured comments of a neighbour. On the fashionable side there is a little fenced-in garden for every family, where fowls walk about pensively and meditate beneath the scarlet-runners (for all the world like me in my garden), and hollyhocks tower above the drying linen, and fuel, stolen from our woods, is stacked for winter use; but on the other side you walk straight out of the door on to manure heaps and pigs.

The street did not look very inviting yesterday, with a lowering sky above, and the wind blowing dust and bits of straw and paper into my face and preventing me from seeing what I knew to be there, a consoling glimpse of green fields and fir woods down at the other end; but I had not been for a long while—we have had such a lovely summer—and something inside me had kept on saying aggressively all the morning, "Elizabeth, don't you know you are due in the village? Why don't you go then? When are you going? Don't you know you *ought* to go? Don't you feel you *must*? Elizabeth, pull yourself together and *go*" Strange effect of a grey sky and a cool wind! For I protest that if it had been warm and sunny my conscience would not have bothered about me at all. We had a short fight over it, in which I got all the knocks, as was evident by the immediate swelling of the bump alluded to above, and then I gave in, and by two o'clock in the afternoon was lifting the latch of the first door and asking the woman who lived behind it what she had given the family for dinner. This, I was instructed on my first round by the Frau Inspector, is the proper thing to ask; and if you can follow it up by an examination of the contents of the saucepan, and a gentle sniff indicative of your appreciation of their savouriness, so much the better. I was diffident at first about this, but the gratification on their faces at the interest displayed is so unmistakable that I never now omit going through the whole business. This woman, the wife of one of the men who clean and feed the cows, has arrived at that enviable stage of existence when her children have all been confirmed and can go out to work, leaving her to spend her days in her clean and empty room in comparative dignity and peace. The children go to school till they are fourteen, then they are confirmed, are considered grown up, and begin to work for wages; and her three strapping daughters were out in the fields yesterday reaping. The mother has a keen, shrewd face, and everything about her was neat and comfortable. Her floor was freshly strewn with sand, her cups and saucers and spoons shone bright and clean from behind the glass door of the cupboard, and the two beds, one for herself and her husband and the other for her three daughters, were more mountainous than any I afterwards saw. The size and plumpness of her feather beds, the Frau Inspector tells me, is a woman's chief claim to consideration from the neighbours. She who can pile them up nearest to the ceiling becomes the principal personage in the community, and a flat bed is a social disgrace. It is a mystery to me, when I see the narrowness of the bedsteads, how so many people can sleep in them. They are rather narrower than what are known as single beds, yet father and mother and often a baby manage to sleep very well in one, and three or four children in the opposite corner of the room in another. The explanation no doubt is that they do not know what nerves are, and what it is to be wakened by the slightest sound or movement in the room and lie for hours afterwards, often the whole night, totally unable to fall asleep again, staring out into the darkness with eyes that refuse to shut. No nerves, and a thick skin—what inestimable blessings to these poor people! And they never heard of either.

I stood a little while talking, not asked to sit down, for that would be thought a liberty, and hearing how they had had potatoes and bacon for dinner, and how the eldest girl Bertha was going to be married at Michaelmas, and how well her baby was getting through its teething.

"Her baby?" I echoed, "I have not heard of a baby?"

The woman went to one of the beds and lifted up a corner of the great bag of feathers, and there, sure enough, lay a round and placid baby, sleeping as sweetly and looking as cherubic as the most legitimate of its contemporaries.

"And he is going to marry her at Michaelmas?" I asked, looking as sternly as I could at the grandmother.

"Oh yes," she replied, "he is a good young man, and earns eighteen marks a week. They will be very comfortable."

"It is a pity," I said, "that the baby did not make its appearance after Michaelmas instead of before. Don't you see yourself what a pity it is, and how everything has been spoilt?"

She stared at me for a moment with a puzzled look, and then turned away and carefully covered the cherub again. "They will be very comfortable," she repeated, seeing that I expected an answer; "he earns eighteen marks a week."

What was there to be said? If I had told her her daughter was a grievous sinner she might perhaps have felt transiently uncomfortable, but as soon as I had gone would have seen for herself, with those shrewd eyes of hers, that nothing had been changed by my denunciations, that there lay the baby, dimpled and healthy, that her daughter was making a good match, that none of her set saw anything amiss, and that all the young couples in the district had prefaced their marriages in this way.

Our parson is troubled to the depths of his sensitive soul by this custom. He preaches, he expostulates, he denounces, he implores, and they listen with square stolid faces and open mouths, and go back to their daily work among their friends and acquaintances, with no feeling of shame, because everybody does it, and public opinion, the only force that could stop it, is on their side. The parson looks on with unutterable sadness at the futility of his efforts; but the material is altogether too raw for successful manipulation by delicate fingers.

"Poor things," I said one day, in answer to an outburst of indignation from him, after he had been marrying one of our servants at the eleventh hour, "I am so sorry for them. It is so pitiful that they should always have to be scolded on their wedding day. Such children—so ignorant, so uncontrolled, so frankly animal— what do they know about social laws? They only know and follow nature, and I would from my heart forgive them all."

"It is *sin*" he said shortly.

"Then the forgiveness is sure."

"Not if they do not seek it."

I was silent, for I wished to reply that I believed they would be forgiven in spite of themselves, that probably they were forgiven whether they sought it or not, and that you cannot limit things divine; but who can argue with a parson? These people do not seek forgiveness because it never enters their heads that they need it. The parson tells them so, it is true, but they regard him as a person bound by his profession to say that sort of thing, and are sharp enough to see that the consequences of their sin, foretold by him with such awful eloquence, never by any chance come off. No girl is left to languish and die forsaken by her betrayer, for the betrayer is a worthy young man who marries her as soon as he possibly can; no finger of scorn is pointed at the fallen one, for all the fingers in the street are attached to women who began life in precisely the same fashion; and as for that problematical Day of Judgment of which they hear so much on Sundays, perhaps they feel that that also may be one of the things which after all do not happen.

The servant who had been married and scolded that morning was a groom, aged twenty, and he had met his little wife, she being then seventeen, in the place he was in before he came to us. She was a housemaid there, and must have been a pretty thing, though there were few enough traces of it, except the beautiful eyes, in the little anxious face that I saw for the first time immediately after the wedding, and just before the weary and harassed parson came in to talk things over. I had never heard of her existence until, about ten days previously, the groom had appeared, bathed in tears,

248

speechlessly holding out a letter from her in which she said she could not bear things any longer and was going to kill herself. The wretched young man was at his wit's end, for he had not yet saved enough to buy any furniture and set up housekeeping, and she was penniless after so many months out of a situation. He did not know any way out of it, he had no suggestions to offer, no excuses to make, and just stood there helplessly and sobbed.

I went to the Man of Wrath, and we laid our heads together. "We do not want another married servant," he said.

"No, of course we don't," said I.

"And there is not a room empty in the village."

"No, not one."

"And how can we give him furniture? It is not fair to the other servants who remain virtuous, and wait till they can buy their own."

"No, certainly it isn't fair."

There was a pause.

"He is a good boy," I murmured presently.

"A very good boy."

"And she will be quite ruined unless somebody—"

"I'll tell you what we can do, Elizabeth," he interrupted; "we can buy what is needful and let him have it on condition that he buys it back gradually by some small monthly payment."

"So we can."

"And I think there is a room over the stables that is empty."

"So there is."

"And he can go to town and get what furniture he needs and bring the girl back with him and marry her at once. The sooner the better, poor girl."

And so within a fortnight they were married, and came hand in hand to me, he proud and happy, holding himself very straight, she in no wise yet recovered from the shock and misery of the last few hopeless months, looking up at me with eyes grown much too big for her face, eyes in which there still lurked the frightened look caught in the town where she had hidden herself, and where fingers of scorn could not have been wanting, and loud derision, and utter shame, besides the burden of sickness, and hunger, and miserable pitiful youth.

They stood hand in hand, she in a decent black dress, and both wearing very tight white kid gloves that refused to hide entirely the whole of the rough red hands, and they looked so ridiculously young, and the whole thing was so wildly improvident, that no words of exhortation would come to my lips as I gazed at them in silence, between laughter and tears. I ought to have told them they were sinners; I ought to have told them they were reckless; I ought to have told them by what a narrow chance they had escaped the just punishment of their iniquity, and instead of that I found myself stretching out hands that were at once seized and kissed, and merely saying with a cheerful smile, "*NunKinder, liebt Euch, und seid brav.*" And so they were dismissed, and then the parson came, in a fever at this latest example of deadly sin, while I, with the want of moral sense so often observable in woman, could only think with pity of their childishness. The baby was born three days later, and the mother very nearly slipped through our fingers; but she was a country girl, and she fought round, and by and by grew young again in the warmth of married respectability; and I met her the other day airing her baby in the sun, and holding her head as high as though she were conscious of a whole row of feather beds at home, every one of which touched the ceiling.

In the next room I went into an old woman lay in bed with her head tied up in bandages. The room had not much in it, or it would have been untidier; it looked neglected and gloomy, and some dirty plates, suggestive of long-past dinners, were piled on the table.

"Oh, such headaches!" groaned the old woman when she saw me, and moved her head from side to side on the pillow. I could see she was not undressed, and had crept under her feather bag as she was. I went to the bedside and felt her pulse—a steady pulse, with nothing of feverishness in it.

"Oh, such draughts!" moaned the old woman, when she saw I had left the door open.

"A little air will make you feel better," I said; the atmosphere in the shut-up room was so indescribable that my own head had begun to throb.

"Oh, oh!" she moaned, in visible indignation at being forced for a moment to breathe the pure summer air.

"I have something at home that will cure your headache," I said, "but there is nobody I can send with it to-day. If you feel better later on, come round and fetch it. I always take it when I have a headache"—("Why, Elizabeth, you know you never have such things!" whispered my conscience, appalled. "You just keep quiet," I whispered back, "I have had enough of you for one day.")—"and I have some grapes I will give you when you come, so that if you possibly can, do."

"Oh, I can't move," groaned the old woman, "oh, oh, oh!" But I went away laughing, for I knew she would appear punctually to fetch the grapes, and a walk in the air was all she needed to cure her.

How the whole village hates and dreads fresh air! A baby died a few days ago, killed, I honestly believe, by the exceeding love of its mother, which took the form of cherishing it so tenderly that never once during its little life was a breath of air allowed to come anywhere near it. She is the watchman's wife, a gentle, flabby woman, with two rooms at her disposal, but preferring to live and sleep with her four children in one, never going into the other except for the christenings and funerals which take place in her family with what I cannot but regard as unnecessary frequency. This baby was born last September in a time of golden days and quiet skies, and when it was about three weeks old I suggested that she should take it out every day while the fine weather lasted. She pointed out that it had not yet been christened, and remembering that it is the custom in their class for both mother and child to remain shut up and invisible till after the christening, I said no more. Three weeks later I was its godmother, and it was safely got into the fold of the Church. As I was leaving, I remarked that now she would be able to take it out as much as she liked. The following March, on a day that smelt of violets, I met her near the house. I asked after the baby, and she began to cry. "It does not thrive," she wept, "and its arms are no thicker than my finger."

"Keep it out in the sun as much as you can," I said; "this is the very weather to turn weak babies into strong ones."

"Oh, I am so afraid it will catch cold if I take it out," she cried, her face buried in what was once a pocket-handkerchief.

"When was it out last?"

"Oh—" she stopped to blow her nose, very violently, and, as it seemed to me, with superfluous thoroughness. I waited till she had done, and then repeated my question.

"Oh—" a fresh burst of tears, and renewed exhaustive nose-blowing.

I began to suspect that my question, put casually, was of more importance than I had thought, and repeated it once more.

"I—can't t-take it out," she sobbed, "I know it—it would die."

"But has it not been out at all, then?"

She shook her head.

"Not once since it was born? Six months ago?"

She shook her head.

"*Poor* baby!" I exclaimed; and indeed from my heart I pitied the little thing, perishing in a heap of feathers, in one close room, with four people absorbing what air there was. "I am afraid," I said, "that if it does not soon get some fresh air it will not live. I wonder what would happen to my children if I kept them in one hot room day and night for six months. You see how they are out all day, and how well they are."

"They are so strong," she said, with a doleful sniff, "that they can stand it."

I was confounded by this way of looking at it, and turned away, after once more begging her to take the child out. She plainly regarded the advice as brutal, and I heard her blowing her nose all down the drive. In June the father told me he would like the doctor; the child grew thinner every day in spite of all the food it took. A doctor was got from the nearest town, and I went across to hear what he ordered. He ordered bottles at regular intervals instead of the unbroken series it had been having, and fresh air. He could find nothing the matter with it, except unusual weakness. He asked if it always perspired as it was doing then, and himself took off the topmost bag of feathers. Early in July it died, and its first outing was to the cemetery in the pine woods three miles off.

"I took such care of it," moaned the mother, when I went to try and comfort her after the funeral; "it would never have lived so long but for the care I took of it."

"And what the doctor ordered did no good?" I ventured to ask, as gently as I could.

"Oh, I did not take it out—how could I—it would have killed it at once—at least I have kept it alive till now." And she flung her arms across the table, and burying her head in them wept bitterly.

There is a great wall of ignorance and prejudice dividing us from the people on our place, and in every effort to help them we knock against it and cannot move it any more than if it were actual stone. Like the parson on the subject of morals, I can talk till I am hoarse on the subject of health, without at any time producing the faintest impression. When things are very bad the doctor is brought, directions are given, medicines made up, and his orders, unless they happen to be approved of, are simply not carried out. Orders to wash a patient and open windows are never obeyed, because the whole village would rise up if, later on, the illness ended in death, and accuse the relatives of murder. I suppose they regard us and our like who live on the other side of the dividing wall as persons of fantastic notions which, when carried into effect among our own children, do no harm because of the vast strength of the children accumulated during years of eating in the quantities only possible to the rich. Their idea of happiness is eating, and they naturally suppose that everybody eats as much as he can possibly afford to buy. Some of them have known hunger, and food and strength are coupled together in their experience—the more food the greater the strength; and people who eat roast meat (oh, bliss ineffable!) every day of their lives can bear an amount of washing and airing that would surely kill such as themselves. But how useless to try and discover what their views really are. I can imagine what I like about them, and am fairly certain to imagine wrong. I have no real conception of their attitude towards life, and all I can do is to talk to them kindly when they are in trouble, and as often as I can give them nice things to eat. Shocked at the horrors that must surround the poor women at the birth of their babies, I asked the Man of Wrath to try and make some arrangement that would ensure their quiet at those times. He put aside a little cottage at the end of the street as a home for them in their confinements, and I furnished it, and made it clean and bright and pretty. A nurse was permanently engaged, and I thought with delight of the unspeakable blessing and comfort it was going to be. Not a baby has been born in that cottage, for not a woman has allowed herself to be taken there. At the end of a year it had to be let out again to families, and the nurse dismissed.

"*Why* wouldn't they go?" I asked the Frau Inspector, completely puzzled. She shrugged her shoulders. "They like their husband and children round them," she said, "and are afraid something will be done to them away from home—that they will be washed too often, perhaps. The gracious lady will never get them to leave their homes."

"The gracious lady gives it up," I muttered.

When I opened the next door I was bewildered by the crowd in the room. A woman stood in the middle at a wash-tub which took up most of the space. Every now and then she put out a dripping hand and jerked a perambulator up and down for a moment, to calm the shrieks of the baby inside. On a wooden bench at the foot of one of the three beds a very old man sat and blinked at nothing. Crouching in a corner were two small boys of pasty complexion, playing with a guinea-pig and coughing violently. The loveliest little girl I have seen for a very long while lay in the bed nearest the door, quite silent, with her eyes closed and her mouth shut tight, as though she were trying hard to bear something. As I pulled the door open the first thing I saw, right up against it, was this set young face framed in tossed chestnut hair. "Why, *Frauchen*," I said to the woman at the tub, "so many of you at home to-day? Are you all ill?" There was hardly standing room for an extra person, and the room was full of steam.

"They have all got the cough I had," she answered, without looking up, "and Lotte there is very bad."

I took Lotte's rough little hand—so different from the delicate face—and found she was in a fever.

"We must get the doctor," I said.

"Oh, the doctor—" said the mother with a shrug, "he's no use."

"You must do what he tells you, or he cannot help you."

"That last medicine he sent me all but killed me," she said, washing vigorously. "I'll never take any more of his, nor shall any child of mine."

"What medicine was it?"

She wiped her hand on her apron, and reaching across to the cupboard took out a little bottle. "I was in bed two days after it," she said, handing it to me—"as though I were dead, not knowing what was going on round me." The bottle had contained opium, and there were explicit directions written on it as to the number of drops to be taken and the length of the intervals between the taking.

"Did you do exactly what is written here?" I asked.

"I took it all at once. There wasn't much of it, and I was feeling bad."

"But then of course it nearly killed you. I wonder it didn't quite. What good is it our taking all the trouble we do to send that long distance for the doctor if you don't do as he orders?"

"I'll take no more of his medicine. If it had been any good and able to cure me, the more I took the quicker I ought to have been cured." And she scrubbed and thumped with astounding energy, while Lotte lay with her little ashen face a shade more set and suffering. The wash-tub, though in the middle of the room, was quite close to Lotte's bed, because the middle of the room was quite close to every other part of it, and each extra hard maternal thump must have hit the child's head like a blow from a hammer. She was, you see, only thirteen, and her skin had not had time to turn into leather.

"Has this child eaten anything to-day?"

"She won't."

"Is she not thirsty?"

"She won't drink coffee or milk."

"I'll send her something she may like, and I shall send, too, for the doctor."

"I'll not give her his stuff."

"Let me beg you to do as he tells you."

"I'll not give her his stuff."

"Was it absolutely necessary to wash to-day?"

"It's the day."

"My good woman," said I to myself, gazing at her with outward blandness, "I'd like exceedingly to tip you up into your wash-tub and thump you as thoroughly as you are thumping those unfortunate clothes." Aloud I said in flute-like tones of conciliation, "Good afternoon."

"Good afternoon," said she without looking up.

Washing days always mean tempers, and I ought to have fled at the first sight of that tub, but then there was Lotte in her little yellow flannel night-gown, suffering as only children can suffer, helpless, forced to patience, forced to silent endurance of any banging and vehemence in which her mother might choose to indulge. No wonder her mouth was shut like a clasp and she would not open her eyes. Her eyebrows were reddish like her hair, and very straight, and her eyelashes lay dusky and long on her white face. At least I had discovered Lotte and could help her a little, I thought, as I departed down the garden path between the rows of scarlet-runners; but the help that takes the form of jelly and iced drinks is not of a lasting nature, and I have but little sympathy with a benevolence that finds its highest expression in gifts of the kind. There have been women within my experience who went down into the grave accompanied by special pastoral encomiums, and whose claims to lady-bountifulness, on closer inquiry, rested solely on a foundation of jelly. Yet nothing in the world is easier than ordering jelly to be sent to the sick, except refraining from ordering it. What more, however, could I do for Lotte than this? I could not take her up in my arms and run away with her and nurse her back to health, for she would probably object to such a course as strongly as her mother; and later on, when she gets well again, she will go back to school, and grow coarse and bouncing and leathery like the others, affording the parson, in three or four years' time, a fresh occasion for grief over deadly sin. "If one could only get hold of the children!" I sighed, as I went up the steps into the schoolhouse; "catch them young, and put them in a garden, with no older people of their own class for ever teaching them by example what is ugly, and unworthy, and gross."

Afternoon school was going on, and the assistant teacher was making the children read aloud in turns. In winter, when they would be glad of a warm, roomy place in which to spend their afternoons, school is only in the morning; and in summer, when the thirstiest after knowledge are apt to be less keen, it is both morning and afternoon. The arrangement is so mysterious that it must be providential. Herr Schenk, the head master, was away giving my babies their daily lessons, and his assistant, a youth in spectacles but yet of pugnacious aspect, was sitting in the master's desk, exercising a pretty turn for sarcasm in his running comments on the reading. A more complete waste of breath and brilliancy can hardly be imagined. He is not yet, however, married, and marriage is a great chastener. The children all stood up when I came in, and the teacher ceased sharpening his wits on a dulness that could not feel, and with many bows put a chair for me and begged me to sit on it. I did sit on it, and asked that they might go on with the lesson, as I had only come in for a minute on my way down the street. The reading was accordingly resumed, but unaccompanied this time by sarcasms. What faces! What dull, apathetic, low, coarse faces! On one side sat those from ten to fourteen, with not a hopeful face among them, and on the other those from six to ten, with one single little boy who looked as though he could have no business among the rest, so bright was he, so attentive, so curiously dignified. Poor children— what could the parson hope to make of beings whose expressions told so plainly of the sort of nature within? Those that did not look dull looked cunning, and all the girls on the older side had the faces of women. I began to feel dreadfully depressed. "See what you have done," I whispered angrily to my conscience—"made me wretched without doing anybody else any good." "The old woman with the headache is happy in the hopes of grapes," it replied, seeking to justify itself, "and Lotte is to have some jelly." "Grapes! Jelly!

Futility unutterable. I can't bear this, and am going home." The teacher inquired whether the children should sing something to my graciousness; perhaps he was ashamed of their reading, and indeed I never heard anything like it. "Oh yes," I said, resigned, but outwardly smiling kindly with the self-control natural to woman. They sang, or rather screamed, a hymn, and so frightfully loud and piercingly that the very windows shook. "My dear," explained the Man of Wrath, when I complained one Sunday on our way home from church of the terrible quality and volume of the music, "it frightens Satan away."

Our numerous godchildren were not in school because, as we have only lived here three years, they are not yet old enough to share in the blessings of education. I stand godmother to the girls, and the Man of Wrath to the boys, and as all the babies are accordingly named after us the village swarms with tiny Elizabeths and Boys of Wrath. A hunchbacked woman, unfit for harder work, looks after the babies during the day in a room set apart for that purpose, so that the mothers may not be hampered in their duties at the farm; they have only to carry the babies there in the morning, and fetch them away again in the evening, and can feel that they are safe and well looked after. But many of them, for some reason too cryptic to fathom, prefer to lock them up in their room, exposed to all the perils that surround an inquiring child just able to walk, and last winter one little creature was burnt to death, sacrificed to her mother's stupidity. This mother, a fair type of the intelligence prevailing in the village, made a great fire in her room before going out, so that when she came back at noon there would still be some with which to cook the dinner, left a baby in a perambulator, and a little Elizabeth of three loose in the room, locked the door, put the key in her pocket, and went off to work. When she came back to get the dinner ready, the baby was still crowing placidly in its perambulator, and the little Elizabeth, with all the clothes burnt off her body, was lying near the grate dead. Of course the mother was wild with grief, distracted, raving, desperate, and of course all the other women were shocked and horrified; but point the moral as we might, we could not bring them to see that it was an avoidable misfortune with nothing whatever to do with the *Finger Gottes*, and the mothers who preferred locking their babies up alone to sending them to be looked after, went on doing so as undisturbed as though what had occurred could in no wise be a lesson to themselves.

"Pray, *Herr Lehrer*, why are those two little boys sitting over there on that seat all by themselves and not singing?" I asked at the conclusion of the hymn.

"That, gracious lady, is the vermin bench. It is necessary to keep—"

"Oh yes, yes—I quite understand—good afternoon. Good-bye, children, you have sung very nicely indeed."

"Now," said I to myself, when I was safely out in the street again, "I am going home."

"Oh, not yet," at once protested my unmanageable conscience; "your favourite old woman lives in the next cottage, and surely you are not going to leave her out?"

"I see plainly," I replied, "that I shall never be quite comfortable till I have got rid of *you*" and in I went to the next house.

The entrance was full of three women—the entrances here are narrow, and the women wide—and they all looked more cheerful than seemed reasonable. They stood aside to let me pass, and when I opened the door I found the room equally full of women, looking equally happy, and talking eagerly.

"Why, what is happening?" I asked the nearest one. "Is there a party?"

She turned round, grinning broadly in obvious delight. "The old lady died in her sleep," she said, "and was found this morning dead in her bed. I was in here only yesterday, and she said—" I turned abruptly and went out again. All those gloating women, hovering round the poor bodythat was clothed on a sudden by death with a wonderful dignity and nobleness, made me ashamed of being a woman. Not a man was there,—clearly a superior race of beings. In the entrance I met the Frau Inspector coming in to arrange matters, and she turned and walked with me a little way.

"The old lady was better off than we thought," she remarked, "and has left a very good black silk dress to be buried in."

"A black silk dress?" I repeated.

"And everything to match in goodness—nice leather shoes, good stockings, under-things all trimmed with crochet, real whalebone corsets, and a quite new pair of white kid gloves. She must have saved for a long time to have it all so nice."

"But," I said, "I don't understand. I have never had anything to do yet with death, and have not thought of these things. Are not people, then, just buried in a shroud?"

"A shroud?" It was her turn not to understand.

"A sheet sort of thing."

She smiled in a highly superior manner. "Oh dear, no," she said, "we are none of us quite so poor as that."

I glanced down at her as she walked beside me. She is a short woman, and carries weight. She was smiling almost pityingly at my ignorance of what is due, even after death, to ourselves and public opinion.

"The very poorest," she said, "manage to scrape a whole set of clothes together for their funerals. A very poor couple came here a few months ago, and before the man had time to earn anything he died. The wife came to me (the gracious lady was absent), and on her knees implored me to give her a suit for him—she had only been able to afford the *Sterbehemd*, and was frantic at the thought of what the neighbours would say if he had nothing on but that, and said she would be haunted by shame and remorse all the rest of her life. We bought a nice black suit, and tie, and gloves, and he really looked very well. She will be dressed to-night," she went on, as I said nothing; "the dressers come with the coffin, and it will be a nice funeral. I used to wonder what she did with her pension money, and never could persuade her to buy herself a bit of meat. But of course she was saving for this. They are beautiful corsets."

"What utter waste!" I ejaculated.

"Waste?"

"Yes—utter waste and foolishness. Foolishness, not to have bought a few little comforts, waste of the money, and waste of the clothes. Is there any meaning, sense, or use whatever in burying a good black silk dress?"

"It would be a scandal not to be buried decently," she replied, manifestly surprised at my warmth, "and the neighbours respect her much more now that they know what nice clothes she had bought for her funeral. Nothing is wanting. I even found a box with a gold brooch in it, and a bracelet."

"I suppose, then, as many of her belongings as will go into the coffin will be buried too, in order to still further impress the neighbours?" I asked—"her feather bed, for instance, and anything else of use and value?"

"No, only what she has on, and the brushes and combs and towels that were used in dressing her."

"How ugly and how useless!" I said with a shiver of disgust.

"It is the custom," was her tranquil reply.

Suddenly an unpleasant thought struck me, and I burst out emphatically,

"Nothing but a shroud is to be put on me."

"Oh no," she said, looking up at me with a face meant to be full of the most reassuring promises of devotion, "the gracious lady may be quite certain that if I am still here she will have on her most beautiful ball dress and finest linen, and that the whole neighbourhood shall see for themselves how well *Herrschaften* know what is due to them."

"I shall give directions," I repeated with increased energy, "that there is only to be a shroud."

"Oh no, no," she protested, smiling as though she were humouring a spoilt and eccentric child, "such a thing could never be permitted. What would our feelings be when we remembered that the gracious lady had not received her dues, and what would the neighbours say?"

"I'll have nothing but a shroud!" I cried in great wrath—and then stopped short, and burst out laughing. "What an absurd and gruesome conversation," I said, holding out my hand. "Good-bye, Frau Inspector, I am sure you are wanted in that cottage."

She made me a curtsey and turned back. I walked out of the village and through the fir wood and the meadow as quickly as I could, opened the gate into my garden, went down the most sheltered path, flung myself on the grass in a quiet nook, and said aloud "Ugh!"

It is a well-known exclamation of disgust, and is thus inadequately expressed in writing.

AUGUST

August 5th.—August has come, and has clothed the hills with golden lupins, and filled the grassy banks with harebells. The yellow fields of lupins are so gorgeous on cloudless days that I have neglected the forests lately and drive in the open, so that I may revel in their scent while feasting my eyes on their beauty. The slope of a hill clothed with this orange wonder and seen against the sky is one of those sights which make me so happy that it verges on pain. The straight, vigorous flower-spikes are something like hyacinths, but all aglow with a divine intensity of brightness that a yellow hyacinth never yet possessed and never will; and then they are not waxy, but velvety, and their leaves are not futile drooping things, but delicate, strong sprays of an exquisite grey-green, with a bloom on them that throws a mist over the whole field; and as for the perfume, it surely is the perfume of Paradise. The plant is altogether lovely—shape, growth, flower, and leaf, and the horses have to wait very patiently once we get among them, for I can never have enough of sitting quite still in those fair fields of glory. Not far from here there is a low series of hills running north and south, absolutely without trees, and at the foot of them, on the east side, is a sort of road, chiefly stones, but yet with patience to be driven over, and on the other side of this road a plain stretches away towards the east and south; and hills and plain are now one sheet of gold. I have driven there at all hours of the day—I cannot keep away—and I have seen them early in the morning, and at mid-day, and in the afternoon, and I have seen them in the evening by moonlight, when all the intensity was washed out of the colour and into the scent; but just as the sun drops behind the little hills is the supreme moment, when the splendour is so dazzling that you feel as though you must have reached the very gates of heaven. So strong was this feeling the other day that I actually got out of the carriage, being impulsive, and began almost involuntarily to climb the hill, half expecting to see the glories of the New Jerusalem all spread out before me when I should reach the top; and it came with quite a shock of disappointment to find there was nothing there but the prose of potato-fields, and a sandy road with home-going calves kicking up its dust, and in the distance our neighbour's *Schloss*, and the New Jerusalem just as far off as ever.

It is a relief to me to write about these things that I so much love, for I do not talk of them lest I should be regarded as a person who rhapsodizes, and there is no nuisance more intolerable than having somebody's rhapsodies thrust upon you when you have no enthusiasm of your own that at all corresponds. I know this so well that I generally succeed in keeping quiet; but sometimes even now, after years of study in the art of holding my tongue, some stray fragment of what I feel does occasionally come out, and then I am at once pulled up and brought to my senses by the well-known cold stare of utter incomprehension, or the look of indulgent superiority that awaits any exposure of a feeling not in the least understood. How is it that you should feel so vastly superior whenever you do not happen to enter into or understand your neighbour's thoughts when, as a matter of fact, your not being able to do so is less a sign of folly in your neighbour than of incompleteness in yourself? I am quite sure that if I were to take most or any of my friends to those pleasant yellow fields they would notice nothing except the exceeding joltiness of the road; and if I were so ill-advised as to lift up a corner of my heart, and let them see how full it was of wonder and delight, they would first look blank, and then decide mentally that they were in the unpleasant situation of driving over a stony road with that worst form of idiot, a bore, and so fall into the mood of self-commiseration which is such a solace to us in our troubles. Yet it is painful being suppressed for ever and ever, and I believe the torments of such a state, when unduly prolonged, are more keenly felt by a woman than a man, she having, in spite of her protestations, a good deal of the ivy nature still left in her, and an unhealthy craving for sympathy and support. When I drive to the lupins and see them all spread out as far as eye can reach in perfect beauty of colour and scent and bathed in the mild August sunshine, I feel I must send for somebody to come and look at them with me, and talk about them to me, and share in the pleasure; and when I run over the list of my friends and try to find one who would enjoy them, I am frightened once more at the solitariness in which we each of us live. I have, it is true, a great many friends—people with whom it is pleasant to spend an afternoon if such afternoons are not repeated often, and if you are careful not to stir more than the surface of things, but among them all there is only one who has, roughly, the same tastes that I have; and even her sympathies have limitations, and she declares for instance with emphasis that she would not at all like to be a goose-girl. I wonder why. Our friendship nearly came to an end over the goose-girl, so unexpectedly inflaming did the subject turn out to be. Of all professions, if I had liberty of choice, I would choose to be a gardener, and if nobody would have me in that capacity I would like to be a goose-girl, and sit in the greenest of fields minding those delightfully plump, placid geese, whiter and more leisurely than the clouds on a calm summer morning, their very waddle in its lazy deliberation soothing and salutary to a fretted spirit that has been too long on the stretch. The fields geese feed in are so specially charming, so green and low-lying, with little clumps of trees and bushes, and a pond or boggy bit of ground somewhere near, and a profusion of those delicate field flowers that look so lovely growing and are so unsatisfactory and fade so quickly if you try to arrange them in your rooms. For six months of the year I would be happier than any queen I ever heard of, minding the fat white things. I would begin in April with the king-cups, and leave off in September with the blackberries, and I would keep one eye on the geese, and one on the volume of Wordsworth I should have with me, and I would be present in this way at the procession of the months, the first three all white and yellow, and the last three gorgeous with the lupin fields and the blues and purples and crimsons that clothe the hedges and ditches in a wonderful variety of shades, and dye the grass near the water in great patches. Then in October I would shut up my Wordsworth, go back to civilised life, and probably assist at the eating of the geese one after the other, with a proper thankfulness for the amount of edification I had from first to last extracted from them.

I believe in England goose eating is held to be of doubtful refinement, and is left to one's servants. Here roast goose stuffed with apples is a dish loved quite openly and simply by people who would consider that the number of their quarterings raises them above any suspicion as to the refinement of their tastes, however many geese they may eat, and however much they may enjoy them; and I remember one lady, whose ancestors, probably all having loved goose, reached back up to a quite giddy antiquity, casting a gloom over a dinner table by removing as much of the skin or crackling of the goose as she could when it came to her, remarking, amidst a mournful silence, that it was her favourite part. No doubt it was. The misfortune was that it happened also to be the favourite part of the line of guests who came after her, and who saw themselves forced by the hard laws of propriety to affect an indifferent dignity of bearing at the very moment when their one feeling was a fierce desire to rise up and defend at all costs their right to a share of skin. She had, I remember, very pretty little white hands like tiny claws, and wore beautiful rings, and sitting opposite her, and free myself from any undue passion for goose, I had leisure to watch the rapid way in which she disposed of the skin, her rings and the whiteness of her hands flashing up and down as she used her knife and fork with the awful dexterity only seen in perfection in the Fatherland. I am afraid that as a nation we think rather more of our eating and drinking than is reasonable, and this no doubt explains why so many of us, by the time we are thirty, have lost the original classicality of our contour. Walking in the streets of a town you are almost sure to catch the word*essen* in the talk of the passers-by; and *das Essen*, combined, of course, with the drinking made necessary by its exaggerated indulgence, constitutes the chief happiness of the middle and lower classes. Any story-book or novel you take up is full of feeling descriptions of what everybody ate and drank, and there are a great many more meals than kisses; so that the novel-reader who expects a love-tale, finds with disgust that he is put off with *menus*. The upper classes have so many other amusements that *das Essen* ceases to be one, and they are as thin as all the rest of the world; but if the curious wish to see how very largely it fills the lives, or that part of their lives that they reserve for pleasure, of the middle classes, it is a good plan to go to seaside places during the months of July and August, when the schools close, and the *bourgeoisie* realises the dream in which it has been indulging the whole year, of hotel life with a tremendous dinner every day at one o'clock.

The April baby was a weak little creature in her first years, and the doctor ordered as specially bracing a seaside resort frequented solely by the middle classes, and there for three succeeding years I took her; and while she rolled on the sands and grew brown and lusty, I was dull, and fell to watching the other tourists. Their time, it appeared, was spent in ruminating over the delights of the meal that was eaten, and in preparing their bodies by gentlest exercise for the delights of the meal that was to come. They passed their mornings on the sands, the women doing fancy work in order that they might look busy, and the men strolling aimlessly about near them with field-glasses, and nautical caps, and long cloaks of a very dreadful pattern reaching to their heels and making them look like large women, called Havelocks,—all of them waiting with more or less open eagerness for one o'clock, the great moment to which they had been looking forward ever since the day before, to arrive. They used to file in when the bell rang with a sort of silent solemnity, a contemplative collectedness, which is best described by the word *recueillement*, and ate all the courses, however many there were, in a hot room full of flies and sunlight.

The dinner lasted a good hour and a half, and at the end of that time they would begin to straggle out again, flushed and using toothpicks as they strolled to the tables under the trees, where the exhausted waiters would presently bring them breakfast-cups of coffee and cakes. They lingered about an hour over this, and then gradually disappeared to their rooms, where they slept, I suppose, for from then till about six a death-like stillness reigned in the place and April and I had it all to ourselves. Towards six, slow couples would be seen crawling along the path by the shore and panting up into the woods, this being the only exercise of the day, and necessary if they would eat their suppers with appreciation; and April and I, peering through the bracken out of the nests of moss we used to make in the afternoons, could see them coming up through the trees after the climb up the cliff, the husband with his Havelock over his arm, a little in front, wiping his face and gasping, the wife in her tight silk dress, her bonnet strings undone, a cloak and an umbrella, and very often a small mysterious basket as well to carry, besides holding up her dress, very stout and very uncomfortable and very breathless, panting along behind; and however much she had to carry, and however fat and helpless she was, and however steep the hill, and however much dinner she had eaten, the idea that her husband might have taken her cloak and her umbrella and her basket and carried them for her would never have struck either of them. If it had by some strange chance entered his head, he would have reasoned that he was as stout as she was, that he had eaten as much dinner, that he was several years older, and that it was her cloak. Logic is so irresistible.

To go on eating long after you have ceased to be hungry has fascinations, apparently, that are difficult to withstand, and if it gives you so much pleasure that the resulting inability to move without gasping is accepted with the meekness of martyrs, who shall say that you are wrong? My not myself liking a large dinner at one o'clock is not a reason for my thinking I am superior to those who do. Their excesses, it is true, are not my excesses, but then neither are mine theirs; and what about the days of idleness I spend, doing nothing from early till late but lie on the grass watching clouds? If I were to murmur gluttons, could not they, from their point of view, retort with conviction fool? All those maxims about judging others by yourself, and putting yourself in another person's place, are not, I am afraid, reliable. I had them dinned into me constantly as a child, and I was constantly trying to obey them, and constantly was astonished at the unexpected results I arrived at; and now I know that it is a proof of artlessness to suppose that other people will think and feel and hope and enjoy what you do and in the same way that you do. If an officious friend had stood in that breathless couple's path and told them in glowing terms how much happier they would be if they lived their life a little more fully and from its other sides, how much more delightful to stride along gaily together in their walks, with wind enough for talk and laughter, how pleasant if the man were muscular and in good condition and the woman brisk and wiry, and that they only had to do as he did and live on cold meat and toast, and drink nothing, to be as blithe as birds, do you think they would have so much as understood him? Cold meat and toast? Instead of what they had just been enjoying so intensely? Miss that soup made of the inner mysteries of geese, those eels stewed in beer, the roast pig with red cabbage, the venison basted with sour cream and served with beans in vinegar and cranberry jam, the piled-up masses of vanilla ice, the pumpernickel and cheese, the apples and pears on the top of that, and the big cups of coffee and cakes on the top of the apples and pears? Really a quick walk over the heather with a wiry wife would hardly make up for the loss of such a dinner; and besides, might not a wiry wife turn out to be a questionable blessing? And so they would pity the nimble friend who wasted his life in taking exercise and missed all its pleasures, and the man of toast and early rising would regard them with profound disgust if simple enough to think himself better than they, and, if he possessed an open mind, would merely return their pity with more of his own; so that, I suppose, everybody would be pleased, for the charm of pitying one's neighbour, though subtle, is undeniable.

I remember when I was at the age when people began to call me *Backfisch*, and my mother dressed me in a little scarlet coat with big pearl buttons, and my eyes turned down because I was shy, and my nose turned up because I was impudent, one summer at the seaside with my governess we noticed in our walks a solitary lady of dignified appearance, who spoke to no one, and seemed for ever wrapped in distant and lofty philosophic speculations. "She's thinking about Kant and the nebular hypothesis," I decided to myself, having once heard some men with long beards talking of both those things, and they all had had that same far-away look in their eyes. "*Qu'est-ce que c'est une hypothese nebuleuse, Mademoiselle?*" I said aloud.

"*Tenez-vous bien, et marchez d'une facon convenable,*" she replied sharply.

"*Qu'est-ce que c'est une hypothese—*"

"*Vous etes trap jeune pour comprendre ces choses.*"

"*Oh alors vous ne savez pas vous-meme!*" I cried triumphantly, "*Sans cela vous me diriez.*"

"*Elisabeth, vous ecrirez, des que nous rentrons, leverbePrier le bon Dieu de m'Aider a ne plus Etre siImpertinente.*"

She was an ingenious young woman, and the verbs I had to write as punishments were of the most elaborate and complicated nature—*Demander pardon pour Avoir Siffle comme un Gaminquelconque, Vouloir ne plus Oublier de Nettoyer mesOngles, Essayer de ne pas tant Aimer les Poudings*, are but a few examples of her achievements in this particular branch of discipline.

That very day at the *table d'hote* the abstracted lady sat next to me. A *ragout* of some sort was handed round, and after I had taken some she asked me, before helping herself, what it was.

"Snails," I replied promptly, wholly unchastened by the prayers I had just been writing out in every tense.

"Snails! *Ekelig.*" And she waved the waiter loftily away, and looked on with much superciliousness at the rest of us enjoying ourselves.

"What! You do not eat this excellent *ragout*?" asked her other neighbour, a hot man, as he finished clearing his plate and had time to observe the emptiness of hers. "You do not like calves' tongues and mushrooms? *Sonderbar.*"

I still can see the poor lady's face as she turned on me more like a tigress than the impassive person she had been a moment before. "*Sieunverschamter Backfisch!*" she hissed. "My favourite dish—I have you to thank for spoiling my repast—my day!" And in a frenzy of rage she gripped my arm as though she would have shaken me then and there in the face of the multitude, while I sat appalled at the consequences of indulging a playful fancy at the wrong time.

Which story, now I come to think of it, illustrates less the tremendous importance of food in our country than the exceeding odiousness of*Backfisch* in scarlet coats.

August 10th.—My idea of a garden is that it should be beautiful from end to end, and not start off in front of the house with fireworks, going off at its farthest limit into sheer sticks. The standard reached beneath the windows should at least be kept up, if it cannot be surpassed, right away through, and the German popular plan in this matter quite discarded of concentrating all the available splendour of the establishment into the supreme effort of carpet-bedding and glass balls on pedestals in front of the house, in the hope that the stranger, carefully kept in that part, and on no account allowed to wander, will infer an equal magnificence throughout the entire domain; whereas he knows very well all the time that the landscape round the corner consists of fowls and dust-bins. Disliking this method, I have tried to make my garden increase in loveliness, if not in tidiness, the farther you get into it; and the visitor who thinks in his innocence as he emerges from the shade of the verandah that he sees the best before him, is artfully conducted from beauty to beauty till he beholds what I think is the most charming bit, the silver birch and azalea plantation down at the very end. This is the boundary of my kingdom on the south side, a blaze of colour in May and June, across which you see the placid meadows stretching away to a distant wood; and from its contemplation the ideal visitor returns to the house a refreshed and better man. That is the sort of person one enjoys taking round—the man (or woman) who, loving gardens, would go any distance to see one; who comes to appreciate, and compare, and admire; who has a garden of his own that he lives in and loves; and whose talk and criticisms are as dew to the thirsty gardening soul, all too accustomed in this respect to droughts. He knows as well as I do what work, what patience, what study and watching, what laughter at failures, what fresh starts with undiminished zeal, and what bright, unalterable faith are represented by the flowers in my garden. He knows what I have done for it, and he knows what it has done for me, and how it has been and will be more and more a place of joys, a place of lessons, a place of health, a place of miracles, and a place of sure and never-changing peace.

Living face to face with nature makes it difficult for one to be discouraged. Moles and late frosts, both of which are here in abundance, have often grieved and disappointed me, but even these, my worst enemies, have not succeeded in making me feel discouraged. Not once till now have I got farther in that direction than the purely negative state of not being encouraged; and whenever I reach that state I go for a brisk walk in the sunshine and come back cured. It makes one so healthy to live in a garden, so healthy in mind as well as body, and when I say moles and late frosts are my worst enemies, it only shows how I could not now if I tried sit down and brood over my own or my neighbour's sins, and how the breezes in my garden have blown away all those worries and vexations and bitternesses that are the lot of those who live in a crowd. The most severe frost that ever nipped the hopes of a year is better to my thinking than having to listen to one malignant truth or lie, and I would rather have a mole busy burrowing tunnels under each of my rose trees and letting the air get at their roots than face a single greeting where no kindness is. How can you help being happy if you are healthy and in the place you want to be? A man once made it a reproach that I should be so happy, and told me everybody has crosses, and that we live in a vale of woe. I mentioned moles as my principal cross, and pointed to the huge black mounds with which they had decorated the tennis-court, but I could not agree to the vale of woe, and could not be shaken in my belief that the world is a dear and lovely place, with everything in it to make us happy so long as we walk humbly and diet ourselves. He pointed out that sorrow and sickness were sure to come, and seemed quite angry with me when I suggested that they too could be borne perhaps with cheerfulness. "And have not even such things their sunny side?" I exclaimed. "When I am steeped to the lips in diseases and doctors, I shall at least have something to talk about that interests my women friends, and need not sit as I do now wondering what I shall say next and wishing they would go." He replied that all around me lay misery, sin, and suffering, and that every person not absolutely blinded by selfishness must be aware of it and must realise the seriousness and tragedy of existence. I asked him whether my being miserable and discontented would help any one or make him less wretched; and he said that we all had to take up our burdens. I assured him I would not shrink from mine, though I felt secretly ashamed of it when I remembered that it was only moles, and he went away with a grave face and a shaking head, back to his wife and his eleven children. I heard soon afterwards that a twelfth baby had been born and his wife had died, and in dying had turned her face with a quite unaccountable impatience away from him and to the wall; and the rumour of his piety reached even into my garden, and how he had said, as he closed her eyes, "It is the Will of God." He was a missionary.

But of what use is it telling a woman with a garden that she ought really to be ashamed of herself for being happy? The fresh air is so buoyant that it lifts all remarks of that sort away off you and leaves you laughing. They get wafted away on the scent of the stocks, and you stand in the sun looking round at your cheerful flowers, and more than ever persuaded that it is a good and blessed thing to be thankful. Oh a garden is a sweet, sane refuge to have! Whether I am tired because I have enjoyed myself too much, or tired because I have lectured the servants too much, or tired because I have talked to missionaries too much, I have only to come down the verandah steps into the garden to be at once restored to quiet, and serenity, and my real and natural self. I could almost fancy sometimes that as I come down the steps, gentle hands of blessing have been laid on my head. I suppose I feel so because of the hush that descends on my soul when I get out of the close, restless house into that silent purity. Sometimes I sit for hours in the south walk by the verandah just listening and watching. It is so private there, though directly beneath the windows, that it is one of my favourite places. There are no bedrooms on that side of the house, only the Man of Wrath's and my day-rooms, so that servants cannot see me as I stand there enjoying myself. If they did or could, I should simply never go there, for nothing is so utterly destructive to meditation as to know that probably somebody inquisitive is eyeing you from behind a curtain. The loveliest garden I know is spoilt to my thinking by the impossibility of getting out of sight of the house, which stares down at you, Argus-eyed and unblinking, into whatever corner you may shuffle. Perfect house and perfect garden, lying in that land of lovely gardens, England, the garden just the right size for perfection, not a weed ever admitted, every dandelion and daisy—those friends of the unaspiring—routed out years ago, the borders exquisite examples of taste, the turf so faultless that you hardly like to walk on it for fear of making it dusty, and the whole quite uninhabitable for people of my solitary tendencies because, go where you will, you are overlooked. Since I have lived in this big straggling place, full of paths and copses where I am sure of being left alone, with wide fields and heath and forests beyond, and so much room to move and breathe in, I feel choked, oppressed, suffocated, in anything small and perfect. I spent a very happy afternoon in that little English paradise, but I came away quite joyfully, and with many a loving thought of my own dear ragged garden, and all the corners in it where the anemones twinkle in the spring like stars, and where there is so much nature and so little art. It will grow I know sweeter every year, but it is too big ever to be perfect and to get to look so immaculate that the diseased imagination conjures up visions of housemaids issuing forth each morning in troops and dusting every separate flower with feather brushes. Nature herself is untidy, and in a garden she ought to come first, and Art with her brooms and clipping-shears follow humbly behind. Art has such a good time in the house, where she spreads herself over the walls, and hangs herself up gorgeously at the windows, and lurks in the sofa cushions, and breaks out in an eruption of pots wherever pots are possible, that really she should be content to take the second place out of doors. And how dreadful to meet a gardener and a wheelbarrow at every turn—which is precisely what happens to one in the perfect garden. My gardener, whose deafness is more than compensated for by the keenness of his eyesight, very soon remarked the scowl that distorted my features whenever I met one of his assistants in my favourite walks, and I never meet them now. I think he must keep them chained up to the cucumber-frames, so completely have they disappeared, and he only lets them loose when he knows I am driving, or at meals, or in bed. But is it not irritating to be sitting under your favourite tree, pencil in hand, and eyes turned skywards expectant of the spark from heaven that never falls, and then to have a man appear suddenly round the corner who immediately begins quite close to you to tear up the earth with his fangs? No one will ever know the number of what I believe are technically known as winged words that I have missed bringing down through interruptions of this kind. Indeed, as I look through these pages I see I must have missed them all, for I can find nothing anywhere with even a rudimentary approach to wings.

Sometimes when I am in a critical mood and need all my faith to keep me patient, I shake my head at the unshornness of the garden as gravely as the missionary shook his head at me. The bushes stretch across the paths, and, catching at me as I go by, remind me that they have not been pruned; the teeming plant life rejoices on the lawns free from all interference from men and hoes; the pinks are closely nibbled off at the beginning of each summer by selfish hares intent on their own gratification; most of the beds bear the marks of nocturnal foxes; and the squirrels spend their days wantonly biting off and flinging down the tender young shoots of the firs. Then there is the boy who drives the donkey and water-cart round the garden, and who has an altogether reprehensible habit of whisking round corners and slicing off bits of the lawn as he whisks. "But you can't alter these things, my good soul," I say to myself. "If you want to get rid of the hares and foxes, you must consent to have wire-netting, which is odious, right round your garden. And you are always saying you like weeds, so why grumble at your lawns? And it doesn't hurt you much if the squirrels do break bits off your firs—the firs must have had that happening to them years and years before you were born, yet they still flourish. As for boys, they certainly are revolting creatures. Can't you catch this one when he isn't looking and pop him in his own water-barrel and put the lid on?"

I asked the June baby, who had several times noticed with indignation the culpable indifference of this boy in regard to corners, whether she did not think that would be a good way of disposing of him. She is a great disciplinarian, and was loud in her praise of the plan; but the other two demurred. "He might go dead in there," said the May baby, apprehensively. "And he is such a naughty boy," said April, who had watched his reckless conduct with special disgust, "that if he once went dead he'd go straight to the *Holle* and stay all the time with the *diable*."

That was the first French word I have heard them say: strange and sulphureous first-fruits of Seraphine's teaching!

We were going round the garden in a procession, I with a big pair of scissors, and the Three with baskets, into one of which I put fresh flowers, and into the others flowers that were beginning to seed, dead flowers, and seed-pods. The garden was quivering in heat and light; rain in the morning had brought out all the snails and all the sweetness, and we were very happy, as we always are, I when I am knee-deep in flowers, and the babies when they can find new sorts of snails to add to their collections. These collections are carried about in cardboard boxes all day, and at night each baby has hers on the chair beside her bed. Sometimes the snails get out and crawl over the beds, but the babies do not mind. Once when April woke in the morning she was overjoyed by finding a friendly little one on her cheek. Clearly babies of iron nerves and pellucid consciences.

"So you do know some French," I said as I snipped off poppy-heads; "you have always pretended you don't."

"Oh, keep the poppies, mummy," cried April, as she saw them tumbling into her basket; "if you picks them and just leaves them, then they ripes and is good for such a many things."

"Tell me about the *diable*," I said, "and you shall keep the poppies."

272

"He isn't nice, that *diable*," she said, starting off at once with breathless eloquence. "Seraphine says there was one time a girl and a boy who went for a walk, and there were two ways, and one way goes where stones is, but it goes to the *lieber Gott*; and the girl went that way till she came to a door, and the *lieber Gott* made the door opened and she went in, and that's the *Himmel*."

"And the boy?"

"Oh, he was a naughty boy and went the other way where there is a tree, and on the tree is written, 'Don't go this way or you'll be dead,' and he said, 'That is one *betise*,' and did go in the way and got to the *Holle*, and there he gets whippings when he doesn't make what the *diable* says."

"That's because he was so naughty," explained the May baby, holding up an impressive finger, "and didn't want to go to the *Himmel* and didn't love glory."

"All boys are naughty," said June, "and I don't love them."

"*Nous allons parler Francais*" I announced, desirous of finding out whether their whole stock was represented by *diable* and *betise*; "I believe you can all speak it quite well."

There was no answer. I snipped off sweet-pea pods and began to talk French at a great rate, asking questions as I snipped, and trying to extract answers, and getting none. The silence behind me grew ominous. Presently I heard a faint sniff, and the basket being held up to me began to shake. I bent down quickly and looked under April's sun-bonnet. She was crying great dreadful tears, and rubbing her eyes hard with her one free hand.

"Why, you most blessed of babies," I exclaimed, kneeling down and putting my arms round her, "what in the world is the matter?"

She looked at me with grieved and doubting eyes. "Such a mother to talk French to her child!" she sobbed.

I threw down the scissors, picked her up, and carried her up and down the path, comforting her with all the soft words I knew and suppressing my desire to smile. "That's not French, is it?" I whispered at the end of a long string of endearments, beginning, I believe, with such flights of rhetoric as priceless blessing and angel baby, and ending with a great many kisses.

"No, no," she answered, patting my face and looking infinitely relieved, "that is pretty, and how mummies always talks. Proper mummies never speak French—only Seraphines." And she gave me a very tight hug, and a kiss that transferred all her tears to my face; and I set her down and, taking out my handkerchief, tried to wipe off the traces of my attempt at governessing from her cheeks. I wonder how it is that whenever babies cry, streaks of mud immediately appear on their faces. I believe I could cry for a week, and yet produce no mud.

"I'll tell you what I'll do, babies," I said, anxious to restore complete serenity on such a lovely day, and feeling slightly ashamed of my uncalled-for zeal—indeed, April was right, and proper mothers leave lessons and torments to somebody else, and devote all their energies to petting—"I'll give a ball after tea."

"*Yes!*" shouted three exultant voices, "and invite all the babies!"

"So now you must arrange what you are going to wear. I suppose you'd like the same supper as usual? Run away to Seraphine and tell her to get you ready."

They seized their baskets and their boxes of snails and rushed off into the bushes, calling for Seraphine with nothing but rapture in their voices, and French and the *diable* quite forgotten.

These balls are given with great ceremony two or three times a year. They last about an hour, during which I sit at the piano in the library playing cheerful tunes, and the babies dance passionately round the pillar. They refuse to waltz together, which is perhaps a good thing, for if they did there would always be one left over to be a wallflower and gnash her teeth; and when they want to dance squares they are forced by the stubbornness of numbers to dance triangles. At the appointed hour they knock at the door, and come in attired in the garments they have selected as appropriate (at this last ball the April baby wore my shooting coat, the May baby had a muff, and the June baby carried Seraphine's umbrella), and, curtseying to me, each one makes some remark she thinks suitable to the occasion.

"How's your husband?" June asked me last time, in the defiant tones she seems to think proper at a ball.

"Very well, thank you."

"Oh, that is nice."

"Mine isn't vely well," remarked April, cheerfully.

"Indeed?"

"No, he has got some tummy-aches."

"Dear me!"

"He was coming else, and had such fine twowsers to wear—pink ones with wibbons."

After a little more graceful conversation of this kind the ball begins, and at the end of an hour's dancing, supper, consisting of radishes and lemonade, is served on footstools; and when they have cleared it up even to the leaves and stalks of the radishes, they rise with much dignity, express in proper terms their sense of gratitude for the entertainment, curtsey, and depart to bed, where they spend a night of horror, the prey of the awful dreams naturally resulting from so unusual a combination as radishes and babies. That is why my balls are rare festivals—the babies will insist on having radishes for the supper, and I, as a decent parent with a proper sense of my responsibilities, am forced accordingly to restrict my invitations to two, at the most three, in a year.

When this last one was over I felt considerably exhausted, and had hardly sufficient strength to receive their thanks with civility. An hour's jig-playing with the thermometer at 90 leaves its marks on the most robust; and when they were in bed, and the supper beginning to do its work, I ordered the carriage and the kettle with a view to seeking repose in the forest, taking the opportunity of escaping before the Man of Wrath should come in to dinner. The weather has been very hot for a long time, but the rain in the morning had had a wonderful effect on my flowers, and as I drove away I could not help noticing how charming the borders in front of the house were looking, with their white hollyhocks, and white snapdragons, and fringe of feathery marigolds. This gardener has already changed the whole aspect of the place, and I believe I have found the right man at last. He is very young for a head gardener, but on that account all the more anxious to please me and keep his situation; and it is a great comfort to have to do with somebody who watches and interprets rightly every expression of one's face and does not need much talking to. He makes mistakes sometimes in the men he engages, just as I used to when I did the engaging, and he had one poor young man as apprentice who very soon, like the first of my three meek gardeners, went mad. His madness was of a harmless nature and took a literary form; indeed, that was all they had against him, that he would write books. He used to sit in the early morning on my special seats in the garden, and strictly meditate the thankless muse when he ought to have been carting manure; and he made his fellow-apprentices unspeakably wretched

275

by shouting extracts from Schiller at them across the intervening gooseberry bushes. Let me hasten to say that I had never spoken to him, and should not even have known what he was like if he had not worn eyeglasses, so that the Man of Wrath's insinuation that I affect the sanity of my gardeners is entirely without justification. The eyeglasses struck me as so odd on a gardener that I asked who he was, and was told that he had been studying for the Bar, but could not pass the examinations, and had taken up gardening in the hope of getting back his health and spirits. I thought this a very sensible plan, and was beginning to feel interested in him when one day the post brought me a registered packet containing a manuscript play he had written called "The Lawyer as Gardener," dedicated to me. The Man of Wrath and I were both in it, the Man of Wrath, however, only in the list of characters, so that he should not feel hurt, I suppose, for he never appeared on the scenes at all. As for me, I was represented as going about quoting Tolstoi in season and out of season to the gardeners—a thing I protest I never did. The young man was sent home to his people, and I have been asking myself ever since what there is about this place that it should so persistently produce books and lunacy?

On the outskirts of the forest, where shafts of dusty sunlight slanted through the trees, children were picking wortleberries for market as I passed last night, with hands and faces and aprons smudged into one blue stain. I had decided to go to a water-mill belonging to the Man of Wrath which lies far away in a clearing, so far away and so lonely and so quiet that the very spirit of peace seems to brood over it for ever; and all the way the wortleberry carpet was thick and unbroken. Never were the pines more pungent than after the long heat, and their rosy stems flushed pinker as I passed. Presently I got beyond the region of wortleberry-pickers, the children not caring to wander too far into the forest so late, and I jolted over the roots into the gathering shadows more and more pervaded by that feeling that so refreshes me, the feeling of being absolutely alone.

A very ancient man lives in the mill and takes care of it, for it has long been unused, a deaf old man with a clean, toothless face, and no wife to worry him. He informed me once that all women are mistakes, especially that aggravated form called wives, and that he was thankful he had never married. I felt a certain delicacy after that about intruding on his solitude with the burden of my sex and wifehood heavy upon me, but he always seems very glad to see me, and runs at once to his fowlhouse to look for fresh eggs for my tea; so perhaps he regards me as a pleasing exception to the rule. On this last occasion he brought a table out to the elm-tree by the mill stream, that I might get what air there was while I ate my supper; and I sat in great peace waiting for the kettle to boil and watching the sun dropping behind the sharp forest me, and all the little pools and currents into which the stream just there breaks as it flows over mud banks, ablaze with the red reflection of the sky. The pools are clothed with water-lilies and inhabited by eels, and I generally take a netful of writhing eels back with me to the Man of Wrath to pacify him after my prolonged absence. In the lily time I get into the miller's punt and make them an excuse for paddling about among the mud islands, and even adventurously exploring the river as it winds into the forest, and the old man watches me anxiously from under the elm. He regards my feminine desire to pick water-lilies with indulgence, but is clearly uneasy at my affection for mud banks, and once, after I had stuck on one, and he had run up and down in great agitation for half an hour shouting instructions as to getting off again, he said when I was safely back on shore that people with petticoats (his way of expressing woman) were never intended for punts, and their only chance of safety lay in dry land and keeping quiet. I did not this time attempt the punt, for I was tired, and it was half full of water, probably poured into it by a miller weary of the ways of women; and I drank my tea quietly, going on at the same time with my interrupted afternoon reading of the *Sorrows of Werther*, in which I had reached a part that has a special fascination for me every time I read it—that part where Werther first meets Lotte, and where, after a thunderstorm; they both go to the window, and she is so touched by the beauties of nature that she lays her hand on his and murmurs "Klopstock,"—to the complete dismay of the reader, though not of Werther, for he, we find, was so carried away by the magic word that he flung himself on to her hand and kissed it with tears of rapture.

I looked up from the book at the quiet pools and the black line of trees, above which stars were beginning to twinkle, my ears soothed by the splashing of the mill stream and the hooting somewhere near of a solitary owl, and I wondered whether, if the Man of Wrath were by my side, it would be a relief to my pleasurable feelings to murmur "Klopstock," and whether if I did he would immediately shed tears of joy over my hand. The name is an unfortunate one as far as music goes, and Goethe's putting it into his heroine's mouth just when she was most enraptured, seems to support the view I sometimes adopt in discoursing to the Man of Wrath that he had no sense of humour. But here I am talking about Goethe, our great genius and idol, in a way that no woman should. What do German women know of such things? Quite untrained and uneducated, how are we to judge rightly about anybody or anything? All we can do is to jump at conclusions, and, when we have jumped, receive with meekness the information that we have jumped wrong. Sitting there long after it was too dark to read, I thought of the old miller's words, and agreed with him that the best thing a woman can do in this world is to keep quiet. He came out once and asked whether he should bring a lamp, and seemed uneasy at my choosing to sit there in the dark. I could see the stars in the black pools, and a line of faint light far away above the pines where the sun had set. Every now and then the hot air from the ground struck up in my face, and afterwards would come a cooler breath from the water. Of what use is it to fight for things and make a noise? Nature is so clear in her teaching that he who has lived with her for any time can be in little doubt as to the "better way." Keep quiet and say one's prayers— certainly not merely the best, but the only things to do if one would be truly happy; but, ashamed of asking when I have received so much, the only form of prayer I would use would be a form of thanksgiving.

SEPTEMBER

September 9th—I have been looking in the dictionary for the English word for *Einquartierung*, because that is what is happening to us just now, but I can find nothing satisfactory. My dictionary merely says (1) the quartering, (2) soldiers quartered, and then relapses into irrelevancy; so that it is obvious English people do without the word for the delightful reason that they have not got the thing. We have it here very badly; an epidemic raging at the end of nearly every summer, when cottages and farms swarm with soldiers and horses, when all the female part of the population gets engaged to be married and will not work, when all the male part is jealous and wants to fight, and when my house is crowded with individuals so brilliant and decorative in their dazzling uniforms that I wish sometimes I might keep a bunch of the tallest and slenderest for ever in a big china vase in a corner of the drawing-room.

This year the manoeuvres are up our way, so that we are blest with more than our usual share of attention, and wherever you go you see soldiers, and the holy calm that has brooded over us all the summer has given place to a perpetual running to and fro of officers' servants, to meals being got ready at all hours, to the clanking of spurs and all those other mysterious things on an officer that do clank whenever he moves, and to the grievous wailings of my unfortunate menials, who are quite beside themselves, and know not whither to turn for succour. We have had one week of it already, and we have yet another before us. There are five hundred men with their horses quartered at the farm, and thirty officers with their servants in our house, besides all those billeted on the surrounding villages who have to be invited to dinner and cannot be allowed to perish in peasant houses; so that my summer has for a time entirely ceased to be solitary, and whenever I flee distracted to the farthest recesses of my garden and begin to muse, according to my habit, on Man, on Nature, and on Human Life, lieutenants got up in the most exquisite flannels pursue me and want to play tennis with me, a game I have always particularly disliked.

There is no room of course for all those extra men and horses at the farm, and when a few days before their arrival (sometimes it is only one, and sometimes only a few hours) an official appears and informs us of the number to be billeted on us, the Man of Wrath has to have temporary sheds run up, some as stables, some as sleeping-places, and some as dining-rooms. Nor is it easy to cook for five hundred people more than usual, and all the ordinary business of the farm comes to a stand-still while the hands prepare barrowfuls of bacon and potatoes, and stir up the coffee and milk and sugar together with a pole in a tub. Part of the regimental band is here, the upper part. The base instruments are in the next village; but that did not deter an enthusiastic young officer from marching his men past our windows on their arrival at six in the morning, with colours flying, and what he had of his band playing their tunes as unconcernedly as though all those big things that make such a noise were giving the fabric its accustomed and necessary base. We are paid six pfennings a day for lodging a common soldier, and six pfennings for his horse—rather more than a penny in English money for the pair of them; only unfortunately sheds and carpentry are not quite so cheap. Eighty pfennings a day is added for the soldier's food, and for this he has to receive two pounds of bread, half a pound of meat, a quarter of a pound of bacon, and either a quarter of a pound of rice or barley or three pounds of potatoes. Officers are paid for at the rate of two marks fifty a day without wine; we are not obliged to give them wine, and if we do they are regarded as guests, and behave accordingly. The thirty we have now do not, as I could have wished, all go out together in the morning and stay out till the evening, but some go out as others come in, and breakfast is not finished till lunch begins, and lunch drags on till dinner, and all day long the dining-room is full of meals and officers, and we ceased a week ago to have the least feeling that the place, after all, belongs to us.

Now really it seems to me that I am a much-tried woman, and any peace I have enjoyed up to now is amply compensated for by my present torments. I believe even my stern friend the missionary would be satisfied if he could know how swiftly his prediction that sorrow and suffering would be sure to come, has been fulfilled. All day long I am giving out table linen, ordering meals, supporting the feeble knees of servants, making appropriate and amiable remarks to officers, presiding as gracefully as nature permits at meals, and trying to look as though I were happy; while out in the garden—oh, I know how it is looking out in the garden this golden weather, how the placid hours are slipping by in unchanged peace, how strong the scent of roses and ripe fruit is, how the sleepy bees drone round the flowers, how warmly the sun shines in that corner where the little Spanish chestnut is turning yellow—the first to turn, and never afterwards surpassed in autumn beauty; I know how still it is down there in my fir wood, where the insects hum undisturbed in the warm, quiet air; I know what the plain looks like from the seat under the oak, how beautiful, with its rolling green waves burning to gold under the afternoon sky; I know how the hawks circle over it, and how the larks sing above it, and I edge as near to the open window as I can, straining my ears to hear them, and forgetting the young men who are telling me of all the races their horses win as completely as though they did not exist. I want to be out there on that golden grass, and look up into that endless blue, and feel the ecstasy of that song through all my being, and there is a tearing at my heart when I remember that I cannot. Yet they are beautiful young men; all are touchingly amiable, and many of the older ones

280

even charming—how is it, then, that I so passionately prefer larks?

We have every grade of greatness here, from that innocent being the ensign, a creature of apparent modesty and blushes, who is obliged to stand up and drain his glass each time a superior chooses to drink to him, and who sits on the hardest chairs and looks for the balls while we play tennis, to the general, invariably delightful, whose brains have carried him triumphantly through the annual perils of weeding out, who is as distinguished in looks and manners as he is in abilities, and has the crowning merit of being manifestly happy in the society of women. Nothing lower than a colonel is to me an object of interest. The lower you get the more officers there are, and the harder it is to see the promising ones in the crowd; but once past the rank of major the air gets very much cleared by the merciless way they have been weeded out, and the higher officers are the very flower of middle-aged German males. As for those below, a lieutenant is a bright and beautiful being who admires no one so much as himself; a captain is generally newly married, having reached the stage of increased pay which makes a wife possible, and, being often still in love with her, is ineffective for social purposes; and a major is a man with a yearly increasing family, for whose wants his pay is inadequate, a person continually haunted by the fear of approaching weeding, after which his career is ended, he is poorer than ever, and being no longer young and only used to a soldier's life, is almost always quite incapable of starting afresh. Even the children of light find it difficult to start afresh with any success after forty, and the retired officer is never a child of light; if he were, he would not have been weeded out. You meet him everywhere, shorn of the glories of his uniform, easily recognisable by the bad fit of his civilian clothes, wandering about like a ship without a rudder; and as time goes on he settles down to the inevitable, and passes his days in a fourth-floor flat in the suburbs, eats, drinks, sleeps, reads the*Kreuzzeitung* and nothing else, plays at cards in the day-time, grows gouty, and worries his wife. It would be difficult to count the number of them that have answered the Man of Wrath's advertisements for book-keepers and secretaries—always vainly, for even if they were fit for the work, no single person possesses enough tact to cope successfully with the peculiarities of such a situation. I hear that some English people of a hopeful disposition indulge in ladies as servants; the cases are parallel, and the tact required to meet both superhuman.

Of all the officers here the only ones with whom I can find plenty to talk about are the generals. On what subject under heaven could one talk to a lieutenant? I cannot discuss the agility of ballet-dancers or the merits of jockeys with him, because these things are as dust and ashes to me; and when forced for a few moments by my duties as hostess to come within range of his conversation I feel chilly and grown old. In the early spring of this year, in those wonderful days of hope when nature is in a state of suppressed excitement, and when any day the yearly recurring miracle may happen of a few hours' warm rain changing the whole world, we got news that a lieutenant and two men with their horses were imminent, and would be quartered here for three nights while some occult military evolutions were going on a few miles off. It was specially inopportune, because the Man of Wrath would not be here, but he comforted me as I bade him good-bye, my face no doubt very blank, by the assurance that the lieutenant would be away all day, and so worn out when he got back in the evening that he probably would not appear at all. But I never met a more wide-awake young man. Not once during those three days did he respond to my pressing entreaties to go and lie down, and not all the desperate eloquence of a woman at her wit's end could persuade him that he was very tired and ought to try and get some sleep. I had intended to be out when he arrived, and to remain out till dinner time, but he came unexpectedly early, while the babies and I were still at lunch, the door opening to admit the most beautiful specimen of his class that I have ever seen, so beautiful indeed in his white uniform that the babies took him for an angel—visitant of the type that visited Abraham and Sarah, and began in whispers to argue about wings. He was not in the least tired after his long ride he told me, in reply to my anxious inquiries, and, rising to the occasion, at once plunged into conversation, evidently realising how peculiarly awful prolonged pauses under the circumstances would be. I took him for a drive in the afternoon, after having vainly urged him to rest, and while he told me about his horses, and his regiment, and his brother officers, in what at last grew to be a decidedly intermittent prattle, I amused myself by wondering what he would say if I suddenly began to hold forth on the themes I love best, and insist that he should note the beauty of the trees as they stood that afternoon expectant, with all their little buds only waiting for the one warm shower to burst into the glory of young summer. Perhaps he would regard me as the

German variety of a hyena in petticoats—the imagination recoils before the probable fearfulness of such an animal—or, if not quite so bad as that, at any rate a creature hysterically inclined; and he would begin to feel lonely, and think of his comrades, and his pleasant mess, and perhaps even of his mother, for he was very young and newly fledged. Therefore I held my peace, and restricted my conversation to things military, of which I know probably less than any other woman in Germany, so that my remarks must have been to an unusual degree impressive. He talked down to me, and I talked down to him, and we reached home in a state of profoundest exhaustion—at least I know I did, but when I looked at him he had not visibly turned a hair. I went upstairs trying to hope that he had felt it more than he showed, and that during the remainder of his stay he would adopt the suggestion so eagerly offered of spending his spare time in his room resting.

At dinner, he and I, quite by ourselves, were both manifestly convinced of the necessity, for the sake of the servants, of not letting the conversation drop. I felt desperate, and would have said anything sooner than sit opposite him in silence, and with united efforts we got through that fairly well. After dinner I tried gossip, and encouraged him to tell me some, but he had such an unnatural number of relations that whoever I began to talk about happened to be his cousin, or his brother-in-law, or his aunt, as he hastily informed me, so that what I had intended to say had to be turned immediately into loud and unqualified praise; and praising people is frightfully hard work—you give yourself the greatest pains over it, and are aware all the time that it is not in the very least carrying conviction. Does not everybody know that one's natural impulse is to tear the absent limb from limb? At half-past nine I got up, worn out in mind and body, and told him very firmly that it had been a custom in my family from time immemorial to be in bed by ten, and that I was accordingly going there. He looked surprised and wider awake than ever, but nothing shook me, and I walked away, leaving him standing on the hearthrug after the manner of my countrymen, who never dream of opening a door for a woman.

The next day he went off at five in the morning, and was to be away, as he had told me, till the evening. I felt as though I had been let out of prison as I breakfasted joyfully on the verandah, the sun streaming through the creeperless trellis on to the little meal, and the first cuckoo of the year calling to me from the fir wood. Of the dinner and evening before me I would not think; indeed I had a half-formed plan in my head of going to the forest after lunch with the babies, taking wraps and provisions, and getting lost till well on towards bedtime; so that when the angel-visitant should return full of renewed strength and conversation, he would find the casket empty and be told the gem had gone out for a walk. After I had finished breakfast I ran down the steps into the garden, intent on making the most of every minute and hardly able to keep my feet from dancing. Oh, the blessedness of a bright spring morning without a lieutenant! And was there ever such a hopeful beginning to a day, and so full of promise for the subsequent right passing of its hours, as breakfast in the garden, alone with your teapot and your book! Any cobwebs that have clung to your soul from the day before are brushed off with a neatness and expedition altogether surprising; never do tea and toast taste so nice as out there in the sun; never was a book so wise and full of pith as the one lying open before you; never was woman so clean outside and in, so refreshed, so morally and physically well-tubbed, as she who can start her day in this fashion. As I danced down the garden path I began to think cheerfully even of lieutenants. It was not so bad; he would be away till dark, and probably on the morrow as well; I would start off in the afternoon, and by coming back very late would not see him at all that day—might not, if Providence were kind, see him again ever; and this last thought was so exhilarating that I began to sing. But he came back just as we had finished lunch.

"The *Herr Lieutenant* is here," announced the servant, "and has gone to wash his hands. The *Herr Lieutenant* has not yet lunched, and will be down in a moment."

"I want the carriage at once," I ordered—I could not and would not spend another afternoon *tete-a-tete* with that young man,—"and you are to tell the *Herr Lieutenant* that I am sorry I was obliged to go out, but I had promised the pastor to take the children there this afternoon. See that he has everything he wants."

I gathered the babies together and fled. I could hear the lieutenant throwing things about overhead, and felt there was not a moment to lose. The servant's face showed plainly that he did not believe about the pastor, and the babies looked up at me wonderingly. What is a woman to do when driven into a corner? The father of lies inhabits corners—no doubt the proper place for such a naughty person.

We ran upstairs to get ready. There was only one short flight on which we could meet the lieutenant, and once past that we were safe; but we met him on that one short flight. He was coming down in a hurry, giving his moustache a final hasty twist, and looking fresher, brighter, lovelier, than ever.

"Oh, good morning. You have got back much sooner than you expected, have you not?" I said lamely.

"Yes, I managed to get through my part quickly," he said with a briskness I did not like.

"But you started so early—you must be very tired?"

"Oh, not in the least, thank you."

Then I repeated the story about the expectant parson, adding to my guilt by laying stress on the inevitability of the expedition owing to its having been planned weeks before. April and May stood on the landing above, listening with surprised faces, and June, her mind evidently dwelling on feathers, intently examined his shoulders from the step immediately behind. And we did get away, leaving him to think what he liked, and to smoke, or sleep, or wander as he chose, and I could not but believe he must feel relieved to be rid of me; but the afternoon clouded over, and a sharp wind sprang up, and we were very cold in the forest, and the babies began to sneeze and ask where the parson was, and at last, after driving many miles, I said it was too late to go to the parson's and we would turn back. It struck me as hard that we should be forced to wander in cold forests and leave our comfortable home because of a lieutenant, and I went back with my heart hardened against him.

That second evening was worse a great deal than the first. We had said all we ever meant to say to each other, and had lauded all our relations with such hearty goodwill that there was nothing whatever to add. I sat listening to the slow ticking of the clock and asking questions about things I did not in the least want to know, such as the daily work and rations and pay of the soldiers in his regiment, and presently—we having dined at the early hour usual in the country—the clock struck eight. Could I go to bed at eight? No, I had not the courage, and no excuse ready. More slow ticking, and more questions and answers about rations and pipeclay. What a clock! For utter laziness and dull deliberation there surely never was its equal—it took longer to get to the half-hour than any clock I ever met, but it did get there at last and struck it. Could I go? Could I? No, still no excuse ready. We drifted from pipeclay to a discussion

285

on bicycling for women—a dreary subject. Was it becoming? Was it good for them? Was it ladylike? Ought they to wear skirts or—? In Paris they all wore—. Our bringing-up here is so excellent that if we tried we could not induce ourselves to speak of any forked garments to a young man, so we make ourselves understood, when we desire to insinuate such things, by an expressive pause and a modest downward flicker of the eyelids. The clock struck nine. Nothing should keep me longer. I sprang to my feet and said I was exhausted beyond measure by the sharp air driving, and that whenever I had spent an afternoon out, it was my habit to go to bed half an hour earlier than other evenings. Again he looked surprised, but rather less so than the night before, and he was, I think, beginning to get used to me. I retired, firmly determined not to face another such day and to be very ill in the morning and quite unable to rise, he having casually remarked that the next one was an off day; and I would remain in bed, that last refuge of the wretched, as long as he remained here.

I sat by the window in my room till late, looking out at the moonlight in the quiet garden, with a feeling as though I were stuffed with sawdust—a very awful feeling—and thinking ruefully of the day that had begun so brightly and ended so dismally. What a miserable thing not to be able to be frank and say simply, "My good young man, you and I never saw each other before, probably won't see each other again, and have no interests in common. I mean you to be comfortable in my house, but I want to be comfortable too. Let us, therefore, keep out of each other's way while you are obliged to be here. Do as you like, go where you like, and order what you like, but don't expect me to waste my time sitting by your side and making small-talk. I too have to get to heaven, and have no time to lose. You won't see me again. Good-bye."

I believe many a harassed *Hausfrau* would give much to be able to make some such speech when these young men appear, and surely the young men themselves would be grateful; but simplicity is apparently quite beyond people's strength. It is, of all the virtues, the one I prize the most; it is undoubtedly the most lovable of any, and unspeakably precious for its power of removing those mountains that confine our lives and prevent our seeing the sky. Certain it is that until we have it, the simple spirit of the little child, we shall in no wise discover our kingdom of heaven.

These were my reflections, and many others besides, as I sat weary at the window that cold spring night, long after the lieutenant who had occasioned them was slumbering peacefully on the other side of the house. Thoughts of the next day, and enforced bed, and the bowls of gruel to be disposed of if the servants were to believe in my illness, made my head ache. Eating gruel *pour la galerie* is a pitiable state to be reduced to—surely no lower depths of humiliation are conceivable. And then, just as I was drearily remembering how little I loved gruel, there was a sudden sound of wheels rolling swiftly round the corner of the house, a great rattling and trampling in the still night over the stones, and tearing open the window and leaning out, there, sitting in a station fly, and apparelled to my glad vision in celestial light, I beheld the Man of Wrath, come home unexpectedly to save me.

"Oh, dear Man of Wrath," I cried, hanging out into the moonlight with outstretched arms, "how much nicer thou art than lieutenants! I never missed thee more—I never longed for thee more—I never loved thee more—come up here quickly that I may kiss thee!—"

October

October 1st.—Last night after dinner, when we were in the library, I said, "Now listen to me, Man of Wrath."

"Well?" he inquired, looking up at me from the depths of his chair as I stood before him.

"Do you know that as a prophet you are a failure? Five months ago to-day you sat among the wallflowers and scoffed at the idea of my being able to enjoy myself alone a whole summer through. Is the summer over?"

"It is," he assented, as he heard the rain beating against the windows.

"And have I invited any one here?"

"No, but there were all those officers."

"They have nothing whatever to do with it."

"They helped you through one fortnight."

"They didn't. It was a fortnight of horror."

"Well. Go on."

"You said I would be punished by being dull. Have I been dull?"

"My dear, as though if you had been you would ever confess it."

"That's true. But as a matter of fact let me tell you that I never spent a happier summer."

He merely looked at me out of the corners of his eyes.

"If I remember rightly," he said, after a pause, "your chief reason for wishing to be solitary was that your soul might have time to grow. May I ask if it did?"

"Not a bit."

He laughed, and, getting up, came and stood by my side before the   fire.

"At least you are honest," he said, drawing my hand through his arm.

"It is an estimable virtue."

"And strangely rare in woman."

"Now leave woman alone. I have discovered you know nothing really of her at all. But *I* know all about her."

"You do? My dear, one woman can never judge the others."

"An exploded tradition, dear Sage."

"Her opinions are necessarily biassed."

"Venerable nonsense, dear Sage."

"Because women are each other's natural enemies."

"Obsolete jargon, dear Sage."

"Well, what do you make of her?"

"Why, that she's a DEAR, and that you ought to be very happy and thankful to have got one of her always with you."

"But am I not?" he asked, putting his arm round me and looking affectionate; and when people begin to look affectionate I, for one, cease to take any further interest in them.

And so the Man of Wrath and I fade away into dimness and muteness, my head resting on his shoulder, and his arm encircling my waist; and what could possibly be more proper, more praiseworthy, or more picturesque?

Vera

by

Elisabeth von Arnim

I

When the doctor had gone, and the two women from the village he had been waiting for were upstairs shut in with her dead father, Lucy went out into the garden and stood leaning on the gate staring at the sea.

Her father had died at nine o'clock that morning, and it was now twelve. The sun beat on her bare head; and the burnt-up grass along the top of the cliff, and the dusty road that passed the gate, and the glittering sea, and the few white clouds hanging in the sky, all blazed and glared in an extremity of silent, motionless heat and light.

Into this emptiness Lucy stared, motionless herself, as if she had been carved in stone. There was not a sail on the sea, nor a line of distant smoke from any steamer, neither was there once the flash of a bird's wing brushing across the sky. Movement seemed smitten rigid. Sound seemed to have gone to sleep.

Lucy stood staring at the sea, her face as empty of expression as the bright blank world before her. Her father had been dead three hours, and she felt nothing.

It was just a week since they had arrived in Cornwall, she and he, full of hope, full of pleasure in the pretty little furnished house they had taken for August and September, full of confidence in the good the pure air was going to do him. But there had always been confidence; there had never been a moment during the long years of his fragility when confidence had even been questioned. He was delicate, and she had taken care of him. She had taken care of him and he had been delicate ever since she could remember. And ever since she could remember he had been everything in life to her. She had had no thought since she grew up for anybody but her father. There was no room for any other thought, so completely did he fill her heart. They had done everything together, shared everything together, dodged the winters together, settled in charming places, seen the same beautiful things, read the same books, talked, laughed, had friends,—heaps of friends; wherever they were her father seemed at once to have friends, adding them to the mass he had already. She had not been away from him a day for years; she had had no wish to go away. Where and with whom could she be so happy as with him? All the years were years of sunshine. There had been no winters; nothing but summer, summer, and sweet scents and soft skies, and patient understanding with her slowness—for he had the nimblest mind—and love. He was the most amusing companion to her, the most generous friend, the most illuminating guide, the most adoring father; and now he was dead, and she felt nothing.

Her father. Dead. For ever.

She said the words over to herself. They meant nothing.

She was going to be alone. Without him. Always.

She said the words over to herself. They meant nothing.

Up in that room with its windows wide open, shut away from her with the two village women, he was lying dead. He had smiled at her for the last time, said all he was ever going to say to her, called her the last of the sweet, half-teasing names he loved to invent for her. Why, only a few hours ago they were having breakfast together and planning what they would do that day. Why, only yesterday they drove together after tea towards the sunset, and he had seen, with his quick eyes that saw everything, some unusual grasses by the road-side, and had stopped and gathered them, excited to find such rare ones, and had taken them back with him to study, and had explained them to her and made her see profoundly interesting, important things in them, in these grasses which, till he touched them, had seemed just grasses. That is what he did with everything,—touched it into life and delight. The grasses lay in the dining-room now, waiting for him to work on them, spread out where he had put them on some blotting-paper in the window. She had seen them as she came through on her way to the garden; and she had seen, too, that the breakfast was still there, the breakfast they had had together, still as they had left it, forgotten by the servants in the surprise of death. He had fallen down as he got up from it. Dead. In an instant. No time for anything, for a cry, for a look. Gone. Finished. Wiped out.

What a beautiful day it was; and so hot. He loved heat. They were lucky in the weather....

Yes, there were sounds after all,—she suddenly noticed them; sounds from the room upstairs, a busy moving about of discreet footsteps, the splash of water, crockery being carefully set down. Presently the women would come and tell her everything was ready, and she could go back to him again. The women had tried to comfort her when they arrived; and so had the servants, and so had the doctor. Comfort her! And she felt nothing.

Lucy stared at the sea, thinking these things, examining the situation as a curious one but unconnected with herself, looking at it with a kind of cold comprehension. Her mind was quite clear. Every detail of what had happened was sharply before her. She knew everything, and she felt nothing,—like God, she said to herself; yes, exactly like God.

Footsteps came along the road, which was hidden by the garden's fringe of trees and bushes for fifty yards on either side of the gate, and presently a man passed between her eyes and the sea. She did not notice him, for she was noticing nothing but her thoughts, and he passed in front of her quite close, and was gone.

But he had seen her, and had stared hard at her for the brief instant it took to pass the gate. Her face and its expression had surprised him. He was not a very observant man, and at that moment was even less so than usual, for he was particularly and deeply absorbed in his own affairs; yet when he came suddenly on the motionless figure at the gate, with its wide-open eyes that simply looked through him as he went by, unconscious, obviously, that any one was going by, his attention was surprised away from himself and almost he had stopped to examine the strange creature more closely. His code, however, prevented that, and he continued along the further fifty yards of bushes and trees that hid the other half of the garden from the road, but more slowly, slower and slower, till at the end of the garden where the road left it behind and went on very solitarily over the bare grass on the top of the cliffs, winding in and out with the ins and outs of the coast for as far as one could see, he hesitated, looked back, went on a yard or two, hesitated again, stopped and took off his hot hat and wiped his forehead, looked at the bare country and the long twisting glare of the road ahead, and then very slowly turned and went past the belt of bushes towards the gate again.

He said to himself as he went: 'My God, I'm so lonely. I can't stand it. I must speak to some one. I shall go off my head——'

For what had happened to this man—his name was Wemyss— was that public opinion was forcing him into retirement and inactivity at the very time when he most needed company and distraction. He had to go away by himself, he had to withdraw for at the very least a week from his ordinary life, from his house on the river where he had just begun his summer holiday, from his house in

London where at least there were his clubs, because of this determination on the part of public opinion that he should for a space be alone with his sorrow. Alone with sorrow,—of all ghastly things for a man to be alone with! It was an outrage, he felt, to condemn a man to that; it was the cruellest form of solitary confinement. He had come to Cornwall because it took a long time to get to, a whole day in the train there and a whole day in the train back, clipping the week, the minimum of time public opinion insisted on for respecting his bereavement, at both ends; but still that left five days of awful loneliness, of wandering about the cliffs by himself trying not to think, without a soul to speak to, without a thing to do. He couldn't play bridge because of public opinion. Everybody knew what had happened to him. It had been in all the papers. The moment he said his name they would know. It was so recent. Only last week....

No, he couldn't bear this, he must speak to some one. That girl,— with those strange eyes she wasn't just ordinary. She wouldn't mind letting him talk to her for a little, perhaps sit in the garden with her a little. She would understand.

Wemyss was like a child in his misery. He very nearly cried outright when he got to the gate and took off his hat, and the girl looked at him blankly just as if she still didn't see him and hadn't heard him when he said, 'Could you let me have a glass of water? I—it's so hot——'

He began to stammer because of her eyes. 'I—I'm horribly thirsty—the heat——'

He pulled out his handkerchief and mopped his forehead. He certainly looked very hot. His face was red and distressed, and his forehead dripped. He was all puckered, like an unhappy baby. And the girl looked so cool, so bloodlessly cool. Her hands, folded on the top bar of the gate, looked more than cool, they looked cold; like hands in winter, shrunk and small with cold. She had bobbed hair, he noticed, so that it was impossible to tell how old she was, brown hair from which the sun was beating out bright lights; and her small face had no colour except those wide eyes fixed on his and the colour of her rather big mouth; but even her mouth seemed frozen.

'Would it be much bother——' began Wemyss again; and then his situation overwhelmed him.

'You would be doing a greater kindness than you know,' he said, his voice trembling with unhappiness, 'if you would let me come into the garden a minute and rest.'

At the sound of the genuine wretchedness in his voice Lucy's blank eyes became a little human. It got through to her consciousness that this distressed warm stranger was appealing to her for something.

'Are you so hot?' she asked, really seeing him for the first time.

'Yes, I'm hot,' said Wemyss. 'But it isn't that. I've had a misfortune—a terrible misfortune——'

He paused, overcome by the remembrance of it, by the unfairness of so much horror having overtaken him.

'Oh, I'm sorry,' said Lucy vaguely, still miles away from him, deep in indifference. 'Have you lost anything?'

'Good God, not that sort of misfortune!' cried Wemyss. 'Let me come in a minute—into the garden a minute—just to sit a minute with a human being. You would be doing a great kindness. Because you're a stranger I can talk to you about it if you'll let me. Just because we're strangers I could talk. I haven't spoken to a soul but servants and official people since—since it happened. For two days I haven't spoken at all to a living soul—I shall go mad——'

His voice shook again with his unhappiness, with his astonishment at his unhappiness.

Lucy didn't think two days very long not to speak to anybody in, but there was something overwhelming about the strange man's evident affliction that roused her out of her apathy; not much,—she was still profoundly detached, observing from another world, as it were, this extreme heat and agitation, but at least she saw him now, she did with a faint curiosity consider him. He was like some elemental force in his directness. He had the quality of an irresistible natural phenomenon. But she did not move from her position at the gate, and her eyes continued, with the unwaveringness he thought so odd, to stare into his.

'I would gladly have let you come in,' she said, 'if you had come yesterday, but to-day my father died.'

Wemyss looked at her in astonishment. She had said it in as level and ordinary a voice as if she had been remarking, rather indifferently, on the weather.

Then he had a moment of insight. His own calamity had illuminated him. He who had never known pain, who had never let himself be worried, who had never let himself be approached in his life by a doubt, had for the last week lived in an atmosphere of worry and pain, and of what, if he allowed himself to think, to become morbid, might well grow into a most unfair, tormenting doubt. He understood, as he would not have understood a week ago, what her whole attitude, her rigidity meant. He stared at her a moment while she stared straight back at him, and then his big warm hands dropped on to the cold ones folded on the top bar of the gate, and he said, holding them firmly though they made no attempt to move, 'So that's it. So that's why. Now I know.'

And then he added, with the simplicity his own situation was putting into everything he did, 'That settles it. We two stricken ones must talk together.'

And still covering her hands with one of his, with the other he unlatched the gate and walked in.

II

There was a seat under a mulberry tree on the little lawn, with its back to the house and the gaping windows, and Wemyss, spying it out, led Lucy to it as if she were a child, holding her by the hand.

She went with him indifferently. What did it matter whether she sat under the mulberry tree or stood at the gate? This convulsed stranger—was he real? Was anything real? Let him tell her whatever it was he wanted to tell her, and she would listen, and get him his glass of water, and then he would go his way and by that time the women would have finished upstairs and she could be with her father again.

'I'll fetch the water,' she said when they got to the seat.

'No. Sit down,' said Wemyss.

She sat down. So did he, letting her hand go. It dropped on the seat, palm upwards, between them.

'It's strange our coming across each other like this,' he said, looking at her while she looked indifferently straight in front of her at the sun on the grass beyond the shade of the mulberry tree, at a mass of huge fuchsia bushes a little way off. 'I've been going through hell—and so must you have been. Good God, what hell! Do you mind if I tell you? You'll understand because of your own——'

Lucy didn't mind. She didn't mind anything. She merely vaguely wondered that he should think she had been going through hell. Hell and her darling father; how quaint it sounded. She began to suspect that she was asleep. All this wasn't really happening. Her father wasn't dead. Presently the housemaid would come in with the hot water and wake her to the usual cheerful day. The man sitting beside her,—he seemed rather vivid for a dream, it was true; so detailed, with his flushed face and the perspiration on his forehead, besides the feel of his big warm hand a moment ago and the small puffs of heat that came from his clothes when he moved. But it was so unlikely ... everything that had happened since breakfast was so unlikely. This man, too, would resolve himself soon into just something she had had for dinner last night, and she would tell her father about her dream at breakfast, and they would laugh.

She stirred uneasily. It wasn't a dream. It was real.

299

'The story is unbelievably horrible,' Wemyss was saying in a high aggrievement, looking at her little head with the straight cut hair, and her grave profile. How old was she? Eighteen? Twenty-eight? Impossible to tell exactly with hair cut like that, but young anyhow compared to him; very young perhaps compared to him who was well over forty, and so much scarred, so deeply scarred, by this terrible thing that had happened to him.

'It's so horrible that I wouldn't talk about it if you were going to mind,' he went on, 'but you can't mind because you're a stranger, and it may help you with your own trouble, because whatever you may suffer I'm suffering much worse, so then you'll see yours isn't so bad. And besides I must talk to some one I should go mad——'

This was certainly a dream, thought Lucy. Things didn't happen like this when one was awake,—grotesque things.

She turned her head and looked at him. No, it wasn't a dream. No dream could be so solid as the man beside her. What was he saying?

He was saying in a tormented voice that he was Wemyss.

'You are Wemyss,' she repeated gravely.

It made no impression on her. She didn't mind his being Wemyss.

'I'm the Wemyss the newspapers were full of last week,' he said, seeing that the name left her unmoved. 'My God,' he went on, again wiping his forehead, but as fast as he wiped it more beads burst out, 'those posters to see one's own name staring at one everywhere on posters!'

'Why was your name on posters?' said Lucy.

She didn't want to know; she asked mechanically, her ear attentive only to the sounds from the open windows of the room upstairs.

'Don't you read newspapers here?' was his answer.

'I don't think we do,' she said, listening. 'We've been settling in. I don't think we've remembered to order any newspapers yet.'

A look of some, at any rate, relief from the pressure he was evidently struggling under came into Wemyss's face. 'Then I can tell you the real version,' he said, 'without you're being already filled up with the monstrous suggestions that were made at the inquest. As though I hadn't suffered enough as it was! As though it hadn't been terrible enough already——'

'The inquest?' repeated Lucy.

Again she turned her head and looked at him. 'Has your trouble anything to do with death?'

'Why, you don't suppose anything else would reduce me to the state I'm in?'

'Oh, I'm sorry,' she said; and into her eyes and into her voice came a different expression, something living, something gentle. 'I hope it wasn't anybody you—loved?'

'It was my wife,' said Wemyss.

He got up quickly, so near was he to crying at the thought of it, at the thought of all he had endured, and turned his back on her and began stripping the leaves off the branches above his head.

Lucy watched him, leaning forward a little on both hands. 'Tell me about it,' she said presently, very gently.

He came back and dropped down heavily beside her again, and with many interjections of astonishment that such a ghastly calamity could have happened to him, to him who till now had never——

'Yes,' said Lucy, comprehendingly and gravely, 'yes—I know—'

—had never had anything to do with—well, with calamities, he told her the story.

They had gone down, he and his wife, as they did every 25th of July, for the summer to their house on the river, and he had been looking forward to a glorious time of peaceful doing nothing after months of London, just lying about in a punt and reading and smoking and resting—London was an awful place for tiring one out—and they hadn't been there twenty-four hours before his wife—before his wife——

The remembrance of it was too grievous to him. He couldn't go on.

'Was she—very ill?' asked Lucy gently, to give him time to recover. 'I think that would almost be better. One would be a little at least one would be a little prepared——'

'She wasn't ill at all,' cried Wemyss. 'She just—died.'

'Oh like father!' exclaimed Lucy, roused now altogether. It was she now who laid her hand on his.

Wemyss seized it between both his, and went on quickly.

He was writing letters, he said, in the library at his table in the window where he could see the terrace and the garden and the river; they had had tea together only an hour before; there was a flagged terrace along that side of the house, the side the library was on and all the principal rooms; and all of a sudden there was a great flash of shadow between him and the light; come and gone instantaneously; and instantaneously then there was a thud; he would never forget it, that thud; and there outside his window on the flags——

'Oh don't—oh don't——' gasped Lucy.

'It was my wife,' Wemyss hurried on, not able now to stop, looking at Lucy while he talked with eyes of amazed horror. 'Fallen out of the top room of the house her sitting-room because of the view—it was in a straight line with the library window—she dropped past my window like a stone—she was smashed—smashed——'

'Oh, don't—oh——'

'Now can you wonder at the state I'm in?' he cried. 'Can you wonder if I'm nearly off my head? And forced to be by myself—forced into retirement for what the world considers a proper period of mourning, with nothing to think of but that ghastly inquest.'

He hurt her hand, he gripped it so hard.

'If you hadn't let me come and talk to you,' he said, 'I believe I'd have pitched myself over the cliff there this afternoon and made an end of it.'

'But how—but why—how could she fall?' whispered Lucy, to whom poor Wemyss's misfortune seemed more frightful than anything she had ever heard of.

She hung on his words, her eyes on his face, her lips parted, her whole body an agony of sympathy. Life—how terrible it was, and how unsuspected. One went on and on, never dreaming of the sudden dreadful day when the coverings were going to be dropped and one would see it was death after all, that it had been death all the time, death pretending, death waiting. Her father, so full of love and interests and plans,—gone, finished, brushed away as if he no more mattered than some insect one unseeingly treads on as one walks; and this man's wife, dead in an instant, dead so far more cruelly, so horribly....

'I had often told her to be careful of that window,' Wemyss answered in a voice that almost sounded like anger; but all the time his tone had been one of high anger at the wanton, outrageous cruelty of fate. 'It was a very low one, and the floor was slippery. Oak. Every floor in my house is polished oak. I had them put in myself. She must have been leaning out and her feet slipped away behind her. That would make her fall head foremost——'

'Oh—oh——' said Lucy, shrinking. What could she do, what could she say to help him, to soften at least these dreadful memories?

'And then,' Wemyss went on after a moment, as unaware as Lucy was that she was tremblingly stroking his hand, 'at the inquest, as though it hadn't all been awful enough for me already, the jury must actually get wrangling about the cause of death.'

'The cause of death?' echoed Lucy. 'But—she fell.'

'Whether it were an accident or done on purpose.'

'Done on——?'

'Suicide.'

'Oh——'

She drew in her breath quickly.

'But—it wasn't?'

'How could it be? She was my wife, without a care in the world, everything done for her, no troubles, nothing on her mind, nothing wrong with her health. We had been married fifteen years, and I was devoted to her—devoted to her.'

He banged his knee with his free hand. His voice was full of indignant tears.

'Then why did the jury——'

'My wife had a fool of a maid—I never could stand that woman—and it was something she said at the inquest, some invention or other about what my wife had said to her. You know what servants are. It upset some of the jury. You know juries are made up of anybody and everybody—butcher, baker, and candle-stick-maker—quite uneducated most of them, quite at the mercy of any suggestion. And so instead of a verdict of death by misadventure, which would have been the right one, it was an open verdict.'

'Oh, how terrible—how terrible for you,' breathed Lucy, her eyes on his, her mouth twitching with sympathy.

'You'd have seen all about it if you had read the papers last week,' said Wemyss, more quietly. It had done him good to get it out and talked over.

He looked down at her upturned face with its horror-stricken eyes and twitching mouth. 'Now tell me about yourself,' he said, touched with compunction; nothing that had happened to her could be so horrible as what had happened to him, still she too was newly smitten, they had met on a common ground of disaster, Death himself had been their introducer.

'Is life all—only death?' she breathed, her horror-stricken eyes on his.

303

Before he could answer—and what was there to answer to such a question except that of course it wasn't, and he and she were just victims of a monstrous special unfairness,—he certainly was; her father had probably died as fathers did, in the usual way in his bed—before he could answer, the two women came out of the house, and with small discreet steps proceeded down the path to the gate. The sun flooded their spare figures and their decent black clothes, clothes kept for these occasions as a mark of respectful sympathy.

One of them saw Lucy under the mulberry tree and hesitated, and then came across the grass to her with the mincing steps of tact.

'Here's somebody coming to speak to you,' said Wemyss, for Lucy was sitting with her back to the path.

She started and looked round.

The woman approached hesitatingly, her head on one side, her hands folded, her face pulled into a little smile intended to convey encouragement and pity.

'The gentleman's quite ready, miss,' she said softly.

III

All that day and all the next day Wemyss was Lucy's tower of strength and rock of refuge. He did everything that had to be done of the business part of death—that extra wantonness of misery thrown in so grimly to finish off the crushing of a mourner who is alone. It is true the doctor was kind and ready to help, but he was a complete stranger; she had never seen him till he was fetched that dreadful morning; and he had other things to see to besides her affairs,—his own patients, scattered widely over a lonely countryside. Wemyss had nothing to see to. He could concentrate entirely on Lucy. And he was her friend, linked to her so strangely and so strongly by death. She felt she had known him for ever. She felt that since the beginning of time she and he had been advancing hand in hand towards just this place, towards just this house and garden, towards just this year, this August, this moment of existence.

Wemyss dropped quite naturally into the place a near male relative would have been in if there had been a near male relative within reach; and his relief at having something to do, something practical and immediate, was so immense that never were funeral arrangements made with greater zeal and energy,—really one might almost say with greater gusto. Fresh from the horrors of those other funeral arrangements, clouded as they had been by the silences of friends and the averted looks of neighbours—all owing to the idiotic jurors and their hesitations, and the vindictiveness of that woman because, he concluded, he had refused to raise her wages the previous month—what he was arranging now was so simple and straightforward that it positively was a pleasure. There were no anxieties, there were no worries, and there was a grateful little girl. After each fruitful visit to the undertaker, and he paid several in his zeal, he came back to Lucy and she was grateful; and she was not only grateful, but very obviously glad to get him back.

He saw she didn't like it when he went away, off along the top of the cliff on his various business visits, purpose in each step, a different being from the indignantly miserable person who had dragged about that very cliff killing time such a little while before; he could see she didn't like it. She knew he had to go, she was grateful and immensely expressive of her gratitude—Wemyss thought he had never met any one so expressively grateful—that he should so diligently go, but she didn't like it. He saw she didn't like it; he saw that she clung to him; and it pleased him.

'Don't be long,' she murmured each time, looking at him with eyes of entreaty; and when he got back, and stood before her again mopping his forehead, having triumphantly advanced the funeral arrangements another stage, a faint colour came into her face and she had the relieved eyes of a child who has been left alone in the dark and sees its mother coming in with a candle. Vera usedn't to look like that. Vera had accepted everything he did for her as a matter of course.

Naturally he wasn't going to let the poor little girl sleep alone in that house with a dead body, and the strange servants who had been hired together with the house and knew nothing either about her or her father probably getting restive as night drew on, and as likely as not bolting to the village; so he fetched his things from the primitive hotel down in the cove about seven o'clock and announced his intention of sleeping on the drawing-room sofa. He had lunched with her, and had had tea with her, and now was going to dine with her. What she would have done without him Wemyss couldn't think.

He felt he was being delicate and tactful in this about the drawing-room sofa. He might fairly have claimed the spare-room bed; but he wasn't going to take any advantage, not the smallest, of the poor little girl's situation. The servants, who supposed him to be a relation and had supposed him to be that from the first moment they saw him, big and middle-aged, holding the young lady's hand under the mulberry tree, were surprised at having to make up a bed in the drawing-room when there were two spare-rooms with beds already in them upstairs, but did so obediently, vaguely imagining it had something to do with watchfulness and French windows; and Lucy, when he told her he was going to stay the night, was so grateful, so really thankful, that her eyes, red from the waves of grief that had engulfed her at intervals during the afternoon—ever since, that is, the sight of her dead father lying so remote from her, so wrapped, it seemed, in a deep, absorbed attentiveness, had unfrozen her and swept her away into a sea of passionate weeping— filled again with tears.

'Oh,' she murmured, 'how *good* you are——'

It was Wemyss who had done all the thinking for her, and in the spare moments between his visits to the undertaker about the arrangements, and to the doctor about the certificate, and to the vicar about the burial, had telegraphed to her only existing relative, an aunt, had sent the obituary notice to *The Times*, and had even reminded her that she had on a blue frock and asked if she hadn't better put on a black one; and now this last instance of his thoughtfulness overwhelmed her.

She had been dreading the night, hardly daring to think of it so much did she dread it; and each time he had gone away on his errands, through her heart crept the thought of what it would be like when dusk came and he went away for the last time and she would be alone, all alone in the silent house, and upstairs that strange, wonderful, absorbed thing that used to be her father, and whatever happened to her, whatever awful horror overcame her in the night, whatever danger, he wouldn't hear, he wouldn't know, he would still lie there content, content....

'How *good* you are!' she said to Wemyss, her red eyes filling. 'What would I have done without you?'

'But what would I have done without *you*?' he answered; and they stared at each other, astonished at the nature of the bond between them, at its closeness, at the way it seemed almost miraculously to have been arranged that they should meet on the crest of despair and save each other.

Till long after the stars were out they sat together on the edge of the cliff, Wemyss smoking while he talked, in a voice subdued by the night and the silence and the occasion, of his life and of the regular healthy calm with which it had proceeded till a week ago. Why this calm should have been interrupted, and so cruelly, he couldn't imagine. It wasn't as if he had deserved it. He didn't know that a man could ever be justified in saying he had done good, but he, Wemyss, could at least fairly say that he hadn't done any one any harm.

'Oh, but you have done good,' said Lucy, her voice, too, dropped into more than ordinary gentleness by the night, the silence, and the occasion; besides which it vibrated with feeling, it was lovely with seriousness, with simple conviction. 'Always, always I know that you've been doing good,' she said, 'being kind. I can't imagine you anything else but a help to people and a comfort.'

And Wemyss said, Well, he had done his best and tried, and no man could say more, but judging from what—well, what people had said to him, it hadn't been much of a success sometimes, and often and often he had been hurt, deeply hurt, by being misunderstood.

And Lucy said, How was it possible to misunderstand him, to misunderstand any one so transparently good, so evidently kind?

And Wemyss said, Yes, one would think he was easy enough to understand; he was a very natural, simple sort of person, who had only all his life asked for peace and quiet. It wasn't much to ask. Vera——

'Who is Vera?' asked Lucy.

'My wife.'

'Ah, don't,' said Lucy earnestly, taking his hand very gently in hers. 'Don't talk of that to-night please don't let yourself think of it. If I could only, only find the words that would comfort you——'

And Wemyss said that she didn't need words, that just her being there, being with him, letting him help her, and her not having been mixed up with anything before in his life, was enough.

'Aren't we like two children,' he said, his voice, like hers, deepened by feeling, 'two scared, unhappy children, clinging to each other alone in the dark.'

So they talked on in subdued voices as people do who are in some holy place, sitting close together, looking out at the starlit sea, darkness and coolness gathering round them, and the grass smelling sweetly after the hot day, and the little waves, such a long way down, lapping lazily along the shingle, till Wemyss said it must be long past bedtime, and she, poor girl, must badly need rest.

'How old are you?' he asked suddenly, turning to her and scrutinising the delicate faint outline of her face against the night.

'Twenty-two,' said Lucy.

'You might just as easily be twelve,' he said, 'except for the sorts of things you say.'

'It's my hair,' said Lucy. 'My father liked—he liked——'

'Don't,' said Wemyss, in his turn taking her hand. 'Don't cry again. Don't cry any more to-night. Come—we'll go in. It's time you were in bed.'

And he helped her up, and when they got into the light of the hall he saw that she had, this time, successfully strangled her tears.

'Good-night,' she said, when he had lit her candle for her, 'good-night, and—God bless you.'

'God bless *you*' said Wemyss solemnly, holding her hand in his great warm grip.

308

'He has,' said Lucy. 'Indeed He has already, in sending me you.' And she smiled up at him.

For the first time since he had known her—and he too had the feeling that he had known her ever since he could remember—he saw her smile, and the difference it made to her marred, stained face surprised him.

'Do that again,' he said, staring at her, still holding her hand.

'Do what?' asked Lucy.

'Smile,' said Wemyss.

Then she laughed; but the sound of it in the silent, brooding house was shocking.

'*Oh*,' she gasped, stopping short, hanging her head appalled by what it had sounded like.

'Remember you're to go to sleep and not think of anything,' Wemyss ordered as she went slowly upstairs.

And she did fall asleep at once, exhausted but protected, like some desolate baby that had cried itself sick and now had found its mother.

IV

All this, however, came to an end next day when towards evening Miss Entwhistle, Lucy's aunt, arrived.

Wemyss retired to his hotel again and did not reappear till next morning, giving Lucy time to explain him; but either the aunt was inattentive, as she well might be under the circumstances in which she found herself so suddenly, so lamentably placed, or Lucy's explanations were vague, for Miss Entwhistle took Wemyss for a friend of her dear Jim's, one of her dear, dear brother's many friends, and accepted his services as natural and himself with emotion, warmth, and reminiscences.

Wemyss immediately became her rock as well as Lucy's, and she in her turn clung to him. Where he had been clung to by one he was now clung to by two, which put an end to talk alone with Lucy. He did not see Lucy alone again once before the funeral, but at least, owing to Miss Entwhistle's inability to do without him, he didn't have to spend any more solitary hours. Except breakfast, he had all his meals up in the little house on the cliff, and in the evenings smoked his pipe under the mulberry tree till bedtime sent him away, while Miss Entwhistle in the darkness gently and solemnly reminisced, and Lucy sat silent, as close to him as she could get.

The funeral was hurried on by the doctor's advice, but even so the short notice and the long distance did not prevent James Entwhistle's friends from coming to it. The small church down in the cove was packed; the small hotel bulged with concerned, grave-faced people. Wemyss, who had done everything and been everything, disappeared in this crowd. Nobody noticed him. None of James Entwhistle's friends happened—luckily, he felt, with last week's newspapers still fresh in the public mind—to be his. For twenty-four hours he was swept entirely away from Lucy by this surge of mourners, and at the service in the church could only catch a distant glimpse, from his seat by the door, of her bowed head in the front pew.

He felt very lonely again. He wouldn't have stayed in the church a minute, for he objected with a healthy impatience to the ceremonies of death, if it hadn't been that he regarded himself as the stage-manager, so to speak, of these particular ceremonies, and that it was in a peculiarly intimate sense his funeral. He took a pride in it. Considering the shortness of the time it really was a remarkable achievement, the way he had done it, the smooth way the whole thing was going. But to-morrow,—what would happen to-morrow, when all these people had gone away again? Would they take Lucy and the aunt with them? Would the house up there be shut, and he, Wemyss, left alone again with his bitter, miserable recollections? He wouldn't, of course, stay on in that place if Lucy were to go, but wherever he went there would be emptiness without her, without her gratefulness, and gentleness, and clinging. Comforting and being comforted,—that is what he and she had been doing to each other for four days, and he couldn't but believe she would feel the same emptiness without him that he knew he was going to feel without her.

In the dark under the mulberry tree, while her aunt talked softly and sadly of the past, Wemyss had sometimes laid his hand on Lucy's, and she had never taken hers away. They had sat there, content and comforted to be hand in hand. She had the trust in him, he felt, of a child; the confidence, and the knowledge that she was safe. He was proud and touched to know it, and it warmed him through and through to see how her face lit up whenever he appeared. Vera's face hadn't done that. Vera had never understood him, not with fifteen years to do it in, as this girl had in half a day. And the way Vera had died,—it was no use mincing matters when it came to one's own thoughts, and it had been all of a piece with her life: the disregard for others and of anything said to her for her own good, the determination to do what suited her, to lean out of dangerous windows if she wished to, for instance, not to take the least trouble, the least thought.... Imagine bringing such horror on him, such unforgettable horror, besides worries and unhappiness without end, by deliberately disregarding his warnings, his orders indeed, about that window. Wemyss did feel that if one looked at the thing dispassionately it would be difficult to find indifference to the wishes and feelings of others going further.

Sitting in the church during the funeral service, his arms folded on his chest and his mouth grim with these thoughts, he suddenly caught sight of Lucy's face. The priest was coming down the aisle in front of the coffin on the way out to the grave, and Lucy and her aunt were following first behind it.

Man that is born of a woman hath but a short time to live, and is full of misery. He cometh up, and is cut down, like a flower; he fleeth as it were a shadow, and never continueth in one stay....

The priest's sad, disillusioned voice recited the beautiful words as he walked, the afternoon sun from the west window and the open west door pouring on his face and on the faces of the procession that seemed all black and white,—black clothes, white faces.

The whitest face was Lucy's, and when Wemyss saw the look on it his mouth relaxed and his heart went soft within him, and he came impulsively out of the shadow and joined her, boldly walking on her other side at the head of the procession, and standing beside her at the grave; and at the awful moment when the first earth was dropped on to the coffin he drew her hand, before everybody, through his arm and held it there tight.

Nobody was surprised at his standing there with her like that. It was taken quite for granted. He was evidently a relation of poor Jim's. Nor was anybody surprised when Wemyss, not letting her go again, took her home up the cliff, her arm in his just as though he were the chief mourner, the aunt following with some one else.

He didn't speak to her or disturb her with any claims on her attention, partly because the path was very steep and he wasn't used to cliffs, but also because of his feeling that he and she, isolated together by their sorrows, understood without any words. And when they reached the house, the first to reach it from the church just as if, he couldn't help thinking, they were coming back from their wedding, he told her in his firmest voice to go straight up to her room and lie down, and she obeyed with the sweet obedience of perfect trust.

'Who is that?' asked the man who was helping Miss Entwhistle up the cliff.

'Oh, a *very* old friend of darling Jim's,' she sobbed,—she had been sobbing without stopping from the first words of the burial service, and was quite unable to leave off. 'Mr.—Mr.—We—We—Wemyss——'

'Wemyss? I don't remember coming across him with Jim.'

'Oh, one of his—his *oldest*—f—fr—friends,' sobbed poor Miss Entwhistle, got completely out of control.

Wemyss, continuing in his rôle of chief mourner, was the only person who was asked to spend the evening up at the bereaved house.

'I don't wonder,' said Miss Entwhistle to him at dinner, still with tears in her voice, 'at my dear brother's devotion to you. You have been the greatest help, the greatest comfort——'

And neither Wemyss nor Lucy felt equal to explanation.

What did it matter? Lucy, fatigued by emotions, her mind bruised by the violent demands that had been made on it the last four days, sat drooping at the table, and merely thought that if her father had known Wemyss it would certainly have been true that he was devoted to him. He hadn't known him; he had missed him by—yes, by just three hours; and this wonderful friend of hers was the very first good thing that she and her father hadn't shared. And Wemyss's attitude was simply that if people insist on jumping at conclusions, why, let them. He couldn't anyhow begin to expound himself in the middle of a meal, with a parlourmaid handing dishes round and listening.

But there was an awkward little moment when Miss Entwhistle tearfully wondered—she was eating blanc-mange, the last of a series of cold and pallid dishes with which the imaginative cook, a woman of Celtic origin, had expressed her respectful appreciation of the occasion—whether when the will was read it wouldn't be found that Jim had appointed Mr. Wemyss poor Lucy's guardian.

'I am—dear me, how very hard it is to remember to say I was—my dear brother's only relative. We belong—belonged—to an exiguous family, and naturally I'm no longer as young as I was. There is only—was only—a year between Jim and me, and at any moment I may be——'

Here Miss Entwhistle was interrupted by a sob, and had to put down her spoon.

'—taken,' she finished after a moment, during which the other two sat silent.

'When this happens,' she went on presently, a little recovered, 'poor Lucy will be without any one, unless Jim thought of this and has appointed a guardian. You, Mr. Wemyss, I hope and expect.'

Neither Lucy nor Wemyss spoke. There was the parlourmaid hovering, and one couldn't anyhow go into explanations now which ought to have been made four days ago.

A dead-white cheese was handed round,—something local probably, for it wasn't any form of cheese with which Wemyss was acquainted, and the meal ended with cups of intensely black cold coffee. And all these carefully thought-out expressions of the cook's sympathy were lost on the three, who noticed nothing; certainly they noticed nothing in the way the cook had intended. Wemyss was privately a little put out by the coffee being cold. He had eaten all the other clammy things patiently, but a man likes his after-dinner coffee hot, and it was new in his experience to have it served cold. He did notice this, and was surprised that neither of his companions appeared to. But there,—women were notoriously insensitive to food; on this point the best of them were unintelligent, and the worst of them were impossible. Vera had been awful about it; he had had to do all the ordering of the meals himself at last, and also the engaging of the cooks.

He got up from the table to open the door for the ladies feeling inwardly chilled, feeling, as he put it to himself, slabby inside; and, left alone with a dish of black plums and some sinister-looking wine in a decanter, which he avoided because when he took hold of it ice clinked, he rang the bell as unobtrusively as he could and asked the parlourmaid in a subdued voice, the French window to the garden being open and in the garden being Lucy and her aunt, whether there were such a thing in the house as a whisky and soda.

The parlourmaid, who was a nice-looking girl and much more at home, as she herself was the first to admit, with gentlemen than with ladies, brought it him, and inquired how he had liked the dinner.

'Not at all,' said Wemyss, whose mind on that point was clear.

'No sir,' said the parlourmaid, nodding sympathetically. 'No sir.'

She then explained in a discreet whisper, also with one eye on the open window, how the dinner hadn't been an ordinary dinner and it wasn't expected that it should be enjoyed, but it was the cook's tribute to her late master's burial day,—a master they had only known a week, sad to say, but to whom they had both taken a great fancy, he being so pleasant-spoken and all for giving no trouble.

Wemyss listened, sipping the comforting drink and smoking a cigar.

Very different, said the parlourmaid, who seemed glad to talk, would the dinner have been if the cook hadn't liked the poor gentleman. Why, in one place where she and the cook were together, and the lady was taken just as the cook would have given notice if she hadn't been because she was such a very dishonest and unpunctual lady, besides not knowing her place—no lady, of course, and never was—when she was taken, not sudden like this poor gentleman but bit by bit, on the day of her funeral the cook sent up a dinner you'd never think of,—she was like that, all fancy. Lucky it

314

was that the family didn't read between the lines, for it began with fried soles——

The parlourmaid paused, her eye anxiously on the window. Wemyss sat staring at her.

'Did you say fried soles?' he asked, staring at her.

'Yes sir. Fried soles. I didn't see anything in that either at first. It's how you spell it makes the difference, Cook said. And the next course was'—her voice dropped almost to inaudibleness—'devilled bones.'

Wemyss hadn't so much as smiled for nearly a fortnight, and now to his horror, for what could it possibly sound like to the two mourners on the lawn, he gave a sudden dreadful roar of laughter. He could hear it sounding hideous himself.

The noise he made horrified the parlourmaid as much as it did him. She flew to the window and shut it. Wemyss, in his effort to strangle the horrid thing, choked and coughed, his table-napkin up to his face, his body contorted. He was very red, and the parlourmaid watched him in terror. He had seemed at first to be laughing, though what Uncle Wemyss (thus did he figure in the conversations of the kitchen) could see to laugh at in the cook's way of getting her own back, the parlourmaid, whose flesh had crept when she first heard the story, couldn't understand; but presently she feared he wasn't laughing at all but was being, in some very robust way, ill. Dread seized her, deaths being on her mind, lest perhaps here in the chair, so convulsively struggling behind a table-napkin, were the beginnings of yet another corpse. Having flown to shut the window she now flew to open it, and ran out panic-stricken into the garden to fetch the ladies.

This cured Wemyss. He got up quickly, leaving his half-smoked cigar and his half-drunk whisky, and followed her out just in time to meet Lucy and her aunt hurrying across the lawn towards the dining-room window.

'I choked,' he said, wiping his eyes, which indeed were very wet.

'Choked?' repeated Miss Entwhistle anxiously. 'We heard a most strange noise——'

'That was me choking,' said Wemyss. 'It's all right—it's nothing at all,' he added to Lucy, who was looking at him with a face of extreme concern.

But he felt now that he had had about as much of the death and funeral atmosphere as he could stand. Reaction had set in, and his reactions were strong. He wanted to get away from woe, to be with normal, cheerful people again, to have done with conditions in which a laugh was the most improper of sounds. Here he was, being held down by the head, he felt, in a black swamp,—first that ghastly business of Vera's, and now this woebegone family.

Sudden and violent was Wemyss's reaction, let loose by the parlourmaid's story. Miss Entwhistle's swollen eyes annoyed him. Even Lucy's pathetic face made him impatient. It was against nature, all this. It shouldn't be allowed to go on, it oughtn't to be encouraged. Heaven alone knew how much he had suffered, how much more he had suffered than the Entwhistles with their perfectly normal sorrow, and if he could feel it was high time now to think of other things surely the Entwhistles could. He was tired of funerals. He had carried this one through really brilliantly from start to finish, but now it was over and done with, and he wished to get back to naturalness. Death seemed to him highly unnatural. The mere fact that it only happened once to everybody showed how exceptional it was, thought Wemyss, thoroughly disgusted with it. Why couldn't he and the Entwhistles go off somewhere to-morrow, away from this place altogether, go abroad for a bit, to somewhere cheerful, where nobody knew them and nobody would expect them to go about with long faces all day? Ostend, for instance? His mood of sympathy and gentleness had for the moment quite gone. He was indignant that there should be circumstances under which a man felt as guilty over a laugh as over a crime. A natural person like himself looked at things wholesomely. It was healthy and proper to forget horrors, to dismiss them from one's mind. If convention, that offspring of cruelty and hypocrisy, insisted that one's misfortunes should be well rubbed in, that one should be forced to smart under them, and that the more one was seen to wince the more one was regarded as behaving creditably,—if convention insisted on this, and it did insist, as Wemyss had been experiencing himself since Vera's accident, why then it ought to be defied. He had found he couldn't defy it by himself, and came away solitary and wretched in accordance with what it expected, but he felt quite different now that he had Lucy and her aunt as trusting friends who looked up to him, who had no doubts of him and no criticisms. Health of mind had come back to him,—his own natural wholesomeness, which had never deserted him in his life till this shocking business of Vera's.

'I'd like to have some sensible talk with you,' he said, looking down at the two small black figures and solemn tired faces that were growing dim and wraith-like in the failing light of the garden.

'With me or with Lucy?' asked Miss Entwhistle.

By this time they both hung on his possible wishes, and watched him with the devout attentiveness of a pair of dogs.

'With you and with Lucy,' said Wemyss, smiling at the upturned faces. He felt very conscious of being the male, of being in command.

It was the first time he had called her Lucy. To Miss Entwhistle it seemed a matter of course, but Lucy herself flushed with pleasure, and again had the feeling of being taken care of and safe. Sad as she was at the end of that sad day, she still was able to notice how nice her very ordinary name sounded in this kind man's voice. She wondered what his own name was, and hoped it was something worthy of him,—not Albert, for instance.

'Shall we go into the drawing-room?' asked Miss Entwhistle.

'Why not to the mulberry tree?' said Wemyss, who naturally wished to hold Lucy's little hand if possible, and could only do that in the dark.

So they sat there as they had sat other nights, Wemyss in the middle, and Lucy's hand, when it got dark enough, held close and comfortingly in his.

'This little girl,' he began, 'must get the roses back into her cheeks.'

'Indeed, indeed she must,' agreed Miss Entwhistle, a catch in her voice at the mere reminder of the absence of Lucy's roses, and consequently of what had driven them away.

'How do you propose to set about it?' asked Wemyss.

'Time,' gulped Miss Entwhistle.

'Time?'

'And patience. We must wait we must both wait p-patiently till time has s-softened——'

She hastily pulled out her handkerchief.

'No, no,' said Wemyss, 'I don't at all agree. It isn't natural, it isn't reasonable to prolong sorrow. You'll forgive plain words, Miss Entwhistle, but I don't know any others, and I say it isn't right to wallow—yes, wallow—in sorrow. Far from being patient one should be impatient. One shouldn't wait resignedly for time to help one, one should up and take time by the forelock. In cases of this kind, and believe me I know what I'm talking about'—it was here that his hand, the one on the further side from Miss Entwhistle, descended gently on Lucy's, and she made a little movement closer up to him—'it is due to oneself to refuse to be knocked out. Courage, spirit, is what one must aim at,—setting an example.'

Ah, how wonderful he was, thought Lucy; so big, so brave, so simple, and so tragically recently himself the victim of the most awful of catastrophes. There was something burly about his very talk. Her darling father and his friends had talked quite differently. Their talk used to seem as if it ran about the room like liquid fire, it was so quick and shining; often it was quite beyond her till her father afterwards, when she asked him, explained it, put it more simply for her, eager as he always was that she should share and understand. She could understand every word of Wemyss's. When he spoke she hadn't to strain, to listen with all her might; she hardly had to think at all. She found this immensely reposeful in her present state.

'Yes,' murmured Miss Entwhistle into her handkerchief, 'yes—you're quite right, Mr. Wemyss—one ought—it would be more—more heroic. But then if one—if one has loved some one very tenderly—as I did my dear brother—and Lucy her most precious father——'

She broke off and wiped her eyes.

'Perhaps,' she finished, 'you haven't ever loved anybody very—very particularly and lost them.'

'Oh,' breathed Lucy at that, and moved still closer to him.

Wemyss was deeply injured. Why should Miss Entwhistle suppose he had never particularly loved anybody? He seemed, on looking back, to have loved a great deal. Certainly he had loved Vera with the utmost devotion till she herself wore it down. He indignantly asked himself what this maiden lady could know of love.

But there was Lucy's little hand, so clinging, so understanding, nestling in his. It soothed him.

There was a pause. Then he said, very gravely, 'My wife died only a fortnight ago.'

Miss Entwhistle was crushed. 'Ah,' she cried, 'but you must forgive me——'

V

Nevertheless he was not able to persuade her to join him, with Lucy, in a trip abroad. She was tirelessly concerned to do and say everything she could that showed her deep sympathy with him in his loss—he had told her nothing beyond the bare fact, and she was not one to read about inquests—and her deep sense of obligation to him that he, labouring under so great a burden of sorrow of his own, should have helped them with such devotion and unselfishness in theirs; but she wouldn't go abroad. She was going, she said, to her little house in London with Lucy.

'What, in August?' exclaimed Wemyss.

Yes, they would be quiet there, and indeed they were both worn out and only wished for solitude.

'Then why not stay here?' asked Wemyss, who now considered Lucy's aunt selfish. 'This is solitary enough, in all conscience.'

No, they neither of them felt they could bear to stay in that house. Lucy must go to the place least connected in her mind with her father. Indeed, indeed it was best. She did so understand and appreciate Mr. Wemyss's wonderful and unselfish motives in suggesting the continent, but she and Lucy were in that state when the idea of an hotel and waiters and a band was simply impossible to them, and all they wished was to creep into the quiet and privacy of their own nest,—'Like wounded birds,' said poor Miss Entwhistle, looking up at him with much the piteous expression of a dog lifting an injured paw.

'It's very bad for Lucy to be encouraged to think she's a wounded bird,' said Wemyss, controlling his disappointment as best he could.

'You must come and see us in London and help us to feel heroic,' said Miss Entwhistle, with a watery smile.

'But I can come and see you much better and easier if you're here,' persisted Wemyss.

Miss Entwhistle, however, though watery, was determined. She refused to stay where she so conveniently was, and Wemyss now considered Lucy's aunt obstinate as well as selfish. Also he thought her very ungrateful. She had made use of him, and now was going to leave him, without apparently giving him a thought, in the lurch.

He was having a good deal of Miss Entwhistle, because during the two days that came after the funeral Lucy was practically invisible, engaged in collecting and packing her father's belongings. Wemyss hung about the garden, not knowing when these activities mightn't suddenly cease and not wishing to miss her if she did come out, and Miss Entwhistle, who couldn't help Lucy in this—no one could help her in the heart-breaking work—naturally joined him.

He found these two days long. Miss Entwhistle felt there was a great bond between herself and him, and Wemyss felt there wasn't. When she said there was he had difficulty in not contradicting her. Not only, Miss Entwhistle felt, and also explained, was there the bond of their dear Jim, whom both she and Mr. Wemyss had so much loved, but there was this communion of sorrow,—the loss of his wife, the loss of her brother, within the same fortnight.

Wemyss shut his mouth tight at this and said nothing.

How natural for her, feeling so sorry for him, feeling so grateful to him, when from a window during those two days she beheld him sitting solitary beneath the mulberry tree, to go down and sit there with him; how natural that, when he got up, made restless, she supposed, by his memories, and began to pace the lawn, she should get up and sympathetically pace it too. She could not let this kind, tender-hearted man—he must be that, or Jim wouldn't have been fond of him, besides she had seen it for herself in the way he had helped her and Lucy—she could not let him be alone with his sad thoughts. And he had a double burden of sad thoughts, a double loss to bear, for he had lost her dear brother as well as his poor wife.

All Entwhistles were compassionate, and as she and Wemyss sat together or together paced, she kept up a flow of gentle loving-kindness. Wemyss smoked his pipe in practically unbroken silence. This was his way when he was holding on to himself. Miss Entwhistle of course didn't know he was holding on to himself, and taking his silence for the inarticulateness of deep unhappiness was so much touched that she would have done anything for him, anything that might bring this poor, kind, suffering fellow-creature comfort—except go to Ostend. From that dreadful suggestion she continued to shudder away; nor, though he tried again, even after all arrangements for leaving Cornwall had been made, would she be persuaded to stay where she was.

Therefore Wemyss was forced to conclude that she was obstinate as well as selfish; and if it hadn't been for the brief moments at meals when Lucy appeared, and through her unhappiness—what she was doing was obviously depressing her very much—smiled faintly at him and always went and sat as near him as she could, he would have found these two days intolerable.

How atrocious, he thought, while he smoked in silence and held on to himself, that Lucy should be taken away from him by a mere maiden lady, an aunt, an unmarried aunt,—weakest and most negligible, surely, of all relatives. How atrocious that such a person should have any right to come between him and Lucy, to say she wouldn't do this, that, or the other that Wemyss proposed, and thus possess the power to make him unhappy. Miss Entwhistle was so little that he could have brushed her aside with the back of one hand; yet here again the strong monster public opinion stepped in and forced him to acquiesce in any plan she chose to make for Lucy, however desolate it left him, merely because she stood to her in the anæmic relationship of aunt.

During two mortal days, as he waited about in that garden so grievously infested by Miss Entwhistle, sounds of boxes being moved and drawers being opened and shut came through the windows, but except at meals there was no Lucy. He could have borne it if he hadn't known they were the very last days he would be with her, but as things were it seemed cruel that he should be left like that to be miserable. Why should he be left like that to be miserable, just because of a lot of clothes and papers? he asked himself; and he felt he was getting thoroughly tired of Jim.

'Haven't you done yet?' he said at tea on the second afternoon of this sorting out and packing, when Lucy got up to go indoors again, leaving him with Miss Entwhistle, even before he had finished his second cup of tea.

'You've no idea what a lot there is,' she said, her voice sounding worn out; and she lingered a moment, her hand on the back of her aunt's chair. 'Father brought all his notes with him, and heaps and heaps of letters from people he was consulting, and I'm trying to get them straight—get them as he would have wished——'

Miss Entwhistle put up her hand and stroked Lucy's arm.

'If you weren't in this hurry to go away you'd have had more time and done it comfortably,' said Wemyss.

'Oh, but I don't want more time,' said Lucy quickly.

'Lucy means she couldn't bear it drawn out,' said Miss Entwhistle, leaning her thin cheek against Lucy's sleeve. 'These

321

things—they tear one's heart. And nobody can help her. She has to go through with it alone.' And she drew Lucy's face down to hers and held it there a moment, gently stroking it, the tears brimming up again in the eyes of both.

Always tears, thought Wemyss. Yes, and there always would be tears as long as that aunt had hold of Lucy. She was the arch-wallower, he told himself, filling his pipe in silence after Lucy had gone in.

He got up and went out at the gate and crossed the road and stood staring at the evening sea. Should he hear steps coming after him and Miss Entwhistle were to follow him even beyond the garden, he would proceed without looking round down to the cove and to the inn, where she must needs leave him alone. He had had enough. That Miss Entwhistle should explain to him what Lucy meant, he considered to be the last straw of her behaviour. Barging in, he said indignantly to himself; barging in when nobody had asked her opinion or explanation of anything. And she had stroked Lucy's face as though Lucy and her face and everything about her belonged to her, merely because she happened to be her aunt. Fancy explaining to him what Lucy really meant, taking upon herself the functions of interpreter, of go-between, when for a whole day and a half before she appeared on the scene—and she had only appeared on it at all thanks to his telegram—Lucy and he had been in the closest fellowship, the closest communion....

Well, things couldn't go on like this. He was not the man to be dominated by a relative. If he had lived in those sensible ancient days when people behaved wholesomely, he would have flung Lucy over his shoulder and walked off with her to Ostend or Paris and laughed at such insects as aunts. He couldn't do that unfortunately, though where the harm would be in two mourners like himself and Lucy going together in search of relief he must say he was unable to see. Why should they be condemned to search for relief separately? Their sorrows, surely, would be their chaperone, especially his sorrow. Nobody would object to Lucy's nursing him, supposing he were dangerously ill; why should she not be equally beyond the reach of tongues if she nursed the bitter wounds of his spirit?

He heard steps coming down the garden path to the gate. There, he thought, was the aunt again, searching for him, and he stood squarely and firmly with his back to the road, smoking his pipe and staring at the sea. If he heard the gate open and she dared to come through it he would instantly walk away. In the garden he had to endure being joined by her, because there he was in the position of guest; but let her try to join him on the King's highway!

Nobody opened the gate, however, and, as he heard no retreating footsteps either, after a minute he began to want to look round. He struggled against this wish, because the moment Miss Entwhistle caught his eye she would come out to him, he felt sure. But Wemyss was not much good at struggling against his wishes,—he usually met with defeat; and after briefly doing so on this occasion he did look round. And what a good thing he did, for it was Lucy.

There she was, leaning on the gate just as she had been that first morning, but this time her eyes instead of being wide and blank were watching him with a deep and touching interest.

He got across the road in one stride. 'Lucy!' he exclaimed. 'You? Why didn't you call me? We've wasted half an hour——'

'About two minutes,' she said, smiling up at him as he, on the other side of the gate, folded both her hands in his just as he had done that first morning; and the relief it was to Wemyss to see her again alone, to see that smile of trust and—surely—content in getting back to him!

Then her face went grave again. 'I've finished father's things now,' she said, 'and so I came to look for you.'

'Lucy, how can you leave me,' was Wemyss's answer to that, his voice vibrating, 'how can you go away from me to-morrow and hand me over again to the torments—yes, torments, I was in before?'

'But I have to go,' she said, distressed. 'And you mustn't say that. You mustn't let yourself be like that again. You won't be, I know— you're so brave and strong.'

'Not without you. I'm nothing without you,' said Wemyss; and his eyes, as he searched hers, were full of tears.

At this Lucy flushed, and then, staring at him, her face went slowly white. These words of his, the way he said them, reminded her—oh no, it wasn't possible; he and she stood in a relationship to each other like none, she was sure, that had ever yet been. It was an intimacy arrived at at a bound, with no preliminary steps. It was a holy thing, based on mutual grief, protected from everything ordinary by the great wings of Death. He was her wonderful friend, big in his simplicity, all care for her and goodness, a very rock of refuge and shelter in the wilderness she had been flung into when he found her. And that he, bleeding as he was himself from the lacerations of the violent rending asunder from his wife to whom he had been, as he had told her, devoted, that he should—oh no, it wasn't possible; and she hung her head, shocked at her thoughts. For the way he had said those words, and the words themselves had reminded her—no, she could hardly bear to think it, but they *had* reminded her of the last time she had been proposed to. The man— he was a young man; she had never been proposed to by any one even approximately Wemyss's age—had said almost exactly that: Without you I am nothing. And just in that same deep, vibrating voice.

How dreadful thoughts could be, Lucy said to herself, overcome that such a one at such a moment should thrust itself into her mind. Hateful of her, hateful....

She hung her head in shame; and Wemyss, looking down at the little bobbed head with its bright, thick young hair bent over their folded hands as though it were saying its prayers,—Wemyss, not having his pipe in his mouth to protect him and help him to hold on to himself, for he had hastily stuffed it in his pocket, all alight as it was, when he saw her at the gate, and there at that moment it was burning holes,—Wemyss, after a brief struggle with his wishes, in which as usual he was defeated, stooped and began to kiss Lucy's hair. And having begun, he continued.

She was horrified. At the first kiss she started as if she had been hit, and then, clinging to the gate, she stood without moving, without being able to think or lift her head, in the same attitude bowed over his and her own hands, while this astonishing thing was being done to her hair. Death all round them, death pervading every corner of their lives, death in its blackest shape brooding over him, and—kisses. Her mind, if anything so gentle could be said to be in anything that sounds so loud, was in an uproar. She had had the complete, guileless trust in him of a child for a tender and sympathetic friend,—a friend, not a father, though he was old enough to be her father, because in a father, however much hidden by sweet comradeship as it had been in hers, there always at the back of everything was, after all, authority. And it had been even more than the trust of a child in its friend: it had been the trust of a child in a fellow-child hit by the same punishment,—a simple fellowship, a wordless understanding.

She hung on to the gate while her thoughts flew about in confusion within her. These kisses—and his wife just dead—and dead so terribly—how long would she have to stand there with this going on—she couldn't lift up her head, for then she felt it would only get worse—she couldn't turn and run into the house, because he was holding her hands. He oughtn't to have—oh, he oughtn't to have—it wasn't fair....

Then—what was he saying? She heard him say, in an absolutely broken voice, laying his head on hers, 'We two poor things—we two poor things'—and then he said and did nothing more, but kept his head like that, and presently, thick though her hair was, through it came wetness.

At that Lucy's thoughts suddenly stopped flying about and were quite still. Her heart went to wax within her, melted again into pity, into a great flood of pitiful understanding. The dreadfulness of lonely grief.... Was there anything in the world so blackly desolate as to be left alone in grief? This poor broken fellow-creature—and she herself, so lost, so lost in loneliness—they were two half-drowned things, clinging together in a shipwreck—how could she let him go, leave him to himself—how could she be let go, left to herself....

'Lucy,' he said, 'look at me——'

She lifted her head. He loosed her hands, and put his arms round her shoulders.

'Look at me,' he said; for though she had lifted her head she hadn't lifted her eyes.

She looked at him. Tears were on his face. When she saw them her mouth began to quiver and twitch. She couldn't bear that.

'Lucy——' he said again.

She shut her eyes. 'Yes'—she breathed, 'yes.' And with one hand she felt along up his coat till she reached his face, and shakingly tried to brush away its tears.

VI

After that, for the moment anyhow, it was all over with Lucy. She was engulfed. Wemyss kissed her shut eyes, he kissed her parted lips, he kissed her dear, delightful bobbed hair. His tears dried up; or rather, wiped away by her little blind, shaking hand, there were no more of them. Death for Wemyss was indeed at that moment swallowed up in victory. Instantly he passed from one mood to the other, and when she finally did open her eyes at his orders and look at him, she saw bending over her a face she hardly recognised, for she had not yet seen him happy. Happy! How could he be happy, as happy as that all in a moment? She stared at him, and even through her confusion, her bewilderment, was frankly amazed.

Then the thought crept into her mind that it was she who had done this, it was she who had transformed him, and her stare softened into a gaze almost of awe, with something of the look in it of a young mother when she first sees her new-born baby. 'So that is what it is like,' the young mother whispers to herself in a sort of holy surprise, 'and I have made it, and it is mine'; and so, gazing at this new, effulgent Wemyss, did Lucy say to herself with the same feeling of wonder, of awe at her own handiwork, 'So that is what he is like.'

Wemyss's face was indeed one great beam. He simply at that moment couldn't remember that he had ever been miserable. He seemed to have his arms round Love itself; for never did any one look more like the very embodiment of his idea of love than Lucy then as she gazed up at him, so tender, so resistless. But there were even more wonderful moments after dinner in the darkening garden, while Miss Entwhistle was upstairs packing ready to start by the early train next morning, and they hadn't got the gate between them, and Lucy of her own accord laid her cheek against his coat, nestling her head into it as though there indeed she knew that she was safe.

'My baby—my baby,' Wemyss murmured, in an ecstasy of passionate protectiveness, in his turn flooded by maternal feeling. 'You shall never cry again never, never.'

It irked him that their engagement—Lucy demurred at first to the word engagement, but Wemyss, holding her tight in his arms, said he would very much like to know, then, by what word she would describe her position at that moment—it irked him that it had to be a secret. He wanted instantly to shout out to the whole world his glory and his pride. But this under the tragic circumstances of their mourning was even to Wemyss clearly impossible. Generally he brushed aside the word impossible if it tried to come between him and the smallest of his wishes, but that inquest was still too vividly in his mind, and the faces of his so-called friends. What the faces of his so-called friends would look like if he, before Vera had been dead a fortnight, should approach them with the news of his engagement even Wemyss, a person not greatly imaginative, could picture. And Lucy, quite overwhelmed, first by his tears and then by his joy, no longer could judge anything. She no longer knew whether it were very awful to be love-making in the middle of death, or whether it were, as Wemyss said, the natural glorious self-assertiveness of life. She knew nothing any more except that he and she, shipwrecked, had saved each other, and that for the moment nothing was required of her, no exertion, nothing at all, except to sit passive with her head on his breast, while he called her his baby and softly, wonderfully, kissed her closed eyes. She couldn't think; she needn't think; oh, she was tired—and this was rest.

But after he had gone that night, and all the next day in the train without him, and for the first few days in London, misgivings laid hold of her.

That she should be being made love to, be engaged, as Wemyss insisted, within a week of her father's death, could not, she thought, be called anything worse than possibly and at the outside an irrelevance. It did no harm to her father's dear memory; it in no way encroached on her adoration of him. He would have been the first to be pleased that she should have found comfort. But what worried her was that Everard—Wemyss's Christian name was Everard—should be able to think of such things as love and more marriage when his wife had just died so awfully, and he on the very spot, and he the first to rush out and see....

She found that the moment she was away from him she couldn't get over this. It went round and round in her head as a thing she was unable, by herself, to understand. While she was with him he overpowered her into a torpor, into a shutting of her eyes and her thoughts, into just giving herself up, after the shocks and agonies of the week, to the blessedness of a soothed and caressed semi-consciousness; and it was only when his first letters began to come, such simple, adoring letters, taking the situation just as it was, just as life and death between them had offered it, untroubled by questioning, undimmed by doubt, with no looking backward but with a touching, thankful acceptance of the present, that she gradually settled down into that placidity which was at once the relief and the astonishment of her aunt. And his letters were so easy to understand. They were so restfully empty of the difficult thoughts and subtle, half-said things her father used to write and all his friends. His very handwriting was the round, slow handwriting of a boy. Lucy had loved him before; but now she fell in love with him, and it was because of his letters.

VII

Miss Entwhistle lived in a slim little house in Eaton Terrace. It was one of those little London houses where you go in and there's a dining-room, and you go up and there's a drawing-room, and you go up again and there's a bedroom and a dressing-room, and you go up yet more and there's a maid's room and a bathroom, and then that's all. For one person it was just enough; for two it was difficult. It was so difficult that Miss Entwhistle had never had any one stay with her before, and the dressing-room had to be cleared out of all her clothes and toques, which then had nowhere to go to and became objects that you met at night hanging over banisters or perched with an odd air of dashingness on the ends of the bath, before Lucy could go in.

But no Entwhistle ever minded things like that. No trouble seemed to any of them too great to take for a friend; while as for one's own dear niece, if only she could have been induced to take the real bedroom and let her aunt, who knew the dressing-room's ways, sleep there instead, that aunt—on such liberal principles was this family constructed—would have been perfectly happy.

Lucy, of course, only smiled at that suggestion, and inserted herself neatly into the dressing-room, and the first weeks of their mourning, which Miss Entwhistle had dreaded for them both, proceeded to flow by with a calm, an unruffledness, that could best be described by the word placid.

In that small house, unless the inhabitants were accommodating and adaptable, daily life would be a trial. Miss Entwhistle well knew Lucy would give no trouble that she could help, but their both being in such trouble themselves would, at such close quarters, she had been afraid, inevitably keep their sorrow raw by sheer rubbing against each other.

To her surprise and great relief nothing of the sort happened. There seemed to be no rawness to rub. Not only Lucy didn't fret—her white face and heavy eyes of the days in Cornwall had gone—but she was almost from the first placid. Just on leaving Cornwall, and for a day or two after, she was a little *bouleversée*, and had a curious kind of timidity in her manner to her aunt, and crept rather than walked about the house, but this gradually disappeared; and if Miss Entwhistle hadn't known her, hadn't known of her terrible loss, she would have said that here was some one who was quietly happy. It was subdued, but there it was, as if she had some private source of confidence and warmth. Had she by any chance got religion? wondered her aunt, who herself had never had it, and neither had Jim, and neither had any Entwhistles she had ever heard of. She dismissed that. It was too unlikely for one of their breed. But even the frequent necessary visits to the house in Bloomsbury she and her father had lived in so long didn't quite blot out the odd effect Lucy produced of being somehow inwardly secure. Presently, when these sad settlings up were done with, and the books and furniture stored, and the house handed over to the landlord, and she no longer had to go to it and be among its memories, her face became what it used to be,—delicately coloured, softly rounded, ready to light up at a word, at a look.

Miss Entwhistle was puzzled. This serenity of the one who was, after all, chief mourner, made her feel it would be ridiculous if she outdid Lucy in grief. If Lucy could pull herself together so marvellously—and she supposed it must be that, it must be that she was heroically pulling herself together—she for her part wouldn't be behindhand. Her darling Jim's memory should be honoured, then, like this: she would bless God for him, bless God that she had had him, and in a high thankfulness continue cheerfully on her way.

Such were some of Miss Entwhistle's reflections and conclusions as she considered Lucy. She seemed to have no thought of the future,—again to her aunt's surprise and relief, who had been afraid she would very soon begin to worry about what she was to do next. She never talked of it; she never apparently thought of it. She seemed to be—yes, that was the word, decided Miss Entwhistle observing her—resting. But resting on what? A second time Miss Entwhistle dismissed the idea of religion. Impossible, she thought, that Jim's girl,—yet it did look very like religion.

There was, it appeared, enough money left scraped together by Jim for Lucy in case of his death to produce about two hundred pounds a year. This wasn't much; but Lucy apparently didn't give it a thought. Probably she didn't realise what it meant, thought her aunt, because of her life with her father having been so easy, surrounded by all those necessities for an invalid which were, in fact, to ordinary people luxuries. No one had been appointed her guardian. There was no mention of Mr. Wemyss in the will. It was a very short will, leaving everything to Lucy. This, as far as it went, was admirable, thought Miss Entwhistle, but unfortunately there was hardly anything to leave. Except books; thousands of books, and the old charming furniture of the Bloomsbury house. Well, Lucy should live with her for as long as she could endure the dressing-room, and perhaps they might take a house together a little less tiny, though Miss Entwhistle had lived in the one she was in for so long that it wouldn't be very easy for her to leave it.

Meanwhile the first weeks of mourning slid by in an increasing serenity, with London empty and no one to intrude on what became presently distinctly recognisable as happiness. She and Lucy agreed so perfectly. And they weren't altogether alone either, for Mr. Wemyss came regularly twice a week, coming on the same days, and appearing so punctually on the stroke of five that at last she began to set her clocks by him.

He, too, poor man, seemed to be pulling himself together. He had none of the air of the recently bereaved, either in his features or his clothes. Not that he wore coloured ties or anything like that, but he certainly didn't produce an effect of blackness. His trousers, she observed, were grey; and not a particularly dark grey either. Well, perhaps it was no longer the fashion, thought Miss Entwhistle, eyeing these trousers with some doubt, to be very unhappy. But she couldn't help thinking there ought to be a band on his left arm to counteract the impression of light-heartedness in his legs; a crape band, no matter how narrow, or a band of black anything, not necessarily crape, such as she was sure it was usual in these circumstances to wear.

However, whatever she felt about his legs she welcomed him with the utmost cordiality, mindful of his kindness to them down in Cornwall and of how she had clung to him there as her rock; and she soon got to remember the way he liked his tea, and had the biggest chair placed comfortably ready for him—the chairs were neither very big nor numerous in her spare little drawing-room—and did all she could in the way of hospitality and pleasant conversation. But the more she saw of him, and the more she heard of his talk, the more she wondered at Jim.

Mr. Wemyss was most good-natured, and she was sure, and as she knew from experience, was most kind and thoughtful; but the things he said were so very unlike the things Jim said, and his way of looking at things was so very unlike Jim's way. Not that there wasn't room in the world for everybody, Miss Entwhistle reminded herself, sitting at her tea-table observing Wemyss, who looked particularly big and prosperous in her small frugal room, and no doubt one star differed from another in glory; still, she did wonder at Jim. And if Mr. Wemyss could bear the loss of his wife to the extent of grey trousers, how was it he couldn't bear Jim's name so much as mentioned? Whenever the talk got on to Jim—it couldn't be kept off him in a circle composed of his daughter and his sister and his friend—she noticed that Mr. Wemyss went silent. She would have taken this for excess of sensibility and the sign of a deep capacity for faithful devotion if it hadn't been for those trousers. Faced by them, it perplexed her.

While Miss Entwhistle was thinking like this and observing Wemyss, who never observed her at all after a first moment of surprise that she should look and behave so differently from the liquid lady of the cottage in Cornwall, that she should sit so straight and move so briskly, he and Lucy were, though present in the body, absent in love. Round them was drawn that magic circle through which nobody and nothing can penetrate, and within it they sat hand in hand and safe. Lucy's whole heart was his. He only had to come into the room for her to feel content. There was a naturalness, a bigness about his way of looking at things that made intricate, tormenting feelings shrink away in his presence ashamed. Quite apart from her love for him, her gratitude, her longing that he should go on now being happy and forget his awful tragedy, he was so very comfortable. She had never met any one so comfortable to lean on mentally. Bodily, on the few occasions on which her aunt was out of the room, he was comfortable too; he reminded her of the very nicest of sofas,—expensive ones, all cushions. But mentally he was more than comfortable, he was positively luxurious. Such perfect rest, listening to his talk. No thinking needed. Things according to him were either so, or so. With her father things had never been either so, or so; and one had had to frown, and concentrate, and make efforts to follow and understand his distinctions, his infinitely numerous, delicate, difficult distinctions. Everard's plain division of everything into two categories only, snow-white and jet-black, was as reposeful as the Roman church. She hadn't got to strain or worry, she had only to surrender. And to what love, to what safety! At night she couldn't go to bed for thinking of how happy she was. She would sit quite still in the little dressing-room, her hands in her lap, and a proverb she had read somewhere running in her head:

When God shuts the door He opens the window.

Not for a moment, hardly, had she been left alone to suffer. Instantly, almost, Everard had come into her life and saved her. Lucy had indeed, as her aunt had twice suspected, got religion, but her religion was Wemyss. Ah, how she loved him! And every night she slept with his last letter under her pillow on the side of her heart.

As for Wemyss, if Lucy couldn't get over having got him he couldn't get over having got Lucy. He hadn't had such happiness as this, of this quality of tenderness, of goodness, in his life before. What he had felt for Vera had not at any time, he was sure, even at the beginning, been like this. While for the last few years—oh, well. Wemyss, when he found himself thinking of Vera, pulled up short. He declined to think of her now. She had filled his thoughts enough lately, and how terribly. His little angel Lucy had healed that wound, and there was no use in thinking of an old wound; nobody healthy ever did that. He had explained to Lucy, who at first had been a little morbid, how wrong it is, how really wicked, besides being intensely stupid, not to get over things. Life, he had said, is for the living; let the dead have death. The present is the only real possession a man has, whatever clever people may say; and the wise man, who is also the natural man of simple healthy instincts and a proper natural shrinking from death and disease, does not allow the past, which after all anyhow is done for, to intrude upon, much less spoil, the present. That is what, he explained, the past will always do if it can. The only safe way to deal with it is to forget it.

'But I don't want to forget mine,' Lucy had said at that, opening her eyes, which as usual had been shut, because the commas of Wemyss's talk with her when they chanced to be alone were his soothing, soporific kisses dropped gently on her closed eyelids. 'Father——'

'Oh, you may remember yours,' he had answered, smiling tenderly down at the head lying on his breast. 'It's such a little one. But you'll see when you're older if your Everard wasn't right.'

To Wemyss in his new happiness it seemed that Vera had belonged to another life altogether, an elderly, stale life from which, being healthy-minded, he had managed to unstick himself and to emerge born again all new and fresh and fitted for the present. She was forty when she died. She had started life five years younger than he was, but had quickly caught him up and passed him, and had ended, he felt, by being considerably his senior. And here was Lucy, only twenty-two anyhow, and looking like twelve. The contrast never ceased to delight him, to fill him with pride. And how pretty she was, now that she had left off crying. He adored her bobbed hair that gave her the appearance of a child or a very young boy, and he adored the little delicate lines of her nose and nostrils, and her rather big, kind mouth that so easily smiled, and her sweet eyes, the colour of Love-in-a-Mist. Not that he set any store by prettiness, he told himself; all he asked in a woman was devotion. But her being pretty would make it only the more exciting when the moment came to show her to his friends, to show his little girl to those friends who had dared slink away from him after Vera's death, and say, 'Look here—look at this perfect little thing—*she* believes in me all right!'

VIII

London being empty, Wemyss had it all his own way. No one else was there to cut him out, as his expression was. Lucy had many letters with offers of every kind of help from her father's friends, but naturally she needed no help and had no wish to see anybody in her present condition of secret contentment, and she replied to them with thanks and vague expressions of hope that later on they might all meet. One young man—he was the one who often proposed to her—wasn't to be put off like that, and journeyed all the way from Scotland, so great was his devotion, and found out from the caretaker of the Bloomsbury house that she was living with her aunt, and called at Eaton Terrace. But that afternoon Lucy and Miss Entwhistle were taking the air in a car Wemyss had hired, and at the very moment the young man was being turned away from the Eaton Terrace door Lucy was being rowed about the river at Hampton Court—very slowly, because of how soon Wemyss got hot—and her aunt, leaning on the stone parapet at the end of the Palace gardens, was observing her. It was a good thing the young man wasn't observing her too, for it wouldn't have made him happy.

'What is Mr. Wemyss?' asked Miss Entwhistle unexpectedly that evening, just as they were going to bed.

Lucy was taken aback. Her aunt hadn't asked a question or said a thing about him up to then, except general comments on his kindness and good-nature.

'What is Mr. Wemyss?' she repeated stupidly; for she was not only taken aback, but also, she discovered, she had no idea. It had never occurred to her even to wonder what he was, much less to ask. She had been, as it were, asleep the whole time in a perfect contentment on his breast.

'Yes. What is he besides being a widower?' said Miss Entwhistle. 'We know he's that, but it is hardly a profession.'

'I—don't think I know,' said Lucy, looking and feeling very stupid.

'Oh well, perhaps he isn't anything,' said her aunt kissing her good-night. 'Except punctual,' she added, smiling, pausing a moment at her bedroom door.

And two or three days later, when Wemyss had again hired a car to take them for an outing to Windsor, while she and Lucy were tidying themselves for tea in the ladies' room of the hotel she turned from the looking-glass in the act of pinning back some hair loosened by motoring, and in spite of having a hairpin in her mouth said, again suddenly, 'What did Mrs. Wemyss die of?'

This unnerved Lucy. If she had stared stupidly at her aunt at the other question she stared aghast at her at this one.

'What did she die of?' she repeated, flushing.

'Yes. What illness was it?' asked her aunt, continuing to pin.

'It—wasn't an illness,' said Lucy helplessly.

'Not an illness?'

'I—believe it was an accident.'

'An accident?' said Miss Entwhistle, taking the hairpin out of her mouth and in her turn staring. 'What sort of an accident?'

'I think a rather serious one,' said Lucy, completely unnerved.

How could she bear to tell that dreadful story, the knowledge of which seemed somehow so intimately to bind her and Everard together with a sacred, terrible tie?

At that her aunt remarked that an accident resulting in death would usually be described as serious, and asked what its nature, apart from its seriousness, had been; and Lucy, driven into a corner, feeling instinctively that her aunt, who had already once or twice expressed what she said was her surprised admiration for Mr. Wemyss's heroic way of bearing his bereavement, might be too admiringly surprised altogether if she knew how tragically much he really had to bear, and might begin to inquire into the reasons of this heroism, took refuge in saying what she now saw she ought to have begun by saying, even though it wasn't true, that she didn't know.

'Ah,' said her aunt. 'Well—poor man. It's wonderful how he bears things.' And again in her mind's eye, and with an increased doubt, she saw the grey trousers.

That day at tea Wemyss, with the simple naturalness Lucy found so restful, the almost bald way he had of talking frankly about things more sophisticated people wouldn't have mentioned, began telling them of the last time he had been at Windsor.

It was the summer before, he said, and he and his wife—at this Miss Entwhistle became attentive—had motored down one Sunday to lunch in that very room, and it had been so much crowded, and the crowding had been so monstrously mismanaged, that positively they had had to go away without having had lunch at all.

'Positively without having had any lunch at all,' repeated Wemyss, looking at them with a face full of astonished aggrievement at the mere recollection.

'Ah,' said Miss Entwhistle, leaning across to him, 'don't let us revive sad memories.'

Wemyss stared at her. Good heavens, he thought, did she think he was talking about Vera? Any one with a grain of sense would know he was only talking about the lunch he hadn't had.

He turned impatiently to Lucy, and addressed his next remark to her. But in another moment there was her aunt again.

'Mr. Wemyss,' she said, 'I've been dying to ask you——'

Again he was forced to attend. The pure air and rapid motion of the motoring intended to revive and brace his little love were apparently reviving and bracing his little love's aunt as well, for lately he had been unable to avoid noticing a tendency on her part to assert herself. During his first eight visits to Eaton Terrace—that made four weeks since his coming back to London and six since the funeral in Cornwall—he had hardly known she was in the room; except, of course, that she *was* in the room, completely hindering his courting. During those eight visits his first impression of her remained undisturbed in his mind: she was a wailing creature who had hung round him in Cornwall in a constant state of tears. Down there she had behaved exactly like the traditional foolish woman when there is a death about,—no common sense, no grit, crying if you looked at her, and keeping up a continual dismal recital of the virtues of the departed. Also she had been obstinate; and she had, besides, shown unmistakable signs of selfishness. When he paid his first call in Eaton Terrace he did notice that she had considerably, indeed completely, dried up, and was therefore to that extent improved, but she still remained for him just Lucy's aunt,— somebody who poured out the tea, and who unfortunately hardly ever went out of the room; a necessary, though luckily a transitory, evil. But now it was gradually being borne in on him that she really existed, on her own account, independently. She asserted herself. Even when she wasn't saying anything—and often she said hardly a word during an entire outing—she still somehow asserted herself.

And here she was asserting herself very much indeed, and positively asking him across a tea-table which was undoubtedly for the moment his, asking him straight out what, if anything, he did in the way of a trade, profession or occupation.

She was his guest, and he regarded it as less than seemly for a guest to ask a host what he did. Not that he wouldn't gladly have told her if it had come from him of his own accord. Surely a man has a right, he thought, to his own accord. At all times Wemyss disliked being asked questions. Even the most innocent, ordinary question appeared to him to be an encroachment on the right he surely had to be let alone.

Lucy's aunt between sips of tea—his tea—pretended, pleasantly it is true, and clothing what could be nothing but idle curiosity in words that were not disagreeable, that she was dying to know what he was. She could see for herself, she said, smiling down at the leg nearest her, that he wasn't a bishop, she was sure he wasn't either a painter, musician or writer, but she wouldn't be in the least surprised if he were to tell her he was an admiral.

Wemyss thought this intelligent of the aunt. He had no objection to being taken for an admiral; they were an honest, breezy lot.

Placated, he informed her that he was on the Stock Exchange.

'Ah,' nodded Miss Entwhistle, looking wise because on this subject she so completely wasn't, the Stock Exchange being an institution whose nature and operations were alien to anything the Entwhistles were familiar with; 'ah yes. Quite. Bulls and bears. Now I come to look at it, you have the Stock Exchange eye.'

'Foolish woman,' thought Wemyss, who for some reason didn't like being told before Lucy that he had the Stock Exchange eye; and he dismissed her impatiently from his mind and concentrated on his little love, asking himself while he did so how short he could, with any sort of propriety, cut this unpleasant time of restricted courting, of never being able to go anywhere with her unless her tiresome aunt came too.

Nearly two months now since both those deaths; surely Lucy's aunt might soon be told now of the engagement. It was after this outing that he began in his letters, and in the few moments he and she were alone, to urge Lucy to tell her aunt. Nobody else need know, he wrote; it could go on being kept secret from the world; but the convenience of her aunt's knowing was so obvious,—think of how she would then keep out of the way, think of how she would leave them to themselves, anyhow indoors, anyhow in the house in Eaton Terrace.

Lucy, however, was reluctant. She demurred. She wrote begging him to be patient. She said that every week that passed would make their engagement less a thing that need surprise. She said that at present it would take too much explaining, and she wasn't sure that even at the end of the explanation her aunt would understand.

Wemyss wrote back brushing this aside. He said her aunt would have to understand, and if she didn't what did it matter so long as she knew? The great thing was that she should know. Then, he said, she would leave them alone together, instead of for ever sticking; and his little love must see how splendid it would be for him to come and spend happy hours with her quite alone. What was an aunt after all? he asked. What could she possibly be, compared to Lucy's own Everard? Besides, he disliked secrecy, he said. No honest man could stand an atmosphere of concealment. His little girl must make up her mind to tell her aunt, and believe that her Everard knew best; or, if she preferred it, he would tell her himself.

Lucy didn't prefer it, and was beginning to feel worried, because as the days went on Wemyss grew more and more persistent the more he became bored by Miss Entwhistle's development of an independent and inquiring mind, and she hated having to refuse or even to defer doing anything he asked, when her aunt one morning at breakfast, in the very middle of apparent complete serene absorption in her bacon, looked up suddenly over the coffee-pot and said, 'How long had your father known Mr. Wemyss?'

This settled things. Lucy felt she could bear no more of these shocks. A clean breast was the only thing left for her.

'Aunt Dot,' she stammered—Miss Entwhistle's Christian name was Dorothy,—'I'd like—I've got—I want to tell you——'

'After breakfast,' said Miss Entwhistle briskly. 'We shall need lots of time, and to be undisturbed. We'll go up into the drawing-room.'

And immediately she began talking about other things.

Was it possible, thought Lucy, her eyes carefully on her toast and butter, that Aunt Dot suspected?

IX

It was not only possible, but the fact. Aunt Dot had suspected, only she hadn't suspected anything like all that was presently imparted to her, and she found great difficulty in assimilating it. And two hours later Lucy, standing in the middle of the drawing-room, was still passionately saying to her, and saying it for perhaps the tenth time, 'But don't you *see*? It's just *because* what happened to him was so awful. It's nature asserting itself. If he couldn't be engaged now, if he couldn't reach up out of such a pit of blackness and get into touch with living things again and somebody who sympathises and—is fond of him, he would die, die or go mad; and oh, what's the *use* to the world of somebody good and fine being left to die or go mad? Aunt Dot, what's the *use*?'

And her aunt, sitting in her customary chair by the fireplace, continued to assimilate with difficulty. Also her face was puckered into folds of distress. She was seriously upset.

Lucy, looking at her, felt a kind of despair that she wasn't being able to make her aunt, whom she loved, see what she saw, understand what she understood, and so be, as she was, filled with confidence and happiness. Not that she was happy at that moment; she, too, was seriously upset, her face flushed, her eyes bright with effort to get Wemyss as she knew him, as he so simply was, through into her aunt's consciousness.

She had made her clean breast with a completeness that had included the confession that she did know what Mrs. Wemyss's accident had been, and she had described it. Her aunt was painfully shocked. Anything so horrible as that hadn't entered her mind. To fall past the very window her husband was sitting at ... it seemed to her dreadful that Lucy should be mixed up in it, and mixed up so instantly on the death of her of her natural protector,—of her two natural protectors, for hadn't Mrs. Wemyss as long as she existed also been one? She was bewildered, and couldn't understand the violent reactions that Lucy appeared to look upon as so natural in Wemyss. She would have concluded that she didn't understand because she was too old, because she was out of touch with the elasticities of the younger generation, but Wemyss must be very nearly as old as herself. Certainly he was of the same generation; and yet behold him, within a fortnight of his wife's most shocking death, able to forget her, able to fall in love——

'But that's *why*—that's *why*,' Lucy cried when Miss Entwhistle said this. 'He *had* to forget, or die himself. It was beyond what anybody could bear and stay sane——'

'I'm sure I'm very glad he should stay sane,' said Miss Entwhistle, more and more puckered, 'but I can't help wishing it hadn't been you, Lucy, who are assisting him to stay it.'

And then she repeated what at intervals she had kept on repeating with a kind of stubborn helplessness, that her quarrel with Mr. Wemyss was that he had got happy so very quickly.

'Those grey trousers,' she murmured.

No; Miss Entwhistle couldn't get over it. She couldn't understand it. And Lucy, expounding and defending Wemyss in the middle of the room with all the blaze and emotion of what was only too evidently genuine love, was to her aunt an astonishing sight. That little thing, defending that enormous man. Jim's daughter; Jim's cherished little daughter....

Miss Entwhistle, sitting in her chair, struggled among other struggles to be fair, and reminded herself that Mr. Wemyss had proved himself to be most kind and eager to help down in Cornwall,—though even on this there was shed a new and disturbing light, and that now that she knew everything, and the doubts that had made her perhaps be a little unjust were out of the way and she could begin to consider him impartially, she would probably very soon become sincerely attached to him. She hoped so with all her heart. She was used to being attached to people. It was normal to her to like and be liked. And there must be something more in him than his fine appearance for Lucy to be so very fond of him.

She gave herself a shake. She told herself she was taking this thing badly; that she ought not, just because it was an unusual situation, be so ready to condemn it. Was she really only a conventional spinster, shrinking back shocked at a touch of naked naturalness? Wasn't there much in what that short-haired child was so passionately saying about the rightness, the saneness, of reaction from horror? Wasn't it nature's own protection against too much death? After all, what was the good of doubling horror, of being so much horrified at the horrible that you stayed rooted there and couldn't move, and became, with your starting eyes and bristling hair, a horror yourself?

Better, of course, to pass on, as Lucy was explaining, to get on with one's business, which wasn't death but life. Still—there were the decencies. However desolate one would be in retirement, however much one would suffer, there was a period, Miss Entwhistle felt, during which the bereaved withdrew. Instinctively. The really bereaved *would* want to withdraw——

'Ah, but don't you *see*,' Lucy once more tried despairingly to explain, 'this wasn't just being bereaved—this was something simply too awful. Of course Everard would have behaved in the ordinary way if it had been an ordinary death.'

'So that the more terrible one's sorrow the more cheerfully one goes out to tea,' said Miss Entwhistle, the remembrance of the light trousers at one end of Wemyss and the unmistakably satisfied face at the other being for a moment too much for her.

'Oh,' almost moaned Lucy at that, and her head drooped in a sudden fatigue.

Miss Entwhistle got up quickly and put her arms round her. 'Forgive me,' she said. 'That was just stupid and cruel. I think I'm hide-bound. I think I've probably got into a rut. Help me out of it, Lucy. You shall teach me to take heroic views——'

And she kissed her hot face tenderly, holding it close to her own.

'But if I could only make you *see*,' said Lucy, clinging to her, tears in her voice.

'But I do see that you love him very much,' said Miss Entwhistle gently, again very tenderly kissing her.

That afternoon when Wemyss appeared at five o'clock, it being his bi-weekly day for calling, he found Lucy alone.

'Why, where——? How——-?' he asked, peeping round the drawing-room as though Miss Entwhistle must be lurking behind a chair.

'I've told,' said Lucy, who looked tired.

Then he clasped her with a great hug to his heart. 'Everard's own little love,' he said, kissing and kissing her. 'Everard's own good little love.'

'Yes, but——' began Lucy faintly. She was, however, so much muffled and engulfed that her voice didn't get through.

'Now wasn't I right?' he said triumphantly, holding her tight. 'Isn't this as it should be? Just you and me, and nobody to watch or interfere?'

'Yes, but——' began Lucy again.

'What do you say? "Yes, but?"' laughed Wemyss, bending his ear. 'Yes without any but, you precious little thing. Buts don't exist for us—only yeses.'

And on these lines the interview continued for quite a long time before Lucy succeeded in telling him that her aunt had been much upset.

Wemyss minded that so little that he didn't even ask why. He was completely incurious about anything her aunt might think. 'Who cares?' he said, drawing her to his heart again. 'Who cares? We've got each other. What does anything else matter? If you had fifty aunts, all being upset, what would it matter? What can it matter to us?'

And Lucy, who was exhausted by her morning, felt too as she nestled close to him that nothing did matter so long as he was there. But the difficulty was that he wasn't there most of the time, and her aunt was, and she loved her aunt and did very much hate that she should be upset.

She tried to convey this to Wemyss, but he didn't understand. When it came to Miss Entwhistle he was as unable to understand Lucy as Miss Entwhistle was unable to understand her when it came to Wemyss. Only Wemyss didn't in the least mind not understanding. Aunts. What were they? Insects. He laughed, and said his little love couldn't have it both ways; she couldn't eat her cake, which was her Everard, and have it too, which was her aunt; and he kissed her hair and asked who was a complicated little baby, and rocked her gently to and fro in his arms, and Lucy was amused at that and laughed too, and forgot her aunt, and forgot everything except how much she loved him.

Meanwhile Miss Entwhistle was spending a diligent afternoon in the newspaper room of the British Museum. She was reading *The Times* report of the Wemyss accident and inquest; and if she had been upset by what Lucy told her in the morning she was even more upset by what she read in the afternoon. Lucy hadn't mentioned that suggestion of suicide. Perhaps he hadn't told her. Suicide. Well, there had been no evidence. There was an open verdict. It had been a suggestion made by a servant, perhaps a servant with a grudge. And even if it had been true, probably the poor creature had discovered she had some incurable disease, or she may have had some loss that broke her down temporarily, and—oh, there were many explanations; respectable, ordinary explanations.

Miss Entwhistle walked home slowly, loitering at shop windows, staring at hats and blouses that she never saw, spinning out her walk to its utmost, trying to think. Suicide. How desolate it sounded on that beautiful afternoon. Such a giving up. Such a defeat. Why should she have given up? Why should she have been defeated? But it wasn't true. The coroner had said there was no evidence to show how she came by her death.

Miss Entwhistle walked slower and slower. The nearer she got to Eaton Terrace the more unwillingly did she advance. When she reached Belgrave Square she went right round it twice, lingering at the garden railings studying the habits of birds. She had been out all the afternoon, and, as those who have walked it know, it is a long way from the British Museum to Eaton Terrace. Also it was a hot day and her feet ached, and she very much would have liked to be in her own chair in her cool drawing-room having her tea. But there in that drawing-room would probably still be Mr. Wemyss, no longer now to be Mr. Wemyss for her—would she really have to call him Everard?—or she might meet him on the stairs—narrow stairs; or in the hall—also narrow, which he would fill up; or on her doorstep she might meet him, filling up her doorstep; or, when she turned the corner into her street, there, coming towards her, might be the triumphant trousers.

No, she felt she couldn't stand seeing him that day. So she lingered forlornly watching the sparrows inside the garden railings of Belgrave Square, balancing first on one and then on the other of those feet that ached.

This was only the beginning, she thought; this was only the first of many days for her of wandering homelessly round. Her house was too small to hold both herself and love-making. If it had been the slender love-making of the young man who was so doggedly devoted to Lucy, she felt it wouldn't have been too small. He would have made love youthfully, shyly. She could have sat quite happily in the dining-room while the suitably paired young people dallied delicately together overhead. But she couldn't bear the thought of being cramped up so near Mr. Wemyss's—no, Everard's; she had better get used to that at once—love-making. His way of courting wouldn't be,—she searched about in her uneasy mind for a word, and found vegetarian. Yes; that word sufficiently indicated what she meant: it wouldn't be vegetarian.

Miss Entwhistle drifted away from the railings, and turning her back on her own direction wandered towards Sloane Street. There she saw an omnibus stopping to let some one out. Wanting very much to sit down she made an effort and caught it, and squeezing herself into its vacant seat gave herself up to wherever it should take her.

It took her to the City; first to the City, and then to strange places beyond. She let it take her. Her clothes became steadily more fashionable the farther the omnibus went. She ended by being conspicuous and stared at. But she was determined to give the widest margin to the love-making and go the whole way, and she did.

For an hour and a half the omnibus went on and on. She had no idea omnibuses did such things. When it finally stopped she sat still; and the conductor, who had gradually come to share the growing surprise of the relays of increasingly poor passengers, asked her what address she wanted.

She said she wanted Sloane Street.

He was unable to believe it, and tried to reason with her, but she sat firm in her place and persisted.

At nine o'clock he put her down where he had taken her up. She disappeared into the darkness with the movements of one who is stiff, and he winked at the passenger nearest the door and touched his forehead.

But as she climbed wearily and hungrily up her steps and let herself in with her latchkey, she felt it had been well worth it; for that one day at least she had escaped Mr. We—— no, Everard.

X

Miss Entwhistle, however, made up her mind very firmly that after this one afternoon of giving herself up to her feelings she was going to behave in the only way that is wise when faced by an inevitable marriage, the way of sympathy and friendliness.

Too often had she seen the first indignation of disappointed parents at the marriages of their children harden into a matter of pride, a matter of doggedness and principle, and finally become an attitude unable to be altered, long after years had made it ridiculous. If the marriages turned out happy, how absurd to persist in an antiquated disapproval; if they turned out wretched, then how urgent the special need for love.

Thus Miss Entwhistle reasoned that first sleepless night in bed, and on these lines she proceeded during the next few months. They were trying months. She used up all she had of gallantry in sticking to her determination. Lucy's instinct had been sound, that wish to keep her engagement secret from her aunt for as long as possible. Miss Entwhistle, always thin, grew still more thin in her constant daily and hourly struggle to be pleased, to enter into Lucy's happiness, to make things easy for her, to protect her from the notice and inquiry of their friends, to look hopefully and with as much of Lucy's eyes as she could at Everard and at the future.

'She isn't simple enough,' Wemyss would say to Lucy if ever she said anything about her aunt's increasing appearance of strain and overwork. 'She should take things more naturally. Look at us.' For it was the one fly in Lucy's otherwise perfect ointment, this intermittent consciousness that her aunt wasn't altogether happy.

And then he would ask her, laying his head on hers as he stood with his arms about her, who had taught his little girl to be simple; and they would laugh, and kiss, and talk of other things.

Miss Entwhistle was unable to be simple in Wemyss's sense. She tried to; for when she saw his fresh, unlined face, his forehead without a wrinkle on it, and compared it in the glass with her own which was only three years older, she thought there must be a good deal to be said for single-mindedness. It was Lucy who told her Everard was so single-minded. He took one thing at a time, she said, concentrating quietly. When he had completely finished it off then, and not till then, he went on to the next. He knew his own mind.

346

Didn't Aunt Dot think it was a great thing to know one's own mind? Instead of wobbling about, wasting one's thoughts and energies on side-shows?

This was the very language of Wemyss; and Miss Entwhistle, after having been listening to him in the afternoon—for every time he came she put in a brief appearance just for the look of the thing, and on the Saturday and Sunday outings she was invariably present the whole time—felt it a little hard that when at last she had reached the end of the day and the harbour of her empty drawing-room she should, through the mouth of Lucy, have to listen to him all the evening as well.

But she always agreed, and said Yes, he was a great dear; for when an only and much-loved niece is certainly going to marry, the least a wise aunt can call her future nephew is a great dear. She will make this warmer and more varied if she can, but at least she will say that much. Miss Entwhistle tried to think of variations, afraid Lucy might notice a certain sameness, and once with an effort she faltered out that he seemed to be a—a real darling; but it had a hollow sound, and she didn't repeat it. Besides, Lucy was quite satisfied with the other.

She used, sitting at her aunt's feet in the evenings—Wemyss never came in the evenings because he distrusted the probable dinner—sometimes to make her aunt say it again, by asking a little anxiously, 'But you *do* think him a great dear, don't you, Aunt Dot?' Whereupon Miss Entwhistle, afraid her last expression of that opinion may have been absent-minded, would hastily exclaim with almost excess of emphasis, 'Oh, a *great* dear.'

Perhaps he was a dear. She didn't know. What had she against him? She didn't know. He was too old, that was one thing; but the next minute, after hearing something he had said or laughed at, she thought he wasn't old enough. Of course what she really had against him was that he had got over his wife's shocking death so quickly. Yet she admitted there was much in Lucy's explanation of this as a sheer instinctive gesture of self-defence. Besides, she couldn't keep it up as a grudge against him for ever; with every day it mattered less. And sometimes Miss Entwhistle even doubted whether it was this that mattered to her at all,—whether it was not rather some quite small things that she really objected to: a want of fastidiousness, for instance, a forgetfulness of the minor courtesies,—the objections, in a word, she told herself smiling, of an old maid. Lucy seemed not to mind his blunders in these directions in the least. She seemed positively, thought her aunt, to take a kind of pride in them, delighting in everything he said or did with the adoring tenderness of a young mother watching the pranks of her first-born. She laughed gaily; she let him caress her openly. She too, thought Miss Entwhistle, had become what she no doubt would say was single-minded. Well, perhaps all this was a spinster's way of feeling about a type not previously met with, and she had got—again she reproached herself—into an elderly groove. Jim's friends,—well, they had been different, but not necessarily better. Mr. Wemyss would call them, she was sure, a finicking lot.

When in October London began to fill again, and Jim's friends came to look her and Lucy up and showed a tendency, many of them, to keep on doing it, a new struggle was added to her others, the struggle to prevent their meeting Wemyss. He wouldn't, she was convinced, be able to hide his proprietorship in Lucy, and Lucy wouldn't ever get that look of tenderness out of her eyes when they rested on him. Questions as to who he was would naturally be asked, and one or other of Jim's friends would be sure to remember the affair of Mrs. Wemyss's death; indeed, that day she went to the British Museum and read the report of it she had been amazed that she hadn't seen it at the time. It took up so much of the paper that she was bound to have seen it if she had seen a paper at all. She could only suppose that as she was visiting friends just then, she chanced that day to have been in the act of leaving or arriving, and that if she bought a paper on the journey she had looked, as was sometimes her way in trains, not at it but out of the window.

She felt she hadn't the strength to support being questioned, and in her turn have to embark on the explanation and defence of Wemyss. There was too much of him, she felt, to be explained. He ought to be separated into sections, and taken gradually and bit by bit,—but far best not to produce him, to keep him from meeting her friends. She therefore arranged a day in the week when she would be at home, and discouraged every one from the waste of time of trying to call on her on other days. Then presently the afternoon became an evening once a week, when whoever liked could come in after dinner and talk and drink coffee, because the evening was safer; made safe by Wemyss's conviction—he hadn't concealed it—that the dinners of maiden ladies were notoriously both scanty and bad.

348

Lucy would have preferred never to see a soul except Wemyss, who was all she wanted, all she asked for in life; but she did see her aunt's point, that only by pinning their friends to a day and an hour could the risk of their overflowing into precious moments be avoided. This is how Miss Entwhistle put it to her, wondering as she said it at her own growing ability in artfulness.

She had an old friend living in Chesham Street, a widow full of that ripe wisdom that sometimes comes at the end to those who have survived marriage; and to her, when the autumn brought her back to London, Miss Entwhistle went occasionally in search of comfort.

'What in the whole world puts such a gulf between two affections and comprehensions as a new love?' she asked one day, freshly struck, because of something Lucy had said, by the distance she had travelled. Lucy was quite a tiny figure now, so far away from her had she moved; she couldn't even get her voice to carry to her, much less still hold on to her with her hands.

And the friend, made brief of speech by wisdom, said: 'Nothing.'

About Wemyss's financial position Miss Entwhistle could only judge from appearances, for it wouldn't have occurred to him that it might perhaps be her concern to know, and she preferred to wait till later, when the engagement could be talked about, to ask some old friend of Jim's to make the proper inquiries; but from the way he lived it seemed to be an easy one. He went freely in taxis, he hired cars with a reasonable frequency, he inhabited one of the substantial houses of Lancaster Gate, and also, of course, he had The Willows, the house on the river near Strorley where his wife had died. After all, what could be better than two houses, Miss Entwhistle thought, congratulating herself, as it were, on Lucy's behalf that this side of Wemyss was so satisfactory. Two houses, and no children; how much better than the other way about. And one day, feeling almost hopeful about Lucy's prospects, on the advantages of which she had insisted that her mind should dwell, she went round again to the widow in Chesham Street and said suddenly to her, who was accustomed to these completely irrelevant exclamatory inquiries from her friend, and who being wise was also incurious, 'What can be better than two houses?'

To which the widow, whose wisdom was more ripe than comforting, replied disappointingly: 'One.'

Later, when the marriage loomed very near, Miss Entwhistle, who found that she was more than ever in need of reassurance instead of being, as she had hoped to become, more reconciled, went again, in a kind of desperation this time, to the widow, seeking some word from her who was so wise that would restore her to tranquillity, that would dispel her absurd persistent doubts. 'After all,' she said almost entreatingly, 'what can be better than a devoted husband?'

And the widow, who had had three and knew what she was talking about, replied with the large calm of those who have finished and can in leisure weigh and reckon up: 'None.'

XI

The Wemyss-Entwhistle engagement proceeded on its way of development through the ordinary stages of all engagements: secrecy complete, secrecy partial, semi-publicity, and immediately after that entire publicity, with its inevitable accompanying uproar. The uproar, always more or less audible to the protagonists, of either approval or disapproval, was in this case one of unanimous disapproval. Lucy's father's friends protested to a man. The atmosphere at Eaton Terrace was convulsed; and Lucy, running as she always did to hide from everything upsetting into Wemyss's arms, was only made more certain than ever that there alone was peace.

This left Miss Entwhistle to face the protests by herself. There was nothing for it but to face them. Jim had had so many intimate, devoted friends, and each of them apparently regarded his daughter as his special care and concern. One or two of the younger ones, who had been disciples rather than friends, were in love with her themselves, and these were specially indignant and vocal in their indignation. Miss Entwhistle found herself in the position she had tried so hard to avoid, that of defending and explaining Wemyss to a highly sceptical, antagonistic audience. It was as if, forced to fight for him, she was doing so with her back to her drawing-room wall.

Lucy couldn't help her, because though she was distressed that her aunt should be being worried because of her affairs, yet she did feel that Everard was right when he said that her affairs concerned nobody in the world but herself and him. She, too, was indignant, but her indignation was because her father's friends, who had been ever since she could remember always good and kind, besides perfectly intelligent and reasonable, should with one accord, and without knowing anything about Everard except that story of the accident, be hostile to her marrying him. The ready unfairness, the willingness immediately to believe the worst instead of the best, astonished and shocked her. And then the way they all talked! Everlasting arguments and reasoning and hair-splitting; so clever, so impossible to stand up against, and yet so surely, she was certain, if only she had been clever too and able to prove things, wrong. All their multitudinous points of view,—why, there was only one point of view about a thing, Everard said, and that was the right one. Ah, but what a woman wanted wasn't this; she didn't want this endless thinking and examining and dissecting and considering. A woman— her very thoughts were now dressed in Wemyss's words—only wanted her man. "'Hers not to reason why,'" Wemyss had quoted one day, and both of them had laughed at his parody, "'hers but to love and—not die, but live.'"

The most that could be said for her father's friends was that they meant well; but oh, what trouble the well-meaning could bring into an otherwise simple situation! From them she hid—it was inevitable—in Wemyss's arms. Here were no arguments; here were no misgivings and paralysing hesitations. Here was just simple love, and the feeling—delicious to her whose mother had died in the very middle of all the sweet early petting, and whose whole life since had been spent entirely in the dry and bracing company of unusually inquisitive-minded, clever men—of being a baby again in somebody's big, comfortable, uncritical lap.

The engagement hadn't leaked out so much as flooded out. It would have continued secret for quite a long time, known only to the three and to the maids—who being young women themselves, and well acquainted with the symptoms of the condition, were sure of it before Miss Entwhistle had even begun to suspect,—if Wemyss hadn't taken to dropping in, contrary to expectations, on the Thursday evenings. Lucy's descriptions of these evenings and of the people who came, and of how very kind they were to her aunt and herself, and how anxious they were to help her, they of course supposing that she was, actually, the lonely thing she would have been if she hadn't had Everard as the dear hidden background to her life—at this point they embraced,—at first amused him, then made him curious, and finally caused him to come and see for himself.

He didn't tell Lucy he was coming, he just came. It had taken him five Thursday evenings of playing bridge as usual at his club, playing it with one hand, as he said to her afterwards, and thinking of her with the other—'You know what I mean,' he said, and they laughed and embraced—before it slowly oozed into and pervaded his mind that there was his little girl, rounded by people fussing over her and making love to her (because, said Wemyss, everybody would naturally want to make love to her), and there was he, the only person who had a right to do this, somewhere else.

So he walked in; and when he walked in, the group standing round Lucy with their backs to the door saw her face, which had been gently attentive, suddenly flash into colour and light; and turning with one accord to see what it was she was looking at behind them with parted lips and eyes of startled joy, beheld once more the unknown chief mourner of the funeral in Cornwall.

Down there they had taken for granted that he was a relation of Jim's, the kind of relative who in a man's life appears only three times, the last of which is his funeral; here in Eaton Terrace they were immediately sure he was not, anyhow, that, because for relatives who only appear those three times a girl's face doesn't change in a flash from gentle politeness to tremulous, shining life. They all stared at him astonished. He was so different from the sorts of people they had met at Jim's. For one thing he was so well dressed,—in the mating season, thought Miss Entwhistle, even birds dress well,—and in his impressive evening clothes, with what seemed a bigger and more spotless shirt-front than any shirt-front they could have imagined, he made them look and feel what they actually were, a dingy, shabby lot.

Wemyss was good-looking. He might be middle-aged, but he was good-looking enough frequently to eclipse the young. He might have a little too much of what tailors call a fine presence, but his height carried this off. His features were regular, his face care-free and healthy, his brown hair sleek with no grey in it, he was clean-shaven, and his mouth was the kind of mouth sometimes described by journalists as mobile, sometimes as determined, but always as well cut. One could visualise him in a fur-lined coat, thought a young man near Lucy, considering him; and one couldn't visualise a single one of the others, including himself, in the room that evening in a fur-lined coat. Also, thought this same young man, one could see railway porters and taxi-drivers and waiters hurrying to be of service to him; and one not only couldn't imagine them taking any notice that wasn't languid and reluctant of the others, including himself, but one knew from personal distressing experience that they didn't.

'My splendid lover!' Lucy's heart cried out within her when the door opened and there he stood. She had not seen him before in the evening, and the contrast between him and the rest of the people there was really striking.

353

Miss Entwhistle had been right: there was no hiding the look in Lucy's eyes or Wemyss's proprietary manner. He hadn't meant to take any but the barest notice of his little girl, he had meant to be quite an ordinary guest—just shake hands and say 'Hasn't it been wet to-day'—that sort of thing; but his pride and love were too much for him, he couldn't hide them. He thought he did, and was sure he was behaving beautifully and with the easiest unconcern, but the mere way he looked at her and stood over her was enough. Also there was the way she looked at him. The intelligences in that room were used to drawing more complicated inferences than this. They were outraged by its obviousness. Who was this middle-aged, prosperous outsider who had got hold of Jim's daughter? What had her aunt been about? Where had he dropped from? Had Jim known?

Miss Entwhistle introduced him. 'Mr. Wemyss,' she said to them generally, with a vague wave of her hand; and a red spot appeared and stayed on each of her cheekbones.

Wemyss held forth. He stood on the hearthrug filling his pipe—he was used to smoking in that room when he came to tea with Lucy, and forgot to ask Miss Entwhistle if it mattered—and told everybody what he thought. They were talking about Ireland when he came in, and after the disturbance of his arrival had subsided he asked them not to mind him but to go on. He then proceeded to go on himself, telling them what he thought; and what he thought was what *The Times* had thought that morning. Wemyss spoke with the practised fluency of a leading article. He liked politics and constantly talked them at his club, and it created vacancies in the chairs near him. But Lucy, who hadn't heard him on politics before and found that she could understand every word, listened to him with parted lips. Before he came in they had been saying things beyond her quickness in following, eagerly discussing Sinn Fein, Lloyd George, the outrageous cost of living—it was the autumn of 1920—turning everything inside out, upside down, being witty, being surprising, being tremendously eager and earnest. It had been a kind of restless flashing round and catching fire from each other,—a kind of kick, and flick, and sparks, and a burst of laughter, and then on to something else just as she was laboriously getting under weigh to follow the last sentence but six. She had been missing her father, who took her by the hand on these occasions when he saw her lagging behind, and stopped a moment to explain to her, and held up the others while she got her breath.

But now came Everard, and in a minute everything was plain. He had the effect on her of a window being thrown open and fresh air and sunlight being let in. He was so sensible, she felt, compared to these others; so healthy and natural. The Government, he said, only had to do this and that, and Ireland and the cost of living would immediately, regarded as problems, be solved. He explained the line to be taken. It was a very simple line. One only needed goodwill and a little common sense. Why, thought Lucy, unconsciously nodding proud agreement, didn't people have goodwill and a little common sense?

At first there was a disposition to interrupt, to heckle, but it grew fainter and soon gave way to complete silence. The other guests might have been stunned, Miss Entwhistle thought, so motionless did they presently sit. And when they went away, which they seemed to do earlier than usual and in a body, Wemyss was still standing on the hearthrug explaining the points of view of the ordinary, sensible business man.

'Mind you,' he said, pointing at them with his pipe, 'I don't pretend to be a great thinker. I'm just a plain business man, and as a plain business man I know there's only one way of doing a thing, and that's the right way. Find out what that way is, and go and do it. There's too much arguing altogether and asking other people what they think. We don't want talk, we want action. I agree with Napoleon, who said concerning the French Revolution, *"Il aurait fallu mitrailler cette canaille."* We're not simple enough.'

This was the last the others heard as they trooped in silence down the stairs. Outside they lingered for a while in little knots on the pavement talking, and then they drifted away to their various homes, where most of them spent the rest of the evening writing to Miss Entwhistle.

The following Thursday evening, her letters in reply having been vague and evasive, they came again, each hoping to get Lucy's aunt to himself, and on the ground of being Jim's most devoted friend ask her straight questions such as who and what was Wemyss. Also, more particularly, why. Who and what he was was of no sort of consequence if he would only be and do it somewhere else; but they arrived determined to get an answer to the third question: Why Wemyss? And when they got there, there he was again; there before them this time, standing on the hearthrug as if he had never moved off it since the week before and had gone on talking ever since.

This was the end of the Thursday evenings. The next one was unattended, except by Wemyss; but Miss Entwhistle had been forced to admit the engagement, and from then on right up to the marriage her life was a curse to her and a confusion. Just because Jim had appointed no guardian in his will for Lucy, every single one of his friends felt bound to fill the vacancy. They were indignant when they discovered that almost before they had begun Lucy was being carried off, but they were horrified when they discovered what Wemyss it was who was carrying her off. Most of them quite well remembered the affair of Mrs. Wemyss's death a few weeks before, and those who did not went, as Miss Entwhistle had gone, to the British Museum and read it up. They also, though they themselves were chiefly unworldly persons who lost money rather than made it, instituted the most searching private inquiries into Wemyss's business affairs, hoping that he might be caught out as such a rascal or so penniless, or, preferably, both, that no woman could possibly have anything to do with him. But Wemyss's business record, the solicitor they employed informed them, was quite creditable. Everything about it was neat and in order. He was not what the City would call a wealthy man, but if you went out say to Ealing, said the solicitor, he would be called wealthy. He was solid, and he was certainly more than able to support a wife and family. He could have been quite wealthy if he had not adopted a principle to which he had adhered for years of knocking off work early and leaving his office at an hour when other men did not,—the friends were obliged to admit that this, at least, seemed sensible. There had been, though, a very sad occurrence recently in his private life,—'Oh, thank you,' interrupted the friends, 'we have heard about that.'

But however good Wemyss's business record might be, it couldn't alter their violent objection to Jim's daughter marrying him. Apart from the stuff he talked, there was the inquest. They were aware that in this they were unreasonable, but they were all too much attached to Jim's memory to be able to be reasonable about a man they felt so certain he wouldn't have liked. Singly and in groups they came at safe times, such as after breakfast, to Eaton Terrace to reason with Lucy, too much worried to remember that you cannot reason with a person in love. Less wise than Miss Entwhistle, they tried to dissuade her from marrying this man, and the more they tried the tighter she clung to him. To the passion of love was added, by their attitudes, the passion of protectiveness, of flinging her body between him and them. And all the while, right inside her innermost soul, in spite of her amazement at them and her indignation, she was smiling to herself; for it was really very funny, the superficial judgments of these clever people when set side by side with what she alone knew,—the tenderness, the simple goodness of her heart's beloved.

Lucy laughed to herself in her happy sureness. She had miraculously found not only a lover she could adore and a guide she could follow and a teacher she could look up to and a sufferer who without her wouldn't have been healed, but a mother, a nurse, and a playmate. In spite of his being so much older and so extraordinarily wise, he was yet her contemporary,—sometimes hardly even that, so boyish was he in his talk and jokes. Lucy had never had a playmate. She had spent her life sitting, as it were, bolt upright mentally behaving, and she hadn't known till Wemyss came on the scene how delicious it was to relax. Nonsense had delighted her father, it is true, but it had to be of a certain kind; never the kind to which the adjective 'sheer' would apply. With Wemyss she could say whatever nonsense came into her head, sheer or otherwise. He laughed consumedly at her when she talked it. She loved to make him laugh. They laughed together. He understood her language. He was her playmate. Those people outside, old and young, who didn't know what playing was and were trying to get her away from him, might beat at the door behind which he and she sat listening, amused, as long as they liked.

'How they all try to separate us,' she said to him one day, sitting as usual safe in the circle of his arm, her head on his breast.

'You can't separate unity,' remarked Wemyss comfortably.

She wanted to tell them that answer, confront them with it next time they came after breakfast, as a discouragement to useless further effort, but she had learned that they somehow always knew when what she said was Everard's and not hers, and then, of course, prejudiced as they were, they wouldn't listen.

'Now, Lucy, that's pure Wemyss,' they would say. 'For heaven's sake say something of your own.'

At Christmas Wemyss had an encounter with Miss Entwhistle, who ever since she had been told of the engagement had been so quiet and inoffensive that he quite liked her. She had seemed to recognise her position as a side-show, and had accepted it without a word. She no longer asked him questions, and she made no difficulties. She left him alone with Lucy in Eaton Terrace, and though she had to go with them on the outings she asserted herself so little that he forgot she was there. But when towards the middle of December he remarked one afternoon that he always spent Christmas at The Willows, and what day would she and Lucy come down, Christmas Eve or the day before, to his astonishment she looked astonished, and after a silence said it was most kind of him, but they were going to spend Christmas where they were.

'I had hoped you would join us,' she said. 'Must you really go away?'

'But——' began Wemyss, incredulous, doubting his ears.

It was, however, the fact that Miss Entwhistle wouldn't go to The Willows; and of course if she wouldn't Lucy couldn't either. Nothing that he said could shake her determination. Here was a repetition, only how much worse—fancy spoiling his Christmas—of her conduct in Cornwall when she insisted on going away from that nice little house where they were all so comfortably established, and taking Lucy up to London. He had forgotten, so acquiescent had she been for weeks, that down there he had discovered she was obstinate. It was a shock to him to realise that her obstinacy, the most obstinate obstinacy he had ever met, might be going to upset his plans. He couldn't believe it. He couldn't believe he wasn't going to be able to have what he wished, and only because an old maid said 'No.' Was the story of Balaam to be reversed, and the angel be held up by the donkey? He refused to believe such a thing possible.

Wemyss, who made his plans first and talked about them afterwards, hadn't mentioned Christmas even to Lucy. It was his habit to settle what he wished to do, arrange all the details, and then, when everything was ready, inform those who were to take part. It hadn't occurred to him that over the Christmas question there would be trouble. He had naturally taken it for granted that he would spend Christmas with his little girl, and of course as he always spent it at The Willows she would spend it there too. All his arrangements were made, and the servants, who looked surprised, had been told to get the spare-rooms ready for two ladies. He had begun to feel seasonable as early as the first week in December, and had bespoken two big turkeys instead of one, because this was to be his first real Christmas at The Willows—Vera had been without the Christmas spirit—and he felt it couldn't be celebrated lavishly enough. Two where there had in previous years been one,—that was the turkeys; four where there had been two,—-that was the plum puddings. He doubled everything. Doubling seemed the proper, even the symbolic expression of his feelings, for wasn't he soon going to be doubled himself? And how sweetly.

Then suddenly, having finished his preparations and proceeding, the time being ripe, to the question of the day of arrival, he found himself up against opposition. Miss Entwhistle wouldn't go to The Willows—incredible, impossible, and insufferable,—while Lucy, instead of instantly insisting and joining with him in a compelling majority, sat as quiet as a mouse.

'But Lucy——' Wemyss having stared speechless at her aunt, turned to her. 'But of course we must spend Christmas together.'

'Oh yes,' said Lucy, leaning forward, 'of course——'

'But of course you must come down. Why, any other arrangement is unthinkable. My house is in the country, which is the proper place for Christmas, and it's your Everard's house, and you haven't seen it yet—why, I would have taken you down long ago, but I've been saving up for this.'

'We hoped,' said Miss Entwhistle, 'you would join us here.'

'Here! But there isn't room to swing a turkey here. I've ordered two, and each of them is twice too big to get through your front door.'

'Oh, Everard—have you actually ordered turkeys?' said Lucy.

She wanted to laugh, but she also wanted to cry. His simplicity was too wonderful. In her eyes it set him apart from criticism and made him sacred, like the nimbus about the head of a saint.

That he should have been secretly busy making preparations, buying turkeys, planning a surprise, when all this time she had been supposing that why he never mentioned The Willows was because he shrank both for himself and for her from the house of his tragedy! There had never been any talk of showing it to her, as there had about the house in Lancaster Gate, and she had imagined he would never go near it again and was probably quietly getting rid of it. He would want to get rid of it, of course,—that house of unbearable memories. To the other one, the house in Lancaster Gate, he had insisted on taking them to tea, and in spite of a great desire not to go, plainly visible on her aunt's face and felt too by herself, it had seemed after all a natural and more or less inevitable thing, and they had gone. At least that poor Vera had only lived there, and not died there. It was a gloomy house, and Lucy had wanted him to give it up and start life with her in a place without associations, but he had been so much astonished at the idea— 'Why,' he had cried, 'it was my father's house and I was born in it!'—that she couldn't help laughing at his dismay, and was ashamed of herself for having thought of uprooting him. Besides, she hadn't known he had been born in it.

The Willows, however, was different. Of that he never spoke, and Lucy had been sure of the pitiful, the delicate reason. Now it appeared that all this time he had just been saving it up as a Christmas treat.

'Oh, Everard——!' she said, with a gasp. She hadn't reckoned with The Willows. That The Willows should still be in Everard's life, and actively so, not just lingering on while house agents were disposing of it, but visited and evidently prized, came upon her as an immense shock.

'I think we can achieve a happy little Christmas for you here,' said her aunt, smiling the smile she smiled when she found difficulty in smiling. 'Of course you and Lucy would want to be together. I ought to have told you earlier that we were counting on you, but somehow Christmas comes on one so unexpectedly.'

'Perhaps you'll tell me why you won't come to The Willows,' said Wemyss, holding on to himself as she used to make him hold on to himself in Cornwall. 'You realise, of course, that if you persist you spoil both Lucy's and my Christmas.'

'Ah, but you mustn't put it that way,' said Miss Entwhistle, gentle but determined. 'I promise you that you and Lucy shall be very happy here.'

'You haven't answered my question,' said Wemyss, slowly filling his pipe.

'I don't think I'm going to,' said Miss Entwhistle, suddenly flaring up. She hadn't flared up since she was ten, and was instantly ashamed of herself, but there was something about Mr. Wemyss——

'I think,' she said, getting up and speaking very gently, 'you'll like to be alone together now.' And she crossed to the door.

There she wavered, and turning round said more gently still, even penitentially, 'If Lucy wishes to go to The Willows I'll—I'll accept your kind invitation and take her. I leave it to her.'

Then she went out.

'That's all right then,' said Wemyss with a great sigh of relief, smiling broadly at Lucy. 'Come here, little love,—come to your Everard, and we'll fix it all up. Lord, what a kill-joy that woman is!'

And he put out his arms and drew her to him.

XII

But Christmas was spent after all at Eaton Terrace, and they lived on Wemyss's turkeys and plum puddings for a fortnight.

It was not a very successful Christmas, because Wemyss was so profoundly disappointed, and Miss Entwhistle had the apologeticness of those who try to make up for having got their own way, and Lucy, who had shrunk from The Willows far more than her aunt, wished many times before it was over that they had after all gone there. It would have been much simpler in the long run, and much less painful than having to look on at Everard being disappointed; but at the time, and taken by surprise, she had felt that she couldn't have borne festivities, and still less could she have borne seeing Everard bearing festivities in that house.

'This is morbid,' he said, when in answer to his questioning she at last told him it was poor Vera's dreadful death there that made her feel she couldn't go; and he explained, holding her in his arms, how foolish it was to be morbid, and how his little girl, who was marrying a healthy, sensible man who, God knew, had had to fight hard enough to keep so—she pressed closer—and yet had succeeded, must be healthily sensible too. Otherwise, if she couldn't do this and couldn't do that because it reminded her of something sad, and couldn't go here and couldn't go there because of somebody's having died, he was afraid she would make both herself and him very unhappy.

'Oh, Everard——' said Lucy at that, holding him tight, the thought of making him unhappy, him, her own beloved who had been through such terrible unhappiness already, giving her heart a stab.

His little girl must know, he continued, speaking with the grave voice that was natural to him when he was serious, the voice not of the playmate but of the man she adored, the man she was in love with, in whose hands she could safely leave her earthly concerns,— his little girl must know that somebody had died everywhere. There wasn't a spot, there wasn't a house, except quite new ones——

'Oh yes, I know—but——' Lucy tried to interrupt.

And The Willows was his home, the home he had looked forward to and worked for and had at last been able to afford to rent on a long lease, a lease so long that it made it practically his very own, and he had spent the last ten years developing and improving it, and there wasn't a brick or a tree in it in which he didn't take an interest, really an almost personal interest, and his one thought all these months had been the day when he would show it to her, to its dear future mistress.

'Oh, Everard—yes—you shall—I want to——' said Lucy incoherently, her cheek against his, 'only not yet—not festivities—please—I won't be so morbid—I promise not to be morbid—but—please——'

And just when she was wavering, just when she was going to give in, not because of his reasoning, for her instincts were stronger than his reasoning, but because she couldn't bear his disappointment, Miss Entwhistle, sure now of Lucy's dread of Christmas at The Willows, suddenly turned firm again and announced that they would spend it in Eaton Terrace.

So Wemyss was forced to submit. The sensation was so new to him that he couldn't get over it. Once it was certain that his Christmas was, as he insisted, spoilt, he left off talking about it and went to the other extreme and was very quiet. That his little love should be so much under the influence of her aunt saddened him, he told her. Lucy tried to bring gaiety into this attitude by pointing out the proof she was giving him of how very submissive she was to the person she happened to live with,—'And presently all my submissiveness will be concentrated on you,' she said gaily.

But he wouldn't be gay. He shook his head in silence and filled his pipe. He was too deeply disappointed to be able to cheer up. And the expression 'happen to live with,' jarred a little. There was an airy carelessness about the phrase. One didn't happen to live with one's husband; yet that had been the implication.

Every year in April Wemyss had a birthday; that is, unlike most people of his age, he regularly celebrated it. Christmas and his birthday were the festivals of the year for Him, and were always spent at The Willows. He regarded his birthday, which was on the 4th of April, as the first day of spring, defying the calendar, and was accustomed to find certain yellow flowers in blossom down by the river on that date supporting his contention. If these flowers came out before his birthday he took no notice of them, treating them as non-existent, nor did he ever notice them afterwards, for he did not easily notice flowers; but his gardener had standing orders to have a bunch of them on the table that one morning in the year to welcome him with their bright shiny faces when he came down to his birthday breakfast, and coming in and seeing them he said, 'My birthday and Spring's'; whereupon his wife—up to now it had been Vera, but from now it would be Lucy—kissed him and wished him many happy returns. This was the ritual; and when one year of abnormal cold the yellow flowers weren't there at breakfast, because neither by the river's edge nor in the most sheltered of the swamps had the increasingly frantic gardener been able to find them, the entire birthday was dislocated. He couldn't say on entering the room and beholding them, 'My birthday and Spring's,' because he didn't behold them; and his wife—that year Vera—couldn't kiss him and wish him many happy returns because she hadn't the cue. She was so much used to the cue that not having it made her forget her part,—forget, indeed, his birthday altogether; and consequently it was a day of the extremest spiritual chill and dinginess, matching the weather without. Wemyss had been terribly hurt. He hoped never to spend another birthday like it. Nor did he, for Vera remembered it after that.

Birthdays being so important to him, he naturally reflected after Miss Entwhistle had spoilt his Christmas that she would spoil his birthday too if he let her. Well, he wasn't going to let her. Not twice would he be caught like that; not twice would he be caught in a position of helplessness on his side and power on hers. The way to avoid it was very simple: he would marry Lucy in time for his birthday. Why should they wait any longer? Why stick to that absurd convention of the widower's year? No sensible man minded what people thought. And who were the people? Surely one didn't mind the opinions of those shabby weeds he had met on the two Thursday evenings at Lucy's aunt's. The little they had said had been so thoroughly unsound and muddled and yet dangerous, that if they one and all emigrated to-morrow England would only be the better. After meeting them he had said to Lucy, who had listened in some wonder at this new light thrown on her father's friends, that they were the very stuff of which successful segregation was made. In an island by themselves, he told her, they would be quite happy undermining each other's backbones, and the backbone of England, which consisted of plain unspoilt patriots, would be let alone. They, certainly, didn't matter; while as for his own friends, those friends who had behaved badly to him on Vera's death, not only didn't he care twopence for their criticisms but he could hardly wait for the moment when he would confound them by producing for their inspection this sweetest of little girls, so young, so devoted to him, Lucy his wife.

He accordingly proceeded to make all the necessary arrangements for being married in March, for going for a trip to Paris, and for returning to The Willows for the final few days of his honeymoon on the very day of his birthday. What a celebration that would be! Wemyss, thinking of it, shut his eyes so as to dwell upon it undisturbed. Never would he have had a birthday like this next one. He might really quite fairly call it his First, for he would be beginning life all over again, and entering on years that would indeed be truthfully described as tender.

So much was it his habit to make plans privately and not mention them till they were complete, that he found it difficult to tell Lucy of this one in spite of the important part she was to play in it. But, after all, some preparing would, he admitted to himself, be necessary even for the secret marriage he had decided on at a registrar's office. She would have to pack a bag; she would have to leave her belongings in order. Also he might perhaps have to use persuasion. He knew his little girl well enough to be sure she would relinquish church and white satin without a murmur at his request, but she might want to tell her aunt of the marriage's imminence, and then the aunt would, to a dead certainty, obstruct, and either induce her to wait till the year was out, or, if Lucy refused to do this, make her miserable with doubts as to whether she had been right to follow her lover's wishes. Fancy making a girl miserable because she followed her lover's wishes! What a woman, thought Wemyss, filling his pipe. In his eyes Miss Entwhistle had swollen since her conduct at Christmas to the bulk of a monster.

Having completed his preparations, and fixed his wedding day for the first Saturday in March, Wemyss thought it time he told Lucy; so he did, though not without a slight fear at the end that she might make difficulties.

'My little love isn't going to do anything that spoils her Everard's plans after all the trouble he has taken?' he said, seeing that with her mouth slightly open she gazed at him in an obvious astonishment and didn't say a word.

He then proceeded to shut the eyes that were gazing up into his, and the surprised parted lips, with kisses, for he had discovered that gentle, lingering kisses hushed Lucy quiet when she was inclined to

365

say, 'But——' and brought her back quicker than anything to the mood of tender, half-asleep acquiescence in which, as she lay in his arms, he most loved her; then indeed she was his baby, the object of the passionate protectiveness he felt he was naturally filled with, but for the exercise of which circumstances up to now had given him no scope. You couldn't passionately protect Vera. She was always in another room.

Lucy, however, did say, 'But——' when she recovered from her first surprise, and did presently—directly, that is, he left off kissing her and she could speak—make difficulties. Her aunt; the secrecy; why secrecy; why not wait; it was so necessary under the circumstances to wait.

And then he explained about his birthday.

At that she gazed at him again with a look of wonder in her eyes, and after a moment began to laugh. She laughed a great deal, and with her arm tight round his neck, but her eyes were wet. 'Oh, Everard,' she said, her cheek against his, 'do you think we're really old enough to marry?'

This time, however, he got his way. Lucy found she couldn't bring herself to spoil his plans a second time; the spectacle of his prolonged silent disappointment at Christmas was still too vividly before her. Nor did she feel she could tell her aunt. She hadn't the courage to face her aunt's expostulations and final distressed giving in. Her aunt, who loomed so enormous in Wemyss's eyes, seemed to Lucy to be only half the size she used to be. She seemed to have been worried small by her position, like a bone among contending dogs, in the middle of different indignations. What would be the effect on her of this final blow? The thought of it haunted Lucy and spoilt all the last days before her marriage, days which she otherwise would have loved, because she very quickly became infected by the boyish delight and excitement over their secret that made Wemyss hardly able to keep still in his chair. He didn't keep still in it. Once at least he got up and did some slow steps about the room, moving with an apparent solemnity because of not being used to such steps, which he informed her presently were a dance. Till he told her this she watched him too much surprised to say anything. So did penguins dance in pictures. She couldn't think what was the matter with him. When he had done, and told her, breathing a little hard, that it was a dance symbolic of married happiness, she laughed and laughed, and flew to hug him.

'Baby, oh, baby!' she said, rubbing her cheek up and down his coat.

'Who's another baby?' he asked, breathless but beaming.

Such was their conversation.

But poor Aunt Dot....

Lucy couldn't bear to think of poor little kind Aunt Dot. She had been so wonderful, so patient, and she would be deeply horrified by a runaway marriage. Never, never would she understand the reason for it. She didn't a bit understand Everard, didn't begin to understand him, and that his birthday should be a reason for breaking what she would regard as the common decencies would of course only seem to her too childish to be even discussed. Lucy was afraid Aunt Dot was going to be very much upset, poor darling little Aunt Dot. Conscience-stricken, she couldn't do enough for Aunt Dot now that the secret date was fixed. She watched for every possible want during their times alone, flew to fetch things, darted at dropped handkerchiefs, kissed her not only at bedtime and in the morning but whenever there was the least excuse and with the utmost tenderness; and every kiss and every look seemed to say, 'Forgive me.'

'Are they going to run away?' wondered Miss Entwhistle presently.

Lucy would have been immensely taken aback, and perhaps, such is one's perversity, even hurt, if she could have seen the ray of hope which at this thought lit her Aunt Dot's exhausted mind; for Miss Entwhistle's life, which had been a particularly ordered and calm one up to the day when Wemyss first called at Eaton Terrace, had since then been nothing but just confused clamour. Everybody was displeased with her, and each for directly opposite reasons. She had fallen on evil days, and they had by February been going on so long that she felt worn out. Wemyss, she was quite aware, disliked her heartily; her Jim was dead; Lucy, her one living relation, so tenderly loved, was every day disappearing further before her very eyes into Wemyss's personality, into what she sometimes was betrayed by fatigue and impatience into calling to herself the Wemyss maw; and her little house, which had always been so placid, had become, she wearily felt, the cockpit of London. She used to crawl back to it with footsteps that lagged more and more the nearer she got, after her enforced prolonged daily outings— enforced and prolonged because the house couldn't possibly hold both herself and Wemyss except for the briefest moments,—and drearily wonder what letters she would find from Jim's friends scolding her, and what fresh arrangements in the way of tiring motor excursions, or invitations to tea at that dreadful house in Lancaster Gate, would be sprung upon her. Did all engagements pursue such a turbulent course? she asked herself,—she had given up asking the oracle of Chesham Street anything because of her disconcerting answers. How glad she was she had never been engaged; how glad she was she had refused the offers she had had when she was a girl. Quite recently she had met one of those would-be husbands in an omnibus, and how glad she was when she looked at him that she had refused him. People don't keep well, mused Miss Entwhistle. If Lucy would only refuse Wemyss now, how glad she would be that she had when she met him in ten years' time in an omnibus.

But these, of course, were merely the reflections of a tired-out spinster, and she still had enough spirit to laugh at them to herself. After all, whatever she might feel about Wemyss Lucy adored him, and when anybody adores anybody as much as that, Miss Entwhistle thought, the only thing to do is to marry and have done with it. No; that was cynical. She meant, marry and not have done with it. Ah, if only the child were marrying that nice young Teddy Trevor, her own age and so devoted, and with every window-sill throughout his house in Chelsea the proper height....

Miss Entwhistle was very unhappy all this time, besides having feet that continually ached. Though she dreaded the marriage, yet she couldn't help feeling that it would be delicious to be able once more to sit down. How enchanting to sit quietly in her own empty drawing-room, and not to have to walk about London any more. How enchanting not to make any further attempts to persuade herself that she enjoyed Battersea Park, and liked the Embankment, and was entertained by Westminster Abbey. What she wanted with an increasing longing that amounted at last to desperation as the winter dragged on, was her own chair by the fire and an occasional middle-aged crony to tea. She had reached the time of life when one likes sitting down. Also she had definitely got to the period of cronies. One's contemporaries—people who had worn the same kinds of clothes as oneself in girlhood, who remembered bishop's sleeves and could laugh with one about bustles—how very much one longed for one's contemporaries.

When, then, Lucy's behaviour suddenly became so markedly attentive and so very tender, when she caught her looking at her with wistful affection and flushing on being caught, when her good-nights and good-mornings were many kisses instead of one, and she kept on jumping up and bringing her teaspoons she hadn't asked for and sugar she didn't want, Miss Entwhistle began to revive.

'Is it possible they're going to run away?' she wondered; and so much reduced was she that she very nearly hoped so.

XIII

Lucy had meant to do exactly as Wemyss said and keep her marriage secret, creeping out of the house quietly, going off with him abroad after the registrar had bound them together, and telegraphing or writing to her aunt from some safe distant place *en route* like Boulogne; but on saying good-night the evening before the wedding day, to her very great consternation her aunt, whom she was in the act of kissing, suddenly pushed her gently a little away, looked at her a moment, and then holding her by both arms said with conviction, 'It's to-morrow.'

Lucy could only stare. She stared idiotically, open-mouthed, her face scarlet. She looked and felt both foolish and frightened. Aunt Dot was uncanny. If she had discovered, how had she discovered? And what was she going to do? But had she discovered, or was it just something she chanced to remember, some engagement Lucy had naturally forgotten, or perhaps only somebody coming to tea?

She clutched at this straw. 'What is to-morrow?' she stammered, scarlet with fright and guilt.

And her aunt made herself perfectly clear by replying, 'Your wedding.'

Then Lucy fell on her neck and cried and told her everything, and her wonderful, unexpected, uncanny, adorable little aunt, instead of being upset and making her feel too wicked and ungrateful to live, was full of sympathy and understanding. They sobbed together, sitting on the sofa locked in each other's arms, but it was a sweet sobbing, for they both felt at this moment how much they loved each other. Miss Entwhistle wished she had never had a single critical impatient thought of the man this darling little child so deeply loved, and Lucy wished she had never had a single secret from this darling little aunt Everard so blindly didn't love. Dear, dear little Aunt Dot. Lucy's heart was big with gratitude and tenderness and pity,—pity because she herself was so gloriously happy and surrounded by love, and Aunt Dot's life seemed, compared to hers, so empty, so solitary, and going to be like that till the end of her days; and Miss Entwhistle's heart was big with yearning over this lamb of Jim's who was giving herself with such fearlessness, all lit up by radiant love, into the hands of a strange husband. Presently, of course, he wouldn't be a strange husband, he would be a familiar husband; but would he be any the better for that, she wondered? They sobbed, and kissed, and sobbed again, each keeping half her thoughts to herself.

This is how it was that Miss Entwhistle walked into the registrar's office with Lucy next morning and was one of the witnesses of the marriage.

Wemyss had a very bad moment when he saw her come in. His heart gave a great thump, such as it had never done in his life before, for he thought there was to be a hitch and that at the very last minute he was somehow not going to get his Lucy. Then he looked at Lucy and was reassured. Her face was like the morning of a perfect day in its cloudlessness, her Love-in-a-Mist eyes were dewy with tenderness as they rested on him, and her mouth was twisted up by happiness into the sweetest, funniest little crooked smile. If only she would take off her hat, thought Wemyss, bursting with pride, so that the registrar could see how young she looked with her short hair,—why, perhaps the old boy might think she was too young to be married and start asking searching questions! What fun that would be.

He himself produced the effect on Miss Entwhistle, as he stood next to Lucy being married, of an enormous schoolboy who has just won some silver cup or other for his House after immense exertions. He had exactly that glowing face of suppressed triumph and pride; he was red with delighted achievement.

'Put the ring on your wife's finger,' ordered the registrar when, having got through the first part of the ceremony, Wemyss, busy beaming down at Lucy, forgot there was anything more to do. And Lucy stuck up her hand with all the fingers spread out and stiff, and her face beamed too with happiness at the words, 'Your wife.'

'"Nothing is here for tears,"' quoted Miss Entwhistle to herself, watching the blissful absorption with which they were both engaged in getting the ring successfully over the knuckle of the proper finger. 'He really *is* a—a dear. Yes. Of course. But how queer life is. I wonder what he was doing this day last year, he and that poor other wife of his.'

When it was over and they were outside on the steps, with the taxi Wemyss had come in waiting to take them to the station, Miss Entwhistle realised that here was the place and moment of good-bye, and that not only could she go no further with Lucy but that from now on she could do nothing more for her. Except love her.

371

Except listen to her. Ah, she would always be there to love and listen to her; but happiest of all it would be for the little thing if she never, from her, were to need either of those services.

At the last moment she put her hand impulsively on Wemyss's breast and looked up into his triumphant, flushed face and said, 'Be kind to her.'

'Oh, Aunt Dot!' laughed Lucy, turning to hug her once more.

'Oh, Aunt Dot!' laughed Wemyss, vigorously shaking her hand.

They went down the steps, leaving her standing alone on the top, and she watched the departing taxi with the two heads bobbing up and down at the window and the four hands waving good-byes. That taxi window could never have framed in so much triumph, so much radiance before. Well, well, thought Aunt Dot, going down in her turn when the last glimpse of them had disappeared, and walking slowly homeward; and she added, after a space of further reflection, 'He really *is* a—a dear.'

XIV

Marriage, Lucy found, was different from what she had supposed; Everard was different; everything was different. For one thing she was always sleepy. For another she was never alone. She hadn't realised how completely she would never be alone, or, if alone, not sure for one minute to the other of going on being alone. Always in her life there had been intervals during which she recuperated in solitude from any strain; now there were none. Always there had been places she could go to and rest in quietly, safe from interruption; now there were none. The very sight of their room at the hotels they stayed at, with Wemyss's suitcases and clothes piled on the chairs, and the table covered with his brushes and shaving things, for he wouldn't have a dressing-room, being too natural and wholesome, he explained, to want anything separate from his own woman—the very sight of this room fatigued her. After a day of churches, pictures and restaurants—he was a most conscientious sightseer, besides being greatly interested in his meals—to come back to this room wasn't rest but further fatigue. Wemyss, who was never tired and slept wonderfully—it was the soundness of his sleep that kept her awake, because she wasn't used to hearing sound sleep so close—would fling himself into the one easy-chair and pull her on to his knee, and having kissed her a great many times he would ruffle her hair, and then when it was all on ends like a boy's coming out of a bath, look at her with the pride of possession and say, 'There's a wife for a respectable British business man to have! Mrs. Wemyss, aren't you ashamed of yourself?' And then there would be more kissing,—jovial, gluttonous kisses, that made her skin rough and chapped.

'Baby,' she would say, feebly struggling, and smiling a little wearily.

Yes, he was a baby, a dear, high-spirited baby, but a baby now at very close quarters and one that went on all the time. You couldn't put him in a cot and give him a bottle and say, 'There now,' and then sit down quietly to a little sewing; you didn't have Sundays out; you were never, day or night, an instant off duty. Lucy couldn't count the number of times a day she had to answer the question, 'Who's my own little wife?' At first she answered it with laughing ecstasy, running into his outstretched arms, but very soon that fatal

373

sleepiness set in and remained with her for the whole of her honeymoon, and she really felt too tired sometimes to get the ecstasy she quickly got to know was expected of her into her voice. She loved him, she was indeed his own little wife, but constantly to answer this and questions like it satisfactorily was a great exertion. Yet if there was a shadow of hesitation before she answered, a hair's-breadth of delay owing to her thoughts having momentarily wandered, Wemyss was upset, and she had to spend quite a long time reassuring him with the fondest whispers and caresses. Her thoughts mustn't wander, she had discovered; her thoughts were to be his as well as all the rest of her. Was ever a girl so much loved? she asked herself, astonished and proud; but, on the other hand, she was dreadfully sleepy.

Any thinking she did had to be done at night, when she lay awake because of the immense emphasis with which Wemyss slept, and she hadn't been married a week before she was reflecting what a bad arrangement it was, the way ecstasy seemed to have no staying power. Also it oughtn't to begin, she considered, at its topmost height and accordingly not be able to move except downwards. If one could only start modestly in marriage with very little of it and work steadily upwards, taking one's time, knowing there was more and more to come, it would be much better she thought. No doubt it would go on longer if one slept better and hadn't, consequently, got headaches. Everard's ecstasy went on. Perhaps by ecstasy she really meant high spirits, and Everard was beside himself with high spirits.

Wemyss was indeed the typical bridegroom of the Psalms, issuing forth rejoicing from his chamber. Lucy wished she could issue forth from it rejoicing too. She was vexed with herself for being so stupidly sleepy, for not being able to get used to the noise beside her at night and go to sleep as naturally as she did in Eaton Terrace, in spite of the horns of taxis. It wasn't fair to Everard, she felt, not to find a wife in the morning matching him in spirits. Perhaps, however, this was a condition peculiar to honeymoons, and marriage, once the honeymoon was over, would be a more tranquil state. Things would settle down when they were back in England, to a different, more separated life in which there would be time to rest, time to think; time to remember, while he was away at his office, how deeply she loved him. And surely she would learn to sleep; and once she slept properly she would be able to answer his loving questions throughout the day with more real *élan*.

But,—there in England waiting for her, inevitable, no longer to be put off or avoided, was The Willows. Whenever her thoughts reached that house they gave a little jump and tried to slink away. She was ashamed of herself, it was ridiculous, and Everard's attitude was plainly the sensible one, and if he could adopt it surely she, who hadn't gone through that terrible afternoon last July, could; yet she failed to see herself in The Willows, she failed altogether to imagine it. How, for instance, was she going to sit on that terrace,—'We always have tea in fine weather on the terrace,' Wemyss had casually remarked, apparently quite untouched by the least memory—how was she going to have tea on the very flags perhaps where.... Her thoughts slunk away; but not before one of them had sent a curdling whisper through her mind, '*The tea would taste of blood.*'

Well, this was sleeplessness. She never in her life had had that sort of absurd thought. It was just that she didn't sleep, and so her brain was relaxed and let the reins of her thinking go slack. The day her father died, it's true, when it began to be evening and she was afraid of the night alone with him in his mysterious indifference, she had begun thinking absurdly, but Everard had come and saved her. He could save her from this too if she could tell him; only she couldn't tell him. How could she spoil his joy in his home? It was the thing he loved next best to her.

As the honeymoon went on and Wemyss's ecstasies a little subsided, as he began to tire of so many trains—after Paris they did the châteaux country—and hotels and waiters and taxis and restaurants, and the cooking which he had at first enjoyed now only increased his longing at every meal for a plain English steak and boiled potatoes, he talked more and more of The Willows. With almost the same eagerness as that which had so much enchanted and moved her before their marriage when he talked of their wedding day, he now talked of The Willows and the day when he would show it to her. He counted the days now to that day. The 4th of April; his birthday; on that happy day he would lead his little wife into the home he loved. How could she, when he talked like that, do anything but pretend enthusiasm and looking forward? He had apparently entirely forgotten what she had told him about her reluctance to go there at Christmas. She was astonished that, when the first bliss of being married to her had worn off and his thoughts were free for this other thing he so much loved, his home, he didn't

375

approach it with more care for what he must know was her feeling about it. She was still more astonished when she realised that he had entirely forgotten her feeling about it. It would be, she felt, impossible to shadow his happiness at the prospect of showing her his home by any reminder of her reluctance. Besides, she was certainly going to have to live at The Willows, so what was the use of talking?

'I suppose,' she did say hesitatingly one day when he was describing it to her for the hundredth time, for it was his habit to describe the same thing often, 'you've changed your room——?'

They were sitting at the moment, resting after the climb up, on one of the terraces of the Château of Amboise, with a view across the Loire of an immense horizon, and Wemyss had been comparing it, to its disadvantage, when he recovered his breath, with the view from his bedroom window at The Willows. It wasn't very nice weather, and they both were cold and tired, and it was still only eleven o'clock in the morning.

'Change my room? What room?' he asked.

'Your—the room you and—the room you slept in.'

'My bedroom? I should think not. It's the best room in the house. Why do you think I've changed it?' And he looked at her with a surprised face.

'Oh, I don't know,' said Lucy, taking refuge in stroking his hand. 'I only thought——'

An inkling of what was in her mind penetrated into his, and his voice went grave.

'You mustn't think,' he said. 'You mustn't be morbid. Now Lucy, I can't have that. It will spoil everything if you let yourself be morbid. And you promised me before our marriage you wouldn't be. Have you forgotten?'

He turned to her and took her face in both his hands and searched her eyes with his own very solemn ones, while the woman who was conducting them over the castle went to the low parapet, and stood with her back to them studying the view and yawning.

'Oh, Everard—of course I haven't forgotten. I've not forgotten anything I promised you, and never will. But—have I got to go into that bedroom too?'

He was really astonished. 'Have you got to go into that bedroom too?' he repeated, staring at the face enclosed in his two big hands. It looked extraordinarily pretty like that, like a small flower in its delicate whiteness next to his discoloured, middle-aged hands, and her mouth since her marriage seemed to have become an even more vivid red than it used to be, and her eyes were young enough to be made more beautiful instead of less by the languor of want of sleep. 'Well, I should think so. Aren't you my wife?'

'Yes,' said Lucy. 'But——'

'Now, Lucy, I'll have no buts,' he said, with his most serious air, kissing her on the cheek, she had discovered that just that kind of kiss was a rebuke. 'Those buts of yours butt in——'

He stopped, struck by what he had said.

'I think that was rather amusing—don't you?' he asked, suddenly smiling.

'Oh yes—very,' said Lucy eagerly, smiling too, delighted that he should switch off from solemnity.

He kissed her again,—this time a real kiss, on her funny, charming mouth.

'I suppose you'll admit,' he said, laughing and squeezing up her face into a quaint crumpled shape, 'that either you're my wife or not my wife, and that if you're my wife——'

'Oh, I'm *that* all right,' laughed Lucy.

'Then you share my room. None of these damned new-fangled notions for me, young woman.'

'Oh, but I didn't mean——'

'What? Another but?' he exclaimed, pouncing down on to her mouth and stopping it with an enormous kiss.

'*Monsieur et Madame se refroidiront,*' said the woman, turning round and drawing her shawl closer over her chest as a gust of chilly wind swept over the terrace.

They were honeymooners, poor creatures, and therefore one had patience; but even honeymooners oughtn't to wish to embrace in a cold wind on an exposed terrace of a château round which they were being conducted by a woman who was in a hurry to return to the preparation of her Sunday dinner. For such purposes hotels were provided, and the shelter of a comfortable warm room. She had supposed them to be *père et fille* when first she admitted them, but was soon aware of their real relationship. '*Il doit être bien riche,*' had been her conclusion.

'Come along, come along,' said Wemyss, getting up quickly, for he too felt the gust of cold wind. 'Let's finish the château or we'll be late for lunch. I wish they hadn't preserved so many of these places—one would have been quite enough to show us the sort of thing.'

'But we needn't go and look at them all,' said Lucy.

'Oh yes we must. We've arranged to.'

'But Everard——' began Lucy, following after him as he followed after the conductress, who had a way of darting out of sight round corners.

'This woman's like a lizard,' panted Wemyss, arriving round a corner only to see her disappear through an arch. 'Won't we be happy when it's time to go back to England and not have to see any more sights.'

'But why don't we go back now, if you feel like it?' asked Lucy, trotting after him as he on his big legs pursued the retreating conductress, and anxious to show him, by eagerness to go sooner to The Willows than was arranged, that she wasn't being morbid.

'Why, you know we can't leave before the 3rd of April,' said Wemyss, over his shoulder. 'It's all settled.'

'But can't it be unsettled?'

'What, and upset all the plans, and arrive home before my birthday?' He stopped and turned round to stare at her. 'Really, my dear——' he said.

She had discovered that my dear was a term of rebuke.

'Oh yes—of course,' she said hastily, 'I forgot about your birthday.'

At that Wemyss stared at her harder than ever; incredulously, in fact. Forgot about his birthday? *Lucy* had forgotten? If it had been Vera, now—but Lucy? He was deeply hurt. He was so much hurt that he stood quite still, and the conductress was obliged, on discovering that she was no longer being followed, to wait once more for the honeymooners; which she did, clutching her shawl round her abundant French chest and shivering.

What had she said, Lucy hurriedly asked herself, nipping over her last words in her mind, for she had learned by now what he looked like when he was hurt. Oh yes,—the birthday. How stupid of her. But it was because birthdays in her family were so unimportant, and nobody had minded whether they were remembered or not.

'I didn't mean that,' she said earnestly, laying her hand on his breast. 'Of course I hadn't forgotten anything so precious. It only had—well, you know what even the most wonderful things do sometimes—it—it had escaped my memory.'

'Lucy! Escaped your memory? The day to which you owe your husband?'

Wemyss said this with such an exaggerated solemnity, such an immense pomposity, that she thought he was in fun and hadn't really minded about the birthday at all; and, eager to meet every mood of his, she laughed. Relieved, she was so unfortunate as to laugh merrily.

To her consternation, after a moment's further stare he turned his back on her without a word and walked on.

Then she realised what she had done, that she had laughed—oh, how dreadful!—in the wrong place, and she ran after him and put her arm through his, and tried to lay her cheek against his sleeve, which was difficult because of the way their paces didn't match and also because he took no notice of her, and said, 'Baby—baby—were his dear feelings hurt, then?' and coaxed him.

But he wouldn't be coaxed. She had wounded him too deeply,—laughing, he said to himself, at what was to him the most sacred thing in life, the fact that he was her husband, that she was his wife.

'Oh, Everard,' she murmured at last, withdrawing her arm, giving up, 'don't spoil our day.'

Spoil their day? He? That finished it.

He didn't speak to her again till night. Then, in bed, after she had cried bitterly for a long while, because she couldn't make out what really had happened, and she loved him so much, and wouldn't hurt him for the world, and was heart-broken because she had, and anyhow was tired out, he at last turned to her and took her to his arms again and forgave her.

'I can't live,' sobbed Lucy, 'I can't live—if you don't go on loving me—if we don't understand——'

'My little Love,' said Wemyss, melted by the way her small body was shaking in his arms, and rather frightened, too, at the excess of her woe. 'My little Love don't. You mustn't. Your Everard loves you, and you mustn't give way like this. You'll be ill. Think how miserable you'd make him then.'

And in the dark he kissed away her tears, and held her close till her sobbing quieted down; and presently, held close like that, his kisses shutting her smarting eyes, she now the baby comforted and reassured, and he the soothing nurse, she fell asleep, and for the first time since her marriage slept all night.

XV

Early in their engagement Wemyss had expounded his theory to Lucy that there should be the most perfect frankness between lovers, while as for husband and wife there oughtn't to be a corner anywhere about either of them, mind, body, or soul, which couldn't be revealed to the other one.

'You can talk about everything to your Everard,' he assured her. 'Tell him your innermost thoughts, whatever they may be. You need no more be ashamed of telling him than of thinking them by yourself. He *is* you. You and he are one in mind and soul now, and when he is your husband you and he will become perfect and complete by being one in body as well. Everard—Lucy. Lucy—Everard. We shan't know where one ends and the other begins. That, little Love, is real marriage. What do you think of it?'

Lucy thought so highly of it that she had no words with which to express her admiration, and fell to kissing him instead. What ideal happiness, to be for ever removed from the fear of loneliness by the simple expedient of being doubled; and who so happy as herself to have found the exactly right person for this doubling, one she could so perfectly agree with and understand? She felt quite sorry she had nothing in her mind in the way of thoughts she was ashamed of to tell him then and there, but there wasn't a doubt, there wasn't a shred of anything a little wrong, not even an unworthy suspicion. Her mind was a chalice filled only with love, and so clear and bright was the love that even at the bottom, when she stirred it up to look, there wasn't a trace of sediment.

But marriage—or was it sleeplessness?—completely changed this, and there were perfect crowds of thoughts in her mind that she was thoroughly ashamed of. Remembering his words, and whole-heartedly agreeing that to be able to tell each other everything, to have no concealments, was real marriage, the day after her wedding she first of all reminded him of what he had said, then plunged bravely into the announcement that she'd got a thought she was ashamed of.

Wemyss pricked up his ears, thinking it was something interesting to do with sex, and waited with an amused, inquisitive smile. But Lucy in such matters was content to follow him, aware of her want of experience and of the abundance of his, and the thought that was worrying her only had to do with a waiter. A waiter, if you please.

Wemyss's smile died away. He had had occasion to reprimand this waiter at lunch for gross negligence, and here was Lucy alleging he had done so without any reason that she could see, and anyhow roughly. Would he remove the feeling of discomfort she had at being forced to think her own heart's beloved, the kindest and gentlest of men, hadn't been kind and gentle but unjust, by explaining?

Well, that was at the very beginning. She soon learned that a doubt in her mind was better kept there. If she brought it out to air it and dispel it by talking it over with him, all that happened was that he was hurt, and when he was hurt she instantly became perfectly miserable. Seeing, then, that this happened about small things, how impossible it was to talk with him of big things; of, especially, her immense doubt in regard to The Willows. For a long while she was sure he was bearing her feeling in mind, since it couldn't have changed since Christmas, and that when she arrived there she would find that he had had everything altered and all traces of Vera's life there removed. Then, when he began to talk about The Willows, she found that such an idea as alterations hadn't entered his head. She was to sleep in the very room that had been his and Vera's, in the very bed. And positively, so far was it from true that she could tell him every thought and talk everything over with him, when she discovered this she wasn't able to say more than that hesitating remark on the château terrace at Amboise about supposing he was going to change his bedroom.

Yet The Willows haunted her, and what a comfort it would have been to tell him all she felt and let him help her to get rid of her growing obsession by laughing at her. What a comfort if, even if he had thought her too silly and morbid to be laughed at, he had indulged her and consented to alter those rooms. But one learns a lot on a honeymoon, Lucy reflected, and one of the things she had learned was that Wemyss's mind was always made up. There seemed to be no moment when it was in a condition of becoming, and she might have slipped in a suggestion or laid a wish before him; his plans were sprung upon her full fledged, and they were unalterable. Sometimes he said, 'Would you like——?' and if she didn't like, and answered truthfully, as she answered at first before she learned not to, there was trouble. Silent trouble. A retiring of

Wemyss into a hurt aloofness, for his question was only decorative, and his little Love should instinctively, he considered, like what he liked; and there outside this aloofness, after efforts to get at him with fond and anxious questions, she sat like a beggar in patient distress, waiting for him to emerge and be kind to her.

Of course as far as the minor wishes and preferences of every day went it was all quite easy, once she had grasped the right answer to the question, 'Would you like?' She instantly did like. 'Oh yes— *very* much!' she hastened to assure him; and then his face continued content and happy instead of clouding with aggrievement. But about the big things it wasn't easy, because of the difficulty of getting the right flavour of enthusiasm into her voice, and if she didn't get it in he would put his finger under her chin and turn her to the light and repeat the question in a solemn voice,—precursor, she had learned, of the beginning of the cloud on his face.

How difficult it was sometimes. When he said to her, 'You'll like the view from your sitting-room at The Willows,' she naturally wanted to cry out that she wouldn't, and ask him how he could suppose she would like what was to her a view for ever associated with death? Why shouldn't she be able to cry out naturally if she wanted to, to talk to him frankly, to get his help to cure herself of what was so ridiculous by laughing at it with him? She couldn't laugh all alone, though she was always trying to; with him she could have, and so have become quite sensible. For he was so much bigger than she was, so wonderful in the way he had triumphed over diseased thinking, and his wholesomeness would spread over her too, a purging, disinfecting influence, if only he would let her talk, if only he would help her to laugh. Instead, she found herself hurriedly saying in a small, anxious voice, 'Oh yes—*very* much!'

'Is it possible,' she thought, 'that I am abject?'

Yes, she was extremely abject, she reflected, lying awake at night considering her behaviour during the day. Love had made her so. Love did make one abject, for it was full of fear of hurting the beloved. The assertion of the Scriptures that perfect love casteth out fear only showed, seeing that her love for Everard was certainly perfect, how little the Scriptures really knew what they were talking about.

Well, if she couldn't tell him the things she was feeling, why couldn't she get rid of the sorts of feelings she couldn't tell him, and just be wholesome? Why couldn't she be at least as wholesome about going to that house as Everard? If anybody was justified in shrinking from The Willows it was Everard, not herself. Sometimes Lucy would be sure that deep in his character there was a wonderful store of simple courage. He didn't speak of Vera's death, naturally he didn't wish to speak of that awful afternoon, but how often he must think of it, hiding his thoughts even from her, bearing them altogether alone. Sometimes she was sure of this, and sometimes she was equally sure of the very opposite. From the way he looked, the way he spoke, from those tiny indications that one somehow has noticed without knowing that one has noticed and that are so far more revealing and conclusive than any words, she sometimes was sure he really had forgotten. But this was too incredible. She couldn't believe it. What had perhaps happened, she thought, was that in self-defence, for the preservation of his peace, he had made up his mind never to think of Vera. Only by banishing her altogether from his mind would he be safe. Yet that couldn't be true either, for several times on the honeymoon he had begun talking of her, of things she had said, of things she had liked, and it was she, Lucy, who stopped him. She shrank from hearing anything about Vera. She especially shrank from hearing her mentioned casually. She was ready to brace herself to talk about her if it was to be a serious talk, because she wanted to help and comfort him whenever the remembrance of her death arose to torment him, but she couldn't bear to hear her mentioned casually. In a way she admired this casualness, because it was a proof of the supreme wholesomeness Everard had attained to by sheer courageous determination, but even so she couldn't help thinking that she would have preferred a little less of just this kind of wholesomeness in her beloved. She might be too morbid, but wasn't it possible to be too wholesome? Anyhow she shrank from the intrusion of Vera into her honeymoon. That, at least, ought to be kept free from her. Later on at The Willows....

Lucy fought and fought against it, but always at the back of her mind was the thought, not looked at, slunk away from, but nevertheless fixed, that there at The Willows, waiting for her, was Vera.

XVI

Those who go to Strorley, and cross the bridge to the other side of the river, have only to follow the towpath for a little to come to The Willows. It can also be reached by road, through a white gate down a lane that grows more and more willowy as it gets nearer the river and the house, but is quite passable for carts and even for cars, except when there are floods. When there are floods this lane disappears, and when the floods have subsided it is black and oozing for a long time afterwards, with clouds of tiny flies dancing about in it if the weather is at all warm, and the shoes of those who walk stick in it and come off, and those who drive, especially if they drive a car, have trouble. But all is well once a second white gate is reached, on the other side of which is a gravel sweep, a variety of handsome shrubs, nicely kept lawns, and The Willows. There are no big trees in the garden of The Willows, because it was built in the middle of meadows where there weren't any, but all round the iron railings of the square garden—the house being the centre of the square—and concealing the wire netting which keeps the pasturing cows from thrusting their heads through and eating the shrubs, is a fringe of willows. Hence its name.

'A house,' said Wemyss, explaining its name to Lucy on the morning of their arrival, 'should always be named after whatever most insistently catches the eye.'

'Then oughtn't it to have been called The Cows?' asked Lucy; for the meadows round were strewn thickly as far as she could see with recumbent cows, and they caught her eye much more than the tossing bare willow branches.

'No,' said Wemyss, annoyed. 'It ought not have been called The Cows.'

'No—of course I didn't mean that,' she said hastily.

Lucy was nervous, and said what first came into her head, and had been saying things of this nature the whole journey down. She didn't want to, she knew he didn't like it, but she couldn't stop.

They had just arrived, and were standing on the front steps while the servants unloaded the fly that had brought them from the station, and Wemyss was pointing out what he wished her to look at and admire from that raised-up place before taking her indoors. Lucy was glad of any excuse that delayed going indoors, that kept her on the west side of the house, furthest away from the terrace and the library window. Indoors would be the rooms, the unaltered rooms, the library past whose window..., the sitting-room at the top of the house out of whose window..., the bedroom she was going to sleep in with the very bed.... It was too miserably absurd, too unbalanced of her for anything but shame and self-contempt, how she couldn't get away from the feeling that indoors waiting for her would be Vera.

It was a grey, windy morning, with low clouds scurrying across the meadows. The house was raised well above flood level, and standing on the top step she could see how far the meadows stretched beyond the swaying willow hedge. Grey sky, grey water, green fields,—it was all grey and green except the house, which was red brick with handsome stone facings, and made, in its exposed position unhidden by any trees, a great splotch of vivid red in the landscape.

'Like blood,' said Lucy to herself; and was immediately ashamed.

'Oh, how bracing!' she cried, spreading out her arms and letting the wind blow her serge wrap out behind her like a flag. It whipped her skirt round her body, showing its slender pretty lines, and the parlourmaid, going in and out with the luggage, looked curiously at this small juvenile new mistress. 'Oh, I love this wind—don't take me indoors yet——'

Wemyss was pleased that she should like the wind, for was it not by the time it reached his house part, too, of his property? His face, which had clouded a little because of The Cows, cleared again.

But she didn't really like the wind at all, she never had liked anything that blustered and was cold, and if she hadn't been nervous the last thing she would have done was to stand there letting it blow her to pieces.

'And what a lot of laurels!' she exclaimed, holding on her hat with one hand and with the other pointing to a corner filled with these shrubs.

'Yes. I'll take you round the garden after lunch,' said Wemyss. 'We'll go in now.'

'And—and laurustinus. I love laurustinus——'

'Yes. Vera planted that. It has done very well. Come in now——'

'And—look, what are those bare things without any leaves yet?'

'I'll show you everything after lunch, Lucy. Come in——' And he put his arm about her shoulders, and urged her through the door the

385

maid was holding open with difficulty because of the wind.

There she was, then, actually inside The Willows. The door was shut behind her. She looked about her shrinkingly.

They were in a roomy place with a staircase in it.

'The hall,' said Wemyss, standing still, his arm round her.

'Yes,' said Lucy.

'Oak,' said Wemyss.

'Yes,' said Lucy.

He gazed round him with a sigh of satisfaction at having got back to it.

'All oak,' he said. 'You'll find nothing gimcrack about *my* house, little Love. Where are those flowers?' he added, turning sharply to the parlourmaid. 'I don't see my yellow flowers.'

'They're in the dining-room, sir,' said the parlourmaid.

'Why aren't they where I could see them the first thing?'

'I understood the orders were they were always to be on the breakfast-table, sir.'

'Breakfast-table! When there isn't any breakfast?'

'I understood——'

'I'm not interested in what you understood.'

Lucy here nervously interrupted, for Everard sounded suddenly very angry, by exclaiming, 'Antlers!' and waving her unpinned-down arm in the direction of the——

'Yes,' said Wemyss, his attention called off the parlourmaid, gazing up at his walls with pride.

'What a lot,' said Lucy.

'Aren't there. I always said I'd have a hall with antlers in it, and I've got it.' He hugged her close to his side. 'And I've got you too,' he said. 'I always get what I'm determined to get.'

'Did you shoot them all yourself?' asked Lucy, thinking the parlourmaid would take the opportunity to disappear, and a little surprised that she continued to stand there.

'What? The beasts they belonged to? Not I. If you want antlers the simple way is to go and buy them. Then you get them all at once, and not gradually. The hall was ready for them all at once, not gradually. I got these at Whiteley's. Kiss me.'

This sudden end to his remarks startled Lucy, and she repeated in her surprise—for there still stood the parlourmaid 'Kiss you?'

'I haven't had my birthday kiss yet.'

'Why, the very first thing when you woke up——'

'Not my real birthday kiss in my own home.'

She looked at the parlourmaid, who was quite frankly looking at her. Well, if the parlourmaid didn't mind, and Everard didn't mind, why should she mind?

She lifted her face and kissed him; but she didn't like kissing him or being kissed in public. What was the point of it? Kissing Everard was a great delight to her. A mixture of all sorts of wonderful sensations, and she loved to do it in different ways, tenderly, passionately, lingeringly, dreamily, amusingly, solemnly; each kind in turn, or in varied combinations. But among her varied combinations there was nothing that included a parlourmaid. Consequently her kiss was of the sort that was to be expected, perfunctory and brief, whereupon Wemyss said, 'Lucy——' in his hurt voice.

She started.

'Oh Everard—what is it?' she asked nervously.

That particular one of his voices always by now made her start, for it always took her by surprise. Pick her way as carefully as she might among his feelings there were always some, apparently, that she hadn't dreamed were there and that she accordingly knocked against. How dreadful if she had hurt him the very first thing on getting into The Willows! And on his birthday too. From the moment he woke that morning, all the way down in the train, all the way in the fly from the station, she had been unremittingly engaged in avoiding hurting him; an activity made extra difficult by the unfortunate way her nervousness about the house at the journey's end impelled her to say the kinds of things she least wanted to. Irreverent things; such as the silly remark on his house's name. She had got on much better the evening before at the house in Lancaster Gate where they had slept, because gloomy as it was it anyhow wasn't The Willows. Also there was no trace in it that she could see of such a thing as a woman ever having lived in it. It was a man's house; the house of a man who has no time for pictures, or interesting books and furniture. It was like a club and an office mixed up together, with capacious leather chairs and solid tables and Turkey carpets and reference books. She found it quite impossible to imagine Vera, or any other woman, in that house. Either Vera had spent most of her time at The Willows, or every trace of her had been very carefully removed. Therefore Lucy, helped besides by extreme fatigue, for she had been sea-sick all the way from Dieppe to Newhaven, Wemyss having crossed that way because he was fond of the sea, had positively been unable to think of Vera in those surroundings and had dropped off to sleep directly she got there and had slept all night; and of course being asleep she naturally hadn't said anything she oughtn't to have said, so that her first appearance in Lancaster Gate was a success; and when she woke next morning, and saw Wemyss's face in such unclouded tranquillity next to hers as he still slept, she lay gazing at it with her heart brimming with tender love and vowed that his birthday should be as unclouded throughout as his dear face was at that moment. She adored him. He was her very life. She wanted nothing in the world except for him to be happy. She would watch every word. She really must see to it that on this day of all days no word should escape her before it had been turned round in her head at least three times, and considered with the utmost care. Such were her resolutions in the morning; and here she was not only saying the wrong things but doing them. It was because she hadn't expected to be told to kiss him in the presence of a parlourmaid. She was always being tripped up by the unexpected. She ought by now to have learned better. How unfortunate.

'Oh Everard—what is it?' she asked nervously; but she knew before he could answer, and throwing her objections to public caresses to the winds, for anything was better than that he should be hurt at just that moment, she put up her free arm and drew his head down and kissed him again,—lingeringly this time, a kiss of tender, appealing love. What must it be like, she thought while she kissed him and her heart yearned over him, to be so fearfully sensitive. It made things difficult for her, but how much, much more difficult for him. And how wonderful the way his sensitiveness had developed since marriage. There had been no sign of it before.

Implicit in her kiss was an appeal not to let anything she said or did spoil his birthday, to forgive her, to understand. And at the back of her mind, quite uncontrollable, quite unauthorised, ran beneath these other thoughts this thought: 'I am certainly abject.'

This time he was quickly placated because of his excitement at getting home. 'Nobody can hurt me as you can,' was all he said.

'Oh but as though I ever, ever mean to,' she breathed, her arm round his neck.

Meanwhile the parlourmaid looked on.

'Why doesn't she go?' whispered Lucy, making the most of having got his ear.

'Certainly not,' said Wemyss out loud, raising his head. 'I might want her. Do you like the hall, little Love?'

'*Very* much,' she said, loosing him.

'Don't you think it's a very fine staircase?'

'*Very* fine,' she said.

He gazed about him with pride, standing in the middle of the Turkey carpet holding her close to his side.

'Now look at the window,' he said, turning her round when she had had time to absorb the staircase. 'Look—isn't it a jolly window? No nonsense about that window. You can really see out of it, and it really lets in light. Vera'—she winced—'tried to stuff it all up with curtains. She said she wanted colour, or something. Having got a beautiful garden to look out at, what does she try to do but shut most of it out again by putting up curtains.'

The attempt had evidently not succeeded, for the window, which was as big as a window in the waiting-room of a London terminus, had nothing to interfere with it but the hanging cord of a drawn-up brown holland blind. Through it Lucy could see the whole half of the garden on the right side of the front door with the tossing willow hedge, the meadows, and the cows. The leafless branches of some creeper beat against it and made a loud irregular tapping in the pauses of Wemyss's observations.

'Plate glass,' he said.

'Yes,' said Lucy; and something in his voice made her add in a tone of admiration, 'Fancy.'

Looking at the window they had their backs to the stairs. Suddenly she heard footsteps coming down them from the landing above.

'Who's that?' she said quickly, with a little gasp, before she could think, before she could stop, not turning her head, her eyes staring at the window.

'Who's what?' asked Wemyss. 'You do think it's a jolly window, don't you, little Love?'

The footsteps on the stairs stopped, and a gong she had noticed at the angle of the turn was sounded. Her body, which had shrunk together, relaxed. What a fool she was.

'Lunch,' said Wemyss. 'Come along—but isn't it a jolly window, little Love?'

'*Very* jolly.'

He turned her round to march her off to the dining-room, while the housemaid, who had come down from the landing, continued to beat the gong, though there they were obeying it under her very nose.

'Don't you think that's a good place to have a gong?' he asked, raising his voice because the gong, which had begun quietly, was getting rapidly louder. 'Then when you're upstairs in your sitting-room you'll hear it just as distinctly as if you were downstairs. Vera——'

But what he was going to say about Vera was drowned this time in the increasing fury of the gong.

'Why doesn't she leave off?' Lucy tried to call out to him, straining her voice to its utmost, for the maid was very good at the gong and was now extracting the dreadfullest din out of it.

'Eh?' shouted Wemyss.

In the dining-room, whither they were preceded by the parlourmaid, who at last had left off standing still and had opened the door for them, as Lucy could hear the gong continuing to be beaten though muffled now by doors and distance, she again said, 'Why doesn't she leave off?'

Wemyss took out his watch.

'She will in another fifty seconds,' he said.

Lucy's mouth and eyebrows became all inquiry.

'It is beaten for exactly two and a half minutes before every meal,' he explained.

'Oh?' said Lucy. 'Even when we're visibly collected?'

'She doesn't know that.'

'But she saw us.'

'But she doesn't know it officially.'

'Oh,' said Lucy.

'I had to make that rule,' said Wemyss, arranging his knives and forks more accurately beside his plate, 'because they would leave off beating it almost as soon as they'd begun, and then Vera was late and her excuse was that she hadn't heard. For a time after that I used to have it beaten all up the stairs right to the door of her sitting-room. Isn't it a fine gong? Listen——' And he raised his hand.

'*Very* fine,' said Lucy, who was thoroughly convinced there wasn't a finer, more robust gong in existence.

'There. Time's up,' he said, as three great strokes were followed by a blessed silence.

He pulled out his watch again. 'Let's see. Yes—to the tick. You wouldn't believe the trouble I had to get them to keep time.'

'It's wonderful,' said Lucy.

The dining-room was a narrow room full of a table. It had a window facing west and a window facing north, and in spite of the uninterrupted expanses of plate glass was a bleak, dark room. But then the weather was bleak and dark, and one saw such a lot of it out of the two big windows as one sat at the long table and watched the rolling clouds blowing straight towards one from the north-west; for Lucy's place was facing the north window, on Wemyss's left hand. Wemyss sat at the end of the table facing the west window. The table was so long that if Lucy had sat in the usual seat of wives, opposite her husband, communication would have been difficult,— indeed, as she remarked, she would have disappeared below the dip of the horizon.

'I like a long table,' said Wemyss to this. 'It looks so hospitable.'

'Yes,' said Lucy a little doubtfully, but willing to admit that its length at least showed a readiness for hospitality. 'I suppose it does. Or it would if there were people all round it.'

'People? You don't mean to say you want people already?'

'Good heavens no,' said Lucy hastily.' Of course I don't. Why, of course, Everard, I didn't mean that,' she added, laying her hand on his and smiling at him so as to dispel the gathering cloud on his face; and once more she flung all thoughts of the parlourmaid to the winds. 'You know I don't want a soul in the world but you.'

'Well, that's what I thought,' said Wemyss, mollified. 'I know all I want is you.'

(Was this same parlourmaid here in Vera's time? Lucy asked herself very privately and unconsciously and beneath the concerned attentiveness she was concentrating on Wemyss.)

'What lovely kingcups!' she said aloud.

'Oh yes, there they are—I hadn't noticed them. Yes, aren't they? They're my birthday flowers.' And he repeated his formula: 'It's my birthday and Spring's.'

But Lucy, of course, didn't know the proper ritual, it being her first experience of one of Wemyss's birthdays, besides having wished him his many happy returns hours ago when he first opened his eyes and found hers gazing at him with love; so all she did was

391

to make the natural but unfortunate remark that surely Spring began on the 21st of March,—or was it the 25th? No, that was Christmas Day—no, she didn't mean that——

'You're always saying things and then saying you didn't mean them,' interrupted Wemyss, vexed, for he thought that Lucy of all people should have recognised the allegorical nature of his formula. If it had been Vera, now,—but even Vera had managed to understand that much. 'I wish you would begin with what you do mean, it would be so much simpler. What, pray,*do* you mean now?'

'I can't think,' said Lucy timidly, for she had offended him again, and this time she couldn't even remotely imagine how.

XVII

He got over it, however. There was a particularly well-made soufflé, and this helped. Also Lucy kept on looking at him very tenderly, and it was the first time she had sat at his table in his beloved home, realising the dreams of months that she should sit just there with him, his little bobbed-haired Love, and gradually therefore he recovered and smiled at her again.

But what power she had to hurt him, thought Wemyss; it was so great because his love for her was so great. She should be very careful how she wielded it. Her Everard was made very sensitive by his love.

He gazed at her solemnly, thinking this, while the plates were being changed.

'What is it, Everard?' Lucy asked anxiously.

'I'm only thinking that I love you,' he said, laying his hand on hers.

She flushed with pleasure, and her face grew instantly happy. 'My Everard,' she murmured, gazing back at him, forgetful in her pleasure of the parlourmaid. How dear he was. How silly she was to be so much distressed when he was offended. At the core he was so sound and simple. At the core he was utterly her own dear lover. The rest was mere incident, merest indifferent detail.

'We'll have coffee in the library,' he said to the parlourmaid, getting up when he had finished his lunch and walking to the door. 'Come along, little Love,' he called over his shoulder.

The library....

'Can't we—don't we—have coffee in the hall?' asked Lucy, getting up slowly.

'No,' said Wemyss, who had paused before an enlarged photograph that hung on the wall between the two windows, enlarged to life size.

He examined it a moment, and then drew his finger obliquely across the glass from top to bottom. It then became evident that the picture needed dusting.

'Look,' he said to the parlourmaid, pointing.

The parlourmaid looked.

'I notice you don't say anything,' he said to her after a silence in which she continued to look, and Lucy, taken aback again, stood uncertain by the chair she had got up from. 'I don't wonder. There's nothing you can possibly say to excuse such carelessness.'

'Lizzie——' began the parlourmaid.

'Don't put it on to Lizzie.'

The parlourmaid ceased putting it on to Lizzie and was dumb.

'Come along, little Love,' said Wemyss, turning to Lucy and holding out his hand. 'It makes one pretty sick, doesn't it, to see that not even one's own father gets dusted.'

'Is that your father?' asked Lucy, hurrying to his side and offering no opinion about dusting.

It could have been no one else's. It was Wemyss grown very enormous, Wemyss grown very old, Wemyss displeased. The photograph had been so arranged that wherever you moved to in the room Wemyss's father watched you doing it. He had been watching Lucy from between those two windows all through her first lunch, and must, flashed through Lucy's brain, have watched Vera like that all through her last one.

'How long has he been there?' she asked, looking up into Wemyss's father's displeased eyes which looked straight back into hers.

'Been there?' repeated Wemyss, drawing her away for he wanted his coffee. 'How can I remember? Ever since I've lived here, I should think. He died five years ago. He was a wonderful old man, nearly ninety. He used to stay here a lot.'

Opposite this picture hung another, next to the door that led into the hall,—also a photograph enlarged to life-size. Lucy had noticed neither of these pictures when she came in, because the light from the windows was in her eyes. Now, turning to go out through the door led by Wemyss, she was faced by this one.

It was Vera. She knew at once; and if she hadn't she would have known the next minute, because he told her.

'Vera,' he said, in a matter-of-fact tone, as it were introducing them.

'Vera,' repeated Lucy under her breath; and she and Vera—for this photograph too followed one about with its eye—stared at each other.

It must have been taken about twelve years earlier, judging from the clothes. She was standing, and in a day dress that yet had a train to it trailing on the carpet, and loose, floppy sleeves and a high collar. She looked very tall, and had long thin fingers. Her dark hair was drawn up from her ears and piled on the top of her head. Her face was thin and seemed to be chiefly eyes,—very big dark eyes that stared out of the absurd picture in a kind of astonishment, and her mouth had a little twist in it as though she were trying not to laugh.

Lucy looked at her without moving. So this was Vera. Of course. She had known, though she had never constructed any image of her in her mind, had carefully avoided doing it, that she would be like that. Only older; the sort of Vera she must have been at forty when she died,—not attractive like that, not a young woman. To Lucy at twenty-two, forty seemed very old; at least, if you were a woman. In regard to men, since she had fallen in love with some one of forty-five who was certainly the youngest thing she had ever come across, she had rearranged her ideas of age, but she still thought forty very old for a woman. Vera had been thin and tall and dark in her idea of her, just as this Vera was thin and tall and dark; but thin bonily, tall stoopingly, and her dark hair was turning grey. In her idea of her, too, she was absent-minded and not very intelligent; indeed, she was rather troublesomely unintelligent, doing obstinate, foolish things, and at last doing that fatal, obstinate, foolish thing which so dreadfully ended her. This Vera was certainly intelligent. You couldn't have eyes like that and be a fool. And the expression of her mouth,—what had she been trying not to laugh at that day? Did she know she was going to be enlarged and hang for years in the bleak dining-room facing her father-in-law, each of them eyeing the other from their walls, while three times a day the originals sat down beneath their own pictures at the long table and ate? Perhaps she laughed, thought Lucy, because else she might have cried; only that would have been silly, and she couldn't have been silly,—not with those eyes, not with those straight, fine eyebrows. But would she, herself, presently be photographed too and enlarged and hung there? There was room next to Vera, room for just one more before the sideboard began. How very odd it would be if she were hung up next to Vera, and every day three times as she went out of the room was faced by Everard's wives. And how quaint to watch one's clothes as the years went by leaving off being pretty and growing more absurd. Really for such purposes one ought to be just wrapped round in a shroud. Fashion didn't touch shrouds; they always stayed the same. Besides, how suitable, thought Lucy, gazing into her dead predecessor's eyes; one would only be taking time by the forelock....

'Come along.' said Wemyss, drawing her away, 'I want my coffee. Don't you think it's a good idea,' he went on, as he led her down the hall to the library door, 'to have life-sized photographs instead of those idiotic portraits that are never the least like people?'

'Oh, a *very* good idea,' said Lucy mechanically, bracing herself for the library. There was only one room in the house she dreaded going into more than the library, and that was the sitting-room on the top floor,—her sitting-room and Vera's.

'Next week we'll go to a photographer's in London and have my little girl done,' said Wemyss, pushing open the library door, 'and then I'll have her exactly as God made her, without some artist idiot or other coming butting-in with his idea of her. God's idea of her is good enough for me. They won't have to enlarge much,' he laughed, 'to get *you* life-size, you midge. Vera was five foot ten. Now isn't this a fine room? Look—there's the river. Isn't it jolly being so close to it? Come round here—don't knock against my writing-table, now. Look—there's only the towpath between the river and the garden. Lord, what a beastly day. It might just as easily have been a beautiful spring day and us having our coffee out on the terrace. Don't you think this is a beautiful look-out,—so typically English with the beautiful green lawn and the bit of lush grass along the towpath, and the river. There's no river like it in the world, is there, little Love. Say you think it's the most beautiful river in the world'— he hugged her close—'say you think it's a hundred times better than that beastly French one we got so sick of with all those châteaux.'

'Oh, a *hundred* times better,' said Lucy.

They were standing at the window, with his arm round her shoulder. There was just room for them between it and the writing-table. Outside was the flagged terrace, and then a very green lawn with worms and blackbirds on it and a flagged path down the middle leading to a little iron gate. There was no willow hedge along the river end of the square garden, so as not to interrupt the view,—only the iron railings and wire-netting. Terra-cotta vases, which later on would be a blaze of geraniums, Wemyss explained, stood at intervals on each side of the path. The river, swollen and brown, slid past Wemyss's frontage very quickly that day, for there had been much rain. The clouds scudding across the sky before the wind were not in such a hurry but that every now and then they let loose a violent gust of ram, soaking the flags of the terrace again just as the wind had begun to dry them up. How could he stand there, she thought, holding her tight so that she couldn't get away, making her look out at the very place on those flags not two yards off....

But the next minute she thought how right he really was, how absolutely the only way this was to do the thing. Perfect simplicity was the one way to meet this situation successfully; and she herself was so far from simplicity that here she was shrinking, not able to bear to look, wanting only to hide her face,—oh, he was wonderful, and she was the most ridiculous of fools.

She pressed very close to him, and put up her face to his, shutting her eyes, for so she shut out the desolating garden with its foreground of murderous flags.

'What is it, little Love?' asked Wemyss.

'Kiss me,' she said; and he laughed and kissed her, but hastily, because he wanted her to go on admiring the view.

She still, however, held up her face. 'Kiss my eyes,' she whispered, keeping them shut. 'They're tired——'

He laughed again, but with a slight impatience, and kissed her eyes; and then, suddenly struck by her little blind face so close to his, the strong light from the big window showing all its delicate curves and delicious softnesses, his Lucy's face, his own little wife's, he kissed her really, as she loved him to kiss her, becoming absorbed only in his love.

'Oh, I love you, love you——' murmured Lucy, clinging to him, making secret vows of sensibleness, of wholesomeness, of a determined, unfailing future simplicity.

'Aren't we happy,' he said, pausing in his kisses to gaze down at what was now his face, for was it not much more his than hers? Of course it was his. She never saw it, except when she specially went to look, but he saw it all the time; she only had duties in regard to it, but he was on the higher plane of only having joys. She washed it, but he kissed it. And he kissed it when he liked and as much as ever he liked. 'Isn't it wonderful being married,' he said, gazing down at this delightful thing that was his very own for ever.

'Oh—wonderful!' murmured Lucy, opening her eyes and gazing into his.

Her face broke into a charming smile. 'You have the dearest eyes,' she said, putting up her finger and gently tracing his eyebrows with it.

Wemyss's eyes, full at that moment of love and pride, were certainly dear eyes, but a noise at the other end of the room made

Lucy jump so in his arms, gave her apparently such a fright, that when he turned his head to see who it was daring to interrupt them, daring to startle his little girl like that, and beheld the parlourmaid, his eyes weren't dear at all but very angry.

The parlourmaid had come in with the coffee; and seeing the two interlaced figures against the light of the big window had pulled up short, uncertain what to do. This pulling up had jerked a spoon off its saucer onto the floor with a loud rattle because of the floor not having a carpet on it and being of polished oak, and it was this noise that made Lucy jump so excessively that her jump actually made Wemyss jump too.

In the parlourmaid's untrained phraseology there had been a good deal of billing and cooing during luncheon, and even in the hall before luncheon there were examples of it, but what she found going on in the library was enough to make anybody stop dead and upset things,—it was such, she said afterwards in the kitchen, that if she didn't know for a fact that they were really married she wouldn't have believed it. Married people in the parlourmaid's experience didn't behave like that. What affection there was was exhibited before, and not after, marriage. And she went on to describe the way in which Wemyss—thus briefly and irreverently did they talk of their master in the kitchen—had flown at her for having come into the library. 'After telling me to,' she said. 'After saying, "We'll 'ave coffee in the library."' And they all agreed, as they had often before agreed, that if it weren't that he was in London half the time they wouldn't stay in the place five minutes.

Meanwhile Wemyss and Lucy were sitting side by side in two enormous chairs facing the unlit library fire drinking their coffee. The fire was only lit in the evenings, explained Wemyss, after the 1st of April; the weather ought to be warm enough by then to do without fires in the daytime, and if it wasn't it was its own look-out.

'Why did you jump so?' he asked. 'You gave me such a start. I couldn't think what was the matter.'

'I don't know,' said Lucy, faintly flushing. 'Perhaps'—she smiled at him over the arm of the enormous chair in which she almost totally disappeared—'because the maid caught us.'

'Caught us?'

'Being so particularly affectionate.'

'I like that,' said Wemyss. 'Fancy feeling guilty because you're being affectionate to your own husband.'

'Oh, well,' laughed Lucy, 'don't forget I haven't had him long.'

'You're such a complicated little thing. I shall have to take you seriously in hand and teach you to be natural. I can't have you having all sorts of finicking ideas about not doing this and not doing the other before servants. Servants don't matter. I never consider them.'

'I wish you had considered the poor parlourmaid,' said Lucy, seeing that he was in an unoffended frame of mind. 'Why did you give her such a dreadful scolding?'

'Why? Because she made you jump so. You couldn't have jumped more if you had thought it was a ghost. I won't have your flesh being made to creep.'

'But it crept much worse when I heard the things you said to her.'

'Nonsense. These people have to be kept in order. What did the woman mean by coming in like that?'

'Why, you told her to bring us coffee.'

'But I didn't tell her to make an infernal noise by dropping spoons all over the place.'

'That was because she got just as great a fright when she saw us as I did when I heard her.'

'I don't care what she got. Her business is not to drop things. That's what I pay her for. But look here—don't you go thinking such a lot of tangled-up things and arguing. Do, for goodness sake, try and be simple.'

'I feel *very* simple,' said Lucy, smiling and putting out her hand to him, for his face was clouding. 'Do you know, Everard, I believe what's the matter with me is that I'm *too* simple.'

Wemyss roared, and forgot how near he was getting to being hurt. 'You simple! You're the most complicated——'

'No I'm not. I've got the untutored mind and uncontrolled emotions of a savage. That's really why I jumped.'

'Lord,' laughed Wemyss, 'listen to her how she talks. Anybody might think she was clever, saying such big long words, if they didn't know she was just her Everard's own little wife. Come here, my little savage—come and sit on your husband's knee and tell him all about it.'

He held out his arms, and Lucy got up and went into them and he rocked her and said, 'There, there—was it a little untutored savage then——'

But she didn't tell him all about it, first because by now she knew that to tell him all about anything was asking for trouble, and second because he didn't really want to know. Everard, she was beginning to realise with much surprise, preferred not to know. He was not merely incurious as to other people's ideas and opinions, he definitely preferred to be unconscious of them.

This was a great contrast to the restless curiosity and interest of her father and his friends, to their insatiable hunger for discussion, for argument; and it much surprised Lucy. Discussion was the very salt of life for them,—a tireless exploration of each other's ideas, a clashing of them together, and out of that clashing the creation of fresh ones. To Everard, Lucy was beginning to perceive, discussion merely meant contradiction, and he disliked contradiction, he disliked even difference of opinion. 'There's only one way of looking at a thing, and that's the right way,' as he said, 'so what's the good of such a lot of talk?'

The right way was his way; and though he seemed by his direct, unswerving methods to succeed in living mentally in a great calm, and though after the fevers of her father's set this was to her immensely restful, was it really a good thing? Didn't it cut one off from growth? Didn't it shut one in an isolation? Wasn't it, frankly, rather like death? Besides, she had doubts as to whether it were true that there was only one way of looking at a thing, and couldn't quite believe that his way was invariably the right way. But what did it matter after all, thought Lucy, snuggled up on his knee with one arm round his neck, compared to the great, glorious fact of their love? That at least was indisputable and splendid. As to the rest, truth would go on being truth whether Everard saw it or not; and if she were not going to be able to talk over things with him she could anyhow kiss him, and how sweet that was, thought Lucy. They understood each other perfectly when they kissed. What, indeed, when such sweet means of communion existed, was the good of a lot of talk?

'I believe you're asleep' said Wemyss, looking down at the face on his breast.

'Sound,' said Lucy, smiling, her eyes shut.

'My baby.'

'My Everard.'

XVIII

But this only lasted as long as his pipe lasted. When that was finished he put her off his knee, and said he was now ready to gratify her impatience and show her everything; they would go over the house first, and then the garden and outbuildings.

No woman was ever less impatient than Lucy. However, she pulled her hat straight and tried to seem all readiness and expectancy. She wished the wind wouldn't howl so. What an extraordinary dreary place the library was. Well, any place would be dreary at half-past two o'clock on such an afternoon, without a fire and with the rain beating against the window, and that dreadful terrace just outside.

Wemyss stooped to knock out the ashes of his pipe on the bars of the empty grate, and Lucy carefully kept her head turned away from the window and the terrace towards the other end of the room. The other end was filled with bookshelves from floor to ceiling, and the books, in neat rows and uniform editions, were packed so tightly in the shelves that no one but an unusually determined reader would have the energy to wrench one out. Reading was evidently not encouraged, for not only were the books shut in behind glass doors, but the doors were kept locked and the key hung on Wemyss's watch-chain. Lucy discovered this when Wemyss, putting his pipe in his pocket, took her by the arm and walked her down the room to admire the shelves. One of the volumes caught her eye, and she tried to open the glass door to take it out and look at it. 'Why,' she said surprised, 'it's locked.'

'Of course,' said Wemyss.

'Why but then nobody can get at them.'

'Precisely.'

'But——'

'People are so untrustworthy about books. I took pains to arrange mine myself, and they're all in first-class-bindings and I don't want them taken out and left lying anywhere by Tom, Dick, and Harry. If any one wants to read they can come and ask me. Then I know exactly what is taken, and can see that it is put back.' And he held up the key on his watch-chain.

'But doesn't that rather discourage people?' asked Lucy, who was accustomed to the most careless familiarity in intercourse with books, to books loose everywhere, books overflowing out of their shelves, books in every room, instantly accessible books, friendly books, books used to being read aloud, with their hospitable pages falling open at a touch.

'All the better,' said Wemyss. '*I* don't want anybody to read my books.'

Lucy laughed, though she was dismayed inside. 'Oh Everard—' she said, 'not even me?'

'You? You're different. You're my own little girl. Whenever you want to, all you've got to do is to come and say, "Everard, your Lucy wants to read," and I'll unlock the bookcase.'

'But—I shall be afraid I may be disturbing you.'

'People who love each other can't ever disturb each other.'

'That's true,' said Lucy.

'And they shouldn't ever be afraid of it.'

'I suppose they shouldn't,' said Lucy.

'So be simple, and when you want a thing just say so.' Lucy said she would, and promised with many kisses to be simple, but she couldn't help privately thinking it a difficult way of getting at a book.

'Macaulay, Dickens, Scott, Thackeray, British Poets, English Men of Letters, *Encyclopædia Britannica*—I think there's about everything,' said Wemyss, going over the gilt names on the backs of the volumes with much satisfaction as he stood holding her in front of them. 'Whiteley's did it for me. I said I had room for so and so many of such and such sizes of the best modern writers in good bindings. I think they did it very well, don't you little Love?'

'*Very* well,' said Lucy, eyeing the shelves doubtfully.

She was of those who don't like the feel of prize books in their hands, and all Wemyss's books might have been presented as prizes to deserving schoolboys. They were handsome; their edges—she couldn't see them, but she was sure—were marbled. They wouldn't open easily, and one's thumbs would have to do a lot of tiring holding while one's eyes tried to peep at the words tucked away towards the central crease. These were books with which one took no liberties. She couldn't imagine idly turning their pages in some lazy position out on the grass. Besides, their pages wouldn't be idly turned; they would be, she was sure, obstinate with expensiveness, stiff with the leather and gold of their covers.

Lucy stared at them, thinking all this so as not to think other things. What she wanted to shut out was the wind sobbing up and down that terrace behind her, and the consciousness of the fierce intermittent squalls of rain beating on its flags, and the certainty that upstairs.... Had Everard *no* imagination, she thought, with a sudden flare of rebellion, that he should expect her to use and to like using the very sitting-room where Vera——

With a quick shiver she grabbed at her thoughts and caught them just in time.

'Do you like Macaulay?' she asked, lingering in front of the bookcase, for he was beginning to move her off towards the door.

'I haven't read him,' said Wemyss, still moving her.

'Which of all these do you like best?' she asked, holding back.

'Oh, I don't know,' said Wemyss, pausing a moment, pleased by her evident interest in his books. 'I haven't much time for reading, you must remember. I'm a busy man. By the time I've finished my day's work, I'm not inclined for much more than the evening paper and a game of bridge.'

'But what will you do with me, who don't play bridge?'

'Lord, you don't suppose I shall want to play bridge now that I've got you?' he said. 'All I shall want is just to sit and look at you.'

She turned red with swift pleasure, and laughed, and hugged the arm that was thrust through hers leading her to the door. How much she adored him; when he said dear, absurd, simple things like that, how much she adored him!

'Come upstairs now and take off your hat,' said Wemyss. 'I want to see what my bobbed hair looks like in my home. Besides, aren't you dying to see our bedroom?'

'Dying,' said Lucy, going up the oak staircase with a stout, determined heart.

The bedroom was over the library, and was the same size and with the same kind of window. Where the bookcase stood in the room below, stood the bed: a double, or even a treble, bed, so very big was it, facing the window past which Vera—it was no use, she couldn't get away from Vera—having slept her appointed number of nights, fell and was finished. But she wasn't finished. If only she had slipped away out of memory, out of imagination, thought Lucy ... but she hadn't, she hadn't—and this was her room, and that intelligent-eyed thin thing had slept in it for years and years, and for years and years the looking-glass had reflected her while she had dressed and undressed, dressed and undressed before it—regularly, day after day, year after year—oh, what a trouble—and her thin long hands had piled up her hair—Lucy could see her sitting there piling it on the top of her small head—sitting at the dressing-table in the window past which she was at last to drop like a stone—horribly—ignominiously—all anyhow—and everything in the room had been hers, every single thing in it had been Vera's, including Ev——

Lucy made a violent lunge after her thoughts and strangled them.

Meanwhile Wemyss had shut the door and was standing looking at her without moving.

'Well?' he said.

She turned to him nervously, her eyes still wide with the ridiculous things she had been thinking.

'Well?' he said again.

She supposed he meant her to praise the room, so she hastily began, saying what a good view there must be on a fine day, and how very comfortable it was, such a nice big looking-glass—she loved a big looking-glass—and such a nice sofa—she loved a nice sofa—and what a very big bed—and what a lovely carpet——

'Well?' was all Wemyss said when her words came to an end.

'What is it, Everard?'

'I'm waiting,' he said.

'Waiting?'

'For my kiss.'

She ran to him.

'Yes,' he said, when she had kissed him, looking down at her solemnly, '*I* don't forget these things. *I* don't forget that this is the first time my own wife and I have stood together in our very own bedroom.'

'But Everard I didn't forget—I only——'

She cast about for something to say, her arms still round his neck, for the last thing she could have told him was what she had been thinking—oh, how he would have scolded her for being morbid, and oh, how right he would have been!—and she ended by saying as lamely and as unfortunately as she had said it in the château of Amboise—'I only didn't remember.'

Luckily this time his attention had already wandered away from her. 'Isn't it a jolly room?' he said. 'Who's got far and away the best bedroom in Strorley? And who's got a sitting-room all for herself, just as jolly? And who spoils his little woman?'

Before she could answer, he loosened her hands from his neck and said, 'Come and look at yourself in the glass. Come and see how small you are compared to the other things in the room.' And with his arms round her shoulders he led her to the dressing-table.

'The other things?' laughed Lucy; but like a flame the thought was leaping in her brain, 'Now what shall I do if when I look into this I don't see myself but Vera? It's *accustomed* to Vera....'

'Why, she's shutting her eyes. Open them, little Love,' said Wemyss, standing with her before the glass and seeing in it that though he held her in front of it she wasn't looking at the picture of wedded love he and she made, but had got her eyes tight shut.

With his free hand he took off her hat and threw it on to the sofa; then he laid his head on hers and said, 'Now look.'

Lucy obeyed; and when she saw the sweet picture in the glass the face of the girl looking at her broke into its funny, charming smile, for Everard at that moment was at his dearest, Everard boyishly loving her, with his good-looking, unlined face so close to hers and his proud eyes gazing at her. He and she seemed to set each other off; they were becoming to each other.

Smiling at him in the glass, a smile tremulous with tenderness, she put up her hand and stroked his face. 'Do you know who you've married?' she asked, addressing the man in the glass.

'Yes,' said Wemyss, addressing the girl in the glass.

'No you don't,' she said. 'But I'll tell you. You've married the completest of fools.'

'Now what has the little thing got into its head this time?' he said, kissing her hair, and watching himself doing it.

'Everard, you must help me,' she murmured, holding his face tenderly against hers. 'Please, my beloved, help me, teach me——'

'That, Mrs. Wemyss, is a very proper attitude in a wife,' he said. And the four people laughed at each other, the two Lucys a little quiveringly.

'Now come and I'll introduce you to your sitting-room,' he said, disengaging himself. 'We'll have tea up there. The view is really magnificent.'

XIX

The wind made more noise than ever at the top of the house, and when Wemyss tried to open the door to Vera's sitting-room it blew back on him.

'Well I'm damned,' he said, giving it a great shove.

'Why?' asked Lucy nervously.

'Come in, come in,' he said impatiently, pressing the door open and pulling her through.

There was a great flapping of blinds and rattling of blind cords, a whirl of sheets of notepaper, an extra wild shriek of the wind, and then Wemyss, hanging on to the door, shut it and the room quieted down.

'That slattern Lizzie!' he exclaimed, striding across to the fireplace and putting his finger on the bell-button and keeping it there.

'What has she done?' asked Lucy, standing where he had left her just inside the door.

'Done? Can't you see?'

'You mean'—she could hardly get herself to mention the fatal thing—'you mean—the window?'

'On a day like this!'

He continued to press the bell. It was a very loud bell, for it rang upstairs as well as down in order to be sure of catching Lizzie's ear in whatever part of the house she might be endeavouring to evade it, and Lucy, as she listened to its strident, persistent summons of a Lizzie who didn't appear, felt more and more on edge, felt at last that to listen and wait any longer was unbearable.

'Won't you wear it out?' she asked, after some moments of nothing happening and Wemyss still ringing.

He didn't answer. He didn't look at her. His finger remained steadily on the button. His face was extraordinarily like the old man's in the enlarged photograph downstairs. Lucy wished for only two things at that moment, one was that Lizzie shouldn't come, and the other was that if she did she herself might be allowed to go and be somewhere else.

'Hadn't—hadn't the window better be shut?' she suggested timidly presently, while he still went on ringing and saying nothing—'else when Lizzie opens the door won't all the things blow about again?'

He didn't answer, and went on ringing.

Of all the objects in the world that she could think of, Lucy most dreaded and shrank from that window; nevertheless she began to feel that as Everard was engaged with the bell and apparently wouldn't leave it, it behoved her to put into practice her resolution not to be a fool but to be direct and wholesome, and go and shut it herself. There it was, the fatal window, huge as the one in the bedroom below and the one in the library below that, yawning wide open above its murderous low sill, with the rain flying in on every fresh gust of wind and wetting the floor and the cushions of the sofa and even, as she could see, those sheets of notepaper off the writing-table that had flown in her face when she came in and were now lying scattered at her feet. Surely the right thing to do was to shut the window before Lizzie opened the door and caused a second convulsion? Everard couldn't, because he was ringing the bell. She could and she would; yes, she would do the right thing, and at the same time be both simple and courageous.

'I'll shut it,' she said, taking a step forward.

She was arrested by Wemyss's voice. 'Confound it!' he cried. 'Can't you leave it alone?'

She stopped dead. He had never spoken to her like that before. She had never heard that voice before. It seemed to hit her straight on the heart.

'Don't interfere,' he said, very loud.

She was frozen where she stood.

'Tiresome woman,' he said, still ringing.

She looked at him. He was looking at her.

'Who?' she breathed.

'You.'

Her heart seemed to stop beating. She gave a little gasp, and turned her head to right and left like something trapped, something searching for escape. Everard—where was her Everard? Why didn't he come and take care of her? Come and take her away—out of that room—out of that room——

There were sounds of steps hurrying along the passage, and then there was a great scream of the wind and a great whirl of the notepaper and a great blowing up on end off her forehead of her short hair, and Lizzie was there panting on the threshold.

'I'm sorry, sir,' she panted, her hand on her chest, 'I was changing my dress——'

'Shut the door, can't you?' cried Wemyss, about whose ears, too, notepaper was flying. 'Hold on to it—don't let it go, damn you!'

'Oh—oh——' gasped Lucy, stretching out her hands as though to keep something off, 'I think I—I think I'll go downstairs——'

And before Wemyss realised what she was doing, she had turned and slipped through the door Lizzie was struggling with and was gone.

'Lucy!' he shouted, 'Lucy! Come back at once!' But the wind was too much for Lizzie, and the door dragged itself out of her hands and crashed to.

As though the devil were after her Lucy ran along the passage. Down the stairs she flew, down past the bedroom landing, down past the gong landing, down into the hall and across it to the front door, and tried to pull it open, and found it was bolted, and tugged and tugged at the bolts, tugged frantically, getting them undone at last, and rushing out on to the steps.

There an immense gust of rain caught her full in the face. Splash—bang—she was sobered. The rain splashed on her as though a bucket were being emptied at her, and the door had banged behind her shutting her out. Suddenly horrified at herself she turned quickly, as frantic to get in again as she had been to get out. What was she doing? Where was she running to? She must get in, get in— before Everard could come after her, before he could find her standing there like a drenched dog outside his front door. The wind whipped her wet hair across her eyes. Where was the handle? She couldn't find it. Her hair wouldn't keep out of her eyes; her thin serge skirt blew up like a balloon and got in the way of her trembling fingers searching along the door. She must get in—before he came—what had possessed her? Everard—he couldn't have meant—he didn't mean—what would he think—what*would* he think—oh, where was that handle?

Then she heard heavy footsteps on the other side of the door, and Wemyss's voice, still very loud, saying to somebody he had got with him, 'Haven't I given strict orders that this door is to be kept bolted?'—and then the sound of bolts being shot.

'Everard! Everard!' Lucy cried, beating on the door with both hands, 'I'm here—out here—let me in—Everard! Everard!'

But he evidently heard nothing, for his footsteps went away again.

Snatching her hair out of her eyes, she looked about for the bell and reached up to it and pulled it violently. What she had done was terrible. She must get in at once, face the parlourmaid's astonishment, run to Everard. She couldn't imagine his thoughts. Where did he suppose she was? He must be searching the house for her. He would be dreadfully upset. Why didn't the parlourmaid come? Was she changing her dress too? No—she had waited at lunch all ready in her black afternoon clothes. Then why didn't she come?

Lucy pulled the bell again and again, at last keeping it down, using up its electricity as squanderously as Wemyss had used it upstairs. She was wet to the skin by this time, and you wouldn't have recognised her pretty hair, all dark now and sticking together in lank strands.

Everard—why, of course—Everard had only spoken like that out of fear—fear and love. The window—of course he would be terrified lest she too, trying to shut that fatal window, that great heavy fatal window, should slip.... Oh, of course, of course—how could she have misunderstood—in moments of danger, of dreadful anxiety for one's heart's beloved, one did speak sharply, one did rap out commands. It was because he loved her so *much*.... Oh, how lunatic of her to have misunderstood!

At last she heard some one coming, and she let go of the bell and braced herself to meet the astonished gaze of the parlourmaid with as much dignity as was possible in one who only too well knew she must be looking like a drowning cat, but the footsteps grew heavy as they got nearer, and it was Wemyss who, after pulling back the bolts, opened the door.

'Oh Everard!' Lucy exclaimed, running in, pursued to the last by the pelting rain, 'I'm so glad it's you—oh I'm so sorry I——'

Her voice died away; she had seen his face.

He stooped to bolt the lower bolt.

'Don't be angry, darling Everard,' she whispered, laying her arm on his stooping shoulder.

Having finished with the bolt Wemyss straightened himself, and then, putting up his hand to the arm still round his shoulder, he removed it. 'You'll make my coat wet,' he said; and walked away to the library door and went in and shut it.

For a moment she stood where he had left her, collecting her scattered senses; then she went after him. Wet or not wet, soaked and dripping as she was, ridiculous scarecrow with her clinging clothes, her lank hair, she must go after him, must instantly get the horror of misunderstanding straight, tell him how she had meant only to help over that window, tell him how she had thought he was saying dreadful things to her when he was really only afraid for her safety, tell him how silly she had been, silly, silly, not to have followed his thoughts quicker, tell him he must forgive her, be patient with her, help her, because she loved him so much and she knew—oh, she knew—how much he loved her....

Across the hall ran Lucy, the whole of her one welter of anxious penitence and longing and love, and when she got to the door and turned the handle it was locked.

He had locked her out.

XX

Her hand slid slowly off the knob. She stood quite still. How *could* he.... And she knew now that he had bolted the front door knowing she was out in the rain. How *could* he? Her body was motionless as she stood staring at the locked door, but her brain was a rushing confusion of questions. Why? Why? This couldn't be Everard. Who was this man—pitiless, cruel? Not Everard. Not her lover. Where was he, her lover and husband? Why didn't he come and take care of her, and not let her be frightened by this strange man....

She heard a chair being moved inside the room, and then she heard the creak of leather as Wemyss sat down in it, and then there was the rustle of a newspaper being opened. He was actually settling down to read a newspaper while she, his wife, his love—wasn't he always telling her she was his little Love?—was breaking her heart outside the locked door. Why, but Everard—she and Everard; they understood each other; they had laughed, played together, talked nonsense, been friends....

For an instant she had an impulse to cry out and beat on the door, not to care who heard, not to care that the whole house should come and gather round her naked misery; but she was stopped by a sudden new wisdom. It shuddered down on her heart, a wisdom she had never known or needed before, and held her quiet. At all costs there mustn't be two of them doing these things, at all costs these things mustn't be doubled, mustn't have echoes. If Everard was like this he must be like it alone. She must wait. She must sit quiet till he had finished. Else—but oh, he *couldn't* be like it, it *couldn't* be true that he didn't love her. Yet if he did love her, how could he ... how could he....

She leaned her forehead against the door and began softly to cry. Then, afraid that she might after all burst out into loud, disgraceful sobbing, she turned and went upstairs.

But where could she go? Where in the whole house was any refuge, any comfort? The only person who could have told her anything, who could have explained, who *knew*, was Vera. Yes—she would have understood. Yes, yes—Vera. She would go to Vera's room, get as close to her mind as she could,—search, find something, some clue....

411

It seemed now to Lucy, as she hurried upstairs, that the room in the house she had most shrunk from was the one place where she might hope to find comfort. Oh, she wasn't frightened any more. Everything was trying to frighten her, but she wasn't going to be frightened. For some reason or other things were all trying together to-day to see if they could crush her, beat out her spirit. But they weren't going to....

She jerked her wet hair out of her eyes as she climbed the stairs. It kept on getting into them and making her stumble. Vera would help her. Vera never was beaten. Vera had had fifteen years of not being beaten before she—before she had that accident. And there must have been heaps of days just like this one, with the wind screaming and Vera up in her room and Everard down in his— locked in, perhaps—and yet Vera had managed, and her spirit wasn't beaten out. For years and years, panted Lucy—her very thoughts came in gasps—Vera lived up here winter after winter, years, years, years, and would have been here now if she hadn't— oh, if only Vera weren't dead! If *only, only* Vera weren't dead! But her mind lived on—her mind was in that room, in every littlest thing in it——

Lucy stumbled up the last few stairs completely out of breath, and opening the sitting-room door stood panting on the threshold much as Lizzie had done, her hand on her chest.

This time everything was in order. The window was shut, the scattered notepaper collected and tidily on the writing-table, the rain on the floor wiped up, and a fire had been lit and the wet cushions were drying in front of it. Also there was Lizzie, engaged in conscience-stricken activities, and when Lucy came in she was on her knees poking the fire. She was poking so vigorously that she didn't hear the door open, especially not with that rattling and banging of the window going on; and on getting up and seeing the figure standing there panting, with strands of lank hair in its eyes and its general air of neglect and weather, she gave a loud exclamation.

'Lumme!' exclaimed Lizzie, whose origin and bringing-up had been obscure.

She had helped carry in the luggage that morning, so she had seen her mistress before and knew what she was like in her dry state. She never could have believed, having seen her then all nicely fluffed out, that there was so little of her. Lizzie knew what long-haired dogs look like when they are being soaped, and she was also familiar with cats as they appear after drowning; yet they too surprised her, in spite of familiarity, each time she saw them in these circumstances by their want of real substance, of stuffing. Her mistress looked just like that,—no stuffing at all; and therefore Lizzie, the poker she was holding arrested in mid-air on its way into its corner, exclaimed Lumme.

Then, realising that this weather-beaten figure must certainly be catching its death of cold, she dropped the poker and hurrying across the room and talking in the stress of the moment like one girl to another, she felt Lucy's sleeve and said, 'Why, you're wet to the bones. Come to the fire and take them sopping clothes off this minute, or you'll be laid up as sure as sure——'and pulled her over to the fire; and having got her there, and she saying nothing at all and not resisting, Lizzie stripped off her clothes and shoes and stockings, repeating at frequent intervals as she did so, 'Dear, dear,' and repressing a strong desire to beg her not to take on, lest later, perhaps, her mistress mightn't like her to have noticed she had been crying. Then she snatched up a woollen coverlet that lay folded on the end of the sofa, rolled her tightly round in it, sat her in a chair right up close to the fender, and still talking like one girl to another said, 'Now sit there and don't move while I fetch dry things—I won't be above a minute—now you promise, don't you——' and hurrying to the door never remembered her manners at all till she was through it, whereupon she put in her head again and hastily said, 'Mum,' and disappeared.

She was away, however, more than a minute. Five minutes, ten minutes passed and Lizzie, feverishly unpacking Lucy's clothes in the bedroom below, and trying to find a complete set of them, and not knowing what belonged to which, didn't come back.

Lucy sat quite still, rolled up in Vera's coverlet. Obediently she didn't move, but stared straight into the fire, sitting so close up to it that the rest of the room was shut out. She couldn't see the window, or the dismal rain streaming down it. She saw nothing but the fire, blazing cheerfully. How kind Lizzie was. How comforting kindness was. It was a thing she understood, a normal, natural thing, and it made her feel normal and natural just to be with it. Lizzie had given her such a vigorous rub-down that her skin tingled. Her hair was on ends, for that too had had a vigorous rubbing from Lizzie, who had taken her apron to it feeling that this was an occasion on which one abandoned convention and went in for resource. And as Lucy sat there getting warmer and warmer, and more and more pervaded by the feeling of relief and well-being that even the most wretched feel if they take off all their clothes, her mind gradually calmed down, it left off asking agonised questions, and presently her heart began to do the talking.

She was so much accustomed to find life kind, that given a moment of quiet like this with somebody being good-natured and back she slipped to her usual state, which was one of affection and confidence. Lizzie hadn't been gone five minutes before Lucy had passed from sheer bewildered misery to making excuses for Everard; in ten minutes she was seeing good reasons for what he had done; in fifteen she was blaming herself for most of what had happened. She had been amazingly idiotic to run out of the room, and surely quite mad to run out of the house. It was wrong, of course, for him to bolt her out, but he was angry, and people did things when they were angry that horrified them afterwards. Surely people who easily got angry needed all the sympathy and understanding one could give them,—not to be met by despair and the loss of faith in them of the person they had hurt. That only turned passing, temporary bad things into a long unhappiness. She hadn't known he had a temper. She had only, so far, discovered his extraordinary capacity for being offended. Well, if he had a temper how could he help it? He was born that way, as certainly as if he had been born lame. Would she not have been filled with tenderness for his lameness if he had happened to be born like that? Would it ever have occurred to her to mind, to feel it as a grievance?

The warmer Lucy got the more eager she grew to justify Wemyss. In the middle of the reasons she was advancing for his justification, however, it suddenly struck her that they were a little smug. All that about people with tempers needing sympathy,—who was she, with her impulses and impatiences—with her, as she now saw, devastating impulses and impatiences—to take a line of what was very like pity. Pity! Smug, odious word; smug, odious thing. Wouldn't she hate it if she thought he pitied her for her failings? Let him be angry with her failings, but not pity her. She and her man, they needed no pity from each other; they had love. It was impossible that anything either of them did or was should *really* touch that.

Very warm now in Vera's blanket, her face flushed by the fire, Lucy asked herself what could really put out that great, glorious, central blaze. All that was needed was patience when he.... She gave herself a shake,—there she was again, thinking smugly. She wouldn't think at all. She would just take things as they came, and love, and love.

Then the vision of Everard, sitting solitary with his newspaper and by this time, too, probably thinking only of love, and anyhow not happy, caused one of those very impulses to lay hold of her which she had a moment before been telling herself she would never give way to again. She was aware one had gripped her, but this was a good impulse,—this wasn't a bad one like running out into the rain: she would go down and have another try at that door. She was warmed through now and quite reasonable, and she felt she couldn't another minute endure not being at peace with Everard. How silly they were. It was ridiculous. It was like two children fighting. Lizzie was so long bringing her clothes; she couldn't wait, she must sit on Everard's knee again, feel his arms round her, see his eyes looking kind. She would go down in her blanket. It wrapped her up from top to toe. Only her feet were bare; but they were quite warm, and anyhow feet didn't matter.

So Lucy padded softly downstairs, making hardly a sound, and certainly none that could be heard above the noise of the wind by Lizzie in the bedroom, frantically throwing clothes about.

She knocked at the library door.

Wemyss's voice said, 'Come in.'

So he had unlocked it. So he had hoped she would come.

He didn't, however, look round. He was sitting with his back to the door at the writing-table in the window, writing.

'I want my flowers in here,' he said, without turning his head.

So he had rung. So he thought it was the parlourmaid. So he hadn't unlocked the door because he hoped she would come.

But his flowers,—he wanted his birthday flowers in there because they were all that were left to him of his ruined birthday.

When she heard this order Lucy's heart rushed out to him. She shut the door softly and with her bare feet making no sound went up behind him.

He thought the parlourmaid had shut the door, and gone to carry out his order. Feeling an arm put round his shoulder he thought the

415

parlourmaid hadn't gone to carry out his order, but had gone mad instead.

'Good God!' he exclaimed, jumping up.

At the sight of Lucy in her blanket, with her bare feet and her confused hair, his face changed. He stared at her without speaking.

'I've come to tell you—I've come to tell you——'she began.

Then she faltered, for his mouth was a mere hard line.

'Everard, darling,' she said entreatingly, lifting her face to his, 'let's be friends—please let's be friends—I'm so sorry—so sorry——'

His eyes ran over her. It was evident that all she had on was that blanket. A strange fury came into his face, and he turned his back on her and marched with a heavy tread to the door, a tread that made Lucy, for some reason she couldn't at first understand, think of Elgar. Why Elgar? part of her asked, puzzled, while the rest of her was blankly watching Wemyss. Of course: the march: *Pomp and Circumstance.*

At the door he turned and said, 'Since you thrust yourself into my room when I have shown you I don't desire your company you force me to leave it.'

Then he added, his voice sounding queer and through his teeth, 'You'd better go and put your clothes on. I assure you I'm proof against sexual allurements.'

Then he went out.

Lucy stood looking at the door. Sexual allurements? What did he mean? Did he think—did he mean——

She flushed suddenly, and gripping her blanket tight about her she too marched to the door, her eyes bright and fixed.

Considering the blanket, she walked upstairs with a good deal of dignity, and passed the bedroom door just as Lizzie, her arms full of a complete set of clothing, came out of it.

'Lumme!' once more exclaimed Lizzie, who seemed marked down for shocks; and dropped a hairbrush and a shoe.

Disregarding her, Lucy proceeded up the next flight with the same dignity, and having reached Vera's room crossed to the fire, where she stood in silence while Lizzie, who had hurried after her and was reproaching her for having gone downstairs like that, dressed her and brushed her hair.

She was quite silent. She didn't move. She was miles away from Lizzie, absorbed in quite a new set of astonished, painful thoughts.

But at the end, when Lizzie asked her if there was anything more she could do, she looked at her a minute and then, having realised her, put out her hand and laid it on her arm.

'Thank you *very* much for everything,' she said earnestly.

'I'm terribly sorry about that window, mum,' said Lizzie, who was sure she had been the cause of trouble. 'I don't know what come over me to forget it.'

Lucy smiled faintly at her. 'Never mind,' she said; and she thought that if it hadn't been for that window she and Everard— well, it was no use thinking like that; perhaps there would have been something else.

Lizzie went. She was a recent acquisition, and was the only one of the servants who hadn't known the late Mrs. Wemyss, but she told herself that anyhow she preferred this one. She went; and Lucy stood where she had left her, staring at the floor, dropping back into her quite new set of astonished, painful thoughts.

Everard,—that was an outrage, that about sexual allurements; just simply an outrage. She flushed at the remembrance of it; her whole body seemed to flush hot. She felt as though never again would she be able to bear him making love to her. He had spoilt that. But that was a dreadful way to feel, that was destructive of the very heart of marriage. No, she mustn't let herself,—she must stamp that feeling out; she must forget what he had said. He couldn't really have meant it. He was still in a temper. She oughtn't to have gone down. But how could she know? All this was new to her, a new side of Everard. Perhaps, she thought, watching the reflection of the flames flickering on the shiny, slippery oak floor, only people with tempers should marry people with tempers. They would understand each other, say the same sorts of things, tossing them backwards and forwards like a fiery, hissing ball, know the exact time it would last, and be saved by their vivid emotions from the deadly hurt, the deadly loneliness of the one who couldn't get into a rage.

Loneliness.

She lifted her head and looked round the room.

No, she wasn't lonely. There was still——

Suddenly she went to the bookshelves, and began pulling out the books quickly, hungrily reading their names, turning over their pages in a kind of starving hurry to get to know, to get to understand, Vera....

XXI

Meanwhile Wemyss had gone into the drawing-room till such time as his wife should choose to allow him to have his own library to himself again.

For a long while he walked up and down it thinking bitter things, for he was very angry. The drawing-room was a big gaunt room, rarely used of recent years. In the early days, when people called on the newly arrived Wemysses, there had been gatherings in it,— retaliatory festivities to the vicar, to the doctor, to the landlord, with a business acquaintance or two of Wemyss's, wife appended, added to fill out. These festivities, however, died of inanition. Something was wanting, something necessary to nourish life in them. He thought of them as he walked about the echoing room from which the last guest had departed years ago. Vera, of course. Her fault that the parties had left off. She had been so slack, so indifferent. You couldn't expect people to come to your house if you took no pains to get them there. Yet what a fine room for entertaining. The grand piano, too. Never used. And Vera who made such a fuss about music, and pretended she knew all about it.

The piano was clothed from head to foot in a heavy red baize cover, even its legs being buttoned round in what looked like Alpine Sport gaiters, and the baize flap that protected the keys had buttons all along it from one end to the other. In order to play, these buttons had first to be undone,—Wemyss wasn't going to have the expensive piano not taken care of. It had been his wedding present to Vera—how he had loved that woman!—and he had had the baize clothes made specially, and had instructed Vera that whenever the piano was not in use it was to have them on, properly fastened.

What trouble he had had with her at first about it. She was always forgetting to button it up again. She would be playing, and get up and go away to lunch, or tea, or out into the garden, and leave it uncovered with the damp and dust getting into it, and not only uncovered but with its lid open. Then, when she found that he went in to see if she had remembered, she did for a time cover it up in the intervals of playing, but never buttoned all its buttons; invariably he found that some had been forgotten. It had cost £150. Women had no sense of property. They were unfit to have the charge of valuables. Besides, they got tired of them. Vera had actually quite soon got tired of the piano. His present. That wasn't very loving of her. And when he said anything about it she wouldn't speak. Sulked. How profoundly he disliked sulking. And she, who had made such a fuss about music when first he met her, gave up playing, and for years no one had touched the piano. Well, at least it was being taken care of.

From habit he stooped and ran his eye up its gaiters.

All buttoned.

Stay—no; one buttonhole gaped.

He stooped closer and put out his hand to button it, and found the button gone. No button. Only an end of thread. How was that?

He straightened himself, and went to the fireplace and rang the bell. Then he waited, looking at his watch. Long ago he had timed the distances between the different rooms and the servants' quarters, allowing for average walking and one minute's margin for getting under way at the start, so that he knew exactly at what moment the parlourmaid ought to appear.

She appeared just as time was up and his finger was moving towards the bell again.

'Look at that piano-leg,' said Wemyss.

The parlourmaid, not knowing which leg, looked at all three so as to be safe.

'What do you see?' he asked.

The parlourmaid was reluctant to say. What she saw was piano-legs, but she felt that wasn't the right answer.

'What do you *not* see?' Wemyss asked, louder.

This was much more difficult, because there were so many things she didn't see; her parents, for instance.

'Are you deaf, woman?' he inquired.

She knew the answer to that, and said it quickly. 'No sir,' she said.

'Look at that piano-leg, I say,' said Wemyss, pointing with his pipe.

It was, so to speak, the off fore-leg at which he pointed, and the parlourmaid, relieved to be given a clue, fixed her eye on it earnestly.

'What do you see?' he asked. 'Or, rather, what do you not see?'

The parlourmaid looked hard at what she saw, leaving what she didn't see to take care of itself. It seemed unreasonable to be asked to look at what she didn't see. But though she looked, she could see nothing to justify speech. Therefore she was silent.

'Don't you see there's a button off?'

The parlourmaid, on looking closer, did see that, and said so.

'Isn't it your business to attend to this room?'

She admitted that it was.

'Buttons don't come off of themselves,' Wemyss informed her.

The parlourmaid, this not being a question, said nothing.

'Do they?' he asked loudly.

'No sir,' said the parlourmaid; though she could have told him many a story of things buttons did do of themselves, coming off in your hand when you hadn't so much as begun to touch them. Cups, too. The way cups would fall apart in one's hand——

She, however, merely said, 'No sir.'

'Only wear and tear makes them come off,' Wemyss announced; and continuing judicially, emphasising his words with a raised forefinger, he said: 'Now attend to me. This piano hasn't been used for years. Do you hear that? Not for years. To my certain knowledge not for years. Therefore the cover cannot have been unbuttoned legitimately, it cannot have been unbuttoned by any one authorised to unbutton it. Therefore——'

He pointed his finger straight at her and paused. 'Do you follow me?' he asked sternly.

The parlourmaid hastily reassembled her wandering thoughts. 'Yes sir,' she said.

'Therefore some one unauthorised has unbuttoned the cover, and some one unauthorised has played on the piano. Do you understand?'

'Yes sir,' said the parlourmaid.

'It is hardly credible,' he went on, 'but nevertheless the conclusion can't be escaped, that some one has actually taken advantage of my absence to play on that piano. Some one in this house has actually dared——'

'There's the tuner,' said the parlourmaid tentatively, not sure if that would be an explanation, for Wemyss's lucid sentences, almost of a legal lucidity, invariably confused her, but giving the suggestion for what it was worth. 'I understood the orders was to let the tuner in once a quarter, sir. Yesterday was his day. He played for a hour. And 'ad the baize and everything off, and the lid leaning against the wall.'

True. True. The tuner. Wemyss had forgotten the tuner. The tuner had standing instructions to come and tune. Well, why couldn't the fool-woman have reminded him sooner? But the tuner having tuned didn't excuse the parlourmaid's not having sewn on the button the tuner had pulled off.

He told her so.

'Yes sir,' she said.

'You will have that button on in five minutes,' he said, pulling out his watch. 'In five minutes exactly from now that button will be on. I shall be staying in this room, so shall see for myself that you carry out my orders.'

'Yes sir,' said the parlourmaid.

He walked to the window and stood staring at the wild afternoon. She remained motionless where she was.

What a birthday he was having. And with what joy he had looked forward to it. It seemed to him very like the old birthdays with Vera, only so much more painful because he had expected so much. Vera had got him used to expecting very little; but it was Lucy, his adored Lucy, who was inflicting this cruel disappointment on him. Lucy! Incredible. And she to come down in that blanket, tempting him, very nearly getting him that way rather than by the only right and decent way of sincere and obvious penitence. Why, even Vera had never done a thing like that, not once in all the years.

'Let's be friends,' says Lucy. Friends! Yes, she did say something about sorry, but what about that blanket? Sorrow with no clothes on couldn't possibly be genuine. It didn't go together with that kind of appeal. It was not the sort of combination one expected in a wife. Why couldn't she come down and apologise properly dressed? God, her little shoulder sticking out—how he had wanted to seize and kiss it ... but then that would have been giving in, that would have meant her triumph. Her triumph, indeed—when it was she, and she only, who had begun the whole thing, running out of the room like that, not obeying him when he called, humiliating him before that damned Lizzie....

He thrust his hands into his pockets and turned away with a jerk from the window.

There, standing motionless, was the parlourmaid.

'What? You still here?' he exclaimed. 'Why the devil don't you go and fetch that button?'

'I understood your orders was none of us is to leave rooms without your permission, sir.'

'You'd better be quick then,' he said, looking at his watch. 'I gave you five minutes, and three of them have gone.'

She disappeared; and in the servants' sitting-room, while she was hastily searching for her thimble and a button that would approximately do, she told the others what they already knew but found satisfaction in repeating often, that if it weren't that Wemyss was most of the week in London, not a day, not a minute, would she stay in the place.

'There's the wages,' the cook reminded her.

Yes; they were good; higher than anywhere she had heard of. But what was the making of the place was the complete freedom from Monday morning every week to Friday tea-time. Almost anything could be put up with from Friday tea-time till Monday morning, seeing that the rest of the week they could do exactly as they chose, with the whole place as good as belonging to them; and she hurried away, and got back to the drawing-room thirty seconds over time.

Wemyss, however, wasn't there with his watch. He was on his way upstairs to the top of the house, telling himself as he went that if Lucy chose to take possession of his library he would go and take possession of her sitting-room. It was only fair. But he knew she wasn't now in the library. He knew she wouldn't stay there all that time. He wanted an excuse to himself for going to where she was. She must beg his pardon properly. He could hold out—oh, he could hold out all right for any length of time, as she'd find out very soon if she tried the sulking game with him—but to-day it was their first day in his home; it was his birthday; and though nothing could be more monstrous than the way she had ruined everything, yet if she begged his pardon properly he would forgive her, he was ready to take her back the moment she showed real penitence. Never was a woman loved as he loved Lucy. If only she would be penitent, if only she would properly and sincerely apologise, then he could kiss her again. He would kiss that little shoulder of hers, make her pull her blouse back so that he could see it as he saw it down in the library, sticking out of that damned blanket—God, how he loved her....

XXII

The first thing he saw when he opened the door of the room at the top of the house was the fire.

A fire. He hadn't ordered a fire. He must look into that. That officious slattern Lizzie——

Then, before he had recovered from this, he had another shock. Lucy was on the hearthrug, her head leaning against the sofa, sound asleep.

So that's what she had been doing,—just going comfortably to sleep, while he——

He shut the door and walked over to the fireplace and stood with his back to it looking down at her. Even his heavy tread didn't wake her. He had shut the door in the way that was natural, and had walked across the room in the way that was natural, for he felt no impulse in the presence of sleep to go softly. Besides, why should she sleep in broad daylight? Wemyss was of opinion that the night was for that. No wonder she couldn't sleep at night if she did it in the daytime. There she was, sleeping soundly, completely indifferent to what he might be doing. Would a really loving woman be able to do that? Would a really devoted wife?

Then he noticed that her face, the side of it he could see, was much swollen, and her nose was red. At least, he thought, she had had some contrition for what she had done before going to sleep. It was to be hoped she would wake up in a proper frame of mind. If so, even now some of the birthday might be saved.

He took out his pipe and filled it slowly, his eyes wandering constantly to the figure on the floor. Fancy that thing having the power to make or mar his happiness. He could pick that much up with one hand. It looked like twelve, with its long-stockinged relaxed legs, and its round, short-haired head, and its swollen face of a child in a scrape. Make or mar. He lit his pipe, repeating the phrase to himself, struck by it, struck by the way it illuminated his position of bondage to love.

All his life, he reflected, he had only asked to be allowed to lavish love, to make a wife happy. Look how he had loved Vera: with the utmost devotion till she had killed it, and nothing but trouble as a reward. Look how he loved that little thing on the floor.

423

Passionately. And in return, the first thing she did on being brought into his home as his bride was to quarrel and ruin his birthday. She knew how keenly he had looked forward to his birthday, she knew how the arrangements of the whole honeymoon, how the very date of the wedding, had hinged on this one day; yet she had deliberately ruined it. And having ruined it, what did she care? Comes up here, if you please, and gets a book and goes comfortably to sleep over it in front of the fire.

His mouth hardened still more. He pulled the arm-chair up and sat down noisily in it, his eyes cold with resentment.

The book Lucy had been reading had dropped out of her hand when she fell asleep, and lay open on the floor at his feet. If she used books in such a way, Wemyss thought, he would be very careful how he let her have the key of his bookcase. This was one of Vera's,—Vera hadn't taken any care of her books either; she was always reading them. He slanted his head sideways to see the title, to see what it was Lucy had considered more worth her attention than her conduct that day towards her husband. *Wuthering Heights.* He hadn't read it, but he fancied he had heard of it as a morbid story. She might have been better employed, on their first day at home, than in shutting herself away from him reading a morbid story.

It was while he was looking at her with these thoughts stonily in his eyes that Lucy, wakened by the smell of his pipe, opened hers. She saw Everard sitting close to her, and had one of those moments of instinctive happiness, of complete restoration to unshadowed contentment, which sometimes follow immediately on waking up, before there has been time to remember. It seems for a wonderful instant as though all in the world were well. Doubts have vanished. Pain is gone. And sometimes the moment continues even beyond remembrance.

It did so now with Lucy. When she opened her eyes and saw Everard, she smiled at him a smile of perfect confidence. She had forgotten everything. She woke up after a deep sleep and saw him, her dear love, sitting beside her. How natural to be happy. Then, the expression on his face bringing back remembrance, it seemed to her in that first serene sanity, that clear-visioned moment of spirit unfretted by body, that they had been extraordinarily silly, taking everything the other one said and did with a tragicness....

Only love filled Lucy after the deep, restoring sleep. 'Dearest one,' she murmured drowsily, smiling at him, without changing her position.

He said nothing to that; and presently, having woken up more, she got on to her knees and pulled herself across to him and curled up at his feet, her head against his knee.

He still said nothing. He waited. He would give her time. Her words had been familiar, but not penitent. They had hardly been the right beginning for an expression of contrition; but he would see what she said next.

What she said next was, 'Haven't we been silly,'—and, more familiarity, she put one arm round his knees and held them close against her face.

'We?' said Wemyss. 'Did you say we?'

'Yes,' said Lucy, her cheek against his knee. 'We've been wasting time.'

Wemyss paused before he made his comment on this. 'Really,' he then said, 'the way you include me shows very little appreciation of your conduct.'

'Well, *I've* been silly then,' she said, lifting her head and smiling up at him.

She simply couldn't go on with indignations. Perhaps they were just ones. It didn't matter if they were. Who wanted to be in the right in a dispute with one's lover? Everybody, oh, but everybody who loved, would passionately want always to have been in the wrong, never, never to have been right. That one's beloved should have been unkind,—who wanted that to be true? Who wouldn't do anything sooner than have not been mistaken about it? Vividly she saw Everard as he was before their marriage; so dear, so boyish, such fun, her playmate. She could say anything to him then. She had been quite fearless. And vividly, too, she saw him as he was when first they met, both crushed by death,—how he had comforted her, how he had been everything that was wonderful and tender. All that had happened since, all that had happened on this particular and most unfortunate day, was only a sort of excess of boyishness: boyishness on its uncontrolled side, a wave, a fit of bad temper provoked by her not having held on to her impulses. That locking her out in the rain,—a schoolboy might have done that to another schoolboy. It meant nothing, except that he was angry. That about sexual allure——oh, well.

425

'I've been very silly,' she said earnestly.

He looked down at her in silence. He wanted more than that. That wasn't nearly enough. He wanted much more of humbleness before he could bring himself to lift her on to his knee, forgiven. And how much he wanted her on his knee.

'Do you realise what you've done?' he asked.

'Yes,' said Lucy. 'And I'm so sorry. Won't we kiss and be friends?'

'Not yet, thank you. I must be sure first that you understand how deliberately wicked you've been.'

'Oh, but I haven't been deliberately wicked!' exclaimed Lucy, opening her eyes wide with astonishment. 'Everard, how can you say such a thing?'

'Ah, I see. You are still quite impenitent, and I am sorry I came up.'

He undid her arm from round his knees, put her on one side, and got out of the chair. Rage swept over him again.

'Here I've been sitting watching you like a dog,' he said, towering over her, 'like a faithful dog while you slept, waiting patiently till you woke up and only wanting to forgive you, and you not only callously sleep after having behaved outrageously and allowed yourself to exhibit temper before the whole house on our very first day together in my home—well knowing, mind you, what day it is—but when I ask you for some sign, some word, some assurance that you are ashamed of yourself and will not repeat your conduct, you merely deny that you have done anything needing forgiveness.'

He knocked the ashes out of his pipe, his face twitching with anger, and wished to God he could knock the opposition out of Lucy as easily.

She, on the floor, sat looking up at him, her mouth open. What could she do with Everard? She didn't know. Love had no effect; saying she was sorry had no effect.

She pushed her hair nervously behind her ears with both hands. 'I'm sick of quarrels,' she said.

'So am I,' said Wemyss, going towards the door thrusting his pipe into his pocket. 'You've only got yourself to thank for them.'

She didn't protest. It seemed useless. She said, 'Forgive me, Everard.'

'Only if you apologise.'

'Yes.'

'Yes what?' He paused for her answer.

'I do apologise.'

'You admit you've been deliberately wicked?'

'Oh yes.'

He continued towards the door.

She scrambled to her feet and ran after him. 'Please don't go,' she begged, catching his arm. 'You know I can't bear it, I can't bear it if we quarrel——'

'Then what do you mean by saying "Oh yes," in that insolent manner?'

'Did it seem insolent? I didn't mean—oh, I'm so tired of this——'

'I daresay. You'll be tireder still before you've done. *I* don't get tired, let me tell you. You can go on as long as you choose,—it won't affect me.'

'Oh do, do let's be friends. I don't want to go on. I don't want anything in the world except to be friends. Please kiss me, Everard, and say you forgive me——'

He at least stood still and looked at her.

'And do believe I'm so, so sorry——'

He relented. He wanted, extraordinarily, to kiss her. 'I'll accept it if you assure me it is so,' he said.

'And do, do let's be happy. It's your birthday——'

'As though I've forgotten that.'

He looked at her upturned face; her arm was round his neck now. 'Lucy, I don't believe you understand my love for you,' he said solemnly.

'No,' said Lucy truthfully, 'I don't think I do.'

'You'll have to learn.'

'Yes,' said Lucy; and sighed faintly.

'You mustn't wound such love.'

'No,' said Lucy. 'Don't let us wound each other ever any more, darling Everard.'

'I'm not talking of each other. I'm talking at this moment of myself in relation to you. One thing at a time, please.'

'Yes,' said Lucy. 'Kiss me, won't you, Everard? Else I shan't know we're really friends.'

He took her head in his hands, and bestowed a solemn kiss of pardon on her brow.

She tried to coax him back to cheerfulness. 'Kiss my eyes too,' she said, smiling at him, 'or they'll feel neglected.'

He kissed her eyes.

'And now my mouth, please, Everard.'

He kissed her mouth, and did at last smile.

'And now won't we go to the fire and be cosy?' she asked, her arm in his.

'By the way, who ordered the fire?' he inquired in his ordinary voice.

'I don't know. It was lit when I came up. Oughtn't it to have been?'

'Not without orders. It must have been that Lizzie. I'll ring and find out——'

'Oh, don't ring!' exclaimed Lucy, catching his hand,—she felt she couldn't bear any more ringing. 'If you do she'll come, and I want us to be alone together.'

'Well, whose fault is it we haven't been alone together all this time?' he asked.

'Ah, but we're friends now—you mustn't go back to that any more,' she said, anxiously smiling and drawing his hand through her arm.

He allowed her to lead him to the arm-chair, and sitting in it did at last feel justified in taking her on his knee.

'How my own Love spoils things,' he said, shaking his head at her with fond solemnity when they were settled in the chair.

And Lucy, very cautious now, only said gently, 'But I never *mean* to.'

XXIII

She sat after that without speaking on his knee, his arms round her, her head on his breast.

She was thinking.

Try as she might to empty herself of everything except acceptance and love, she found that only her body was controllable. That lay quite passive in Wemyss's arms; but her mind refused to lie passive, it would think. Strange how tightly one's body could be held, how close to somebody else's heart, and yet one wasn't anywhere near the holder. They locked you up in prisons that way, holding your body tight and thinking they had got you, and all the while your mind—you—was as free as the wind and the sunlight. She couldn't help it, she struggled hard to feel as she had felt when she woke up and saw him sitting near her; but the way he had refused to be friends, the complete absence of any readiness in him to meet her, not half, nor even a quarter, but a little bit of the way, had for the first time made her consciously afraid of him.

She was afraid of him, and she was afraid of herself in relation to him. He seemed outside anything of which she had experience. He appeared not to be—he anyhow had not been that day—generous. There seemed no way, at any point, by which one could reach him. What was he *really* like? How long was it going to take her really to know him? Years? And she herself,—she now knew, now that she had made their acquaintance, that she couldn't at all bear scenes. Any scenes. Either with herself, or in her presence with other people. She couldn't bear them while they were going on, and she couldn't bear the exhaustion of the long drawn-out making up at the end. And she not only didn't see how they were to be avoided—for no care, no caution would for ever be able to watch what she said, or did, or looked, or, equally important, what she didn't say, or didn't do, or didn't look—but she was afraid, afraid with a most dismal foreboding, that some day after one of them, or in the middle of one of them, her nerve would give out and she would collapse. Collapse deplorably; into just something that howled and whimpered.

This, however, was horrible. She mustn't think like this. Sufficient unto the day, she thought, trying to make herself smile, is the whimpering thereof. Besides, she wouldn't whimper, she wouldn't go to pieces, she would discover a way to manage. Where there was so much love there must be a way to manage.

He had pulled her blouse back, and was kissing her shoulder and asking her whose very own wife she was. But what was the good of love-making if it was immediately preceded or followed or interrupted by anger? She was afraid of him. She wasn't in this kissing at all. Perhaps she had been afraid of him unconsciously for a long while. What was that abjectness on the honeymoon, that anxious desire to please, to avoid offending, but fear? It was love afraid; afraid of getting hurt, of not going to be able to believe whole-heartedly, of not going to be able—this was the worst—to be proud of its beloved. But now, after her experiences to-day, she had a fear of him more separate, more definite, distinct from love. Strange to be afraid of him and love him at the same time. Perhaps if she didn't love him she wouldn't be afraid of him. No, she didn't think she would then, because then nothing that he said would reach her heart. Only she couldn't imagine that. He *was* her heart.

'What are you thinking of?' asked Wemyss, who having finished with her shoulder noticed how quiet she was.

She could tell him truthfully; a moment sooner and she couldn't have. 'I was thinking,' she said, 'that you are my heart.'

'Take care of your heart then, won't you?' said Wemyss.

'We both will,' said Lucy.

'Of course,' said Wemyss. 'That's understood. Why state it?'

She was silent a minute. Then she said, 'Isn't it nearly tea-time?'

'By Jove, yes,' he exclaimed, pulling out his watch. 'Why, long past. I wonder what that fool—get up, little Love—' he brushed her off his lap—'I'll ring and find out what she means by it.'

Lucy was sorry she had said anything about tea. However, he didn't keep his finger on the bell this time, but rang it normally. Then he stood looking at his watch.

She put her arm through his. She longed to say, 'Please don't scold her.'

'Take care,' he said, his eyes on his watch. 'Don't shake me——'

She asked what he was doing.

'Timing her,' he said. 'Sh—sh—don't talk. I can't keep count if you talk.'

She became breathlessly quiet and expectant. She listened anxiously for the sound of footsteps. She did hope Lizzie would come in time. Lizzie was so nice,—it would be dreadful if she got a scolding. Why didn't she come? There—what was that? A door going somewhere. Would she do it? Would she?

Running steps came along the passage outside. Wemyss put his watch away. 'Five seconds to spare,' he said. 'That's the way to teach them to answer bells,' he added with satisfaction.

'Did you ring, sir?' inquired Lizzie, opening the door.

'Why is tea late?'

'It's in the library, sir.'

'Kindly attend to my question. I asked why tea was late.'

'It wasn't late to begin with, sir,' said Lizzie.

'Be so good as to make yourself clear.'

Lizzie, who had felt quite clear, here became befogged. She did her best, however. 'It's got late through waiting to be 'ad, sir,' she said.

'I'm afraid I don't follow you. Do you?' he asked, turning to Lucy.

She started. 'Yes,' she said.

'Really. Then you are cleverer than I am,' said Wemyss.

Lizzie at this—for she didn't want to make any more trouble for the young lady—made a further effort to explain. 'It was punctual in the library, sir, at 'alf-past four if you'd been there to 'ave it. The tea was punctual, sir, but there wasn't no one to 'ave it.'

'And pray by whose orders was it in the library?'

'I couldn't say, sir. Chesterton——'

'Don't put it on to Chesterton.'

'I was thinking,' said Lizzie, who was more stout-hearted than the parlourmaid and didn't take cover quite so frequently in dumbness, 'I was thinking p'raps Chesterton knew. I don't do the tea, sir.'

'Send Chesterton,' said Wemyss.

Lizzie disappeared with the quickness of relief. Lucy, with a nervous little movement, stooped and picked up *Wuthering Heights*, which was still lying face downward on the floor.

'Yes,' said Wemyss. 'I like the way you treat books.'

She put it back on its shelf. 'I went to sleep, and it fell down,' she said. 'Everard,' she went on quickly, 'I must go and get a handkerchief. I'll join you in the library.'

'I'm not going into the library. I'm going to have tea here. Why should I have tea in the library?'

'I only thought as it was there——'

'I suppose I can have tea where I like in my own house?'

'But of course. Well, then, I'll go and get a handkerchief and come back here.'

'You can do that some other time. Don't be so restless.'

'But I—I *want* a handkerchief this minute,' said Lucy.

'Nonsense; here, have mine,' said Wemyss; and anyhow it was too late to escape, for there in the door stood Chesterton.

She was the parlourmaid. Her name has not till now been mentioned. It was Chesterton.

'Why is tea in the library?' Wemyss asked.

'I understood, sir, tea was always to be in the library,' said Chesterton.

'That was while I was by myself. I suppose it wouldn't have occurred to you to inquire whether I still wished it there now that I am not by myself.'

This floored Chesterton. Her ignorance of the right answer was complete. She therefore said nothing, and merely stood.

But he didn't let her off. 'Would it?' he asked suddenly.

'No sir,' she said, dimly feeling that 'Yes sir' would land her in difficulties.

'No. Quite so. It wouldn't. Well, you will now go and fetch that tea and bring it up here. Stop a minute, stop a minute—don't be in such a hurry, please. How long has it been made?'

'Since half-past four, sir.'

'Then you will make fresh tea, and you will make fresh toast, and you will cut fresh bread and butter.'

'Yes sir.'

'And another time you will have the goodness to ascertain my wishes before taking upon yourself to put the tea into any room you choose to think fit.'

'Yes sir.'

She waited.

He waved.

She went.

'That'll teach her,' said Wemyss, looking refreshed by the encounter. 'If she thinks she's going to get out of bringing tea up here by putting it ready somewhere else she'll find she's mistaken. Aren't they a set?*Aren't* they a set, little Love?'

'I—don't know,' said Lucy nervously.

'You don't know!'

'I mean, I don't know them yet. How can I know them when I've only just come?'

'You soon will, then. A lazier set of careless, lying——'

'Do tell me what that picture is, Everard,' she interrupted, quickly crossing the room and standing in front of it. 'I've been wondering and wondering.'

'You can see what it is. It's a picture.'

'Yes. But where's the place?'

'I've no idea. It's one of Vera's. She didn't condescend to explain it.'

'You mean she painted it?'

'I daresay. She was always painting.'

Wemyss, who had been filling his pipe, lit it and stood smoking in front of the fire, occasionally looking at his watch, while Lucy stared at the picture. Lovely, lovely to run through that door out into the open, into the warmth and sunshine, further and further away....

It was the only picture in the room; indeed, the room was oddly bare,—a thin room, with no carpet on its slippery floor, only some infrequent rugs, and no curtains. But there had been curtains, for there were the rods with rings on them, so that somebody must have taken Vera's curtains away. Lucy had been strangely perturbed when she noticed this. It was Vera's room. Her curtains oughtn't to have been touched.

The long wall opposite the fireplace had nothing at all on its sand-coloured surface from the door to the window except a tall narrow looking-glass in a queerly-carved black frame, and the picture. But how that one picture glowed. What glorious weather they were having in it! It wasn't anywhere in England, she was sure. It was a brilliant, sunlit place, with a lot of almond trees in full blossom,—an orchard of them, apparently, standing in grass that was full of little flowers, very gay little flowers, of kinds she didn't know. And through the open door in the wall there was an amazing stretch of hot, vivid country. It stretched on and on till it melted into an ever so far away lovely blue. There was an effect of immense spaciousness, of huge freedom. One could feel oneself running out into it with one's face to the sun, flinging up one's arms in an ecstasy of release, of escape....

'It's somewhere abroad,' she said, after a silence.

'I daresay,' said Wemyss.

'Used you to travel much?' she asked, still examining the picture, fascinated.

'She refused to.'

'She refused to?' echoed Lucy, turning round.

She looked at him wonderingly. That seemed not only unkind of Vera, but extraordinarily—yes, energetic. The exertion required for refusing Everard something he wanted was surely enormous, was surely greater than any but the most robust-minded wife could embark upon. She had had one small experience of what disappointing him meant in that question of Christmas, and she hadn't been living with him then, and she had had all the nights to recover in; yet the effect of that one experience had been to make her give in at once when next he wanted something, and it was because of last Christmas that she was standing married in that room instead of being still, as both she and her Aunt Dot had intended, six months off it.

'Why did she refuse?' she asked, wondering.

Wemyss didn't answer for a moment. Then he said, 'I was going to say you had better ask her, but you can't very well do that, can you.'

Lucy stood looking at him. 'Yes,' she said, 'she does seem extraordinarily near, doesn't she. This room is full——'

'Now Lucy I'll have none of that. Come here.'

He held out his hand. She crossed over obediently and took it.

He pulled her close and ruffled her hair. He was in high spirits again. His encounters with the servants had exhilarated him.

'Who's my duddely-umpty little girl?' he asked. 'Tell me who's my duddely-umpty little girl. Quick. Tell me——' And he caught her round the waist and jumped her up and down.

Chesterton, bringing in the tea, arrived in the middle of a jump.

XXIV

There appeared to be no tea-table. Chesterton, her arms stretched taut holding the heavy tray, looked round. Evidently tea up there wasn't usual.

'Put it in the window,' said Wemyss, jerking his head towards the writing-table.

'Oh——' began Lucy quickly; and stopped.

'What's the matter?' asked Wemyss.

'Won't it—be draughty?'

'Nonsense. Draughty. Do you suppose I'd tolerate windows in my house that let in draughts?'

Chesterton, resting a corner of the tray on the table, was sweeping a clear space for it with her hand. Not that much sweeping was needed, for the table was big and all that was on it was the notepaper which earlier in the afternoon had been scattered on the floor, a rusty pen or two, some pencils whose ends had been gnawed as the pencils of a child at its lessons are gnawed, a neglected-looking inkpot, and a grey book with *Household Accounts* in dark lettering on its cover.

Wemyss watched her while she arranged the tea-things.

'Take care, now—take care,' he said, when a cup rattled in its saucer.

Chesterton, who had been taking care, took more of it; and *le trop* being *l'ennemi du bien* she was so unfortunate as to catch her cuff in the edge of the plate of bread and butter.

The plate tilted up; the bread and butter slid off; and only by a practised quick movement did she stop the plate from following the bread and butter and smashing itself on the floor.

'There now,' said Wemyss. 'See what you've done. Didn't I tell you to be careful? It isn't,' he said, turning to Lucy, 'as if I hadn't *told* her to be careful.'

Chesterton, on her knees, was picking up the bread and butter which lay—a habit she had observed in bread and butter under circumstances of this kind—butter downwards.

'You will fetch a cloth,' said Wemyss.

'Yes sir.'

'And you will cut more bread and butter.'

435

'Yes sir.'

'That makes two plates of bread and butter wasted to-day entirely owing to your carelessness. They shall be stopped out of your—— Lucy, where are you going?'

'To fetch a handkerchief. I must have a handkerchief, Everard. I can't for ever use yours.'

'You'll do nothing of the kind. Lizzie will bring you one. Come back at once. I won't have you running in and out of the room the whole time. I never knew any one so restless. Ring the bell and tell Lizzie to get you one. What is she for, I should like to know?'

He then resumed and concluded his observations to Chesterton. 'They shall be stopped out of your wages. That,' he said, 'will teach you.'

And Chesterton, who was used to this, and had long ago arranged with the cook that such stoppages should be added on to the butcher's book, said, 'Yes sir.'

When she had gone—or rather withdrawn, for a plain word like gone doesn't justly describe the noiseless decorum with which Chesterton managed the doors of her entrances and exits—and when Lizzie, too, had gone after bringing a handkerchief, Lucy supposed they would now have tea; she supposed the moment had at last arrived for her to go and sit in that window.

The table was at right angles to it, so that sitting at it you had nothing between one side of you and the great pane of glass that reached nearly to the floor. You could look sheer down on to the flags below. She thought it horrible, gruesome to have tea there, and the very first day, before she had had a moment's time to get used to things. Such detachment on the part of Everard was either just stark wonderful—she had already found noble explanations for it—or it was so callous that she had no explanation for it at all; none, that is, that she dared think of. Once more she decided that his way was really the best and simplest way to meet the situation. You took the bull by the horns. You seized the nettle. You cleared the air. And though her images, she felt, were not what they might be, neither was anything else that day what it might be. Everything appeared to reflect the confusion produced by Wemyss's excessive lucidity of speech.

'Shall I pour out the tea?' she asked presently, preparing, then, to take the bull by the horns; for he remained standing in front of the fire smoking in silence. 'Just think,' she went on, making an effort to be gay, 'this is the first time I shall pour out tea in my——'

She was going to say 'My own home,' but the words wouldn't come off her tongue. Wemyss had repeatedly during the day spoken of his home, but not once had he said 'our' or 'your'; and if ever a house didn't feel as if it in the very least belonged, too, to her, it was this one.

'Not yet,' he said briefly.

She wondered. 'Not yet?' she repeated.

'I'm waiting for the bread and butter.'

'But won't the tea get cold?'

'No doubt. And it'll be entirely that fool's fault.'

'But——' began Lucy, after a silence.

'Buts again?'

'I was only thinking that if we had it now it wouldn't be cold.'

'She must be taught her lesson.'

Again she wondered. 'Won't it rather be a lesson to us?' she asked.

'For God's sake, Lucy, don't argue. Things have to be done properly in my house. You've had no experience of a properly managed household. All that set you were brought up in—why, one only had to look at them to see what a hugger-mugger way they probably lived. It's entirely the careless fool's own fault that the tea will be cold. *I* didn't ask her to throw the bread and butter on the floor, did I?'

And as she said nothing, he asked again. 'Did I?' he asked.

'No,' said Lucy.

'Well then,' said Wemyss.

They waited in silence.

Chesterton arrived. She put the fresh bread and butter on the table, and then wiped the floor with a cloth she had brought.

Wemyss watched her closely. When she had done—and Chesterton being good at her work, scrutinise as he might he could see no sign on the floor of overlooked butter—he said, 'You will now take the teapot down and bring some hot tea.'

'Yes sir,' said Chesterton, removing the teapot.

A line of a hymn her nurse used to sing came into Lucy's head when she saw the teapot going. It was:

What various hindrances we meet—

and she thought the next line, which she didn't remember, must have been:

Before at tea ourselves we seat.

But though one portion of her mind was repeating this with nervous levity, the other was full of concern for the number of journeys up and down all those stairs the parlourmaid was being obliged to make. It was—well, thoughtless of Everard to make her go up and down so often. Probably he didn't realise—of course he didn't—how very many stairs there were. When and how could she talk to him about things like this? When would he be in such a mood that she would be able to do so without making them worse? And how, in what words sufficiently tactful, sufficiently gentle, would she be able to avoid his being offended? She must manage somehow. But tact—management—prudence—all these she had not yet in her life needed. Had she the smallest natural gift for them? Besides, each of them applied to love seemed to her an insult. She had supposed that love, real love, needed none of these protections. She had thought it was a simple, sturdy growth that could stand anything.... Why, here was the parlourmaid already, teapot and all. How very quick she had been!

Chesterton, however, hadn't so much been quick as tactful, managing, and prudent. She had been practising these qualities on the other side of the door, whither she had taken the teapot and quietly waited with it a few minutes, and whence she now brought it back. She placed it on the table with admirable composure; and when Wemyss, on her politely asking whether there were anything else he required, said, 'Yes. You will now take away that toast and bring fresh,' she took the toast also only as far as the other side of the door, and waited with it there a little.

Lucy now hoped they would have tea. 'Shall I pour it out?' she asked after a moment a little anxiously, for he still didn't move and she began to be afraid the toast might be going to be the next hindrance; in which case they would go round and round for the rest of the day, never catching up the tea at all.

But he did go over and sit down at the table, followed by her who hardly now noticed its position, so much surprised and absorbed was she by his methods of housekeeping.

'Isn't it monstrous,' he said, sitting down heavily, 'how we've been kept waiting for such a simple thing as tea. I tell you they're the most slovenly——'

There was Chesterton again, bearing the toast-rack balanced on the tip of a respectful ringer.

This time even Lucy realised that it must be the same toast, and her hand, lifted in the act of pouring out tea, trembled, for she feared the explosion that was bound to come.

How extraordinary. There was no explosion. Everard hadn't—it seemed incredible—noticed. His attention was so much fixed on what she was doing with his cup, he was watching her so carefully lest she should fill it a hair's-breadth fuller than he liked, that all he said to Chesterton as she put the toast on the table was, 'Let this be a lesson to you.' But there was no gusto in it; it was quite mechanical.

'Yes sir,' said Chesterton.

She waited.

He waved.

She went.

The door hadn't been shut an instant before Wemyss exclaimed, 'Why, if that slovenly hussy hasn't forgotten——' And too much incensed to continue he stared at the tea-tray.

'What? What?' asked Lucy startled, also staring at the tea-tray.

'Why, the sugar.'

'Oh, I'll call her back—she's only just gone——'

'Sit down, Lucy.'

'But she's just outside——'

'Sit *down*, I tell you.'

Lucy sat.

Then she remembered that neither she nor Everard ever had sugar in their tea, so naturally there was no point in calling Chesterton back.

'Oh, of course,' she said, smiling nervously, for what with one thing and another she was feeling shattered, 'how stupid of me. We don't want sugar.'

Wemyss said nothing. He was studying his watch, timing Chesterton. Then when the number of seconds needed to reach the kitchen had run out, he got up and rang the bell.

In due course Lizzie appeared. It seemed that the rule was that this particular bell should be answered by Lizzie.

'Chesterton,' said Wemyss.

In due course Chesterton appeared. She was less composed than when she brought back the teapot, than when she brought back the toast. She tried to hide it, but she was out of breath.

'Yes sir?' she said.

Wemyss took no notice, and went on drinking his tea.

439

Chesterton stood.

After a period of silence Lucy thought that perhaps it was expected of her as mistress of the house to tell her about the sugar; but then as they neither of them wanted any....

After a further period of silence, during which she anxiously debated whether it was this that they were all waiting for, she thought that perhaps Everard hadn't heard the parlourmaid come in; so she said—she was ashamed to hear how timidly it came out— 'Chesterton is here, Everard.'

He took no notice, and went on eating bread and butter.

After a further period of anxious inward debate she concluded that it must after all be expected of her, as mistress of the house, to talk of the sugar; and the sugar was to be talked of not because they needed it but on principle. But what a roundabout way; how fatiguing and difficult. Why didn't Everard say what he wanted, instead of leaving her to guess?

'I think——' she stammered, flushing, for she was now very timid indeed, 'you've forgotten the sugar, Chesterton.'

'Will you not interfere!' exclaimed Wemyss very loud, putting down his cup with a bang.

The flush on Lucy's face vanished as if it had been knocked out. She sat quite still. If she moved, or looked anywhere but at her plate, she knew she would begin to cry. The scenes she had dreaded had not included any with herself in the presence of servants. It hadn't entered her head that these, too, were possible. She must hold on to herself; not move; not look. She sat absorbed in that one necessity, fiercely concentrated. Chesterton must have gone away and come back again, for presently she was aware that sugar was being put on the tea-tray; and then she was aware that Everard was holding out his cup.

'Give me some more tea, please,' he said, 'and for God's sake don't sulk. If the servants forget their duties it's neither your nor my business to tell them what they've forgotten,—they've just got to look and see, and if they don't see they've just got to stand there looking till they do. It's the only way to teach them. But for you to get sulking on the top of it——'

She lifted the teapot with both hands, because one hand by itself too obviously shook. She succeeded in pouring out the tea without spilling it, and in stopping almost at the very moment when he said, 'Take care, take care—you're filling it too full.' She even succeeded after a minute or two in saying, holding carefully on to her voice to keep it steady, 'I'm not—sulking. I've—got a headache.'

And she thought desperately, 'The only thing to be done with marriage is to let it wash over one.'

XXV

For the rest of that day she let it wash; unresistingly. She couldn't think any more. She couldn't feel any more,—not that day. She really had a headache; and when the dusk came, and Wemyss turned on the lights, it was evident even to him that she had, for there was no colour at all in her face and her eyes were puffed and leaden.

He had one of his sudden changes. 'Come here,' he said, reaching out and drawing her on to his knee; and he held her face against his breast, and felt full of maternal instincts, and crooned over her. 'Was it a poor little baby,' he crooned. 'Did it have a headache then——' And he put his great cool hand on her hot forehead and kept it there.

Lucy gave up trying to understand anything at all any more. These swift changes,—she couldn't keep up with them; she was tired, tired....

They sat like that in the chair before the fire, Wemyss holding his hand on her forehead and feeling full of maternal instincts, and she an unresisting blank, till he suddenly remembered he hadn't shown her the drawing-room yet. The afternoon had not proceeded on the lines laid down for it in his plans, but if they were quick there was still time for the drawing-room before dinner.

Accordingly she was abruptly lifted off his knee. 'Come along, little Love,' he said briskly. 'Come along. Wake up. I want to show you something.'

And the next thing she knew was that she was going downstairs, and presently she found herself standing in a big cold room, blinking in the bright lights he had switched on at the door.

'This,' he said, holding her by the arm, 'is the drawing-room. Isn't it a fine room.' And he explained the piano, and told her how he had found a button off, and he pointed out the roll of rugs in a distant corner which, unrolled, decorated the parquet floor, and he drew her attention to the curtains,—he had no objections to curtains in a drawing-room, he said, because a drawing-room was anyhow a room of concessions; and he asked her at the end, as he had asked her at the beginning, if she didn't think it a fine room.

Lucy said it was a very fine room.

'You'll remember to put the cover on properly when you've finished playing the piano, won't you,' he said.

'Yes I will,' said Lucy. 'Only I don't play,' she added, remembering she didn't.

'That's all right then,' he said, relieved.

They were still standing admiring the proportions of the room, its marble fireplace and the brilliancy of its lighting—'The test of good lighting,' said Wemyss, 'is that there shouldn't be a corner of a room in which a man of eighty can't read his newspaper'—when the gong began.

'Good Lord,' he said, looking at his watch, 'it'll be dinner in ten minutes. Why, we've had nothing at all of the afternoon, and I'd planned to show you so many things. Ah,' he said, turning and shaking his head at her, his voice changing to sorrow, 'whose fault has that been?'

'Mine,' said Lucy.

He put his hand under her chin and lifted her face, gazing at it and shaking his head slowly. The light, streaming into her swollen eyes, hurt them and made her blink.

'Ah, my Lucy,' he said fondly, 'little waster of happiness—isn't it better simply to love your Everard than make him unhappy?'

'Much better,' said Lucy, blinking.

There was no dressing for dinner at The Willows, for that, explained Wemyss, was the great joy of home, that you needn't ever do anything you don't want to in it, and therefore, he said, ten minutes' warning was ample for just washing one's hands. They washed their hands together in the big bedroom, because Wemyss disapproved of dressing-rooms at home even more strongly than on honeymoons in hotels. 'Nobody's going to separate me from my own woman,' he said, drying his hands and eyeing her with proud possessiveness while she dried hers; their basins stood side by side on the brown mottled marble of the washstand. 'Are they,' he said, as she dried in silence.

'No,' said Lucy.

'How's the head?' he said.

'Better,' she said.

'Who's got a forgiving husband?' he said.

'I have,' she said.

'Smile at me,' he said.

She smiled at him.

At dinner it was Vera who smiled, her changeless little strangled smile, with her eyes on Lucy. Lucy's seat had its back to Vera, but

443

she knew she had only to turn her head to see her eyes fixed on her, smiling. No one else smiled; only Vera.

Lucy bent her head over her plate, trying to escape the unshaded light that beat down on her eyes, sore with crying, and hurt. In front of her was the bowl of kingcups, the birthday flowers. Just behind Wemyss stood Chesterton, in an attitude of strained attention. Dimly through Lucy's head floated thoughts: Seeing that Everard invariably spent his birthdays at The Willows, on that day last year at that hour Vera was sitting where she, Lucy, now was, with the kingcups glistening in front of her, and Everard tucking his table napkin into his waistcoat, and Chesterton waiting till he was quite ready to take the cover off the soup; just as Lucy was seeing these things this year Vera saw them last year; Vera still had three months of life ahead of her then, three more months of dinners, and Chesterton, and Everard tucking in his napkin. How queer. What a dream it all was. On that last of his birthdays at which Vera would ever be present, did any thought of his next birthday cross her mind? How strange it would have seemed to her if she could have seen ahead, and seen her, Lucy, sitting in her chair. The same chair; everything just the same; except the wife. 'Souvent femme varie,' floated vaguely across her tired brain. She ate her soup sitting all crooked with fatigue ... life was exactly like a dream....

Wemyss, absorbed in the scrutiny of his food and the behaviour of Chesterton, had no time to notice anything Lucy might be doing. It was the rule that Chesterton, at meals, should not for an instant leave the room. The furthest she was allowed was a door in the dark corner opposite the door into the hall, through which at intervals Lizzie's arm thrust dishes. It was the rule that Lizzie shouldn't come into the room, but, stationary on the other side of this door, her function was to thrust dishes through it; and to her from the kitchen, pattering ceaselessly to and fro, came the tweeny bringing the dishes. This had all been thought out and arranged very carefully years ago by Wemyss, and ought to have worked without a hitch; but sometimes there were hitches, and Lizzie's arm was a minute late thrusting in a dish. When this happened Chesterton, kept waiting and conscious of Wemyss enormously waiting at the end of the table, would put her head round the door and hiss at Lizzie, who then hurried to the kitchen and hissed at the tweeny, who for her part didn't dare hiss at the cook.

To-night, however, nothing happened that was not perfect. From the way Chesterton had behaved about the tea, and the way Lizzie had behaved about the window, Wemyss could see that during his four weeks' absence his household had been getting out of hand, and he was therefore more watchful than ever, determined to pass nothing over. On this occasion he watched in vain. Things went smoothly from start to finish. The tweeny ran, Lizzie thrust, Chesterton deposited, dead on time. Every dish was hot and punctual, or cold and punctual, according to what was expected of it; and Wemyss going out of the dining-room at the end, holding Lucy by the arm, couldn't but feel he had dined very well. Perhaps, though, his father's photograph hadn't been dusted,—it would be just like them to have disregarded his instructions. He went back to look, and Lucy, since he was holding her by the arm, went too. No, they had even done that; and there was nothing further to be said except, with great sternness to Chesterton, eyeing her threateningly, 'Coffee at once.'

The evening was spent in the library reading Wemyss's school reports, and looking at photographs of him in his various stages,— naked and crowing; with ringlets, in a frock; in knickerbockers, holding a hoop; a stout schoolboy; a tall and slender youth; thickening; still thickening; thick,—and they went to bed at ten o'clock.

Somewhere round midnight Lucy discovered that the distances of the treble bed softened sound; either that, or she was too tired to hear anything, for she dropped out of consciousness with the heaviness of a released stone.

Next day it was finer. There were gleams of sun; and though the wind still blew, the rain held off except for occasional spatterings. They got up very late—breakfast on Sundays at The Willows was not till eleven—and went and inspected the chickens. By the time they had done that, and walked round the garden, and stood on the edge of the river throwing sticks into it and watching the pace at which they were whirled away on its muddy and disturbed surface, it was luncheon time. After luncheon they walked along the towpath, one behind the other because it was narrow and the grass at the sides was wet. Wemyss walked slowly, and the wind was cold. Lucy kept close to his heels, seeking shelter under, as it were, his lee. Talk wasn't possible because of the narrow path and the blustering wind, but every now and then Wemyss looked down over his shoulder at her. 'Still there?' he asked; and Lucy said she was.

They had tea punctually at half-past four up in Vera's sitting-room, but without, this time, a fire—Wemyss had rectified Lizzie's tendency to be officious—and after tea he took her out again to show her how his electricity was made, while the gardener who saw to the machinery, and the boy who saw to the gardener, stood by in attendance.

There was a cold sunset,—a narrow strip of gold below heavy clouds, like a sullen, half-open eye. The prudent cows dotted the fields motionlessly, lying on their dry bite of grass. The wind blew straight across from the sunset through Lucy's coat, wrap herself in it as tightly as she might, while they loitered among outhouses and examined the durability of the railings. Her headache, in spite of her good night, hadn't gone, and by dinner time her throat felt sore. She said nothing to Wemyss, because she was sure she would be well in the morning. Her colds never lasted. Besides she knew, for he had often told her, how much he was bored by the sick.

At dinner her cheeks were very red and her eyes very bright.

'Who's my pretty little girl,' said Wemyss, struck by her.

Indeed he was altogether pleased with her. She had been his own Lucy throughout the day, so gentle and sweet, and hadn't once said But, or tried to go out of rooms. Unquestioningly acquiescent she had been; and now so pretty, with the light full on her, showing up her lovely colouring.

'Who's my pretty little girl,' he said again, laying his hand on hers, while Chesterton looked down her nose.

Then he noticed she had a knitted scarf round her shoulders, and he said, 'Whatever have you got that thing on in here for?'

'I'm cold,' said Lucy.

'Cold! Nonsense. You're as warm as a toast. Feel my hand compared to yours.'

Then she did tell him she thought she had caught cold, and he said, withdrawing his hand and his face falling, 'Well, if you have it's only what you deserve when you recollect what you did yesterday.'

'I suppose it is,' agreed Lucy; and assured him her colds were all over in twenty-four hours.

Afterwards in the library when they were alone, she asked if she hadn't better sleep by herself in case he caught her cold, but Wemyss wouldn't hear of such a thing. Not only, he said, he never

446

caught colds and didn't believe any one else who was sensible ever did, but it would take more than a cold to separate him from his wife. Besides, though of course she richly deserved a cold after yesterday—'Who's a shameless little baggage,' he said, pinching her ear, 'coming down with only a blanket on——' somehow, though he had been so angry at the time, the recollection of that pleased him— he could see no signs of her having got one. She didn't sneeze, she didn't blow her nose——

Lucy agreed, and said she didn't suppose it was anything really, and she was sure she would be all right in the morning.

'Yes—and you know we catch the early train up,' said Wemyss. 'Leave here at nine sharp, mind.'

'Yes,' said Lucy. And presently, for she was feeling very uncomfortable and hot and cold in turns, and had a great longing to creep away and be alone for a little while, she said that perhaps, although she knew it was very early, she had better go to bed.

'All right,' said Wemyss, getting up briskly. 'I'll come too.'

XXVI

He found her, however, very trying that night, the way she would keep on turning round, and it reached such a pitch of discomfort to sleep with her, or rather endeavour to sleep with her, for as the night went on she paid less and less attention to his requests that she should keep still, that at about two o'clock, staggering with sleepiness, he got up and went into a spare room, trailing the quilt after him and carrying his pillows, and finished the night in peace.

When he woke at seven he couldn't make out at first where he was, nor why, on stretching out his arm, he found no wife to be gathered in. Then he remembered, and he felt most injured that he should have been turned out of his own bed. If Lucy imagined she was going to be allowed to develop the same restlessness at night that was characteristic of her by day, she was mistaken; and he got up to go and tell her so.

He found her asleep in a very untidy position, the clothes all dragged over to her side of the bed and pulled up round her. He pulled them back again, and she woke up, and he got into bed and said, 'Come here,' stretching out his arm, and she didn't come.

Then he looked at her more closely, and she, looking at him with heavy eyes, said something husky. It was evident she had a very tiresome cold.

'What an untruth you told me,' he exclaimed, 'about not having a cold in the morning!'

She again said something husky. It was evident she had a very tiresome sore throat.

'It's getting on for half-past seven,' said Wemyss. 'We've got to leave the house at nine sharp, mind.'

Was it possible that she wouldn't leave the house at nine sharp? The thought that she wouldn't was too exasperating to consider. He go up to London alone? On this the first occasion of going up after his marriage? He be alone in Lancaster Gate, just as if he hadn't a wife at all? What was the good of a wife if she didn't go up to London with one? And all this to come upon him because of her conduct on his birthday.

'Well,' he said, sitting up in bed and looking down at her, 'I hope you're pleased with the result of your behaviour.'

448

But it was no use saying things to somebody who merely made husky noises.

He got out of bed and jerked up the blinds. 'Such a beautiful day, too,' he said indignantly.

When at a quarter to nine the station cab arrived, he went up to the bedroom hoping that he would find her after all dressed and sensible and ready to go, but there she was just as he had left her when he went to have his breakfast, dozing and inert in the tumbled bed.

'You'd better follow me by the afternoon train,' he said, after staring down at her in silence. 'I'll tell the cab. But in any case,' he said, as she didn't answer, 'in *any* case, Lucy, I expect you to-morrow.'

She opened her eyes and looked at him languidly.

'Do you hear?' he said.

She made a husky noise.

'Good-bye,' he said shortly, stooping and giving the top of her head a brief, disgusted kiss. The way the consequences of folly fell always on somebody else and punished him.... Wemyss could hardly give his *Times* the proper attention in the train for thinking of it.

That day Miss Entwhistle, aware of the return from the honeymoon on the Friday, and of the week-end to be spent at The Willows, and of the coming up to Lancaster Gate early on the Monday morning for the inside of the week, waited till twelve o'clock, so as to allow plenty of time for Wemyss no longer to be in the house, and then telephoned. Lucy and she were to lunch together. Lucy had written to say so, and Miss Entwhistle wanted to know if she wouldn't soon be round. She longed extraordinarily to fold that darling little child in her arms again. It seemed an eternity since she saw her radiantly disappearing in the taxi; and the letters she had hoped to get during the honeymoon hadn't been letters at all, but picture postcards.

A man's voice answered her,—not Wemyss's. It was, she recognised, the voice of the pale servant, who with his wife attended to the Lancaster Gate house. They inhabited the basement, and emerged from it up into the light only if they were obliged. Bells obliged them to emerge, and Wemyss's bath and breakfast, and after his departure to his office the making of his bed; but then the shades gathered round them again till next morning, because for a long while now once he had left the house he hadn't come back till after they were in bed. His re-marriage was going to disturb them, they were afraid, and the pale wife had forebodings about meals to be cooked; but at the worst the disturbance would only be for the three inside days of the week, and anything could be borne when one had from Friday to Monday to oneself; and as the morning went on, and no one arrived from Strorley, they began to take heart, and had almost quite taken it when the telephone bell rang.

It didn't do it very often, for Wemyss had his other addresses, at the office, at the club, so that Twite, wanting in practice, was not very good at dealing with it. Also the shrill bell vibrating through the empty house, so insistent, so living, never failed to agitate both Twites. It seemed to them uncanny; and Mrs. Twite, watching Twite being drawn up by it out of his shadows, like some quiet fish sucked irresistibly up to gasp on the surface, was each time thankful that she hadn't been born a man.

She always went and listened at the bottom of the kitchen stairs, not knowing what mightn't happen to Twite up there alone with that voice, and on this occasion she heard the following:

'No, ma'am, not yet, ma'am.'

'I couldn't say, ma'am.'

'No, no news, ma'am.'

'Oh yes, ma'am, on Friday night.'

'Yes, ma'am, first thing Saturday.'

'Yes, it is, ma'am—very strange, ma'am.'

And then there was silence. He was writing, she knew, on the pad provided by Wemyss for the purpose.

This was the most trying part of Twite's duties. Any message had to be written down and left on the hall table, complete with the time of its delivery, for Wemyss to see when he came in at night. Twite was not a facile writer. Words confused him. He was never sure how they were spelt. Also he found it very difficult to remember what had been said, for there was a hurry and an urgency about a voice on the telephone that excited him and prevented his giving the message his undivided attention. Besides, when was a message not a message? Wemyss's orders were to write down messages. Suppose they weren't messages, must he still write? Was this, for instance, a message?

He thought he had best be on the safe side, and laboriously wrote it down.

Miss Henwissel rang up sir to know if you was come and if so when you was coming and what orders we ad and said it was very strange 12.15.

He had only just put this on the table and was about to descend to his quiet shades when off the thing started again.

This time it was Wemyss.

'Back to-night late as usual,' he said.

'Yes sir,' said Twite. 'There's just been a——'

But he addressed emptiness.

Meanwhile Miss Entwhistle, after a period of reflection, was ringing up Strorley 19. The voice of Chesterton, composed and efficient, replied; and the effect of her replies was to make Miss Entwhistle countermand lunch and pack a small bag and go to Paddington.

Trains to Strorley at that hour were infrequent and slow, and it wasn't till nearly five that she drove down the oozy lane in the station cab and, turning in at the white gate, arrived at The Willows. That sooner or later she would have to arrive at The Willows now that she was related to it by marriage was certain, and she had quite made up her mind, during her four weeks' peace since the wedding, that she was going to dismiss all foolish prejudices against the place from her mind and arrive at it, when she did arrive, with a stout heart and an unclouded countenance. After all, there was much in that *mot* of her nephew's: 'Somebody has died everywhere.' Yet, as the cab heaved her nearer to the place along the oozy lane, she did wish that it wasn't in just this house that Lucy lay in bed. Also she had misgivings at being there uninvited. In a case of serious illness naturally such misgivings wouldn't exist; but the maid's voice on the telephone had only said Mrs. Wemyss had a cold and was staying in bed, and Mr. Wemyss had gone up to London by the usual train. It couldn't be much that was wrong, or he wouldn't have gone. Hadn't she, she thought uneasily as she found herself uninvited within Wemyss's gates, perhaps been a little impulsive? Yet the idea of that child alone in the sinister house——

She peered out of the cab window. Not at all sinister, she said, correcting herself severely; all most neat. Perfect order. Shrubs as they should be. Strong railings. Nice cows.

The cab stopped. Chesterton came down the steps and opened its door. Nice parlourmaid. Most normal.

'How is Mrs. Wemyss?' asked Miss Entwhistle.

'About the same I believe, ma'am,' said Chesterton; and inquired if she should pay the man.

Miss Entwhistle paid the man, and then proceeded up the steps followed by Chesterton carrying her bag. Fine steps. Handsome house.

'Does she know I'm coming?'

'I believe the housemaid did mention it, ma'am.'

Nice roomy hall. With a fire it might be quite warm. Fine windows. Good staircase.

'Do you wish for tea, ma'am?'

'No thank you. I should like to go up at once, if I may.'

'If you please, ma'am.'

At the turn of the stairs, where the gong was, Miss Entwhistle stood aside and let Chesterton precede her. 'Perhaps you had better go and tell Mrs. Wemyss I am here,' she said.

'If you please, ma'am.'

Miss Entwhistle waited, gazing at the gong with the same benevolence she had brought to bear on everything else. Fine gong. She also gazed at the antlers on the wall, for the wall continued to bristle with antlers right up to the top of the house. Magnificent collection.

'If you please, ma'am,' said Chesterton, reappearing, tiptoeing gingerly to the head of the stairs.

Miss Entwhistle went up. Chesterton ushered her into the bedroom, closing the door softly behind her.

Miss Entwhistle knew Lucy was small, but not how small till she saw her in the treble bed. There really did appear to be nothing of her except a little round head. 'Why, but you've shrunk!' was her first exclamation.

Lucy, who was tucked up to her chin by Lizzie, besides having a wet bandage encased in flannel round her throat, could only move her eyes and smile. She was on the side of the bed farthest from the door, and Miss Entwhistle had to walk round it to reach her. She was still hoarse, but not as voiceless as when Wemyss left in the morning, for Lizzie had been diligently plying her with things like hot honey, and her face, as her eyes followed Miss Entwhistle's approach, was one immense smile. It really seemed too wonderful to be with Aunt Dot again; and there was a peace about being ill, a relaxation from strain, that had made her quiet day, alone in bed, seem sheer bliss. It was so plain that she couldn't move, that she

452

couldn't do anything, couldn't get up and go in trains, that her conscience was at rest in regard to Everard; and she lay in the blessed silence after he left, not minding how much her limbs ached because of the delicious tranquillity of her mind. The window was open, and in the garden the birds were busy. The wind had dropped. Except for the birds there was no sound. Divine quiet. Divine peace. The luxury of it after the week-end, after the birthday, after the honeymoon, was extraordinary. Just to be in bed by oneself seemed an amazingly felicitous condition.

'Lovely of you to come,' she said hoarsely, smiling broadly and looking so unmistakably contented that Miss Entwhistle, as she bent over her and kissed her hot forehead, thought, 'It's a success. He's making her happy.'

'You darling little thing,' she said, smoothing back her hair. 'Fancy seeing you again like this!'

'Yes,' said Lucy, heavy-eyed and smiling. 'Lovely,' she whispered, 'to see you. Tea, Aunt Dot?'

It was evidently difficult for her to speak, and her forehead was extremely hot.

'No, I don't want tea.'

'You'll stay?'

'Yes,' said Miss Entwhistle, sitting down by the pillow and continuing to smooth back her hair. 'Of course I'll stay. How did you manage to catch such a cold, I wonder?'

She was left to wonder, undisturbed by any explanations of Lucy's. Indeed it was as much as Lucy could manage to bring out the most necessary words. She lay contentedly with her eyes shut, having her hair stroked back, and said as little as possible.

'Everard—' said Miss Entwhistle, stroking gently, 'is he coming back to-night?'

'No,' whispered Lucy contentedly.

Aunt Dot stroked in silence.

'Has your temperature been taken?' she asked presently.

'No,' whispered Lucy contentedly.

'Oughtn't you—' after another pause 'to see a doctor?'

'No,' whispered Lucy contentedly. Delicious, simply delicious, to lie like that having one's hair stroked back by Aunt Dot, the dear, the kind, the comprehensible.

'So sweet of you to come,' she whispered again.

Well, thought Miss Entwhistle as she sat there softly stroking and watching Lucy's face of complete content while she dozed off even after she was asleep the corners of her mouth still were tucked up in a smile—it was plain that Everard was making the child happy. In that case he certainly must be all that Lucy had assured her he was, and she, Miss Entwhistle, would no doubt very quickly now get fond of him. Of course she would. No doubt whatever. And what a comfort, what a relief, to find the child happy. Backgrounds didn't matter where there was happiness. Houses, indeed. What did it matter if they weren't the sort of houses you would, left to yourself, choose so long as in them dwelt happiness? What did it matter what their past had been so long as their present was illuminated by contentment? And as for furniture, why, that only became of interest, of importance, when life had nothing else in it. Loveless lives, empty lives, filled themselves in their despair with beautiful furniture. If you were really happy you had antlers.

In this spirit, while she stroked and Lucy slept, Miss Entwhistle's eye, full of benevolence, wandered round the room. The objects in it, after her own small bedroom in Eaton Terrace and its necessarily small furniture, all seemed to her gigantic. Especially the bed. She had never seen a bed like it before, though she had heard of such beds in history. Didn't Og the King of Bashan have one? But what an excellent plan, for then you could get away from each other. Most sensible. Most wholesome. And a certain bleakness about the room would soon go when Lucy's little things got more strewn about,—her books, and photographs, and pretty dressing-table silver.

Miss Entwhistle's eye arrived at and dwelt on the dressing-table. On it were two oval wooden-backed brushes without handles. Hairbrushes. Men's. Also shaving things. And, hanging over one side of the looking-glass, were three neckties.

She quickly recovered. Most friendly. Most companionable. But a feeling of not being in Lucy's room at all took possession of her, and she fidgeted a little. With no business to be there whatever, she was in a strange man's bedroom. She averted her eyes from Wemyss's toilet arrangements, they were the last things she wanted to see; and, in averting them, they fell on the washstand with its two basins and on an enormous red-brown indiarubber sponge. No such sponge was ever Lucy's. The conclusion was forced upon her that Lucy and Everard washed side by side.

From this, too, she presently recovered. After all, marriage was marriage, and you did things in marriage that you would never dream of doing single. She averted her eyes from the washstand. The last thing she wanted to do was to become familiar with Wemyss's sponge.

Her eyes, growing more and more determined in their benevolence, gazed out of the window. How the days were lengthening. And really a beautiful look-out, with the late afternoon light reflected on the hills across the river. Birds, too, twittering in the garden,—everything most pleasant and complete. And such a nice big window. Lots of air and light. It reached nearly to the floor. Two housemaids at least, and strong ones, would be needed to open or shut it,—ah no, there were cords. A thought struck her: This couldn't be the room, that couldn't be the window, where——

She averted her eyes from the window, and fixed them on what seemed to be the only satisfactory resting-place for them, the contented face on the pillow. Dear little loved face. And the dear, pretty hair,—how pretty young hair was, so soft and thick. No, of course it wasn't the window; that tragic room was probably not used at all now. How in the world had the child got such a cold. She could hear by her breathing that her chest was stuffed up, but evidently it wasn't worrying her, or she wouldn't in her sleep look so much pleased. Yes; that room was either shut up now and never used, or—she couldn't help being struck by yet another thought—it was a spare room. If so, Miss Entwhistle said to herself, it would no doubt be her fate to sleep in it. Dear me, she thought, taken aback.

But from this also she presently recovered; and remembering her determination to eject all prejudices merely remarked to herself, 'Well, well.' And, after a pause, was able to add benevolently, 'A house of varied interest.'

455

XXVII

Later on in the dining-room, when she was reluctantly eating the meal prepared for her—Lucy still slept, or she would have asked to be allowed to have a biscuit by her bedside—Miss Entwhistle said to Chesterton, who attended her, Would she let her know when Mr. Wemyss telephoned, as she wished to speak to him.

She was feeling more and more uneasy as time passed as to what Everard would think of her uninvited presence in his house. It was natural; but would he think so? What wasn't natural was for her to feel uneasy, seeing that the house was also Lucy's, and that the child's face had hardly had room enough on it for the width of her smile of welcome. There, however, it was,—Miss Entwhistle felt like an interloper. It was best to face things. She not only felt like an interloper but, in Everard's eyes, she was an interloper. This was the situation: His wife had a cold—a bad cold, but not anything serious; nobody had sent for his wife's aunt; nobody had asked her to come; and here she was. If that, in Everard's eyes, wasn't being an interloper Miss Entwhistle was sure he wouldn't know one if he saw one.

In her life she had read many books, and was familiar with those elderly relatives frequently to be met in them, and usually female, who intrude into a newly married *ménage* and make themselves objectionable to one of the parties by sympathising with the other one. There was no cause for sympathy here, and if there ever should be Miss Entwhistle would certainly never sympathise except from a neutral place. She wouldn't come into a man's house, and in the very act of being nourished by his food sympathise with his wife; she would sympathise from London. Her honesty of intention, her single-mindedness, were, she knew, complete. She didn't feel, she knew she wasn't, in the least like these relatives in books, and yet as she sat in Everard's chair—obviously it was his; the upholstered seat was his very shape, inverted—she was afraid, indeed she was certain, he would think she was one of them.

There she was, she thought, come unasked, sitting in his place, eating his food. He usedn't to like her; would he like her any the better for this? From a desire not to have meals of his she had avoided tea, but she hadn't been able to avoid dinner, and with each dish set before her—dishes produced surprisingly, as she couldn't but observe, at the end of an arm thrust to the minute through a door—she felt more and more acutely that she was in his eyes, if he could only see her, an interloper. No doubt it was Lucy's house too, but it didn't feel as if it were, and she would have given much to be able to escape back to London that night.

But whatever Everard thought of her intrusion she wasn't going to leave Lucy. Not alone in that house; not to wake up to find herself alone in that house. Besides, who knew how such a chill would develop? There ought of course to have been a doctor. When Everard rang up, as he would be sure to the last thing to ask how Lucy was, she would go to the telephone, announce her presence, and inquire whether it wouldn't be as well to have a doctor round in the morning.

Therefore she asked Chesterton to let her know when Mr. Wemyss telephoned; and Chesterton, surprised, for it was not Wemyss's habit to telephone to The Willows, all his communications coming on postcards, paused just an instant before replying, 'If you please, ma'am.'

Chesterton wondered what Wemyss was expected to telephone about. It wouldn't have occurred to her that it might be about the new Mrs. Wemyss's health, because he had not within her recollection ever telephoned about the health of a Mrs. Wemyss. Sometimes the previous Mrs. Wemyss's health gave way enough for her to stay in bed, but no telephoning from London had in consequence taken place. Accordingly she wondered what message could be expected.

'What time would Mr. Wemyss be likely to ring up?' asked Miss Entwhistle presently, more for the sake of saying something than from a desire to know. She was going to that telephone, but she didn't want to, she was in no hurry for it, it wasn't impatience to meet Wemyss's voice making her talk to Chesterton; what was making her talk was the dining-room.

For not only did its bareness afflict her, and its glaring light, and its long empty table, and the way Chesterton's footsteps echoed up and down the uncarpeted floor, but there on the wall was that poor thing looking at her, she had no doubt whatever as to who it was standing up in that long slim frock looking at her, and she was taken aback. In spite of her determination to like all the arrangements, it did seem to her tactless to have her there, especially as she had that trick of looking so very steadily at one; and when she turned her eyes away from the queer, suppressed smile, she didn't like what she saw on the other wall either,—that enlarged old man, that obvious progenitor.

Having caught sight of both these pictures, which at night were much more conspicuous than by day, owing to the brilliant unshaded lighting, Miss Entwhistle had no wish to look at them again, and carefully looked either at her plate or at Chesterton's back as she hurried down the room to the dish being held out at the end of the remarkable arm; but being nevertheless much disturbed by their presence, and by the way she knew they weren't taking their eyes off her however carefully she took hers off them, she asked Chesterton what time Wemyss would be likely to telephone merely in order to hear the sound of a human voice.

Chesterton then informed her that her master never did telephone to The Willows, so that she was unable to say what time he would.

'But,' said Miss Entwhistle, surprised, 'you have a telephone.'

'If you please, ma'am,' said Chesterton.

Miss Entwhistle didn't like to ask what, then, the telephone was for, because she didn't wish to embark on anything even remotely approaching a discussion of Everard's habits, so she wondered in silence.

Chesterton, however, presently elucidated. She coughed a little first, conscious that to volunteer a remark wasn't quite within her idea of the perfect parlourmaid, and then she said, 'It's owing to local convenience, ma'am. We find it indispensable in the isolated situation of the 'ouse. We gives our orders to the tradesmen by means of the telephone. Mr. Wemyss installed it for that purpose, he says, and objects to trunk calls because of the charges and the waste of Mr. Wemyss's time at the other end, ma'am.'

'Oh,' said Miss Entwhistle.

'If you please, ma'am,' said Chesterton.

Miss Entwhistle said nothing more. With her eyes fixed on her plate in order to avoid those other eyes, she wondered what she had better do. It was half-past eight, and Everard hadn't rung up. If he were going to be anxious enough not to mind the trunk-call charge he would have been anxious enough before this. That he hadn't rung up showed he regarded Lucy's indisposition as slight. What, then, would he say to her uninvited presence there? Nothing, she was afraid, that would be really hospitable. And she had just eaten a pudding of his. It seemed to curdle up within her.

458

'No, *no* coffee, thank you,' she said hastily, on Chesterton's inquiring if she wished it served in the library. She had had dinner because she couldn't help herself, urged to it by the servants, but she needn't proceed to extras. And the library,—wasn't it in the library that Everard was sitting the day that poor smiling thing ... yes, she remembered Lucy telling her so. No, she would not have coffee in the library.

But now about telephoning. Really the only thing to do, the only way of dignity, was to ring him up. Useless waiting any more for him to do it; evidently he wasn't going to. She would ring him up, tell him she was there, and ask—she clung particularly to the doctor idea, because his presence would justify hers if the doctor hadn't better look in in the morning.

Thus it was that, sitting quiet in their basement, the Twites were startled about nine o'clock that evening by the telephone bell. It sounded more uncanny than ever up there, making all that noise by itself in the dark; and when, hurrying up anxiously to it, Twite applied his ear, all that happened was that an extremely short-tempered voice told him to hold on.

Twite held on, listening hard and hearing nothing.

'Say 'Ullo, Twite,' presently advised Mrs. Twite from out of the anxious silence at the foot of the kitchen stairs.

"Ullo,' said Twite half-heartedly.

'Must be a wrong number,' said Mrs. Twite, after more silence. "Ang it up, and come and finish your supper.'

A very small voice said something very far away. Twite strained every nerve to hear. He hadn't yet had to face a trunk call, and he thought the telephone was fainting.

"Ullo?' he said anxiously, trying to make the word sound polite.

'It's a wrong number,' said Mrs. Twite, after further waiting. "Ang it up.'

The voice, incredibly small, began to talk again, and Twite, unable to hear a word, kept on saying with increasing efforts to sound polite, "Ullo?'Ullo?'

"Ang it up,' said Mrs. Twite, who from the bottom of the stairs was always brave.

'That's what it is,' said Twite at last, exhausted. 'It's a wrong number.' And he went to the writing-pad and wrote:

A wrong number rang up sir believed to be a lady 9.10.

So Miss Entwhistle at the other end was defeated, and having done her best and not succeeded she decided to remain quiescent, at any rate till the morning. Quiescent and uncritical. She wouldn't worry; she wouldn't criticise; she would merely think of Everard in those terms of amiability which were natural to her.

But while she was waiting for the call in the cold hall there had been a moment when her fixed benevolence did a little loosen. Chesterton, seeing that she shivered, had suggested the library for waiting in, where she said there was a fire, but Miss Entwhistle preferred to be cold in the hall than warm in the library; and standing in that bleak place she saw a line of firelight beneath a door, which she then knew must be the library. Accordingly she then also knew that Lucy's bedroom was exactly above the library, for looking up she could see its door from where she stood; so that it was out of that window.... Her benevolence for a moment did become unsteady. He let the child sleep there, he made the child sleep there....

She soon, however, had herself in hand again. Lucy didn't mind, so why should she? Lucy was asleep there at that moment, with a look of complete content on her face. But there was one thing Miss Entwhistle decided she would do: Lucy shouldn't wake up by any chance in the night and find herself in that room alone,—window or no window, she would sleep there with her.

This was a really heroic decision, and only love for Lucy made it possible. Apart from the window and what she believed had happened at it, apart from the way that poor thing's face in the photograph haunted her, there was the feeling that it wasn't Lucy's bedroom at all but Everard's. It was oddly disagreeable to Miss Entwhistle to spend the night, for instance, with Wemyss's sponge. She debated in the spare-room when she was getting ready for bed—a small room on the other side of the house, with a nice high window-sill—whether she wouldn't keep her clothes on. At least then she would feel more strange, at least she would feel less at home. But how tiring. At her age, if she sat up all night—and in her clothes no lying down could be comfortable—she would be the merest rag next morning, and quite unable to cope on the telephone with Everard. And she really must take out her hairpins; she couldn't sleep a wink with them all pressing on her head. Yet the familiarity of being in that room among the neckties without her hairpins.... She hesitated, and argued, and all the while she was slowly taking out her hairpins and taking off her clothes.

At the last moment, when she was in her nightgown and her hair was neatly plaited and she was looking the goodest of tidy little women, her courage failed her. No, she couldn't go. She would stay where she was, and ring and ask that nice housemaid to sleep with Mrs. Wemyss in case she wanted anything in the night.

She did ring; but by the time Lizzie came Miss Entwhistle, doubting the sincerity of her motives, had been examining them. Was it really the neckties? Was it really the sponge? Wasn't it, at bottom, really the window?

She was ashamed. Where Lucy could sleep she could sleep. 'I rang,' she said, 'to ask you to be so kind as to help me carry my pillow and blankets into Mrs. Wemyss's room. I'm going to sleep on the sofa there.'

'Yes ma'am,' said Lizzie, picking them up. 'The sofa's very short and 'ard, ma'am. 'Adn't you better sleep in the bed?'

'No,' said Miss Entwhistle.

'There's plenty of room, ma'am. Mrs. Wemyss wouldn't know you was in it, it's such a large bed.'

'I will sleep on the sofa,' said Miss Entwhistle.

XXVIII

In London Wemyss went through his usual day, except that he was kept longer than he liked at his office by the accumulation of business and by having a prolonged difference of opinion, ending in dismissal, with a typist who had got out of hand during his absence to the extent of answering him back. It was five before he was able to leave—and even then he hadn't half finished, but he declined to be sacrificed further—and proceed as usual to his club to play bridge. He had a great desire for bridge after not having played for so long, and it was difficult, doing exactly the things he had always done, for him to remember that he was married. In fact he wouldn't have remembered if he hadn't felt so indignant; but all day underneath everything he did, everything he said and thought, lay indignation, and so he knew he was married.

Being extremely methodical he had long ago divided his life inside and out into compartments, each strictly separate, each, as it were, kept locked till the proper moment for its turn arrived, when he unlocked it and took out its contents,—work, bridge, dinner, wife, sleep, Paddington, The Willows, or whatever it was that it contained. Having finished with the contents, the compartment was locked up and dismissed from his thoughts till its turn came round again. A honeymoon was a great shake-up, but when it occurred he arranged the date of its cessation as precisely as the date of its inauguration. On such a day, at such an hour, it would come to an end, the compartments would once more be unlocked, and regularity resumed. Bridge was the one activity which, though it was taken out of its compartment at the proper time, didn't go into it again with any sort of punctuality. Everything else, including his wife, was locked up to the minute; but bridge would stay out till any hour. On each of the days in London, the Mondays to Fridays, he proceeded punctually to his office, and from thence punctually to his club and bridge. He always lunched and dined at his club. Other men, he was aware, dined not infrequently at home, but the explanation of that was that their wives weren't Vera.

The moment, then, that Wemyss found himself once more doing the usual things among the usual surroundings, he felt so exactly as he used to that he wouldn't have remembered Lucy at all if it hadn't been for that layer of indignation at the bottom of his mind. Going up the steps of his club he was conscious of a sense of hard usage, and searching for its cause remembered Lucy. His wife now wasn't Vera, and yet he was to dine at his club exactly as if she were. His wife was Lucy; who, instead of being where she ought to be, eagerly awaiting his return to Lancaster Gate—it was one of his legitimate grievances against Vera that she didn't eagerly await—she was having a cold at Strorley. And why was she having a cold at Strorley? And why was he, a newly-married man, deprived of the comfort of his wife and going to spend the evening exactly as he had spent all the evenings for months past?

Wemyss was very indignant, but he was also very desirous of bridge. If Lucy had been waiting for him he would have had to leave off bridge before his desire for it had been anything like sated,— whatever wives one had they shackled one,—and as it was he could play as long as he wanted to and yet at the same time remain justly indignant. Accordingly he wasn't nearly as unhappy as he thought he was; not, at any rate, till the moment came for going solitary to bed. He detested sleeping by himself. Even Vera had always slept with him.

Altogether Wemyss felt that he had had a bad day, what with the disappointment of its beginning, and the extra work at the office, and no decent lunch 'Positively only time to snatch a bun and a glass of milk,' he announced, amazed, to the first acquaintance he met in the club. 'Just fancy, only time to snatch——' but the acquaintance had melted away and losing rather heavily at bridge, and going back to Lancaster Gate to find from the message left by Twite that that annoying aunt of Lucy's had cropped up already.

Usually Wemyss was amused by Twite's messages, but nothing about this one amused him. He threw down the wrong number one impatiently,—Twite was really a hopeless imbecile; he would dismiss him; but the other one he read again. 'Wanted to know all about us, did she. Said it was very strange, did she. Like her impertinence,' he thought. She had lost no time in cropping up, he thought. Of how completely Miss Entwhistle had, in fact, cropped he was of course unaware.

Yes, he had had a bad day, and he was going to have a lonely night. He went upstairs feeling deeply hurt, and winding his watch.

But after much solid sleep he felt better; and at breakfast he said to Twite, who always jumped when he addressed him, 'Mrs. Wemyss will be coming up to-day.'

Twite's brain didn't work very fast owing to the way it spent most of its time dormant in a basement, and for a moment he thought—it startled him that his master had forgotten the lady was dead. Ought he to remind him? What a painful dilemma.... However, he remembered the new Mrs. Wemyss just in time not to remind him, and to say 'Yes sir,' without too perceptible a pause. His mind hadn't room in it to contain much, and it assimilated slowly that which it contained. He had only been in Wemyss's service three months before the Mrs. Wemyss he found there died. He was just beginning to assimilate her when she ceased to be assimilatable, and to him and his wife in their quiet subterraneous existence it had seemed as if not more than a week had passed before there was another Mrs. Wemyss. Far was it from him to pass opinions on the rapid marriages of gentlemen, but he couldn't keep up with these Mrs. Wemysses. His mind, he found, hadn't yet really realised the new one. He knew she was there somewhere, for he had seen her briefly on the Saturday morning, and he knew she would presently begin to disturb him by needing meals, but he easily forgot her. He forgot her now, and consequently for a moment had the dreadful thought described above.

'I shall be in to dinner,' said Wemyss.

'Yes sir,' said Twite.

Dinner. There usedn't to be dinner. His master hadn't been in once to dinner since Twite knew him. A tray for the lady, while there was a lady; that was all. Mrs. Twite could just manage a tray. Since the lady had left off coming up to town owing to her accident, there hadn't been anything. Only quiet.

He stood waiting, not having been waved out of the room, and anxiously watching Wemyss's face, for he was a nervous man.

Then the telephone bell rang.

Wemyss, without looking up, waved him out to it and went on with his breakfast; and after a minute, noticing that he neither came back nor could be heard saying anything beyond a faint, propitiatory "Ullo,' called out to him.

'What is it?' Wemyss called out.

'I can't hear, sir,' Twite's distressed voice answered from the hall.

'Fool,' said Wemyss, appearing, table-napkin in hand.

'Yes sir,' said Twite.

He took the receiver from him, and then the Twites—Mrs. Twite from the foot of the kitchen stairs and Twite lingering in the background because he hadn't yet been waved away—heard the following:

'Yes yes. Yes, speaking. Hullo. Who is it?'

'What? I can't hear. What?'

'Miss who? En—oh, good-morning, How distant your voice sounds.'

'What? Where? *Where?*'

'Oh really.'

Here the person at the other end talked a great deal.

'Yes. Quite. But then you see she wasn't.'

More prolonged talk from the other end.

'What? She isn't coming up? Indeed she is. She's expected. I've ordered——'

'What? I can't hear. The doctor? You're sending for the doctor?'

'I daresay. But then you see I consider it isn't.'

'I daresay, I daresay. No, of course I can't. How can I leave my work——'

'Oh, very well, very well. I daresay. No doubt. She's to come up for all that as arranged, tell her, and if she needs doctors there are more of them here anyhow than—what? Can't possibly?'

'I suppose you know you're taking a great deal upon yourself unasked——'

'What? What?'

A very rapid clear voice cut in. 'Do you want another three minutes?' it asked.

He hung up the receiver with violence. 'Oh, damn the woman, damn the woman,' he said, so loud that the Twites shook like reeds to hear him.

At the other end Miss Entwhistle was walking away lost in thought. Her position was thoroughly unpleasant. She disliked extraordinarily that she should at that moment contain an egg and some coffee which had once been Wemyss's. She would have breakfasted on a cup of tea only, if it hadn't been that Lucy was going to need looking after that day, and the looker-after must be nourished. As she went upstairs again, a faint red spot on each cheek, she couldn't help being afraid that she and Everard would have to exercise patience before they got to be fond of each other. On the telephone he hardly did himself justice, she thought.

Lucy hadn't had a good night. She woke up suddenly from what was apparently a frightening dream soon after Miss Entwhistle had

465

composed herself on the sofa, and had been very restless and hot for a long time. There seemed to be a great many things about the room that she didn't like. One of them was the bed. Probably the poor little thing was bemused by her dream and her feverishness, but she said several things about the bed which showed that it was on her mind. Miss Entwhistle had warmed some milk on a spirit-lamp provided by Lizzie, and had given it to her and soothed her and petted her. She didn't mention the window, for which Miss Entwhistle was thankful; but when first she woke up from her frightening dream and her aunt hurried across to her, she had stared at her and actually called her Everard—her, in her meek plaits. When this happened Miss Entwhistle made up her mind that the doctor should be sent for the first thing in the morning. About six she tumbled into an uncomfortable sleep again, and Miss Entwhistle crept out of the room and dressed. Certainly she was going to have a doctor round, and hear what he had to say; and as soon as she was strengthened by breakfast she would do her duty and telephone to Everard.

This she did, with the result that she returned to Lucy's room with a little red spot on each cheek; and when she looked at Lucy, still uneasily sleeping and breathing as though her chest were all sore, the idea that she was to get up and travel to London made the red spots on Miss Entwhistle's cheeks burn brighter. She calmed down, however, on remembering that Everard couldn't see how evidently poorly the child was, and told herself that if he could he would be all tenderness. She told herself this, but she didn't believe it; and then she was vexed that she didn't believe it. Lucy loved him. Lucy had looked perfectly pleased and content yesterday before she became so ill. One mustn't judge a man by his way with a telephone.

At ten o'clock the doctor came. He had been in Strorley for years, and was its only doctor. He was one of those guests who used to dine at The Willows in the early days of Wemyss's possession of it. Occasionally he had attended the late Mrs. Wemyss; and the last time he had been in the house was when he was sent for suddenly on the day of her death. He, in common with the rest of Strorley, had heard of Wemyss's second marriage, and he shared the general shocked surprise. Strorley, which looked such an unconscious place, such a torpid, unconscious riverside place, was nevertheless intensely sensitive to shocks, and it hadn't at all recovered from the shock of that poor Mrs. Wemyss's death and the very dreadful

466

inquest, when the fresh shock of another Mrs. Wemyss arriving on the scene made it, as it were, reel anew, and made it reel worse. Marriage so quickly on the heels of that terrible death? The Wemysses were only week-enders and summer holiday people, so that it wasn't quite so scandalous to have them in Strorley as it would have been if they were unintermittent residents, yet it was serious enough. That inquest had been in all the newspapers. To have a house in one's midst which produced doubtful coroner's verdicts was a blot on any place, and the new Mrs. Wemyss couldn't possibly be anything but thoroughly undesirable. Of course no one would call on her. Impossible. And when the doctor was rung up and asked to come round, he didn't tell his wife where he was going, because he didn't wish for trouble.

Chesterton—how well he remembered Chesterton; but after all, it was only the other day that he was there last—ushered him into the library, and he was standing gloomily in front of the empty grate, looking neither to the right nor to the left for he disliked the memories connected with the flags outside the window, and wishing he had a partner because then he would have sent him instead, when a spare little lady, bland and pleasant, came in and said she was the patient's aunt. An educated little lady; not at all the sort of relative he would have expected the new Mrs. Wemyss to have.

There was a general conviction in Strorley that the new Mrs. Wemyss must have been a barmaid, a typist, or a nursery governess,—was, that is, either very bold, very poor, or very meek. Else how could she have married Wemyss? And this conviction had reached and infected even the doctor, who was a busy man off whom gossip usually slid. When, however, he saw Miss Entwhistle he at once was sure that there was nothing in it. This wasn't the aunt of either the bold, the poor, or the meek; this was just a decent gentlewoman. He shook hands with her, really pleased to see her. Everybody was always pleased to see Miss Entwhistle, except Wemyss.

'Nothing serious, I hope?' asked the doctor.

Miss Entwhistle said she didn't think there was, but that her nephew——

'You mean Mr. Wemyss?'

She bowed her head. She did mean Mr. Wemyss. Her nephew. Her nephew, that is, by marriage.

'Quite,' said the doctor.

Her nephew naturally wanted his wife to go up and join him in London.

'Naturally,' said the doctor.

And she wanted to know when she would be fit to go.

'Then let us go upstairs and I'll tell you,' said the doctor.

This was a very pleasant little lady, he thought as he followed her up the well-known stairs, to have become related to Wemyss immediately on the top of all that affair. Now he would have said himself that after such a ghastly thing as that most women——

But here they arrived in the bedroom and his sentence remained unfinished, because on seeing the small head on the pillow of the treble bed he thought, 'Why, he's married a child. What an extraordinary thing.'

'How old is she?' he asked Miss Entwhistle, for Lucy was still uneasily sleeping; and when she told him he was surprised.

'It's because she's out of proportion to the bed,' explained Miss Entwhistle in a whisper. 'She doesn't usually look so inconspicuous.'

The whispering and being looked at woke Lucy, and the doctor sat down beside her and got to business. The result was what Miss Entwhistle expected: she had a very violent feverish cold, which might turn into anything if she were not kept in bed. If she were, and with proper looking after, she would be all right in a few days. He laughed at the idea of London.

'How did you come to get such a violent chill?' he asked Lucy.

'I don't—know,' she answered.

'Well, don't talk,' he said, laying her hand down on the quilt—he had been holding it while his sharp eyes watched her—and giving it a brief pat of farewell. 'Just lie there and get better. I'll send something for your throat, and I'll look in again to-morrow.'

Miss Entwhistle went downstairs with him feeling as if she had buckled him on as a shield, and would be able, clad in such armour, to face anything Everard might say.

'She likes that room?' he asked abruptly, pausing a moment in the hall.

'I can't quite make out,' said Miss Entwhistle. 'We haven't had any talk at all yet. It was from that window, wasn't it, that——?'

'No. The one above;'

'The one above? Oh really.'

'Yes. There's a sitting-room. But I was thinking whether being in the same bed—well, good-bye. Cheer her up. She'll want it when she's better. She'll feel weak. I'll be round to-morrow.'

He went out pulling on his gloves, followed to the steps by Miss Entwhistle.

On the steps he paused again. 'How does she like being here?' he asked.

'I don't know,' said Miss Entwhistle. 'We haven't talked at all yet.'

She looked at him a moment, and then added, 'She's very much in love.'

'Ah. Yes. Really. I see. Well, good-bye.'

He turned to go.

'It's wonderful, wonderful,' he said, pausing once more.

'What is wonderful?'

'What love will do.'

'It is indeed,' agreed Miss Entwhistle, thinking of all it had done to Lucy.

He seemed as if he were going to say something more, but thought better of it and climbed into his dogcart and was driven away.

XXIX

Two days went by undisturbed by the least manifestation from Wemyss. Miss Entwhistle wrote to him on each of the afternoons, telling him of Lucy's progress and of what the doctor said about her, and on each of the evenings she lay down on the sofa to sleep feeling excessively insecure, for how very likely that he would come down by some late train and walk in, and then there she would be. In spite of that, she would have been very glad if he had walked in, it would have seemed more natural; and she couldn't help wondering whether the little thing in the bed wasn't thinking so too. But nothing happened. He didn't come, he didn't write, he made no sign of any sort. 'Curious,' said Miss Entwhistle to herself; and forbore to criticise further.

They were peaceful days. Lucy was getting better all the time, though still kept carefully in bed by the doctor, and Miss Entwhistle felt as much justified in being in the house as Chesterton or Lizzie, for she was performing duties under a doctor's directions. Also the weather was quiet and sunshiny. In fact, there was peace.

On Thursday the doctor said Lucy might get up for a few hours and sit on the sofa; and there, its asperities softened by pillows, she sat and had tea, and through the open window came the sweet smells of April. The gardener was mowing the lawn, and one of the smells was of the cut grass; Miss Entwhistle had been out for a walk, and found some windflowers and some lovely bright green moss, and put them in a bowl; the doctor had brought a little bunch of violets out of his garden; the afternoon sun lay beautifully on the hills across the river; the river slid past the end of the garden tranquilly; and Miss Entwhistle, pouring out Lucy's tea and buttering her toast, felt that she could at that moment very nearly have been happy, in spite of its being The Willows she was in, if there hadn't, in the background, brooding over her day and night, been that very odd and disquieting silence of Everard's.

As if Lucy knew what she was thinking, she said—it was the first time she had talked of him—'You know, Aunt Dot, Everard will have been fearfully busy this week, because of having been away so long.'

'Oh of course,' agreed Miss Entwhistle with much heartiness. 'I'm sure the poor dear has been run off his legs.'

'He didn't—he hasn't——'

Lucy flushed and broke off.

'I suppose,' she began again after a minute, 'there's been nothing from him? No message, I mean? On the telephone or anything?'

'No, I don't think there has—not since our talk the first day,' said Miss Entwhistle.

'Oh? Did he telephone the first day?' asked Lucy quickly. 'You never told me.'

'You were asleep nearly all that day. Yes,' said Miss Entwhistle, clearing her throat, 'we had a—we had quite a little talk.'

'What did he say?'

'Well, he naturally wanted you to be well enough to go up to London, and of course he was very sorry you couldn't.'

Lucy looked suddenly much happier.

'Yes,' said Miss Entwhistle, as though in answer to the look.

'He hates writing letters, you know, Aunt Dot,' Lucy said presently.

'Men do,' said Miss Entwhistle. 'It's very curious,' she continued brightly, 'but men *do*.'

'And he hates telephoning. It was wonderful for him to have telephoned that day.'

'Men,' said Miss Entwhistle, 'are very funny about some things.'

'To-day is Thursday, isn't it,' said Lucy. 'He ought to be here by one o'clock to-morrow.'

Miss Entwhistle started. 'To-morrow?' she repeated. 'Really? Does he? I mean, ought he? Somehow I had supposed Saturday. The week-end somehow suggests Saturdays to me.'

'No. He—we,' Lucy corrected herself, 'come down on Fridays. He's sure to be down in time for lunch.'

'Oh is he?' said Miss Entwhistle, thinking a great many things very quickly. 'Well, if it is his habit,' she went on, 'I am sure too that he will. Do you remember how we set our clocks by him when he came to tea in Eaton Terrace?'

Lucy smiled, and the remembrance of those days of love, and of all his dear, funny ways, flooded her heart and washed out for a moment the honeymoon, the birthday, everything that had happened since.

Miss Entwhistle couldn't but notice the unmistakable love-look. '*Oh* I'm so glad you love each other so much,' she said with all her heart. 'You know, Lucy, I was afraid that perhaps this house——'

She stopped, because adequately to discuss The Willows in all its aspects needed, she felt, perfect health on both sides.

'Yes, I don't think a house matters when people love each other,' said Lucy.

'Not a bit. Not a bit,' agreed Miss Entwhistle. Not even, she thought robustly, when it was a house with a recent dreadful history. Love—she hadn't herself experienced it, but what was an imagination for except to imagine with?—love was so strong an armour that nothing could reach one and hurt one through it. That was why lovers were so selfish. They sat together inside their armour perfectly safe, entirely untouchable, completely uninterested in what happened to the rest of the world. 'Besides,' she went on aloud, 'you'll alter it.'

Lucy's smile at that was a little sickly. Aunt Dot's optimism seemed to her extravagant. She was unable to see herself altering The Willows.

'You'll have all your father's furniture and books to put about,' said Aunt Dot, continuing in optimism. 'Why, you'll be able to make the place really quite—quite——'

She was going to say habitable, but ate another piece of toast instead.

'Yes, I expect I'll have the books here, anyhow,' said Lucy. 'There's a sitting-room upstairs with room in it.'

'Is there?' said Miss Entwhistle, suddenly very attentive.

'Lots of room. It's to be my sitting-room, and the books could go there. Except that—except that——'

'Except what?' asked Miss Entwhistle.

'I don't know. I don't much want to alter that room. It was Vera's.'

'I should alter it beyond recognition,' said Miss Entwhistle firmly.

Lucy was silent. She felt too flabby, after her three days with a temperature, to engage in discussion with anybody firm.

'That's to say,' said Miss Entwhistle, 'if you like having the room at all. I should have thought——'

'Oh yes, I like having the room,' said Lucy, flushing.

Then it was Miss Entwhistle who was silent; and she was silent because she didn't believe Lucy really could like having the actual room from which that unfortunate Vera met her death. It wasn't natural. The child couldn't mean it. She needed feeding up. Perhaps they had better not talk about rooms; not till Lucy was stronger. Perhaps they had better not talk at all, because everything they said was bound in the circumstances to lead either to Everard or Vera.

'Wouldn't you like me to read aloud to you a little while before you go back to bed?' she asked, when Lizzie came in to clear away the tea-things.

Lucy thought this a very good idea. 'Oh do, Aunt Dot,' she said; for she too was afraid of what talking might lead to. Aunt Dot was phenomenally quick. Lucy felt she couldn't bear it, she simply couldn't bear it, if Aunt Dot were to think that perhaps Everard.... So she said quite eagerly, 'Oh do, Aunt Dot,' and not until she had said it did she remember that the books were locked up, and the key was on Everard's watch-chain. Then she sat looking up at Aunt Dot with a startled, conscience-stricken face.

'What is it, Lucy?' asked Miss Entwhistle, wondering why she had turned red.

Just in time Lucy remembered that there were Vera's books. 'Do you mind very much going up to the sitting-room?' she asked. 'Vera's books——'

Miss Entwhistle did mind very much going up to the sitting-room, and saw no reason why Vera's books should be chosen. Why should she have to read Vera's books? Why did Lucy want just those, and look so odd and guilty about it? Certainly the child needed feeding up. It wasn't natural, it was unwholesome, this queer attraction she appeared to feel towards Vera.

She didn't say anything of this, but remarked that there was a room called the library in the house which suggested books, and hadn't she better choose something from out of that,—go down, instead of go up.

Lucy, painfully flushed, looked at her. Nothing would induce her to tell her about the key. Aunt Dot would think it so ridiculous.

'Yes, but Everard——' she stammered. 'They're rather special books—he doesn't like them taken out of the room——'

'Oh,' said Miss Entwhistle, trying hard to avoid any opinion of any sort.

'But I don't see why you should go up all those stairs, Aunt Dot darling,' Lucy went on. 'Lizzie will, won't you, Lizzie? Bring down some of the books—any of them. An armful.'

Lizzie, thus given *carte blanche*, brought down the six first books from the top shelf, and set them on the table beside Lucy.

Lucy recognised the cover of one of them at once, it was *Wuthering Heights*.

473

Miss Entwhistle took it up, read its title in silence, and put it down again.

The next one was Emily Brontë's collected poems.

Miss Entwhistle took it up, read its title in silence, and put it down again.

The third one was Thomas Hardy's *Time's Laughing-Stocks*.

Miss Entwhistle took it up, read its title in silence, and put it down again.

The other three were Baedekers.

'Well, I don't think there's anything I want to read here,' she said.

Lizzie asked if she should take them away then, and bring some more; and presently she reappeared with another armful.

These were all Baedekers.

'Curious,' said Miss Entwhistle.

Then Lucy remembered that she, too, beneath her distress on Saturday when she pulled out one after the other of Vera's books in her haste to understand her, to get comfort, to get, almost she hoped, counsel, had felt surprise at the number of Baedekers. The greater proportion of the books in Vera's shelves were guide-books and time-tables. But there had been other things,—'If you were to bring some out of a different part of the bookcase,' she suggested to Lizzie; who thereupon removed the Baedekers, and presently reappeared with more books.

This time they were miscellaneous, and Miss Entwhistle turned them over with a kind of reverential reluctance. That poor thing; this day last year she was probably reading them herself. It seemed sacrilege for two strangers.... Merciful that one couldn't see into the future. What would the poor creature have thought of the picture presented at that moment,—the figure in the blue dressing-gown, sitting in the middle of all the things that had been hers such a very little while before? Well, perhaps she would have been glad they weren't hers any longer, glad that she had finished, was done with them. These books suggested such tiredness, such a—yes, such a wish for escape.... There was more Hardy,—all the poems this time in one volume. There was Pater—*The Child in the House* and *Emerald Uthwart*—Miss Entwhistle, familiar with these, shook her head: that peculiar dwelling on death in them, that queer, fascinated inability to get away from it, that beautiful but sick wistfulness no, she certainly wouldn't read these. There was a book called *In the Strange South Seas*; and another about some island in the Pacific;

474

and another about life in the desert; and one or two others, more of the flamboyant guide-book order, describing remote, glowing places....

Suddenly Miss Entwhistle felt uncomfortable. She put down the book she was holding, and folded her hands in her lap and gazed out of the window at the hills on the other side of the river. She felt as if she had been prying, and prying unpardonably. The books people read,—was there ever anything more revealing? No, she refused to examine Vera's books further. And apart from that horrible feeling of prying upon somebody defenceless, upon somebody pitiful, she didn't wish to allow the thought these books suggested to get any sort of hold on her mind. It was essential, absolutely essential, that it shouldn't. And if Lucy ever——

She got up and went to the window. Lucy's eyes followed her, puzzled. The gardener was still mowing the lawn, working very hard at it as though he were working against time. She watched his back, bent with hurry as he and the boy laboriously pushed and pulled the machine up and down; and then she caught sight of the terrace just below, and the flags.

This was a dreadful house. Whichever way one looked one was entangled in a reminder. She turned away quickly, and there was that little loved thing in her blue wrapper, propped up on Vera's pillows, watching her with puzzled anxiety. Nothing could harm that child, she was safe, so long as she loved and believed in Everard; but suppose some day—suppose gradually—suppose a doubt should creep into her mind whether perhaps, after all, Vera's fall ... suppose a question should get into her head whether perhaps, after all, Vera's death——?

Aunt Dot knew Lucy's face so well that it seemed absurd to examine it now, searching for signs in its features and expression of enough character, enough nerves, enough—this, if there were enough of it, might by itself carry her through—sense of humour. Yes, she had a beautiful sweep of forehead; all that part of her face was lovely—so calm and open, with intelligent, sweet eyes. But were those dear eyes intelligent enough? Was not sweetness really far more manifest in them than intelligence? After that her face went small, and then, looking bigger than it was because of her little face, was her kind, funny mouth. Generous; easily forgiving; quick to be happy; quick to despair,—Aunt Dot, looking anxiously at it, thought she saw all this in the shape of Lucy's mouth. But had the child strength? Had she the strength that would be needed equally—supposing that doubt and that question should ever get into her head—for staying or for going; for staying or for running ... oh, but running, running, for her very *life*....

With a violent effort Miss Entwhistle shook herself free from these thoughts. Where in heaven's name was her mind wandering to? It was intolerable, this tyranny of suggestion in everything one looked at here, in everything one touched. And Lucy, who was watching her and who couldn't imagine why Aunt Dot should be so steadfastly gazing at her mouth, naturally asked, 'Is anything the matter with my face?'

Then Miss Entwhistle managed to smile, and came and sat down again beside the sofa. 'No,' she said, taking her hand. 'But I don't think I want to read after all. Let us talk.'

And holding Lucy's hand, who looked a little afraid at first but soon grew content on finding what the talk was to be about, she proceeded to discuss supper, and whether a poached egg or a cup of beef-tea contained the greater amount of nourishment

XXX

Also she presently told her, approaching it with caution, for she was sure Lucy wouldn't like it, that as Everard was coming down next day she thought it better to go back to Eaton Terrace in the morning.

'You two love-birds won't want me,' she said gaily, expecting and prepared for opposition; but really, as the child was getting well so quickly, there was no reason why she and Everard should be forced to begin practising affection for each other here and now. Besides, in the small bag she brought there had only been a nightgown and her washing things, and she couldn't go on much longer on only that.

To her surprise Lucy not only agreed but looked relieved. Miss Entwhistle was greatly surprised, and also greatly pleased. 'She adores him,' she thought, 'and only wants to be alone with him. If Everard makes her as happy as all that, who cares what he is like to me or to anybody else in the world?'

And all the horrible, ridiculous things she had been thinking half an hour before were blown away like so many cobwebs.

Just before half-past seven, while she was in her room on the other side of the house tidying herself before facing Chesterton and the evening meal she had reduced it to the merest skeleton of a meal, but Chesterton insisted on waiting, and all the usual ceremonies were observed—she was startled by the sound of wheels on the gravel beneath the window. It could only be Everard. He had come.

'Dear me,' said Miss Entwhistle to herself,—and she who had planned to be gone so neatly before his arrival!

It would be idle to pretend that she wasn't very much perturbed,—she was; and the brush with which she was tidying her pretty grey hair shook in her hand. Dinner alone with Everard,— well, at least let her be thankful that he hadn't arrived a few minutes later and found her actually sitting in his chair. What would have happened if he had? Miss Entwhistle, for all her dismay, couldn't help laughing. Also, she encouraged herself for the encounter by remembering the doctor. Behind his authority she was secure. She had developed, since Tuesday, from an uninvited visitor into an indispensable adjunct. Not a nurse; Lucy hadn't at any moment been positively ill enough for a nurse; but an adjunct.

She listened, her brush suspended. There was no mistaking it: it was certainly Everard, for she heard his voice. The wheels of the cab, after the interval necessary for ejecting him, turned round again on the drive, crunching much less, and went away, and presently there was his well-known deliberate, heavy tread coming up the uncarpeted staircase. Thank God for bedrooms, thought Miss Entwhistle, fervently brushing. Where would one be without them and bathrooms,—places of legitimate lockings-in, places even the most indignant host was bound to respect?

Now this wasn't the proper spirit in which to go down and begin getting fond of Everard and giving him the opportunity of getting fond of her, as she herself presently saw. Besides, at that very moment Lucy was probably in his arms, all alight with joyful surprise, and if he could make Lucy so happy there must be enough of good in him to enable him to fulfil the very mild requirements of Lucy's aunt. Just bare pleasantness, bare decency would be enough. She stoutly assured herself of her certainty of being fond of Everard if only he would let her. Sufficiently fond of him, that is; she didn't suppose any affection she was going to feel for him would ever be likely to get the better of her reason.

Immediately on Wemyss's arrival the silent house had burst into feverish life. Doors banged, feet ran; and now Lizzie came hurrying along the passage, and knocked at the door and told her breathlessly that dinner would be later not for at least another half hour, because Mr. Wemyss had come unexpectedly, and cook had to——

She didn't finish the sentence, she was in such a hurry to be off.

Miss Entwhistle, her simple preparations being complete, had nothing left to do but sit in one of those wicker work chairs with thin, hard, cretonne-covered upholstery, which are sometimes found in inhospitable spare-rooms and wait.

She found this bad for her *morale*. There wasn't a book in the room, or she would have distracted her thoughts by reading. She didn't want dinner. She would have best liked to get into the bed she hadn't yet slept once in, and stay there till it was time to go home, but her pride blushed scarlet at such a cowardly desire. She arranged herself, therefore, in the chair, and, since she couldn't read, tried to remember something to say over to herself instead, some poem, or verse of a poem, to take her attention off the coming dinner; and she was shocked to find, as she sat there with her eyes shut to keep out the light that glared on her from the middle of the ceiling, that she could remember nothing but fragments: loose bits floating derelict round her mind, broken spars that didn't even belong, she was afraid, to any really magnificent whole. How Jim would have scolded her,—Jim who forgot nothing that was beautiful.

By nature cool, in pious habits bred,
She looked on husbands with a virgin's dread....

Now where did that come from? And why should it come at all?

Such was the tone and manners of them all
No married lady at the house would call....

And that, for instance? She couldn't remember ever having read any poem that could contain these lines, yet she must have; she certainly hadn't invented them.

And this,—an absurd German thing Jim used to quote and laugh at:

Der Sultan winkt, Zuleika schweigt,
Und zeigt sich gänzlich abgeneigt....

Why should a thing like that rise now to the surface of her mind and float round on it, while all the noble verse she had read and enjoyed, which would have been of such use and support to her at this juncture, was nowhere to be found, not a shred of it, in any corner of her brain?

What a brain, thought Miss Entwhistle, disgusted, sitting up very straight in the wickerwork chair, her hands folded in her lap, her eyes shut; what a contemptible, anæmic brain, deserting her like this, only able to throw up to the surface when stirred, out of all the store of splendid stuff put so assiduously into it during years and years of life, couplets.

A sound she hadn't yet heard began to crawl round the house, and, even while she wondered what it was, increased and increased till it seemed to her at last as if it must fill the universe and reach to Eaton Terrace.

It was that gong. Become active. Heavens, and what activity. She listened amazed. The time it went on! It went on and on, beating in her ears like the crack of doom.

When the three great final strokes were succeeded by silence, she got up from her chair. The moment had come. A last couplet floated through her brain,—her brain seemed to clutch at it:

479

Betwixt the stirrup and the ground
She mercy sought, she mercy found....

Now where did that come from? she asked herself distractedly, nervously passing one hand over her already perfectly tidy hair and opening the door with the other.

There was Wemyss, opening Lucy's door at the same moment.

'Oh how do you do, Everard,' said Miss Entwhistle, advancing with all the precipitate and affectionate politeness of one who is greeting not only a host but a nephew.

'Quite well thank you,' was Everard's slightly unexpected reply; but logical, perfectly logical.

She held out her hand and he shook it, and then proceeded past her to her bedroom door, which she had left open, and switched off the light, which she had left on.

'Oh I'm sorry,' said Miss Entwhistle.

'That,' she thought, 'is one to Everard.'

She waited for his return, and then walked, followed by him in silence, down the stairs.

'How do you find Lucy?' she asked when they had got to the bottom. She didn't like Everard's silences; she remembered several of them during that difference of opinion he and she had had about where Christmas should be spent. They weighed on her; and she had the sensation of wriggling beneath them like an earwig beneath a stone, and it humiliated her to wriggle.

'Just as I expected,' he said. 'Perfectly well.'

'Oh no—not perfectly well,' exclaimed Miss Entwhistle, a vision of the blue-wrapped little figure sitting weakly up against the pillows that afternoon before her eyes. 'She is better to-day, but not nearly well.'

'You asked me what I thought, and I've told you,' said Wemyss.

No, it wouldn't be an impulsive affection, hers and Everard's, she felt; it would, when it did come, be the result of slow and careful preparation,—line upon line, here a little and there a little.

'Won't you go in?' he asked; and she perceived he had pushed the dining-room door open and was holding it back with his arm while she, thinking this, lingered.

'That,' she thought, 'is another to Everard,'—her second bungle; first the light left on in her room, now keeping him waiting.

She hurried through the door, and then, vexed with herself for hurrying, walked to her chair with almost an excess of deliberation.

'The doctor——' she began, when they were in their places, and Chesterton was hovering in readiness to snatch the cover off the soup the instant Wemyss had finished arranging his table-napkin.

'I wish to hear nothing about the doctor,' he interrupted.

Miss Entwhistle gave herself pains to be undaunted, and said with almost an excess of naturalness, 'But I'd like to tell you.'

'It is no concern of mine,' he said.

'But you're her husband, you know,' said Miss Entwhistle, trying to sound pleasant.

'I gave no orders,' said Wemyss.

'But he had to be sent for. The child——'

'So you say. So you said on the telephone. And I told you then you were taking a great deal on yourself, unasked.'

Miss Entwhistle hadn't supposed that any one ever talked like this before servants. She now knew that she had been mistaken.

'He's your doctor,' said Wemyss.

'My doctor?'

'I regard him entirely as your doctor.'

'I wish, Everard,' said Miss Entwhistle politely, after a pause, 'that I understood.'

'You sent for him on your own responsibility, unasked. You must take the consequences.'

'I don't know what you mean by the consequences,' said Miss Entwhistle, who was getting further and further away from that beginning of affection for Everard to which she had braced herself.

'The bill,' said Wemyss.

'Oh,' said Miss Entwhistle.

She was so much surprised that she could only ejaculate just that. Then the idea that she was in the act of being nourished by Wemyss's soup seemed to her so disagreeable that she put down her spoon.

'Certainly if you wish it,' she said.

'I do,' said Wemyss.

The conversation flagged.

Presently, sitting up very straight, refusing to take any notice of the variety and speed of the thoughts rushing round inside her and determined to behave as if she weren't minding anything, she said in a very clear little voice which she strove to make sound pleasant, 'Did you have a good journey down?'

'No,' said Wemyss, waving the soup away.

481

This as an answer, though no doubt strictly truthful, was too bald for much to be done with it. Miss Entwhistle therefore merely echoed, as she herself felt foolishly, 'No?'

And Wemyss confirmed his first reply by once more saying, 'No.'

The conversation flagged.

'I suppose,' she then said, making another effort, 'the train was very full.'

As this was not a question he was silent, and allowed her to suppose.

The conversation flagged.

'Why is there no fish?' he asked Chesterton, who was offering him cutlets.

'There was no time to get any, sir,' said Chesterton.

'He might have known that,' thought Miss Entwhistle.

'You will tell the cook that I consider I have not dined unless there is fish.'

'Yes sir,' said Chesterton.

'Goose,' thought Miss Entwhistle.

It was easier, and far less nerve-racking, to regard him indulgently as a goose than to let oneself get angry. He was like a great cross schoolboy, she thought, sitting there being rude; but unfortunately a schoolboy with power.

He ate the cutlets in silence. Miss Entwhistle declined them. She had missed her chance, she thought, when the cab was beneath her window and all she had to do was to lean out and say, 'Wait a minute.' But then Lucy,—ah yes, Lucy. The minute she thought of Lucy she felt she absolutely must be friends with Everard. Incredible as it seemed to her, and always had seemed from the first, that Lucy should love him, there it was,—she did. It couldn't be possible to love him without any reason. Of course not. The child knew. The child was wise and tender. Therefore Miss Entwhistle made another attempt at resuscitating conversation.

Watching her opportunity when Chesterton's back was receding down the room towards the outstretched arm at the end, for she didn't mind what Wemyss said quite so acutely if Chesterton wasn't looking, she said with as natural a voice as she could manage, 'I'm very glad you've come, you know. I'm sure Lucy has been missing you very much.'

'Lucy can speak for herself,' he said.

Then Miss Entwhistle concluded that conversation with Everard was too difficult. Let it flag. She couldn't, whatever he might feel able to do, say anything that wasn't polite in the presence of Chesterton. She doubted whether, even if Chesterton were not there, she would be able to; and yet continued politeness appeared in the face of his answers impossible. She had best be silent, she decided; though to withdraw into silence was of itself a humiliating defeat.

When she was little Miss Entwhistle used to be rude. Between the ages of five and ten she frequently made faces at people. But not since then. Ten was the latest. After that good manners descended upon her, and had enveloped her ever since. Nor had any occasion arisen later in her life in which she had even been tempted to slough them. Urbane herself, she dwelt among urbanities; kindly, she everywhere met kindliness. But she did feel now that it might, if only she could so far forget herself, afford her solace were she able to say, straight at him, 'Wemyss.'

Just that word. No more. For some reason she was dying to call him Wemyss without any Mr. She was sure that if she might only say that one word, straight at him, she would feel better; as much relieved as she did when she was little and made faces.

Dreadful; dreadful. She cast down her eyes, overwhelmed by the nature of her thoughts, and said No thank you to the pudding.

'It is clear,' thought Wemyss, observing her silence and her refusal to eat, 'where Lucy gets her sulking from.'

No more words were spoken till, dinner being over, he gave the order for coffee in the library.

'I'll go and say good-night to Lucy,' said Miss Entwhistle as they got up.

'You'll be so good as to do nothing of the sort,' said Wemyss.

'I—beg your pardon?' inquired Miss Entwhistle, not quite sure she could have heard right.

At this point they were both just in front of Vera's portrait on their way to the door, and she was looking at each of them, impartially strangling her smile.

'I wish to speak to you in the library,' said Wemyss.

'But suppose I don't wish to be spoken to in the library?' leapt to the tip of Miss Entwhistle's tongue.

There, however, was Chesterton,—checking, calming.

So she said, instead, 'Do.'

XXXI

She hadn't been into the library yet. She knew the dining-room, the hall, the staircase, Lucy's bedroom, the spare-room, the antlers, and the gong; but she didn't know the library. She had hoped to go away without knowing it. However, she was not to be permitted to.

The newly-lit wood fire blazed cheerfully when they went in, but its amiable light was immediately quenched by the electric light Wemyss switched on at the door. From the middle of the ceiling it poured down so strongly that Miss Entwhistle wished she had brought her sun-shade. The blinds were drawn, and there in front of the window was the table where Everard had sat writing—she remembered every word of Lucy's account of it on that July afternoon of Vera's death. It was now April; still well over three months to the first anniversary of that dreadful day, and here he was married again, and to, of all people in the world, her Lucy. There were so many strong, robust-minded young women in the world, so many hardened widows, so many thick-skinned persons of mature years wanting a comfortable home, who wouldn't mind Everard because they wouldn't love him and therefore wouldn't feel,—why should Fate have ordered that it should just be her Lucy? No, she didn't like him, she couldn't like him. He might, and she hoped he was, be all Lucy said, be wonderful and wholesome and natural and all the rest of it, but if he didn't seem so to her what, as far as she was concerned, was the good of it?

The fact is that by the time Miss Entwhistle got into the library she was very angry. Even the politest worm, she said to herself, the most conciliatory, sensible worm, fully conscious that wisdom points to patience, will nevertheless turn on its niece's husband if trodden on too heavily. The way Wemyss had ordered her not to go up to Lucy.... Particularly enraging to Miss Entwhistle was the knowledge of her weak position, uninvited in his house.

Wemyss, standing on the hearthrug in front of the blaze, filled his pipe. How well she knew that attitude and that action. How often she had seen both in her drawing-room in London. And hadn't she been kind to him? Hadn't she always, when she was hostess and he was guest, been hospitable and courteous? No, she didn't like him.

She sat down in one of the immense chairs, and had the disagreeable sensation that she was sitting down in Wemyss hollowed out. The two little red spots were brightly on her cheekbones,—had been there, indeed, ever since the beginning of dinner.

Wemyss filled his pipe with his customary deliberation, saying nothing. 'I believe he's enjoying himself,' flashed into her mind. 'Enjoying being in a temper, and having me to bully.'

'Well?' she asked, suddenly unbearably irritated.

'Oh it's no good taking that tone with me,' he said, continuing carefully to fill his pipe.

'Really, Everard,' she said, ashamed of him, but also ashamed of herself. She oughtn't to have let go her grip on herself and said, 'Well?' with such obvious irritation.

The coffee came.

'No thank you,' said Miss Entwhistle.

He helped himself.

The coffee went.

'Perhaps,' said Miss Entwhistle in a very polite voice when the door had been shut by Chesterton, 'you'll tell me what it is you wish to say.'

'Certainly. One thing is that I've ordered the cab to come round for you to-morrow in time for the early train.'

'Oh thank you, Everard. That is most thoughtful,' said Miss Entwhistle. 'I had already told Lucy, when she said you would be down to-morrow, that I would go home early.'

'That's one thing,' said Wemyss, taking no notice of this and going on carefully filling his pipe. 'The other is, that I don't wish you to see Lucy again, either to-night or before you go.'

She looked at him in astonishment. 'But why not?' she asked.

'I'm not going to have her upset.'

'But my dear Everard, don't you see it will upset her much more if I don't say good-bye to her? It won't upset her at all if I do, because she knows I'm going to-morrow anyhow. Why, what will the child think?'

'Oblige me by allowing me to be the best judge of my own affairs.'

'Do you know I very much doubt if you're that,' said Miss Entwhistle earnestly, really moved by his inability to perceive consequences. Here he had got everything, everything to make him happy for the rest of his life,—the wife he loved adoring him, believing in him, blotting out by her mere marrying him every doubt as to the exact manner of Vera's death, and all he had to do was to be kind and ordinarily decent. And poor Everard—it was absurd of her to mind for him, but she did in fact at that moment mind for him, he seemed such a pathetic human being, blindly bent on ruining his own happiness—would spoil it all, inevitably smash it all sooner or later, if he wasn't able to see, wasn't able to understand....

Wemyss considered her remark so impertinent that he felt he would have been amply justified in requesting her to leave his house then and there, dark or no dark, train or no train. And so he would have done, if he hadn't happened to prefer a long rather than a short scene.

'I didn't ask you into my library to hear your opinion of my character,' he said, lighting his pipe.

'Well then,' said Miss Entwhistle, for there was too much at stake for her to allow herself either to be silenced or goaded, 'let me tell you a few things about Lucy's.'

'About Lucy's?' echoed Wemyss, amazed at such effrontery. 'About my wife's?'

'Yes,' said Miss Entwhistle, very earnestly. 'It's the sort of character that takes things to heart, and she'll be miserable— miserable, Everard, and worry and worry if I just disappear as you wish me to without a word. Of course I'll go, and I promise I'll never come again unless you ask me to. But don't, because you're angry, insist on something that will make Lucy extraordinarily unhappy. Let me say good-night to her now, and good-bye to-morrow morning. I tell you she'll be terribly worried if I don't. She'll think'— Miss Entwhistle tried to smile—'that you've turned me out. And then, you see, if she thinks that, she won't be able——'Miss Entwhistle hesitated. 'Well, she won't be able to be proud of you. And that, my dear Everard—'she looked at him with a faint smile of deprecation and apology that she, a spinster, should talk of this— 'gives love its deepest wound.'

Wemyss stared at her, too much amazed to speak. In his house.... In his own house!

'I'm sorry,' she said, still more earnestly, 'if this annoys you, but I do want—I really do think it is very important.'

There was then a silence during which they looked at each other, he at her in amazement, she at him trying to hope,—hope that he would take what she had said in good part. It was so vital that he should understand, that he should get an idea of the effect on Lucy of just that sort of unkind, even cruel behaviour. His own happiness was involved as well. Tragic, tragic for every one if he couldn't be got to see....

'Are you aware,' he said, 'that this is my house?'

'Oh Everard——' she said at that, with a movement of despair.

'Are you aware,' he continued, 'that you are talking to a husband of his wife?'

Miss Entwhistle said nothing, but leaning her head on her hand looked at the fire.

'Are you aware that you thrust yourself into my house uninvited directly my back was turned, and have been living in it, and would have gone on indefinitely living in it, without any sanction from me unless I had come down, as I did come down, on purpose to put an end to such an outrageous state of affairs?'

'Of course,' she said, 'that is one way of describing it.'

'It is the way of every reasonable and decent person,' said Wemyss.

'Oh no,' said Miss Entwhistle. 'That is precisely what it isn't. But,' she added, getting up from the chair and holding out her hand, 'it is your way, and so I think, Everard, I'll say good-night. And good-bye too, for I don't expect I'll see you in the morning.'

'One would suppose,' he said, taking no notice of her proffered hand, for he hadn't nearly done, 'from your tone that this was your house and I was your servant.'

'I assure you I could never imagine it to be my house or you my servant.'

'You made a great mistake, I can tell you, when you started interfering between husband and wife. You have only yourself to thank if I don't allow you to continue to see Lucy.'

She stared at him.

'Do you mean,' she said, after a silence, 'that you intend to prevent my seeing her later on too? In London?'

'That, exactly, is my intention.'

Miss Entwhistle stared at him, lost in thought; but he could see he had got her this time, for her face had gone visibly pale.

'In that case, Everard,' she said presently, 'I think it my duty——'

'Don't begin about duties. You have no duties in regard to me and my household.'

'I think it my duty to tell you that from my knowledge of Lucy——'

'Your knowledge of Lucy! What is it compared to mine, I should like to know?'

'Please listen to me. It's most important. From my knowledge of her, I'm quite sure she hasn't the staying power of Vera.'

It was now his turn to stare. She was facing him, very pale, with shining, intrepid eyes. He had got her in her vulnerable spot he could see, or she wouldn't be so white, but she was going to do her utmost to annoy him up to the last.

'The staying power of——?' he repeated.

'I'm sure of it. And you must be wise, you must positively have the wisdom to take care of your own happiness——'

'Oh good God, you preaching woman!' he burst out. 'How dare you stand there in my own house talking to me of Vera?'

'Hush,' said Miss Entwhistle, her eyes shining brighter and brighter in her white face. 'Listen to me. It's atrocious that I should have to, but nobody ever seems to have told you a single thing in your life. You don't seem to know anything at all about women, anything at all about human beings. How could you bring a girl like Lucy—any young wife—to this house? But here she is, and it still may be all right because she loves you so, if you take care, if you are tender and kind. I assure you it is nothing to me how angry you are with me, or how completely you separate me from Lucy, if only you are kind to her. Don't you realise, Everard, that she may soon begin to have a baby, and that then she——'

'You indelicate woman! You incredibly indecent, improper——'

'I don't in the least mind what you say to me, but I tell you that unless you take care, unless you're kinder than you're being at this moment, it won't be anything like fifteen years this time.'

He repeated, staring, 'Fifteen years this time?'

'Yes. Good-bye.'

And she was gone, and had shut the door behind her before her monstrous meaning dawned on him.

Then, when it did, he strode out of the room after her.

She was going up the stairs very slowly.

'Come down,' he said.

She went on as if she hadn't heard him.

'Come down. If you don't come down at once I'll fetch you.'

This, through all her wretchedness, through all her horror, for beating in her ears were two words over and over again, *Lucy, Vera—Lucy, Vera* struck her as so absurd, the vision of herself, more naturally nimble, going on up the stairs just out of Wemyss's reach, with him heavily pursuing her, till among the attics at the top he couldn't but run her to earth in a cistern, that she had great difficulty in not spilling over into a ridiculous, hysterical laugh.

'Very well then,' she said, stopping and speaking in a low voice so that Lucy shouldn't be disturbed by unusual sounds, 'I'll come down.' And shining, quivering with indomitableness, she did.

She arrived at the bottom of the stairs where he was standing and faced him. What was he going to do? Take her by the shoulders and turn her out? Not a sign, not the smallest sign of distress or fear should he get out of her. Fear of him in relation to herself was the last thing she would condescend to feel, but fear for Lucy—for Lucy.... She could very easily have cried out because of Lucy, entreated to be allowed to see her sometimes, humbled herself, if she hadn't gripped hold of the conviction of his delight if she broke down, of his delight at having broken her down, at refusing. The thought froze her serene.

'You will now leave my house,' said Wemyss through his teeth.

'Without my hat, Everard?' she inquired mildly.

He didn't answer. He would gladly at that moment have killed her, for he thought he saw she was laughing at him. Not openly. Her face was serious and her voice polite; but he thought he saw she was laughing at him, and beyond anything that could happen to him he hated being defied.

He walked to the front door, reached up and undid the top bolt, stooped down and undid the bottom bolt, turned the key, took the chain off, pulled the door open, and said, 'There now. Go. And let this be a lesson to you.'

'I am glad to see,' said Miss Entwhistle, going out on to the steps with dignity, and surveying the stars with detachment, 'that it is a fine night.'

He shut and bolted and locked and chained her out, and as soon as he had done, and she heard his footsteps going away, and her eyes were a little accustomed to the darkness, she went round to the back entrance, rang the bell, and asked the astonished tweeny, who presently appeared, to send Lizzie to her; and when Lizzie came, also astonished, she asked her to be so kind as to go up to her room

489

and put her things in her bag and bring her her hat and cloak and purse.

'I'll wait here in the garden,' said Miss Entwhistle, 'and it would be most kind, Lizzie, if you were rather quick.'

Then, when she had got her belongings, and Lizzie had put her cloak round her shoulders and tried to express, by smoothings and brushings of it, her understanding and sympathy, for it was clear to Lizzie and to all the servants that Miss Entwhistle was being turned out, she went away; she went away past the silent house, through the white gate, up through the darkness of the sunken oozy lane, out on to the road where the stars gave light, across the bridge, into the village, along the road to the station, to wait for whatever train should come.

She walked slower and slower.

She was extraordinarily tired.

XXXII

Wemyss went back into the library, and seeing his coffee still on the chimney-piece he drank it, and then sat down in the chair Miss Entwhistle had just left, and smoked.

He wouldn't go up to Lucy yet; not till he was sure the woman wasn't going to try any tricks of knocking at the front door or ringing bells. He actually, so inaccurate was his perception of Miss Entwhistle's character and methods, he actually thought she might perhaps throw stones at the windows, and he decided to remain downstairs guarding his premises till this possibility became, with the lapse of time, more remote.

Meanwhile the fury of his indignation at the things she had said was immensely tempered by the real satisfaction he felt in having turned her out. That was the way to show people who was master, and meant to be master, in his own house. She had supposed she could do as she liked with him, use his house, be waited on by his servants, waste his electric light, interfere between him and his wife, say what she chose, lecture him, stand there and insult him, and he had showed her very quickly and clearly that she couldn't. As to her final monstrous suggestion, it merely proved how completely he had got her, how accurately he had hit on the punishment she felt most, that she should have indulged in such ravings. The ravings of impotence, that's what that was. For the rest of his life, he supposed, whenever people couldn't get their own way with him, were baffled by his steadfastness and consequently became vindictive, they would throw that old story up against him. Let them. It wouldn't make him budge, not a hair's-breadth, in any direction he didn't choose. Master in his own house,—that's what he was.

Curious how women invariably started by thinking they could do as they liked with him. Vera had thought so, and behaved accordingly; and she had been quite surprised, and even injured, when she discovered she couldn't. No doubt this woman was feeling considerably surprised too now; no doubt she never dreamt he would turn her out. Women never believed he would do the simple, obvious thing. And even when he warned them that he would, as he could remember on several occasions having warned Vera—indeed, it was recorded in his diary—they still didn't believe it. Daunted themselves by convention and the fear of what people might think,

491

they imagined that he would be daunted too. Then, when he wasn't, and it happened, they were surprised; and they never seemed to see that they had only themselves to thank.

He sat smoking and thinking a long time, one ear attentive to any sounds which might indicate that Miss Entwhistle was approaching hostilely from outside. Chesterton found him sitting like that when she came in to remove the coffee cup, and she found him still sitting like that when she came in an hour later with his whisky.

It was nearly eleven before he decided that the danger of attack was probably over; but still, before he went upstairs, he thought it prudent to open the window and step over the sill on to the terrace and just look round.

All was as quiet as the grave. It was so quiet that he could hear a little ripple where the water was split by a dead branch as the river slid gently along. There were stars, so that it was not quite dark; and although the April air was moist it was dry under foot. A pleasant night for a walk. Well, he would not grudge her that.

He went along the terrace, and round the clump of laurustinus bushes which cloaked the servants' entrance, to the front of the house.

Empty. Nobody still lingering on the steps.

He then proceeded as far as the white gate, holding her capable of having left it open on purpose,—'In order to aggravate me,' as he put it to himself.

It was shut.

He stood leaning on it a minute listening, in case she should be lurking in the lane.

Not a sound.

Satisfied that she had really gone, he returned to the terrace and re-entered the library, fastening the window carefully and pulling down the blind.

What a relief, what an extraordinary relief, to have got rid of her; and not just for this once, but for good. Also she was Lucy's only relation, so there were no more of them to come and try to interfere between man and wife. He was very glad she had behaved so outrageously at the end saying that about Vera, for it justified him completely in what he had done. A little less bad behaviour, and she would have had to be allowed to stay the night; still a little less, and she would have had to come to The Willows again, let alone having a free hand in London to influence Lucy when he was at his club playing bridge and unable to look after her. Yes; it was very satisfactory, and well worth coming down day earlier for.

He wound up his watch, standing before the last glimmerings of the fire, and felt quite good-humoured again. More than good-humoured,—refreshed and exhilarated, as though he had had a cold bath and a thorough rub-down. Now for bed and his little Love. What simple things a man wanted,—only his woman and peace.

Wemyss finished winding his watch, stretched himself, yawned, and then went slowly upstairs, switching off the lights as he went.

In the bedroom there was a night-light burning, and Lucy had fallen asleep, tired of waiting for Aunt Dot to come and say good-night, but she woke when he came in.

'Is that you, Aunt Dot?' she murmured, even through her sleepiness sure it must be, for Everard would have turned on the light.

Wemyss, however, didn't want her to wake up and begin asking questions, so he refrained from turning on the light.

'No, it's your Everard,' he said, moving about on tiptoe. 'Sh-sh, now. Go to sleep again like a good little girl.'

Through her sleepiness she knew that voice of his; it meant one of his pleased moods. How sweet of him to be taking such care not to disturb her ... dear Everard ... he and Aunt Dot must have made friends then ... how glad she was ... wonderful little Aunt Dot ... before dinner he was angry, and she had been so afraid ... afraid ... what a relief ... how glad....

But Lucy was asleep again, and the next thing she knew was Everard's arm being slid under her shoulders and she being drawn across the bed and gathered to his breast.

'Who's my very own baby?' she heard him saying; and she woke up just enough sleepily to return his kiss.

Made in United States
Orlando, FL
20 December 2022

27429085R00270